Books by Henrietta Buckmaster

LET MY PEOPLE GO

DEEP RIVER

FIRE IN THE HEART

BREAD FROM HEAVEN

AND WALK IN LOVE

ALL THE LIVING

ALL THE LIVING

ALL THE LIVING

*A Novel of One Year in the Life of
William Shakespeare*

by HENRIETTA BUCKMASTER

"*To him that is joined to
all the living there is
hope: for a living dog is
better than a dead lion.*"

ECCLESIASTES

RANDOM HOUSE / NEW YORK

First Printing

© Copyright, 1962, by Henrietta Buckmaster

All rights reserved under International and Pan-American Copyright Conventions. Published in New York by Random House, Inc., and simultaneously in Toronto, Canada, by Random House of Canada, Limited.
Library of Congress Catalog Card Number: 62-17164
Manufactured in the United States of America by Kingsport Press, Inc.

Design by George Salter

For JOSEPH BALFIOR

AUTHOR'S NOTE

Since most commentators and critics of Shakespeare have drawn upon their imaginations, and since the universality of the plays prompts the most subjective responses, I do not feel that anything has been invented out of context in this novel.

We know a good deal about William Shakespeare, a man profoundly shaped by his times—and I say this in spite of those malcontents the Baconians, the Oxfordians, the Marlovians, and the supporters of Queen Elizabeth as "the true Shakespeare." (Why is the fact of genius airily put aside?)

Out of a plethora of books, all appreciated and valued in one way or another, the most indispensable proved to be John Stowe's *Survey of London; Shakespeare's England*, two volumes of essays by distinguished contributors; *Shakespeare*, by John Middleton Murry; *Stratford*, by E. C. Fripp; *The Meaning of Shakespeare*, by H. W. Goddard; *As They Liked It*, by Alfred Harbage; *Shakespeare*, by M. E. Reese; *The Essence of Shakespeare's Sonnets*, by Edward Huebler; and the theatre chapters of *Shakespeare Without Tears*, by Margaret Webster.

I have tried to use no words not indigenous to the times, and if any have slipped in, it is not the fault of Bartlett's *Complete Concordance to the Dramatic Works of Shakespeare*, or of *Shakespeare's Glossary*, by C. T. Onions, or of *A Dictionary of Early English*, by Joseph T. Shipley, or of Schmidt's *Lexicon*— or of the King James Version of the Holy Bible.

Since no one has an exact knowledge of the dimensions, or even the appearance of the Globe Theatre, I have felt free to speculate, and my speculations are based on the practical needs of actors and management—as well as on some of the provocative assumptions of Dr. Leslie Hotson in his latest book *The Wooden O*.

Whatever its shape, the Globe was a "temple in a green field" where a great poet spoke for humanity.

DRAMATIS PERSONAE

In London

William Shakespeare
Augustine Phillips
Richard Burbage
William Sly   *Housekeepers of the Globe:*
Thomas Pope   *Joint owners of the lease and property*
Robert Armin
Henry Condell
John Heminges

Ned Shakespeare
Sam
Jamie   *Apprentices*
Edmans

Gib, *a Johnny Factotum*

John Marston
Thomas Dekker   *Playwrights*

The Old Man

Jasper Shore, *a brothel-keeper*

Lord Hunsdon, *the Lord Chamberlain*
Sir Edmund Tilney, *Master of the Revels*

Lord William, *a fair youth*
The Earl of Rutland
The Earl of Essex   *Great Lords*
The Earl of Southampton
Lord William Herbert

Sir Thomas Levenson
Sir Roderick Parry
Robin Catesby
Edward Bushell   *Dependants and Followers*
John Florio   *of the Lords*
Sir Gelly Meyrick
Sir Charles Davers
Lord Monteagle

William Camden, *Clarenceux King-of-Arms*

Sir Piers Dalglish, *the Queen's spy*

Sir Fulke Greville, *the Queen's ear*

In Stratford

Tom Greene, *a Shakespeare cousin*
John Shakespeare, *Will's father*
Gilbert Shakespeare, *his brother*
Richard Quiney, *High Bailiff*
Hamnet Sadler, *a neighbor*
Thomas Rogers, *a butcher*
Philip Rogers, *an apothecary*
Henry Walker, *chief alderman*
Abineck Newhall, *constable*
Meekins, *beadle*
Thomas Adrian Quiney, *Richard's son*
The Rev. Mr Byfield, *vicar of Holy Trinity Church*
John Hall, *physician*

John Coombs, *the richest man in Stratford*

Nicholas Smith *and* Michael Hart, *boys.*

Sir Robert Throgmorton of Coughton Court

Sir Edward Greville: The Black Lord

WOMEN *in London and Stratford*

Anne Shakespeare	Mrs Heminges
The Lady	Mrs Burbage
The Queen	Mrs Nell
Mary Shakespeare	
Joan Hart, *her daughter*	The Waiting Woman
	Tib a Prior, *a country girl*
Judith and Susanna,	Nan Fuller, *a hired girl*
daughters of Will	
	Judith Sadler
The Lady's sister	Elizabeth Quiney

xii

BOOK ONE

CHAPTER *One*

ALL was bright sunlight . . .

The sun had risen like glorious Phoebus, galloped across the sky without impediment of cloud, and was now sinking with effulgent regret.

Will, who had ridden away from Stratford that morning, paused at the turn of the road to give attention to the rosy light of the sunset on the plastered walls of the inn. He sat for a moment watching the birds fly to their nests in the thatched roof and listened to their adieux to the day. A clash of protesting noise came from one nest. He smiled and touched his horse.

Around the turn of the road he came to the yard of the Aylesbury inn. The confraternity that would be waiting for him here was made of good fellows, one to all. O, hail and dear love!

A window in the inn was thrown open and he saw Gus Phillips lean out, Gus Phillips, lank as a bone, gaunt as righteousness, loping and sinewy, the best man in the world for kept confidences and good faith. He waved and Gus shook his long arms and shouted to the room within, "Here is Will! Welcome! Welcome! Welcome!"

As though the words were made flesh and blood, the welcomers appeared, streaming into the yard. Will shouted to their shouts. John Heminges, as massive as Jove, led the flock. Will seized his hand.

"Jacko—dear fellow—" He struggled with his horse, which

had reared on its hind legs and was flailing in dismay. "Dickon—take care!" But Burbage seized the bridle and flashed at Will a look of elegant command.

"Oh, let me serve you, old boy, till we've got you used to city ways again."

"Then give me your hand!" said Will. "And Willy Sly—and Hal—!" A tidy descent was out of the question, though the stable boy had the horse under control. "Well, well, well, well, lads. Jesu, if you'd put me down, I'd find my feet. Ned, good lad!"

Heminges exercised a powerful restraint. He pulled at a few shoulders. He intervened with an impressive sonority which his stutter merely embellished and reinforced. "Give Will his fffeet. Cccome. Inside all."

Burbage swore at a slough which had taken his boot up to the ankle. He kicked at a few other ankles in a friendly way, saying, "Godamercy, let him live. It's his right."

"Ah," said Will, standing at last. He ran his hand over his thin auburn hair and laughed with such infectious joy that Rob Armin, their best clown, crowed like chanticleer and turned a cartwheel through the door.

The stable boy, grinning, took away his horse. Will put his hands on the shoulders of Gus Phillips and his own brother, Ned, and shook them back and forth.

"So, let me have a look. By Gis, as ugly as ever. Lovamercy, I am glad to see you both. Safe with wise men at the last."

The public room was filled with the life of the leaping fire. In the fireplace, two spits were turning the supper. The landlord wiped his hands on the sides of his breeches, and kissed Will on both cheeks. The landlord's wife and his daughter came up for their kisses. The ale boy shook his hand and shocked up his own hair with delighted embarrassment. Two strangers knocked out their pipes by the fire and took keen note of a change in the air. The dog barked. The parrot screamed. Off in the stable, the horses whinnied. A little wind sprang up. The night descended.

Across the width of the room a line of fine fellows had been stretched in comic show by John Heminges, who acted as drill master: the players, the bound brotherhood, the tall, the short, the plain, the handsome, the men, the lads.

Will walked gravely down the line shaking hands and bending his ear for the name of each.

"Will Sly, sir," said Sly, the expression on his comely face as bold as a thief's. "Young, handsome, and very talented. Best in tragedy, comedy, history, good at kissing, sir, being so handsome. Also very fine—sir, sir, you'll miss a good bet if you pass me by!"

"And much trouble, likewise," said Will, "being so handsome." He moved to the small man next in line. "You, sir?"

"Tom Pope, please you, sir, my face is said to be against me, sir, but, begging your pardon, sir, I'm very well liked as old ladies, sir, old gentlemen, and the lower nobility. I'm thirty-four years old, sir, and I've got a good roar that can sound like a lion, and my falsetto is—oh, sir, just one chance!"

The landlord and the ale boy were quiet as mice as they set up the trestle tables, but they were grinning all over their faces. The two strangers, waiting dinner, carefully watched a behavior somewhat outside their normal experience.

"Rob Armin, your lordship, I can take off six coats most *humorously*, sir, and I've got very sound ideas about the gist of a joke, as for example, sir, there were two clowns, sir, and a cow-maid—well, I must say it seems very funny to me, sir!"

Henry Condell struggled for a moment, then fell into the swing. "Well, I like brave men, Will—and I feel myself when I've got a mighty line to say—and Will, oh, Will—I was thy Mark Antony this summer. God, I'd give my heart for such again."

"Ah, Hal, there's a greeting I can bear with me!" Holding Condell with one hand, he reached for Gus Phillips with the other; Gus, the *rara avis* of friends, thin as a poker, kinder than judgment day. "And this cudgel or staff—or be it a man? I pinch it but it does not cry out."

Gus crowded his arms against his long, thin sides and drew down his narrow face and boomed in a deep, sad voice, "Oh, I can most cleverly play a stave or a stick, sir, if that suits your poetical needs in a narrow place. Also, in tragical-comical-histori-

3

cal-pastoral vein, you'd have a hard time to do better than me, sir. Now these lads, sir—speak up, boys—tell the kind employer— apprentices, sir—"

"Best in the business, sir," said Sam, "for young friends and warlike noises and carrying things."

"And wives . . ." said Ned, with a sad look at his brother.

"And comic maids," said Edmans capering.

"And the ladies Mr Burbage loves," said Jamie, who was as fair as the day.

Last there was Jacko Heminges, standing apart, tickled with his own joke. Will grasped his hand. "And you, sir?"

The Jovian head looked down on Will. The nose slightly twitched while the pale blue eyes stared without a bat of the lids. "I keep you all out of gaol, Wwwilly-boy, as you dear lads know, and cccount the receipts correctly after you've all had a go at the sums. And if there's anything else you'd like to ask me, feel quite fffree to do so."

The line behind him chorused, "For Jacko is our God; he makes all things beautiful and the rough places plain."

"Oh, heaven and hell," cried the landlord, rushing forward, "no blasphemy for the love of God, my friends!"

Burbage would not stand in such a row, not he, but he joined the chorus by pounding the arm of his chair and crying softly, "Oyez, oyez." One foot was propped against a stool. His fine traveling clothes showed no seam of dust. With his beard newly trimmed, a small fresh ruff at his neck, himself sniffing a poncet box, he looked up at Will with a shrewd merriment.

Will went down on his knees before him. "And you, I take it, sir, play only kings of England or nobility of the higher rank. This is all very fine indeed, but how much money have we made by your scramble through the shires?"

"In Jesu's name," said Dickon Burbage, with a wild bright glance at all, "hark to the fellow who's lain comfortably at home while we've toiled in the summer heat."

Will pushed away Dickon's foot and sat down on the stool. "Never mind that. I've toiled through summer sweat to trim a part to cover up thy paunch." He struck cheerfully at Burbage's middle.

4

Burbage did not stir. He said lazily, "I'faith, *you* look too sleek and bonnied by the sun. By heaven, you must put out the brightness of your hair; the color's far too gay for a sober man of thirty-six, and your look's too merry. What do you play, sir?"

"Attendance on you, my satrap."

"Have you trimmed nice parts for all? Forget about my middle! What did you cook this summer—laughter or tears?"

"Oh, melancholic smiles."

"Read it!"

"On an empty stomach? God's teeth, man!" Will slapped Dickon's kicking foot and stood up. "Mistress—!"

The landlord's wife wiped her hot, smiling face. "Three minutes, sir." They loosened their knives to be ready without delay. The young boys thrust plates under the dripping spits and were hustled into service by the landlady, who cried over her shoulder, "That was a rare treat, sir."

"Oh, they're rare spirits, mistress," Will said. "Gentlemen all and monsters of zeal—sell their own mothers for a good part—but not sell each other, eh, my nobles, one for all? Or has some awful temptation laid its horny hands on you while my back's been turned? Wear you some new visage of old Adam?"

Sly put his hand on Will's shoulder. " 'We are constant as the northern star of whose true fix'd and resting quality there is no fellow in the firmament. The skies are painted with unnumbered sparks—' "

"Hum! Well done," said Will. "How does Dickon fancy such a ringing Caesar?"

"Poorly," said Dickon. "But knows how to pull out the ropes if he climbs too high."

The Welsh stranger sharpened his knife on the hearthstone so that he might ask the landlady in a loud whisper, "Is that so, just? I'm thinking they will be murdering each other."

Will laughed aloud. Sly sent his dagger up to the hilt under Will's arm. The landlady said, "God bless you, Davy, it's all coarse spirits—the result, you might say, of being torn asunder for these many a weeks."

Burbage wrinkled his brow and smiled privately. The firelight on his face showed the kings, the princes, the bold brave lovers,

Will thought, and over them all, Richard Burbage. His nose was large, his mouth thin, his face pockmarked and sunbrowned. The key to kings and lovers lay in the eyes. They were subtle beyond expression. Behind the heavy lids, a world designed and occupied by him went on.

He rose and rumpled Will's hair. "Good parts, old boy, or, by Hercules, we'll carve you up for dinner."

Will put up a restraining hand. "My pate's not so well covered it can be pushed about by any thoughtless hand."

But Burbage patted his crown again. "Good parts—or else I'll swear you stayed in bed all summer."

Will said, "Blessed Mary!" in a wry and comic voice, but he knew he had not spoken soon enough to conceal the naked look in his eyes. Dickon might not perceive, but Gus would. His glance slipped to Gus.

Gus's narrow, cragged face had great sweetness in the mouth and eyes. He put his hand on Will's arm and said in his deep way, "It's never quite the same without you, Will. Our taskmasters, rain and heat and petty officialdom, spare no rod. And the dust— oh, Jethro, we're made of half the topsoil of the Midlands!"

Heminges snorted. "Tttaskmasters! Who requires the sssun to be gentle, and the rrrain to fall only when he's sssafely indoors? Lllord Bbburbage here."

"Ah," said Will Sly, "yet who requires the best beds for all, God bless his gentlemanly soul, but this our mortal god!"

"Hah!" said Heminges. "Who is it must dddouse the sssun, ttturn off the rrrain, set up the ssstage, crimp the feathers, remember the parts, and double for all in the end?"

The chorus answered him, "Father Jehovah!"

Heminges was not really angry, but he made a good show. Will's glance leaped. "Oh, I've lived in the shadow of that greatness, Jacko. I've shared those grand and wily processions into town, all drums and banners and Mister Marquess Burbage demanding the best beds for all, God bless him indeed."

"If I may say so," said the subject himself, "you've all nicely profited from my creature concerns. Those delectable smells that our dear mistress here" (he kissed the landlord's wife) "com-

6

mands from the pot are my happy conceits. Is that not so, my love?"

She giggled. "I'd never have dreamed of such victuals meself, sir!"

The dishes were rattling onto the table, and the boys had already straddled the benches. Burbage sat at the head of the table. "Come, all. Knives out." He bowed his elegant head. "For this food we thank Thee, God Almighty."

Ned pushed his way to sit next to Will, not rudely but insistently, so that Hal Condell found himself moved down a seat. But Condell was good-natured; he smiled sideways at Ned, and even turned him around by the shoulders so that Will could inspect him. "See a man, Will? Where, i'faith, is thy baby brother?"

Ned reddened and muttered, half-smiling, "Hell, I'm eighteen."

Will said, "Was he handy and obedient, Hal?"

Condell put a fist at Ned's jaw. "Best 'prentice ever."

Ned asked softly, "How's home? How's our mother and father? How's Anne?"

"Well. Well. All send love. Truth, the summer has made you a man. Are you happy in mind, lad?"

Ned shrugged, turned away his head, and then turned swiftly back, smiling a little. This was a dark brother, Will thought with a sudden pang—a dark soul, a lad who rarely smiled. He lacked an appetite for life. He was wary of life. Myself at eighteen? Will thought as he said, "Please pass the sallet." He reflected that at eighteen he had had too great an appetite for trial and error, but he too had had a dark soul. He made a joke, but underneath his thoughts ran on, and he put something choice on Ned's plate from his to show his care and love.

"Tell me of home," Ned said.

"By-and-by, dear lad."

"Home is best."

"Say you so now? You were tearing wild to leave it."

Private conversations were blown to kingdom come. Will was the center. He gladly played the part of the loved one returned. He gladly bore all the jokes at himself. All remembrances, all that was wry, dry, sardonic in their pilgrimage of artifice along the

7

lanes and rutted roads of England, all straw beds and feather beds, all complaisant maids and wives, all authorities and admirers were translated for his special benefit.

Will Sly leaned past John Heminges' heaving shoulders to fix Will with hard opaque eyes and pin down a joke forever. All touched Will by voice or hand as though he were a good-luck piece, and he responded with quick gay love.

His light clear complexion and bright hair, the copper lights in his hazel eyes, the lips which, by nature, turned upward and not down, all gave vivacity and worked in his favor when his thoughts were heavy. The two strangers who sat at the table, a lawyer journeying to Oxford, and a drover from Wales who most times slept out with his cattle but had a fierce chill and had come in for the warmth, listened with candid attention.

Burbage gave several sudden raps with his knuckles. He spoke directly to Will. "This is all very gay, but some gall is mixed in it. Times are bad. There's much poverty. Moreover, in Buckden and Kettering we were forbidden to play."

"In God's name, why?" Will cried.

"A change of wind. Reformers in the town places."

Will whistled.

"And, moreover, we need Gib, our Johnny Factotum. Who, by hell, left him behind? The curtains fell down once—it's no sauce for your goose to laugh, Willy Sly! It was I, by God, who had to fight my way out to the daylight again, and *these* yokels laughed louder, Will, than the ones who paid for the fun. Hark to them now! Miscreants! Time-servers! Gib would have put up the curtains to stay."

When Will stopped laughing he said, "Gib can be toted along right enough, but who is going to pull down the curtain on town officials?"

"There are wwways, I've got no doubt, Will," said Heminges. "GGGus and I are crafty when it comes to sixpence in the till."

"Oh, that's God's truth!" said Burbage, falling into laughter, "I'm fond of business too, but they—they'd be stewards for the devil if we'd allow."

"Is there much money in your business?" asked the lawyer carefully.

Burbage stared at him a moment. "For us, sir, with the help of God and the Lord Chamberlain—who as you know manages the domestic affairs of her Majesty the Queen—there is a very fine flow of that useful commodity of exchange that oils the lamps and keeps good will flowing between buyer and seller."

"You're rich," said the lawyer.

"Aye," said Burbage.

Condell leaned across Ned, whom neither love nor money would move, and said in his heavy handsome voice, "It's been fine—a fair time. No grumble." He sat thinking for a moment, his large hands splitting an apple. He flashed a sudden whole look at Will. "Interesting to deal with officials, see fat heads yield. I'd like to have a hand at business when we get to London."

"Would you now, Hal?" said Will. "Jacko and Gus will revere you for those simple words."

The lawyer had fallen into a whispered colloquy with Burbage which was broken by many lewd and private guffaws. Will did not touch his ale. He believed that by sufficient display of a quick bright spirit he would conceal any disquiet. He thought in sudden panic, I am precisely halfway between Stratford and London. To go forward or back is now the same thing.

Condell had turned away, but now he looked again at Will with his commonplace eyes in his handsomely commonplace face. "I know I am a simple fellow. I am glad to be again with thee who makes things bright."

This was so unexpected that Will felt a piercing leap of tears. But he smiled—and his smile always came so merrily that he seldom smiled alone.

"Oh, Hal, I think no one of us would do less for another than for himself. We're bound together, are we not, in some love that is, by heaven, most wondrous."

Sly, listening, said tartly, "I'll be sobbing milk and water soon." He was a little tipsy and so a little bellicose and showing-off. Stirring the sweet scent of the rushes on the floor, he jumped to his feet, struck Rob Armin a blow, and then crouched with his sword. Armin's expression did not change but he made a comic leap in the air and armed himself with the poker.

From foolish actions they fell into foolish declamations.

" 'Duke! Royal lecher! Go, gray-haired adultery!' "

" 'Foolish wench, what hast thou done? That, alas, which cannot be undone and therefore I fear me undone.' "

The fooling was infectious. Tom Pope and Sam and the younger boys were struck down by the same disease. The drover came out of his fever clouds to guffaw. The lawyer, though somewhat more critical, was perfectly happy to be given gratis what many men paid for in coin of the realm. Condell leaped over the bench and entered the fray. Roars and falsettos, the clang of poker and sword, set the dog to barking, the parrot to screaming, and the landlord's wife and daughter into tears of laughter.

Will watched sideways over his shoulder, with no special feeling save that the good fellows were at it, but Burbage suddenly shook the whole bench. He roared like the wind, a splendid primordial sound. He moved his short body with a beautiful grace, and his words rang.

"God's 'ounds! Clowns and bumpkins! Fools and clods! Good only for acting in the straw! More of that and I'll cut you down and send you home. Lie to! Fall out! Hell's damnation, never did I see such rank duplicity! Betray us all! Mountebanks!"

Will Sly found his voice. He said in his hard, no-quarter way, "You're drunk."

"Drunk, he says! Would God you were as drunk as I, Will Sly, and then you'd have some sense of what the actor owes his art! Tom Pope—and oh, you wicked boys! Rapine of noble words. Capers. I'll beat you well!" and he flew at them with blows and gestures.

Will looked at Ned and Ned slyly smiled. Heminges had gotten to his feet and was forcefully interjecting his masterful stutters. He grasped Dickon with one hand and cuffed little Edmans with the other. "Dddickon, not so hhhot. God's bbblood—we'll all lose country ways soon enough!"

"They love country ways!" Dickon shouted. "Tear a passion to tatters and they've reached the top of their bent!"

Sly knocked the poker from Armin's hand and patted him on the head with the flat of his sword. Burbage looked at Will. Entreaty was in his eyes, unbeknownst to himself. It was profound and unspeakable. He made a gesture that elicited some of the splendor, terror and simplicity of the man within.

Will rose. How well he knew the man and his art could not be separated. He too was his art, though one confessed this only in the language of heart and sensibility. For all that each man was himself alone, each man was the others' as well. This was the paradox.

Will put his arm through Dickon's, and he heard the faint heave of a sigh and saw the sweat standing suddenly on Dickon's brow. Dickon said on a falling voice, "It is the actor's craft to enter and interfere with the life of a character, but this is rape—"

Will replied, "Let us sit down and say what must be mended, for, sure, the country has a loosening way. But by all the holy martyrs, Dickon, we trust each other or we fall apart. Now let us make our supplications to the creative imagination."

"Games and sport, Dickon," Sly murmured. "When I catch my breath, I'll give you *The Siege of Cadiz* to make thy fell of hair rise up and tears course down thy cheeks."

Dickon sank into his chair and beat a measure on the edge of the table. "When I hear your voices ragged, and all your niceties forgotten, and gestures coarse—and art condemned—oh, Jesu, then I think: What will our enemies plan when they see our crudy ways?" He shivered.

Heminges patted Edmans and gave him an apple. The lawyer looked very knowing, and the drover forgot his chill. The landlord took down his pipe and sat beside Phillips, sharing puffs.

Dickon looked fleetingly at Will and sideways at Heminges. He said, "I'll chill your bones with present prophecy—if we are not better than the best two days from now." In a laden voice he spoke their doom. "*Edward Alleyn. Now* start up in wrath and terror."

Tom Pope blew out his flabby cheeks. "The *spit* rises in *me* mouth . . ."

"By Lucifer," said Dickon softly, his glance sweeping all the faces, "when you make fools of yourselves, the thought of Alleyn rears before me like a specter out of hell. There, in his great barn of a theatre, his hireling imps are dancing to what tune? What tune? Public approbation—crowds—the tune of dancing pennies! While we, poor louts, trudge the country lanes and—"

"Oh, Dickon, come down, come down!" said Gus Phillips in his deep and quiet way. "We trudge because we choose to do so—or have you second thoughts of filthy London in the summer? And wherever we are, we are the best in England. The Queen's own sword will not be more keen and polished than we, when the time comes."

"And it is not Alleyn who is called the mortal god of London, but Burbage," Sly said craftily.

Dickon needed a few more such words of consolation. He said angrily, "Every damn playwriting pimp has sold his sweet whoring words to Alleyn, I have no doubt, while we've been gone—and our dear good Will must break his heart to make three plays out of one tattered shroud to keep our nakedness from showing."

Dear good Will asked mildly, "Who says Alleyn has not slept straight through the summer, or died of the plague?"

"Alleyn! Hah! He never sleeps night or day. And will never die! He spends his time casting magic charms against us. I know those charms—infallible bat's blood written on parchment—" Burbage's own blood was rising again.

"Peace, Dickon," said Will rather tiredly, "let thy superstitions lie. I will not share crude fears—" he smiled very faintly— "subtle ones are good enough."

Dickon was indeed a little drunk. He flung out the beautiful net of his voice and drew them all in to sweet and sour reflections on life. The lawyer surreptitiously wrote down epigrams that he could adjust to High Table talk at Oxford. Will put his head down on his folded arms and winked at Phillips. The landlord took down one of the trestle tables but did not wish to disturb Will with the other. In the corner, Ned and Sam played at knucklebones, and young Jamie went to sleep with his head on Father Heminges' shoulder.

Will had winked because Phillips was his truest friend. Yet his heart was barren. Sly took a lute from the wall and played a sweet

sad air that ringed with light the room. The drover sang with it
in such a tender melancholic voice that the landlady wept for all
discarded sons and cast-off maidens. Darkness deepened. Night
was heavy. Men should be asleep. The dog slept. Dickon, in
iambic pentameter, spoke a fond farewell to all lovers, and in his
voice was such a wanton beauty that the pulses danced. Yet Will
wished all to remain at an absolute point of perfect non-feeling:
it was safest and best.

. . . Actors were the very distillation of sight, sense, power—
the abstract, the mirror—but not life, not life itself . . . in God's
name, so let it be. Then no pain from yesterday or fear from tomorrow could take him unawares . . . Will drifted, half-hearing.
Dickon's voice sank to the rich diapason that he employed for
parental or uxorial tributes. Nothing would stop him now. Will
sighed. Dickon would pump out a steady flow into which each
might dip his hands and bless himself. The lute played on. Will
could bear no more.

Burbage's uxorial tributes slipped into plaintive recollections of
a feather bed and his round rosy Winifred. Will lifted his chin
against his folded arms and said in a careful voice, "You've no
fear the wizard Alleyn has crept into thy bed with his great
spells?"

Burbage was wide awake and on his feet. "Will! The wife of
my bosom and the mother of my children—!"

Will dropped his head again. "*O puritas, nomen tuum maritus
est!*" he murmured. His eyes were on the lawyer.

"*Ecce?*" asked the lawyer with a thin smile.

Will did not raise his head but addressed this stranger with
careful sleepiness. "This is an evil world, my friend, and we must
guard each other's honor."

"Excellent sound advice, sir. God give you a quiet night."

Ned squatted down beside Will. "There was a quilt Mother
was to send . . ."

"In my saddlebag." He buried his face in his arms.

Gus stood beside him for a moment, and then turned to wake
the sleeping boys. Dickon was now ready for bed, alone, since his
sweet Winifred would tomorrow be gathered to his arms. Sly

made certain signs to the landlord's daughter but she shook her head.

Will did not stir, though in the blackness of his hideaway, his eyes were open.

The bright day is done and we are for the dark—

O fear, blind and headlong, do not make my bed in hell!

CHAPTER *Two*

THE next day was Sunday. It was autumn, the year 1600. London lay sixty miles to the southeast. The rain straggled down.

Breakfast finished, twelve men and boys shouted, cursed, grumbled and mounted their horses. Heminges, his face weathered by wind, sun, and compassion, roamed up and down in the mud, attentive to the woes of early morning. Gus Phillips paid the landlord, examined the state of the carts that bore their gear, and burrowed Edmans, the littlest boy, under a shelter of boxes. His long sad face was alive with the rain. When he mounted his horse, he said firmly, "God bless the day. Where is Will?"

The landlord stood in the doorway and called anxiously, "You'll sure go to church? Law will take after me if you dunt."

Burbage laid his hand on his heart. "Never fear. Where is Will?"

"He forgot the saddlebag," Ned cried, dripping and prancing but with some cheerful expectations of the future. "With our bread and butter in it."

"Merciful mother of God, the play!" cried Burbage. "My ears are drooping like a jackass, Ned, to hear those first lines of consolation. Do they sound like shillings?" Ned pranced and showed off. "What is it like?"

"The play? I don't know. Gay, he says."

"Gay. Is that all?"

14

Ned said pertly, "Nobody's asked my thoughts before. Gay. Maybe full of naughty sayings."

Will came out in haste and mounted his horse, apologizing with little jokes. The lawyer joined the landlord in the doorway. The players waved to the landlord and the lawyer and picked their way through the mud to the muddy road.

Apples lay rotting on the ground. Sheep with matted fleece huddled beneath the trees. The drenched cowmaid drew milk from slippery udders and cast a sodden look at them. A homeless man peered out from the ditch where he had drawn broken boughs beneath and above him.

They passed through a forest on the edge of the village, and shouted to dishearten any highwayman not cowed by the weather. Sly, unshaven and sleepy, sang a song.

> "When I was and a little tiny boy
> With a hey, ho, the wind and the rain,
> A foolish thing was but a toy
> For the rain it raineth every day."

Some might call it a rough land, Will thought, with straggly heaths and briary commons and marshy wastes and all these great forests, but he and his called it home and England.

When the sun came out the rain was forgotten. They shouted to the sun, and pulled out their pistols before they came to the next forest. Henry Condell, two pistols gripped with his bridle, rode with an athletic flourish. Ned made charges at trees, pointing his pistol and making up couplets. Heminges broke out a staff, twelve feet in length topped by a pike, and they all pretended to scatter. The carts and wagons rattled and bounced behind them on the vile road, and Edmans uttered such mournful cries that he was hauled from his burrow.

Sheep stood in flocks on the hillsides, and black-and-white houses thrust themselves up from the fields. By the roadside last flowers took on a new brightness.

At last Dickon called in the sweet music of his voice, "Will, soul, the fruit of thy solemn summer will make us laugh again—is that the truth?"

"The new play? Oh, in a melancholic sort of way."

"Hum. Read it as we ride."

"It will keep."

"Why do you put me off?"

"Ho-ho!" replied Will. "Search this riddle for the wisdom of the world!"

Gus said softly to Will, "Aye—why?"

Will frowned and blew out his cheeks. Dickon waited for a moment and then, scarcely raising his voice, asked over his shoulder, "Who makes the play, you or I?"

Sly laughed. "Hark to the two! That means we're almost home."

Burbage turned in his saddle to look at Will, whose bright eyes were waiting. Dickon's lips were thin but his expression was deep and amused. "Who taught you all you know?" he asked.

Will said with a heavenly smile, "God," and crossed himself.

Dickon stared, then he snorted a laugh and pulled his horse away from a rut. "I taught you, fool. There'd be no play without an actor. Give me some gibberish Persian and I'll drown the stage in thy tears."

A solitary horse in a field galloped along with them for a distance, and the journeying horses rolled their eyes toward him as they troughed up the mud. Dickon lifted his effortless voice. "Will, soul, no more laughter."

"None?"

The clown Armin cried, "You'd knock down my house?"

Dickon held up his hand. "I've thought and said naught. All through the summer—up and down this vile country and now to London. In London, who is our greatest enemy?"

"Lady Poverty."

"Be serious!"

Sly said obediently, "Edward Alleyn."

"And who, again, is Edward Alleyn?"

"Edward Alleyn is an actor who pitifully strives to be as great as Richard Burbage."

"No wizard?" Will asked.

Dickon made a gesture of reproach and went on with his

catechizing. "And how does Edward Alleyn fool people in this manner?"

"By drawing deluded playgoers into his own drafty barn of a theatre where he lampoons nature with such plucked chickens as Hieronimo in *The Spanish Tragedy* by Thomas Kyd," Sly piped and broke down in laughter.

Dickon nodded with a gleam in his eye. "Well learned. Well spoken."

Phillips then obliged with a brief demonstration.

> "On every side drop captains on the ground,
> And soldiers, some ill-maimed, some slain outright,
> Here falls a body sindered from his head:
> There legs and arms lie bleeding on the grass
> Mingled with weapons and unboweled steeds,
> That scattering o'erspread the purple plain
> Till Don Andrea—"

"In a nutshell," said Burbage. He shifted in his saddle. "Alleyn has taken food from our mouths with such asscry. 'Arms and legs lie bleeding on the grass.' Fie! Fie! Who'd weep at that? But hark." He lifted his voice:

> "Pardon me, Julius! Here wast thou bay'd, brave hart;
> Here didst thou fall, and here thy hunters stand,
> Sign'd in thy spoil and crimson'd in thy lethe.
> O world, thou wast the forest to this hart;
> And this indeed, O world, the heart of thee!
> How like a deer strucken by many princes
> Dost thou here lie!

"I've observed how young and old have wept at that—dead Caesar. Will, *thy* Caesar. Wait, Will, speak not. These are days for weeping. Times are out of joint. In the fatness of these pursy days, virtue begs of vice its pardon. And know this—men are as the time is."

He sat with one hand on his hip as his horse labored through the slough. "There are many alarums abroad. Signs in the skies. Have you considered the year? It is a remarkable conjunction of sevens and nines in the Queen's life—and name me figures more mysterious than these. Now we must face it. We are honored and we are rich, but we are also mortal."

"Hell's buckets, but Alleyn has griped thee good!" said Rob Armin with an angry laugh.

Dickon said, "He walks on my grave."

Phillips gave a laugh of amazement. "But Alleyn is merely a businessman. He has no powerful patron as we have."

Dickon turned like a flame and fixed Gus with his eyes. "Let Jacko and you be as good businessmen!"

In a thunder of stutters, Heminges took offense. "Wwwho wwwould—God's bbblessed—"

"And I'll butter thy woe," said Dickon, unmoved. "The Queen's as good a businessman as Alleyn—she wants the best, yet we must pay the bills. Now, answer my question—what play do we own that's made up of profound heaves and sighs to which Will can add his great magic before which I bow my head—"

"Well, God's wonders—!" said Will.

"—and so throw down our gage to Alleyn."

Gus shrugged to Sly, and Sly blew out his lips.

Heminges ventured, "*Tttitus Andronicus?*"

"No," said Will.

"*Ttthomas Lord Cccromwell?*"

"No," said Sly.

Condell swept out his arm and unfurled his manly voice. " 'His antique sword rebellious to his arm lies where it falls, repugnant to command—' "

"By Gis!" cried Dickon joyfully. "The very thing! Thomas Kyd's old champing steed, *Hamlet's Revenge!* Hal, I kiss you!"

Sly sighed and practiced a speech sotto voce. Burbage rode with his hand on Condell's shoulder. "If Alleyn can have Kyd's old *Hieronimo*, by Jove, I can have Kyd's old Hamlet-revenge-revenge made conjunctive to these times," he cried. "Will, dear soul, mend it. Stretch it to our measure! The wise and melancholy Saturn is now ascendant in the heavens, and that is a good omen for witty men like our sweet Will."

Will made a sour face. "Doctor that poor dead Kyd's miserable play? Oh, Dickon—"

18

"Come, come, Will-good-heart. You've brought to life worse than *Hamlet's Revenge.*"

"Look you, Dickon, Kyd's play is a very sorry thing. It aches, all its hinges creak, it keens—"

Dickon turned around to look at him in astonishment. "But this is your excellence, dear boy—make, mend, patch, do—and, by God, make excellent serviceable plays." He caught a glimpse and added with his own true grace, "And remain a poet, for all."

Will smiled at him, not taken in.

"Dickon, you're mad, north-northwest."

"Never mind that. I can tell a play from a plangency, however the wind blows."

Will said slyly, "No laughter at all?"

Burbage bared his teeth in a smile. "Does Alleyn laugh?"

Armin slithered his horse up a rut to Will's side. "Defend clowns, Will!"

"Be calm, dear fool," Will replied. "I hold thee dear for thy kind of laughter—so free of foolish capers."

"'Hamlet—*revenge*,'" said Tom Pope to Will Sly, rolling his eyes. "'I am the ghost of thy fither, doomed to walk abroad—'"

"Nay, dunce," Sly protested with a great yawn, "thou art made too much of beef to be a ghost. What shall we make Tom, all? That tricking gamester, sweet Ophelia's father?" He trilled falsetto, "'O, O, sweet majesty of Denmark—'"

Condell, exercising his sword arm in his relentless virile youth, ventured a deep hope that his own gifts might, this time, carry him on the floodwaters of the play. "For," said he, "I *have* tasted Mark Antony."

The day grew brighter. Some rode on the bank to set their pace faster. Some declaimed old Hamlet speeches out of Kyd, some sang sweet and sad songs. Will was silent. The others gave and received thoughts and admonitions so that their fellowship fitted together like the door to its frame.

They clattered through a village and over a bridge. A sabbath-watcher shouted a kindly warning of hell. They swept off their hats.

As they came into a beech forest, mysterious and beautiful as a cavern under the sea, and as filled with danger, Burbage said to Will, "You have not said a word, dear soul. Is it agreed? We will shake out Kyd's old *Hamlet's Revenge* into the bright day of Shakespeare—and meet our great rival on his own ground?"

Will replied after a moment, "I will bear it some thought."

"Odds, man, that's no answer."

Will smiled at Dickon. "It's a fair answer, dear soul. I wish to laugh: you say *no laughter*. Well, I must plan its obsequies with decent care."

Rob Armin muttered, "Holy martyrs, pray for me."

Burbage turned back with a shrug that almost carried away his ears. He said sharply to Armin, "Give us a song." He had learned the provoking science of waiting for Will.

The only traveler who passed was a journeyman carpenter. They nodded to each other and he joined in a verse of the song for the space of his passage.

Gus Phillips dropped back to Will's side. "Must you have laughter?"

Will looked at him with his swift and nimble glance. All the planes of his face were alive. "Hell, no!"

Gus waited a moment. "Yet I think this setting of thyself against Dickon is more than a game."

A state, a condition, something more subtle and elusive than thought, wiped out Will's natural expression. What Phillips saw, at that instant, was as wide and defensive as a moat.

Will made a joke and his quick-moving glance went over fields and road. Gus shrugged and whistled. Then he looked at the pale face and the queer shrouded eyes and remembered how he loved this man, and how all sins lay upon all men to their doom or salvation. He thought of his own sins, grievous and faulty, of the bright day and the wary adder, of life and the mystery of death.

He took off his hat to the russet trees and thanked God that all were alive though their sap had run out. He turned his long tanned face to that chalice of eternity, the sky. Presently he glanced sideways at Will.

Will was watching him with a guarded yet avid gaze that

dropped away in the view of the other. Gus smiled and whistled again. Heminges called back, "Think you we are on the rrright rrroad?"

"Road? Jesu!" cried Sly.

Jamie's voice piped, "There be the sun, sir, straight in its course."

Burbage swore and pressed on through the trough that passed for a road.

Gus said, "I've not seen you for three months. Honey Will, gentle Will, merry Will—all intact. Yet the eyes of my great love see a man who has changed."

Will did not reply. They entered a wood. The vile road had become less than a cart track, overdone by the thick woods, for who but a painted fool would leave his own fields to go six miles into a foreign land? He did not reply until they came to the open again. Then he said, "I suppose no other man has ever known the secrets of my heart as you." Yet he shook his head. "No. No words are best. Silence. Ask me no questions."

Gus said nothing. An old farm lay by the road, of the honied Cotswold color—near as old as King Henry V—bustling in its venerable life with children, byre, dovecote and barn, at peace with the days and the seasons.

Gus said, "Silence is golden. But speech is better for this load on your heart—"

Will made a good effort to laugh. "It's light as a dream . . . Do you believe in dreams, Gus?"

"What was thy dream?"

"Are they real?"

Gus shrugged and lifted his brown face again to the sun. "As real as our thoughts, I daresay."

Will said, "I am not superstitious as Dickon is." He took off his hat and pretended that the sun was his be-all. They had come to the end of the village which had, between the first old farm and the last old cottage—in the conjunction of these mucky times—crumbled and died. It was like a man hale above the waist and sickening below. Grass grew in the door of the church and all its windows were sightless. Will shivered and Gus waited.

21

"I dreamed I stood beside my wife to say goodbye. I dreamed while still in Stratford. There was the house, there the open door. But in the dream I was, at the same time, sitting on my horse saying goodbye to myself in the door. And in the door was not myself but my cousin Tom, who stood with his arm about my wife's waist. They were laughing at me. And all about them were sudden flowers, monstrous, sick and evil like no flowers of God."

Gus spoke after a moment. "And you, in your dream?"

"I, riding away, ploughed myself underground . . ."

"And when you waked from your dream?"

"I have not waked."

Gus looked at him and said boldly, "Will, friend, what has happened that you should dream in such a way?"

Will gave no answer save his speaking face.

"Who is this cousin?" asked Gus.

"A Warwick man. On my father's side a cousin in some degree. Five years ago he entered Middle Temple. Last year he was called to the Bar, though for a year he will be my steward. We've been friends of a kind."

"He gave up the law to be thy steward?" Gus asked in some astonishment.

"He said he was a countryman at heart. When I bought land and a great house he asked to serve me." His glance slipped to Gus, and he said ironically, "Perhaps he took a closer look at my wife."

"I do not know your wife," said Gus, "save as your wife . . . is your dream against her? Has she abused you in some way?" He wondered if Will had heard him, for Will had turned away. "Was your good wife not glad to have you home?"

Will nodded. Then he shook his head. "Do not ask me. She is what she is: it is I who have the devil. I will not say one word against her. I married in haste and perchance she regrets in leisure. We have two children and a dead son, a fine house, and an ape on my back. I am Anyman."

"I fancy not. For you are Will, and even the ape commands your regard."

"Everywhere my son was dead . . ."

22

"Aye. It comes more hard for thinking time has eased the grief. Two years dead—nay, scarcely two! That is short time for time to work. Think on it—*there* is the cause of your sadness. If you would wear a dark mind, see how your fears are disguised."

"Did my son Hamnet die because of his father's sins, or his mother's?"

"In God's name, who knows now?"

Will said with no special stress, "The time comes in a man's life when he must know himself or die. Glad or sad, peace or war, the time is his."

Gus was cautious, his gray eyes, unblinking, turned to Will. "Are we our own priests?"

"All the times that one is afraid of the dark and of dreams comes back to me . . . Gus, I am not a weak man."

"Is that my cue?"

"No one knows me as well as you."

"Then I testify to your strength."

"But I am very ill served, Gus . . ."

"By your dream?"

Will did not speak for a moment. "By my conscience."

A hill shut them from the others. The sound of viols and flutes, and the boys' singing voices, floated back sweet as apples on the air. Gus looked at Will, and what he saw made him speak with agitation. "Will, in the name of God, speak out! Say what it is!"

Will turned the full life of his eyes on Gus.

"You've forgotten, man, who lies in wait in London?"

Gus frowned and stared. "Lies in wait—holy Mother of God —no, Will! In all good conscience—!"

"Conscience—my very word, you see."

"Will, she is a little squeaking girl with the heart of an earwig!"

"Say on."

Gus said urgently, "She is a Duke's daughter and a Marquess' sister, and a Queen's Maid, though she has the manners of a trull, and there's an end."

Will frowned and turned away his head, yet he nodded. Gus's voice took on a deeper urgency. "You had no right or privilege in the first place with a lady born as high as she—though a trollop, as I'm a Christian man. And by God's mercy she left you for one of her own degree. Though it cut you to the heart, bless God, and *there's* an end!"

This time Will did not nod. He sat like a stone and the planes of his cheeks were stiffened.

Gus's face took on his agitation. "Let the man keep her who took her! Think of him—my God!—thy patron, a lord, Lord William. By hell, he can injure us all if he choose! I don't trust the look of your face! Hell's buckets, you told me she was gone forever!"

Will barely opened his lips. "She is gone . . . but she is there."

"Has she written you? Has she sent for you? Is this her devising, not yours?"

Will slowly shook his head.

"Then what have you done?"

Will's lips scarcely moved. "I think of her. St Anthony in the desert did not have such thoughts . . ."

After a moment Gus gave a short laugh. "Well then, by St Priapus, douse the shutters! Oh, Will, Will—look you—thy own patron! Oh, be friends with form and order! She is out of thy star. Oh, to kiss and roll about is no great sin—at least we're all such sinners—but to be so enthralled, why, this outtops all reason!"

Will smiled at him faintly. "By my own strength, I'll not give in."

Gus blew out his breath. "Well, bolster this strength stoutly, man, and think, if all else fails, of mortal sin."

Will smiled more openly.

"—And of the sacred bonds of marriage, for the body's honor and the soul's wholesomeness! Will, I know you for what you are, a just and loving man—and there's your strength. What is your fear?"

Will did not answer for some time. When he replied, he did so with a composure that he knew was false. "By our blessed Lord, I know not what to say. Must I *word* it?"

"Speak."

"I am corrupted by spells, by mischiefs manifold and sorceries terrible."

Gus thought he did not hear—or heard some simile such as poets make. "Witchcraft?" he said at length in bewilderment. Then he said gently, "We are reasonable, unsuperstitious men. Yet I suppose there are some matters that lie beyond our reason."

Will spoke with sudden violence, "Summer storms and winter ravages—not all the whips of heaven are large enough to punish the poor body."

"Dost thou love thy wife?" Gus asked abruptly.

Then Will crumpled. "Oh, there's a mischief-breeder, Gus! Oh, a very telling, vexatious mischief-breeder, Gus. Dost thou love *thy* wife?"

"Most times."

They rode past a field where men were cutting thatch. Then Will saw the serpent that had been waiting.

For his marauding heart there had been a judgment. Were his wife to succumb to the common lust of humankind, then he would have no more a wife; the land would be desolate, no homes be there, only bracken and brambles and the wide world. *My mistress is the wide world. There armies roam at will.* Ah, on this awful dictum he would bring his craftiness to bear . . . Ah, lawless, murdering marauders of the heart. Lust's as near to murder as flame to smoke—murder murders peace and love. Oh, the witch was an infection in the blood. Had she caused it so? Had he brought home to his wife a plague to which his wife had sickened?

Tom had taken his place in the doorway of his dream—or was it a dream? Did he wish to call some other man a sinner and not himself? Lord William had injured his dignity but Tom could injure his soul. Was it not a wife's vow to stay alive till death? Shall I ask: Have you betrayed me? But women will say anything. If carnality raged in me, why not in her? But she is my wife! God, I will punish home . . . Nay, I will weep no more!

Gus said, "Thy complexion's changed, thy breath comes hard. Once I saw a man behave in such a manner who was indeed bewitched. Let me inquire, with the greatest care, whether she practices a black art."

"The little earwig? Not for the world!"

"There's a coven said to be at Westminster. It reaches close to the Queen."

"Gus, give me your word you will make no inquiries!"

"But think you, a witch was burned a Michaelmas ago for casting spells on a man."

Will said softly, "If I have been bewitched, I will drive a stake through my own heart."

Their friends were a vivid shape against the road ahead, their clothes as bright as flowers. The music of the pipes and viols came as fresh and innocent as the day. In the distance church bells began to ring. Ned separated himself from those ahead and rode back. Will watched him coming . . . himself in his youth? He waved Ned back but Ned came on.

"Hurry," Ned shouted, "church is not waiting!"

The bells were ringing with incredible speed, gaiety and brilliance. They rose to a crescendo of sound and played upon the nerves till one could scarcely endure this heavenly rapture. Glory, glory, glory, glory, glory, angels besieging the ramparts of God . . . The air splintered.

Will lifted his head. He was shriven by the sound. Though hell gaped, the terrifying mystery of man's fall and his search for redemption seemed on the verge of an answer. Were the bells to ring again, his eyes might see into heaven and hell.

Gus said thinly, "I do not know why I should be, or thou, or he, or she, unless to find some answer."

Will was stung with love. He put out his hand to Gus. "God dare not despise us!"

"Hurry—hurry!" called Ned.

The others had dismounted and tied their horses before the church. Burbage stood with his hand shielding his eyes for the laggards. His relief showed in his impatience.

"Go to, go to! Thou art so late we must tiptoe," he cried, moving with a clatter toward the church door.

Will paused and looked at the little church. He put his hand on

Gus. "In truth, the old fellows built the chancel askew. See how it tips by a little?"

Gus replied, "Thus the Redeemer's head sank on one side as he gave up the ghost."

"Truly, Gus?"

"So it is said."

"Hah! Sweet and merciful."

CHAPTER *Three*

AS they rode through the hills of Hampstead and saw the River Thames curling through the city aqueous in the twilight, Will said to himself, She was an infection in the blood. The blood is cleared. I am no more infected or humiliated. God be with me.

This was a bargain for the safety of home.

They came through the melancholy villages above the city where autumn seemed more inexorable than in the country. When the descending road hid the river the city men rode forward with lighted spirits, the countrymen withdrew, in heart, to hills and meadows. Will thought of green fields.

Farmhouses yielded to burghers' homes. The meadows stretched out into vegetable gardens for London. Burbage signaled for them to throw back their cloaks and display their livery as the Lord Chamberlain's Men. They also shook out their banners, so that the city which was their demesne might lose no occasion to honor them. It was a duty to the Lord Chamberlain and to each other.

In the clutter of roads converging on London they were greeted. Some cheers were perfunctory, some were whole-hearted, some were injunctions against sinning, shamming, and all the works of the devil.

They came past Tyburn Tree. In the heavy end of the day, a body swung there like a last leaf on a tree. Some of the exhalation of the crowd which had witnessed this hanging still fretted the air.

27

A gaggle of boys was shaking the Tree. They shouted when the body stirred. As the riders passed, a raven moved smoothly out of the sky and sank onto the dead shoulder where both swung together as the bird cleaned its feathers.

At the village of St-Giles-in-the-Fields, they turned toward Holborn and came to the cluster of houses around the Inns of Court. The city bells were ringing, and over all was the master tolling of Paul's. Here their admirers were thick as the grass. Young lawyers, young clerks, young students, young gents, young nobles, and men in their prime threw up their hats with huzzas when they saw them. The more limber ran by the side of the horses asking impudent questions.

Will and Condell and Heminges bowed to them with their own courtesy. Armin and Pope bowed in a farrago of clowning. Burbage, for whom the shouts were the loudest, bowed with a shrewd mixture of great noble and humble, hearty friend.

The cheers for Burbage were still ringing in their ears when they passed over Holborn Bridge and heard other cries. "I strike! Dog, move! Thou spawn of Cecil, yield thy place!"

"Not for great Earl Essex, by Our Lady's lap!"

These servants of great lords blocked the road to all, and fell upon each other with swords and staves. Some citizens shrieked, others slammed their doors. The Lord Chamberlain's Men scattered down the closest street.

"Hot! Hot!" said Dickon when they reassembled. He called to a passerby. "What is the history of the times? Which great servants are set on which?"

The man who wore a clerk's dress grimaced. "Tomorrow who knows? Today the Lord Essex challenges man and the devil, and Cecil replies for the Queen."

"Has the great Earl lost the Queen?"

The man shrugged. "Some say yes, some no. His servants claim the streets."

"Well, well."

As they came up Newgate Street, where Giltspur and Old Bailey crossed, the bells of St Sepulcher clanged out for vespers. The handsome arch of Newgate leaned heavily against the evening sky. The prison within the walls showed feeble slits of light. Both within and without men greeted this last hour of day with great earthly noise, as though heaven or hell would claim them with the fall of the night.

Here the players divided, Dickon, Heminges, Condell, Armin and Sly, Jamie and Sam turning north toward Aldermansbury and Shoreditch. Filling the road, while a carter shrieked and a coachman demanded a right of way, they said goodbye as though they might not meet again. Who knows where death lurks? Yet Dickon took a lien on the future. He threw his arms about Will.

"The *Hamlet*," he said loudly above the street din. "Give not too much thought, soul. Do the birds, when they sing?"

Will smiled. "Ah, butty, the birds need not sing in iambic pentameter."

Dickon laughed. "We have come back to Greatness, soul. Do not confuse her with blind Fortune." He thrust his heel in his horse's side, but then he halted again. "Give me this *What-You-Will*. I'll read it tonight."

Will fished in his saddlebag and came up with the play. Dickon weighed it and grinned. "Worth three hundred pounds?"

"Oh, more, if you do not tear the wings off my words."

Dickon knew how to answer this. He said soothingly, "I'll make you a fine play, Will, with a new beginning, middle and end. Now, let us meet at nine." He groaned. "Jacko, there's Lord Hunsdon first. You'll not fail me? You'll meet me there to pay our duty to him at his breakfast?"

Jacko, sitting massively, said, "Who'll wake me up?"

Dickon touched his horse. "You've got twelve children and a wife." He began kissing his fingers, "And I, I—oh, Winifred, Winifred, stir not, thy lover approaches!"

Condell also looked cheerful. He asked Heminges, "Do you think my baby will know me after three months?"

"I've got no dddoubt. If she don't, your wife will."

Condell looked at Will.

"Oh, aye, count on one or the other," Will said. He thought that all except Sly and the 'prenticed boys were going to their own well-furnished homes and loving families. Pope, too, was going to a house that he had filled with homeless children, and Gus would find a wife and five children, some grief and some joy. Only Will and Ned were bound for a lodging where a whore lived above them and one below. Will had a perverse thought. Go far enough with Dickon and he would come to the house and gardens of Lord William. What was Lord William doing, the sweet corrupt youth?

He clanged shut the door on such thought.

He turned with Pope and Gus through Newgate and struggled for passage against the traffic which wished to be locked in or locked out of the City. Vendors cried their last cries. Mechanicals, wearing the signs of their professions, skipped around the legs of gentlemen's horses; the twilight dimmed only a bit of the silk scarlet and gold of the riders.

Will opened his soul to the city, the dark and the light of his soul. The noises of nightfall were a din in his ears: the bells that clanged, the horsemen who cried out against the footmen, and the walkers who cursed the riders, while those who cursed at the Lord Chamberlain's Men sent their hate to batter his mind: *Dangerous traps of Satan, lying in wait for the unwary. Gaudy evil! Sin and sinners!*

In Cheapside, the bright painted houses glowed in the last of the day, and the commotion in stalls and shops, the rattles, the thuds, the clashing, the cries, would be reproduced in the morning. The live meat in the Shambles was bellowing and stamping. The scolding bell of St Mary-le-bow's searched and found all. With the dusk deepening, they hurried to elude curfew. The Watch, with rattle and club, began to cry out his warnings.

Will and Ned, Gus, Pope and Edmans plunged into the purgatorial warren of alleys running down to the river. Here they were cramped in their riding. They furled their banners and loosened their daggers, while Ned and Edmans ran to sit on the carts where they rattled, rich and exposed in the rear.

Once they heard the cry of "Clubs!" and a scream and a scuffle. Fine houses were passed, crouching behind their closed shutters to wait out the night. Street lights were scarce and watchmen forgot to replenish those that were spent. Lanterns appeared in the dusk, bobbing for home. As night deepened, only a fool or a rogue would stay where death lurked. Will ground his teeth and longed for a door of his own to close.

The city woke to hell in the dark. The hell of a violent arm, a voice, of running feet, of subtle allusions, ghost-ridden by poverty—no supper, no bed—by the black underlinings of grief, by the bitter formlessness of drink, all of which the black night embraced without comfort or surcease.

The night compounded the terrible smells. The stench was stirred in the refuse heaps by a constant rustle of life. Dogs, cats, and rats, starving, hoped for a means to live, but with a sudden shriek, death came at the jaws of another.

Will heard these sounds, and the sounds of their horses' feet, with a black heart. Oh, God, the price of singing was to become the song. The price of the cat's life was to become the death of the cat. In his soul he knew that no cry or pain or joy had life apart from him.

Yet jogging past London Stone in the moments before curfew, hurrying to pass over the bridge before the gates were bolted, he thought that life could not be commented upon with how-many words, but must be lived whatever its name or nature. A choice, was there a choice? Not as there might be choice between tree or man, but choice as imagination informed fact and as insight superseded the irreconcilable.

He distrusted words. Words pounded in his head. He never yet had heard that the bruised heart was mended through the ear. He distrusted thought. He distrusted London. His heart pounded under his chin. The country road in the rain and the sun and I both skeptical and credulous—where are they now? He distrusted blood and the stars. He distrusted night and, even more, he distrusted day.

All this hung on the edge of his mind like a gibbet at sunset. He was a recounter of life yet he was enshrouded by panic: a man is understood by his paradoxes. He was dismayed at himself and groped for good sense. He hated London! Well, swallow the bad taste and go on.

The City, harassing players, had driven them to the suburbs.

They entered upon London Bridge as the City gates were being heaved into place. The cart barely scraped by the close buildings. In this narrow tunnel of road, stretching from shore to shore, with the steep dank buildings rising above them arched by stout timbers, the cobblestones echoed the horses' hoofs against the walls, and the noise returned trebled by the pushing tide thundering around the arches.

At the end of the bridge, the keeper was calling for them to come faster. Above were the dark, beating wings of scavenging birds rising and settling on the bridge towers. A traitor's head, and treason had a hundred names to the Queen, was impaled no doubt on the tower pikes. The head might have remained unobserved had it not been for the whirring wings of death's harbingers. Oh, welcome home!

Will was a little surprised at his bitterness. Though London was filth and noise and panic, it was also keenness and praise and good hearts. Panic? That was a strange word to use. He regarded his thoughts with deep suspicion. What's in thy hideaway, Will? Speak up, man, for thou art no fool.

They turned into Bankside. They went past the Clink where an occasional glow encircled a gentleman-prisoner with enough money for candles. They went, still silent, past St Saviour's Church, and past the Bishop of Winchester's palace and his great park, under the broody walls of which nestled the brothels owned by his lordship. They were sharp with screams, lights, and men, though some of the drabs sat in the evening calling to passersby, and sang out to the players as old friends returning home.

Gus, Will, and Pope greeted these friends, exchanged pleasant obscenities, caught the children who ran to them crying, "What have you brought me!" and held them against the sides of their beasts for a trot.

They crossed over the ditches stirred by the tide, passed the tenements that stretched as far as Lambeth Marsh. The fog was beginning to settle. This morning in Oxfordshire was a year away.

Phillips said good night and turned off for Horseshoe Court. Will thought *wife* as one might think *primrose* or *green*. He thought *home*. It created a sense; it moved the air like a measure of music. The night was a tunnel without beginning or end. In the tunnel was filth, drunkenness, whoring, and prisons.

They left the river. They turned up Maid Lane, and there the eight-sided theatre rose up before them in the field.

Will's heart bounded. Fears, sins, and bitterness did not lie in that mysterious temple in the green fields. Imagination has healed wounds before. It has more redemptive powers than the prayers of the saints, he thought.

The fields stretched south as far as they could see. A windmill here and there was antediluvian against the sky. In these fields, the maypoles would be set in the spring. The marshes lay to the east, where lived the heron and duck and where the curlew cried.

Will lingered and looked, though the fog was spreading in from the river. Tom Pope said in his housewifely way, "How shall we care for the carts? Lock them up in their old nursery or let them bide at the inn?"

Will said, "I have a mind to unlock our door and go in. Let us put them away in their shed."

Pope was pleased. The carts had served them well and should be made content as were their horses and lads. Will unlocked the side door of the theatre, and while Pope ordered about his lads with endearments and patted the sides of the carts, Will went on and stood in the pit.

Above him was the open sky, around him the empty galleries, before him the stage and the mysterious recesses that were the world in fact and fancy. In the darkness and the emptiness he was a king.

He leaned against a pillar, bearing himself hard yet thinking with cool joy that in the beginning was the Word. Therefore something in the word must be blessed, although to such an obscure conclusion one brought some caution . . . for the word also meddled, it raked at men's lives; the malice of the word joined with its mercy to put out the light. He hated malice. He loved mercy. He would no more blow out a man's light than he would quench the smoking flax.

I can be more sharp with myself than any man alive, but in the end do I do more than cleave the sea with a sword?

Then, because he fancied that she jigged across the stage, her brocaded skirts in her hands, her little feet quick as mice, he said aloud, smiling faintly, "Nay, do not come. Do not call me. I forbid you. I will not come. I see you now as death and evil, and I am a sensible man."

A lantern danced. A hoarse ironic voice spoke from the stage. "Oh, king of smiles. *Omnia abeunt in mysterium.* Nay, I hear you, for I hear all."

Will frowned and peered with narrowed eyes. "Oh, Gib!" he said. The upturned corners of his mouth became a smile. "You have not been knocked on the head or stabbed in the back, thank God. How goes the world?"

"It wears, sir, as it grows." Gib remained on the stage, so Will went down to him. Once Gib had had a last name, but no one remembered it now. He was Johnny Factotum who held the prompt book and all the plays together, who made the winds blow on the stage and sent up smoke and ghosts from the cellarage.

He now sat on his heels at the edge of the stage so that his face was not far above Will's. The lantern stood beside him. He was dark, raw, and handsome in a brutal offhand way. Something unfinished was about him: his smile was sideways and there was a splintered light in his eyes. He dangled a letter between his first and second fingers.

"This pulsing, scented, heavy missive came for you. See how it quivers. It was sealed with such urgency that I ran like a hind when I saw your lights."

Foolish panic mocked at Will. He did not look at the letter. He continued to smile at Gib. "It is yours, Gib."

Gib poked at his face with his black gaze. "Feel it coiling, burning, promising. Take it."

Will turned away. Gib wagged the letter briskly.

"Come, come. What good are women save to ride to business?" He wagged the letter again and threw it at Will's feet. Will picked it up and read in the lantern light: "Come tonight. The garden gate is open. I kiss the inside of your mouth."

Anger modulated his dismay. Yet his hands began to tremble. Gib stood up, watching him with a rough compassion.

34

Will turned away, turned back, glanced at Gib. Then he slowly shredded the letter. He thrust the shreds into his pouch and looked at Gib. Gib had not taken his eyes from him. After a moment, Gib grunted and said, "Welcome, traveler. Have you heard the chimes at midnight? Have you done wild things?"

"Oh, we've been merry. The others have brought back honor, too, and money." Will blinked and frowned. "Well, who stole, who fornicated, who bargained for his soul while we were gone?"

"The world. But more to the point are the remnants left us by the Queen's censor of Middleton's play."

"Damnation! When I read it it would have passed through the most pusillanimous keyhole of censor!"

"Well, times have changed, old boy. Treason or discontent or whoremongering or poverty or some other such engines of the devil are churning like a dairymaid. Each time Lord Essex is a spoiled brat to the Queen, the censor falls into a swoon and cuts off another privy part of the old war horse. Then it falls to me to get it hobbling once again."

"Poor Gib. Give it me tomorrow and I will see how we can fool the censor."

Gib said wryly, "Jonson is in gaol again."

"Poor Ben. Was it a word or a blow? Who else is with him?"

"Dekker slipped through like a heifer bitten by the breeze, but Chapman—" Will laughed. Gib looked at him curiously. "I sometimes think you are the only playwright who's not been gaoled."

Will touched Gib on the arm and said gaily, "We have both been gaoled, Gib, though we knew it not until we tried the door. Why should I laugh at others? My door is fast locked. Is not yours?"

Gib's expression did not change. His lips still curved upward at one side and his eyes said nothing. "Why is it fast locked, Will?"

"Mortality. Mortality," Will said with a wide smile.

Gib's gaze did not waver. In it was the pity and the malice that sharpens such a man's curiosity. "Then are all men in gaol."

"Truly, as you say, dear master, *omnia abeunt in mysterium*."

Gib emitted a little snorting laugh. Will looked at him for a

35

moment, a crooked friend who loved and hated in equal measure. He pressed his hand and turned away, glancing up at the foggy sky.

"Dickon wants Kyd's old *Hamlet's Revenge* made afresh."

"Not bad. Will you do it?"

"Oh, aye. The ladder of life may be full of rotten rungs, but I climb on, cheerful, nimble, clean, obedient."

"What if it break?"

"Then I fall up into heaven."

"I would not so deceive myself."

Will held out his hand. "Do you think so? Good night, friend. Why, you—as I—have neither youth nor age. We are, as it were, an after-dinner sleep, dreaming on both."

Will called out to Pope, "Do not fall into the river, Tom! Draw on my right arm. Ned! Edmans!"

"Here."

"Hitch yourselves to the other side. Now off we go!"

In the fog they heard the scratching of boats against the river steps but could not see the river. They clung together. Their voices were hollow. Pope was happy. "God's mercies never fail. At least we get no daggers in our backs on such a night."

"Tom, tomorrow we try our breaths on *The Merchant of Venice*. And in the evening we will read this new great play."

"*What-You-Will?*"

"Aye."

The rattle of the Watch and the Watch's voice were close at hand. "What's your business!"

"To squeak like a mouse and roar like a lion. What's your, Affabel?"

Affabel, the Watch, loomed through the murk to shake their hands in welcome and breathe of onions. "Take care," he said, "lads a' come all the way from Saffron Hill to stir some mischief. It's filthy times."

" 'Ods me," said Pope, "we live in the skirts of the town and skirts are filthy. God go wi' 'ee."

Will said, "Would you say this is your turning, Tom?"

Pope answered cheerfully, "Oh, I'd say this might be hell for all I know. But I'll try my soul."

"So, good night."

"Good night . . ."

"Good night . . ."

Will and Ned went on in silence. They could hear the singing in the brothels and a constable waking some indignant householder to make sure he was at home. Ned, swinging the lantern, said, "Mind the ditch," and there they were.

They went into their tenement, decently kept, thank God, the refuse swept out of the hall and a lock on the door. First step up and all was well. The landlady heard them and came to her door with a candle.

"Welcome, old friends," she said.

Ned and Will paused on the stairs while she and Will spoke up and down to each other on the welfare of each. She asked after his wife and both of his daughters. Will thought that, with the light shining on her, she was a pretty woman, and she thought, for the hundredth time, that he was the beautifulest man she had ever known, though in truth it might be only his kindness which made him seem so.

"All's well, then, and good night," she said and turned back. "Come in tomorrow and we will have a pot of ale and some gossip."

"That I will. Many thanks, Mrs Nell."

She waited, with her candlelight, till they had reached the first floor. As Will fumbled at his door, she heard the voice of their neighbor, the old man, the sorcerer, and she made a furtive sign of the cross.

The old man said, "Thou art safe home, honored friend, beloved of Hermes Trismegistus."

Ned went into their room to set down the lantern and to light a candle. Will stood by the stair well to ask the old man how he did, how were his mice and his owl. The huge old man smiled with all his face and searched Will's countenance as though trying

37

to recall something already well known. His voice was rich as the sea.

"My angels have unlocked new treasures since last we met," he said in his gentle thunder. "Come you in and let me tell you."

"I've ridden since daybreak. Let me come tomorrow."

"Ah, tomorrow," the old man said, as though eternity were spoken of.

Will went into the old man's room.

The old man closed the door, even against Ned who had come into the doorway. He said, with his hand on Will's arm, "Last night you and I were summoned in our dreams, but since you were not present, I am now constrained to say a word to you. So must I close the door. So must we speak alone."

"I saw you not," said Will, always obliged to answer this powerful old man in his own terms.

"Aye, because you did not heed the call. My angels have showed to me the secret of the mind speaking to the mind. Let me tell you that where I go at night is heaven and hell. I cannot speak for other men, but for my single self I would as lief be blotted out as stumble blindly or by fortuity. I have brought myself, by potions and my will, so close to death that I may say I've oped the portals of eternity. Last night—"

Will stirred. He too had dreamed last night. He said these were too many dreams for him. The old man stopped like a hawk on the wing. He looked at Will for a moment with brilliant eyes, and then he slowly nodded.

"I have gone in and out of death so often it holds no fears." He added hastily, ". . . not that I see you dead! Well then, wait awhile." But he asked, because curiosity was his nature, "Are you afraid to know what is seen and heard in a new world?"

Will smiled. "Afraid? . . . well, let us fence with terms, old friend. Now, *afraid*—"

"Nay, your mind is very dear to me; we will not fence. In that sweet transparency where time and space both yield, I see you as clearly as I see myself, and for this reason speak."

Will was moved with a caution that came down on him like an

icy bath. He was astonished. In this sanctuary of Hermes Trismegistus where only good was transacted, what was lying in wait for him so close upon his return? That good caution should be more pertinent than the cause itself, filled him with an even wilier amazement.

He sat down, in speech and action self-restrained, and said, "Good old friend, in this sanctuary—" and his bright look went about the room with its alchemical retorts, its astrological and mystical charts, and its benign animals—"one is frightened only if one is afraid of God."

The old man's laugh rumbled far away. "Then you are afraid of God? Yet the Babe of Bethlehem is sweet as honey."

There was a faded grandeur about the old man. His velvet coat was threadbare but gleaming crimson. His hair and beard were white, his eyes younger than a newborn child's. Some said he was not a Christian and dealt with familiar spirits, but the old man said God was Truth and that this embraced the Bethlehem Babe and all else. This might not be an ecclesiastical answer, but it held the same balm as Christmas songs with their "sweet babe" and "hushabye" and "joy to the world," and Will could no more turn away from a man who dared angelic flights than he could turn away from a girl making posy chains.

Yet he found that he was bracing himself like a schoolboy before the Heavenly Master, and was surprised how tired he was, how unprepared and apprehensive. He tried to find his customary calm, and stumbled on it briefly by thinking with amusement that King Saul must have felt some such peevish astoundment when the ghost of Samuel interfered with his rest. He said with a laugh, attempting to balance the occasion, "My wise friend, you must agree that a man who forces the gates of heaven and hell awes the reason and puts to flight the imagination."

The old man studied Will for a moment, and said with a smile, "Love looks not with the eyes but with the mind. Be not afraid."

Will reached out his finger to the little owl who was like a dumpling girl. If he had the wit of his apprehension he would not linger. The owl climbed upon his hand and ruffled her feathers. "These little beasts of thy love know no fear. Why should I?" A mouse scampered up his arm. "The mouse shall lie down with the owl . . ."

"Let us speak what we feel, not what we ought to say."

Will faced the old man abruptly. "Say what it is you must. I am turned to hear."

The solid blackness of the old man's eyes was deceptive. There seemed no iris, yet as Will looked, a small brilliance gleamed and grew larger. He put out his large steady hand, and spoke with sudden animation. "You are in deadly danger, friend."

"Of what, in the name of God?"

The old man sat down on the edge of a chest and gathered his worn crimson skirts about him. "When memory enters ancient night and moves beneath the waters of the mind, question becomes answer, betrayal is kept faith. Black is indeed white."

Will was seized by irrational panic. The panic mounted like a stormy sea. He fell into a rage. "Though I have nightly dreamed of encounters between myself and me, if what you say is true, then I stand more naked than a man unclothed. I say it is untrue!"

The old man hesitated, and then he added with a little sidelong look, "I know what you are thinking now; that many doorways open onto the garden of evil and which one will you dare."

The garden . . . Will was drenched in sweat.

"No, not so, in God's name!"

He sat on a three-legged stool, the owl on his arm, and, in the light of the single candle, stared at the old man.

The old man said softly, "Eros was an ancillary god. He did not rule in Olympus."

Will got slowly to his feet and coaxed the bird to her perch. Then he hesitated as though uncertain why he moved. He said in a light voice, "The garden does not tempt me."

He went toward the door but he looked back. The old man's gentle ironic eyes were fixed on him. "Be cheerful, friend. Even through the hollow eyes of death I see life peering."

Will stood between the two closed doors in the darkness.

What garden? The garden where hung the fruit of Hesperides?

He felt her flesh press against him, body to body, mouth to mouth.

He turned in the dark and opened the door of the old man's room. He held out the shreds of her letter. "Which is the sin and which the sinner?" The old man, who had not moved from the chest, merely looked at him. "Exorcise me this and I will go wherever your angels lead."

Will spoke in a white voice but the old man made no move. "Then bless me," Will said boldly, "and I will do the cursing."

He held the shreds of paper in the candleflame until they nipped his fingers.

CHAPTER *Four*

WILL moved in the cold morning light. He opened his eyes. Ned, on the same pillow, was watching him.

For a moment they looked at each other, all eyes. Will was defenseless with sleep. Then, pierced with uneasiness, he came awake. The questions in his brother's eyes were like primal forces: fire, thirst, tempest, frost. God's eyes. Will shut them out.

The city was waking. A scream, not of terror or pain, drew the street together like the strings of a purse. He had burned the letter, expelled the evil spirit and had the victory.

Below on the river was the sound of oars and of watermen's voices. The church bells began to ring with a loud purposefulness, not with that rapturous tongue of angels heard on the country road—yesterday? Paul's bell reverberated across the river.

Will listened for a moment, and said, because the victory was his, "Welladay—day . . . day." Ned stirred slightly, putting his arms behind his head. "Ned, zure we must stand on hoin legs, else no wool ull be soun in Warwickshire."

Ned turned his unblinking eyes.

"So, up!" said Will and flung off the covers. He put on his clothes and Ned watched him without moving, his head lifted by his folded arms. Will, dressed save for his jacket, said, "Up, up," and plucked away the pillow.

Ned, bare as a thrush, crossed his legs and continued his reflections. Ned seldom smiled. Ah, I used to smile. At twenty? At twenty, I had a babe. A golden child to be carried through the fields and by the river, while my wife gathered wild berries and fed us both. He shook the bed.

"Up, up," Ned murmured, then looked at Will with moody eyes. "Why?"

"Lad, do not play with me. We are men who work to live."

Ned said in a low voice, "I'll not play Calpurnia."

Will did not reply for a moment. He set out the mugs and cut the bread. Then a provoking anger seized him. "Your articles of apprenticeship are to me. I am your master."

The moody mercurial silence of this boy spread like a slow tide and became the substance of the room. His eyes flickered to Will. He blinked and the delicate skin beneath his eyes looked very white. "I am a man," he said softly, as though this answered both himself and Will.

"Who doubts it?"

Then, since Ned did not reply, Will asked again gently, "If you be so divided, why did you come back with me, old lad? This year and last?"

"Because you did—master."

Will smiled. He looked at this long fair brother with a lasting affection. He shook the bed. "I wish there were no ages between eighteen and twenty-three. Or that youth slept out the rest. Why does Calpurnia sit so ill?"

"Because I am a man?"

"Lad, lad, passion is both man and woman. Think of Jamie. What would I be without him for maiden passion?"

Ned muttered, "He's not yet a man."

Will laughed a little and kicked at the bed. "Up, up. Poor old boy, are you no longer young enough to have innocence with its humanity, or old enough to understand? Will you love?"

Ned's eyes opened suddenly.

"Then take off your swaddling clothes else I must treat you as a babe."

Ned looked at him with solemn eyes and said with an inflec-

42

tion almost as ironic as Will's, "I came back because I was our family's babe. Why did *you* come, long ago?"

Will poured out their ale. "Imagination," he replied at length.

Ned sat up and laughed. "Do not fob me off. You came the way I came—because you'd burst apart unless you did. And now you're famous, old, and rich, and what have you got?" Will waited, and Ned looked at him distractedly. "I don't know what you've got—I look about—I don't know!" He got up swiftly and struggled with his clothes. "In Stratford, something—but here? And what will *I* have?"

Will sat so silent that Ned looked at him over his shoulder. Will smiled. "Well, you can with careful saving buy a store, as Jacko Heminges has in Shoreditch, and set a wife to keep it."

Ned tried to put on his shoe and, growing impatient, hopped on one foot to pick up his mug of ale. Will spoke for him after a moment. "You're half ashamed of our cry of players; your heart's not here. And then imagination speaks through you in such large fair terms that you're no longer Ned. To play a woman—where's there shame in that? Shall I cancel your articles and you go home to Stratford, and keep a store with our father and marry a wife our mother will select?"

Ned muttered over the top of his mug, "She did not select yours."

"Shall I send you home?"

"Did you go home?"

"Dear lad, we are not one. Each sets his course."

"Did our mother select your wife?"

"I did not answer you, and I will not now, for you bait me and I will not rise."

Ned said softly, "I love Anne. I know she was got with child by you and she much older. Why do you put me off?"

"Why do you ask such questions now? You are breeding mischief."

"Mischief?" Ned looked at Will without guile. "What has happened? I was not home like you. You'll not talk of it. I want to know."

Will said sharply, "In the name of God, try me no further!"

43

Now all Ned's tossed and woeful looks gave way to bewilderment. He sat very still, with rumpled hair, sipping his ale and stealing glances at Will. Will, seeing him from the side of his eye, laughed in spite of himself. "All is well at home. All love you. All love me. The sun shines there. Soon the snow will fall."

Ned said softly, "It is unjust. You were there and you tell me nothing."

Will's anger rose intemperately, but instantly he put it down. If he could not justify his anger then he must not yield to it. "All's the same, dear lad. No difference. Each in his place. Though I did forget—Nan Fuller sent a token." He rose to get a ribbon bow.

Ned sat with it in his hands, looking at it broodingly. "I'm not witty and dissembling as you are—oh, that is not meant offensively!—but I am like you, and that is when we quarrel."

After a moment Will said gently, "Dear heart, you are a golden lad. Yet make sure that your resolution has no rotten canvas in it, else you will be tossed and helpless with only rage against the sea, and must come to any port to mend your sails."

"Like you?" said Ned irrepressibly.

Will rose abruptly. "Finish up and let us go. Else I will beat you till you hobble."

Ned said with an anger as swift as his brother's, "Take your Calpurnias to kingdom come! They cannot fool me any more!"

Will cried, "Boy, boy, did we invent the stories of our lives?"

Ned's fingers fumbled at his jacket. "I'll not give it!"

"What, lad?"

Ned snatched up his shoes and struck at himself. "Me, me, me, me!" He flung open the door and ran down the stairs.

Me, ah me, ah me. Will whistled through his teeth. Me, me, me, at eighteen or at six and thirty.

But it was more than that. He stood by the table leaning heavily on his hands. Too many questions had been asked. Why of him, a man so resolute to be elusive? Why now?

He stood motionless, compelled against his will to think of home.

Stratford, in its small and homely ways, its careful daring and its confined recklessness, was like a painted cloth against the wall. Fix your eyes upon it long enough, and its blunt and simple lines will say: This is reality, this is your life from birth to death.

He took up his hat and went down the stairs. When the door would not open readily, he struck at it and got a splinter in his hand.

It was strange that he could not precisely remember Anne, how she looked. Ah, there were her eyes, strange oblong eyes, and her slow smile.

Where Ned, in his anger, had gone was worth a shrug . . . yet Will yearned to know. Where would I go? Where would my son have gone had he not gone into the cold ground?

The day was unfolding. In the morning light, only the dirty river, sweet Thames, looked immortal. He stood near an open ditch, but he took no notice of the stench, for the river calmed him. It was already crowded with boats but less dangerous than the streets. The early sun caught at their sails.

He drew out the splinter and sucked the side of his hand. He waved to the women who had waded beyond the mud of low tide and were washing clothes in deeper water. They called to him that he looked well; was he happy? In the tenements and brothels along the river, life was waking shrilly. A man appeared in the doorway behind him, yawned, and, buttoning up his clothes, started on a sleepy lurch for a pail of water. Will crossed the ditch to stand on the wharf, and one of the watermen hurried to untie his boat.

"Not now," said Will. "Good friend, how goes the world?"

"Older by half. And thine?"

"Ah, my world is but a word put into a breath."

Another waterman, dressed in his sailor's blouse and his loose breeches, coarse hose and flat shoes, fitted cap and flat hat, was fishing from his boat. He called across, "By cock's bones, it's fine weather for friars. Will there be crowds and crowds today to welcome you back? What will you play?"

"*The Merchant of Venice.*"

"Good enough."

"What brings thee business best: comedy or tragedy, friend?"

"Crowds."

Will laughed, but the waterman said sharply, "If we suffer, you suffer, so who laughs? Who cares for us? Who cares for you?" He swept his bare arm toward the other side of the river. "Those great palaces, look you, lapping at our river, giving not a farthing for our suffering. Great Essex smelling so sweet, and great Earl Pembroke and little Lord Cecil, and all else—all the way to the Queen!" His jabbing finger marked the palaces to the bend of the river. "They care better for their dogs, though, by hell, their dogs suffer too!"

"We bear it or we change it," Will said.

The waterman looked up at him. "Aye. You're not one of the great. You care. We know it, all. A caring man, we call you."

"Do you, now?" said Will, pleased. "Aye, I care." He stood for a moment longer on the river wall watching an old woman bent double, groping in the mud for coal or wood, rope or bones. As he watched, she held up her hand with gibbers of delight, showing a copper nail. She held her basket breast high as she struggled toward the landing stairs, her torn garments stiff with slime and scarcely covering her.

Will went down the steps to give her a hand, but she hunched away her shoulders until she heard his voice.

"You?" she said, and gave a cackle. She held up her basket. "Feast won, fast lost." He tore away a brass button from his doublet and put it into her basket. She crowed like a cock, her old throat shaking to the sound. Then she kissed his hand, leaving slime up over his cuff.

"Well, missus, where's thy son to keep thee out of the cold mud?"

"Dead drunk."

"The button's not for him to sell."

"Aye. God 'ove 'ee. Bless 'ee—bless 'ee!"

"Fair weather after thee!"

He dipped his hand into the river to wash it clean of slime, and crouched there on the steps for a moment, looking toward London Bridge. Bearing its load of houses, it seemed to float diaphanous in the misty light. And the river, sweet Thames, was a clear excellent highway out of the filthy warrens and murderous lanes of the city. Three swans drifted by, careless but expectant, and the waterman who sat at Will's feet broke up part of his bread and threw it to them.

"Ah, they feed me, when worst comes to worst, yielding those great necks."

"Gaol for thee."

"Not too bad a place when the winter winds blow down the river."

Will asked with curiosity, "Think you not the Queen feels our hunger?"

The waterman thrust out his lips, grimaced, shrugged. "She suffered once—not a clean petticoat, 'tis said, but to all her gilded cods, poor forked man's no better than a radish! Eat him and belch."

Will stood up, shaking dry his hands. All these, watermen, women, and swans, the great palaces on the far bank, the breweries, the wharfs and the Steelyard of the merchants, there side by side, and St Paul's rising behind like a strange old bird, measured and defined this world that was grafted on him. The other river, Avon, wandering through meadows, had the same dayspring upon it, the same sun. The same humanity. The same wonder. Might it be the same world?

A midden cart creaked past with its load of garbage and its cloud of flies. The old soldier driving it had lost half his face for the Queen. He greeted Will with a crack of the whip. As Will passed, the load of stench was heaved into the river.

Will went along the river wall as far as the Paris Garden Stairs, where he stood for a moment watching the barge of a great noble family pass in the river. Its standard and the bright livery of its rowers were like flower petals against the river mist. Music came across the water from players behind the curtains. Will watched its course, as allusive as thought.

He whistled reflectively. Bear this and bear all. He jangled coins in his pocket and kicked at trash in his way. Outside the Cardinal's Cap, the brothel's boy servants were playing with tops. Will stopped to watch and advise. And then he turned over a keg to sit for a while and chat with a beggar who was disguising his child's leg with pustulant sores. Other beggars, crippled and verminous, sat against the brothel wall eating their bread. They held out their hands for a greeting, not a coin. He kissed an old woman who could not see him but knew his voice. All, all had, as he, seen the spider steeped in their drink.

The stench rose from the beggars and from the bear garden nearby. In the bear garden, the barking of dogs and the huddled sounds of the bulls and the bears compounded a misery.

A heron suddenly rose overhead, and he watched its flight to the marsh. The high tide covered now the coarse grass and reeds of the marsh, but it was there, to be thought of . . . the home of wild fowl.

He rose, too mindful of the vile world to be at ease. The river flowed on, unmoved by this day in which animals would be torn to death, thus rendering some men insensible to the sharp barbs within their own selves. He said goodbye and broke to a run. But the rank smell of the garden followed him all the way to the Globe.

Well, so be it. Man was the human condition. The incongruities of that paragon of animals became the quintessence of dust. To understand this was to pluck out a mystery. On the edge of the field he stopped. A few late cornflowers were here as lovely as Homer's sea.

He found Gus Phillips in the Housekeepers' Room, computing figures and adding new ones. His keen, tanned face was gray in the early light. His eyes were opaque. He had looked up with a deep frown, but the frown passed when he saw Will.

Will sat down opposite and drew to himself a schedule of figures. "Could it be that thirty and six are magic numbers, and so explain a world part jaundiced?"

Gus looked up. Then he smiled with half his mouth. "I am three and thirty years old. Is that also a conjunction of magic to explain what's ill about *my* heart?"

Will laughed and picked up his pen. "In the cold light of London morning, I see us as we are, men of small account. The world is made up of high and low, and we are low. Will you, in good stomach, say Amen?"

"Amen." Gus added a figure, scratched it out, added another. "God jokes with us," said Will and rose to walk about.

Gus watched him. "Have you ever thought how often you write of banishment? Kings banished, Proteus banished, Romeo, princes banished. From what? Hearth and home. I come home to London, you do not. You come to banishment. Sit you down and mend these figures for me."

Will leaned over to study the figures.

"How are Agnes and the little ones?"

Gus gave a groan of melancholic protest. " 'Those dulcet sounds in break of day that creep into the dreaming bridegroom's ear and summon him to marriage . . .' "

"Aye, that is the play today, but not your part. But, the little ones were glad to see you?"

"Oh, they! We kissed and kissed. They had cold little knees and I warmed them, all in my lap." Gus's rare sweet smile studied the table for a moment. "Oh, she was glad." He smiled faintly. "It is only that she has been so ill used so young and fair with three. Another serving maid will mend her hurt."

"Dear Gus. You, of all men, should have a loving, tender wife."

Gus made a rueful gesture. "I reckon that I got what I bargained for."

Outside a bolt was drawn with a clatter, and then came the sound of footsteps and voices. Will went to the door and set it open. In a moment Sly and Condell, leaping up the stairs four at a time, catapulted into the room. Presently Armin and Pope, embracing cordially in the doorway, efficiently blocked each other's entrance.

Will Sly was handsome and snapping today. He said cheerfully, "All but my first three lines have gone gone gone. What comes after, 'Let me play the fool'? Hal can't remember no more than me."

Will tossed him the play roll. "Why, next you say, 'My little body is aweary of this world.' "

Even Condell laughed. He went to the table and saw the foolscap. "Ah, schedules, plans, money, plans, money, money. Beautiful."

Sly let the roll unwind to the door and held it high above his shoulder, humming to himself. "Ah, I remember it all, and every other part as well. When shall we begin?" He wound up the roll.

Pope said tartly, "When Lord Chamberlain Hunsdon gets done asking foolish questions of Dickon and Jacko."

Will said, "How are all wives and chicks?"

"Oh, very well," said Condell quickly. "My Elizabeth—" A slow smile went over his face, but he said no more. Then to show how well he felt, he swept Sly off his feet and shook him in the air. "This fool thinks he will not marry. God save him."

"Put me down," Sly said calmly, "or I'll kick you where you'll be no more use as husband." Condell lowered him hastily. "Bring me Elizabeth's sister, and I'll marry her."

"But she's got none!"

"Then I am safe." Sly brushed himself and linked his arm with Pope's. "Coom along, dear old Tom. You'll explain all things to me. It's line six from the bottom I can't quite get the hang of. You'll say it's really my mother I'm missing when I forget it and that'll set everything right. 'Master young man, I pray you, which is the way to master Jew's?'"

Phillips replied in an offhand piping voice, not looking up, "'Do I look like a cudgel or a hovel-post, a staff or a prop? Do you not know me, father?'"

Will intervened with a clatter. "This is too rich a sauce. You'll all sicken your lines!"

But Sly, firmly propelling Pope, who was shaking with laughter, said back to Will, his black eyes full of mirth, "'It's a wise father that knows his own child.'" Then he returned. "Are you bustling in buskin today, Will?"

"Not if five penances and ten Pater Nosters have worked as they should."

"Ah, Will, whatever sort of actor will you make, man, denying your gifts?"

"Your questions are slyer than your name, dear soul."

Sly laughed. "Nay, you be not too bad an actor, if we make enough hurly-burly to drown out your voice."

Armin said, "Oh, come, come, Willy Sly, be done."

Sly protested, "He knows I love him, hey, Will? Then who plays Antonio?"

"Hal."

Condell looked up to see if anyone wished to make what of this.

Sly whistled. "By St Genesius who prays for actors! Can ye wear a fashionable melancholy, Hal? The black velvet cloak with the crimson sleeves has suffered a hurt."

"Aye, that I know." Then Condell addressed Phillips, with a side look at Sly. "It's three pounds, thirteen and six due on its refurbishing. Will Sly gave it a dunking last spring."

Sly grimaced, shrugged, made a penitential gesture, and disappeared. Phillips wrote it down. "—and sixpence. Pay it out today, Hal, from the receipts."

"Aye. Before he dunks it again. At the Fortune, Alleyn'd have fined Sly most the price of the cloak."

"Oh, Alleyn's a tyrant and moneylender," Gus said cheerfully. "Sly owns that cloak as much as you or I. Sly'll pay up for you if you split your fine breeches."

"Me?" Condell looked incredulous. Then he saw he was being chivvied and smoothed himself down. "What gets into Sly?"

"Tearing high spirits," Will said, sucking his pen. "No wife."

"I'faith," said Condell, gravely considering the shape of his legs, "she *was* right glad to see me."

"And the baby?"

"You know, she looks just like her mother," he reflected. "Tonight there's a churchwardens' meeting. Will I be wanted here?"

Will smiled. "No, we'll listen to the midnight bells for thee."

"Ah, the bells." It was a shy smile on his large handsome face. Then he added in a burst of happiness, "That's another reason Elizabeth is such a good wife. She doesn't mind the midnight frolics in no way."

When Burbage and Heminges arrived there was one minute to spare. This minute was used to convey Lord Hunsdon's greetings, which Dickon delivered in a brisk, precise duplication of the Lord Chamberlain's voice and manner. Then, without pausing for breath, he cried, "Why are we waiting? Men and boys, smartly now! Up and about!" He clapped his hands and stamped his foot, and then he could not keep himself from laughing. "Are we mad to go on this afternoon? We've not done the *Merchant* for six months. Do we remember a third of our parts?"

Will said with an awful look, "We will!"

As they went down the narrow stairs to the stage, each took note of the dust in corners, of cobwebs, wormholes, or any evidences of poor housewifery. Gus drew in and out the curtains of the doorway to see what dust could be shaken out.

Will saw Ned sitting on a stool, his lips moving, a play roll in his hands, a deep crease between his eyes. Will touched his shoulder, and glanced down at the roll. "Prince Hal. Why not thy part today, dear lad?" Ned hunched his shoulders. "By God, you are a baboon, Ned!" He was still sore and annoyed when he looked about at the players whom they had left behind in London, and who were now eager to be harnessed once again. But he put on a good face and greeted them all, going from one to the other, as Gus was doing, and Heminges and Burbage, shaking hands and inquiring after their health.

"Where's Gib?" Will asked at last.

Gib, patiently waiting against the door, said, "Close as thy shadow."

"Good. So then, Dickon?"

Dickon wished Ned's stool and courteously extracted it. Then to Condell he said with a brisk wave of his hand, "Proceed, my lord."

Condell said promptly with no inflection, " 'In sooth, I know not why I am so sad: it wearies me; you say it wearies you . . .' " and so on until it was Sam's turn to say, " 'Your mind is tossing on the ocean.' "

"More mmmmercifully, Sam," said Heminges, his master. "Salerio is cccheering his friend."

"And, Sam, forget not the position of hand and arm," Will said. "Good lad. Hal, might it not be proper to advance there by a pace, and still hold thy position? Much better. Gus, the Jew has been waiting for such a time as this . . .".

The rehearsal's only flaw was that each remembered words and gestures differently. This led to a courteous lunacy, for everyone was good-humored and quite adamant about his own memory until capitulation came suddenly on a second thought.

"Nay, what a fool! Sure as my life, he came as you say . . ."

"But now I know certainly that I played this above looking down. Gib, made you no marks? Were you asleep?"

They were irreproachably courteous while outcrying each other. Gus picked up his viol and played softly to himself. In the end, Heminges enforced discipline. "Will wrote a ppplay that is ppproof against all fffools save ourselves. Let him tell us what is bbbest."

So Will made a firm selection from the plethora of remembrance, and each was glad to have his giddy moment brought back to the fold, though with a few backward looks.

". . . as I do remember, things went poor in that scene, Jacko. Did we not mend something there, Gib?"

"I do know that Sly's hat looked like a pancake, and how could I have seen that except from above?"

Will whistled amiably.

"Perhaps he was on his knees, praying to remember his part."

Will stood up and put aside his stool. "If there were five ounces of brain amongst us, butties, we'd all be on our knees for a space. Every man is an ass out of harness. Nay, sweet friends, have not the sullens. Let us sit down and render a just account to ourselves. Now, no one here is more nor less than an actor, whether he be the great Dickon, or our Jamie whose voice is uncracked. Sit here, Jamie, and pipe for us a soft little tune. Now. We are the best players in England. We are good friends. We bear each others' fardels. We are also feared. We can make a fool of a man quicker than he can of himself. Good. So we must rehearse again from the start. And, I pray you, forget the country ways of your summer. Dickon was right. You take to them as ducks do to water. Yet it is the actor's craft to charm into life, to transmute and communicate the image of drama. And you lads, Jamie, Sam, Edmans, Ned—your voices, your manners, your movements—I recommend a diligent study," and he made a farcical face. "Let discretion be your master, all. Now, once more, I beg you, fast but well spoken."

So it went until noon. Will blew hot and cold on his author's patience. "This is not *my* play," he was heard to mutter dolefully once or twice, but when a gesture or an inflection translated an intuition or an innocence, he struck his hands together and embraced the nearest man.

Gus sat on the steps leading down to the tiring room studying his lines when he was not speaking the words of Shylock. On the stage, Burbage now and then exercised the splendor of his voice, but mostly he kept it at a walk, though he made gestures so beautiful that they went beyond all formal expression. Jamie, who was Portia, was so radiant that even Sly put his arm around the boy's shoulder. Armin unleashed a bit of business for Young Gobbo which Dickon expunged before a moment had passed with no ill-feeling on either side.

Ned played Nerissa with a calculated stiffness. Will demonstrated to him how to walk, to hold his skirts, to curtsey, but Ned held doggedly to his stiffness, stumbled, fell, and then looked straight at Will, and said, "Play it yourself."

For propriety's sake, Will boxed his ears.

The sun stood straight above the open roof. The porter moved about the pit, throwing rushes on the ground and giving his advice.

When the last word had been spoken, they stood uneasily looking at Will. Burbage, hoping to cast the first vote, said, "Well spoken, well acted. A bit more nimbleness in the kneejoint of words, but that is all." Then he too glanced at Will and did not hurry away to the dinner that now took his thoughts.

Will expelled a deep sigh, smiled and stood up. "By the Lord," he said devoutly, "we are the best even when we are the worst. Sam, give over Salerio. Is that a hard thing to ask? Gib must play him. We cannot do without Gib in the trial of the Jew. He must be on the stage where every last man can hear his promptings."

Dickon flew into a rage. "Death and damnation! I told you, lumpkins, fools! Oh, we are undone—quite undone!"

Will said patiently, "We'll button ourselves up in time, Dickon. But for tomorrow, I recommend *Julius Caesar*, which, God willing, must be fresh in your country minds."

"Will, soul," Sly coaxed, "take on you the Prince of Arragon—you've got such elegant manners—and then I'll have only Gratiano to remember."

"No, let it be." Will laughed. "Look fresh and merrily, my lads. The world is not lost! Good hearts, I trust you all. Now let us go over a few matters. Gib, could not we have a bench for the Jew in this scene? Gus, what of that? Shall we fiddle with your speech? Make it more to the point?"

"I've fiddled as it is," said Gus. "I think it wants going back."

"Nay, it needs shaping more to yourself. Dickon, you've made fresh marks in the casket scene. Very pleasing."

Dickon, still flushed and uneasy, cleared his brow miraculously and made a jerky little bow.

"Jacko, I will mend that speech of yours where your old stammer will not give you rest."

" 'Ttttwas trying to remember where I moved."

"Never mind." Will rolled up the play and slapped it against his leg. "If anyone says we lack perfection of form, butties, we will say Praise God, we have something far better than that: we are resourceful and undaunted. Now go and pray. Gib, a word with you."

Gib took shape at Will's side. Dickon said, "Will, a word with *you*. We're not going to prayer but to thy new play. We'll read it at dinner. Time hath a whip at our backs. The play must go on this day week."

Will rolled his eyes. "Well, what about it, Dickon?"

"About it? Oh, rare. Too much laughter, and not enough lines for me; too many jokes at the expense of our friends. Pope will get carried away by what's set down for him, and Gus will make a great ninny of Malvolio." He burst out laughing and put his arms around his bridling friends. "But after we've taken it apart and put it together, it will serve."

Will looked at Gib. "We are as moonstruck, Gib, as Starvling, else how could we put up with such a foolish life?"

"Oh, at supper, after the cries for Burbage, and the shouts for all others," Gib mocked, "Dickon will preen, and Sly will caper, and you will grin like a fool."

"If the miracle does not happen, and we gibber instead?"

Gus answered drily, "When the saints were banished of England, St Genesius hid."

Will laughed. "You hear, Gib? For the sake of St Genesius, write the plot large on a board and hang it in the tiring room where we can see it plain."

"Shall I put sound notations on it as well?"

"Does it help? What do you say, all?"

"Oh," Hal said, "sometimes we can hear stamping or noisy business when we cannot hear the words."

"As you say. Well, Johnny Factotum, lug us all, keep it going, even if you must dance a jig in the middle."

Gib nodded. He might indeed have to dance a jig.

CHAPTER *Five*

DINNER finished, Dickon said, "Well, what think you, Jacko, Sly, will we grow rich from this new jocundity of Will's?"

Heminges said, "It is good all around—good for us, a good play. Faith, I lllove you, Will! You go hand in hand with nature and money in the box!"

Will smiled and patted him. "Tasty words, Jacko. For them much thanks." He rose.

"Will, a moment." Dickon cleaned his knife and put it in his belt. "The new *Hamlet*. Shall we say meet tomorrow and all give our thoughts? Agreed all? I know what we must have: whatever outstares Alleyn. Will, there is a way to use the ghost which can *dumbfound London*."

"There's a smear on thy cheek, Dickon. There, dear old boy," Will said.

Dickon hissed in his breath and then laughed craftily. "Never mind." He took a handful of figs. "John Marston would write this in a flash of lightning."

"Good. Set him on it."

"And have him run straight to Alleyn for a fatter fee?"

Heminges linked his arm with Burbage's. "Dickon, lad, you do suffer. Will'll ease thy pain; he always has. Come now, wwwalk and tttalk with me."

Will loitered, crossing the field. Ned drew up, his hands in his breeches. Will said, "You're a fool to be rude to me at rehearsals."

Ned said, "I burst."

"There's your swordplay and singing—bad—and the Five Positions not yet learned. You are far from a man of gentle ways and pleasing voice."

"Ah, that comes!"

"If you do not act the fool!"

Ned said very low, "If we do *Julius Caesar* tomorrow, I'll not be womanized."

Will smiled at him in a studying way. "If you would learn, dear lad, what women have to teach us you'd make a better man."

"What kind of women?" said Ned carefully.

"Valiant, witty ones—the best there are."

"In London there are tarts and foists."

After a moment, Will said with ironic tenderness, "I see now you have too fine a beard for Nerissa."

Ned said huskily, "What shall I play tomorrow?"

"What will you love? For love you must. Cinna the Poet?"

Ned struggled honorably to think of himself as loving Cinna the Poet.

The Globe pennant had been raised to the flagpole on the roof and snapped in the wind. Up from the river, across the fields, the crowds were swelling, all kinds of men and women, all degrees, lords and apprentices. Ned said in a voice oddly like Will's, "I would be very thankful to play Cinna the Poet."

"Take him in your mind then," said Will as he bowed to a playgoer who had nudged his neighbor and cast looks at Will.

Having bowed once, he bowed again and again. Some thrust out their hands silently, some called him by name. He was all

57

smiles and bows and love. He did indeed love them. The color mounted in Ned's cheeks. His eyes were bright. Hands were thrust to him also, and he bloomed and bowed. Will said, bowing, "Then Cinna let it be."

Cresting themselves up from the river like damask swans, or like great birds spreading their satin wings, came nobility and their masked ladies. A rustle of scent went by and Will suddenly drew in his breath. The smell had assaulted him. Of all the senses smell was the greatest conjurer. Taking him unguarded, the strong sweet perfume raised a ghost. He forgot Ned, he forgot the crowds that knew and watched him. He turned like a mechanical man. The rustle went by, a gentleman he scarcely knew, but the scent had done its work. The scent had been the scent Lord William had always worn.

I am ashamed, Will said urgently to himself. What strange fits and starts are these? Lord William was no longer either friend or enemy, merely a man who had seduced his mistress. Yet Will stood for a moment longer like a man recovering his balance in a high wind.

Lord William was the youth who had courted him like Jupiter with a shower of golden coins and praise. Lord William was the youth who had courted him for the mind's love and the honor of poets. Lord William was the youth who knew that a woman, a wife, a servant, even friends could be commanded but a poet never.

Lord William was the youth to whom he had confided his midwinter madness and whom he had asked to speak a word in his favor to his mistress the witch.

That was all done with now, all, all the madness that now seemed a fevered sleep enjoined by spirits terrible and all the spelling charms of the body and such daubery. For only through such witchery of lust, he told himself ferociously, could he have lost all sense of the world's fixed stars of season, form, office, custom of men and planets.

He looked at Ned not seeing him. He who should have been on guard morning, noon and night, knowing so well the world and the flesh, caught by a scent! He had exorcised a letter but not the man who had walked in, at his own request, taken his lady by the hand and, with smiles and bows, led her off to bed.

It was no breach of faith, he told himself. Lord William is a sensualist as common to the times as poetry or the Indies. Lord William is as high above me as the stars and took a lady of his own orbit. Equal with equal copulating is no breach of faith.

Will felt like a man who had forgotten the loss of a leg until he tried to stand on it.

Humiliation had been the cruelest blow of all. That he who knew so well how to live within the formal and ordained structure of class and degree had so yielded to his mind's confusion— he could scarcely yet believe that he had done it. She and Lord William had not humiliated Will: I did it to myself.

Lord William was lust in persona!

Will turned back toward the river. But there before him was the Earl of Rutland debouching from his boat. Lord Rutland was Lord William's cousin. Will rubbed his hand violently over his face. By Venus, Cupid, and Priapus, I forgave the seducer in three summer sonnets—though, stupid youth, how could he know what I forgave?

"And he replied in alexandrines that were not bad, not bad at all!"

"Who?" Ned, enthralled and dismayed, had been watching his brother's face.

Will looked at him sharply and tried to lash his foundering thoughts. "Run, let us run! Some men are fools by birth and some by education. But the saddest are those who instruct themselves in nonsense like your brother."

"What has happened?" cried Ned, running beside him.

"Mad boy, the play cannot start without us!"

"Will!" Ned grasped his arm. "If I have offended, I ask thy pardon, and that thou put it down to—to—oh, whatever thy love says."

"Oh, Ned. And I, thy pardon—!"

Will went at a stumble up to the Housekeepers' Room. There, cribbed, confined, he would be safe. He sank onto a stool and looked at the wall. He heaved out a laugh. Safe? There was no danger that he did not have fully in hand! He sat there shaking with laughter, and rose only to lock the door.

Promptly at three, a shutter opened high overhead, the Globe's trumpets sounded, a kettledrum crashed, and Gus's voice spoke like God in the country plays.

"Good people of London, and high-born gentles, all. Know ye that we, the players of the Lord Chamberlain, will play, with your gracious permission, the comedy of *The Merchant of Venice* by William Shakespeare. In it will be said many wise things, and some merry, and a new song, never heard before, will be sung. Now frame your minds to mirth and merriment, which bars a thousand harms and lengthens life, good gentles, all."

Will, his head comically in his hands, said aloud, "Witty, wise, and merry—that is me." Then he heard Hal Condell's voice far away.

" 'In sooth, I know not why I am so sad . . .' "

And presently he heard the stormy shouts, applause, and stamping that greeted Burbage. He drew in his breath and rose to unlock the door.

Yes, Dickon had it best. Among the Inns of Court, and the courtiers, and all the fashionable world, was a saying, "He is not a gentleman who does not know Dick Burbage." Whoever you might have been born, still not a *gentleman* until Dick Burbage, son of a joiner, out of Warwickshire, lent you some of his luster. Burbage, transforming and illuminating, bore a faint resemblance to God.

A resemblance not to a peer—for nothing could alter the fact that he was, by law, a vagabond—but to God.

Of no one else could this be said: not of Alleyn, nor of himself, whatever his private struggle with the nobility. This was a nice reflection, objective and ironical enough to restore his equilibrium. In time, a flourish of trumpets closed the first scene, and in a moment Gus Phillips appeared, bearded and gabardined.

He did not sit down but stood in the door saying, "The galleries are filled, and the twelve-penny rooms. All the stools on the stage have been sold. For that we'll offer no thanks, since

Lord Ashley has filled them with a party that will stick in our throats."

"What else can you expect from a come-lately lord. He's still too near to trade to behave with decorum," said Will, sardonic with his newly memorized humility. "But I fancy Jacko has his eye on him." Then he asked calmly, "Who sits in the Lords' Rooms?"

"There is a rumor that Lord Essex inquired of a friend's friend what the bill of fare would be, and, by God, a prodigious light of greatness is playing over the left Room today. I think it does not come from Lord Southampton alone."

"Ah. He is here? An old patron returned. And who else?"

Gus said briefly, "Lord William."

"And who else?"

Gus turned his long bony face and said with a thin smile, "Are you asking about the witch? Ask outright. And then I can say I did not ascertain, being a prudent man."

Will looked down at the paper before him and blew out his cheeks.

"Curtain-drawer forgot his mask." Gus laughed. "There was a shock to see a strange bare face on the stage. Gib gave him what-for and tied it on for Judgment Day." He listened for a moment, his head turned aside. "I must be gone. Ah, one more thing— that money-gatherer by the stairs must be watched. I saw him scratch his head and drop a coin down his neck." He shook out his gabardine, and Will heard him going down the stairs.

Will rose and leaned against the window, looking at the sweet river which made smallness of fears. Once, as a boy, he had run away to Naseby to find where the Avon came up from the caves of the earth, and he had walked by a trickle till it turned to a stream that, a river at length, led him home.

His father had beaten him, but later owned that to follow all the way home was a rare summat . . . For the Thames he would walk on his knees to the Cotswolds, praying each step of the way, if it would bring the innocence back to his heart.

He picked up a pen to lay out the schedule to talk over with

Gus. The laughter and clapping, the raised voice of Burbage, came to him like the sounds of the sea. He heard another scene come to an end, and presently Gus returned. This time he took off his robe and laid it carefully by. He sat down facing Will, and drew the ledger toward him. Then he remembered something and stood up abruptly.

"This was sent you by Gib."

It was a letter. In familiar broad calligraphy it read, "If you come not tonight I will harry your soul."

All of her he could remember—all, at that instant—body, smell and tone of voice.

"God's body," said Gus, seeing his face, "I did not know what I was handing you."

Will shook his head. He folded up the letter and thrust it aside; he began to speak to Gus of the schedule. But he got no further than the length of three breaths before he stood up and walked about.

"Gus, I have exorcised by fire and water. But I have not cut out my guts, and that is where I love her. Can I live if I cut them out?"

Gus made an effort. "Your philosophy . . ."

"A stale dish on a cold platter!"

Gus watched him do nothing and did nothing himself, though he scratched his pen up and down.

At length Will laid both hands flat on the table.

"Give me leave. Have patience."

"Holy Child, I say nothing!"

Will drew a sheet of paper toward him and took up his pen. He hesitated only once or twice. When he had finished he glanced at Gus, who could not, for his life, pretend to an interest in business. Will read aloud:

"Thou blind fool, Love, what dost thou to mine eyes
That they behold, and see not what they see?
They know what beauty is, see where it lies,
Yet what the best is take the worst to be.
If eyes, corrupt by over-partial looks,
Be anchor'd in the bay where all men ride,

Why of eyes' falsehood hast thou forged hooks,
Whereto the judgment of my heart is tied?
Why should my heart think that a several plot,
Which my heart knows the wide world's common place?
Or mine eyes seeing this, say this is not,
To put fair trust upon so foul a face?
   In things right true my heart and eyes have erred,
   And to this false plague are they now transferred."

Gus did not speak for a moment, then he said with a valiant calm, "You call her a whore."

"Yes."

"The bay where all men ride. She will kill you for it."

"No, I will kill her if necessary."

"Think—oh, think again! Her rich kinsmen—and Lord William!"

"Gus, some things can only be borne with a killing."

"Or gaol!"

"It is done."

"What?"

"I will be free."

Gus reached across for the poem and tore it up. "There is your warranty of freedom." Will beat softly on the table.

"Your incontinence is now with words!" Gus cried.

Will took the torn pieces and fitted them together. Then he wrote them out again on a fresh sheet. Gus set his lips.

Will struck a flint and lit the candle. "Incontinent? Not at all." He took the letter and burned it. He smiled at Gus. "I aroint the witch." Under the candleflame he sealed the poem.

Gus scarcely looked up from the study of his laced fingers. "As a woodcock to thine own springes . . . poor fool."

Will went down the stairs and stood back of the stage where two limp actors sat against a post, and two others stood, their cheeks together, whispering in each other's ears. He pushed aside a curtain and mounted a few steps of the ladder which led to the stage. The curtains, forming a room in Portia's home, concealed him, but he could see Gib behind the property rack where his voice would be available to any actor who stepped back for a prompting. Will heard the sweet music of Jamie's androgynous voice, " 'Let it presage the ruin of your love, and be my vantage to exclaim on you,' " and Burbage's reply, " 'Madam, you have bereft me of all words; only my blood speaks to you in my veins.' "

When the scene ended, stagemen came onto the stage to hang a painted canvas of a street in Venice, and Gib came to the ladder. Will put the sealed letter into his hand.

"See that my lady has this."

A voice, not an actor's, rang out profanely.

"Lord Ashley," said Gib, "enacting a lordling." Will looked about and stepped aside for Heminges, dressed as Old Gobbo, to mount the ladder hastily.

Gib fumbled at the seal. "Women are fools," he offered. "I will sit you down to a tale sometime—"

"Not I," said Will. "What are the demands on your prompting?"

"Mr Burbage forgot, but no one knew. Mr Heminges groped and mumbled but all believed him. For the next scene, pray to the devil."

At a flourish of trumpets, Gus Phillips passed them and went onto the stage. The audience caterwauled. His altered voice came back harsh with passion. " 'I'll have my bond, speak not against my bond!' " Gib motioned to a stageman and gave him the sealed poem while he found his place in the prompt book.

Heminges came down the ladder, a massive grip on the sleeve of Lord Ashley but his manner smiling. Lord Ashley was stout and drunk and filled with dislike of all lower orders.

"The Jew is a dog," he said, speaking louder than Gus.

"Aye," said Heminges richly.

"He is a wolf! Hang him!"

"Aye."

"I have him on the hip!"

"Another gentleman has him on the hip, sir. Leave it to him."

Lord Ashley struggled for a moment. Heminges drew him with composure across the pit and to the Lords' Door. Their voices rose clearly above Gus's, which fell to a staying silence.

"Who is it? Dare I trust him?"

"God's mercy, my lord. It is the Lord Gratiano assisted by the Lord Bassanio and the Lord Antonio."

"Friends of mine?"

"Aye, bosom friends. There you are, my lord, safe in the hands of your mother." All waited till Lord Ashley's servant had taken him in charge, and then Gus's voice was heard again.

Will returned to the stairs which led to the Housekeepers' Room. He paused halfway up and opened the door to the gallery.

Some in the audience were coughing from the fumes of tobacco, some were cracking nuts, some were loudly telling their neighbors what should be watched on the stage. Orange and nut sellers were relentlessly hawking, and sellers of books were still pursuing the literate. A brace of nobles made a noisy return to their seats on the stage. These latter play-lovers shifted their stools, talked among themselves, lighted their pipes, examined the actors with sudden icy languor, and yawned till all their blackened teeth showed.

Will stood behind two masked women. He stared at those lords on the stage, at their earrings, their pearl necklaces, their beards of fantastical shapes and dyed however they chose. Then he lifted his eyes to the Lords' Rooms.

There, leaning on the window frame of the Room to the right, sat the Earl of Southampton in the sunlight of white satin and jewels, his fair hair reaching his shoulders. Will's eyes lingered for a moment . . . His first patron, his first tutor in the necromancy of privilege and position. They too had been twin souls, Will thought with affectionate irony. To this Earl he had dedicated his published poems.

Rest in peace.

It was the other Room which commanded him now. There in a consummation of black velvet and jewels, his dark hair reaching his shoulders, his head as erect as a heron's and crowned by a jeweled hat, sat Lord William, the very compendium of that power, place, and prerogative which had been an intellectual abstraction until this moment.

Will studied the narrow, proud, beautiful face of him who had given him patronage, honor, and now his own pride. . . . Incontinent with words? He smiled. He was made continent by pride.

Love was a rebus, a play on words. Sensuality was all that was held in common by high and low, and even that in differing aspect. For the lady's sensuality had been demanding, Will's presumptuous, and Lord William's careless and taking.

Only humanity had been injured.

Will turned and, unnoticed, flexed his stiff body. He had expelled all evil spirits. He stood on a rock that nothing could shake.

Above all, lest he forget, he too was a gentleman, his status lawfully affirmed with sealing wax and ribbons, coat of arms, and coin of the realm exchanged. He could greet that splendid youth, leaning on the edge of the window ineluctable as day, with a calmness and courtesy that was unshaken of motion.

The lordlings on the stage had stopped their card game and were counseling Bassanio and Antonio on the proper treatment of Jews. One picked up a rush and tickled Gus when he drew near. Will knew by the jerk of his head that Gus was provoked. Will narrowed his eyes. He knew the true names and titles of Tybalt, Proteus, Gratiano, and all the play-nobles who walked onto this stage out of life.

Gus Phillips loved this Jew. " 'I'll not be made a soft and dull-eyed fool.' " With what wounded humanity did Gus invest him. He placed on all the words of Shylock a triple meaning: sinner, victim, and survivor.

Some in the gallery were calling for quiet, for the penny-payers in the pit were stamping and dancing, crowding around the edge of the stage, one catching Gus by the ankle, one setting his dog to bite at his heels. Yet tomorrow they would weep with Caesar.

He looked a last time at the Lords' Room—the Room which concerned him (let Lord Southampton be his own star to whoever sat concealed behind him)—and he itemized what he must remember: there sits a man who holds much power to injure me; he is hot-tempered, his appetites may be called impersonal and fastidious lusts.

Will studied him a moment longer for his own self-respect and equilibrium.

A woman's white hand moved out of the curtained shadows and rested on Lord William's shoulder. The young man barely turned his head and his listening expression scarcely altered. His eyes remained fixed on the stage and his lips moved in the briefest answer. Lord Rutland, bright as a macaw, cried out something, but Lord William quieted him with a swift move of his hand.

Oh, Will, remember all this well! Lord William loves my words, the best part of me. I, in turn, have given this lord a true Christian love, for I have seen him as a man. Let this suffice and so move on, for the longer you, a fool, stand here, the more will your murderous poem, your eyes watching the white hand, your art tongue-tied by authority, bite like fleas on a dog and you'll scratch to no purpose.

He moved. His hands were wet. The outer mechanics of this inner truth became crude and clanging. Lord William's full glory blazed as though Will had been vouchsafed a vision. On second thought, it was clear he must avoid Lord William at all costs today.

Lord William evidently felt some intensity which drew his attention from the stage. He frowned and glanced about him. Suddenly those dark brilliant eyes looked straight across the gallery.

On the stage, a nobleman's watch struck loudly.

Will drew back. One of the lads ran past him to warn the musicians above of their cue.

In the Housekeepers' Room, Heminges had wedged his large form between the table and the wall and there he was reading with moving lips the schedules that had been drawn. He lifted his brows at Will. Will sat down across from him and took out his dagger. He tapped it against the edge of the table and smiled at Heminges. "Dear old master." Heminges pushed forward the bags that held the day's receipts.

"Well, soul, count up."

He emptied one bag. After a moment Will untied the other. Will said, "Let us give Hal Condell charge of our play rolls. That will be one less task for Gib, and Hal has a taste for common sense and keeping shop."

"So? Good. I too have got a mmmind to shape him up."

In the distance the music of Belmont gave place to the voice of Gus speaking the epilogue. Heminges divided the computations, so much for the shareholders, so much set aside for the wages, so much for Sly's cloak, so much for the poor.

The noise of the jig, and Armin's falsetto, came up to them as Heminges put his mark to the last division. Gus's voice rose in thanks and farewell as Will agreed with the sum.

"A fffull house," said Heminges. "We're ppproperly home." Then he raised his brows and listened. Playgoers, released from confinement, burst like a dam. He rose and stood by the window waving his fingers to their backs as they hurried across the field to the river where the boatmen had already set up their cries. "God bless thee, lambs, come again."

The bells of Southwark clanged, and Paul's across the river, a tone out of place, took up the call for vespers. Daniel, the curtain-drawer, fighting his mask, came with a gift and a message for Will.

"This purse yere from my lord Southampton, and a cob calls hisself Sir Giles Harcourt sends to speak with ye."

For a moment Will held the silk purse on his palms and then he laid it down by Heminges with a pat. "Shall we or shall we not help Sir Giles?" he asked with a laugh.

"If they're in gggood condition only," Heminges said, looking over the top of his spectacles.

Sir Giles was a young man who danced up and down in the sun and spoke in a terrible hurry.

"Ah, there you are—ah, yes. Ah, they're fine smallclothes and a doublet and a cloak and—ah, yes—hosen—all complete—bought last week—won't sell them for nothing, but devil's teeth, what will you give me?"

"How oft have they been worn, sir?"

"Not over once. No wine spilled, no dagger holes—"

"Five pounds."

68

"Done for six."

"Sir, we had two elegant outfits of you a fortnight ago."

"Ah, God's murder, give me the five. Send tonight. Give me the five now."

"By your leave, sir, money and goods at the same time."

Sir Giles swore and trotted off to find his servant. Gib, coming to Will, said, "You have been sent for to the Lords' Rooms."

"Which lord?"

"Lord William."

"Presently."

"Presently is soon said."

"Gib!"

A flower and feather of lordlings bore past on their way to the river. They did not speak to Will nor he to them, for some wore such an excellent shine that they could scarcely see their own image in their own brightness.

Lord William's brilliance was of a different metal. Will had been wise to have his second thought. An encounter must be avoided as though his hope of salvation rested on this abstinence.

"Why do you wait?" Will asked. "I will come by-and-by."

"That too is easily said."

"In the name of God, what is it, Gib!"

"It is you—your face! Confound them. Let them go!"

"Let who go?"

Gib hesitated. "That skinny little heifer and her friend."

"Thou elvish-marked abortive rag of honor—!"

Gib said hotly, "Have it your way!" and turned abruptly.

Will sucked in his breath noisily and took a strong grasp of Gib. "Forgive me. I ask your pardon. Has he sent in the name of both? Do both wait for me?"

Gib's hard, shining eyes saw into Will.

"Calm yourself. He put her in his wherry, under his pennant, with his rowers making toward Whitehall."

Will's hand tightened on Gib. "Befriend me again, Gib. Take whatever reply suits your discretion best. I will not come to him. Say I am sick."

"I'll say you've fallen into a fit," said Gib drily.

Gib broke to a run and Will turned away, whistling through his teeth.

With no deep surprise at fate's caprice, he saw Lord William coming down the path toward him.

CHAPTER *Six*

THEIR eyes were on one another. In remote and individual regions faint shocks were noted, inexplicable to Lord William's unclouded brows, clear as lightning to Will.

Will came to a halt some distance from this fair youth whose hand flew out like a bird. Will bowed.

For a moment Lord William did not speak. Then he said, "The exact—the ineffable word—to magnify the meeting of poets, it eludes me! I came to look for you. And by the holy mercies, you rise before me!"

Will touched the jeweled hand and his natural warmth could not be repressed. "How does your lordship for this many a day?"

"Well, well!" Lord William grasped not only Will's hand but also his arm. "Oh, I have hungered in thy absence. A man's love and friendship are like a house; all manner of things come in and out but the love remains sure. A man's love to a man has truth and strength. Oh, I see you now as though new-perceived, your humane gaze, your movements forever arm-in-arm with life!"

Will wondered if this youth had no heart or too much sensibility. Which was it, and which had he forgiven?

No more be griev'd at that which thou hast done . . .

Take all my loves, my love, yea, take them all . . .

Loving offenders, thus I will excuse ye:
Thou dost love her, because thou know'st I love her . . .

Lord William waited eagerly and Will summoned up his careful schooling. "My lord, your merit has my duty strongly knit to show me worthy of your sweet respect."

"Ah." The youth turned his face this way and that to the

70

setting sun as though calling up spirits unseen. "Shall I tell you what was in my heart before I saw you coming down this path? I thought that poetry is the elixir, the bread of life. He who has a poet for a friend has been brushed by immortality. Nay, you have been my father; it is you who fertilized my soul. Yet standing alone I was washed by a sudden fear. I heard the beating of wings which belonged to no earthly bird. Intuitions, intimations, wild surmise—" He lifted his hands in their scented gloves. "Lo, they passed, and my heart ached." His hot dark eyes were smoldering, his hands were as swift as birds. "And then I saw you."

He was taller than Will. He looked down at him, and he smiled. "I love poets more than I love women, for they feed my soul and thus lead me faster to heaven." The color mounted in his cheeks. "Dear master, can a poet be separated from his poem? By heaven, you're scarce a man—more a thought, more a synonym for pure meter!"

Will knew that nods and smiles and murmurous sounds would serve him for some time. His heart was neither cold nor warm, it merely beat. Yet compassion was not absent; this youth, the seducer, had called him *father*. Some jokes are made in heaven. The beardless face and tender worldly mouth were as expressive as a running brook. The hands spread and moved, unaffected by his gloves: hands, whether in marble or bronze or skeleton, or living ones in motion, might be called Lord William's devoted obsession. Will listened and murmured and marshaled all his itemized remembrance for his defense:

This youth was the heir of a third earl, paternal grandson of one of those industrious and serviceable men whom the Tudors had ennobled, but son, on his mother's side, of a family that owed its origin to King Henry III. At ten he had caught the Queen's fancy, at eleven he had startled his father with a Greek ode composed by himself, at twelve he had disarmed a famous swordsman, at fifteen he had come down from the University and had also killed a man. At eighteen he had sired three children by three women. At twenty-three he had given to Will an aquamarine set in gold filigree and a gold-handled dagger, thus establishing his patronage. At twenty-four years and six months, he had reached out his hand for the lady.

71

At his present age, twenty-five, he commanded without speaking; his train of followers who dined with him, trooped after him in the street, marked his enthusiasm in the theatre and applauded as they saw fit, were composed of young men with titles equal to or older than his own, but it was he who ruled. The average Englishman was short and swarthy; Lord William was tall, slender, dark, and beautiful, with princely manners and exquisite form.

On his black velvet doublet diamonds were sewn. On his legs were boots of the softest leather which rose to his thighs. Above them great puffed hose blossomed like flowers and around his head bloomed a stiffened collar like a calyx. Beneath the collar hung a necklace of gigantic pearls, and in one ear lobe hung a great pear pearl. Yet he was no hermaphrodite, Will knew to his blessing. In this age of paradox, he might dress as gaudily as a woman and be a man, be both brutal and kind, coarse and delicate, might chain violent activity to a motionless pleasure, and the effect would be as clear as logic, an aspect of that singularity of the human equation.

Will's smile flashed. How glittering and taking was the paradox of the human equation! Lord William, caught in a reel of hyperboles, saw the smile and laughed, a sound charming in its youth and lack of artifice. O God forgive all us fat geese, Will thought, and yet I will be most crafty, sir, until I know the rules of this game.

Lord William took him by the arm and raised a call. His cousin, the Earl of Rutland, answered the sound like a tame hawk, and thrust his head around the theatre door. Lord William, his bird in hand, started toward the river.

"Wait! Wait!" called Rutland, half in and half out the door. "Heigh-ho, lads—Will Herbert, come quickly. Tom, whip thy ass!" and then he motioned frantically to Lord William. "Wait—wait—there's still Dickon and Sly!"

"No," said Lord William proceeding across the field, his color high, "we are on our way. Here's all that counts for good measure."

Will made a wary joke and Lord William laughed again. One

hand still held to Will, and his happy flow of words became as charming and ingenious as a work of art. He paused for nothing; in a narrow alley a woman stumbled over a doorway to get out of his path, and her curses followed them.

Lord William said in his high clear voice, "I have had an ornament made, set in three rows of pearls, with my portrait in little. My servant has it in his purse. It is for thee, my heart's friend. Do you know why? Hark.

> What hast thou then more than thou hadst before?
> No love, my love, that thou mayst true love call;
> All mine was thine before thou hadst this more.
> Then if for my love thou my love receivest,
> I cannot blame thee, for my love thou usest;
> But yet be blam'd, if thou thyself deceivest
> By wilful taste of what thyself refusest.
> I do forgive thy robb'ry, gentle thief,
> Although thou steal all my poverty;
> And yet love knows it is a greater grief
> To bear love's wrong than hate's known injury.
> Lascivious grace, in whom all ill well shows,
> Kill me with spites; yet we must not be foes."

Will heard with no change of countenance. With an unwelcome clarity he remembered the sacrificial energy that had set down this poem and sent it from Stratford on a summer day that should have been devoted to reinvesting his lost manliness. Instead he had yielded to the sickly need to please, a need that fed the very ill which should have been interred with hasty obsequies.

"It was a fair day, three months ago, when it came to my hands," Lord William said in his artful voice. "I had been hawking and my mind was filled with rhyming thoughts of my sweet haggard. All fled. I committed thy poem to my heart; I abstained from all food till it was mine."

Will studied him. *Heard you nothing? Heard you no cry?* He struck a smiling blow. "It is rarely that a poet hears his poems spoken with such indigitation."

73

It was said so sweetly that Lord William's startled gaze had no place to rest. Then, with shining animation, Will talked of woes and wonders that perplexed the poet, of etymologies, syntax, gallimaufrey, compoundage and antonyms till Lord William could only nod and nod. It was a nice revenge, though taken against the wrong man. I am my own culprit.

Behind them the others were strung out like a necklace: Rutland, Sly, and Sir Thomas Levenson running to keep up with themselves, Burbage and Lord Herbert quiet and firm in the rear, the lords' servants following with their lords' swords, themselves heavily armed.

Lord William's barge, painted with garlands and gilded, his pennant at the stern, the rowers in pied-green livery, rocked with the tide. Lord William stood with his foot on the wale and motioned off Rutland and Sir Thomas Levenson.

"I'll have none but the great poet of England. Take thou the boat."

Rutland cursed cheerfully and hitched Sly and Sir Thomas aboard. The waterman cried, "Eastward ho!" as a greeting to Will and to Sly, and waited till the caparisoned barge of Lord William had pushed onto the river. Then the others followed, merry as roses. Rutland possessed himself of the waterman's lute and began the sad song of *Hero and Leander*.

The sun setting behind Westminster filled the sky with gold. In the palaces along the riverbanks, lights were appearing like beacons: on the river stairs, goings and comings marked the end of day. All the great ships below London Bridge stirred with the evening breeze, and all the little boats between the bridge and the bend in the river danced as though an angel had brought them good news.

Lord William sat in his plumed and jeweled splendor grasping the side of the barge. He looked up the river, and turned his head to look down, and lifted his face to the golden streamers of cloud. Will thought, *In action, how like an angel.* His irony mounted. Action meant gesture and appearance, meant stance, poise, animation of body into which is fused the very soul of the man. Action meant the use of voice and limbs in playacting. By inexorable

74

logic, Will stripped Lord William of animate power and made him a part of the illusion, a heart of the seeming.

Lord William was crying, "Ah, there is no other place in all the world where God has so set his seal," and he looked wonderfully young as he spoke. "Behold our ships going to the edge of the world, Englishmen hold the universe in their hands."

It was a quickening cry. Will's nimble and piercing glance saw what Lord William saw. Lord William's voice, lifted against the river traffic, was youthfully shrill, "There is nothing we cannot do! Tell me of new wonders to test my wonder."

Will called in reply, though the mockery in his tone was lost, "New heavens, new hells?"

The bells on both sides of the river were ringing their endless reminder of men's need for redemption.

Lord William replied gaily, "New fashions, new laws, new elements, new poems, new sermons!"

"Charity cold," Will said, looking beyond London Bridge where, Gib had told him, a sea-thief had died yesterday at Wapping Stairs under three tides in his chains. "Nothing good but by imputation, justice disannulled, the moral abandoned."

"Speak clearly, master," Lord William cried. "I cannot quite hear you."

"Ah, the right is wrong, the straight crooked. Find out for yourself."

"Still your voice goes on the wind!" But Lord William had perhaps caught a word or two, for he looked now at Will with a puzzled frown as though a trusted hand had left him to founder. He called sharply to Rutland, "Sing something else, you fool: that breaks my heart. Sing *O Mistress Mine*."

It was Burbage, in Lord Herbert's painted boat, who replied with the song. The rowers set their strokes to his fine voice, and they all joined in the chorus. Will lowered his head and smiled. He who spits against the wind, spits in his own face.

They came ashore at the Three Cranes tavern. Little boys held the boats steady, held tenaciously, like hawsers, although the liveried men tried to push them away. Beyond them on the hill loomed St Paul's, its blackened stump of a tower lowering over

75

the warren of dwellings that ran to the river. Lord William dismissed his barge, but his servant, with his master's sword, stayed close at hand. Rutland, Sly, and Levenson sprang ashore, and Rutland continued to pluck at the lute till the waterman reclaimed his instrument.

Lord William had walked a pace ahead and now stood looking up the river, his expression changed.

"I feel," he said, "a change of wind. I feel that you have flicked at me. I feel a strange disquiet." His dark eyes moved suddenly to Will and his stiffened hand rubbed the diamonds on his doublet. "Yet is it not I who determine a change of wind and others who agree?" He asked in a low voice, "Do you not love me?"

Will saw him as he might never see him again: a little frightened. Standing against the evening sky, his hauteur was unbowed but in his eyes was a sudden desolation. At that moment Will saw how hopeless it was to lay his burden on another man. Lord William had been shielded from all pain. He lived in a solipsistic world, the lord and owner of his face. Will thanked his angels that he himself could feel both fright and pain.

Will answered gently. "Does truth change with alteration? I think not."

"Altered? Who? Thou or I?" He was still troubled.

Will could not resist a thrust for himself, but so benign that its point could pierce unnoticed. "Why, the eagle that was swallowed up by the sun, my lord."

Lord William frowned. Who could take offense at comparison to sun or eagle? He hesitated for a moment longer. He half drew a ring from his finger, then he thrust it back. An alteration came to his expression. He flung his arm across Will's shoulder. He had a little dagger of his own.

"Poets are England's glory," he said with a bell-tone in his voice. ". . . thou, Plautus of our time . . ."

Will bowed his head to hide a smile; he could not for the life of him withhold his admiration for the precise counterthrust, even though its purpose might be to cut him down. Plautus! In Lord William's world, a writer of plays was not a poet. This was very devious and clever. I am a poet by sufferance only; my trade is

76

plays. I am a gentleman by sufferance only; my status is at the mercy of lords and law. It was so subtle and wicked that he looked at Lord William with new eyes. Lord William was watching him with sixteen generations cooling his gaze, though his smile was tender.

All foolery was past. Mutual courtesy was the only emotion permitted lord, lady, or player. As surely as Lord William knew the names of all his forebears, so did he know how to keep a man like Will in his place.

Will bowed.

They might sup, get drunk, go arm-in-arm with perfect ease and intimacy (save he must never call Lord William by his Christian name), but let this Plautus with his quasi-coat of arms take one step across the bound that custom set as dark and absolute as God's watch of man, and he would find a humiliation more soul-burning than if his breeches tumbled down.

It was not easy to know when the dark bound had been passed. And why in hell's name did he care! He watched a flock of scavenging birds rise untidily with cries of anger at each other. To care was to immure himself in his brain and so waste night, day, and time. With or without the favor of this noble effigy of gilded generations (and his sideways glance immured Lord William), he was still a lamb of God. Was this heartless? No. I am a poet; that is God's gift to me; all else is the world's comment and caprice.

How relentless and infallible must be the study which taught one how to love one's enemies. What disdain of power yet what balance; for to lose a master, one must not gain a foe. He could hear Dickon say, *Does the mouth tear the hand for lifting food to its face?*

This youth was also the lamb of God. Let me strip him to the soul, where we are equal.

Lord William, so sensitive to a change of air, and richer in craft than innocence, took Will's arm and talked suddenly of the countryside, of a spring day when all the lambs were on the hillside and the blossoms on the trees, present dissension wiped out by two shepherds blowing on their pipes.

77

Lord William slipped his party into Five Foot Lane and, by a skillful use of alleys, into Knightrider's Street. The traffic-glutted streets required all one's ingenuity. Around the conduits and the bakeshops women clogged the roads with gossip. Street musicians filled the mouths of alleys. Carriers' carts and coaches would neither retreat nor give way, and coachmen and carters rose to shrill invectives. Noise was as omnipresent as the air: the shopkeepers' stout-voiced callers, the beggars with their clappers, the cries of vendors, the scandals shouted as newssheets, the filthy jokes flung at strangers, wove a net of noise to catch and trip them all.

They passed over Walbrook ditch. The sewage had choked the wooden pipe and overflowed the street; they stepped aside and went on. For some time the noble lords had held their poncet boxes to their noses, but now, in compassion, Lord William bought bouquets of rosemary for the others.

In St Paul's Churchyard, the booksellers were closing their booths, but Lord William sent his servant to halt a man who had a volume on which he had set his heart. Will looked up at the fire-blackened stump of the tower and wandered off where it led. When Lord William turned to him for his opinion he would not be at hand.

He had healthier friends in the ragtag of the cathedral. Not a vendor nor bookseller failed to call out to him, welcoming him back, nor he to answer. His nimble spirit freshened. There was not one here he did not value higher than a lord: the impecunious gentlemen who hung about the nave of the church hoping so cheerfully for invitations to a meal—they would repay with wit and good heart; the coney-catchers who wore parsley in their hats as impudent proof of their power to pluck their poor human rabbits—they winked at him and in full light picked the purses of the two-legged country coneys who gaped in all innocence at the carnal hurly-burly. Honest men all.

Here in the aisles were the mercers' stalls, and the drapers' stalls and the goldsmiths'—merchants wearing their hats in church. They loudly called their wares, and greeted him, using the font or the tombs as change counters. Ale and beer were sold, and kisses. Apprentices looking for work, soldiers looking for patrons, clerks looking for fees, whores looking for lovers, all cried their needs under the roof of the church.

The organ began to play. It had no effect upon the roar of tongues and feet. When the choristers raised their voices to sing the vespers, they remained as remote as angels.

But Will listened, reaching through the carnal noise.

Oh, the tawny smells of countryside, the fragrant colors of the winter meadows, the titmouse singing in the dry hedge—his wife standing in the door. His wife . . .

He looked at her fleetingly in his mind's eye and turned away. But he felt her looking at him still, and with a lurch of heart he stared up at the blackened roof . . . She had known him from childhood. She had known his wild dreaming youth. She had loved, yielded, married, and obeyed. . . . Oh, hateful sin, grounded on sinful loving. Oh, those sealed false bonds of love which robbed a marriage bed of its revenues . . . if penalty was the size of sin, then she must despise, ridicule, and cuckold him.

He heard Rutland calling his name, and Rutland's running steps. The Earl talked twelve to the dozen about a book of love that a bookseller had hidden under his counter and would not sell for bribe or honest money.

Rutland led Will out of church. "He says not even to the Queen's grace would he dare to sell it," he cried in his bright quick way, "and then he whets me so with part tellings and sketches of the hand that I'm half mad with twitches. What can I set on him to make him give it up?"

"A hundred gold nobles."

Rutland laughed. "Fie, for that I'd write my own love-book." He offered a sweet. "Of writing, I've something to ask, now we're alone. It is—how shall I say—a joke, a jest, a jingle, a lampoon. Will you do it for me?"

"Against whom, my lord?"

The Earl did not reply for a moment. Then he said softly, "No one known to you."

"Then I do not hate him. No, my lord."

The Earl did not look at him. "I'll pay you well."

"Pardon me, no, my lord."

79

Rutland took it in good nature. He called up his servant with his sword, and used it to whiffle their way through the crowds of Newgate Street. "Hell's breeches," he shouted cheerfully, "my cousin knows all the short ways. We should have held to him." He looked over his shoulder at Will. "How did you step on his toes? He went off in a thunder saying I could bring you or not as I chose."

Will made a contingent gesture. Rutland drew him down a side tunnel and laughed. "I'd pay to see that again—himself so out of face. Tell me, my friend, is he through with the lady thy woman?"

It was a blow made gross by its carelessness. Even Rutland looked startled on second thought.

"Godamercy, did I raise a ghost? Well, never mind. It's more likely she'll tire of him first." Then, pricked by some kindness to scramble on, he asked with a side glance of his little blue eyes, "Why ever did you set him on her—aye, I know all, he talks to me waking and asleep. By God's cock, you know how he uses women, else you've spent your time blindly as his bosom friend."

Still Will did not answer, and Rutland said after a moment in a thoughtful voice, "Yet, by the devil's codpiece, it is piquant. My grandmother had a groom who lay with my aunt. That was a merry-do, for they loved not wisely but very well. He was whipped and she sent to a nunnery. Oh, oh—I am a great fool but I mean it kindly—some must be whipped but not all, 'fore God! And your lady will go to no nunnery, unless it be the London kind where two pairs of shoes stand beside the bed."

He could not stop talking, having confounded even his own kindliness. "You could have trusted a woman to me, for I know about the heart though you may not think so. My cousin knows only horning and hot backs." Pulling desperately at the reins of his indiscretion, he brought himself to a slow halt. "Though his lute music is uncommon good. Are his poems equal?"

Will spoke with an effort. "Very fine."

In a voice made gentle by his good heart, Rutland said, "He honors you as he honors no other man . . . But that does not say what I mean very well."

A man with a basket on a stick went crying past them. "Bread for the poor prisoners of Newgate, for Christ Jesus' sake!" Rutland put his fingers in his purse to give out a penny. They passed through Newgate, and from the grates and holes of the prison in the wall they heard the lamentations of the prisoners. "One penny, for Christ His sake, to buy some bread, to buy some bread!"

Will tossed all his pennies through the grate. By that movement the stench seemed to rise and mingle with the stench of the street.

Lust and violence, rape and war, like knife and fork, lie down together. For a moment Will's gloved hand covered the lower part of his face, his rosemary forgotten.

Two horsemen filled the street and the Earl, forced back against the city walls, cursed at one of them by name. The horseman turned and waved his riding stick in glad surprise.

Will longed to feel his way home like a blind man. Rutland had a tight grip on his arm and leaned against him as he cleaned off his breeches where the horsemen had fouled them. Then Rutland found that some nip had cut his breeches and taken his purse. He swore and burst into laughter.

"By Jove, it's that foist, Nick Jennings, and his woman. I saw them yonder. See, they use no tools. Did you ever see so neat a nip?" He stood for a moment holding out his pantaloon, lost in admiration. Then he fastened his hand on Will's sleeve and, starting on, knocked others into the gutter as was only fair all around.

Will said quietly, "By your leave, my lord, I will not go on. I am indeed not well."

Rutland looked at him, full of surprise, and then sharp suspicion, and then compassion. He stopped short. "If you do not, you will put me to great confusion. For I must then say to my cousin that I have injured you and that will compound his anger."

"You have not injured me, my lord. My indiscretion is my enemy."

Rutland stood soberly in the middle of the street where the houses met overhead and eternal gloom lay below. He put his hand under Will's arm and jigged it up and down gently. "You deal with yourself too unkindly. The blood rages, we purge ourselves. Well, we are men. Praise God we're not eunuchs." He glanced at Will. "No, I will not be put off. You must come and soothe his anger in your way. God's teeth, man, what are women but orchards and fields. You pick them and plough them." He started on abruptly. His compassion, which was of a simple kind, had done what it could.

Will hesitated. For that brief moment, in the bustle of Holborn, he dwelt in a region of choice: he could suit himself or he could suit a belted earl.

He lingered as long as he dared, playing with fancies.

CHAPTER *Seven*

THEY came into the Paschal Lamb together.

Lord William sat facing the door, his passionate passivity (the paradox that enhanced this paradoxical youth) confounded now by an outraged pride. It was as plain as words. He stared at the two, he offered no greeting. His stare was hard as flint. His hand flew to the jewels on his breast.

Rutland, pausing to select a pipe from the rack on the wall, said, "A bum-bailiff stopped me with a writ. Will talked him from the writ and me from striking him dead."

Will felt a crow of awful laughter. Was the world, thank God, made up of lies juggling with lies? For if the heart saw only the heart, or thought addressed truth, where could Will hide? He shook hands with Lord Herbert, pulled at Sly's forelock, and bowed with playful formality to Burbage.

Lord William's expression cleared at his cousin's words. He rose and put his hand on Will's shoulder, to draw him toward the seat at his left hand.

At his right was a man whose hand Will seized and wrung.

"By heaven, sir, how do you do, most honored sir?"

"Well, most well and heartily, good sir, and greetings to you with my heart!" And then they both fell silent, smiling, for Lord William, between them, created an inhibition. Yet their relation to each other was, Will thought, far deeper than either's to Lord William. This was a man endowed. His name was William Camden. Nature had domed his brow, rendered his voice so portentous that his Yea or his Nay was enough, and then seen to it that he was small, brisk, and genial. He had written in Latin *A True and Royal History of England,* which had made such a subtle defense of the old Queen's actions that they seemed the acts of God. Moreover, he wrote of England as a part of the world, not as an island fog-enshrouded in the North Sea. He loved plays and he heard music, and he held poets in high regard, as his smiles and nods to Will affirmed.

But more relevant to the moment was his authority as Clarenceux King-of-Arms, which had granted and confirmed to John Shakespeare, father of William, the shield and coat of arms that made a gentleman: viz., in a field of gold upon a bend sable a spear of the first the point upward headed argent.

Though such a shield was nothing to be trusted in a crisis—viz. this past hour's dilemma—yet to preside at the fabrication of that quasi-species, a gentleman, entailed an intimacy as deep as a doctor's. They continued to smile and duck in little bows, and ask half-questions and receive part replies, for nothing more could be attempted with Lord William's hands on each.

However, bows and smiles served them well enough, for Will had a present need to draw assurance that Plautus was a man of sensibility. Why had he not said Seneca? He muffled a laugh. He would ask his lordship.

But at the moment Lord William required an absolute concentration, for he was consulting with the landlord on the proper diet for an ill man of sanguine humor. It took Will a moment to understand that this man was himself.

The landlord, washed and brushed to a lustrous consistency, his rat-colored stockings tight and smooth, his shoes shining, was well informed of the esoterics of food. He understood with great nicety the relation of time to the four elements and the four humors in their particularity to food, and Lord William shot at Will frequent little glances to judge his susceptibility to heron, porpoise, congers, anchovies in wine, roasted apple, beer, cheat, manchet, and cheese, as each was considered and decided on.

While this ceremonial proceeded, Will, glancing at Camden across the huge sleeve of Lord William, heard him say *Stratford* without opening his mouth. This mixed joy with despair, but mostly joy, for Stratford was a fact not a dream. Stratford was a house built in honor, was gardens and orchards, barns and lands; Stratford confirmed without a doubt that Will was husband, father, son.

"There," said Lord William drawing off his gloves, "you have put yourself in my care, and I will care for thee."

Down the table, Burbage and Lord Herbert had their heads together, and Sly and Lord Rutland were playing darts with the center board. The other guests were three modest baronets who suggested a close affinity with a fashionable torpor but gave their orders for supper with alacrity.

The Paschal Lamb was filled, but Lord William's table drew the honeybees. A noise of fiddlers snatched up three-legged stools and put them close by the fireplace, and a singing boy took his place behind them, all as close as hope to a lord and his purse. Lord William paid no conscious heed but his body and his breath appeared to mingle with the music.

The figures in the painted hangings on the wall quickened in the light, and the eyes of one glittered as though through a peephole a man was peering out. Will nodded and winked, turning himself slightly in his seat away from Lord William to watch that glittering eye. Though I am here a legal vagabond, he confided to it, while at the same time he smiled, nodded and joked with his friends, have I not cut the golden jesses that held me to Lord William? 'Fore God, do not my lands and barns, my pleasant walks and orchards say I am free of all servility?

Lord William raised his hand to the white-aproned waiter. "And garlick on the salad, but not for him." He then loosened his dagger and put it by his right hand, and took his napkin from its case in his pocket and laid out his golden toothpick.

The noise of fiddlers and the singing boy were adamant as stone to keep their petition in Lord William's ear. They gave no ground, though they sat in the way of the waiters who cursed and kicked them covertly.

Lord William sighed contentedly, shifted his feet so that the rushes on the floor sent up a fragile scent of lavender, bowed his magnificent hat, and said grace. Scarcely had he picked up his knife before a fellow with keen eyes and a smell of poverty knelt and slipped a poem between his right hand and Camden. The fellow said softly, "I cast myself at your lordship's feet and beg for your name on this poem."

Lord William glanced at the sheet held to his eyes by the shaking hand, and struck it with the back of his fist.

"I pay only for quality."

The fellow pled in a low voice, but Lord William shook his head and called to his cousin Rutland while the fellow still begged. Without warning, the fellow turned his eyes on Will and in them was all the pain and loss of gouged sight.

Will gave a little grunt. He could not look at the fellow. To see him as a man violated humanity. To see him as a man lay too close to the nerve, and marked that great gulf between those who had and those who had not. Those who had crossed the gulf dared not look back at those who had not. There, but for the grace of God, go I. But by turning away his eyes he had wounded himself in a way no balm could heal.

He sat there answering some syllogism of Lord Herbert's with a witty splicing of words, though he could not keep his sliding eyes from the poet who loitered, with a baited look, studying the Earl of Rutland.

Will also looked at the Earl of Rutland for a moment. How crookedly the young Earl's cheek and mouth were joined. Then with great deliberation he looked at Lord William, and saw the skull beneath the beauty. Finally with the same calm, he turned his eyes on the others, one by one: Camden, intellect rampant; Lord Herbert, a deadly nightshade of a youth; Sir Thomas Levenson, who stole other men's jokes and reputations; Burbage, Sly, jolly, jolly; one called Sir Piers Dalglish, who, judging from his suit of solemn black, was patron of the cult of Melancholy;

one called Sir Roderick Parry, unplumbed; one called William Shakespeare, unfathomed. All weaving glances in and out that entangled them in some relentless pattern.

It was a moment made of stone. Within the grip of this world were all functions and movements arranged and ordained; within this prescribed and merciless armillary of custom and convention was crooked the genius, Man.

He dropped his gaze to the bare boards of the table, simple, scrubbed, themselves, and honorable.

Speech flowed through Lord William, whose shoulders moved, whose hand became even more articulate, whose brows were raised, who clutched the pearls at his throat. His ornamented speech came to an unfinished epigram: "Plain dealing is a jewel—" which he offered to Will with a touch of urgency as he opened his spice box to add keenness to his sack.

Will saw the hungry poet staring down at Rutland. "But they that use it," said Will, "will die beggars."

Camden smiled slightly and glanced at the fair young lord to offer whatever disinterested comfort might be required. Will wondered whether the lady-witch would reply to his sonnet. He did not know which he dreaded most, a reply or no reply. But if he did not first punish her, then she would be very hot to punish him, and his soul was sick for peace.

"Ah," Lord William said, "beggars only if they eschew the constancy of friendship."

Will smiled. "But look you, my good lord, how friendship is constant in all things save the office and affairs of love."

Lord William drew his brows together and a slow color mounted in his cheeks. He glanced piercingly at Will and then sideways at Camden and then beyond at whoever might have heard. Rutland had heard. A look of bald humor flashed but was kindly put out. He closed one eyelid at Will and tossed his cousin a sweet to suck. Will thought: When did she receive the sonnet? Did she read it aloud? Did Rutland observe any change in her manner? He watched as Rutland pushed away the poet. The man stood isolated, in a kind of desolate dignity, the poem stiff in his hand.

Will rose, beckoned the man, drew him into the corridor. In silence he read the poem. Forced into a formal meter, it strove to beat its way into a wild conjugation of forces. Will stood silent for a moment, the words of the poem fluttering like a bird in his mind. The poet fastened on him an angry look. At length Will nodded. He stared at the poet and the poet stared at him.

"I will do what I can," Will said and fished out a coin. "I am no better off than you save that lords protect me for the moment. Do not be too nice. Keep at them, and I will do so too."

The anger in the poet's eyes did not abate. He took the coin without a word.

Will returned to his place at the table. Lord William watched him with a frown. The frown said a man might be sick but he must not be ambiguous.

Will had no comfort for him. Will had given this youth a meticulous devotion; he owed no more. He was twelve years older. Lord William had called him *father*. He would bide his time and extract a miraculous draught of fishes for the hungry poet. So much was owed to Will.

He drew out his stool so that he might have a word with Camden. Camden inclined his ear.

"Tell me, sir: What makes a gentleman?"

Camden raised his bushy brows, and a peculiar look came on his face, composed of caution and amazement. His lips parted but he said nothing, and then a glance of perfect shrewdness leveled the space between them.

"Like yourself, sir?"

"Very like myself. What do you see when you look at me?"

Camden's short, spare body was very erect. The mighty dome of his brow was smooth as silk. "I see an amalgam, a man supple but not sinuous, gentle but not sharp, self-possessed but not thrusting himself forward, sanguine but not choleric, keen but not sharp, a concinnity of parts like an instrument in tune."

Camden spoke with such sweet composure that for a moment Will did not laugh. Then he did.

"That is a very artful answer, dear sir, but not what I had in mind."

Camden went on quietly, "Whatever there may be of tumults, cataracts and insurrections within thy private kingdom, I know not. Only the eye of heaven knows."

"You will say no more?"

Camden put up his hand to stroke his beard and thus muffle his words. "Sir, I am the priest of many mysteries. Probe them not. As a man, I seek a just account of men, and yet how intemperate, shifting, and unjust are all the forces of the world."

Will wished that he had not asked his question, for the answer had been no reply, and had left him with the uneasy sense of a gentleman teetering on an heraldic bough. What was Camden not saying? He returned the look with a half frown and a tight smile, and then brought himself and his stool to his former place, no better off than before.

Lord William, the turn of his head indicating that he was aware of both men behind his back, summoned up his authority like a dinner. In a loud clear voice he announced that he would set the subject for discussion: it would be the metaphysics of cosmography. He took off his hat, stroked his lovelocks for a moment, replaced his hat, glanced sideways at Will, whispered, "How are you feeling?" and gestured to Rutland, who gave indications of speech.

Rutland ventured onto the slippery ice of man's divided nature. He kept his balance by recollecting for their benefit a poem much admired by metaphysicians. " 'I know the heavenly nature of my mind, But 'tis corrupted both in wit and will . . . I know I am one of nature's little kings, Yet to the least and vilest things am thrall . . . and, to conclude, I know myself a man, Which is a proud and yet a wretched thing.' "

Will ran his fingers through his hair and glanced at Lord William. The poet stood by the door quietly tossing up the coin, his expression washed with hunger and contempt. Lord William's eyes were roaming and his left hand lay on the back of Will's chair. He listened to Sir Thomas Levenson, who looked wonderfully young and hopeful as he cried, "Nay, am not I—man—the noblest substance in all the universe—noble in reason, infinite in faculty?"

But this Sir Piers rejected in a dark voice, his eyes on Lord William only: "Yet vile and abject unless he raise himself above humanity."

Sir Thomas rallied, and spoke out of no text but with great animation of the vitality of men and the sensuality of women. Sir Piers shrugged and said that this had nothing to do with the metaphysics of cosmography.

The poet looked suddenly at Will, smiled with the side of his mouth, spat, and disappeared.

Sir Roderick Parry, sitting beside Will, had been silent, his eyes closed, as he swayed slightly with the singing boy. Now he opened his eyes and fixed them with a living blueness on Will. He said in a soft singsong, "I could tell thee tales a hundred."

"In God's name, do!" said Will. "If they be true tales of men and women."

"Aye," said Sir Roderick, "of men who bleed and women who weep."

"Yet to ask questions of heaven is divine," Will said after a moment. "Could there be such another time or place in the history of the world?" He looked about. "Yet I would mend the looks of these so that, if cut, they bled . . ."

Sir Roderick looked at him obliquely and smiled faintly. The reflectiveness remained in his eyes. Will turned away to the painted hanging where the tribulation of Susanna with the elders was set forth. . . . He wondered with sudden fear how the lady-witch would strike. . . . Alas, poor old men, their rectitude and sobriety wantonly displaced by quivering thighs and shaking breasts. He gave them his warm sympathy.

As his eyes traveled over the painted cloth, he saw his friend John Marston sitting below the least elder, and there, below the painted bush which hid Susanna, was Thomas Dekker. They were not dressed as gentlemen, but were shaven, decent, sentient, watching Lord William's friends with fixed attention.

Marston wrote plays like a filthy angel and Dekker like a seraphic devil, and they lived where five shillings was a king's ransom. Will saluted them, from his secure place, with a modest gesture.

No change came on Marston's saturnine face, but Dekker's moon-face unclouded, and he rose with his tankard in hand. Then Marston rose also, and obeying what life had taught him— to take the field with a rush—came swiftly across the room and interrupted cosmography with a greeting abrupt and rude.

He spoke directly to Will in a loud voice over the heads of the others. "Why took you—like a foolish Christian—comfort and consolation to Ben in prison? Know you not that he used me unendurably?"

"I took no comfort to Ben in prison."

"Ah, then you're a liar too!" He shook Burbage's chair.

"Oh, Jack!"

Lord William covered half his face with his hand so that he might remain half concealed from this fracas.

Dekker strolled over smiling, his eyes cold, a careful conciliation in the spacing of his nods and glances.

"At thy merry murdering again?" he asked of no one in particular.

"Jack, you are a fool," said Will mildly. "What man knows more of guile and craft than you, or puts it on the line with fewer emendations?" He laughed without rancor. "Then consider Ben for what he is, and let all who have borne his rudeness unite in a great day of forgiveness."

Dekker said smoothly, "Oh, I concur in that. Such a great throwing about of brains requires a fine last scene and kisses all round."

Camden said drily, "Jonson knows his Latin."

"Aye, but no English!" Marston cried, kicking Burbage's chair till Dickon rose with great courtesy and offered it to him. "And 'fore God, I am an Englishman and want no other language." He sat down, and Dickon stood for a moment, looking at him with wry amusement, and then found another seat.

"So are we all Englishmen," said Will, "and play with words to see what shapes and cunning ways they yield." He smiled slightly. "And so does Ben for all his pompous learning. Come, Jack, be generous."

Marston sat down and stroked the length of his nose with his black-rimmed finger, staring at Will. "Ben knows that you're a fool. He knows that you undertake nothing; have no ingenuity, rework old saws."

"Then it is I you hate, not Jonson," said Will.

"I hate all boys who lead an easy life! You sit like a king on Bankside because you hold shares in a theatre which caters to the wind and the rain."

"Well, God save me from those theatres that are closed on top like the minds that write for them."

"Ah," said Dekker, now himself wounded. "Blackfriars has given us a shilling or two, Will, when the Globe turned us away."

Marston rattled a tankard. "When an inferior playwright has no one above him, cannot he call the tunes?"

Lord William said, "Enough. We would not bear thee, Mr Marston, did we not remember thy certain wit. Speak like an Englishman."

Marston looked angry—that is, more angry than before—for Lord William's tone was the one he used to a servant. But he replied as though not wishing to cut off his nose to spite his face.

"What else is there, my lord, but hot words and kissing our thumbs? No offense."

"See that that is so."

"You also write political tracts if I am not misinformed," Sir Piers said over the rim of his pot.

Then Marston grew a mottled shade, with anger or fear no one could tell, and reached forward to smite the table.

"He lies, he lies, who says I am not a loyal Christian Englishman!"

Sir Piers sucked at his lips and closed his eyes. Marston struck again.

"Hear me!"

"I hear."

Sir Roderick laughed abruptly for Will to hear. "I am not a loyal Christian Englishman. I am Welsh and I thank God."

This made Will gay. "My great granddad was named ap Griffin—so will you have me?"

Sir Roderick shook with laughter. "Ah, we will make these

English quail. There's none can be put over us. We're the lost tribe of Israel, God's own chosen!"

Will said, half gay, half grave, "You have given me myself, sir. Now I will study to like me." For indeed this kind Welshman had, for one moment, set the sky without planets and the wind from the south.

Marston's voice came as though a passion of strangulated thoughts were fighting their way out to die. Why need he hate so much Dickon, Sly, himself? Let him hate the lords who kept witty men alive only to buy them cheap. Dickon, Sly, himself knew the exhaustion of fear. They stood with their kind even when bludgeoning each other. But to drag the entrails of a soul into the presence of men who had no knowledge of hungry despair and were concerned only with stars and heavenly bodies and special rhymes and the best gilt to use on books, and whether a viol was best made in France or in Italy, was to degrade himself and them.

Rutland motioned to Dekker, and Will heard him say softly, "Tell thy friend to come and see me." But Burbage said loudly, "Peace, in God's name. I thought Alleyn and the Fortune had you by the throat. Am I wrong? Are you free?"

"Free as a dog hanging from a tree. That strangury, that filth, Alleyn emits his urine drop by drop. Twice he's disbanded the actors in the last six months to tighten his hold over the poor devils by engaging them at lower terms. And towards us—"

"Then you are tied," Burbage murmured. "What can we do?"

"Look you, the Fortune keeps a tireman to remake old costumes when they fall apart. So do they bind us to make marketable commodities out of trash. Four pounds Alleyn gave me for the last play, and I owe him six."

"So?"

"Now he has set five of us miserable, spavined no-men to write each an act, which for me and him"—he jerked his head toward Dekker—"is as easy as pissing. But we will draw it out, and he will not know that the time has been spent writing for you."

Dekker added drily, "For it is such a nice thing to be in the company of successful men."

Burbage opened both hands and held them wide. His manner was as cold and correct as Lord Herbert's. "Alleyn will learn."

"He will learn if you tell him."

"Come fair and square. Then we'll pay you openly," Will said.

Marston stared at Will, one eyelid drooping more than the other, the lines across his forehead as fixed as wood. "May the eternal ineffectual priapism seize you," he said with a nasty violence.

Lord William let his hand fall heavily on the table. Dekker's eyes slid from face to face. "Hold there, Jack—" he said. But Will replied calmly, "Thy good wish, amended somewhat, might be a blessing, Jack."

Burbage murmured an effectual lively sound, well shaped and given forth with a cunning inflection. His rage he would save for his own kind.

Sly said, "Keep your curses for your enemies, Jack. We'll set you to work but not like a mouse in a hole. Come forth. Be a cat."

The red light was still there in Marston's eyes, but some of the violence had drained from his voice. "Aye, from a safe port it's easy to give good advice. That's a fine doublet you have on, and I mark that the collar has not been worn before."

"Let be, Jack," said Dekker, sensibly bored. "These men know thy tongue."

"I wish one or two things clear in my mind. Who rules at the Globe?"

"We all," said Burbage, Sly, and Will.

"Not he alone who swells the stage night after night with his stealings from other men?"

"Will Shakespeare?" asked Will.

Then Marston laughed. He seemed at that moment to put off his nastiness. His face cleared, his hand did not shake. Yet even so, he was not pleasant as other men.

"Ah, Will, as Ben says, perhaps thou art a better actor of parts than a writer of plays. If Ben laughed at thy *Julius Caesar* as a poor thing of no worth, everyone knew it. It was not done in a corner. I'll write thee a grand part and then London will not be able to hold both thee and Dickon."

"Well, we both thank thee."

"Hah!" said Sir Roderick to Will, "that *was* a pelting. This weather be not kind." Then he laughed a little. "In the old days, when the sea got too rough, the good Welsh put axe and spear in hand and waded into the briny deep, taking arms against it. But it's never been said that the sea was alarmed." He waved his hand toward Marston. "Ah, look you, my heart aches for the fellow. 'Tis like a Welshman he is, come to ravenous London."

Then Sir Roderick looked silently at Will for a moment, and said, "Lift *your* heart, friend. In Wales there's naught but love of words. There you'd be a king."

"For that, many thanks."

After a moment, Sir Roderick said softly, "Our smallness is fit into the place designed for it by the highest point. Our lord here, look you, feeds you from his plate but as *he* wills to do so. And list you to the music. That is a sweet song of death of which we are so enamoured. And look you, there is no honor among the great, only self-interest and intrigue which gamble with men's lives and peace." With his bright blue eyes, he studied Will again. "But I am not done in by that. Nor you neither."

Will frowned and smiled and looked at him. "Say on."

"Well, is it not a marvel how this terrible great world cannot daunt that rare creature, man?"

Lord William had been conducting his class with a stern hand, vexed that Will had added only here and there. He offered Will his golden toothpick. The fruit went from hand to hand. The maid called them all "love" and poured fresh sack. Camden had drawn out his chair till he was able to lean by Will's shoulder and say, "Our English language, think you, sir, as fluent as Latin, say you not, sir? as courteous as Spanish? Nay, have we not beautifuler words than all, sir? We make it as we speak it, and you, good friend—"

What he meant to say was left unfinished, for Rutland's voice rose sharply. "That is a lie!"

Lord William's eyes opened wide, and Will too perceived that some dangerous charge and thrust had taken place, for Rutland had jumped to his feet.

Sir Piers was his antagonist. That black knight was smiling slightly and toying with his wine, his eyes fixed on Rutland as though each move were an open book. Lord William frowned and looked at Will and Will at him. Both now recognized Sir Piers.

They recognized him by certain incontrovertible signs and suspicions inhering in these troubled times. Sir Piers was not some hanger-on of Lord Herbert, as Will had imagined, but was a Cecil agent, a spy for the Queen.

Lord William examined his dagger with his fingers as he measured the heat of the quarrel.

"Say 'honorificabilitudinatibus,' Roger," he commanded his cousin softly.

Rutland answered angrily, "I am not drunk. Nor am I an enemy of any man in power. Nor will I have my free tongue plucked about."

"Why, who does that will find us fierce as lions," said Lord William softly.

Sir Piers, not amending his smile in any way, said, "In the skies, princes' fortunes may be read. Last July, we trembled at the sun's eclipse until the astrologers put our minds at rest. The astrologers spoke in the Queen's favor, and her loyal subjects must say Amen. But Lord Rutland chooses to interpret these signs of heaven in a different way."

Rutland spoke furiously. "You set on me with innuendo and head shakings and little jokes!"

"Ah, no, my lord, that is where your temper outreached your judgment."

Rutland stamped and grasped his dagger. Sir Piers went on, still faintly smiling, though not with his cold eyes, "You said we must loose the bonds of custom and let men of youthful daring shape the destinies of England; that an old woman could not stem the dangers of a civil war, and that it was high time—"

"In God's name," cried Rutland, pale as death, "I said none of these things as you have put them!"

"But as *you* put them, they are the same."

Sir Piers's cold eyes moved to each in turn. He said calmly, "I fancy there is no man present *save myself alone* who is not a kinsman or friend to the Earl of Essex."

Lord William opened his mouth, but any prudent man would know that words were pointless. To denounce Essex was insane, for none here would believe that he did so with his heart. To defend the man whom the Queen had loved would be an even wilder folly. Will's glance leaped from one face to another.

Sir Piers knew, and all here, that not one could lift a hand against him at this moment. Later, on the dark street, he would have his own allies. He was quite safe. He had done all he needed. Will's eyes remained on him the longest and Sir Piers was drawn to give him back his gaze. Will's lips turned up but not at Sir Piers; at fretted Fortune. London was a cauldron of perfidy against the Queen, and each man weighed, according to his own temperament, the deadly dangers. An old Queen might be dying and her caprices fan the coal of civil war, but there were still the rack, the screws, the slow fire, the disembowelments, and the powerful men who fixed her policies. And informers everywhere.

In that queer silence, Marston's laugh broke like cracking glass. At this Rutland, with prodigious self-mastery, put away his dagger and flung out his hands.

"Alas, my friends, pity me. I was born under the choleric planet." It was said with such pride, however, that neither pity nor forbearance was required. Sir Piers did not move. Camden, Will, Burbage, and Sly sat like men on painted cloths.

These terrible, glittering, and unruly men invited terrible and glittering falls. Will slipped a glance at Lord William, dressed like a popinjay, yet canny and alert, and at Rutland with his girlish hair and his strong arm, and at Herbert, smooth and dimpled, his full lips like a stone flower, and saw them for a moment as the old Queen had seen her subjects high and low when she had called them the "ungovernable beasts of England."

Well, she had been angry, and recognized her own Englishness in her people. Will, too, was English. He thought of home.

Camden was watching calmly, his little gray eyes almost closed as he turned the core of an apple round and round in his fingers. He had sewn up the history of this turbulent isle. All knew that one might be a nonconformist in the mind, if proportion, priority, and order remained undisturbed in the outer frame of things. But treason—the word, treason—hovered in the room.

Will sought and found Camden's eyes again. We are, he thought, two men who look for a super-sensible judgment to spare us some of the logic of these troubled times. Camden passed a small hand across his large domed head; Will watched him steadfastly. Treason . . . there was also treason to good sense, treason to humanity . . .

Will was suddenly compassionate of Lord William's opening and closing hand. He spoke as an older man to a younger.

"Sir, you would have known it had this been your time to fight."

Lord William turned his eyes and Will fancied that he was close to tears. "Aye, that is well said." He nodded several times, and after a moment pushed himself from the table. The others slowly rose also. Lord William picked up his dagger.

Lord William's servant brought his cloak and received his purse for payment, whereupon the fiddlers and the singing boy sprang from their places. Lord William linked his arm with Rutland's and, with a gesture of his jeweled glove, drew his friends into a circle.

Sir Piers, in his black cloak and his black plumed hat and his fashionable melancholy, was ignored. Lord William succeeded in divesting him, for that moment, of all plan and purpose. Those who commanded the moment were in a better position to command the hour as well.

Marston and Dekker had detached themselves from any association with high places and high falls. Only one of their own kind would have seen the derision behind their careful looks. Will paused beside them, smiling and stroking the top of the chair. Dekker smiled in reply and said softly, "He will snap his fingers for thee in a moment."

Marston said with harsh merriment, "Man will break out, despite philosophy."

97

"Praise God, in the world of high and low, we are very low, where only dog eats dog," murmured Dekker.

"Come to the Globe and we will talk as you like," Will said. Dekker raised his eyebrows and inclined his head. Marston hastily poured the dregs from several tankards into one pot. "You do not romanticate us as some kind of squalid aliens to your sinecured society?"

Will said patiently, "Oh, Jack, give over."

Dekker said with a good temper, "We thank you, Will."

Will hesitated, but Lord William's servant appeared in the doorway and snapped his fingers.

Camden stood just outside the door calmly drawing on his gloves.

"Well, sir, we are all ships at sea whose only purpose is a safe port."

"Aye, good sir," Will replied. "I pray that your port and mine will be the same happy haven."

Lord William stood in a defense of lanterns. He held out his hand to Will and drew him to his side. "Ah, I love thee with a perfect love," he said. "Let nothing come between us." He drew the ring from his gloved hand and put it on Will's hand. "Wait on me tomorrow and I will also give you the ornament I told you of." He mounted the horse which his servants had brought.

Burbage, Sly, and Will embraced each other, and in this threefold clasp, Burbage relieved himself of a volley of epithets. Then he and Sly, with Camden and Sir Thomas, set out, walking by Lord William's horse, while the armed and mounted servants fell in behind.

Lord Herbert stood in his own ring of lanterns and armed men. He said in his soft voice that the city being so black and dangerous, he would set Will across the river in his own wherry. So Will went with him and Sir Roderick through the night smells and sounds down to the river, past Blackfriars Theatre to Baynard's Castle. There at his own gate, Lord Herbert, as silent and flower-mouthed as ever, took leave of Will.

It was Sir Roderick who clasped Will by the hand and said, "In *The Black Book of Carmarthen* it says, 'Three things are lovable in man: peace, wisdom, and kindness.' Good night, my friend."

Will replied to him in Welsh, "Good night. God bless you."

Thus at the end he found himself alone on the river. Watermen in the livery of Herbert's father, the Earl of Pembroke, rowed him swiftly among the dark shapes of the boats.

Moving on the surface of the water, silent and black as hell, he might be in the midst of death. With a sigh and a breath, alone and at peace, he started softly to sing: "*My hand becomes my destiny. I am no man's fool.*"

The wherry drew up at the wharf.

But irony comes home to roost. When he had said *I am no man's fool,* he had neglected to add, *and no woman's neither.*

She was waiting when he opened the door of his room.

CHAPTER *Eight*

SHE was dressed as a boy. She had been running, and the smell of her body, as she sprang toward him, spoke such a power of nature that words died on his lips.

What words? *Go away. Welcome.* Had he not heard her footsteps in his dread? In a suffocating revelation he wondered in what fool's blindness he had lived these past months to think that he could be free of her . . . or wished to be.

For a moment he could not turn this sudden roaring surge into thought and so control it. God or devil! here was neither wit, nor logic, choice, idea, mind—only invocation.

Though she was dressed as a boy, she was so female that he was stirred, there and then, past enduring. Not female in outer ways of breasts and hips, but in some emanation, some promise, some such appeal to all the senses of copulation that beauty would have been a disservice, and she had no beauty.

She smiled and put her hands on him. "Kiss me," she said.

Then, in a measure, he came to himself. He shook his head and went past her, leaving open the door. Where was Ned? He prayed to hear him leaping up the stairs. He sat down in the window embrasure, his arms across his chest, smiling with the warmth he gave the dog, the cat, the tree, the river. He half listened to the sounds of night to detach himself from the room, but he did not take his eyes from her, for his vaunted strength would lie in his watchfulness.

Her black hair was electric and spirited and fell over her brow. Her little face was flat and square with a small flat nose as delicate and curious as a young cat's. Her eyes were round and sleepy, her mouth wide and prone to laughter. But in the narrow black eyebrows and the squared lines of cheek, and the indentations of mouth, was a sensuality so subtle it could scarcely be measured. Even the tips of her ears, and her nape where it vanished into her hair were voluptuous, as though every portion half concealed about her was half-revealed. Her boy's clothes did not impede her. Her body moved in them with no self-consciousness; she pranced on her short lovely legs looking at things which did not concern her yet eagle-eyed toward him. At length, beckoning with all her fingers, she said, from a distance, "Come and kiss me."

This time he did not trouble to reply or to shake his head. He merely looked at her with a smile. Now he must feed himself with cold thoughts, for they would be her enemy. Life had not taught him candor when he should be wary. The body in the boy's clothes, the smell of woman, said that he had only the briefest time in which to confirm his resolution. She closed the door.

When she had been out of sight, he had made her as wicked as sin, as black as hell. Yet she was unchanged. He was perversely shocked; his own pain seemed now humiliating. She was gay and prancing as though she had no heart, or as though time had been obliterated. For thus had she pranced and shed an innocence over their first meeting, a spring before the last. While she smiled, he engaged in the risky and involuntary enterprise of remembering that time.

Some river entertainment, at the end of Lent, had been planned by the Marquess, her brother, for the Queen. The River Thames and the sea into which it flowed were to hail Gloriana. The barges of the Queen's great nobles, bearing fantastical edifices of grottoes and sunken caverns and palaces beneath the sea, as well as grassy mounds and riverbanks, were to move before the barge on which her Majesty would be enthroned.

Noble peers and ladies would grace these edifices as water deities, spritely majesties of air and sun, who had come to pay their tribute in masque and verse to the Queen of All the Elements.

Water would be thrust up into the air by cunning devices, and after dark a display of fireworks would simulate the tribute of the firmament. All to cost three thousand pounds.

The Lord Chamberlain had required Will and Dickon Burbage to smooth rough corners and encourage clear, loud speech.

So it happened that while the noble lords and ladies were being coaxed to move and speak like water gods, the most gifted and carefree of them all proved to be the little water sprite who was the Marquess' sister. She had pranced and danced behind the others in an abandon as irrepressible as sunlight on the water. That she was her brother's sister and a Queen's Maid in no way affected her ambition: let the ladies who loved themselves above all others be the queens and goddesses. Behind their backs, she could sing and kiss, prance and dance to her heart's content.

Will was enchanted; as enchanted as a countryman is by the spring and a shepherd by new lambs. All his sweetness and his merriment came out to meet her, and all his elegance paid court to the lady.

For underneath her guise of water sprite was her antithesis, and this the worldly part of his mind recognized as a measure of her charm. Yet he felt no qualms. The more sophisticated game of who is she and who am I was touched on so lightly that it merely added piquancy to the occasion. The pleasant spring hours on the river, when he and Dickon made certain that her Majesty would not be deprived of a single tribute, passed with all the innocence of good intentions and of music.

The Queen had been delighted. The Marquess, with large tact, had recognized the Earl of Essex' precedent rights on such occasions and relinquished to him the part of Neptune, while he himself assumed the lesser robes of River Thames. This pleased the

Queen, and her old raddled face was alight with smiles and laughter to see her sweet Robin as a king who could not harm herself. Her beautiful voice called across the water to greet and thank her compeers of air and sea.

All would have been concluded with the fireworks, and all participants gone home to their rightful hopes and happiness, had the lady not in a waiting moment asked Will to read her one of his poems. She wept and kissed him, and thus the net was slipped beneath his feet.

With the first season of their passion, all the unaffected gaiety, the merry sweetness, the childlike teasing of dull care had seemed perfection. But time and events showed a truer face, and in a delayed, protesting way, he became incredulous that he had been so simple. Then it was too late.

Her self-will was their undoing. It stopped at nothing till she had her way. But then she did not want what she had wanted, and yet she would not let it go for it was hers and must submit to all her changing whims. So her vital force became her wantonness. Her impetuosity became her arrogance. Her teasing of dull care became cruel coldness to unsatisfied desire, and the tender embassy of love sank down to death.

He, in his turn, had gored himself and sold cheap what was most dear. At last, all that remained had been his desperate need and her compelling wickedness that took the cruel revenge of promising all and withholding everything.

The fevered body that nursed its own disease had, like a lunatic, begged some mercy through Lord William, but in such ambiguous terms that any action was an answer. Such madness was, however, its own undoing, and now he sat in the window embrasure a resolute, free, and honest man—if he did not stir one inch.

In her boy's clothes she sat against the edge of the table and gossiped artfully, sang a song, and told a joke so adroitly that he laughed in spite of himself.

"Hah!" she cried, lifting herself to the table, "I knew you were not a log of wood."

He made an ejaculation that committed him to nothing. He was aware that she was studying him intently, her round chin resting in her white collar. Her eyes were so black they seemed without expression. She said tenderly, "How you hate me. I must do the wooing."

He looked toward the closed door and listened for Ned's footsteps on the stairs. He looked into the black night and weighed the sound of raised voices and a sharp amorous cry. Then he looked again at her who was rank with guile. He said (although he was not sure that it was wise to speak at all), "Lady, let us not talk of things past and done."

Scarcely had he said it than he knew himself a fool. He turned away his head so that she would not see. But she saw all.

"Past and done?" She laughed. "Oh, no—that is not my will toward Will."

She gazed at him with greedy gentleness, and after a moment pushed herself from the chest and knelt beside him. She put her hands on his hands where they clutched at his arms.

"I see I have been most careless of your heart. What could I do? Could I tell you that you misjudged me altogether?"

"Let us not talk of it."

"It was you spoke first." And there she had him.

He said after a long pause, "I have naught in the world to speak against Lord William."

She put her cheek against his arm. "But against me—?"

He moved suddenly so that she fell back against her heels. Her eyelids drooped and she sat thus as though she had planned it. She said with a little smile, "Why do you not believe me? Why do you believe evil people who would impugn the Virgin Mary?"

The light made tender the corners of her eyes, softened her wiry hair. All this laid a great burden on him. Men had resisted women before, but at that moment he found it difficult to remember what forces had been called to their aid. She could both unman and violate him. She could reverse the positions of man and woman, overwhelm, outrage, and plunder him.

His thoughts were bitter, charmless, heavy.

She persisted, watching him carefully. "Why do you so?"
"Because I know you."

Her lips quivered for a moment as though she wished to laugh. She looked at the floor but her eyelids were alive with vivacity. She glanced up at him and said simply, "You sent him to me. You knew what he fancied in women. He laid such hands on me as never did a man before. What could I do?"

He stared at her for a moment, and then he laughed to redress the balance. Presently she touched his hand and played with his fingers. "Forgive me," she said softly. "Pray for me. It is my nature. Pity me."

He tried to outwit her by asking with equal simplicity, "Why do you distress yourself? There was no honor between us, hence there is no dishonor now. I wish to make quietus of that which was never truly mine. I am a married man and I regret my adultery."

She stroked his hand again with one finger. "Why," she asked softly, "did you then send me that wicked sonnet in such a rage?"

He tried to remember. Every spot he touched in his mind or his soul was bruised. He looked at her with the only feeling he could trust, a narrow, cramped, cautious pain. She bore his look boldly, hiding nothing. At length he said hoarsely, "Thou art a whitely wanton, with two pitch balls in thy face for eyes . . ."

Her eyelids flickered, showing that she did not fancy that especially, but she said nothing. Then she stroked his hand again, and after a moment he abruptly drew away his hand, stood up, and moved beyond her reach.

She said very low, "Can you not understand how fears come on me, and I must ask one man or another to assuage them?" The brisk little voice was thin as paper. "I have been frightened all my livelong days. Only servants in a castle and I, a child, alone. When my father came I made him carry me always in his arms, even when I was no more a child, and when he stroked me I was not afraid."

Will paced carefully along the lines of a floor board, concentrating with all his power. The thin little voice curled round his head like smoke. There was one way he could deal with this: pour wax in the vents of his ears.

"Is there any woman not afraid?" she asked him on a rising voice.

He answered huskily, "I know naught of this."

"Aye, to be a woman is not a man's fate."

Then an impersonal rhetorical outrage broke through his silence. "You dishonor women!"

She was unaffectedly surprised. "Dishonor women? Not I. It is men, and to what use they bind us. And what they will and will not have from women."

"You jig, you mock, you lisp, you call your wantonness your ignorance! God has graced women. I'll have none of your lies."

She sat there on her heels, kicked and trodden, looking younger than his daughters. "Perhaps God has given women some merit in your eyes, but not in the eyes of courtly men."

She said it so simply that his heart was touched. His pacing stopped, and he stood staring out the dark window. In all humanity he knew that her sorcery and spells were those of flesh and blood, and so to heap abuse on her alone was untrue and base. Yet if he conceded one feather's weight in the scales that balanced this account, he would be undone. *Just go, go, go away.*

Behind him she was very silent. A fly buzzing was lost in the curtains of the bed. She asked softly, "Shame? Does not thy desire at this moment pander reason?"

He heard her in a terrible rage. "You pursue life so that you may be thrown to the ground. You drink my blood," he said hoarsely.

"Must naught be said of you? You have pilfered from my body."

"Never without your leave!"

She rose up slowly from the ground. He heard her move and he gripped the window edge. How well her daring matched his caution, her desire his withholding. In the window glass he saw her raise her arms above her head, clasp her fingers, and sway back and forth. He heard her humming. Then she stamped. He was startled but he did not turn. She said in a mild tone, "Women are very shocking to men. I will go. We will be friends another day."

"Aye, go. For if you stay I will say many vile and frightful things that should not be said or heard. I know thy body—I know the price it claims." His voice was low, as though vile and frightful things were a sadness, not a sin.

Her eyes moved from one small thing to another; her hand picked up the snuff box and the candle snuffer, as though she meant to idle out this storm and not go at all.

He felt his weakness run like sweat down his back. The leech he had applied seemed to infect his blood rather than to clear it. He wondered, in a flash of mordancy, how many shapes and adumbrations mortal man allowed himself before he welcomed the grave to put an end to the joke of mortality.

He turned, steadying himself against the carved side of the window, and said to her, face to face, still in that quiet voice, "Do you think there is no price to pay for our sin, and nothing that I'll extract from you for kicking at my heart as you have done? Nay, more, rending my entrails, hour by hour? You sway me from the likeness of a man. You are the evilest thing that hath possessed my life. If I could slake my rage on you I'd do it."

As he spoke he saw the look in her eyes, and the light that slowly dawned. Not the light that he intended, of abasement, or even anger. He knew while he poured out his words like bitter refuse that he had created a strange tautness in her. She knew too much of his meaning. She knew more than his words revealed. His fingers gripped the window edge, a round smooth feminine rise of carving. For a moment the woman was wiped out. She was only a metaphor. Why, in justice, should he attack her when it was himself deceiving himself at prayer that was the guilty one?

He looked at her small firm body which had no trace of poetry except good health, standing awkwardly because he had caught her in an unguarded moment, at her coarse hair and her opaque eyes black as the badge of hell. He saw her and he did not see her. She was imperious, lawless, passionate, proud; her soul was equivocal.

He could believe for a flashing moment that he had wrested her will from her; that she would not recoil. But too late he feared his own conclusions; he had set no guard for them, and she had seen the expression in his eyes.

She swept off her man's hat and threw it violently on the floor. She shook out her hair that he had once called the color of mourning. The force of anger was there, yet he could not be sure of its truth; was it true? When she turned on him it was like an assault. "Now behold—look—and see me!"

He did see her, without changing his expression. She walked back and forth before him, with no lightness. When she trod, she trod on the ground, her arches and toes alive to her step.

He strove for calmness. She said imperiously, "You have spoke daggers past all endurance."

"I would they were daggers," he answered bitterly.

"Then kill me. Aye, do it. Do it!" She flew at him and dragged his dagger from his belt. "Do it!" She thrust the handle toward him. He looked at it, and then he pushed away her hand. In a violent splendid gesture she slashed at her doublet, opening it wide and causing herself to cry out slightly where the point drew blood on her breast.

"Oh, foolish woman." He seized her hand and shook the dagger from it. Then, seeing her skin with the bleeding scratch, he whispered, "You gore and whore a man—I'd have your life."

"Take it!" she screamed. He held her with both hands and shook her back and forth, her head jerking as harsh little cries were shaken from her. She tore at him spiritedly till, in a cold rush of distaste, he saw how noxious and brutal were their acts.

He let her go, and she fell. She scrambled quickly to her feet and flew at him again in a frenzy of kicks and blows.

"Let be," he said harshly. He held her with a strong grasp, for a moment plundered of words. Then he gasped, "We are a corruption in the other's blood. Let us know it and abstain."

"I spit at you!" she cried in a thin wail, and did spit at him. "Do you dare put hands on me—you common fellow!"

He struck her then, but he caught her, and he groaned for poor humanity. Yet humanity was now the devil's advocate. He was scarcely aware he still held her till he saw into the blackness of her eyes. And then he could not let her go until he had in some way enforced his resolution.

He knew he was using words as desperate means to drive her off; he held her because in defense of himself he feared to let her go. "A woman may be a man's, but not her appetites!"

"What is that to thee?" Her words were like the rushing of wind. She flung against him with her body, an agile lashing impact that was mindless. "Oh, men, hot as monkeys—salt as wolves in pride—I will bear no more!" Yet her struggling was a ritual.

He cried out against the storm that had now struck his heart. "I will speak until I am done."

"Let me go," she moaned.

"I believe in your witchcraft," he cried in agony. "Have you kissed the devil's ass?"

"Ah, la," she sighed, and without warning she gave up all resistance. She turned her hands till they clasped his as soft as cloud. "What shall I say? I am what I am?"

He trembled, clutching for his balance. He held her still, as though holding her gave him leave to hate her. "Has my lord not stabbed you well in my absence? Do not take the time to lie to me!"

Then he could no longer bear to touch or hold her. The sound of his pacing filled his ears as though all the house shook to his secret. "What follows after? Nothing? Why, then, the world is nothing, and men and women nothing put to nothing. God, oh, God—"

She stood there in the center of the room, her hands half raised as though he had not slipped away from them; her voice was low and sweet. "Is nothing nothing when I leave him and come to thee who spills such dirty water on me?"

"It is all I have to give thee—dirty water." He heard his voice, he heard how strained it was, how lost in governance. He foundered, he stopped before her, his knuckles white beside his thighs. "If he breaks a lance with every woman, what is that to me?"

Her abrupt gesture was merciless; she stripped herself of her slashed doublet and kicked it against the wall. Yet her queer little harsh voice was tender. "I am not every woman. On every woman you would not spill your anger."

He gazed at the open shirt and the little breasts.

"Here is a tragedy of love," she said, in a small voice. "I hurt you so that you may hurt me, for that is the ecstasy of love. How can we reach each other except by pain? How can we make our bodies one except by pain? I long to be thy body. Is this not the very ecstasy of love? Else I am sick. And you are sick. And we are destroyed."

He said hoarsely, "Oh, from what power have you this power? You give the lie to my true sight. Oh, your worst exceeds the best." He took her in his arms and buried his face against her neck. "How ugly thou art, thou little school of night. Who taught thee how to make me love thee when I hate thee more and more?"

She closed her hand over the back of his neck. Now he was mortgaged to whatever she desired. "Ah," she whispered. "What do you say now?"

Her voraciousness was an art. She became all kiss, all mouth, all prone desire. She made a bed the promise of all bliss. He wanted most of all to punish her, and she wished to be punished, and this required a violence in extremity.

She moaned, making wild strange sounds, part of laughter. He held her fast, but in time she beat upon him as though she would go mad if held or if released. He spoke and spoke to her in sounds too soft for words, watching her face beneath him, as voracious as she to know all that she felt.

She fought and deepened the excitement, for in the strangled cries and the convulsive movements was a violence of rapine, war and plunder.

When the blood was satiated and the field was quiet, all that lived behind his closed lids were great blinding lights. He was a king. He was a son of giants. He was a victor. All the earth was full of spring.

She was a fact, she was his love, his body—he had no thought. All other times she had demeaned and unmanned him, but not now! Where was remorse or dismay! He had no thought with which to question or strength to dwell one moment from this moment. There was no past.

She stirred, and slowly twisted up her hair into a roll. He put his arms about her. She laughed and kissed him, and began to dress herself. He would not open his eyes; all the white lights changed to color as the door opened and Ned stood on the threshold.

Now he could no longer pretend that time had not caught up with him, but he could ignore it for this moment, and the next. Ned did not cross into the room. He stood neither coming nor going, his expression too young to be dissembling.

The lady rose and did not look back at Will. She put her hand on Ned's arm, and rubbed it up and down his sleeve. Then she went on those steady little feet, running down the stairs.

Ned turned his head toward the dark stairs. The street door closed. As he turned to look at Will, her running footsteps grew fainter.

Will frowned till his whole brow was contracted. Ned stood for some time fingering the curtains of the bed, looking at his own white knuckles. Will did not speak.

Ned's voice cracked. "A pretty mocking. Was Troy thus?" Then he tugged at the curtains till they fell across the bed, and turned abruptly toward the door. "Go to hell."

"Ned, Ned—!"

Ned put his hand on the door. "Burn there, thou—appetite."

"Come back."

"No," said Ned.

"Ned, come back!"

Ned shut the door, but he looked at Will with such proud and baleful eyes that Will saw himself when young and stupid.

"Are you my conscience, boy?"

Ned pounded against the posts of the bed. "Be up, for shame —oh, shame!"

Will slowly rose. Ned drove with his dagger at the bed posts. Will took the dagger from him. Then Ned struck at him and Will seized his wrists.

Will said not a word. Ned struck him with his foot. Will was light as air, all feeling and no thought; he could carry the world and not feel it.

Ned wrenched himself free and threw open the door. Will said out of old habit, "Where are you going?"

Ned shouted, "An honest tearsheet is an honest woman for a man without a wife. But a man who whores against the best woman in the world, he's a devil in human shape!"

The slamming of the door remained in Will's ears . . . but in another life, another life. This life hung suspended, troubleless, and free; it had no past or future.

CHAPTER *Nine*

WILL wakened before dawn and reached for sleep again. Hammering had waked him. He heard it now as though someone were building a ladder to heaven. Then a voice, fresh with life, shouted, "Stop that noise!" and on this edge of sleep, he also heard a faraway cry, "Help, help!"

He stirred. Help, oh, ministering angels. The hammering came from the old man across the hall. If the hammering would stop, Will was confident that he would find himself on the verge of the inmost soul, the exploration of which would end all doubts.

But the hammering continued, and that feeble sense that makes cowards of mortal men, locked the door and sat mute and waiting. *Help, oh, help,* far away on the edge of the world. He buried his face. The hammering continued. Ned was not in the bed. Will rose unwillingly.

Thought was established again, in the dim early morning, but it was kept rigorously in a small locked closet of his brain. All else partook of lightness, of that *eúphoros* of the Greeks whereby man might bask with the immortals. With the coming of the day, some weight would surely tread upon him like a heavy housewife, but the balm remain.

He did not think; he merely dwelt with feeling, standing by

the window with an idleness so intent that it was able to partake of each action in the early street and be untouched.

The day brightened. Women went to the river to wash their clothes, men called to each other, a cat chased a dog. Suddenly he drew a deep cavernous breath as from the depths of the earth. He moved. He put his hand on the table and slowly sat down. Well, day, day—

An inkwell, pen, paper, and a ragged prompter's copy of Kyd's *Hamlet's Revenge* lay together. Close by his hand lay a copy of Cardan's *De Consolatione*. Many men in this troubled age had sought its consolation. With the same withdrawn intentness, he read this book as he had read the street; he read it in his memory through the closed covers.

"Before a man can act boldly he must master his own soul.

"His reason must rule. He must possess himself of that calmness which is only derived from self-knowledge and self-control.

"He must be unmoved by the event.

"He must choose right from wrong, honor from venality.

"He must acquire the courage to act, to suffer and to be calm.

"To these principles no man of sensibility opposeth himself."

And he must know that adultery and murder are two sides of the same coin . . .

This would not be found in *De Consolatione*. It had slipped through the wicket like a beggar at the wedding feast.

Now he roused himself by the strong good sense that was the measure of his balm. Words were crude; they violated the subtlety of facts. A man could sicken himself with thought. *Lie thou still. There's nothing either good or bad but thinking makes it so.* His good sense was filled with such good reason that he was bathed in sweat when he discovered that he had merely turned a knife within himself.

Well, a man must live until he die!

Adultery and murder: words, words, words! Where was Ned? Ned had enacted the world shattering Eden's bliss. Where was Ned, who must have faith to balance his own portentous quest for sinlessness?

Murder and adultery are the sins without forgiveness. The two are one. Yet why, he asked himself with the clear shallowness that was common sense, should such disparities be made the same? The walls did not reply, nor the table, nor the floor, nor the book, nor his gently swinging foot. Nor his heart. It came of itself, the reply. *Because they are unkind.*

How he laughed at this: that he, who magnified a universal compassion, should be caught in his own trap. *None can be called deformed but the unkind.* He had said that?

He left his chair—but where had he to go? He was a man who planned his own philosophy and argued for his salvation in words so subtle and selected that priest and prelate were confounded. Why, surely he was as well equipped to alter things in his own behalf as that heathen philosopher who, when he wished to eat a grape, put it to his mouth and opened his lips.

In the odd arrested silence and clear bateless light of the room, he felt himself stumbling out of the house into a legend of his own devising.

Who has usurped my life that I must live so many different parts?

When men bask with the gods, feelings are cool until they are hot. To freeze Priapus must surely be the way to God. Good. A little colder and all will be well.

But then, with that divinity of hell which must be some part of heaven, the door opened onto the Warwickshire sunlight. He sighed, for the chill had not quite eaten its way to his heart.

All the circular reasonings, all the symmetrical answers fell away. In a stark, stripped way he felt relief.

He sat down again slowly and looked steadfastly at his wife with his mind's eye. Are you mine?

The cart of the water carrier had gone by. The odd beating of air, as powerful as the passing of Elijah's chariot, had tokened the scavenging birds who bore away garbage and refuse.

He stood for a moment outside his door. What had the old man built during the night? In his crystal bowl would Ned be found? The silence was apocalyptic and Will hurried down the stairs.

He scuffed at the lane, he breathed deeply the fetid air. The bells of morning were stirring the horizon near and far. To promise a beauteous day and send a man forth without his cloak into black clouds . . . to heal the wound and leave the shame uncured . . . to put a brand, a blister, upon the honest skin between the brows where character was writ—why, that was to ransom life for jests.

A man's real curse was not concupiscence, but that he thought too much. For such a man is apt to find himself in the dead center where no one hears his cries for help. Yet does the world grant an honest choice?

Against the natural man were stumbling fools, priest and pedant, were lust, brutality, and all the toys of desperation. Ah, but there was a heart to the matter, and when the rank deposit of strophe and metaphor had been spaded off, the truth of love-and-live would prance and sing.

He longed to go to sleep again where paradise had been secure.

There were three hundred ale houses and five prisons and two dozen brothels, and all the pustules and French sicknesses thereof, within the sweep of his arms.

Here, in Southwark, was the foul excrescence of London, pushed to the edge of the city. Yet honest men and women lived here too, and children played, his friends and neighbors.

He went to the Cardinal's Cap for his breakfast. It was a hothouse open day and night. Here no one questioned sin or venality since it paid the rent and the taxes. This was his home. He was a very proud man who had received a prophecy last night, and must now defy the auguries of doom.

Before the cleaning maid began her day, the smells assaulted. The air reeked with vomit and illicity, the rushes were soaked with spilt drink and sluttery. He reared his head and covered his nose with his hand. He rose and set open the door to the morning air.

Before he had finished his pottage and ale, he called for pen and ink. The tapster was a shock-headed, potato-nosed fellow whom curiosity had not abandoned in this rude life, and he set down the pen and ink with interest.

"A play," he said as one who had paid for his ticket many

times and had rights in this matter, "there's heap I could put you to . . . marry, dogs bait bears, two-legged ones!" He laughed so that all the gaps in his teeth showed. "Right here! I put my stakes to be merry, old bear and all."

"I'll stake your merriment," said Will, "but your feast will be a fast. It will all come to hot ice. Will you have it so?"

The tapster laughed again, not quite sure of himself. "Well," he said. "I'll split a gut laughing at fast or feast if you'll write it down"

He went off in a hurry, for a sailor customer whose pantaloons had been stolen was pounding on a table and shouting for some kind of justice. Will smoothed out the old Kyd script. He would have to mend its torn pages before he could read it properly. By Lord Lucifer, he'd make it a sullen requital of wrongs and cut back all niceties. No play would keep counsel; it would tell all.

"God is your only jig-maker," he called out to the tapster, but the tapster was shouting at the sailor, "Out. We'll have no rutters here, bare-arsed. This is an honest bawdy house. Out! Out!"

When he returned he brought Will a free gift of ale so that he might lean his hands on the table and complain of the lawbreakers who tear a poor whore's dress but slobber for their own panta loons.

Will could not keep himself from a joke. "Bawdery is a lawful trade?"

"If the law would allow it, sir. Consider—weigh this now, sir— be this not monstrous bad faith: here we have a coop of the best night birds, sir, well washed, used to rough handling, who go at it with good heart and canvas well, and constable every night say he'll call up the law if we don't scrape on his palm. Or sailors, look you, bring back their mates for trouble till we have such din that constable says, 'Well, well, what about it!' Mr Shore, now—"

But Mr Shore, the proprietor, called him away in an angry voice to care for some break-out of trouble elsewhere, and Mr Shore himself stood with his ruff in hand to inveigh at the times.

"One more dead man, Will," he said, "and we're undone."

"What does the Bishop say to the cold corpse?"

" 'Jasper Shore, where's my rent!' " He put on his ruff. "Look you, Will, it's a foul world, and I know it well. My Dorothy's an honest woman. Why not more respectability then, and less trouble, you ask? Well, I look at this tutored world. The world thinks and I think too that till you geld and spay all the youth of the city, we are in business. Hell, 'tis the Bishop's in business! Look you! Poor parish widows, where does he send 'em? Here to me— here! So they'll get some money for the church plate on Sunday. By St Charity, call me a fleshmonger if you like, but it's the devil's own hypocrisy which calls me panderer while seeking the fruits of the pandering. Come now, be honest, Will."

Will smiled at him. He ran his hand through his thinning hair. "Oh, rebellion of a codpiece, Jasper! We're all honest men and women, true-blue to sin."

Shore pressed him, not satisfied. "Poverty and lechery are the curse of Adam. Can they be put off till the resurrection?"

Will picked up the lute in place of answer, and struck a chord for calm and refreshment. Jasper Shore went to sell a neighbor's child a pot of ale to carry home, and a sleepy young tearsheet slipped onto the bench by Will to drink her beer and listen to the music. She blinked her lids and presently put her arms on the table and her sleepy head on them. He took his pen and started to write.

She giggled. "It dances fast as a foiner."

He rubbed her cheek gently with the feathers of his pen and smiled at her. "Wilt thou learn thy a's and b's from me, little heifer?"

"Pooh, not me." She rubbed her nose against her arm. "Faith, I'm no fool to want to read. Art thou writin' down words I'll stand to hear?"

"God knows."

"A play, that's what I fancy." Her voice piped. "Stand! Hold! Avaunt! And all the gold coins they throw about! Geld a codpiece, be they real?"

"No, love. Here, go eat this orange and get some color in thy little cheeks, for I must write down some ugly thoughts."

She was not offended. There was a stupid sluttery in her prettiness. She wandered off out of doors, tearing the skin from the orange.

Jasper Shore came back, on the bias, as it were, for the day was getting on.

"One more thing tell me! Who is not a bawd between gold and want?"

Will was suddenly angry. "Let's have no sanctified bawds! Nor, by the same virtue, no gilded monsters so deformed that nothing's left of man." He looked at Shore's hard, cold eyes. "If I be such a monster then whip me. And I'll whip thee."

"Thanks. I have enough of the law."

"Oh, Jasper, it's a steep and thorny path to heaven; we feel no prick as yet. Let's call us what we are, sinners and doubledealers."

Shore did not care for this. He shrugged. He called the tapster angrily and went back to business. Business eddied about Will. He paid it no more heed. Writing words was a very cunning hideaway. Sometime later he looked at his watch and left.

He went to the tenement where lived Pope with his adopted children, poor orphans all.

A wreath of children's faces told him that Dada was still rehearsing and would not be home till night, then they would have eels for supper and baked prunes and dragon's wings, *and up and up* in their imagination, till they and Will all toppled into laughter.

He went on to dinner at the Falcon, where he found his friends. The Falcon was an honest inn, no whore-house. It was as familiar as his own room. Let this be his home.

He found all who had been rehearsing that day's play of *Julius Caesar*, and a scene or two of tomorrow's old get-penny *A Warning to Fair Women*, in the crook of the parlor where the waiters had set up their tables as they did each day. And Ned, why, Ned was here as naturally as fine weather, here where he should be, learning Cinna the Poet . . . a foolish untoward poet who died because he could not prove he was a poet. But never mind. Ned was healthy, strong, alive, angry, busy, himself in all his parts. Will could live again, and bask a little.

He put his hand on Ned's shoulder, but Ned did not look up

or speak. Even so, Will sank into a chair with a relief that was close to weakness. These others, these friends, these men of temptations and tempers—we belong together in sickness and health. With them was a bond strong as a marriage.

Sly called out, "Fiddle all morning, while we worked?"

Will snapped his fingers and stood up. He jiggled Dickon's chair and then he opened a mullioned window to hear the shouts of children playing on the scaly shore of low tide.

Heminges stood beside him to say that Sir Edmund Tilney, the Master of the Revels, had commanded himself and Condell to Clerkenwell that evening. He talked for a moment of getting a good copy of *What-You-Will* registered tomorrow at the Stationers' to protect them, for "by the rood, it's a choice play and some will soon steal it."

Will said he would keep on fiddling while Jacko worked so well.

"I fancy we'll be rich this season," Heminges mused without a stutter. "Though I feel much melancholy in the air, signs say all is favorable."

Will was pleased, smiled, spoke his satisfaction.

"Rebecca says for us another store in Sssshoreditch. Wise wwwwife, by Gis. I have never heard that people stop bbbbuying when they are gloomy," Heminges said.

Condell had gone onto the river wall to run up and down athletically. He believed very heartily in the body's fitness, but he came now to stand below the window and remind Jacko of certain postponed business with the Master of the Revels which they must raise that evening. "He'd be pleased if we forgot, but it's our money."

"Aye, good Hal! Put those figures in thy head and hold them there!"

"Oh, I've never let them go," said Condell, and ran another heat.

Dickon called them peremptorily to table. The boys sat at the foot, Edmans, the youngest, next to Heminges, who would mind his manners and give him choice bits. Will felt his mouth full of sweetness as he shook out his napkin. An uncommon thing had been built on this trust and love. No theatre in London, or the whole world, was knit so strong nor bound together with such good reasons. This was a mansion in heaven. Indeed, *this* was his home.

Heminges had scarcely said grace, the gray-clay pots of ale been lifted, and the joint carved, before Dickon called them to order. He was rehearsal-bright with that hard square intelligence that was as intuitive as a shaft of light. His glance darted here and there, gathering in, missing nothing, his manner carefully calm because faced with a time of creation.

He said, "We need four new plays, but by God's mercy only two revivals if all goes well. If not, we need more in a hurry. We have this *What-You-Will* by our Shake-Shaft here—unless the Revels wish it kept for the Queen. Tony Munday's play goes to rehearsal in the morning, and we will bring out *The Merry Wives* for playing Friday, and *A Warning for Fair Women* to-morrow. Let us this week yield Thursday to Paris Garden and the bears."

Phillips said sharply, "I'll not step aside for bear-baiting."

"The law says nothing should interfere on Thursday with the baiting," Dickon said without much spirit.

"We agreed to demur. I demur. It's a shocking bad business all around."

"I stand with Gus. It's a nice law to break."

Dickon shrugged. "Well, then, Chapman promises that he will be ready by Friday. God knows how we will piece out the matter with Ben in gaol." He reflected for a moment, listening sharp-eyed to Sly's vehement and good-natured gaol sentence of Ben, and said merely, "Ah, he writes as well in gaol as without. But never mind—all these pace out the time till Will is ready. Five weeks, say you, Will, to give us this *Hamlet?*"

Will frowned and poked at his meat. Five weeks was a fair time. He did not know why he frowned and hesitated. Out of the great conglomeration of things which had come upon him—which he did not wish to sort out—he could not confuse his work. It lay on the lawful side of his life and was not, for his soul's sake, to be entangled with hesitations or equivocation.

He nodded, and then he shrugged, smiling.

Dickon pushed away his half-finished plate and wiped his mouth. "Less noise at the end of the table. When you have finished, lads, go out for a game."

Heminges whispered to Edmans, "Drink up thy ale. Here's thy napkin. Mind the time, lads. Keep trimmed."

Sam and Ned took seats closer, though Ned would not sit next his brother. Dickon was tapping out his thoughts at the tips of his fingers.

"Now, how shall he mend old *Hamlet's Revenge*. Revenge is hollow, think you not, in the old fashion. A ghost we must have, but in a new way. Amorous, think you?"

"Oh, amorous, sure," said Sly promptly, "ghosts and girls."

"Jamie is deft, we can use him more than we do, with good taste, while he is still young enough to be a sweet lass."

Gus said, "We want blood, love, a touch of madness, verse, dynastic intrigue, enough lines for us all to speak, satire for the educated, ribaldry for the one-shilling admissions, and something fashionable for the Lords' Rooms." He burst out laughing. "Hammer it up, Will, like our good fellow!"

Will smiled again and let his hand rise and fall on the table.

"That's not so far off the mark," said Pope, a little afraid of a joke at a serious moment. "Mixed well, cooked well, it should nourish us for thirteen or twenty performances. For the benefit of all, eh, Will?"

Will made a courteous grimace.

"Aye, one pampers him now," said Dickon with a powerful light of affection, "for who knows our faults as he and, like a kind nurse, sets us forth in the best way." Dickon sat there in his strong grace, as easy as a cat, the subtle watchful eyes behind the heavy lids seeing all, his beautiful fingers spreading and closing on the table.

"Oh, God!" said Will with a laugh.

Dickon narrowed his eyes and went on implacably. "Look you, we must think of ourselves; the old parts are outgrown. Or wilt thou take this into account, Will, and alter us felicitously? I, now, I am no longer a stripling."

Will considered Dickon with a half-smile. "Thou wilt do. Thou wilt have rest here and there and fight a duel in bits and pieces."

Burbage laughed. No one in London could fight a duel better in one piece than he. "So be it. We will have revenge, satire, stoicism for fashion, and good parts for all in five weeks. Now speak up. Will must have strong thoughts from us all." He reached for an orange.

Gus said after a moment, "I think it is folly to tell Will his business."

Burbage was startled. "But his business is ours."

"Ah, but do we not trust him?"

Dickon's eyes rounded. "Hah, but does he not trust us?" He turned his eyes to Will and glanced at him with that subtle attentiveness which underlay all his louder speeches. "Hah, Will?"

Will passed his hand over his mouth and said through his fingers, "Before God, I am exceedingly weary. Triviality with no thought"—he shrugged—"*tant pis;* but revenge—for revenge one needs words and thought. Set Marston to work, I pray you; set him to work for natural revenge and good parts for all." A vigorous silence fell. He glanced at them with a glint of humor. "We put in a get-penny four weeks from now, and Marston will be ready a fortnight later."

The silence was so reverberate that he looked about with his gold-flecked eyes and added stubbornly, "If I beat up Kyd and Shakespeare like a bowl of eggs, what will we have? Dickon outstaring Alleyn. It wearies me. It must soon weary you. We must keep Dickon mindful of his greatness—stand between him and his folly." He grinned and dropped his lids.

Burbage was angry. His anger was like a flame darting up when the brazier lid was lifted, but concealed when the lid was put on again, as his good sense prompted now.

From the side of his eye Will saw Gus watching him.

"I am mindful of our obligation to each other," Will said. "I'll cook and season and trim and shape any get-penny that's intended for laughter—but do not ask me to touch revenge."

Burbage said, "But we ask only a *play*," and twisted the love-lock at his temple.

Heminges frowned and set his knife this way and that, and then looked at Will with a glance as penetrating as a good magistrate's. Armin cleared his throat, thought better of the attempt, and exercised his eyebrows up and down.

Will said, "Whatever fetters the spirit is evil; I think revenge comes from the devil. What is a ghost?" He saw their astonishment.

"What has this to do with a play dead in three years?" Dickon asked with false gentleness.

Will hesitated. Then his glance took them all in. He replied lightly, "I am a man, then I am a poet. Last of all I write plays. Surely this is no queerer than green geese and jam?"

Dickon frowned more deeply and pared a nail with his knife. Condell drew in his breath to speak, but Will, examining an apple with makeshift intentness, said, well aware of ironic overtones, "Has not man a counter to fate? Revenge is against nature."

"Oh, damn nature then!" Dickon cried.

Will shifted and brushed his clothes and counted the strong bond that held them together. He needed them now as a child needs a mother.

He begged. "I proposed Marston in no idleness. I implore you —Marston! let me do something else."

"Marston hates actors," Armin said, his brows bristling.

Sly tipped up his handsome face. "He called me a painted monster. And Jacko a peasant." Heminges belched on cue.

Will said, "He hates himself."

Pope cried, "Who would not—a University man, writing lasciviousness for the Blackfriar Children to act!"

"By God, Will!" Burbage exclaimed, "why not a ghost? This makes me mad!" He was gaily annoyed and swung his foot rapidly. "Make it the ghost of old Falstaff. 'I am thy father's ghost. Blessed are they that have been my friends, and revenge on the lord chief justice!' "

Heminges frowned and worked his mouth. "Our Will is a ggglory. He is our happy imitator of nature, a most gggentle expressor. I pray God his hand and mind are nnnever bbbad friends of each other."

"Well, by my faith," said Dickon. But he seized his authority quickly and pointed his finger at Will. "We have never asked anything of you but actable plays with good parts. We've never failed you, nor you us."

Will said quickly, "I'll prune and polish and make you laugh. Rob will be fool to Dickon's gaudy knight. No get-penny—I'll make you such a dish of laughter that Alleyn will lie down and die in solemn rage. But do not ask me for this *Hamlet!*"

There was silence. Who could be really displeased with wit and laughter? Armin was singing under his breath. Gus said, "Here is my leave, Will. Give me thy hand."

Burbage said drily, "Gus, soul, Will need not plead."

Heminges muttered, "Whatever he wants, I gggive him."

Sly, demonstrating a series of correct bows for Sam, said, "The handsome ghost of William Sly will trip with many mirth-provoking falls."

Dickon said, "The cupboard with the ghosts is closed. Will has decided. Now. Dekker proposed this morning a lampoon on Ben Jonson. What do you say to that?"

But Gib came for them at that moment in peremptory anger. He said the time was close, were they mad?—and jiggled chairs and drew them from the table when a man left his seat by an inch. Two great lords had already spread their feathers by the stage door.

Ned did not loiter with his brother. He ran after Sam to perform the ritual of knocking him down. It was Gus who walked with Will. He said nothing but Will sensed he gave him brief sidelong looks. At length Gus said softly, "There *is* a coven of witches close by Westminster, as I thought."

Will smiled. "And she is one?"

"I did not say so," Gus answered carefully.

"Ah, do not fool with me. I will tell you that all her spells are honest spells, and I'm an honest man again."

Gus was very careful. "What do you mean by that?"

"That conscience doth make cowards, that the day is full of sunlight, that women—all women—are the very instruments of life."

123

Gus looked at the ground as he walked, and did not nod to the two lords who sat in the sunlight. "Poor dog," he said.

Will was not angry. He had had such thoughts as these himself when he had set himself against old Adam. And, who knows, they might come again. But not now, not for a space of bliss.

As Several Noble Romans, in *Julius Caesar,* Will effected slight changes during the afternoon and was often on the stage. The sky above the open roof was bluer than cornflowers and the sun shone with vigorous good will into the eyes of the cheaper seats but spared the lords on the stage. Will knew, with a sweet congestion of the air about his heart, that she was here today. Ned died with great effectiveness as Cinna the Poet. There was much to be said for the congruities of life.

At length when the jig had been danced, Will stood by the tiring-room ladder, wiping the paint from his face and waiting for the lords to descend, and his lady. To see her was all he wished, to exchange some words that would dissemble what they must not show and yet would be a perfect acrostic of themselves.

The lords descended. With the jewels, colors, clothes, scents, swords, and high voices, the tiring room and the open space beyond were as fashionable as a palace. Here Burbage ruled as indisputably as Lord William. Burbage was dressed in silver armor and trunk hose of quilted satin. Lord William wore a doublet of Genoa velvet in a violet shade and trunk hose of silver cloth. Burbage's court was held with Lord Herbert at his right hand, and there was not even a subtle discrepancy between them save that one was nineteen and would soon be Earl of Pembroke and the other thirty-three and a gentleman by knack and sufferance.

Lord William's court was held with Will as center, but presently Will, with a gesture of such refined equivocation that any reason could be deduced, melted away. She was waiting for him somewhere, the clever girl, the little water sprite. He went to the stairs which led to the Housekeepers' Room.

There, in the corridor, a rush light burned in a sconce. On the dim stairs, he saw her kissing Sly.

He laughed. His brain was safe and his feelings all his own. Here was some game he must play. Sly moved first and pushed her from him. At that she turned. A wide childish smile came upon her face, and her flat black eyes leapt into life. She looked from one man to the other, making a little sound in her throat. She laughed again, and drew Sly by the hand to Will. In her farthingale and stiff bodice, her jeweled gloves and feathered hat, her painted face, and with the heavy emanation of musk, the metamorphosis was compelling, as though all bone and structure was familiar, but the appearance changed.

Sly broke away from her as she brought him up to Will. His face had reddened. He muttered some apology or assorted explication, and fled up the stairs. She smiled at Will.

"Friends all," she said.

"What game is this called?" he asked.

She smiled widely. "Why, God-made-lips-for-kissing."

"Mine and yours for kissing," he said.

She looked at him obliquely, and there was a cool speculation behind her kohl-painted eyes. "I'll not lead apes in hell," she said softly.

He tried to laugh, but his throat was clogged by his heart, which seemed to have left its accustomed place. "Sweet heart, only virgins lead apes in hell. You need have no fear." His thoughts were seeping out of that little closet in his mind where he had locked them well. But he'd seal it yet. "Tell me that thou art honest, and give me no reason to see otherwise, and I'll believe thee for blind Cupid's sake."

She looked at him in a veiled way and stroked the stiff brocade on her bosom. "Thou hast but one wit. I've halted all the rest."

He frowned and turned away. This was like an old play, one line remembered from the last. Well, tear it up and write anew! He looked at her briefly, and smiled, knowing that the man who doubts puts himself to his own purgation. She gave him back a smile, but he had seen this look before: her little chin doubled into her ruff, her eyes as cool and brutal as a child's waiting for a grown man to make a fool of himself. He took her hand.

"I beg you," he said softly, "be true to Lord William and to me. Faithfulness to two has more merit than faithlessness to three."

Her smile grew, her painted eyes were fixed on him with a simple curiosity.

"By God," she said, at length, "I do believe you are a man in love." She struggled for a moment with a laugh, and then she spilled it gay and incredulous.

He grew fiery red and his eyes stung. He struggled for a moment, then he said in a rage, "You are worse than Circe who turned men into swine."

He knew that someone stood behind him, but he had not the will to turn. When Gib, and not a stranger, spoke close to his ear, he felt a pitiful relief.

"Lord William is asking for both of you, wherever you may be. He knows not where."

She looked from one to the other with her black eyes as sharp as a monkey's and her laughter trembling.

"Tell Lord William," she said to Gib, "that a man of improvident jealousy is wearing suddenly a look of such astonished innocence that I must see this comedy to an end."

Gib did not stir. She made a little impatient shuffling of her feet. "I'd rather a crow cawed at me than a man in love." She was restless and entrapped, for the two stood between her and the door. Will said softly, "I'll go mad if you play the faithless heart."

She replied with an inexplicable gentleness, "Let thy wife hear thee speak such a huge translation of hypocrisy."

He took her arm in a savage grip. "Press not my patience nor my pain, which is too deep for pity."

"Oh, strike me and be damned!" She wrenched her arm from his grip. "What I wish I'll give, naught else!"

She pressed by Gib so imperiously that he fell back, and she went on through the door.

"Hot, hot," said Gib. "Hot blood, hot deeds."

Will turned on him fiercely. "I wish thou wert a dog. Then I might love thee!"

Gib hitched his shoulders. "She uses thee and then she leaves thee with all this hot blood."

Will sat down abruptly on the stairs. "Gib, in God's mercy, kill me."

"Not on my life."

"I wear my wits in my belly and my guts in my head!" Gib shifted his feet. "You speak like an ass."

Will covered his face with his hands. After a moment he lifted his head and looked at Gib in the flickering light. "Why should I do without her?"

Gib was careful to answer nothing.

"We are too nice," Will said thinly. "That is against nature. We corrupt ourselves opposing nature. What do you say?"

"That you dare not keep him waiting any longer."

Will drove his breath through his teeth. He rose suddenly. "Well, why are you holding the door? Let us go in." He stood before Gib looking into his sardonic face.

Gib's black eyes were cold as buttons. He smiled after a moment, and then straightened his body. "God speed the day thy mind is clear again so that I can at least water an ass at it."

"Gib, if I want her—!"

"Take her, but do not keep him waiting any longer."

Will wiped his face with the napkin. Last night he had set a course. To vacillate was to rehearse anew all the doubts and pains, to freshen conscience and show himself a man so infirm of purpose that he might with greater profit stand upon a roof and be a weathercock.

"I cannot live by thinking!"

Gib made no answer.

"Quarter thought, Gib, and what do you have? One part wisdom, and three parts coward."

Gib said, "Run with this fever and finish its course. Do what you must. Get in there *politicly*. For I pray God that habit will wrench awe from fools."

He waited grimly till Will had brushed his sleeve and set his collar straight.

She was standing close by Lord William but joking with Rutland. Her curled and bejeweled hair under the little hat was stiff as wires. Her small painted face had no expression, though when she saw Will a certain wariness came on it. But Rutland added something to what he had said and she laughed. Then Rutland saw Will standing close by, and simple good will rushed to his face.

Will was aware that Lord William was favoring Dickon with a courteous peroration on dramatic axioms, Aristotelian syllogisms, and a somewhat bizarre resolution for the death of Cassius. When he turned his splendid height and gave his hand to Will, his speech did not falter. This was the perfect protection for Will's bold design.

Will took her hand to kiss it. He said softly, "Madam, because you are an honest woman, somewhat given to lying, I've translated your merry ways out of false honesty into English. Will you hear, now or another time?"

She said nothing. Her hand was stiff and her expression guarded. Rutland said, as softly as Will had spoken, "Here's a wit of cheveril!"

"Not so pliant as cheveril, my lord," said Will sharply, "for my lady knows that an honest man will speak for himself when a fool will not. Shall I speak, madam?"

Her eyes remained black as jet, but she raised her brows with some kind of consent.

"In good English, thy merry ways are murderous. I bought my wit dearly, and I'll not sell it for thy false trade. I'll have my bargain."

She remained stiff as stays for a moment longer, and then she turned to Lord William and said loudly, "My lord, this man is thy servant, is he not?" She spoke loudly, and this made Lord William frown. Dickon, who had been replying to Lord William, worked a few mellifluous sounds to a conclusion.

"Oh, the servant of the muse, dear lady!" Lord William said.

"I mean, at thy beck and call!"

Now Lord William himself grew cautious. His reply was softly given.

"A poet, madam, comes at no one's—"

"God's lid! Such shilly-shally! He hath spoken like a saucy lackey and, under that guise, plays the knave."

Lord William was decisively unused to any form of rudeness, and his flush and flashing eyes showed that a woman's rudeness was as intolerable as a man's. He pressed his lips. But in a public theatre, before public servants, such a charge could not be ignored. He had one simple obligation as reflex as a sneeze. He spoke exactly what he should, no more.

"Sir, thou art in no condition to offend this lady. Thy duty is toward her and to acquiesce in all. Thus is your duty also paid to me. Ask the lady's pardon."

All heard. It was a public rebuke. Lord William had raised his voice into that vexatious silence. Ned, standing by the door, heard; Gib, putting away helmets and swords, heard. Condell, changing his clothes, and the rush boy, and the man who pulled down the pennant, heard.

The color left Will's face and he drew away. Lord William seemed to feel a momentary pang of deep confusion. It was incontrovertible that to offend her was to gibe at the speciality of rule, at degree, priority, and place; was to gibe at himself! Yet Will had withdrawn his arm.

"This thou knowest right well!" Lord William said to him with a poorly controlled agitation. "Reprove not my love by thy disclaimer. Why dost thou withdraw?"

For a moment Will made no reply. Then he bowed in answer.

The lords and friends, Levenson, Meyrick, Cuffe exchanged subtle looks and arranged their own epigrams to suit the moment. Lord William was too careful a young man to examine a shift in the wind too directly. He scarcely glanced at the lady, having concern only for Will's expression, all tone and texture.

She gave a small husky laugh, and Rutland was plainly enthralled by her actions, as who would not be, looking as she did: so without malice and yet so cruel.

The silence was like a hangman's hood. It was she who broke it. She said to Will, "You have not asked my pardon."

"Madam, I humbly ask your pardon."

She put out her hand to him and, as his lips touched the soft glove, she played a tarradiddle with his fingers. Lord William broke into a rush of fanciful and amusing speech. He included all. He then summoned his servant, who, reading his mind, handed him a jeweled pendant from his pouch.

Lord William gave it to Will. "And my love toward you."

The lady took up her mask and put it over her eyes. She was smiling to all. The withdrawal was executed with large style, and appropriate thanks were suggested to actors, musicians, tire men, rush boys and all.

Burbage and Heminges accompanied the great ones to the door.

Will did not move. He would have to crack his inflexible bones to make them obey. Gus stood beside him. His face was drawn. He said softly, "I did not kill him."

Will laughed. "Oh, *you* have too clear a mind to yield to folly."

Dickon returned. His face, well boned, decisive, very human, wore the expression of a man who had eaten something that disagreed with him. Heminges also came back and gave, somehow, the impression of an old staked bear. He stood swaying a little, not looking at Will, but saying off to a chair, "I will kkknot his uuuurinals around his hhhead."

At that moment, Rutland appeared at the actors' door and beckoned Will. He stood frowning as he drew and sheathed his dagger. When Will came up, he put his hand on Will's arm.

"I have been thinking. It is well known that love-sickness comes from too much black bile. It enters through the eyes, goes through the sluices into the veins, enters the liver—well, all this you know. What I wish to say is, you must take care. I have a doctor—very skillful. He will be honored. I will pay his account. *I* will be honored—" He was suddenly dismayed and embarrassed. "It is such a stupid illness. It humiliates."

Will thanked him. He felt an unwilling tenderness toward this youth.

CHAPTER *Ten*

SO, Will concluded, there is no real choice. Amen. Let there be no self-reproaches, no backward looks. Let there be no delusive fancy that bestial oblivion would bring any mercy.

Yet when Will Sly came to him, his lively face furrowed with his need to ask forgiveness, he scarcely allowed him to speak. He listened to a few disjointed words, and then he lashed him with the vulgarest speech he knew. He saw dimly Sly's sullen, almost tearful look, and felt a remorse he could not act upon.

One must be a free soul whatever the odds. One must preserve a freedom of choice even though the reality disputed the ambition.

How?

All duty, dogma, obligation that did not arise from one's own nature was a ghost-demon, and a rational man rose in rebellion. How?

The days were filled with autumn mists. Lord William sent another gift, and for several days his servant brought at nine each morning samples of his lordship's poetry and requests that "my master in these lines" speak candidly. He begged and then he commanded Will to come to him, but Will replied that all the new plays exacted his first duty.

After two days, he won back Ned.

They rehearsed the new play *What-You-Will* (or *Twelfth Night*, since the Master of the Revels had agreed that it would be appropriate for the Christmas season). Will detested it. Such a trifling of man with woman, and of woman with man . . . how could the fools bear such pains of unrequitement? Dickon, rehearsing Jamie, evoked all Viola's rueful sweetness and caused Will to sit down, in his Sea Captain's costume, his head in his hands, and think what a dunce he had been to give so much of his heart to these witty loving golden girls of his imagination. They would no longer serve. They were too far from pain.

Only Gus Phillips knew of the sucking holes that filled his mind.

Gus said angrily, "Remember, she has nothing to give. You cast away nothing if you cast her away. See her as she is. She is cruel so that she may give herself some feeling—unless, Christ save us, she is not human and has no blood!"

"*Revenge!*" Will laughed suddenly. "What could I make out of that old *Hamlet* when I know of no revenge to take on this poor forked radish that is me?"

Lord Rutland remembered his quarrel with Sir Piers, and Sir Piers did not forget. A follower of each was killed in the streets. Thus each warned the other.

On a day of drenching rain Lord Rutland sent for Will. He expressed his sympathy that his doctor's ministrations had been unavailing—aye, he had inquired. He was full of active graces, adages on women, artlessness. He paced about and shocked up his fair hair with his fingers. At length he came to the point.

The realm must be stabilized, the succession assured, the old Queen persuaded to recognize the only man she could trust, her dearest Robin, Earl of Essex. The people of London loved him as much as the Queen. They trusted his loyalty and knew that no other man loved her Grace as did he.

The people, however, were confused by the foxes which gnawed the roots of her power: Cecil, Raleigh, and Cobham. Strong and vigorous tracts, cogently argued, were necessities now. It would be worth a pound if Will would write one.

Will listened, hearing the rolling drums of his own rebellion. He listened to Rutland in silence though a crow of laughter broke in his vitals.

When Rutland had finished he walked up and down, his little blue eyes fixed on Will. Will sat swinging his crossed leg, his expression impassive. Oh, to be sure, he'd strike a blow for Will against authority! He rose and went to Rutland's desk and, in a wild humor, wrote out a doggerel verse.

He handed it to Rutland, who read it, guffawed, looked sharply at Will, read it again and tried to stifle his laughter.

"But this is not the cogent reasoning—"

"This is very cogent, my lord, for the sticks and stones of London."

"A reasoning, reasonable set of reasons—"

Will shook his head. Rutland glanced again at the verse and heaved with laughter. He opened a drawer and took out a purse. Will refused any payment.

His self-compensation lingered for some time. Walking home in the heavy rain, with water dripping from his hat brim, he laughed aloud once or twice. Even in so slight a thing as this, he found the pleasure of knowing that it was good and hit the mark. A very cogent good reason for being friends with words! He told no one.

It was not the danger which made him cautious. It was the lone bold need to strike a blow for himself against authority. He did not think of any danger.

A heavy fog settled on the city and on his brain. He scarcely noticed which was which. He trimmed and fashioned, rehearsed and kept store, counted receipts and enjoyed the view of impenetrable fog, eschewed all ale at dinner and at supper for the nightmares that it brought, patched matters up with Sly so that they embraced with old affection, and, to sum up, fancied that by a legerdemain so skillful that Ares must be his guardian angel, he would live until he died. He blessed the fog. It was such a right and proper state for man.

From noon till dark, men could scarcely find their way. Torches were never put out on London Bridge, and aldermen and burgesses were required to set a light before their doors. But no gleam, day or night, penetrated the supernatural atmosphere.

Preachers said some great evil had been done which made men fit only for such murk. Constables were increased, and the nights were shaken with their staves knocking against the walls of houses and with their cries of *Murder!*, both as futile as the lights. No plays were given, for none cared to hazard the trip across the river nor the dangers of the thieves who came up in swarms from the Isle of Dogs, and down from Islington. Nor, for that matter, could they see the actors on the stage.

Ned and Sam went into Surrey to cut wood for their fires. And Will, left alone, was touched with madness.

He sat in his room into which the fog drifted through the locked window, and he stabbed his pen at the table. Five, six, seven days had gone by, nine, ten, three weeks since she had diddled her fingers in his palm. Humiliation? Oh, that's the Latin word for dunderhead! In plain English, he was prepared like Doctor Faustus to sell his soul. To be disenthralled of his sin he would have to sell himself to God, but God would not buy such a bit of carrion flesh. It was as though increase of appetite grew by feeding on his thoughts.

He sent her a sonnet:

> Being your slave, what should I do but tend
> Upon the hours and times of your desire? . . .
> Nor dare I question with my jealous thought
> Where you may be, or your affairs suppose,
> But, like a sad slave, stay and think of nought
> Save where you are how happy you make those.
> So true a fool is love that in your will,
> Though you do anything, he thinks no ill.

She sent him a topaz in reply, effective against the passionate lunatic, frenzy, melancholy, and such madness as frantic lust.

He gave the topaz to the little tearsheet at the Cardinal's Cap. And then, to flagellate himself as any decent sinner must, he sent another sonnet:

> That god forbid that made me first your slave
> I should in thought control your times of pleasure,
> Or at your hand th' account of hours to crave,
> Being your vassal bound to stay your leisure!
> O, let me suffer, being at your beck,
> Th' imprison'd absence of your liberty,
> And patience, tame to sufferance, bide each check
> Without accusing you of injury.
> Be where you list; your charter is so strong
> That you yourself may privilege your time
> To what you will; to you it doth belong
> Your self to pardon of self-doing crime.
> I am to wait, though waiting so be hell;
> Not blame your pleasure, be it ill or well.

All his clever twistings, he told himself, had been the unnatural man's attempt to refute nature. Oh, God, was not all nature witchcraft, and all nature natural? He wanted her, and nature put no choice.

By Eros, she had rapturized humiliation by those playful touches on his hand!

Well, then! Well, then! Will would once more step forth to

whip hypocrisy! He drew in his breath gustily and made the floor boards creak as he hailed the day.

All was well. All was as it was and as it must be.

Did she hate men and devour them? If it were so, and he had only a poor remembrance, that did not make her less qualified in amorous arts, less constant in pleasure, or less attemptable.

The fog was in his mouth and nose. He could not see the street. He heard the muffled cries of the Watch and his nervous bell. He heard citizens calling to each other to be led home. But he was alive. All her promises coursed through his veins. He laughed aloud, he sang, he danced as he played a galliard on his lute.

Banished? The damned used that word in hell; howlings attended it. But he—he was not banished! He was alive, not wasted by remorse or unnatural suspirations.

That she had sent him no word merely piqued him on. He had more rights in her than a king in his kingdom. War took by assault, and this was the war of Venus and Mars who made of their coition Eros, the love god.

He took warning from his blunder that had brought on her rage. He had been masterful then but a fool. Now he would play a fool but be the master.

No one should summon her but himself.

If the god of nature were with him this night, she would not be attending on the Queen. He looked for omens. When the permission of blood and will conjoined, then intent was irresistible.

Let witchcraft join with beauty, lust with both.

Only the unnatural man sat down and wept.

He went below and knocked at Mrs Nell's door. When she opened it, he asked that her son take a message. She hesitated because of the fearful night, but when the boy heard that he would be given a ducat and a ride with Gabe Holmes, the cleverest waterman of all, he would not be held at home. And when his mother knew he was to go to the Queen's palace of Whitehall, she was touched with greatness.

She pressed Will to linger with her, and she gave him some parry to drink. He was lightheaded with joy.

Whether his lady came or not would in no way affect the outcome. Nothing could withstand his desire for more than a space. All would tumble as had his poor sick unnatural self.

Mrs Nell was a bright, pretty woman with a decent way to make in a parish of whores. She was a loving woman, though not in the way of Venus. He held such women in high regard. They kept life in the frozen earth. They were both good and blessed.

He was happy, and the two chatted like old friends of this one's business and that one's health, and of a marriage made in heaven against terrible odds; of a poor man's great good fortune who had found a royal in the street—nay, thou rogue, a gold royal with the Queen's inscription—and had thus a dowry for his blind but beautiful daughter. Mrs Nell would soon be going back to Suffolk where she came from, for her aunt had died and left her a farm.

Jolly, very jolly. He kissed her. Such women deserved a place in heaven before they died. He knew she had taken no money from the poor sick whore upstairs, but had given her food instead.

Presently he felt he must be alone to wait. She said that she would send her son to him the moment he returned.

He lay on his bed in the dark, his arms folded back of his head, and thought how man was an animal and happiest when he did not strive for godliness. He may even have slept, for animals sleep much and are much benefited. Yet he was wide awake and in a furious bliss when a knock came on his door.

It was Wat, the son, and he was alone. He gave Will a letter. Will begged him for a candle, and stood in the fuming black trying to feel the words through the page as Wat ran for the light.

The boy stood watching, not lubricously, but because he had so much to think about as he linked this man, his old friend, with the palace of Whitehall. Will, not looking up, put his arm about Wat's shoulder and thanked him out the door.

It was not that she had written much, but he wished it printed on his mind. "Praise be the gods for foul weather that thou dost think of me. Yet I'll not come to thee at thy command. The garden gate is open."

He paused outside the old man's door, greatly prompted to say his own words back to him—of doors that opened onto the garden of life. But the old man lived in another part of his sensibility.

The foul weather protected private deeds. Neither good nor evil could be seen; in the fog there was no past or future.

Gabe Holmes grumbled at being roused from his fire again, but he was, in fact, glad for the fare. It was an inching journey across the invisible river, and Gabe said he might be Charon on the Styx and hoped that Will was not bound for hell. Gabe had sailed with Drake in the golden days when the whole world was filled with hope and daring; he had fought at Cadiz with Lord Essex. Now he showed his skill.

They did not talk, for the fog crowded into their mouths and, moreover, they needed their four eyes and their ten senses for the journey.

"I be not going around in circles," Gabe said at last, "but where else I know not." Then they heard a man call and knew they were close to some shore. Gabe was not unduly vain that he had brought them straight to the stairs at Whitehall.

It was a Queen's man who had called, having heard the shipping of oars. But he did not question them, for these were public stairs.

The garden gate was west of the river wall, and Will groped his way. After an eternity of stop and start, his hand found the bend in the wall which turned and led him to the gate. He knocked. It was opened by an inch, and a voice said, "Who's that?"

He went up a private staircase—the waiting woman frisking ahead with a rustle of skirts—down an empty hall, to his lady's rooms.

He went to her straight. There was no moment even of greeting. He took her in his arms. "To exorcise thee is to conjure thee," he said between kisses, "thou excellent piece of fresh witchcraft."

"Hotly, hotly," she said with a running laugh. "Stand off or I will beat thee."

"Why should I stand off?" he said. "That is not why I came."

"Ah yes," she said, picking up her little fan and holding it before her like a dagger. "Why didst thou come?" And then she burst into such gay laughter that he laughed with her. The waiting woman standing by the door sniggered.

"To lay down the treasures of my body for thy fee is to be no better than a whore. There is another price I'll have," she said.

"Name it."

She was dressed in the white brocade of the Queen's Maid, with not many jewels since the Queen liked jewels best on herself. Her face was painted white with ceruse, her eyes were lined in kohl and her lips had red dye on them. The room was heavy with perfume, as though to fool the fog. It was his world only by diligent study.

"By-and-by," she said.

He walked up and down looking at her, and she bore his scrutiny with her dyed lips smiling and her kohled eyes showing little expression. His decision had been to play the fool but be the master. He was excellent at picking up his lines.

She gestured to her waiting woman, who brought a cup of wine.

"Now thou wilt tell me what there is to have and love in me, and I will add it up to see my price."

He answered, "I cannot see thy face with all that paint upon it."

"Never mind. Thou wilt tell me."

"Very well." He paced for a moment longer looking at her. "I hate thee, for when thou dost frown on me, then do I spend revenge upon myself though I am innocent."

"Item."

"I hate thee, because for thy sake I tyrannize on those I call my friends."

"Item."

"I worship those parts of thee that my wit sees clearly are defects."

"That is love!"

"I censure falsely what I see aright. I've sworn thee fair, but thou art black as night."

"Love—I think."

"The more I hear and see that gives true cause of hate, the more I love thee."

"Oh, my bonny lad!"

"Thy worst exceeds my best."

"Excellent, excellent."

"Thou dost give the lie to my true sight, and make me call the day the night."

"Ho-hum."

"I am a child, and only thou canst stop my crying."

She had sat very still as he moved before her, his mobile face making no secret of himself. Now she said nothing but put up her hands to the diamonded caul on her hair. Her maid sprang forward and lifted off the caul. The lady sat for a moment longer, tapping her fan on her arm, and then she rose.

Her maid stood vivid and attentive. The lady gestured again and smiled at Will. The maid took off her mistress' gown. Beneath was her kirtle in two parts of skirt and bodice. The maid began the labor of unfastening pins and ties, while the lady stood rubbing at her red lips and studying Will with smiles as though he were a new lover.

Beneath the kirtle was a French hooped skirt, padded and stiffened around the hips, and a bodice busked and laced. The maid took off her lady's sleeves, her skirt and bodice. The lady smiled and flung her fan at him. Her arms were now bare and as tempting as marchpane.

Then the maid unbound her petticoat, and the lady stepped out in her chemise. The maid, as smiling as her mistress, stood with the petticoat across her arm.

The lady took off her own shoes and stockings. Her voice was muffled by her bent position, but he heard her, though there was much pounding in his ears.

"Dost thou say I am not what I am? Then I am not; I am someone else. My life stands in the level of thy dreams." She pranced on her bare feet, and lifted her chemise.

Underneath were a boy's fitted pantaloons.

He frowned and caught his lip. Half of her was woman and half was not. She kept her side glance fixed on him.

"Since I live in thy dreams, thou art helpless," she said softly. "See thy helplessness, poor fool."

He said through ground teeth, "Very well—I am thy fool—but debase me quickly."

She gestured again to her giggling maid, who took off her own dress, her kirtle and petticoat. "Now put these on," she said to him.

He hesitated, he started to protest, but since he had forsworn his reason, what choice had he? He slowly picked up the dress.

The maid, tall and ungainly, capered in her chemise, but her mistress snapped her fingers. Will, with shaking hands, grinning like a fool, put on the woman's clothes as the lady put on a shirt and doublet. All he said was, "I'll not have thy painted face with me."

"Nor I thy man's. Cover thyself." She flung a mantilla to him as her maid poured water into a bowl. The maid scrubbed away her lady's paint, looking at him meanwhile with a steady grin.

He was nothing. He was hidden from the world and from himself. He stood with the lace covering his head and face, and the gown covering his body. He had forfeited himself. He felt a pang, but somewhere else. Manhood was somewhere else. Thought was somewhere else. But nature kept her own fires glowing, for nature was not fooled.

The lady took up a hat. She stood in front of him, so close that her breath stirred the mantilla. "We'll ride where I say, and spend the night and day in joy of each other." Then she laughed, tweaking and straightening the mantilla. He heard the maid laugh too as the door closed.

What is done cannot be undone; it is past now, and yet it is not past. I will not keep my word!

Yet—yet—God, Jesu, he thought going after her down the stairs. Be resolute, whether it be ill or well. Stay thy course or call thyself a hopeless lump of indecisive matter not fit for the dung heap.

She had laid her plans. A servant with two horses was waiting at the door she opened. The fog rushed to meet them. The horses snorted and jangled in a murk that frightened them, and the servant hastily ducked indoors again. She spoke calmingly to her horse, and turned its head toward the westward gate. His horse followed with a jerk; they were roped together against the mischance of the fog.

Paving bricks sounded beneath the hooves. When the bricks gave way to unpaved road, he knew that they had passed Westminster. It was mad and dangerous; he heard her laugh. His horse had a woman's saddle, and he found it hard to keep his seat.

She sang and asked riddles, but he did not answer. She cursed him, and when he did not reply to her curses, she laughed. She said, "Do not be offended. I know thou art a man," and laughed again, putting out her hand to caress him.

"The fog will ease somewhat across the river." He asked her how she would know the river until they fell in. "The devil has given me eyes," she said. With some awe he believed her, for, although none could distinguish one blur from another, she said, "This is Chelsea," and, "This is Chiswick," and suddenly, "Here now, somewhere—"

She got off her horse and he heard her stumbling in the fog. He called after her but she said, "Ah, here it is!" When she mounted her horse she turned its head toward the river and led him across a rustic bridge.

On the Surrey side, the fog did somewhat abate. After a mile or so they could see each other as dark shapes. The horses grew calmer, and she sent out her breath in a long hum. He said resolutely, "Stop. I will no longer wear this dress."

But she laughed and struck his horse. "Nay, that's my price."

It was all perversely artful, as ensnaring as the skirts around his feet: humiliation diminished by the conditions of adventure she imposed: free spirits mocking custom, souls full of daring.

In the simplest, most harmonious manner, she said, "Why there's a moon," and so it was, scudding among the clouds. As they rode, her odd little hoarse voice set all things in happy place. She spoke of all the ways that he had made her happy, and in this she was most crafty indeed. So crafty that, for all his rare knowledge of her, he still could marvel that one woman had such voluptuous gifts. Anguish, remorse, futility, had no more substance than the shadows designed by children's fingers to play against a wall.

He saw windmills slowly turning in the faint light, the creaking of their vanes sympathetic and domestic. A sleepy bird called, and a dog made a careful inquiry of the dark.

It was the simplicity which both rocked him to rest and started him awake at the same time. Her copulating voice had become as reassuring as true love. She truly cared for nothing but his love, she said. She regretted all the torments she had wished on him but they came from love. "Pity my waywardness!"

She set out her remorse so touchingly, her promises were so clear and simple, that only a hard heart could stay unmoved. The night was full of gentleness, sounds were all safe and sleepy, the luminous sky was filled with the music heard in silence, and all the reaches of the moon were filled with harmony. He felt the flapping of his woman's dress against his heels.

Without warning, she spoke of his wife. It was so well contrived, however, in this trusting world of two, that it scarcely touched him. Perhaps he felt some distaste at her questions but not enough to make the distaste real.

"How does she look? Is she fat or thin? How old is she? Does she rail at you, and you at her? Do you write poems to her? Do you love her?"

He answered on a wave of little sounds, "—um-hum-hum— forty-four—fair—" and she laughed with a greedy gaiety. "Why, she's a woman for another man, not thee!"

He felt that he must answer this, that his honor was engaged, but no words were right.

At last they came to an inn. She jumped from her horse and pounded on the door. After a time a sleepy servant opened to them and grinned at her as though he knew her. In the low, smoky public room, she threw aside her hat and said, "Bring us food and cider, and make the bed."

The sleepy servant saw Will. He worked his nose and guffawed. The lady too was watching Will. She tried to swallow her laughter, but she failed. She and the servant laughed together.

Will said nothing. He tore off the dress and flung it into the fire.

She dismissed the servant hastily and came to Will. She embraced him, she pressed herself against him and lifted her face. He hated her but he could not afford such a luxury. The gay little face with the kitten eyes was his own passion; her body became his; where starting flesh began its pleasure and found its pain was here. He groaned and kissed her.

But without warning she flung herself away. She kicked at the fire, she kicked at the settle, she kicked at the bitch and her puppies who lay near the fire, she looked sideways at Will.

"This place is hell!" she cried suddenly, throwing up her arms. "It's a midden heap. It will not do. Come!"

"No, I will not move."

"It jars on me! It's all awry. I will not stay!" She danced about, shrugging and shuddering, watching him.

"I beg you," he said desperately, "you have used me very poorly."

"Ah, but I shall use you very well. Trust me."

He wet his lips. He had hobbled his reason and left it tied at home. The servant came in with a tray of food. She ran at him crying, "Take off that vile stuff! Be gone!" The servant gaped, off balance with the loaded tray. She took some money from her purse and threw it on the tray. "There. Go!"

When he had stumbled out, she flung herself in Will's arms. "Oh, pity me. Care for me. Take me home."

"I will not."

"Oh, beast! Oh, ape! Thou dost take myself from me! Thou dost rob me of myself. Oh, it is monstrous! A woman is pillaged. I give no consent!"

Her agitation was angry and terrible, but his agitation was equally terrible and quiet. She looked at him suddenly, a queer deep inspection, and then said in a hard voice, "Well, thou art to wait, though waiting so be hell. I care not, if you but suffer."

He replied tonelessly, "I will not wait."

Something came over her then that he had never seen before. She was ugly and she was defeated.

Defeated? Hah! Defeat to win. In an angry venom she jerked him to the room she seemed to know so well.

Though he had what he wished, he did not wish it at all, for it was a stale rite, so sullen, hopeless, and degrading that he cursed her. Listening to him, she stared at the ceiling. Then as though by some resurgence of her powerful will, the ugliness faded, the flat dull face resumed a liveliness, as a tide covers again an exposed beach. She wept: true or false? Because she felt some guilt, or because she did not know what else to do to fill the time? He hated her coldly and calmly. Her wanton spirit looked out of every joint and motive of her body, but could not again deceive him.

Yet her weeping, always so penitential, teased some remnant of Christian hope. He said, "There, there," as though she were a child. She took advantage of him, teasing him again, but he stood up.

"I would to God you had never been born. We will go."

"Yes," she replied briskly. "I have had enough."

CHAPTER *Eleven*

SHE had handed him a gown, but it was he himself who had put it on with his own hands.

With a clarity that a sick man brings to his life, he saw that the disguise and the reality must be keenly parted; the seeming and the truth. *Seems. I know not seems. I know what is:* myself, unpurged but repentant, my self-respect torn but still my own, my fears and my temptations well marked and apprehended.

I scarcely knew myself until this moment and now, in God's name, I must love the man within so that I may lead him into the day again. Somewhere, untrammeled and undisguised, is the strength of life.

He wrote down, "Poor soul, the center of my sinful earth . . . within be fed, without be rich no more. So shalt thou feed on Death that feeds on men, and Death, once dead, there's no more dying then." Oh, the death of Death, a consummation devoutly to be wished.

He had one safe and certain joy: a power of words. Without it he would be tongueless, earless, armless; with it, he sustained a loving heart, agony, passionate intuition, but no weakness. Even the poems to her, of self-debasement, and the formal praises to Lord William confirmed a kind of strength, for their emotional cost computed up a gain.

In the Housekeepers' Room he studied Gus and Jacko, "Good friends, I need you."

Jacko said, "Ah?" and Gus, "Here we are."

"Let us find Dickon, and eat our dinner together."

Jacko's eyes grew bright. "I'll wwwhistle him up."

The four sat in the Falcon by the window looking on the foggy river. Dickon was filled with irritation at the weather, lost receipts; filled with gaiety because one day the sun would shine again, one day it would be spring. He had no intention of letting chance play any part in this confabulation now, but he did not press Will save to have more pie, more cheese, more jokes. At length Will put away his knife.

He leaned on his elbows; his eyes were on the foggy day. "As we are one and work together, let me heed my portents."

"What portents?" Dickon asked cautiously.

"Why, the portent that came to Brutus who conjectured wrongly that his strength would carry his philosophy. Dickon, think how greatly you could show a man divided, struggling against his soul's perdition: a man more divided than Brutus; indeed, as living men are cut in two."

Dickon made a response that came forth as a grunt. Then he tried a more congenial sound. Will spoke directly to him.

"Think how much more of man there is than a sudden blaze. There are unrequited wrongs and passion, and dreadful choice, and injuries that take more than revenge to set them right. And a man's own base cunning."

He hesitated. Gus shuffled his feet, and Jacko made marks on the table with his knife. Dickon kept his captain's eye on him. Will said slowly, "I do not wish to show cleverness self-defeated, nor even the will impotent. But if I set forth a man dishonest to himself, with only rash and lonely reason left, then we may truly see a human soul adrift."

"Is this—ah, would this be our compendium of ghosts and

145

blood previously called *Hamlet's Revenge?*" Dickon asked carefully.

"Yes."

"Ah. Ghosts and all?"

Will looked at him cheerfully. "I now believe in weird and haunting things that fly by night."

Dickon raised his brows, and then his eyes showed a light of great affection. "Well, let us know more, and we'll give thee our strong thoughts."

"I have strong thoughts aplenty."

"Hum. What has happened to your tongues, you fools? Have you no gifts for Will?"

"I take his gift to us," said Phillips quietly.

Heminges said gruffly, "He hhhath not fffailed us yet."

"Hell's buttons," said Dickon in justified distemper, "can he do no wrong?"

Will looked at him with upturned mouth. "Dickon, you've explored the merry heart and gone to greatness. I'll take you to new fields."

Dickon, not to be outdone, said with humor, "Ah, I'll take you there—poor lame donkey without me on your back." He expelled his breath as though a load had been laid down. "Will, you'll not tweak the censor?"

"No."

"Nor offend the noble lords by a prince too much a man?"

"No."

Dickon then put out his hands in a formal gesture. "I wait."

Will laughed. He stood up and laid his share of payment on the table. "I know what you will all attempt if this *Hamlet* pleases you. You'll cut it about. Each will alter a point, each shape up his speech, each decide, in the end, that it lacks some commodity for him."

Heminges gave a snort of laughter. Dickon said, "In five weeks, Will?"

Will carefully rumpled Dickon's hair. "More likely six or seven."

The fogs lifted and the snows came. The city was quiet because men and carts were muffled by snow. The river froze and there was a cautious going and coming across the gray ice. The watermen's families starved and there was great suffering on every hand. The scavenging birds picked hopelessly at the frozen garbage, and sometimes on still days the pitiful roars of the lions could be heard from the Tower like creatures in a dream. Poor small beasts ran wild with hunger.

Even braziers set at close intervals did little to warm the Globe, and a loud noise of stamping feet interfered with every play.

When *Twelfth Night* was first given the snow had laid a thick blanket on the edge of the stage and a deep pile of snow on the hats and shoulders of the groundlings who stood in the pit, their hands tucked under their arms. On the stage the nobility was wrapped to the nose in furs and huddled over braziers.

But they all liked what they got and clapped their hands. Mrs Burbage and Mrs Heminges stamped their feet and clapped with all the rest.

"Very nice!" said plump and beaming Mrs Heminges later, kissing Will.

"Oh, excellent good merriment," said Mrs Burbage, kissing him. "Hear how they laughed. You've made a nice good part for Dickon, though I fancy he's too fat. Well, I will see."

"Winifred, I love thee!"

She laughed. "Then, sweet friend, kiss me again."

"Honey Will," said Mrs Heminges, "our homes are thine. Come and be merry."

"That I will, dear Rebecca. Kiss the little ones, till I come and give my own."

Heminges, always thinking of new ways to protect their interests, devised strips of woven hemp crossed over and over each other and nailed to the edge of the open roof, with thatch laid sparsely on. But the snow continued to fall, and presently brought down the hemp.

Mrs Nell adopted a homeless waif, half dead with cold. Will looked at the child and at Mrs Nell, and kissed them both.

147

"You are a true woman," he said, and though she might wonder a little at his words, she was not puzzled at his tenderness.

"She hath a name," said Mrs Nell, "but she is so cold she hath forgotten it. So I'll call her Perdita until she recollects herself. In the spring, we'll go to Suffolk."

The days of Christmas came. The icebound barges of the nobles were decked in holly, and all the little boats that could go nowhere had garlands at their prows.

Mrs Nell, with a pink nose, stood nailing holly and bay to her house, and on the windows of the Cardinal's Cap were bay and ivy. All Southwark, for that matter, about the river where the brothels lay, was gay with boughs. Bay and ivy were fastened also to the pump and the standards of the streets. And the old man, Will's neighbor, went carefully down the icy street with a sprig of holly in his hat.

In the Bishop's Church of St Saviour, holy songs could be heard night and day.

On Christmas Eve, Will and Ned, Pope, his apprentices and all his orphans, Gus and his family, went to church. Later, singing songs, they walked as far as the frozen marsh.

" 'Tis said that on this night the bird of dawning singeth without rest," said Pope, "and more, 'tis said no spirit dare stir."

"But witches plenty!" cried Mrs Phillips in her shrill little voice.

"Nay, the time is wholesome, neither planet harms, nor fairy flies, nor witch has power to charm, so hallowed is the night."

Will said softly, "Indeed, I part believe it."

On Twelfth Night they gave their new play in the Great Chamber at the palace, in the warm, reeking atmosphere of the Queen. All the courtiers were dressed in white, but the terrible old lady blazed with jewels and color, and her red wig was like a flame that none could put out. Will's lady was not there. He hoped she was in hell.

Everyone whispered and conjectured, and at the center of all conjecture stood Lord Essex as beautiful and arrogant as Lucifer. He had recently offended the Queen and been confined to Essex House. To bless the season his restraints had been lifted, but she would not have him near her, though no one could tell from her wrinkled glance whether or not he was a fallen angel. Her eyes followed him more than the play.

This rich insatiable world merely confirmed the bad temper of the times.

Rutland was seen more and more in the company of Essex, and Lord William once struck his cousin in public, though he promptly asked his pardon.

Three new plays were enacted at the Globe to offset three put on by Alleyn at the Fortune. At one play Will saw the lady sitting between her brother, the Marquess, and Lord William, and she made a play of her fingers toward him. He took fair warning. While the jig was danced, he fled to the Housekeepers' Room and stood alone in the bitter cold. A brave ass!

Yet in no way could he leave the bitter cold or the dark room black as ignorance. His mind danced. Where is Sly? Where is Lord William? Who does the act of darkness with her? Who will give me an ounce of civet to sweeten my imagination?

Satan's honorable hell is empty, for all the devils are roosting in my brain.

Oh, Will, he reproached himself, teeth chattering in the cold, you are a Christian, you are a man. Must the hell-hated lie try your heart again? In Christ's name, she is my own insensate wickedness, without sex or name unless I call her Weird Woman, Fate.

He stood at the lonely window watching the snow fall on the frozen field across which foes and friends were hurrying home. *To darkness, fleet souls that fly backward, go . . .*

The next day Lord William came to Southwark, having learned that the fall of snow would again close the theatre. His friends were with him: Rutland, Herbert, the lady, the lady's own sister, masked, and, in a great lumbering coach, someone's aunt.

They invaded the street with cries and laughter, with the jingling of silvery bridles, the brilliant pawing of horses, and their own superb arrogance of quilted satin and velvet. Will, looking out the window of his room, saw them.

While three servants ran for Will, Gus, and Sly, Lord William rode fiercely up and down the narrow street, churning the snow, cried on by the shouts of his friends and the lighthearted ladies.

Will watched with stony eyes, his hands behind his back. Here were indeed Fate and the Weird Woman, and the devil in the form of Lord William. He watched their actions as though they belonged to a tale told in the firelight.

Lord William's horse was a great gray stallion which performed heroic feats of equilibrium and challenged the air with its flailing forelegs. Lord William's cheeks were rosy, his eyes like holiday candles, his dark hair tossed in the sun.

So the bait was dangled. Will would not take it.

Lord William's servant came, but Will did not respond to his knock. He remained where he was, a stone man, partly concealed.

Will heard Rutland shout a wager and saw him guide his horse onto the ice. The horse picked its way for a pace or two on the rough ice, and then broke into whinnies. It was more absurd than ten clowns hitting each other with bladders. A servant slid onto the ice and, smirking, led the great horse up the bank. Rutland sat with his arms folded across his chest and mock rage on his face. Lord William shouted that such a horse was afflicted by its color; white horses were under the pallid control of the moon.

The great lords and ladies and the coach took up all the space in the street. The residents had to retreat before the restive horses. Some ventured, because of the terrible cold, to beg of the lords, but they got nothing for their pains. Two children, crying for cold and hunger, begged for the love of God, and the old lady in the coach flung them a penny.

The lady cried, "Oh, la!" in a light voice and struck her foot with her whip, so that her mare danced on the white ground and her long sky-blue skirt whipped like a pennant. Lord Herbert, sitting on his high sorrel horse, leaned his elbow on the top of the coach and exhaled his breath to form clouds. These he pondered with half-closed eyes. Now and then he leaned against the neck of his horse to speak to the aunt within the coach, and then sat erect again to blow more patterns of vapor and to open his blue eyes as wide as he could.

Lord William cried out at the misbegotten laggards, the players, and listened to his servant who had returned without Will. The whole occasion had become a descant, Will now saw, not a tale for firelight: a descant about a Lady incapable of fidelity, therefore blameless, who had seduced a golden lord, and by this means entrapped a clown.

The virtue of such a variation lay in its sentimental comment which allowed Will to see that this scarlet lord might be cold, self-endeared, solipsistic, sensuous, and brutal, but was, in fact, innocent of betrayal—for all that was true between them was their poetry, and this had not been betrayed.

Lord William made an abrupt gesture and dismounted. Will saw him marching across the crusted snow toward him. Will had a ludicrous desire to leap into bed and say that he was sick.

Lord William threw open the door without knocking. He stood smiling, and then he advanced with his arms outstretched.

"Servants are dolts. I come myself, the only proper petitioner."

Will kissed his hand. His answer was more ironic than he intended. "*Laudator temporis acti sum.*"

As they emerged, with Lord William firmly linked to Will, Sly and Gus came down the street, led captive by Lord William's servants, who held the bridles of their horses. Gus's expression was careful; only Sly bounded into the present with no reservations. Lord William mounted his great horse and the two ladies galloped carefully around the three players, striking them lightly with their whips. Will was aware of only one lady, but he did not look at her. He felt the light blows of the whips and smiled in all directions but hers. He hoped that like the baited bear he too might strike a blow.

Lord William gave a bugle-like cry, and lords, ladies, and players turned their horses into the white world under a brilliant sky. They rode in a streaming banner of color, shouting to each other and singing songs of love and winter.

There was something unspeakably dear about the earth transformed by snow with the radiant sky above. The rolling hills of Surrey became a subtle compound of distance, depth and all the innocence of God's seventh day.

Rutland's horse fell, and Rutland did not mount again. Instead he rolled down a hill and made snowballs to fling at the others.

The lady slipped off her horse and, tucking up her skirts, ran over the hard white crust to Rutland, and they rolled in the snow till her mask came off and then they covered each other's face with handfuls of snow.

The old aunt, who was not seen, squealed a protest. Lord William galloped with a slow, labored caution down the slope and stood over the two in the interests of justice. Then he started a hare and called for his bow and arrow.

Rutland leapt to his horse. Sly galloped with him, and the sister armed herself like Diana and ran down the hill.

The lady scrambled up as best she could and started back to her horse. But she was entangled by the snow and, laughing, fell again and again. Will could watch no more and dropped from his horse to give her his hand. She clung to him, merry and spent, her cheeks the color of cherries. She shook out her sodden skirts and fastened them up with a chain.

"You will not hunt, nor will I," she said. "For me a hare is not enough; for you it is too much. What shall we do? Let us skate. Come." From the miraculous hamper in the coach, which had disgorged the bows, now came the skates, and she sat under a frosted willow tree while her servant made them fast.

Will put on his with slow fingers.

She stood up sturdily on the ice, not wavering, and glided toward him with her hands outstretched. He took her hands and, in the quiet concord of skating, they started down the river.

Her merriment dropped away. She looked younger than her own youthfulness. They went swiftly and smoothly in silence. Sly, who had abandoned the hunt, and Gus sped past them racing. Lord Herbert went before them calmly and backward, performing turns, arabesques, and leaps of remarkable skill, and then skated gravely away by himself.

Still they said not a word; they skated for a mile or more. Then she sighed. It was a sad little moan which seemed to come unknown to herself. She pressed his hands and slowed their pace and gradually they came to a slow circular halt.

A bonfire had been lighted by the river wall of a great house and she glided to the bank within the warmth of the fire. Children and servants were tending the fire.

For a long time she stared at the sun, and then she looked at him. Her manner was sober and full of restraint. Clasping her hands against her knees, she spoke.

She loved him. She cared truly for nothing but his love and honor. She regretted bitterly all the torments she had put on him, but they came from fear.

Her little hoarse voice set all things in their place. "I live in many fears. Pity them. Drive them away. Be my own and I will be yours." She put his hand against her cheek. She asked his pardon for all unfaithfulness. "I am as true as truth's simplicity."

He did not know what to say. Simplicity . . . he was the perpetual servant of that simple truth miscalled simplicity. He was a man who, given a moiety, believed with all his heart in the wholesome life. He looked at her askance. In a rapid stream of words, she told of a fiery horse in her childhood which had pawed the air and looked at her with red-hot eyes. It might have trampled her to death, but she had felt how glorious it would be to have it love her, and she put away her fears. She subdued it with endearments and with sugar, and rode it, at length, for its pleasure and hers. Was this not very brave?

She asked it so artlessly that love and pity sprang in him. "But at other times," she went on, quick and sad, "I am not so good or brave, and I do many wicked things for which God doth punish me. But I must feel, else I do not know for sure that I exist or make a mark on others."

She plucked at the side of the bank where stiff grass broke through the snow. "Perhaps one defect will be that corruption which brings me finally to hell. But I must chance or die."

She looked at him and smiled. Against his will he saw her smile as tender, her manner brave. He warned himself against this thought as being far too subtle sweet. He said merely, "Why do you say this now?"

"Because I must cleanse my heart." Her manner was so calm and clear that only an evil man would see dissembling. She was as unassailable and candid as his own daughters.

Because he was a man of healthy spirit, who could not harbor an injury or fail to seize all evidence of hope and wholesomeness, he abruptly cast his dice. He sat down beside her and put his arm about her shoulders as though she were a child. The children minding the bonfire came and sat with them, and Will put his other arm around a little girl.

To call this false was to call primroses sinful. It cast out evil and cleansed the heart. Thank God, thank God, he could love this innocence. He could swear her fair and think her bright, and so confound the powers of the world. For had not God made her a bonny child, and was it not his duty as a Christian man to acknowledge and preserve the grace within?

The snowy riverbank and the bright day were as fixed forever as a painting on a piece of cloth. There it hung in his mind for solace, joy, and reassurance, confirming what he had always known, that there are no tricks in plain and simple truth. He could take care but he would also list the grace within. It was a soothing thought and most pliant.

Only Ned frowned and watched him, seeking for something he was too young to name.

That next Monday, Will was dressed to go onto the stage. As he waited for the trumpets to blow, he heard Ned's voice, high and excited, and saw Ned running through the actors' door. Who was with him? He could not believe his eyes. Tom Greene! Tom —Tom from Stratford! Tom, whom he had last seen in a dream.

Will hardly heard the greeting he gave. Tom Greene in London? What of Stratford?

"In God's name, speak!"

Tom, with Ned crying out like a chorus, raised his brows and shrugged his shoulders and said, "I'faith, i'truth, 'twill keep till later; you are busy, Ned dragged me here against my judgment."

"Speak!" said Will.

It was Ned who shrieked, "Dick Quiney and Henry Walker and Hamnet Sadler and Thomas Rogers have been brought from home *in irons* and lodged right here in Marshalsea prison!"

"No, it is a lie!" said Will, sitting down on the nearest box. "Irons—the best men of Stratford! Tom!"

Tom crooked his lip. "It is because of Sir Edward Greville. Great madman. As lord of the manor, and Stratford's overlord, he claims the right to enclose the verge along the riverbank. Well, it seems that Stratford has an ancient right—you know this before I do—of public pastureland. So, what acts do our gallant friends perform? They take shovels and mattocks and dig up the hedges he's planted."

"Oh, hell!" said Ned, meaning his own exile in London.

Will whooped with laughter. "Tom, I'd give six months of summer to have seen it! Henry, Hamnet, old Rogers, Dick. In their Sunday clothes? How are they now?"

"You'll see. Right perky."

"And you? What have you done?"

"I'm a lawyer, cousin. Have you forgotten? Staple Inn and Middle Temple." He said it with a bite. "When the Council applied to the law against Sir Edward, the Council got clapped in irons. They're a litigious lot, and I'm here to see that no mistake is again made in the law." He smiled at Will. "We all have a mind, I think, to prove that law has been made for man and not man for the law."

"It's a young thought," said Will smiling in his turn. "Therefore it has my blessing."

Ned could scarcely bear his paint and robes for that afternoon. When the performance was over, he and Will went, still in their paint, and talked to their friends behind the bars.

Dick Quiney was Will's dear friend. So too was Hamnet Sadler for whom his dead son had been named. And Rogers was the butcher, a very prime cut of meat! And Henry Walker, a mercer like Quiney, was a gentleman, a churchwarden, and an alderman: they were all his friends, who knew the inside of his home as he did theirs.

"He's a madman, Sir Edward," Quiney said, a little embarrassed, yet not unaware of martyrdom. "He thinks, as lord of the manor, he can take from us our great self-governing charter given us two reigns ago. To compound his mischief, he says we carted off six loads of willow which belonged to him. Indeed we did, and made a good show, for how else can one speak to such a fool?"

Will shouted with pleasure, and they laughed with him behind the bars. Quiney, who was High Bailiff and head man of Stratford, said, "He called it riot, and here we be, at the Queen's mercy."

"Never mind," said Will, "the Queen loves royal prerogative even more than property. She'll sustain a charter." He returned for a further word. "I'll solicit for thee of Fulke Greville. He has the Queen's ear and no love of his cousin. And I'll go bail for thee."

He and Tom were rowed across the river to Whitehall. Tom delivered a brief encomium on the joys of country living in contrast to the devil's misery of this depraved and filthy city. Will did not comment; his thoughts revolved. Tom talked steadily in his heavy grave voice, without looking at Will, of the legalism in this case: what Will's father had counseled (as a former High Bailiff he knew all quiddities and oddities); what his mother had counseled (for she had a shrewder mind than most men's). He gave his own opinion as they were rowed past Middle Temple. Will tried once or twice to ask of wife and daughters, but he could not bring out the words. He would ask Quiney, carefully, in a general way.

Greville's secretary arranged that bail should be granted, and Will put up security. Out came the Stratford men, joking in a studied kind of way, but pleased with themselves nonetheless. Those who had not seen London informed themselves of the sights, but not before Ned had asked a dozen questions about home and games: had the lads from Bidford sent in a challenge yet? Had any thrown the sledge to break the record? Who had made up the sides for football? This year the goals would stretch across the river!

One or another answered all questions, and they told in addition of sicknesses and thefts and the Autumn Fair. While Tom was contentedly lost in the law of it all and the life of the Temple again, Will and Ned took the others to the Tower, where they peered carefully into the pit to see the wild beasts, and then Will hired a wherry to take them down the river as far as Greenwich Palace. There they drifted till they had filled their eyes with one more palace of the Queen and the tall-masted ships from far away.

All the while they talked of Stratford. Oh, it was a bitter winter. A cow had fallen into a pond and they could see her dead eyes staring at them from under the frozen surface! They tapped the sides of the *Golden Hind* rocking at its anchor at Deptford. What things it had seen—crocodiles and sea beasts and men with two heads! They watched birds rise from the Isle of Dogs, and drew close to Wapping Old Stairs, where sea thieves were chained to be killed by the tide.

"Well, bad men must be punished," said Henry sadly.

They drifted around Billingsgate to watch a coal barge fit its way into the wharf, and Quiney said a fourth of the newborn infants had died from the cold and the damp. "What can we do but burn coal tar and pray?"

They lingered down Fleet Street to see the puppet shows and all the strange exhibits . . . a little dragon, a sweet, blinking little beast that had something in its eyes like his little lady, a five-legged calf, an Indian from America, a dead mermaid . . . and lingered in Charing Cross to buy pictures in the picture shops, though painted images created some disharmony in nascent Puritans.

They stayed in London barely a fortnight. Will did not stir from them except to work. He thought of the child-lady, so penitent and tender, but he thought of her safe in some budding grove, fair, fresh and sweet, and there he told her to remain.

Fulke Greville, who was a man very clear in spirit and in love with poetry, used his good offices with the Privy Council. When he sent for Will to tell him this, he used the occasion to talk of the poet's function to examine, without concealment, the baggage of the soul. He lingered over this, and poured two glasses of wine to prolong the time.

Sir Edward had succeeded merely in sending Stratford men to London to remind Will that every Stratford street and lane, each arch of the bridge, each glint of sunshine on church tower was his own. These Stratford men were as well versed in the world as London men, they played their music on village greens or in their parlors, read their Latin or their English, and were perhaps more honorable, for were they not seeking the rights of many, though by no means insensible to the snares laid by humankind?

"Oh, God, and His Jesu, bring me home again!"

It was a strange cry, considering how much at peace he was. The cry had torn from him within the hearing of Ned, who shouted, "Well, who is the bigger fool, you or I? Let's go!"

Will caught his head between his hands and rocked it back and forth.

"Do you dare?" Ned shouted. "No! All trussed up like a fowl for a whore's eating!"

Will did not answer.

He asked no questions about his own home, for it was both too near and too far. He did not want old suspicions vivified, he did not want old emotions wakened. To hear Tom speak of his wife might break the truce with himself. He did not dare, for the lady was stirring in that budding grove.

To love her innocence was to be alive to her and so by slow stages to let her steal into his heart and from his heart through his blood and at length to his mind, which she could infuse in oblique and guileful ways before he was awake.

Yet Tom eyed him in a way that could not be ignored. He let Tom speak. "This is a filthy place to live, with whores and boozies all about and decency outlawed. Surely no man seeks such a life unless the bait is taking."

"What bait?" asked Will carefully.

" 'Tis for you to say."

"I do not like your imputation."

Tom was silent for a moment. "Then I ask your pardon. But what would you think had you the cues given me by one and another?"

Will struck blindly with his words. "Ned is a young fool—!" and thought, And I am a greater one to yield so much.

Tom did not contradict him. But after a moment he said in a somewhat gentler voice, "At home you're a gentleman. See what you are here."

Will wished to God that they were gone—and that he could beat Ned.

As the men of Stratford at length said their goodbyes and started for the boat, Tom held back. He said to Will in his heavy pleasant voice, "You have not asked one question about your wife. Is this not strange?"

"*You* say it!"

Tom looked astonished. "I? Why not I? I sit on guard in your house and keep your ledgers matched. Such silence is unnatural. It's not like you. What shall I tell her?"

"How *is* my wife? How are my chicks? How is my mother, my father, my brother, my sister, my sister's children?"

Tom said severely, "Your wife hath received no word from you."

Will said quickly, "Nor I from her. Why did you not write, since she cannot?"

Then Tom looked at him most oddly. After a moment he said shortly, "Ned has the news. Ask him."

"What news?"

Tom said again sharply, "I like it not!"

"*You* like it not! What news?"

"No news, save doings too small for your nobility."

Will was seized with anger. "What news? How is my wife?" he cried.

"Peace, peace! She is well enough."

Will seized his arm. "What do you wish to say with these ambiguous givings-out? How is my wife?"

Tom, speaking roughly, said, "She will do very well with my support and guidance. She is a wise woman, your wife."

Here was a turnabout. In his mind Will shouted, *All I ask is that the tree be not shaken too soon!*

Let his lady not stir from the frame in which he set her—see her fair and loving, clear and honest, sitting forever beside him on a snowy bank. Let his wife—what in hell's name had Tom lisped, hinted, shaken his head on?

That night he wrote his wife a letter. He sent it to his brother Gilbert, who would read it to her, not Tom.

"Dear Wife. You are much in my thoughts. I greet and embrace you and our daughters. I fancy that winter has laid a heavy

hand on all, but spring will come and glad hearts rejoice. I am
well in health, and so is Ned. Exchange kisses in my name. Your
loving husband."

Then he added a postscript.

"A man and wife being two are one. This is a conundrum. But
since you are a wise woman, as rumor hath it, it will not put you
out."

CHAPTER *Twelve*

A JANUARY spring tantalized. The thaw set in, the ice broke.
Little birds looked for food in a cadenza of twittering. Small
boats dared to creep among the floes. The fog returned.

Will evaded Dickon's questions, for the play had made small
jaunts into nowhere. The words of Sir Fulke Greville reverberated in his mind: *The poet's function is to examine the baggage
of the soul.*

All morning, when he was presumed to be writing at his play,
he dwelt on Brutus' passion and the lonely world in which
Brutus had sought himself.

That afternoon an unsigned verse was fastened to Will's costume. It set forth the coupling of his lady with Sir Piers Dalglish
as though it were a common knowledge. It made no mention of a
snowy bank where children sat.

He held the scrap of paper in his hand for a long time, and
then he tore it up, for his obligation was to keep good faith with
innocence. Yet there was a blur before his eyes.

He stood in darkness for a moment, his thoughts muddy and
confused. Then with great force he compelled himself to go
about his business. He would not join again in that roundelay
. . . *but if innocence were not innocence but a spell cast on the
mind!* No, he was done with double thoughts . . . *yet if innocence is not innocence but the worm in the bud . . . and if craft,
being quicker than innocence, devours the lamb? . . .*

He had set up a loving image with which to cool the imagination and lay thrift upon the conscience, and by hell or heaven, he'd hold his course thereby.

The next day she stood in the tiring room, painted and jeweled, her mask in one hand. She was dressed as brightly as a bird, but a peahen beside Lord William's plumed splendor. She seemed downcast and moody. Will paid his duty to her, but she greeted him with the barest smile and so he withdrew to a distance, where he watched her as he talked with Sir Gelly Meyrick.

Meyrick was a low, rapid murmurer who left his auditor free to pursue his own thoughts. *See how her gaze is chained to Lord William like Andromeda to her rock!* The temperate Will asked why he should watch her so hungrily if he were an honest man; the Will of divided counsel could not take away his eyes.

By Venus' doves, she seemed to plead without her tongue . . . where had he seen that look before? Why, in his own passion, helpless, hopeless, chained.

Sir Gelly became aware that he had no listener. He took offense until his eyes followed Will's, and then he laughed a little.

"God's blood," he murmured, "I'd thank no woman to love me as she loves that man. A leech, no less, save I fancy he is bloodless and so feels no loss."

Will heard and did not hear. He opened his mouth and a strange voice asked, "Has this abject love been well known for long?"

"Oh, what time or matter is in these things?" and Sir Gelly sniggered.

Will saw the hunger on her face as a chart of passion's reefs and shoals. Let a careful mariner be warned by it—and yet it gave great pain. Never had she shown this face to him.

Without warning, Lord William turned his eyes on her, and she opened her mouth as though her breathing were constricted. At that moment she gave all humbleness, all dreadful supplication. She begged not to be cast away. Lord William's glance remained cold yet voluptuous. Never had Will seen her soul before. It was as distraught, lovesick and anguished as his own. Here was her true love in which self-love was lost.

How overthrown was any charge against Sir Piers. As for Will, Will must have been long since cast out—if he had ever had a place.

His first obedient thought was *Rejoice*. He turned away.

How well he had exorcised all evil! When suffering comes, it comes not single but in battalions. I scarcely knew I loved so much. I scarcely knew myself until this moment. Oh, sleep— sleep. He that sleeps feels not the toothache.

It was the best he could muster.

Sleep, thou ape of God.

He stumbled homeward.

A man must know himself or the poet dies.

Counsel terrible and irrefutable, and he did not know how to do or undo it. It pierced the crust of self-will, self-love, self-justification. Yet beneath the broken crust was an inchoate and formless mass, like the primal sea of consciousness.

Yet it was not like the sea, but like doors opening and closing in a great wind.

So Jacob had wrestled with the angel and had said, I will not let thee go until thou bless me. "Bless me!" said Will in a thin voice, "or I curse you."

The sound of a recorder was suddenly as pungent as smell. He was stricken. There must be no music! The music continued. He paced to the window and back. Can a man know himself?

Terra incognita! Death horrible, most horrible, with all thy lusts cut off while in full bloom.

The divided man—here was the ghost! The murdered and the murderer, one. Surely the devil of this knowledge haunts a man from bitterness to madness.

He laughed shakily and stood for some moments fingering his pen and stroking one trembling hand up and down his thigh. He stared at some words he had written down, but he would not be fool enough to read them.

Persistent as dripping water, the sound of the recorder insinuated his mind. He lay on his bed listening, one arm across his eyes.

Life sweet, life heart to heart. After a time he listened for the source of the music, and he lifted his head slightly as he followed it to the old man's room. Old man, unafraid of heaven or hell, knowing the nature of ghosts. The old man was his honor. Could he bear him now? He rose and crossed the hall.

The old man glanced up somewhat startled and then he smiled. In the center of his room was a great round frame which turned upon two firm and immovable hooks opposed to each other. On it, the little owl was riding. Here in this sanctuary of the old man only good was transacted.

Will stopped and stared at this frame of the world and at the two firm and immovable hooks on which it turned. He glanced through the open fretwork of frame at the old man watching him.

"How did you prove that it was round?" Will asked, saying what came first to his mind.

"By three. First I compared it for that likeness which it has with the chief idea, that is to say, the shape of God's Mind which hath neither start nor finish and must therefore be compared to a sphere. Second, by its aptness to move and to contain, for were it not round it would not be so apt to turn nor to contain so much as it doth, since roundness holds in. Third"—and he laughed and held down his cheek to the mouse which sat on his shoulder—"necessity proveth it to be round, for did it have angles and corners it would not turn with such ease, or, in turning about in a jerky way, would leave empty places that nature abhors."

Ah, Will loved him, so beautiful, benign, and unhaunted. "And all this around us?" Will said, giving shape to the empty air.

"The eleven heavens and the spheres, so 'tis said. That I cannot confirm. 'Tis said the first is the sphere of the Moon, the second the sphere of Mercury, the third of Venus, the fourth of the Sun, the fifth of Mars, the sixth of Jupiter, the seventh of Saturn, the eighth of the Fixed Stars, called fixed because they are fastened in this heaven like knots in a garden, the ninth the Crystal Heaven, the tenth, the First Movable of a most clear and pure substance without stars, that moves with equal gait from east to west making a revolution in twenty-four hours. The eleventh the Imperial Heaven that is immovable, the foundation of the world, most round of shape, most great in quantity, most clear in quality and most high in place, for there dwells the Mind of God and all His angels."

Will walked around the globe, and the little owl turned to see him pass and ruffled her feathers when she lost her balance.

"You have not put man in the center of this empty globe," Will said with a smile as he stroked the little owl.

The old man laughed. "Whatever thou seest, it is God I have put there—His sign, His unknowable Name. Thou seest no end."

He rumbled to his feet and, gathering his frayed green velvet about him, came to Will's side. Such a powerful tall old man stood a head above Will even though he stooped a bit. He looked at Will with a slow tenderness, and he touched the sphere so that it moved.

"Is man indeed the center?" he asked, studying Will. "Shall I inquire?" He took up the little owl, who strove mightily to keep her eyelids open. " 'Tis God sent the raven to Elijah, sent Balaam's ass, sent Daniel's lions." He turned the sphere gently. "Man, compounded and formed by God, is the story of the Universal. Is that not so? The bones of thy body—are they not as the rocks and the stones? Thy blood, doth it not resemble those waters which are brooks and rivers and disperse over the earth? Is thy breath not like the air? Is thy natural heat not like the enclosed warmth which the earth hath in itself and thus bring nature to the speedier sprouting of seeds? Are the hairs of the body not like the grass, and thy determination to the wandering and unstable clouds, and thy eyes to the light of the sun and the moon, and thy thoughts to the motion of angels, and thy immortal soul to the image of God?"

He studied Will's face for a moment longer, and as he turned away he said, "Aye, and the tides of thy blood and the tempest in thy members, are they not the earth before the majesty of God is lifted on high?"

Will drew in his breath. He touched the sphere so that it moved. "Yet desires and passions set the course of action. See, my desire moves this. Reason is not the cause."

"Think you so?" The old man looked at him from heavy-lidded

eyes and nodded. "Yet reason masters it." And he stretched out his hand and stopped the movement. He smiled at Will.

The music of the recorder slipped like a rose into the air. Will was startled. He looked, and there in the shadows, in a coign of the wall, he saw a man standing, one leg bent against the wall. Will peered, and then he started and bowed. It was the Earl of Southampton. The Earl came forward, shaking out the recorder and extending his hand. "Thou art well come, old friend," he said in a sweet voice. "Sit thee down. Nay, let me touch that wart upon thy hand for I think thou hast been sent to confirm my fortune."

He was dressed in black; he looked as spangled as the night. Black velvet was sewed with jet and with pearls as lustrous as the moon; a pearl hung from one ear lobe, and great pearls were on his hands. His fair long hair fell to his silvery ruff from beneath a velvet hat with diamonds sewn like stars. The narrow face with full mouth and enigmatic eyes was turned on Will.

He put his hand on Will's, touching the hard spot by Will's second finger, and then emitted such a sigh as might uproot a tree.

"My lord," said Will, "I give you my humble service. I have not seen you for many a day."

"Put away, put away," said the Earl, "by that old woman. Locked up. But now my times have changed! Let me touch you again."

The old man said sternly, "My lord Southampton, do you think, like a boy, that such superstitions will reveal God's mysteries? Will does not bear the plans of God on his hand; they are borne in your heart."

The Earl of Southampton colored and shrugged, and then made a gesture of deprecation. "But the future is so slow in coming," he said in his eager light voice. "To be warned or to go forward—oh, my master"—and he put out his jeweled hand to the old man—"my soul cries out, What must I do? Must I go forward? Must I stand back? Oh, the future is so much more than ourselves."

The old man looked at Will. The Earl said, "Nay, let him stay. His love is old and dear to me." He then turned on Will a sudden sharp and worldly glance, "And he has done some recent service of a doggerel kind," and laughed so that Will remembered that wretched verse. "Though he be no homunculus, we will use him as such."

The old man was as near to anger as Will had ever seen him. He spoke heavily. "It is the wickedness in our own hearts that, when we are sick in fortune, makes the sun, the moon, the stars guilty of our disasters. Look into your heart!"

The Earl stopped. He murmured, "*Stultorum plena sunt omnia*," and he became the image of distress. "Speak not of disasters or you will bring them on my head." He sighed again, angrily this time, and fell to pacing back and forth.

Will, whose curiosity had overmastered him, leaned against the edge of a loaded table, where books, a crystal bowl, hourglasses, and instruments of precision struggled for a place. The Earl said fiercely, "Disaster has banished me from court, though some do whisper that the High and Great One is my mother."

The old man said, "Zut, take care!"

"Nay, I do not credit it, for no mother would treat a son as she do me. Yet were I to know, then I might prove my heirdom—" but even he stepped back from such a burning dream.

The Earl put his hand lightly on the old man's shoulder and laughed a little, and proved by that double gesture why his charm was his fate. "But this is gamesome talk—see, it died with the fall of my breath. It is the other I long for. Tell me of it, I beseech you. What conjunction of fiery planets will set my lord's course and mine?"

Will wondered, What lord, what other? and then, with dismay, he felt the singe of greatness. Those fiery planets were not in the sky. They blazed and cast their light in London, and were the lords Essex and Southampton. He sat very still. The old man did not speak; his eyes were on Southampton. The Earl paced up and down and then stood in front of the old man as impressive as the King of Night.

"Tear it from the depths or the heights," he said lightly. "It is in thy power to do so."

The old man raised his black eyes to the young man's face, but all gentleness had been wiped away.

The Earl cried, "God's death! I can myself somewhat read of heaven and hell, and some spirits come at my bidding. But for all I know they may come from the devil who assumes a pleasing shape." He fell again to pacing, then he drew a pearl ring from his finger and thrust it forward.

"This is thine, whatever is foretold."

The old man said nothing and that black and painful gaze probed and pierced Southampton. At length the old man said in a far-off rumble like the skies speaking, "If this is the reason you came, my lord, you did deceive me."

"No, not I—never! Deceive—never! Speak of another, not me. Not deception. Consider my honor, sir, consider that it is owing to my position that I come to thee."

"Ah, what has reason to do with honor?"

Southampton grew pale and stood staring at the old man. Will, hunched over his own arms, marked how the Earl's color came and went and yet the old man sat still. Thus souls, rather than kingdoms, were won and lost; thus the ambiguities of men set the appearance against the fact.

Southampton said in a low voice, "Why do you set yourself against me?"

In a moment the old man replied, "Because I will not put truth into a box."

Southampton turned angrily away. He stared at Will, though Will felt he did not see him.

"Well, there are others. You are not the only one who reads the future." He snatched at his heavy cloak and drew on his gloves so roughly that he loosened a jewel and flung it on the floor. "But I have trusted you with certain matters that should stay with us." He stood with his teeth sunk into his lower lip until the lip was white. "If we cannot make her see, what choice have we but discontent and strife and civil war?" He swung around and cried, "I would trust him with my wife, my heir, my lands, my hope, my honor! If my great lord Essex falls I fall with him.

Surely for him there is a comet in the sky, or in the conjunction of my planets some word of his. I beg you, sir, I beg you! Have I ever begged before? Why do you deny me this?" He turned on Will. "Why does he? What do I ask that I should be denied?"

His oddities of manner dropped from him. The pale strange eyes and the narrow face became the signs of a man beset. Perhaps this was what the old man had been waiting for. He moved in his chair. He put back his head, closed his eyes, and said quietly, "When one takes away the veil of life, it is partly good and partly bad because we know so little what we do. This may be knowledge at the price of moral loss, and it is a heavy matter for those who see both right and wrong—but dimly, in a maze."

The Earl said hoarsely, "You did once cast my horoscope, though I never asked you what it read."

"Aye. And let us beware of what such matters unleash within our own o'erteeming fancies."

"Tell me!"

The old man was stubborn as a tree. "Astrology is the foolish daughter of a wise mother. Ask me not."

The Earl stretched out both hands toward the crystal bowl. "Gaze into your magic crystal. I will be satisfied."

"Nay, nor that neither." The old man sat with his elbows on the arms of the chair, his fingers against his cheeks.

Southampton said then with passionate irony, "Bring up the ghost of my father!"

The old man sighed. "I have touched on all these ways," he said, and something heavy clouded his voice, "and knowing them, I disknow them here and now." Southampton covered his face with his gloved hands and groaned. This touched a wellspring in the old man. He got up and handed the Earl a drink.

"What is this?"

"Wisdom," the old man said.

The Earl drank it eagerly. The old man stood touching the open sphere. "I will say this. You have told me of a certain month and day. By a computation which has no concourse with devils, I have learned that near that day the sun will be eclipsed." Southampton started forward. The old man went on, "To me this is a natural phenomenon due to the passing back and forth of planets, but to the ignorant it can signify some grave foretelling. Know this and act wisely."

Southampton could scarcely speak. "The sun eclipsed. Gloriana covered by the watery star." He looked with a wild grace at Will. "It is the moon that is the Earl of Essex' sign. What you have done for us must be multiplied a thousandfold. You will rise with us." Southampton grasped Will's arms and shook him back and forth. "And Raleigh and Cobham and the dwarf Cecil will fall." Then he turned and, taking off the pearl ring, put it with both hands into the old man's hand.

But the old man would not take it. It lay on his stiff distended palm.

"Take it, my lord. It will give no joy." He was so adamant that, in some dismay, Southampton took it back. Southampton looked from one to the other, knew that he had finished here, and could not wait to be gone. With scarcely another word he went out the door.

The old man was more shaken than Will had ever seen him. He stood like a moss-covered boulder in the center of the room. At that moment he partook of some of that conjunction of elements in man, air, fire, water.

"How wantonly we pluck at the unknown," he said in a quiet voice. "Men insure against calamity and run to embrace her." His indignation was mounting. "Why, men strive more to avoid death than to stay alive. That young man is in love with death, though he believes in a life of torment after death. And thou hast in some manner most foolishly insulted life. What hast thou done?"

Will said with a half smile, "We are all men on double business bent. To go and come."

"Nay, to go—to go—as men of single mind!"

Will touched the arabesque of the world, and said to its airy nothing, "Yet 'tis from our beggar's bodies that our heroes draw their shadows."

The old man looked at him sharply, and a smile returned. "Very well. I will think on the paradox of ourselves as beggars and of our heroes who shadow our lives most carelessly, being so in love with death."

Will asked with a smile, "What did you give him to drink?"

"Some quieting herbs which wear their own signs upon them." He studied Will. "Do you too think I am a practitioner of arts inhibited and unwarranted?"

Will embraced him and laughed. "You are my unbeveled edge."

He had not asked how one disposed of a ghost.

CHAPTER *Thirteen*

FROM that day, rumors shot into the air like fireworks.

To Will it seemed as though Southampton had set fire to the squibs when he closed the door of the old man's room. Will was very glad of all overt dangers, for they buried with solid heavy spades of earthy reckonings the deep and knotted pains that were the soul's danger. *Pax vobiscum:* die immured.

In the Falcon, in the tiring room, in the Paschal Lamb, in the Cardinal's Cap, rumors heaved and swelled. No one put a name to them, although in the tiring room a whisper rattled like dry bones that the Earl of Rutland had some special mark upon him, whether good or bad none chose to say. And this, of course, with no effort at all, reached out a bony arm and embraced Lord William.

It was a very dangerous thing to be a lord. Many studied how they might draw attention to their lowliness.

Some believed that plans had been completed—by whom?—to seize the court, the Tower, the City, so that the Queen would be compelled to give that change of government that the lords Essex and Southampton were thought to wish. Some said James of Scotland knew these plans and gave his blessing, for would he not then be a mile closer to the crown of England?

Lord William, attending each new play, gave no hint of a perturbed spirit, and Lord Rutland had at one moment a good-natured jollity about him, at another the look of having eaten fire.

"Well, it does not concern us," Burbage said, with no connecting word before or after, and yet each understood his meaning. Of course Burbage was no man's fool. He did not really mean what he said.

Will had put from his mind that doggerel verse. Even when he saw Rutland it brought nothing but a faint remembrance of pleasure. But after Southampton, a certain foreboding troubled him.

One day he and John Heminges came from the Stationers' Hall. A stolen version of *Twelfth Night* was being put about, and they had taken some steps to insure their rights. As they passed through the bedlam of Paul's Churchyard, a ferrety fellow slipped out from a stall and plucked Will by the sleeve. He showed his broken teeth in a smile of great comradeship.

He was an itinerant printer, a man who did salacious ballads and seditious tracts, and had already had his right hand cut off. In the freemasonry of the printed word, where the censor was both God and the devil and a sensible man sang a black-and-white mass to suit all, this one-handed fellow was not an outcast. True, one did not sit down for an ale with him, but one let him live.

Will slowed his pace, and Heminges looked sideways from his kind eyes. The fellow said nothing; he continued to smile, and then sang under his breath:

"Gulled England boasts three lords of warp and woof,
There's Raleigh, the fox, false Cob, and the dwarf.
They weave a wondrous web for a cold north king
That twines the feebling, flattered Queen Bee in."

Will groaned, then he laughed, then he plucked away his sleeve. What a fool he had been to compound such a joke.

"No!" he said explosively.

The fellow laughed and said, "It's a secret. I'll keep faith."

"No!" Will said, laughing, and yet he felt the sweat on his brow. He tore away his sleeve and broke into a run. Heminges with a fervent inquiry ran along with him.

"Will, what did he mean?"

"No," Will said, and then, safe out of Paul's, he slowed his pace and wiped his brow. "Lord, what a pelting. Well, never mind."

Heminges, his face drained of color, caught Will's arm and

forced him to a halt. He whispered in a dying voice, "Holy Mother, Will, was it you who wrote that wicked verse?"

But Will would yield nothing. He laughed and went faster than Heminges. He was torn with embarrassment, remorse, caution, and laughter.

In the tiring room that night, when he drew near to Rutland, Heminges came and stood by them like God the Father listening.

"It was a rash foolish thing," Will said, "to give a name to that printer. Your lordship knows—"

Rutland embraced him. "I said nothing. Some hint perhaps but I said nothing."

"I was a fool," said Will with perfect candor.

"Zut," said Rutland. "There's no harm. I'll close his mouth."

Will glanced then like a guilty boy at Heminges. Heminges pressed his lips tightly and turned massively away. His only comment came obliquely. After the play, when they met for an ale, he said, "Thou art a strange bird, Will. None other here leaves his nest so empty. Thou hast not a chick nor a wife with thee. It is against nature. It leads to rash deeds and to sickness."

Next day Burbage caught Will by the arm, his face brimming with laughter.

"Ben Jonson's out of gaol," he said, "and he has beaten Dekker to it!"

"Hah?"

"He heard that Dekker planned to write a play for us and hold him up to fun. So he's already written his reply for Blackfriars, though, by the mass, it's no reply, coming as it does before the question."

Will laughed. "Bold Ben."

"So Tom Dekker's will be the reply, and like two gamecocks, we and the Children will fight it out till we are surfeited with blood and money and can, politicly, ignore these star-crossed days."

"Thank God for playwrights and their low ways."

Dickon then put his hand on Will's arms and gazed deep into his eyes without a word.

"No," Will whispered, "it is not ready."

Dickon laughed and put his arm about Will's shoulder. "If thou but knew my thirst to play thy prince! Ah! Thou hast kept me from the wine of princes since Hal."

Will embraced him. "My thirst is not thine. I do not feel it." Yet, in fact, he felt a very great longing for that world of private joy where, out of the rare compendium of remembrance and intuition—shaped by the inner sight, conjured by the voice unheard—some measure of truth set him in fresh and spacious fields.

And, in truth, he longed to see Dickon step forth as the Prince, for he alone would make tangible and direct all that was inner and surmised.

In the City many people spoke with a wild half-knowledge of the eclipses of last summer and the days of reckoning that were now upon them. For the prophecy had pointed to an event that would unfold some time between 10 January 1601 and 12 July 1603. To the judicious this seemed to leave a wide range for the imagination; to the imaginative and superstitious, it meant seizing the present disquiet and wrenching a prophecy from it.

It became a murmur behind all speech, an excitement that gave impulse to wayward acts, a coloration and a smell that transformed the commonplace. Will said very little, for he was allied with the judicious, but his nerves crawled.

There were barely concealed meetings in Drury House, Southampton's home, and the Earl of Essex was said to have made a terrible joke on the Queen's conditions for favor and forgiveness. He said "her conditions are as crooked as her carcass." Since this woman loved him, how could she bear to learn of such cruel words?

On the first Friday in February, the players gave an old trifling comedy by some forgotten author, calculated to soothe Dickon's nerves. Lord William was present as though he had no other place to go. In all his silken splendor, he seemed young and desperate. His urbanity lay on him like a thin layer of dust. His cousin Rutland was not with him, though Gib, who was vulpine with sharp-toothed and angry conjectures, said that Lord William had sent

Sir Thomas Levenson to search for Lord Rutland and had not once looked at the stage for watching the doors and entrances. To this Will added, for his own consideration, the somber, sinister figure of Sir Piers Dalglish, playing cards on the stage with a friend. His presence swelled into a great brooding bird of prey.

Each nut that cracked, each foot that shuffled, each raised voice was both itself and the beast beneath the skin. Before the epilogue and the jig, Lord William descended to the tiring room, his face stripped of all expression save alarm, and that most imperfectly disguised.

He came straight to Will, his hand outstretched to take Will's arm, his pupils dilated so that his eyes were very dark.

"Where is my cousin Roger?"

"I do not know, my lord."

He shook Will's arm and stared at him.

"Will, Will, find him for me."

"My dear lord, where shall we look?"

Lord William stared at him, still clutching at his arm. "Why is Burbage so flushed and hot? He will call thee in a moment. Do not go."

"Nay, my lord, he will come to us."

"Do not listen. Some madman will try to persuade thee to perform thy play of *King Richard II*. Even if it be my cousin, do not yield. Hear me? Do not yield!"

"My good lord, why should we perform an old play, out of fashion?"

"Did the Queen not say that Richard was herself? Did she not? 'I am Richard. Knowest thou not?'"

"That was a time past, my lord, when a contentious book by Hayward roused her anger. She did not speak of my play."

"But Hayward wrote his book of Richard, and Richard will serve again as proxy for Elizabeth. A new Bolingbroke is rising up." Will fell very silent. The jig and the song had ended, and they heard the shufflings of three thousand people going home. To be disguised, to be a player, might hide him and his friends for a time.

Lord William still held him by the arm. He did not look at Will, but at Burbage and the men around him. Burbage had not let go his role in the play. Even his voice still partook of it, as though standing between him and the impossible world.

"There stands Gelly Meyrick. It will be he, mark my words. He is Essex' boyhood friend." He looked suddenly at Will. "Thou rash fool. Thou hast already compounded mischief for my cousin!"

This made Will angry. To be pushed this way and that should not be required of any man. He had no doubt that Lord William was talking of that cursed doggerel. Then Lord William's tone brightened as suddenly as it had darkened. "Oh, Will, I love thee. My love for thee is as fair as the bright inlays of heaven. Hayward is in the Tower now, didst thou not hear? Thou must prize thyself and dodge trouble."

Will was startled. "But for two years Hayward's book has been dragged about and no conclusions reached!"

"Well, they have now decided. The book was dedicated to the Earl of Essex. What will a foolish old woman make of thy play if Bolingbroke stalks about this stage again?"

"We are not playing *Richard!*"

Lord William took away his hand and shrugged.

"I wooed the Queen this morning with a game of ivory counters which spelled out her greatness and glory. But she scarcely noted, staring at me instead." He pressed trembling fingers against his eyes. "By our Lord Christ, I wish I knew nothing, and I wish I did not care."

Dickon had left Phillips and Sir Gelly Meyrick and Sir Gelly's friends. His eyes were on Will. His expression was closed shut like a box; neither his mouth nor his eyes nor his movements had any language. He came across to Will like a fine machine, the breastplate over his doublet gleaming in the torchlight, and sweat on his painted brow.

Lord William spoke before Burbage could say a word. "Do not trust Meyrick. He is a fowler's net. Ask him where is my cousin. Will, do not listen."

Burbage stood like a replica of himself, though his eyes were bright and searching.

"My lord," he said, "Sir Gelly Meyrick has spoken for Lord Essex."

Lord William delivered himself to his fear and his fury. He strode halfway across the room and said so loudly that all could hear him, "Traitors! rogues! They lay snares for honest men because they fear a tired old woman!"

Neither the Queen nor Lord Essex would care too much for such words. Yet no one spoke, for caution was first nature to both lords and commons. Sir Gelly beat at the pummel of his sword so that the sword jerked up and down under the skirt of his cloak. He asked in a courteous murmur what roguery there was (he carefully avoided treason) in a performance of *King Richard II?*

At this, Will seized Dickon's shoulder. Dickon nodded. "Tomorrow night—it is asked for."

"Why? Why?"

Sir Gelly replied that it was the will of the Earl of Essex.

"That is not sufficient, sir!" Will answered. "It is too old. We will lose by it."

"His lordship hankers for it like a child for sweets."

Will persisted doggedly, "We cannot afford to do so old a play."

There was a thorny silence. States of power are like the tides. A man may be innocent and yet be dragged by them this way and that. Sir Gelly stared at him, for he was not at his best when begging. He replied carelessly, still waggling his sword, but his expression had hardened. "My lords Essex and Southampton will assure you against failure."

Phillips attempted what he could do. "Our posters for tomorrow are printed."

Sir Gelly turned white. "Tomorrow his lordship requires the play." He glanced with a quick frown at Will, Burbage, Phillips, and the others. "It is a fancy, a fancy as strong as iron." He added after a moment, "That is why you are here, players, to satisfy iron fancies. We will give you forty shillings, more than your ordinary. You will have the play in good order and well spoken, and new posters will be printed."

Lord William spoke loudly. "Gelly Meyrick, where is my cousin?"

"Which cousin, sir?"

"You know right well which cousin I mean."

"Well, there is Lord Southampton who is a cousin of thine, and Lord Rutland who is a cousin of thine. You will find them together at Essex House."

Lord William turned away blackly. Sir Piers was standing ten feet away, unseen until this moment. His large hat shadowed his impassive face. It might seem he had nothing to record against Lord William, but Lord William, like an angry dog turning this way and that to find a quarrel, took three steps and struck Sir Piers in the face with his glove.

Well, that was that. Friends would support, honor be sustained, peace officers hoodwinked, and the combatants brought together in secret. Some felt a sigh of relief, for the prospect of lawbreaking offered far less danger than treason.

Sir Gelly bit the side of his finger, but since he could not be a friend to either side, he resumed his own business. He drew on his gloves.

"It is agreed. I will pay you the sum tomorrow."

Will said, "Sir, it is not agreed. Hayward is in the Tower. This is not a time to play *King Richard II*."

Sir Gelly grew white as a corpse. He glittered at Will through narrowed lids. "If you resist us, I am told to command you to Essex House."

Will turned away. "So be it. Gus, let us fetch our cloaks. Dickon . . ."

On the stairs they stood huddled one above another. "There is nothing we can do or say." Will smoothed and smoothed at the side of his cheek. "We must go. You, Dickon, see the Lord Chamberlain, and tell him lightly, as though the matter's of little consequence, what we are compelled to do. Lightly—"

"Oh, yes," said Dickon, knowing who would be crushed between two powerful forces if it were not lightly done.

Will said in imitation of Meyrick, "That is why we are here, we players, to satisfy forty shillings." He gave his knuckles a sudden blow against the wall. "Well, by our reversed pride, we hold ourselves as men. You have a good way with Lord Hunsdon, Dickon, and Gus and I will speak between the eyes to these other lords."

Dickon was too politic even in this safe womb of stair well to do more than curse softly under his breath. But Gus was aroused. Gus had a way of measuring madness and stripping it of both poetry and moonshine. He did so now in a few words.

They set off across the field, Sir Gelly well in advance, not looking back. The Earl of Essex' barge knocked at the wharf. They clambered in without grace. No one spoke.

Will and Gus sat swaying to the counterforce of boat and river as though here was the same counterforce between the humanist's perfect world and the actualities. In another boat someone was singing a hymn of Tallis, and to Will it had a mournful charm. In the twilight, the palaces seemed strongholds of legends, invincible to reason.

Near the Temple Stairs, they turned toward the shore. The great water gates of Essex House opened, and they passed under the elaborate entrance into the quiet shoal by the steps.

CHAPTER *Fourteen*

SIR GELLY slipped and scrambled up the water steps before the others, and went at a little dogtrot toward the palace. He paid no further attention to Gus and Will who after a moment went through the garden to the servants' door.

Will despised, he was afraid, he was helpless, yet he was a man. He knew it must all be written on his face. Gus, he saw, had studied how to clear himself of all expression.

The garden covered a great space and was an artful complication of paths, borders and beds. A slender dog came up to them, trailing a broken silver chain. Gus laid his hand on its muzzle and it looked at them with melancholy eyes. In the west, at the bend of the river, the towers and gables of Whitehall loomed against the evening sky. There she sat, the grim, dying, splendid old woman who had given glory to England and love to this lord.

This large, sprawling and ugly palace, with its recollection of ecclesiastical splendor, had a passionate life as Essex' little kingdom which, by virtue of his ambition and his ardor, he had enlarged to mean *England*.

East of his gardens lay the gardens of the Temple and west, beyond the lane, lay the lowering and regal grandeur of Arundel House where the Earls of Arundel lived. Growing up around the palace, like the needs of humanity, were the stables, the spicery, the chandlery, the laundry, the boiling house, the woodyard, the slaughterhouse, all redolent with smells and sound and servants.

Will and Gus knew by instinct the way to the servants' arch. A steward stood in the doorway with a bag of coins from which he was paying men with hampers of capon and geese. He nodded at Gus and Will, and they went on into the drafty reach of halls and stairways.

Somewhere a man was whistling. He was whistling the tune of the doggerel. If Will heard this doggerel in hell it would be his worst affliction. Preparations for supper were going forward. In the vast vaulted kitchen, the aromatic smells, the heat, the clanging of pots, the shouted orders, the cooks and maidservants and men servants, were a world of might in miniature. A clerk of the kitchen stared at them, and seeing they had no business with him went past them brusquely, for the bake house, the buttery, the wafery, the confectionary, the ewery, the larder, the poultry house, the scalding house, the pantry and the scullery were all included in the rise and fall of his sun.

At any moment during the next two hours his lordship might call for his supper and the supper of three hundred friends. The stewards were accountable and therefore on edge.

A chamberlain, sent by Sir Gelly, led them up the wide stone stairs under the low fanned roof and down a gallery of linenfold paneling and dark portraits. Low-ceiled corridors went off like garden paths, and from a room nearby a love song was being played on a lute. Its tender sadness was poignant and impersonal.

At last they came to the great library. The chamberlain opened the door and stood aside.

This room was the pure and concentrated essence of that substance *gentleman*, Will reflected. Here, two hundred in the living flesh glittered and gleamed. Here too were all the magnificent ambiguities of behavior in this age of dark and light—learning, art, intrigue, ambition, power, beauty, force.

One wall was covered with shelves of books: books in vellum and velvet, books with ornate metal clasps, plain ones and jewel-studded ones, books in English, Italian, French, German, Latin, Greek, and Hebrew. Here were also shapes of ships, and Roman heads in marble, artful heads in painted plaster, and curious ornaments of silver. On the other walls were tapestries of inexpressible richness. There was also a portrait of the Queen.

The chairs were carved with an intensity that covered all the surfaces. On the floor were not the rushes of ordinary men but carpets of ardent colors and deep texture.

The Earl of Southampton, who was sitting like a kinglet, held out his hand for Will to kiss. He held a sheet of writing in his hand, and tapped it fretfully.

"The scansion is poor and the thought hath a limp," he said to Sir Gelly leaning over his shoulder. "Felicity is quite thrown down." He handed the sheet to Will in an absent way, and Will handed it back after a moment, for the poem was in Italian.

Meyrick was inclined to protest, but the Earl gave his sudden full attention to Will, as though recalling with a start the reason for his presence.

"The play," he said. "By such obliqueness will we find our course." He hesitated for a moment. "It is a whim." He smiled. He did not suggest that Sir Gelly had failed in his mission; indeed, Sir Gelly gave no special sign of recollecting Will. "I have a great longing to see the play—as great as Lord Essex' longing."

Will looked swiftly about. He caught Gus's eye. In this great room reeking of power, they two were of no consequence. Yet danger and disaster lay in that play at this time with these men to applaud. In a hard, truculent way, Will marveled that a play of his should be so infected. Yet he must answer, and he frowned.

Rutland saved him. Rutland stood suddenly beside him, looking down at his kneeling figure. He put his hand on Will's shoulder, playfully pushing him back and forth. "Why, Will, you are holden here by old ties, are you not? Can you resist them? How goes my cousin? Will you carry a letter back to him?"

"If I may heal a breach by doing so, my lord."

"Breach? Why, there's no breach save that between spring and summer." And he went away cheerfully, although Will was quite sure his paleness was unnatural to him.

Southampton was talking to someone else, and Will glanced from the side of his eye at Gus. Their legs ached from their kneeling. Will stood up and Gus rose a moment after, and, to take the measure of their own forebodings, they looked hastily about this seat of power to see who else was here.

There was Giovanni Florio, whose presence cast no special light since he was a tutor in the household, although a man of prodigious learning. There was Ned Bushell, gentleman usher to Essex, who was of no great consequence save that he came from Warwickshire and was in some way a cousin's cousin to Dick Quiney.

There was also Sir John Harington, but that gave no answer, either, for he was the Queen's godson. There too was Henry Cuffe, a headstrong and unruly man, but he was secretary to the Earl of Essex, and Sir Christopher Blount was his stepfather. However, Lord Monteagle and the Earl of Bedford, and Sir Charles Davers whose life Essex had saved, were less easily reconciled to a domestic pattern. There were also Robert Catesby and Francis Tresham, ambitious and daring men, always in danger, and Sir Edward Baynham, who had set himself at the head of a coven of roaring youth in the City calling themselves the Damned Crew.

All these pieces put together spelt out turbulence and trouble. These men composed a private army of swordsmen; they were bold confident fellows, men who had railed against place and authority. They were brilliant, restless, and without scruple. Each spoke his mind as plainly and foully as a footpad.

To Will, fate hung over all and all must surely feel it in nerve ends and imagination. For several moments he studied Catesby's arrogant beauty and imperious gestures as he talked with Bushell. They were Warwickshire born and bred. Will, as son of the High Bailiff of Stratford, had known them and their imprudence all his life, and now he barely smiled when Catesby hailed him from a distance.

The rich, dense, dark-brown-and-crimson atmosphere of this room began to oppress him. It was the dark brown and crimson of powerful anger, high ways, passionate doings, set to the blazing fire, the heat and the light of a hundred candles. The ground for action might not be worth a straw, yet who among these would debate the question of a straw if honor were their cause?

One woman was in the room: Essex' sister, Lady Rich. Sitting in a window embrasure, she played the zither, while Lord Mountjoy, her lover, clad in yellow satin, accompanied her on a lute. It was a calming and domestic scene but somehow very evil.

Will chewed at his lip. He stood back to back with Gus. Before him was the conjunction of power. How could they escape killing? If the heavens themselves observed degree, priority, and place, office and custom before the sun, how could two poor and helpless men fall out of their place without a death? Or would he and Gus, by their very lowliness, somehow slip through the jointures of degree?

Within his hearing someone said that Raleigh must be killed. Catesby said it. The word hung there like the words of a song. Catesby then spoke to Will in his bold, handsome way, recalling for some capricious reason a boyhood sport. Will replied that Catesby had been very bold and commanding in their boyhood, but he hoped that the boiled brains of youth had given place to a dish more fit for men. Catesby laughed and eyed Will for a moment.

Southampton raised his head and looked at Will in that detached fashion which so imposed on a man's individuality. He beckoned and Will again knelt beside him. He spoke of the dear love that had always lain between them, the love of men so different from the love of women; indeed, what nobler word was there than friendship which could only exist between men who, lofty and passionate, brought sacrifices to its altar.

His lordship's gaze wandered now and then, not from inattention but because he must be aware of all the shifting currents of this room. He had put his hand on Will's arm, and his grasp tightened whenever his gaze turned away. A servant at the sideboard was pouring wine into crystal glasses. The Earl gave Will no occasion to reply. His long silky hair, and the cool voluptuousness of his features had some quality of legend. He said, although his eyes turned to a flurry of movement at the end of the room, " 'Thou hast taught the dumb on high to sing and heavy ignorance aloft to fly, have added feathers to the learned's wing and given to grace a double majesty.' " He then looked full at Will and sighed. "Such words are jewels locked within my heart."

Will groaned within himself. God damn words. Words written down long ago had no right to stir a dull allegiance. Yet he smiled and bowed and took care not to add a further word.

"And so it is," said the Earl on a long light sigh, "that you must add feathers to our purpose, and let your *Richard* sing us aloft like angels. Burbage, our mortal god of London, will play the king?"

Will whistled up his resolution. "Dear my lord, let us not hazard an undertaking so ripe with danger."

Southampton stared at him in the odd way which seemed to look straight through him. "Danger? Who gave you leave to use that word to me?"

Will said boldly in his soft voice, "Is not danger susceptible to all men?"

A servant took away their glasses, pouring off the dregs and wiping them, there and then, to replace upon the sideboard. Southampton twisted a lock of his long hair. "Aye, 'tis dangerous to go abroad, for who may not strike you down in the street? May not your boat leak and you drown? Speak of honor, not of danger."

Will persisted. "We players, good my lord, cannot afford too much of honor." The Earl rallied him then, not as though he recognized any need to beg, but as though an agreement made by mutual consent was more propitious than one taken by coercion.

"Presently my lord of Essex will come in, and his fancy to see this play is even sharper than mine own. If there is some inconvenience to you in it, he will pay."

183

"My lord, permit us to give a private performance, here in the Great Hall, or in whatsoever hall you designate."

A slow anger grew behind the Earl's calm eyes.

"Why do you resist me?" he asked softly. "By what perverseness do you show such disobedience?"

"Perverseness it is not, my lord. I appeal to your own calmness of mind." He added with a certain slyness, *"Suivez raison,"* which was the motto of the Earl's family. "As for obedience, this we owe to the Queen. Hayward has been sent to the Tower for writing of Richard's submission to Bolingbroke. Were my name Richard, I would cast it off tonight."

"It is neither your name nor mine nor his; it is merely a name and English and meant for our use." Someone had brought him a plate of food, and he turned from Will to accept it in one hand and more wine in the other. Thus provided, he seemed at a disadvantage; someone used the occasion to speak hissingly and at length into his face. The Earl listened, his only movement to put down the glass on a table.

Giovanni Florio drew near and looked down at Will. His dark face and eyes were smiling. Will rose.

"Well, we are met again," Florio said. "How many years is it since we sat in a bower in Hampshire, both on the business of teaching his lordship?"

"When he was eighteen and I nine years less than my present age," Will said with a smile. "But you have kept in his lordship's service better than I."

"Ah, because my Greek is indispensable and my French is perfection. What could you teach but syntax and rhetoric? And I am not careless of trifles as you have been. I labor to be a Vulcan who may hatchet a Minerva from that Jupiter's big brain. Call him Jupiter and who's amiss?" He went on streaming talk as a sower streams seeds, not looking to see which took root. "This is not a gulf to be bridged by genius, for who is genius, you or I, to trust ourselves to a *swaying swayingest* bridge between us and high nobility? Ah, as things are and as they ought to be, where's the consequence? But I know my worth and thou knowest thine and it is *silverest silver* to their gilded gold, for we take most apt and cunning thoughts in all languages and speech and dangle them like honeysuckles to their bees. And then one thanks them, *best-best benefactors, best most loved-loving patron,* and goes on about one's humble way."

He did not lower his voice, and yet no one seemed to take his ornate words amiss, for Florio's manner had its own prerogative. "Ah, I've wept, I've sweated, and I've gone on, till now I stand at bay, still resolute John Florio. But thou—thou hast the look of an exhausted stag, not resolute in any way. Take my counsel—"

"No," said Will, "I take my own. What do you make of all these roiling gentlemen and this fierce blaze?"

"Shall I tell thee, in a whisper?" But he did not lower his voice. "Here are all Caesar's conspirators save one. They stand at the base of Pompey's statue. Some are moved by hate and some by greed, some by love, envy, or mischief, and one or two by justice. And when the absent lord comes in, then we will see stars fall in Rome."

Will was not comforted. He said wryly, "I have heard many words from you in the years of our knitted lives. I would I could make something of them now."

Florio looked at him hard for a moment and then smiled with one corner of his mouth. He reached out and drew Gus in. "So you may if you will listen to me carefully. I have nothing to say —and here I quote the great Montaigne—entirely, simply, and with solidity of myself *without* confusion, disorder, blending, mingling, nor in one word. However, were I to say what life should be (caught as we are in this great coil of power and we poor geese), I should say that there is nothing so sweet in life as a quiet rest and gentle sleep, that sleep without dreams. That is what I say, and I am glad that I can talk and talk and so do nothing. But your play is a keystone, and I am very glad that it will not be I who puts it in its place."

Gus said softly, "How will they use it?"

Florio played for a moment with the edge of Will's white collar. Then he leaned forward and whispered to them, "So you have agreed?"

Will looked at him with a wild glance. "There is an upper and a nether millstone. At the moment we see not how to avoid one or the other. What would you say?"

Florio sighed and his black eyes were sad and deep. "The play will set forth for the people of London that kings have been held by their subjects and compelled to yield in their designs. It says that kings are but men—or women. Without the play, who may say this and not be hanged? Thy play will make visible and animate that certain high lords merely follow in a sovereign's footsteps; that is to say, King Henry IV's. Does that compound treason? It is very sinuous, but the reason weaves to its source at last."

Will exclaimed, "Such words are no rivals to the spring! We do not thank you for them." And then he calmed his tone, for this man had warned them well. "Sweet friend, we three stand between power and power. It is very hard on simple men who would be glad to eat their bread in peace."

Florio put his hands on Will's shoulders, kissed him on both cheeks, and saluted Gus as well.

"Keep your head, rouse your wits, and let the great fall."

Gus said, "Hush!" sharply, but Florio merely laughed and lifted his finger. "Hark, I hear Greatness drawing near!"

There were indeed sounds of rustling, as though the sea were moving back or the air were stirred by a thousand wings. Voices were lifted. Eyes turned in one direction. A door was flung back. Servants with candelabras entered. Finally, like planets circling the great sun itself, appeared a pride of gentlemen, and the tall princely figure of Essex himself.

Oh, here was a lord! Will, for all his careful watch, could not remain unmoved. Here was an age's glory: the perfect man endowed with all the gifts of nature and of civilization.

He was dressed in white and silver, his scabbard and his shoes were of white velvet, his jerkin white satin lined with silver, embroidered with gold, his beauty as glistening as his jeweled doublet, and his manner as golden as his sword. All this, in the hour past, had feasted the old Queen's eyes.

He was a being so gifted that he needed no Mephistopheles to increase his splendor, and for a moment Will allowed himself to be caught up in the harmony of such a figure. A paragon, an expectancy, a rose of the fair state, the observed of all observers.

He came forward swiftly with his long stride, talking to the lord at his side. Southampton had risen with a plate of food still in his hand and this he thrust at the nearest, Will. His expression lighted as though the day had come, and when he went up to Essex, he put his arm about his shoulder.

Lady Rich stopped her playing and ran to her brother. He paid no special heed to any; to all he gave his sun. The impetuous and melancholy spirit of this man was as visible as his outward form, for in glance, manner, words, tone were, most cunningly intermixed, ambition, erudition, piety, and lasciviousness.

"Ah, is that not a *man?*" said Florio with a suggestion of laughter, "Mark him well. How tall he stands. His hair is the color of the sun, his eyes as black as night. Is this not how the gods appeared—say, Jupiter?" Will smiled at him and made a gesture that begged for moderation. But Florio went on more softly now. "How can a man looking as he does be harassed? Nay, let me talk. You will be glad of it by-and-by. Some say he has never fallen sick, nor failed in anything on which he set his mind, nor felt any penetrating misery or afflictive pain." When Florio spoke of his health, Essex showed his fine teeth in a smile, and when he spoke of his immunity to affliction, Essex laughed aloud.

"But see how swiftly laughter goes, and how noble is his frown. The landscape of the face has its days and hours. Behold: the twilight and soon the dark."

Now the Earl paid greater heed to those about him. He embraced his sister. They stood not five paces away, and Will saw the bold arched nose, the swelling beneath the eyes, and the piercing gaze that wavered without warning.

"And so he speaks."

Will said drily, "You are as good as a chorus."

"Hush."

The speech of this triumphant being was no declamation of an angel. The voice was hoarse, and passion was indicated by an inchoate stream of words. "Raleigh and Cobham, Raleigh and Cobham," he repeated as though conjuring two powerful incubi, "they are the ones who will kill me. I name our enemies."

"*We will kill them!*"

187

"Nay, today was I crossed by a demon. We must think on this warning before we set our course."

Rutland spoke somewhat harshly, "What demon? Raleigh?"

"It took the form of a wild horse in the street. None saw it save myself."

"None?"

"None."

"Yet you did not fall down dead when it crossed you, which you should have done had it been sent by the devil."

Essex looked at Rutland with a wild surmise. "Ah, I had not thought of that. But still is it very dangerous. The sour humor roused by it must pass away before we move in safety."

Blount, his stepfather, spoke roughly. "My lord, they will act before we do. They have seen our hands."

"How so? Not so! What have they seen? In the Council I spoke defiantly, but no more than is fitting for a man as ill used as I have been."

"Did the Queen speak a word for thee today, Robin?" Southampton asked.

"Not by a sound, though, by God, her eyes did speak. As will her tongue when I have proved that no man in England may be trusted save I alone."

What lights can play on such a scene? thought Will, and what does one make of power knee to knee with power? Gus covered the lower part of his face with his hand; Will stood, his arms folded close to his chest, observing how the world creates such a man as Essex, and how such a man creates his own world. Here was mood and impulse, face and body one, vivid, distracted, disintegrating in hopeless destiny. Will fancied that he saw Essex crumpling as he stood, so ruthless and so bated that he knew not whether to go or come. This man believed in demons and in spirits from another world; he saw by the light of lightning and was surely a little mad.

How well he knew such a man—almost as well as himself, Will thought ironically. This man was his own demon; his superb uncertainty was his supreme distinction. In the widening circle of the men about him, his princely bearing yielded and was recovered. Essex was now suspicious, now incredulous; fidelity and honor were words that glowed like rotten wood.

Here was a man whose battles would not stay won. Here was a man who had reached the headwaters of the Styx. Here was a man who, passionate and headstrong, rushed blindly to his fate. Will knew of such another man.

A log fell apart with a great shower of sparks, and the heat flared up for a moment intolerably. Someone kicked back the log and the two earls, like pistils in a flower, stood alone.

Essex' stepfather, Blount, said, "Robin, it is you must speak the word *On!*"

It seemed as though Essex were struggling in some way to shield himself, for he cried out suddenly, "Happy were I, if I could finish forth my fate, and when I die, find my tomb to be the bush where harmless Robin resteth with the thrush."

Sir Christopher made a move of raw impatience, and Essex thrust out his hand. But the gesture was unfulfilled; he put his cheek against the dark hair of his sister and closed his eyes.

She tightened her arm about him, and all the gentlemen stirred with that disquiet which marks any variation from a head-long course. Some exchanged looks, making their plans in their glances. Without warning, Essex opened his eyes straight at Will.

"Ah," he said, and made an importunate gesture. "Think you not that we can do all things? Is this not the age of all possibility?"

He waited with such solicitation that Will was obliged to answer.

"It is so held, my lord."

"Ah, so held by what fate, what stars? Nay, by what reason? Or is man, in the perfection of nature, in the likeness of his Maker, able to do all things? What do you say?" the Earl looked about him with his despairing puffy eyes, as though this time he wished no answer. Then he pronounced his own doom. "The people love me."

Southampton stood close to Will and close to Essex, and he put a hand on the arm of both. "Robin, the players are your dear servants. They will enact *King Richard II*, and that will set our minds at rest."

Gus made a noisy move. The tears came into Essex' eyes and he nodded his head. "Good. Now I know that God will speak. We will see and hear."

He kissed Southampton on both cheeks and then held out his hand to Will.

Retreat was now cut off for the players. Protest could only be made by an authority higher than their own. Will kissed the hands of the two earls.

Southampton was watching Will with an adamantine gaze. He said clearly, "Thou wilt not lose by this."

Essex turned away as though his spirit had been refreshed. He drew after him four-fifths of the gentlemen. Southampton said to Gus, still without a smile, "My love to thee. I will requite thee." He made a sign to Sir Charles Davers, who went ahead of them toward the door. As Davers called to a chamberlain, he drew forth a purse. "This is for you." He gave it to Gus. "By-and-by you will be paid more."

The chamberlain took them to the gateway on the Strand and thrust them out onto the dark street without a word. Across the road was the church of St Clement Danes, and they turned toward Temple Bar, stumbling a little in the dark and from their thoughts.

A shouting group in the livery of a great lord went by with torches which lighted a head impaled on Temple Bar. Gus hissed and stumbled.

Will took his arm. "We are not worth a beheading."

They passed under the three-gated arch of Temple Bar and observed with mixed feelings the domestic light of the printer who lived there. "Purveyor of words, foe of the peaceful mind," Will muttered. "Which is the turning for Whitefriar Steps?"

"The next lane. If Lord Hunsdon forbid the play, will we be two against Dickon?"

"Nay, we will be three against the world."

They went by lighted houses to the Temple Gardens and down the lane which led to the river.

"We have sold cheap what is most dear!"

"Ah? Two gentlemen possess alternatives against the high nobility?" Gus asked with passionate irony.

"I'll impaste thy questions," Will answered savagely. "We're gentlemen by sufferance only. Our coats of arms are paper." The boatman pushed onto the river.

Gus laughed faintly. "To which may be added," he said, clutching the side of the boat, for a high wind had sprung up, "Dog eat dog till all topples down."

CHAPTER *Fifteen*

DICKON had returned from Lord Hunsdon. He listened to Will and Gus in silence, and then he shrugged.

"Well, fall to. Who knows the parts?"

Will asked urgently, "What did Lord Hunsdon say?"

"He said very craftily that we should proceed."

Gus said, "God's death!" and Condell cursed and began rummaging among their rolls for the text of the play.

"By God, treat our old horse as a get-penny, and some of the onus will be taken off," said Burbage in a dark fury. He tossed a script to Ned. "Learn Bagot in any scrambled way."

They went about their business darkly, even Heminges snapping at his friends, and Sly vicious. Those who remembered remembered, and those with new parts huddled over new lines.

They worked through the night. The boys who played the ladies were frightened and sleepy, and Gus spent much time with an arm across the shoulder of his apprentice to give him courage.

Ned was both lowering and excited. Will listened to Ned's lines and to Ned's questions. "What has gone wrong? What are we doing? Will there be danger? Sweet, sweet brother, tell me, for the love of Jesus!"

"Who knows?" Will answered. "We may be kicked and cuffed; we may be overlooked."

Only Condell grew calmer as the night went on. He would be Bolingbroke for the first time, and though he might die for it, with what glorious words would he expire: "Then, England's ground, farewell; sweet soil, adieu! My mother, and my nurse, that bears me yet! Where'er I wander, boast of this I can; Though banish'd, yet a trueborn Englishman."

Pope, who played John of Gaunt and who sucked at a tooth rather than cry out his perturbation, came to Will at one point and asked if it would not be wise to change a line, for Gaunt condemned the leasing out of England to Richard's favorites, and was not that what the Queen did for *her* favorites? Since Gaunt was the father of the usurper Bolingbroke, was this not a reproach to the Queen?

Will, who also had turned this over like a sore tooth, said that seldom could he speak his mind of treasons to the common man, that he had done so here, and if the Queen saw it as a rebuke then she saw true for once in her self-willed life.

Pope groaned and went back to the comfort of his aching tooth.

They worked through the morning. During the time a servant came from Lord William with a letter. It was agitated, spattered with ink stains from a pen that had written too fast, and asked, with little regard for spelling, what was toward? Had they heeded his warning? Had Will seen his cousin? *Beware, beware, beware* in a dozen ways.

Will was too weary to answer discreetly. "Tell him," he told the servant, "that we are all leaping into the custard this afternoon —or it may turn into Jack Drum's Entertainment and we'll all be cudgeled through the door."

The servant was too proud a young man to laugh at this, but he raised his brows.

By dinnertime they were indifferent to death or disaster. Will slept with his head on the table, whereas Burbage sat stiff as a king to defy his fatigue.

"The gggreat dddanger," said Heminges, "is that Will hhholds the mmmirrror up to nature as no other playwright dddoes in London. Sweet tttongue, alas."

"By hell," said Dickon, directing his anger, "that tongue is too nimble by far!" He covered his face with his hands in a gesture of unexpected poignancy.

Gus, looking out the window of the Falcon during dinner, saw a wherry draw to the wharf, and he said in a flat voice that the birds of prey were gathering. They peered through the window and saw Essex' friends, his evil geniuses, Lord Monteagle, Sir Christopher Blount, Sir Gelly and Sir Jocelyn Meyrick, Mr Ellys Jones, Mr Edward Bushell, Mr Robert Catesby and Sir Charles Davers aiding each other to the enterprise of debouching. The Globe men watched them like judges and looked from one to the other, saying what they thought with no fear of contradiction.

It was not fear so much as anger which possessed them—anger that they were the ones who'd be whipped. As for fear, Lord Hunsdon had sent a deputy that morning to inquire of their health, speak of the good weather, wish them success; two-faced words to be read according to their tempers. Their legal status as vagabonds was, in normal times, veiled by success and money. Now only the Lord Chamberlain's self-interest stood between them and the beadle's whip. It was not a fortifying thought.

When Sir Charles Davers and Lord Monteagle entered the Falcon briskly, no player stood up. It was a small thing, but it served.

Sir Charles inquired with a steady smile if each man understood his role in relation to the higher scheme of the day. Burbage answered with a cold courtesy, Will, drowsy-eyed, with a disarming forthrightness that Richard was his bastard whom he disowned, Sly with an impudence close to rudeness. Sir Charles lost his smile and Lord Monteagle fooled with his sword. Each man stood forth in his own naked soul at that moment.

The gentlemen coldly told the players to hasten to their play of "the killing of King Richard II." They themselves took their places in the sun outside the lords' entrance, and watched from under their heavy shading hats the ordinary people of London trailing across the field, unaware of themselves in any historic context.

The theatre pennant was raised. The actors put paint on their faces and Burbage assumed the scarlet robe that served for all kings. His chain of office caught on the king's crown, and he tore at it in a blazing rage, with sudden tears in his eyes.

Gib was everywhere, perfectly controlled and ruthlessly controlling, the book never out of his hand. He made certain that each actor had his wig, his sword, his spear, his cloak, or his woman's gear, made certain that the musicians understood what music must follow what spoken cues, and that the means to effect the sound of clanging gates were in the right place for himself to handle. In passing Will, he looked him in the eye and said, "God's fools."

When the theatre's trumpet sounded, Gus, Dickon, and Will embraced each other and made a swift round of the tiring room, pressing the hands of the actors and wishing them good stomach with their lines.

Then Burbage and Pope climbed onto the ladder, and Condell and Will, who was Mowbray, waited on the ladder to follow.

Will consoled himself that most actors were philosophers of disassociation. He heard Sly's ugly temper vanish in Hotspur, and Gus dissolve his anxieties into the Earl of Northumberland, and Dickon forget his lines.

Dickon was adept at sounds in place of meaning, and he sang his way with such meticulous gestures from one scene to the next that few were the wiser. But his face, stripped to the bone as it seemed to his friends, told the truth of his agitation.

Before Will departed the stage as Mowbray, he glanced at the Lords' Rooms and saw Davers and Monteagle, the Meyricks, all in their places. Robert Catesby and Henry Cuffe were sitting on the stage. The light of the torches showed visages as watchful and impassive as those of Satan's minions. It seemed to Will that they glanced only now and then at the actors, that their eyes were fixed on the audience.

The audience was gay and pleased with this old surprise. They cried out to their favorites—for each actor had his coterie to whom he bowed when the applause deserved it—and all was as innocent as an April day of any fateful purpose. During an interval, Meyrick descended the steps to that private world under the stage and said coldly to Burbage, "You are not making your lines clear. Let it be heard when the king agrees to his deposition."

Burbage replied with his sharp silence and cold eyes, and Meyrick clambered up the steps again not quite clear what had been said or answered.

Will sat under the stage, his eyes closed, listening to the return of Richard from Ireland, and preparing himself to appear now as the Duke of York. Suddenly he was shaken vigorously. Gib's fingers dug into his arm, though Gib said nothing; close behind him were two muffled figures. Hah! Will thought, rising slowly. Life holds such perfect entrances and exits that life is far better than a play.

The Earl of Southampton removed the folds of scarf from his face and smiled at Will somewhat distantly, and then the Earl of Essex unveiled himself. How insufferably beautiful they were; the very halls of heaven and hell seemed scarcely fit for such flashing men. Their superb bearing and divine effrontery almost reconciled Will to the tyrant Custom.

Essex looked about him. "I do not wish to be seen but to see," he said in his hoarse voice. "Where is a private place?"

"There is no private place, my lord," said Will, "save a little knothole that I myself use now and then."

The Earl made a gesture of assent and came after Will, trailing his long cloak up the ladder, through the property rack, to the inner stairs that were the Housekeepers' own. There he bent his tall figure and managed, by that special dispensation granted him, to look like a mariner with his spyglass rather than a boy at a peephole.

From the musicians' gallery the drums and trumpets brayed out the entrance of the king, the banners broke in all their colors on the stage, and Will, smothering his deep misgivings, ran to join the entrance of Bolingbroke, who had come to claim his stolen crown. Presently Richard would appear on the balcony above the stage, and then the purpose of the great nobles here today would be set forth to the people of London. Will alone knew of the dark, fateful eye that watched for their response through a little hole.

The scene advanced. The men in the Lords' Rooms were sitting forward, prepared to enlarge that moment when Bolingbroke knelt down before the king whom he had toppled and, reaching for the crown, said, "My gracious lord, I come but for mine own." The words were spoken: *my own.*

The gentlemen in the Lords' Rooms discharged the ordnance

of their applause. The audience looked about in some surprise and clapped in a disordered way.

The fateful scene was over. A slight sense of emptiness ensued. The gentlemen studied the effect in whispered colloquies. Each subsequent word of Bolingbroke was underlined by their applause. The audience fell in with spirit, glad to have their money's worth. With the surrender of the crown and Richard's tears, a decent silence came with some awe, till a fellow in the pit began to sing that doggerel verse.

At this Dickon lost hold of himself. He came to the edge of the stage and cried in a thunderous voice, "None of that! None of that! We'll have no sedition here!"

When the scene was over, Will went to the Earl of Essex, who stood away from the peephole, his back to the wall, a carven figure within which dwelt a man of burning eyes.

He gave no sign of seeing Will, and Will stared at him for a moment, cutting into his soul this image of thwarted power and ambition—the world's image, in degree and scope.

Essex moved and his eyes lighted on Will. He nodded several times and came slowly down the steps.

"Aye," he said, "aye, it was well done. Mark you, how they cried out." He smiled at Will as he descended, and his smiling deepened. He stood a step or two above Will, his fine head and excited eyes turned downward. "Audacity is all."

Will said nothing. The Earl laid his hand on Will's shoulder as he passed. He said in his hoarse whisper, "Yet, will I not be Bolingbroke. I will merely take her by surprise and oblige her to listen to the truth."

The play came to an end. Sir Gelly gave them two pounds and reproved Burbage for his reproof. The players dispersed, anxious for the solitude of their private thoughts. Will went to his room and sat at his table. Across the river, light blazed in the palaces, and on the river a barge of the Lord Mayor, with gilt-carved bow and liveried rowers, was moving toward Whitehall. He felt a crushing need to be master of these high times.

Night had fallen when Lord William's steward scratched at his door.

The steward was a cool, private-faced man with discerning eyes and none of the divided manner that many servants of great nobles showed to a player. He said, "Good evening, sir. My lord has sent me to speak about tomorrow."

"Tomorrow?"

"In his lordship's view it would be well for you to have a deposition ready, setting forth the whole course of events, and testifying to the true occurrences that you saw last night in Essex House."

"I saw naught, sir."

"Ah? Will anyone believe you, sir?"

"I saw life enacted."

"And treason against the Queen's grace?"

"I saw no treason—" Will hesitated, and the steward watched him with a sidelong gaze. "I saw men—a man—driven to extremities of purpose."

The steward said with no inflection, "My lord has sent you his message. It is well sent." He turned as though to go, and then he looked back at Will and returned to put a hand on his arm. "Let me add, sir—for it is no secret—that the Queen sent for Lord Essex to the Privy Council not two hours past. Since my lord has good reason to believe that my lord of Essex was, at that moment, returning from a performance of *King Richard II*, he requires me to tell you further that Lord Essex refused to go to the Queen; that he begged all his friends to sleep at Essex House, that he has barred the gates and water gate and doors, and now he sits trapped in his own double chains."

The steward said it sadly, as though he had seen many grand acts of great men lead to perdition. Will was moved. He walked up and down before the steward. "Alas, alas, a noble mind cast down. This is greatness in extremity!"

The steward made a slight deprecating movement. "A man is often blind to all *but* his extremity. This can be his ruin when every second thought should be his honor."

Will smiled at this man who had something very human behind his gaze.

"Shall I tell you what I make of honor, sir?" he said. "The

same as did old Falstaff: 'Can honor set to a leg. Nor an arm. Nor take away the grief of a wound? No.' " Will spoke very directly to some pellucid quality in this man. "All that is noble is that reward that comes to each regardless of his rank who of his own free will hazards all he has for the common weal. Must we cast away those who do not find this common weal? I think our hearts must be thoroughfares for all who are God's own, whether saint or sinner."

The steward studied him a moment with his kindly eyes. His voice was gentle though his words were safe. "I doubt if my lord or those in authority, sir, would fancy such an answer."

He reached into his purse and handed Will a coin from his lord. "The deposition, sir?"

"I'll think on it. My thanks to you."

He sat down at his table again, though the air was very fretted and his thoughts were torn by princes and greatness and state policies. He had promised no deposition; there was no great thing to fear. He thought of revenge and of greatness disjoined, and of ghosts.

He sat with his arms on the table staring at the candle, rolling his pen between his fingers. True passion is the wide arc of feeling. It fills the wastes of shame, it cancels ambiguities. All color, sound, shape that he had put away in his remembrance was his to draw upon.

He sat quietly for a long time. From awareness to imagination to words set down, from the profundity and sound of words to the acuteness of the actor, from metaphysics to good parts . . . there was in this course no mystery save the mystery of the craftsman. And then he fell to a profounder thought of Essex trapped like a beast in his own chains, of Southampton and Rutland, Ned Bushell, Catesby, Florio, not abstracts but flesh and blood and apprehensive. And he thought of many forms of death.

He thought of night. *'Tis now struck twelve . . . And I am sick at heart . . . What art thou that usurp'st this time of night, together with that fair and warlike form in which the majesty of buried Denmark did sometimes march?*

Usurp . . . aye, there's the word.

Usurp my honor, life, ambition, true passion; usurp man, his office and his self-containment.

He thought of the wind. It howled on the battlements of Elsinore no less than within a man's heart.

The next day was Sunday. Ned and he ate breakfast, though Ned ate mostly at the side of his finger, so stirred was he by the events and rumors in which he himself had shared last night in Southwark and along the Strand.

Florio came while they still sat at breakfast, a pale dragging figure asking with flowery and circuitous speech for haven. His liquid eyes were ringed and heavy. He too had seen events. Yet he was very much a man; he would not pretend that all was well.

" 'Twas scarce nine o'clock, I fancy, when Sir Charles Davers said that entrance to the Queen's presence was barred to Essex men, and then our mightiest lord was quite beside himself. Never did I see such rage, never, never. I thought he'd dash away his brains. He addressed all his gentlemen with wild gestures, tossing his head this way and that like a lion. He told how he had been abused and lied about, how his heart was pure, how he had been denied this right and that. And then he stood by the gate to the Strand and shouted to the populace—oh, saints, oh, gods, I hear it now!—that no man bore so much ill use from those who would sell the Queen to Spain as he, and he said Raleigh had a Spanish heart. By-and-by Lord Southampton had to draw him back. It was a fearful sight, for my dear lord Essex was weeping like a child.

"Then came four great Officers of State and knocked to know the reason why he would not attend the Council and why this mighty gathering of prime gentlemen defied the Queen's peace. Then there was much crying within the courtyard, some shouting, 'Kill them!' some shouting 'Cast the Great Seal out the window!' Well, my lord seized the Officers of State and called through a wicket that they must be locked up and held as hostages. And then he called all his gentlemen, and said that they and he must march on the City. At that point, my friend, the porter at the gate, slipped me through.

"For who am I that I should be caught in this mighty moil?

Though no danger lurks with me or thee, it's safer, safest, to be with our own kind—simple simple hearts with no aspiring greatness. Indeed, indeed, I never heard a word from him that might be turned to treason. Alas, didst thou? Why, how can treason come from mouths so steeped in poetry as were our two great lords', who brought us safely home when we were lost in the world's great poverty? Why, you have praised the lord Southampton, and I have blessed their names in the view of all, again and again. And yet you know, oh, Jesu—" and he buried his face in his hands and wept.

Ned rubbed hard at the side of his face. Will took Florio by the arm and led him to a chair.

"Nay," Florio wept, "I cannot stay within this house. Nor yet at church. Will you not walk with me somewhere that men have not infected?"

"Aye, that I will."

Will charged Ned to find Pope and Phillips in church and hold together in case of need. For who knew what this day would bring?

Ned would do anything asked of him if he were not confined!

Will put his arm through Florio's and they passed through the crowded streets, to reach the country lanes back of the marshes. Florio drew away from the raw humanity but Will drew him forward.

"Where's thy pity?" Will asked gently. "All these take violence as a cat takes cream. Let them teach us."

Jasper Shore stood in the doorway of the Cardinal's Cap, and said to Will with an anxious scowl that trouble was in the air.

"Sunday morning after Saturday night," said Will, nodding wisely. But Jasper Shore grunted that he knew very well Sunday followed Saturday: this was something else again. The tears overflowed on Florio's face.

The maimed soldier who drove the midden cart wore a flowering coltsfoot in his hat. He said, "What's possessed the bells? Hark how they fret!"

"Sunday bells," said Will.

"Nay. I've heard such only when the cannon followed."

Florio protested to Will, "Why do you deny their questions? Do you think it will postpone our destiny?"

"I do not know our destiny," Will said quietly.

"I will tell you," said Florio and he did, as though he had an ague of the tongue.

They came into the quiet lanes where snowdrops were in bud, and he set forth how men like him and Will could be caught in great falls and how it could affect their hearts and bodies. He staggered now and then, for fear had hold of him.

They went as far as a moated manor house, and then they turned back to sit by a fishpond in the sun while Florio talked of doom and destiny, and Will watched insects skim the water and fish rise to seize them.

Florio was no coward, Will thought. He was a man profoundly at odds with his own philosophy, a man caught in the current of a great amiss, both innocent and victim. And so am I! Florio turned his sad Italian eyes and said if a man's mind cannot master the mortal world, what hope has he in the immortal? Need a man yield to the chaotic urgencies of the world which shifted with the wind and had no more substance than the blown dust?

Will replied that to him character and destiny were one. He heard a mistle thrush sing; the hints of spring were all about. He said gently that the art of knowing and feeling sorrow was made pregnant to good pity.

Presently Florio was quieted and wondered if they would escape the great net that would be flung today.

"I doubt it not," Will replied, though his tone lacked some assurance. "And I think that we should now return and face ourselves like men. Time must friend or end."

"And poets are but men in fact," Florio said. Will shrugged good-naturedly. Florio smiled. "You love better to be a poet than be called one." Will embraced him, laughing.

"I'll not forget thee, Will."

"Nor I, thee."

In the Falcon, Pope, Gus, and Sly were sitting by the window dressed in their plainest clothes, as though to stress their obscurity. The air was sharp. The wrong word would acquire a cutting edge. A servant dropped a tray of dishes, and startled shrieks and curses drove the poor fellow from the room. It also released a cacophony of questions from one stranger to another. Since Will and Florio were the latest to come in, they were presumed to know the most. They were anathematized by a distraught fellow when they had nothing to add to the end of the world.

"I am amazed," said Will to all, "no archangel has blown for judgment. What do we fear?"

"The Spaniards," said Pope in a doomed voice, his round face flabby. "Essex has sold us to the Spaniards . . ."

"Oh, God's ground, thou art sensible and miss all sense!"

Sly chewed on his mustache. "I lost six pounds at gleek last night betting it was not the Spanish."

"It is the Irish," said Gus with the shadow of a smile. "And Dickon and Jacko are our hostages."

"Where are they? Why are they not here?" Will asked.

Gus took out a pack of cards. "I will wager that Lord Hunsdon sent for them." Sly clicked his fingers and Gus dealt him a hand.

"Where then are Condell and Armin?"

"In the Tower," said Pope in a tombed voice.

"Well, by hell, the way we're looked at, I might believe it. Are we lepers? See how they draw away. Sir, have we offended you?"

The man to whom he spoke started and stared. In answer he cried to the room, "Look you! Corruption sits upon their brows!"

"Are you mad?" Gus asked courteously.

"Why did you play the killing of King Richard?"

"Oh, base fool!"

"Know you not, see, that by royal proclamation Essex has been made a traitor, and all with him?"

Gus put down his cards and crossed himself. Sly blinked several times and looked slidingly at all the faces. Pope died over his folded hands. Will thought ironically, Nerveless Will, speak again on man and his destiny.

Florio said so softly his voice had scarcely any tone, "Where shall we go? Must we hide?"

Gus stood up by the window. His face was drawn. Across the river came the sound of shouting near the wharf at Queen's

Hythe. Below them on the riverbank, where the tide had bared the scaly shore, was closer shouting of boys at play.

The man who had treated them as lepers drew near with his pot of ale. He pushed at Gus and cried, "You're servants and small men. You can be dropped through a dunghole and who cares!"

"Shut your mouth," Sly shouted, "or I will stop it!"

"Be quiet, in God's name," said Gus. "Listen!"

The shouts across the river and the shouts of Southwark fisherman dragging in a net of fish and the shouts of a fight on the river wall below the Falcon mingled in a distracting medley. Gus leaned far out the window to distinguish the shouts from Queen's Hythe.

A boat moved out of Queen's Hythe; under the glint of many oars it turned up the river at great speed. The shouting did not stop.

"Merrymakers," said Pope, not moving from the table. "Let's swear, drink, dance," and he made a dunce cap from his napkin and put it on.

Gus, looking at each in turn, sat down at the table, his back to the window. The stranger leaned on his shoulder and said, "Let their quillers cheat the devil how they may—ha-ha—cat will mew and dog will have his day!"

Sly told, over his shoulder, that the boat was drawing through the water gate of Essex House. "Perhaps we have watched great events," he said sardonically.

Then Will lost his composure, which had been held together by a weak resolution. He snatched up his hat and said he meant to find Heminges in hell or prison. "But here they are," he added softly, and rubbed his wet brow with his napkin.

Burbage was running up the river steps ahead of Jacko. He came straight into the Falcon, talking as he entered.

"By God, he raised the siege and it's all over! What will they do with him?"

"Tell all quietly and in order," said Gus.

"Quietly! There's no order! Look, look at my cloak!" and he displayed it torn in many places. "Done at Paul's church. The man is mad or we are mad, or the whole world's lost its mind!"

"Speak what happened," Will said firmly.

"In hell's name, who knows? What we *saw*—"

"What you saw, then."

"We heard too," said Jacko, "that two hundred prime gentlemen came out of Essex House—"

"—marching down the Strand and Fleet"—Burbage's fever was in his tongue—"calling out that they would be murdered by Raleigh and Cobham, God's wounds! Bedford and Rutland— Rutland, mind you!—Southampton, Essex, all walking to raise a siege, shouting to people—quite mad!"

"This we *heard*," said Jacko carefully, looking around at friends and strangers.

"By Hercules, we saw them too. They came into the City by Ludgate with swords and pistols, and then they raised Essex' standard. Jesu, like the siege of Cadiz!"

"Go on."

"Folk, coming out of Paul's," said Heminges, "were—"

"Nay, who is telling this?" Dickon asked, not unkindly but in perturbation.

"We ourselves saw him!"

"Aye. We saw him. We saw him. On Cheapside we saw him, great Essex, his face streaming with sweat. He turned his head this way and that like a hunted creature, and he cried some word that sounded like *For the Queen! A plot is laid for my life!* But no one could make sense of what he wanted. Many were his friends but what could they do? To have raised a sword arm in that crowd would have been to cut oneself. He knew—he knew he was lost." Dickon sat down abruptly. "Well, there it is. City heralds followed almost on his heels . . . Greatness fallen. They promised a thousand pounds to anyone who would take my lord, and pardon to those who forsook him. This in the City—so my lord was betrayed even before he came—"

"Call him not *thy* lord," said Sly angrily.

"Well, what shall I call him? Lucifer, who when he falls can never hope again?"

Will said quietly, "Call him by his name. Robin Devereux came

204

to the citizens of London who love him well, but they lifted no hand to give him what he rashly asked. That is the simple story."

"Aye, the rest—" Dickon ran his fingers through his hair, and looked at Heminges. "Well, we came to Paul's—he was already in retreat. At the word traitor, many slipped away of those two hundred, and put on cloaks, it's said, to disguise themselves. A few stayed by, fifty perhaps. He had counted surely on his friend that sheriff Smith in Gracechurch Street to give him arms and men. The sheriff failed him though he gave a drink of water. When we saw him, his countenance was ghastly. Of an armorer he was begging arms. The man said he had no arms for him. 'Not for me, Pickering?' he answered in a tone to wring thy heart."

Sly said, "Not mine. Remember that, Dickon."

Dickon looked at him with hate. He would not go on. Jacko, mastering his stammer, told the rest. "Ludgate was locked. Tom Levenson's brother, John—one we know!—was going home to his own house in Ludgate from the sermon in Paul's church denouncing the Earl, we now hear, betrayed before he came, as Dickon says—well, Tom's brother was compelled by the Bishop standing there on the steps of the church to draw the chain across the sssstreet. And he was told to command pikemen and musketeers, come from God knows where, and hold the street."

"When the Earl, proud as St George," Dickon interrupted, "asked permission to leave the City, and he asked it in a most seemly way, he was refused. Never did I see a man more proudly humbled. No one dared to raise a sound. Treason—oh, blessed Saviour, to be hanged and cut down while still alive and have thy innards ripped away while thy heart still beats—"

"Be silent!" Will cried.

Dickon said softly, "No man is such a thief to honor as to suffer so. Well, we saw him, as though his whole life was written on his face. All his hopes and now his death. People stared in silence and I think their hearts were torn. When he stood for a moment and reached out his hands to them, some had the grace to sob." He looked about at them. "We saw Ned Bushell go pray passage of Levenson. We stood as close as you. We heard him say, 'I tell you that my lord says he will and must pass and that he will pass by you as a true servant of her Majesty and a friend of the State, and that he only seeketh to suppress the tyranny of those who have sold and betrayed the State to the Spaniard.' "

Jacko murmured, "Well learned and well spoken, Dickon."

"Then one shouted 'Shoot,' and the pistols were discharged and answered by what shot the muskets had, and forthwith Sir Christopher Blount charged with his sword and hacked at the chain till the sparks flew. He was shouting . . ." He passed his hand over his face and asked in a shaking voice, "What was he shouting, Jacko?"

"*Saw, saw, saw! Tray! Tray! Shoot!*" Jacko cried.

"And some of the Earl's men got between the post and the chains and drove among the pikes and halberds. Sir Christopher spouted blood from the face and young Mr Tracy, the Earl's page, dropped dead. The shouting never ceased—it was like wild Irish cries. On both sides were dead and dying, though Ned Bushell still fought like a decent man, and Robin Catesby was crying '*Ça, ça, Tirez!*' though bleeding from a hundred wounds. Ah, well, then he summoned together those who were left—some twoscore were all, I'd say, left of our brave band—"

"When did we put on Essex livery?" Sly asked coldly.

Burbage stared at him. Will said, "Nay, Will Sly, this is terrible, grand poetry. With grace be silent."

But Sly was nervous and sat biting his lip and impaling Burbage with his eyes.

"Then they went down Friday Street to the river and at Queen's Hythe gave orders to what boats were there to take them to his own water gate. We were in his footsteps down Friday Street—Friday, child of woe."

"So we did partake . . ." said Gus.

"And now," Florio murmured, "we wait."

"Aye," Will said, "we wait."

Crowds had gathered on Bankside. Will moved his chair so that he might see out the window over their heads. This coign of vantage was crowded by a dozen others. It seemed as though news was plucked visibly from the air. The excitement was as clear as the sweat on a man's brow. The crowd along the bank made sound without sense. Children leapt up and down. A man and a woman danced, and someone with a viol struck up a tune. One boy fell into the river and swam about for a time diving for pennies which he could not find. The song of Essex when he returned from Ireland went from voice to voice but it died away on the nudges of careful men when they saw the black pacing figure of the canon of St Saviour's—he was the Bishop of Winchester's man and thus guardian of established orthodoxies.

Condell came up hurriedly from a boat, crying to them at the window, "What, all here? Have we not a play to give? Has the whole world gone mad?"

Someone in the crowd shrilled, "Wilt thou play another killing?" And someone else cried, "Who cares for tinsel crowns today?"

"Who indeed?" Gus muttered.

"Come along," said Heminges, "tinsel's no more rrridiculous than mmmen!"

As they left the inn to cross the field, a blaze and a roar came from a barge drifting before Essex House.

In the theatre were a handful of spectators, and even they wished to have a part in both worlds. They shouted through the performance, seizing words of the bawdy old comedy enacted, and twisting them to other meanings. Those few gentlemen with seats on the stage talked steadily of cliques and court and treason, laying loud wagers as events thrust themselves into the Globe. There was no restraint of customers. They flung themselves out-of-doors whenever their imaginations rang a tocsin, and on each return to their seats, they shouted louder than the actors.

At one point, Will from old habit glanced at the Lords' Rooms. There, with a palpable shock, he saw Sir Piers Dalglish sitting in his plumed splendor and on either side of him, bolt upright, masked, his own lady and her sister. They were like three figures in a puppet show. They sat so still and wooden that Will forgot his lines and was recalled to himself by Gib's hissed counsel.

When he came off the stage he leaned against a post to collect himself. What spying-out engaged Sir Piers? Was she there compelled and helpless, or was she demonstrating to the world (that is, Sir Piers) that she was ready to betray a lover? What would he do?

Gus, on his way to the stage, stopped by him. Will said, "What will he do, thinkst thou?"

"Who?"

"The plumed serpent of the Queen."

"Oh, him." Gus laughed. "Build more bad accounts against himself in heaven." Gus went onto the stage.

During a sennet between scenes, the three left the box and came down into the tiring room. Will was caught in all his sore suspicions. Sir Piers nodded, and the ladies stood stiff as stays, their hands flat against their farthingales, as alike as two peas behind their masks.

None spoke. Sir Piers tapped his poncet box and said in his slow, cool way, "It is much regretted that thy noble friends have not come here today."

"My noble friends?" said Will.

"To withdraw their high and mightiness on such a day shows either excessive fear of her gracious Majesty or a guilty part in seditious acts."

"I know nothing, nothing, nothing," said Will, trying to give a reading that was neither too bold nor too indifferent.

"Well, if you know nothing, you are of nothing use to the Queen," and Sir Piers smiled slightly. The lady's sister laughed, but Will's lady did not move in any way.

She was so plain and cold, so dull of spirit, so empty in her gestures that Will scarcely knew her. She acknowledged him in no fashion, her face was turned slightly from him, and through the eye slots of her mask he could see that she was looking everywhere but in his direction.

Her sister, on the other hand, was gay and quizzical, calling him "Mister Shakespeare" with each sentence, and putting bold questions to him of plays and players. When Sir Piers said with an ambiguous smile, "Well, the Queen knows all," and moved to go, Will's lady promptly put her hand on Sir Piers's arm, and went with no look to right or left.

Will found his hands cold. By St Priapus, he had at last attained the dignity of hating her!

Actors' voices tolled on, chorused by the Southwark bells which had begun a doleful clanging. The insistence of the bells put an end to the play, for the audience ran from the theatre and did not return. All, that is, save two grizzled barons who held their seats on the stage while they laid wagers on the bells. Will asked if they wished the jig.

"By the death, no! I wager those bells are rung by hotbloods who have climbed the steeple."

"Very likely, sir."

"Yet what will this day bring? Will we die when it is over? Tails we die before the week is out!"

Will left them to go and wash his face.

The men of the Globe stood in the field in the twilight debating: Should Burbage, Heminges, Armin, and Condell go home across the river? Disjoin? Nay. Then the Southwark men must come with them. Nay. They returned to the Falcon.

The tables had not been taken down and Florio still sat with the cold dinner before him. The twilight had darkened the river, and in a congested voice he told the terrible tales that had been shouted through the window, or that he had gathered in brief forays of his own.

All was over. That was certain.

Artillery, shot from the Queen's barge under the command of the Lord Admiral and from the roofs of houses and of St Clement Danes by Lord Burghley had brought the Earl to submission. But he had paced the roof for a long time, his tall figure seen by all. He had waved his sword and shouted an all-hail and a kiss to the City. At length his wife and sister were seen to plead with him, and in the light of smoky torches he had conferred, there on the lead, with the Queen's voice, Sir Fulke Greville.

It burned the heart. In the sight of London had come another of the Queen's barges, and the Earl had stepped aboard. The lords Southampton, Rutland, and Monteagle, all mighty lords until this moment, had followed him.

The excitement still roared. Tidings passed from mouth to mouth up the riverbank told of their proud debarkment at Lambeth Palace into custody of the Archbishop of Canterbury. Ah,

209

those churchly men, who always fiddled with the people's will!

Will, clawed and raked by the lady *et* Sir Piers, or the lady *cum* Sir Piers, or the lady conjunctive to Sir Piers, heard the sounds and furies as scabrous part-music, sung, played, chanted, and enacted by demons against infernal lights. Filthy acts called for filthy actors, whores and foists.

The stews and tenements had emptied. Clients paid their whores to stay with them while they scanned the river and waited for fresh rumors. Even the prisoners in the Clink pounded on their shutters and shouted over the river, and in the great park of the Bishop's palace were mysterious lights: marsh lights of evil spirits?

A barge illumined with many lanterns came suddenly to the wharf by the inn. A shout went up, and foists and honest citizens danced with excitement in the smoky torchlight. Debouching was a company in the Lord Constable's livery, pikemen and musketeers. Dickon pressed against Will to peer with him into the gloom.

The pikemen lowered their pikes at the crowd crying, "On the Queen's business!" and ruthlessly forced a path.

"By God," said Dickon, "who are they bearing hugger-mugger in this fashion? Where to, Affabel?" he called discreetly to the constable who stood below.

"Marshalsea," said the constable, shrugging, "or the Clink, since they were not weighed into the river."

"As God's my witness," said Will softly, "I'll swear that one passing is Ned Bushell."

Heminges said, "I am sick—I am sick," and indeed he looked very ill. Will was suddenly overcome by hunger, shocking hunger. It was that or weep his outcast state, or search out that woman who was the very figure of these deadly times and strike her down. He crammed in his cold dinner. Then Burbage drew in a deep breath, and picked up his knife also, and the others followed. Not a word was said. At length they sighed and wiped their mouths, and Burbage said he must be gone. Florio said he had such an emptiness of spirit, might he stay the night in the company of one of them? It was Heminges who, rousing himself, put an arm about him and took him home to shelter with his own large brood.

So Will was left with Pope. They drank some fresh ale and picked at raisins.

"The end of day . . ."

"Well, we have resolved on courage. Let's be brave," said Pope with flabby gallantry.

Toward ten o'clock a servant in Lord William's livery, and well armed, entered and beckoned Will. The thought leapt: *Enter Destiny.*

He followed the servant, who led him to a shadowed figure standing within the precincts of the Globe.

"I have been searching for you," said Lord William in a whisper. "I did not wish to draw attention to myself."

"How fares my lord?"

"Not by any means at all! My cousin, they have taken him. You must say he never uttered treason, that night by night, in your hearing, he spoke loyally of the Queen."

"My lord, we are most pitifully entangled. We players are tainted fish, trying to sweeten our own smell."

"By the stock and honor of my kin, it will be a sin if you fail him now!"

"My good lord!"

"Do not speak. I'll not allow my choler linked to patience. All is now anger! I'll not excuse injuries to me or mine." He paced up and down. "A hundred have been taken into custody. Who of them will talk? See that you are very prudent when they question you. Say naught against my cousin—nay, more, speak a word for him. I adjure you. Do not fail. In no wise fail." He stood close to Will and said softly, "The Earl—not my cousin, but Essex—has burned all the papers which he carried in a bag about his neck. All is well. He burned most of all the letter from his Majesty of Scotland. Do not fear."

"My lord," Will said desperately, "we are servants and play-actors. We have naught to do with great events."

Lord William laughed a little. "Think you so? What man can say that of himself? He lives, does he not?"

In this crepuscular world, Will saw Lord William's face. He remembered a wax image he had seen which had begun to melt and yet had kept its form. A woman looked so when she had wept too much.

Lord William struck his dagger against the wall of the theatre. "There is no importunity I will not make. Damon ne'er loved Pythias as I love my cousin. There is a Captain Lea—nay, I will not speak of him. Do what you can. I charge you, on your honor."

CHAPTER *Sixteen*

THOSE who slept well that night remembered events with a shock when they woke. Those who slept poorly, as did Will, who had spent all that night writing down part sentences and fragments of men's thoughts, trying to make clear some shred of the human mystery—those non-sleeping men dragged themselves into a familiar day with no shock.

A message came early from Gus that he and Will had been summoned to the Lord Chamberlain's; to his own house, which meant private questions.

They met at the Paris Garden Steps dressed in their liveries as the Lord Chamberlain's Men. They were calm, for their helplessness would not be served by fear. The river was struggling with craft, and it seemed as though the Queen's pennant was on all of them. It was a rainy day, the river pitted with drops.

Gabe Holmes, pulling hard against the tide, still had breath to chivvy them on their plight. A trumpeteer in a noble barge blew a warning as they drew too close, and Gabe loosed a ditchful of oaths, as filthy as the water.

"So do all high-born," he cried to Will and Gus. "They break wind with us and drop us down their privy holes. Nay, thou art in a fair way to be manure that's not even used. Ha, thou hast red lines about thy necks this morning. Thou'lt soon be kicking air. Yet if they send thee dancing into space, what will my trade do? Hah? Tell me that?" With his head turned to maneuver against both tide and the River Fleet, emptying here into the Thames, he shouted, "I was a sailor under Drake and I was promised my guts' worth for every sail I raised. Now? I get a penny for a ride—and my hands, look at my hands! Blessed shit, they fixed that price forty years ago. Can we live on a penny? By St Traveler's Ass, I'd as lief raise a target, for whoso'er will hear of it."

He brought them with scarcely a bump into the stairs at Blackfriars. They gave him threepence each, and he promised them a nosegay at their hanging.

"I'll not go to my hanging or any man's without I eat," said Will, and at a cookshop bought meat pies which they munched going up the hill in the rain.

The theatre at Blackfriars offered a closed face, though some of the child actors were swinging wetly on the gates, and one of them picked up a clod of mud and flung it after Gus.

At the corner Gus stopped to repair the damage to his cloak. At Bridewell's prison a beadle was tying a whore to the back of a cart. He struck her a few blows in a promissory way as his colleague took up the metal basins that would be hammered at the crossroads to call witnesses to the beatings. The rain provoked them all.

Hunsdon House, a few paces on, was half stone, half timber, old-fashioned and commodious, the timber covered with carvings painted and gilded. The porter opened the gate and they went through a low tunnel into a quadrangle. It was unpaved, and rain and horses had churned it into troughs. A horse tethered to a ring gave them a red look. Like my own, Will thought.

They sought out a servant, and the servant gave them, as they fancied, a hangman's glance. He set them waiting in an anteroom where they shook out their cloaks and hats. Spontaneously they clasped hands.

At last the servant returned and they went into Lord Hunsdon's study. He did not turn his eyes to them. A man in poor plain clothes was leaning on his desk, talking rapidly, and another, in sober satin, stood nearby nodding with each syllable. At the window onto Castle Lane stood still another man, and he turned his head slightly to look at them. It was Sir Piers.

Sir Piers nodded and smiled, and the smiling, so unlike his taciturnity, seemed no less unkind than Judas'. He made a movement as though to join them, but at that moment Lord Hunsdon turned to them.

They had known him since he was plain George Carey, cousin to the Queen through her mother, Anne Bullen. A cold man, he was locked to the Queen by ties as strong as steel. As Lord Chamberlain, he ruled the royal household; every detail, every shadow, every light, every footfall, every whispered word belonged, in the end, to him.

He was dressed in black velvet with a lace collar, white as a winding sheet. His soft puffy hands turned over and over a box of sealing string. His blond beard and hair had some gray which scarcely showed. His thin nose was delicate enough to scent and suffer all, but his heavy-lidded eyes, with their guarded and opaque look, set a watch upon that suffering.

He spoke, still without looking at them, and his pale mouth opened sideways, as though one side of his face was immobile.

"Good day to you. The nature of my questioning is private. Your answers will be sifted well and will add to the safety of the realm." Then he looked at them. "The Queen taxes me with questions, and since her wisdom is uncommon, I must know the answers." He addressed himself to Will by a sudden pale pointed glance. "It is you who must give them to me. What mean these lines?"

His gaze was lowered to a paper on his desk and he read slowly, with no stress, in a clear voice. " 'This land of such dear souls . . . is now leas'd out—I die pronouncing it—like to a tenement or pelting farm.' " He glanced up briefly, and Will opened his mouth to speak, but Lord Hunsdon made a gesture and continued. " 'England, bound in with the triumphant sea . . . is now bound in with shame, with inky blots and rotten parchment bonds. That England, that was wont to conquer others, hath made a shameful conquest of itself. Ah, would the scandal vanish with my life, how happy then were my ensuing death.' "

He raised his opaque eyes and waited quietly.

Will heard these words as though new written. He made a strong effort to speak with the same lack of stress as had Lord Hunsdon.

"My lord, these were things said, rightly or wrongly, of King Richard II in his untried youth."

Lord Hunsdon's lips moved slightly. "By the true and living John of Gaunt? Or are they words which you have put into the mouth of this uncle?"

"My lord, I do not know by a syllable which words are my own and which were drawn from chronicles and annals written down by others."

Lord Hunsdon did not take his cold eyes from Will's face. "His Majesty King Richard II was ancestor to her Grace. Some disloyal voices say she places security above chivalry, or leases out the profits on custom to those who have her favor. Is this a coincidence between what is said so rebelliously of the Queen and what you say of King Richard? Do you share in any particular the sentiments put into the mouth of John of Gaunt? Might you not have altered them without offending truth?"

Will moved with caution.

"The Queen in her wisdom has guided us to be a great and peaceful nation. I owe no loyalty but to the Queen."

"Yet the Queen sees herself as though called Richard." Lord Hunsdon hesitated for a moment, and looked at them with a sudden intense personalness which vanished almost as it came. "She was scarcely restrained from having Hayward put to the rack. She wished him to confess that in his book he hinted at her deposition." He stared at them for a moment. "For it is impossible to expunge the dedication of that book: to the Earl of Essex." Then he made a fist of his voice. "What heard you at Essex House? Who did you see? What was said?"

Gus and Will were attuned like two viols. Their responses were concordant.

"My lord, we were there so unwillingly we strove to leave before we came."

"That is not replying. Who did you see?"

"Those lords and gentlemen, my lord, who have been seized."

He stared at them again, and yet with nothing personal in his glance.

Gus spoke urgently, "My lord, since we did not wish to see nor hear nor know nor be there, we were blind men with plugged ears."

"That was poor loyalty to the Queen's security."

"Good my lord, why should it come to us that the Queen was endangered? We thought of our distaste."

"What did you conceive as distasteful in the tragedy of an English king?"

"The urgency, my lord, that required this—old-fashioned play to be done."

"Did that not make you look about? Should you not then in loyalty have listened to all the reasons adducible?" They did not answer. "Who o'erruled your judgment?"

Then Gus said boldly, "It was, I think, my lord, yourself. Burbage brought your reassurance. When we left Essex House we had promised nothing, whatever they might think."

Lord Hunsdon's expression said little. The nostrils quivered and the lips pressed together, but the change was slight. He said quietly, glancing at Will, "We must add to the debit side that three and four years ago you dedicated two published poems to the Earl of Southampton."

"My good lord—"

"Say no more. They are a fact. I will control the recollection if it be within my power." He permitted a moment's humanity. "It is events which catch up men like you, not you, events. I understand. But there is one disquieting fact: the Privy Council's suspicions of my lord of Essex were confirmed by the playing of *King Richard II.*"

"Then may not the playing be called God's sign of warning to her Majesty?" Gus said, his hands clutched behind his back.

Hunsdon answered coldly, "That may be so. I will present it thus." Sir Piers stirred and came forward. Lord Hunsdon glanced at him. "One more question. What have you heard spoken by the Earl of Rutland?"

"My good lord, we players know such peers only as our patrons. We talk of poetry and playacting and how a gesture should be made. We do not share in other things."

"I do not speak of *sharing* but of *overhearing*."

Sir Piers said pleasantly, "You heard his treason at the Paschal Lamb the night I taxed him of it."

"That night we heard high words and some loud exercise on the part of both," Will said.

"My lord," said Gus, "it would be worth our lives to hear and answer such high things. Hard words are spoken in our hearing which become soft words when a cooling follows. It is, I fancy, the nature of greatness to be sanguine and choleric. We live discreetly, and we do not forget at any time to whom we owe our living and our loyalty."

One of Lord Hunsdon's eyelids quivered slightly. Sir Piers spoke again. "There is a rumor that a playwright, known to all, set down a doggerel verse which has plagued the Queen. Know you of this?"

Will tried to read the bland, dark face. But Lord Hunsdon made an angry move and jangled the bell on his desk. "It could be two dozen men or none. I believe, and the Queen believes, that it came from some wretched chapman, so poorly was it put together."

Sir Piers began to speak, but Lord Hunsdon forestalled him. "Go to! We have big fish to catch. The little ones we can scoop up in our hands."

It was clear to Will, to Gus, and to Sir Piers that Lord Hunsdon wished nothing asked or answered in this matter.

"Her Majesty's strength and calmness are unimpaired. I make no doubt she will continue true mistress of herself and of events." He jingled the bell again, and when a secretary came, he said, "My purse."

From the purse he took five shillings and handed them to Gus. As he did so, he said, for what reason they knew not unless it be that he gave and took with the same hand, "The Earls of Essex and Southampton, and my lord Monteagle, were taken to the Tower at dawn today."

Gus bowed and murmured some kind of thanks—for money or for courtesy or for treating them like men, whichever seemed the best. Lord Hunsdon looked at Will as though a shutter had opened slightly. Will asked, "And the others, my lord?"

The shutter closed again. Lord Hunsdon turned away. He said, without looking up from a paper which his secretary had placed, "Good day to you. I pray you, mind carefully your duty to her Grace and to myself."

When they came out onto the street by St Anne's Church, Gus stood for a moment flexing his clutched hands. The rain had stopped. Will said nothing for a pace or two, and then he spoke ferociously. "She would use us as catspaws and informers. She is greedy, vain, cruel—"

"For the love of God! What we think must not be counted." Gus drew Will back, for three horsemen abreast filled the street.

Will said, "I defy authority. I will not yield to the tyrant Custom."

"Oh folderol! He who wishes all smooth as glass will rule us." Gus was remorseless. "And if you or I put our muddy feet on our lord's smooth surface, his fury will not be hot but cold, yet it will sear us all the same. Where will we go now?"

"To Jacko."

"Aye, we need each other."

Gus caught Will's arm to draw him into a narrow street between overhanging houses where apprentices in blue gowns and flat hats were playing a furtive game of ball. There he put both hands on Will's shoulders and held him firmly.

"Hear me. He spared the worst question—of thy foolish verse. Now there must be no hot words nor hot spirits. We must take care, even amongst ourselves, that there be no sudden fires. We will be pulled about. Counsel will be gratis. Our silence can be as good as speech. We are not fools, so let us not behave like fools. Let us be neither servile nor despairing."

Will said, "My passion is very hot!"

"That may be. But let us harbor only what we may in safety hold: a meek tenacity that will see us safely home."

Around conduits and bakeshops, women were talking, and *Es-*

sex was in their voices. Here yesterday his fatal drama had been played out. Will and Gus avoided Paul's churchyard, for they wanted no questions asked by their friends.

In Cheapside the noise was deafening. The ordinary noise of carpenters at work in open shops, strong-voiced apprentices shouting the wares of all their masters, hawkers, beggars, drovers, carters, at war with each other, the doomed bellowing cattle in the Shambles were all augmented by clamorous remembrances. Here, into this welter of life, into this City with its fierce independence, Essex had come seeking his destiny. Had this man seen him and that man turned away his head?

Essex was intensely present to Will, who had spent the night thinking of princes and kings, princes claiming their kingdoms, majesty soiled, men uncertain before their fatal acts. Essex' figure was almost as clear as the bodies around him. Essex had lighted a flame that was quickly put out, yet Will heard his name from a man in a torn jerkin, from a booth-keeper, from a clerk, from the tolling bell of St Mary-le-Bow.

On Cheapside their pocket was any man's, and his spittle theirs, so intimately were they linked. Essex was the lost lover of all . . . Why had he not made clear what he wished?

One man cried across the open kennel in the middle of the street, "He is our Barak, Deborah's mighty man of valor! She cannot give him to the hangman! Our Queen—but he is our general!"

Will lingered by a booth to finger stuff he did not need so that he might hear a man say to a merchant, "He is the Protestant champion of Europe. It is the Spaniards, mark my words, who would have him killed!"

As they passed Goldsmiths' Row, they heard a ballad monger singing discreetly a song made up overnight:

> "Sweet England's pride is gone
> Welladay! Welladay!
> Brave honor grace him still,
> gallantly, gallantly:
> He ne'er did deed of ill,
> well it is known;

But Envy, that foul fiend,
whose malice ne'er did end,
Hath brought true virtue's friend
unto his thrall."

Let him return today, and would he fail?

In this maze of lanes, byways, courts, alleys, passages, where tall warped buildings peered into each other's windows, Essex' name drifted like milkweed.

Will was passionate with wonder and amazement. A fashionable lady lay back in her coach beside a young man who fed sweetmeats into her mouth. The driver lashed at his horses and a drayman and his sleepy horse were knocked aside and the dray broken by the imperious coach.

Had the drayman and the coachman been thinking of Essex?

Gus and Will escaped down Milk Street, for Cheapside would be impassable until the constables had forced a way, and they came, by an alley, into Aldermansbury Street.

Here the cries were muted. This was a quiet genteel parish where Heminges, Condell, and assorted gentry had their homes, gardens, positions, and graves. Parish bells were ringing, but the nearest, the bell of St Mary Aldermansbury, had a light domestic tone for both the quick and the dead.

Heminges' home was comfortable and handsome, half-timbered, with a gabled roof, fine furniture, and cushions striped with cloth of silver on the chairs.

Heminges had twelve children, a wife, three apprentices who were treated as kindly as his children, and now Florio who required careful nursing. Yet he managed all, and the financial affairs of the Globe, and the grocery which his wife supervised in Shoreditch, with a Jovian kindliness of stammers.

His wife Rebecca greeted them with kisses and agitation, for Jacko had taken to his bed with shakings, vomitings and great distemper. "He raves!" she said, her own plump face looking mournfully from one to the other of these friends who were close as a family.

"Out of his mind?" cried Gus, starting toward the stairs.

"Nay, he raves quite like himself—save he's the kindest man in all the world and *never* raves! Nay, he shouts out against God knows who—all who pull down poor men's commerce—some he hates more than others, the ones who smell so sweet. Oh, la is me!"

Gus said, "I will just go up and speak to him quietly."

"Aye, do that, for I will tell you it's the danger to the theatre is his sickness. We've got thirteen children that run and kick," and she put her hands flat on her round belly where the thirteenth grew, "but I'll tell you, *he* has fourteen!" Will put his arm about her shoulders and kissed her cheek. Then she laughed, her agitation calmed. "Nay, fifteen, with that Florio sitting in the kitchen like a monument to his pet dog."

"Shall I see to Florio?" Will said.

"Nay, come you in and eat up for thy strength. Oh, Will, Will, Jacko's such a dear good man, and he says, What will they do without me! and then he struggles up, all shakes and pukes, and then sinks back and asks as sweet as a poor babe however will you live if he dies."

"Oh, we'll not live—but he'll not die!" said Will in great concern.

"Oh, no, no—not unless they kill off that fourteenth child of his."

"Where's my godson? He must go for Burbage!"

"It's a wonder," said Rebecca crisply now, "how twelve children can vanish all at once. Willy!"

It took only a few loud cries to bring the boy named for Will—the two Wills embraced gladly—and send him off for Burbage.

Then Rebecca sat Will firmly in the dining room and sent another child for Florio and filled two mugs with ale. The tablecloth was encrusted with needlework, gilt plate stood on the shelves; the maids who brought in the pastry were neat and clean and gave Will a welcome as warm as Rebecca's. This was the home of a prosperous and loving man—and, Will thought, nodding to Florio, who slipped into the chair beside him, it came from a careful measuring of adversity and human delinquence in one scale, and good sense and mutual felicity in the other . . . as now.

"Ha!" Rebecca laughed, hearing voices on the stairs, "Gus has made my dear man well!"

Jacko came in, pale, his dressing gown wrapped about him, frowning, talking with Gus, sick, but resolutely well. He embraced Will without a word, and sank into a chair as he answered his own questions in a high voice unlike his own.

"It's nothing nnnew, Lord Hunsdon's cccaution. Nor our wwwearisome good sense!"

"Jacko, be calm," said Will, "we need not only good sense but thy food digested, dear Father Jehovah—"

But Heminges took him by the front of his doublet and shook him slightly. "We've never been in gggaol, not oone of us! Is that not a remmmarkable thing? Nnnot for suspicion, nor for debt, nor for drunkenness nor for too much brown paper and old gggginger! We'll give no noble fools a chance to change that."

Will rose and moved about restlessly. At length he stood behind Heminges and put his hands on his shoulders. "I'm gingered enough for gaol at this moment."

Gus said drily, "Nay, we must all be named Caution now."

"Aye, and puke up those wicked men who embroiled us," Heminges said heartily, "and do not you remember the word gaol in any language." He suddenly found his appetite and ate a pastry greedily.

On the sound of raised voices and slammed doors, Burbage came in. He gave the impression of perfect control but none were deceived. Dickon was anguished by fate, the future, his own mercurial temper. He spared no greetings. He said, "Tell me— tell all!"

When he had heard, he sat with his head in his hands, shaking his head back and forth. Heminges went on remorseless as a juggernaut setting out ineluctable expectations if they held to perfect caution and behavior.

Will had no quarrel with this. He was merely angry at the inexorable, baited by the inexplicable. But Dickon moaned, "Six thousand pounds—nay, more," and then they too thought of their investments. As they sat silent, breaking pastry with their fingers and feeding morsels to the children, Will laughed.

"I listened to our play—my *Richard*—as though it were a stranger. Indeed I had half forgot. How do you say it, Dickon, when Richard is alone at the last in his nutshell?"

Dickon did not raise his head. He muttered, " 'I have been studying how I may compare This prison—' Oh, no!"

Will smiled. " 'Oh, no' is not in the line, old lad. How does it go—'have I the daintiness of ear to check time broke in a dis-order'd string—' It goes thusly somehow, and then it comes to 'now hath time made me his numb'ring clock.' " Will rose to walk back and forth and pause by the open mullioned window to glance into the wet garden. "Does not that clock in its finity reveal the infinite?" he asked. "Is not our greatest treasure the relativity which pricks us to eternity?" He looked at them and smiled a little, but he stared longest at the blurred image of gar-den reflected in a polished plate. "We bear our own misfortunes on the back of such as have before endured the like. Do you sup-pose my lord Essex thought on this? Thus plays a great man, in one person, many people, and none content. When crushing penury persuades Richard he was better than a king, then he is kinged again. Is Essex dreaming? Now doth time make man his numbering clock; his sighs, tears, groans are minutes, hours, post-ing to the Queen's joy, while, in truth, he is naught but her Jack o' the clock wearing away his hours."

"Do you think we are comforted by that?" Gus asked quietly.

Will said rather wistfully, "It might comfort some."

Jacko said firmly, "Are we agreed?"

"Agreed on thee?"

"*Agreed.*"

"We are agreed that thou art our shepherd."

Heminges said, wiping his face which had taken back its color, "We are agreed. Naught else matters."

The temper of the City was unsure, and on Tuesday it was put under a strong guard. Bands of militia were summoned from Surrey, Essex, and Middlesex, and camped in the country around Westminster guarding the Court as though, people said, "the Spaniards were in the land."

223

Fair-weather friends of the Globe went to great pains to prove their devotion to caution and Queen. The authorities in the City who hated the theatre used the occasion to point out the evils it bred: disloyalty, pandering, epidemics, idleness, incontinence, inveigling, and alluring of maidens by those young ravens who prowled through the galleries spying for female carrion, the danger from scaffolds, weapons, and gunpowder effects on the stage, from canting and ranting and building chapels to Satan. Not to mention that it was the business of actors to deceive: hence were they all hypocrites, doing no less than the evil of persuading their audience to yield to false passions, false goodness, false riot, and evil, suiting forms to all their conceits.

Slops were poured on them.

Florio was at the theatre as often as Heminges, who seemed to wear him as a sidepiece. By Heminges' metaphor, one more sheep into the fold was merely a consequence of the stormy weather. Florio must observe the rules, that was all: that they were faithful to each other, prudent, discreet, self-respecting. He sat playing softly on a flute, pausing only to tell, in his soft voice, of some monstrous rumor.

Sly came in badly beaten, his face marked. Gib glued on a beard and mended his clothes. The City was pulsing with staves, pikes, pistols, daggers, cudgels. The Watch gave up and sat drinking beer. Dead bodies floated in the river. Southwark spewed out vice and violence as though hell's lid had been taken off. Condell fell into a brawl which tore his clothes. He would not talk of it. He hinted that someone had spoken offensively of Will.

Gus was certain one must not hope too much. In the theatre, at meals, at rehearsals, Gus was apt to wear no expression on his face save the expression of his own gaunt boniness. He said, when Will taxed him with his taciturnity, that he was counting over to himself the great weights of life as they had fallen, how the balance could be set awry by a drop of rain.

Happily, the routine of their days bore them up. They were men who had been secure for a long time. Will dared not say to any that he thanked God his inner commotion was well concealed by this outer chaos.

. . . For none of these events had abated the dull ache that filled his mind and, worse, his heart. That she had never loved him in any way he now believed with that quiet sense of humiliation which was so much worse for not deserving pity. A lofty passion, however illicit it might be, could demand some sympathy to equal its surge of feeling. But to have been only a fowl trussed for a whore's eating—hah, such debasement had best be thrown out with the offal, and there an end! How the fowl must have suffered before its neck was wrung . . .

But to debase himself put no balm on his inward bruises, and he thanked God that these wounds were out of sight to be healed in God's own time Who saw all things.

He spent much time with his play of the Prince of Denmark, thinking of men caught between themselves and some great amiss. It was a secret life.

Sitting one evening in the Falcon, waiting for Dekker and the last part of Dekker's play, each told the others that they must not be afraid. And yet fear was a necessary lubricant to relieve a terrible congestion. When Florio wondered how they would dissemble and thus hide themselves, they answered boldly. But Florio, weaned of all his hyperboles, said sadly, "Yet I will disappear, and you must forget that such a man as I ever lived who loved his lordship." He glanced at Will with his Italian eyes overflowing now with tears. "Ah, tragedy concerneth high fellows: high as the gallows or high as my lord."

Heminges had been waiting for such a moment to ply his Jovian art. "By hell," he said, busily laying a pattern on the table with mugs, napery, knives and spoons, "there are other ttthings to talk about, nigh as important as tthe gallows. There is this rrrakeshell, jack-drums-entertainment of Dekker's." He chuckled, liking to remember bawdy lines in quiet introspection. The others stirred and shifted but Heminges was implacable. "Come. Rehearsals tttomorrow and he has not sssettled this last pppart."

Will said, "Let us mourn awhile in decency high falls and lost innocence."

"Lost inininnocence?" said Jacko in a flat voice. "Lost pppence and pounds. Come. If it's Lllenten fare you want, I ssshan't be wwwith you. Come. Dekker's pppplay."

Dickon sighed. "What does he call it now?" he asked heavily.

"*Satiromastix.*"

"Did the censor expunge the line we talked of?"

"No," said Jacko.

"Then we will expunge it." Dickon drew the sheets toward him. He riffled through them, saying in precisely articulated syllables, "We will expunge everything that later on might pester us."

Jacko was testy. "Wwwipe up. Wwwipe away, but we cccannot give out all the parts till that last ssscene is sssettled."

"So, God's lid, where is Dekker?"

"He was sssent for."

"Send again!"

But Dekker arrived before the boy had more than straightened his stockings and reached for his jerkin. Marston was with him, half drunk, ferociously gay, and Dekker was making angry efforts to shift him away.

Dekker was uneasy, moving his pale eyes and twisting his mouth to one side, as though an equivocal expression would set a fence about him. His fingers trembled, and his anger at Marston spilled over into surliness with the others.

Marston would not go away. He sat down at the table, clattering his chair and reaching out for Jacko's pint pot. He talked steadily in a high voice that gave no quarter.

"By holy testicles, thou art spit carrion, turning round and round to make a roast for doomsday. Nay, 'tis something fine to see proud fellows brought so low. I would not have thy places for a marquisate. By thy new humility, cut me a slice of that roast."

No one moved. Dekker blew out his lips. "Go away, Marston. Business will not keep for fools like thee."

"Fools?" Marston had risen and was cutting an uneven hunk from the roast. With a knife in his hand he was even bolder. "A fool? I see the times as you do not, dissemblers. As Mary was a whore so were your own mothers; nay, you are all bastards to your destiny and have not the wit to see life from beneath, where all velvet leaves look the same."

"Oh, God," Will cried, "thy filth is more than we can bear!"

"Soft, soft! I am spared illusions, and if you call that filth then your fate becomes you, and I promise that that fate will be most horrible. For you have deceived yourselves from first to last, you have no more reckoning of this time—that none of us may so much as raise our voice against church and state and queen and lords as may the devils against his mighty lordship Satan. Do you dare write of anything worth hearing? Do you, Will? Dare? Why the very hounds of hell bay with laughter."

Gus cried, "Jack Marston, we must set a guard for ourselves. Out. Will, take his other arm."

But Marston fought them so fiercely, his hot Italian mother his only parent at such a time, that Will sucked his hand where the knife had grazed it, and Gus sat down to nurse his jaw.

Marston laughed. Then he leaned across the table. "I will speak very softly." And so he did, but sibilating so that his speech became a long hiss. "If Anne Bullen's daughter betrays the Earl of Essex then is she of filthier stock than I suspect. Ask me why."

He paused and swept the table with his black mischievous glance. "Because 'twas she who planned each step that he took. Ask me why." Again he dug them with his eyes. "To distract. There are too many poor, too many hungry, too many famines. Too many storms. Too many thieves in high places. Business is bad. Money's value has sunk. Complaints spread like the French itch. Who knows what the future will hold? Uneasiness is high and low. Will we have more civil war when Bullen's girl dies?" He still held the knife in his hand, and sat down to carve at his meat. "But Essex has made the Spanish scare more frightening than a tart with the scab. And those were her instructions." He began to chew a piece of meat and was obliged to gesture with his knife until he could speak again. "We can only mock at such times if we are decent men, but you and Dekker go on writing your mulish plays as though England were unchanged."

Dekker muttered, "What do you men want from this last part of my play?"

Heminges hurriedly drew it toward him and started to speak, but Marston was quicker than Heminges' stammer.

"I told him what this last scene should be. Make the ass stand for the Queen's Minister and you will have something that your children will praise you for."

"Let the ass stand for the Queen's Minister and we will not be there to have children," said Will into his interlaced hands.

Marston shouted, "Fool! call things by their true names! Ben Jonson understands this. I understand. We are cleverer than you, William, for we bring the boil to a head and let it spew its poison. But thy trumphery devices are too stale to vomit."

Will considered him. "Jack, I do not yield to you. You set forth disease and anger; that's too variable to hit the mark. And thus you roil about, letting obscenity obscure the truth. For truth you have, indeed, and I will be the first to say it. But I require some human dignity."

"What a fool you are. What a vapid dreamer. Be what is! Your bag of skin and bones may try its games of self-delusion, but copulation's all. The rain copulates with the earth and the ape with the she-ape, and what is the raging sea but nature's bowels rumbling with flatulent passion? Oh, you make me mad!"

Will did not answer for a moment. Then he said with a quick light in his eyes, "The middle of humanity thou dost not know, Jack, only the extremity of both ends."

"Well, what is that to thee, Laodicean, neither cold nor hot. Life—and I!—have no time for fools who do not strip life bare. How I'll laugh when you do find at last that the breasts of thy women have all the softness of an old man's penis."

"Lord God," Gus said, "we will bear no more. Lads, out with him."

So five or six—only Burbage and Will did not stir—grasped his arms and thighs. Marston did not resist this time, but he burst out laughing. "Wait—Will knows I love him. All I say is strip thyself to death, and know all. Nay, do not push. Am I not thy old friend who goes and comes as he sees fit? Oh, get thy dirty hands off me! We fellows are nothing, nothing, nothing, and it's best we know it. You are an actor, Will, and I a cobbler of plays. It is only that we piss alike that links us with these others. Yet you trust in high and mightiness, and hide behind your paper walls. *Oh, I am so genteel. Oh, la, la, la, nothing doubt,* says he. But face thyself! We are nature's bawds and we must be as crafty with ourselves as are old bawds with their old faces. Nay, do not push. Unloose me, and I will shake you all by the hand, finish Dickon's ale, and go out as I came in, a man."

His exit had some worth to it, for he managed it alone and on his own terms. When the door had closed, they sat without speaking for a moment. Will was very silent, and the others shaken and unsure. It was Dekker who spoke first, in a low voice, not lifting his eyes from his fingers which crumbled bread.

"He is a wild man, but is he not right? Are you safe?" The others stirred to answer, but Dekker lifted his pale eyes and under wrinkled brows addressed himself to Burbage. "Neither he nor I have even such protection as you have. There's no lord cares for us, and what half-dozen pounds come from a play is all I have in the wide world except my wits."

"Well?" said Dickon coldly. "What are you asking?"

Dekker hesitated for a moment. "Dare I risk myself with you, clouded as you are? I, with only a play between me and the Clink?"

Dickon permitted his outrage to climb into a mighty wave, but Will intervened before the wave could break.

"Tom, you ask a question which is by no means out of place. We answer straight. We do not know what fate may hold, and yet, if ever discretion is proved true, it must be now, for never have men been so discreet even to the losing of their conscience."

Heminges grunted. Burbage said tartly, "Speak in your own name, Will."

Dekker was still frowning, with a pasty look upon his face, but his little eyes were fixed on Will. "We'll not lose our dignity, Tom," Will added, "whatsoever happens. And, Tom, dignity is a great thing for such as we who have none, save as we make it. I fancy dignity may now be even better than safety if we do not flinch or falter with our eyes or speak in little voices." Will smiled. "So let us talk about your last scene as self-respecting cobblers would about their last." He hesitated, and touched the shoulder of Florio, who had been quiet a long time. "And let's be proud to be each other's friends."

Dekker continued to watch him, but his face slowly cleared, so that it became round and stupid rather than lowering. The keenness of his eyes, however, told the story, and he looked toward Heminges and then toward the others.

At length he said, "What is amiss with the last scene?"

It was the fair-weather friends who distressed them most. They were a small corrosive but they wore at the nerves. Certain lords came to the theatre but left without a word. Often they hissed or showed reservations that could only be explained as an expedient wish to set a gulf between themselves and the players.

As for the lady, Will thanked God that he now hated her for his humiliation. Though hatred was not an emotion that left men at their best, it had at least some dignity about it.

His play of *Hamlet* would not let him rest. He might scramble down some words and jokes, and please their sickly coffers—and this was a palpable obligation—but he was plagued by something else: a fierce recalcitrance that defeated his mind, for truth lay just beyond his grasp. Grasp it he must, for health of mind and money.

He sat at his table as though a part of the furniture, and his pen took on its own life. Mortality was his theme. Men had woes beyond desire: hunger, fear, ambition, hopes blighted, themselves the victims of the world's duplicity, their destinies wickedly assailed, their minds divided.

CHAPTER *Seventeen*

SOMEONE scratched at Will's door. He frowned and paid no attention. The scratch persisted and at length he rose. For a moment he did not recognize the livery worn by the youth who stood outside. Then with a start, he perceived a servant of his lady's brother, the Marquess.

The youth handed him a letter. It was from the lady, and she directed him to come to her brother's house. For a moment he stood in some confusion. Why? What does this mean? He opened his mouth to say he was busy, sick, or dead, but the basilisk eyes of the servant saved him from such madness. He said he would come directly.

The youth stepped into his room. Will lifted his brows, but it was clear that his escort had no plan to leave him. Will shaved himself and put on his best clothes in the presence of this silent, watchful youth, and they went together to the landing steps where the boat waited.

The Marquess' home was one of the new and splendid houses between Westminster and St James's Park. At the servants' entrance, the youth gave him to the charge of a steward who took him along light and airy corridors to a room from which the river could be glimpsed.

It was a room of sober splendor, the panels carved in the plain modern way, the hangings rich and thick in folds, the carpet like a garden.

Why here? What fate was here?

Will stood by the window quieting his nerves with the glimpse of river in the noontime light. The whisper of a gown caused him to turn abruptly. There in the dim light she stood smiling slightly.

There was something unfamiliar, fair, incandescent about her. She was dressed in oyster satin, and she seemed very pale in this dark room. Behind her was an open door where a faint light glowed. The whisper of her dress accompanied her as she came to him and held out her hand. He kissed her hand and said nothing. She was subdued and gentle and this put him on his guard.

She walked up and down, her glance always returning to him. At length, holding her hands flat against her farthingale, she said abruptly, "I have been ill."

"Madam!"

"No poems came from you. No conundrums to break the tedium."

"Are you now well?"

She shrugged. "Well enough."

He waited carefully, keeping his eyes on her. In this civilized room, designed by a pragmatic mind, fashioned by the clean honesty of master carpenter and glazier, where the silken cushions on the chairs induced tranquility, and the marble heads of noble Romans regarded mortality with indifference, there was some climate of confessional. She continued to walk up and down.

"Are you very smeared with pitch?" she asked softly.

"Am I what, madam?"

"Smeared with pitch. You should not look at me with such cool cold eyes. I have your heart and you have mine. This warms us."

"In that case, madam," he replied gently, "it should be known that I would not bring to you the smell of pitch."

She hesitated, stroking the satin of her dress. "You are saying you would not willingly harm me. But what if you did so against your will, my Will?"

He frowned and searched her face. He was aware suddenly of the great silence of the house, as though no one moved here but she and himself. The clatter of coaches and horsemen on the street surrounded them like a wall. Where were servants? Where were her brother's children or her brother himself?

"How could I do so against my will?" He was groping for a meaning to this encounter. He marveled again at the living force that gave such mysterious relations to all her ambiguities. She was, in this oddly provocative moment, frail and luminous— healthy and opaque.

She stopped some distance from him and faced him with clasped hands. She raised her voice.

"By events you could harm me!" she said passionately. "By fearful doings, warned of by signs in the skies."

He listened to a dog bark somewhere in the corridor. "Madam," he said gently, "how can fearful signs in the sky affect a man like me? They are reserved for princes."

"Ah!" And then she inexplicably wrung her hands. "You acted

a foolish disloyal play. Mad! It was said moreover that you took money from the Earl of Rutland for some treasonable composition. Is that true? Tell me, on your honor."

His startled silence must have told her what she wished to know. Yet she went on passionately, "I cannot lend myself to thy plays, so publicly, if I do not know!"

He looked at her, for a moment so shocked by the iciness of his suspicions that he dared not trust himself even to a disclaimer. Then he said in a soft rage, "Why do you think that *you* can escape calumny when the innocent cannot?"

"Sir, you offend me!"

"Madam, you offend *me*." He had seen the light beyond the open door obliterated for a moment. He had been treated many ways by her, but he had never believed that she would allow herself to be used as a decoy of state. It did not break his heart but it did unloose his fury.

"Are you honest?"

"What do you mean?" she asked frowning in some agitation.

"Would you sooner transform honesty to a bawd than let the bawd be an honest woman?" She flushed. "Is this a paradox to you?"

"It may be," she faltered.

"Then let it sit in the corner of your mouth to gnaw upon. I am an honest man and I have offended neither myself nor my Queen. If you have a soul you will regret putting me to this purgation." She wrung her hands. "Have you a soul?" He heard a footstep and a door close. He felt a dreary pain. "Oh, my lady, my lady!" He went quickly to the open door and into the room beyond. There a candle burned, as innocent as a choir boy. The room was empty yet he could swear that a scent still lingered, a familiar scent that some man he knew had worn not long ago.

She cried out angrily and seized his arm. "By what right do you act as though you were master here?"

"By my word, lady, I'd liefer be betrayed by a common customer than by one I've loved."

"Oh, you do misjudge me," she cried, and the tears came.

"Do I indeed? Will you swear that you were not sent to spy

me out? Though what you hoped to gain is past my wit to know. Tell me!" He took her wrist.

She hesitated and then she wept. "In God's name, no!" she cried, and for a fraction of a moment he believed her. "*I* do not betray you," she said woefully, "it is thy own rashness puts thee in great danger."

"Yet you have let yourself add to my danger."

"How? How?" When he did not answer, her manner changed. She sank onto a stool and put both hands over her face. Presently she drew a shuddering sigh. She said something so softly that he could not hear.

"What do you say?"

"Do not hate me."

"Hate you?" He let fall her arm and turned away. Yet in his voice was a certain gentleness. "Dear madam, I see thee as thou art, a catspaw to great designs. My honor has not been given away. I ask your pardon. Give me leave to go."

She dropped her hands and looked up forlorn and pale, the tears still on her cheeks, her hair awry. "Alas, alas," she said wanly, "do not go, I beg you. I am most deject and wretched." He had never heard her voice so sad, and he looked down at the bowed head covered with a net of jewels, and the slender nape, as touching as a child's. But he said nothing, reminded that he did not know what made her sad.

She seized his hand and held it. "I have been emptied by my fears." She groaned. "Not for myself . . . but what punishment, what dreadful acts, may lie in wait. Oh, dear heart!" She wept against his arm, holding him like iron prongs. "Dangers . . . oh, we must take heed!"

He felt a far-off tenderness. Solicitude leveled differences and broke up the stony ground. Human beings must keep some good between them. He held her cheek as he would a child's. She said less wanly, "What can you do? Have you betrayed aught?"

"Betrayed?"

"Hast thou let fall anything that might bring him in?"

"Bring who in?"

She raised her little face streaked with her fear. "Why, my lord."

He stood very still. She said gently, "Dear soul, thy fall would be low, his high. Who would be hurt the most?"

"Oh, true. You love him more than your own prudence?"

"Oh." Her cheek fell against his arm. For a long time they were silent. When she spoke he heard her sadness. "I have no rights or power. I was born to be used for others' greatness. I am pawned against the Queen, the knights, the bishops. My name and person are moved from square to square. He is the only man who makes this helplessness a joy. Before him I must be helpless."

She seemed to take some melancholy pleasure in the two meanings of the word. She slipped her hand into Will's. "To marry him would please love and policy . . . but he will not have it." She kissed Will's fingers one by one. He was scarcely aware of her actions. He was thinking of the fresh bruises which had been laid on the old ones. "When he touches me he has perfect power. Even to think of him gives pleasure. Do you know?"

"Yes," said Will and drew away his hand.

"How can you know?" She took his hand again. "But I will have him however he will have me—which is poor indeed. If I did not seize such scraps of joy I would be a puppet. I would go mad."

Will said, "Poor little heart." But he held himself back from saying any more. Presently she looked up at him and a faint smile appeared.

"Ours is a threefold love," she said.

"No, sweet lady, a threefold death."

"I will not have it so." Then she said softly, "Some cannot escape each other—that is, you and I. We are like serpents coiled." He looked at her for a moment, then walked a little from her. When he turned again he saw fear had touched her face, a fear as spontaneous as though her lungs had been deprived of air. "Why do you set yourself against me? Oh, heart, heart!" She leaned across and caught his hand again. "I will not let you go. Some good and bad between us instructs our woes. Deny me not!"

"And die again? Sweet lady, no."

She said in her old peremptory way, "It is for thee to fit consent to my sharp need. Thou wilt save him," she said quietly, digging her nails in his hand.

"Dearest lady, there is naught that I can do!"

"He says you can undo him."

"I cannot do that neither."

She shrieked, "You will save him! You will swear to whatever he tells you!"

He tore away his hand and went quickly to the door. "By your leave, my lady, I will go."

"God damn you! The devil take you!" she screamed. "You will do for him, or I will do you in!"

He was more shaken than he cared to own. That afternoon they gave his own old play of *As You Like It*, and with fingers still trembling he put on his paint. As you like it—never, never in the world of great and small!

Sir Piers Dalglish was at the play. Afterward he spoke to Will, his handsome face, with its short black beard, expressing an equivocal good will. His eyes were neither cold nor hot, merely watchful.

The scent on his clothes was unmistakable.

Ned had fallen in love with a baker's daughter, and the love must play its course. Will went home alone. As he came into the house, Mrs Nell told him that the old man, his neighbor, had been taken away by two of the Queen's soldiers before supper.

"What will they do?" she whispered. "He is such a good old man. I do not believe his black arts."

"Indeed," Will said quickly, "indeed, they are white arts; they are humankind!"

The news perturbed him deeply. He went into the old man's room and sat down with a candle. The motionless animals watched him from their places and he talked with them.

"He will not go to hell, thy master, for heaven longs for him. This is the world's great amiss—that such as he can have his great soul questioned—here is holy ground. It frightens only them who are frightened by a loving God." The little beasts and birds

236

gave no sign of not understanding. He put some food for them. There he sat all night: a vigil of himself enclosing all. The candle guttered and went out. He heard Ned come and go and come again. At dawn he moved his cramped limbs and stood by the window. While the water carts were still rattling, the old man was brought home.

Will said nothing. His relief emptied him. He took the old man's hands and kissed them both. The old man smiled and put his arm around Will. He went, drawing Will, to speak to his live things, yet he stumbled as he did so.

The birds broke their silence, and the little beasts ran up and down. The old man was tired and white, and not inclined to talk.

"Answer only this," said Will at length. "Was it I—or the lord Southampton—who brought you there?"

The old man fondly pressed his shoulder and said in a faint voice, "Who says you or I or the lord Southampton when All is One?"

That day, the mail carrier from Stratford left for Will at the Paschal Lamb a letter and petition from Dick Quiney. The letter said that their great black Lord of the Manor had tried to seize their tithes which had been Stratford's from time immemorial. The petition was for Westminster.

Will's great desire was to remain invisible to officialdom, but whatever Stratford asked he was compelled to do. He went again to Sir Fulke Greville, who sighed with a small flick of humor and said that he would rather Stratford pressed on him than London. For a few moments, in his apartment at Whitehall, they talked of Warwickshire in all seasons and of what must soon be planted in the gardens. Sir Fulke inquired of his father and his mother, of his wife. Then Sir Fulke said, "And of thyself, sir; does the muse Euterpe still love thee?"

For a bare moment Will was silent, and this worldly room and all its works faded away. He said, "Dear sir, there is a single joy that remains I know not how, untouched. It is a burst of light, a drink of water—myself at work."

The kind humane eyes showed how well they understood. Sir

237

Fulke rose and held out his hand. "Dear sir, I pray that nothing amiss ever comes to thee."

On Thursday there was an uprising in the City. Certain apprentices, plotting to raise five thousand men to storm the Tower for Essex, betrayed their plans too soon.

"What will the Queen do if Marston is right?" Gus asked, looking up from the ledger.

"It may be she will fit clemency to honor," Will said. "She has recoiled from killing her favorites."

If Marston were right, and the Queen had set on the insurrection, then she must not let the effects escape her grasp. Yet that night they heard that a Captain Thomas Lea, of a good family, who had been trusted by the Queen in Ireland, was seized at the very door to the room where the Queen, attended only by her ladies, was at dinner. Captain Lea said he had planned to seize the Queen and compel her to sign a warrant freeing Essex and his friends.

Will grew cold. Was not Captain Lea the name spoken by Lord William? And if Lord William were drawn in, then how could any of them escape?

At noon they heard that the Privy Council had begun to examine all who had taken part in the uprising. By midafternoon, Dekker brought them news that a public announcement said that the Earl of Essex had himself attended the performance of *King Richard II.*

That night Ned brought word that their fellow Warwickshire men, Ned Bushell and Robin Catesby, had been taken out of Marshalsea for examination by Lord Hunsdon, by the Lord Keeper Egerton, and by the Lord Admiral.

Ned and Will did not go to bed that night. They sat in a tavern near Marshalsea, talking of this man and that, of kinship and loyalty and of Ned Bushell, gentleman usher to Essex, who was cousin to a cousin of Dick Quiney. All the iniquities of Southwark, all the lurid sin and moral squalor, underlay their question: How could any man have hope before the judgment seat?

At length, in the dark of the night, Bushell was returned to the prison and they saw his face in the light of the torches.

"How looked he—hurt?" Ned asked, running up to Will.

"Nay, I think not."

"Yet he limped," Ned said.

"Nay," said Will sharply, "I saw it not. But he was very pale. And where was Catesby?"

That day they learned that Sir Gelly Meyrick, the boyhood friend of Essex, had been examined: he who had said that his attachment to Robin's fortunes would end but with his life. William Camden brought the news.

Camden—why *Camden?* Will asked himself . . . Camden who had granted and confirmed a shield and coat of arms to make of him a gentleman?

It seemed as though Camden did not look at him, or when he did, looked in a faltering way. Yet Camden had sought him out, searching for him as far as the Falcon, and he had spoken courteously to Ned, though Ned was seldom courteous to anyone these days. Will boldly tried his suspicions and asked what confusion Meyrick had compounded.

"He saith he dined in the company of certain gentlemen well known to us, and that he was a little late in coming to the play on King Henry IV."

"*King Henry IV,* he called it?" Will asked with a little smile. "Not *King Richard II?*"

"No. But concerned with the killing of King Richard II."

Will rose and walked about. "Did he make plain that he begged and we refused?"

"Not that I know of."

"Sir, what will become of us? It seems we are all birds who, struggling to be free, are limned the worser."

Camden rubbed his hand across his dome-like brow. He murmured, barely moving his thin lips, "Yet we are not birds but men and have some element of choice."

"Oh, dear sir, dear sir, speak of that. My soul longs to hear."

Camden smiled. He seemed to be laboring under a weight, and at odds with some part of himself.

Why was it *Camden* who had come? Will saw Camden illumined by fate. His furred velvet, though anachronistic to this heavy day, suited the terrible ornamentation of life, the painful irrelevance of time, place, and destiny.

Will, walking up and down, staring at Camden to extract his meaning, could not displace the firm solid fact of Camden sitting in a chair, his legs apart, his hand closed on the table, his gaze kind but remote, fixed on Will. The simplest of friendships have now and then an element of confrontation. Will sensed that a legitimizing of his own confusion was bearing down like a dark cloud.

He stood close above Camden, so that Camden was obliged to lift his eyes to look at him. "Sir, what else is in your heart to say? I beg you, speak!"

Camden's brows went up like two portcullises. He hesitated, drumming with his fingers. "A stupid foolish matter. A matter of your coat of arms."

"Say on, sir."

"Well, let us go back and recollect that I was honored in the Herald's Office over the heads of men who felt more deserving than myself. Now this has seethed and wracked some men, and York Herald, who is indeed a choleric man, has drawn up a list of grievances." He paused and then with an upward glance of the most courteous diffidence added, "Granting arms to Shakespeare, the player, lives at the head of my offense."

Will was silent for a moment, and then he laughed a little. He resumed his pacing. At length he said, not turning around, "What must you do, sir? Speak. I wish to hear."

"Pray remember that York Herald is a quarrelsome man. He now protests that a man of base rank uses a bearing which is scarce differenced from the shield of the Lords Mauley, an ancient family, it is true." He groaned. "Well, I have demonstrated, and, by my word, I know whereof I speak, that there is a patible difference in the two spears—yours and Lord Mauley's. That is a full answer, but he wishes to do me an ill turn, and in these high times he feels that he is lion rampant." He shook a little at his own small joke. "That the arms were assigned to Shakespeare the player I have disputed—though, my dear sir, I know of no man who does honor greater honor—for it is to your father that they adhere, and he was Majesty's officer and High Bailiff of his town. This by the Queen's gracious example removes any base-born taint, for in our land true gentility is determined by the actions of a man."

"Yet your demonstration is not enough?" Will asked with an impediment in his throat.

"Not quite enough."

Will paused on the other side of the room and looked at him. He laughed again. "So I am now a gentleman teetering on my heraldic branch. And you, good sir, have you acquired some doubts?"

Camden groaned again, a way he had, it seemed, of relieving his congested thoughts.

"No doubts, good sir. Though if your father could obtain some proof that King Henry VII advanced and rewarded his great-grandsire with lands and tenements as we have testified, then I could confound York Herald to my heart's pleasure."

Gentility was so volatile Will marveled that a man gave it importance of any kind. Had he, Will, ever desired this coat of arms? Not he. It was his mother, and then perhaps his father, and all the subtle lures of place and condition. Camden was watching him.

Touch, withdraw, suffer misgivings, come and go but do not attain. Grasp. Be prudent. Be evasive. Will said, "Dear sir, Stratford was burned some years ago. My father says proof perished then. Must I not believe my father?"

Camden made a large gesture and slowly rose. He held out his hand to Will and then, with great courtesy, to Ned, who, scrambling to his feet, knocked over his stool.

"By my troth," he said, with sudden vigor, "it should be a good sport to confound York Herald. Well, we will see!" He held out his hand a second time to Will. "I am not insensible, sir, to the penalty some men extract from themselves if their gentility is confirmed and then taken from them. I beg you, sir, recall that every man is as significant as Adam—and no more."

241

That night an officer of the Privy Council came to Phillips' house. He bore a warrant that called for the examination of Augustine Phillips and William Shakespeare on the following day.

CHAPTER *Eighteen*

THE palace of Whitehall sprawled between Scotland Yard and Canon Row, and the shadows of Westminster fell upon it when the sun was setting. It was a vast teeming warren, lying across the King's Street which ran out of Charing Cross to the cathedral of Westminster, and was a way of common passage.

To the right of the public street were the lodgings of the Queen's nobles, the Queen's tiltyard, cockpit, her tennis courts, her bowling alleys, and a gallery of the palace in which great princes and nobles could stand at the windows and watch the games. To the north lay Saint James's Park.

On the river side of the public road lay the gardens and orchards, the state apartments and the apartments of the Queen. Farther up the road, toward Westminster, a bridge crossed the Long Ditch and led to Canon Row, where lived noblemen of such standing as the Earl of Hertford, the Earl of Derby, and the Earl of Lincoln.

Will and Gus came through the garden and into a courtyard of the palace through a low arch which they stooped to enter. The courtyard was filled with idle servants of great nobles and of the Queen.

They came into the palace without interference, for this was still a public way. Inside the palace they stepped past servants who were gathering stale rushes from the floor and strewing fresh. They knew the way to the Lord Chamberlain's offices, but from there they were sent back toward the privy apartments, and after knocking on this door and that, found what they sought. Halberdiers guarded these inner doors, and here they kicked their heels. But after a time they were brought into a narrow gallery where two men in brown sat on two stools before a table. In a room nearby a virginal was being played, and Will heard it more perfectly than the scratching of the pens.

In his mind only his lady played the virginal. Somewhere in this warren of a palace she lived and breathed.

The brown men were without identity, examiners of the Attorney General, perhaps, for they wrote down legal phrases and were cool and skillful in their questioning. They asked those things which had already been asked, no more. Gus took his oath that Sir Gelly Meyrick had importuned them for a play on the killing of King Richard II: that they had determined to act some other play, but had been tempted by the forty shillings to give Sir Gelly what he asked.

Will swore to the same facts. The sound of the virginal ceased. As the examiners thrust forward the sheets on which they had been writing, and commanded them to fix their signatures, the inner door was opened. One of the brown men, glancing up, smothered an oath and rasped his stool as he rose to his feet. The Queen had entered the room.

As she came forward, she looked not at the examiners but intently at the players. They saw before them the woman they had seen time and again, but saw her afresh: her slender height, her grace, her wrinkled and bedizened face white with paint and red with rouge, her false red hair, the gaps in her yellow teeth—for she was smiling—her dark and beautiful eyes painted with kohl. She said in her fine voice to each correctly, "Master Phillips. Master Shakespeare."

They went down on their knees and there remained. One of the examiners fetched a chair but she declined it. Instead she stood by the window so that half her face was shadowed, and with her long jeweled fingers she tapped occasionally at the glass, reflectively or to join the activity without with the life within.

Lord Hunsdon who had entered after her stood nearby. His skin was stretched tight across his bones; he maintained a stony-faced guard against any involuntary play upon his countenance. His thin mouth was drawn a little to one side and this slight deviation suggested some element of strain which showed nowhere in the cold blue eyes or the elegant impassive hands.

The Queen examined her two master players for a moment. What they could see of her expression, facing the light as they did, was shrewd and close.

Gloriana, Cynthia, Belphoebe, the matchless Oriana, the peerless Lady of the Sea, the superb Phoenix of the World, Eliza their Queen, she who had raised herself and them into the first place of the world, for England was her passion and her creed and to act greatly was to induce greatness: so emotion took them as it does all men at some time when they are least prepared to defend themselves. Will wished to have no trumpet in his heart for this woman who was also Hecate and the Queen of Night, but he felt a strong excitement nonetheless, and he knew by the constant little clearing of Gus's throat that he too was moved.

She said in a light voice, as though she gave her words small weight, "The tree from which so many branches grew has been struck at with a blight." She fixed Phillips with a quizzical look. He knew but one thing to say.

"Madam?"

She went on with a slight smile; not all her words were clear for the empty spaces in her mouth. "I am that tree." She watched them brightly with her lovely eyes. They bowed their heads. "There was also a flame which has been quenched. It can never be rekindled." Her beautiful voice paused. Phillips bowed his head again. She went on, still smiling, "That flame is my lord of Essex, his ambition." They lowered their eyes. In the same sweet voice, without change of modulation, she said, "Are these not aphorisms which have been lived out in our time?"

The smile continued. Hunsdon did not take his eyes from her face while she spoke. The two examiners knelt motionless as wooden figures on which birds might clean their feathers and leave their white mementos.

The Queen said, "The wit of the fox is everywhere. Can you tell me where I may find faithful and virtuous men?" She was driving them sharply and not taking her eyes from them, darting her glance from one man to the other, but fixing it mostly on Phillips.

He was not a swift and witty man, but then he was not an ingenuous man either. He hesitated for a moment, and then he said staunchly, "Why, madam, wherever Englishmen are proud to be themselves."

She looked at him startled, her painted eyes vividly alive. Then she laughed, a merry sound like a young girl's which her old raddled mouth in no way nullified. "Aye," she said. "Aye, well spoken by an Englishman." She tapped on the window, staring down into the courtyard, and then disquiet seized her. She slapped her hands against her farthingale and fell to pacing back and forth. The men watching her were caught in a swift tumult which lacked name or character. She drew a little dagger from her waist and struck at the arras although scarcely giving heart to what she did. At length she paused in the center of the room and stamped her feet, one after the other, almost as though she might begin a dance.

She seemed to be in the sudden grip of an anger that swept and engulfed her. She looked from one to another, and then, without warning, her gaze hooked itself to Will. It seemed to him as though steel pierced and entered him. The pain shocked him into a narrow personal attentiveness.

She advanced on him, walking like a man, her hands still flat against her farthingale, the jewels in her hair and ears moving jerkily. She stopped an arm's length from him and stared down at his face. Her voice was low and cold and she seemed aware of none but Will.

"Those who have spent their time and honesty to buy false hope and shallow praise had best remember, when they cast up their reckoning, that their sum will be the sum of fools because their knavery was not plain from the beginning."

Will studied her painted face for a moment. "Madam, the story of our lives runs on from year to year."

"What do you mean by that?"

"Why, madam, that honest men must face their reckoning as best they can from day to day, and all else besides."

Her painted eyebrows rose and her eyelids narrowed.

"Oh, you have lived long on the almsbasket of words. I am not surprised that you have a fat tongue."

"Madam, in the name of our blessed Lord, my tongue belongs to my sovereign Lady as do the tongues and loyalty of my fellows."

"By God's bones then," she said, "why did you take from its graveclothes *this* play—this play of all, wherein an anointed king—" And then, to his astonishment, her old used-up face showed such sorrow and was so close to tears that he put out his hand involuntarily. "Why? Why?" she whispered. "All these depositions tell me nothing!" and she took the papers from the desk and flung them to the ground. Then she turned on him again with tears in her eyes. "Does not divinity edge a king, God's ewe? Then, to my face, say why you have tampered with divinity and crowned another king while yet the first one lives."

Kneeling there he grappled for an answer. "Ah, madam, do you then call Bolingbroke a king?"

She frowned and sucked in her empty cheeks, trying to spring at his meaning so that it did not spring at her. But in her mind she stumbled and gave him such a look that he spoke on.

"Does the usurper wear the crown in the sight of God? Nay, can his head or heart lie peaceful?"

"Why did you not say so clearly?"

"Madam, by your gracious leave, I did. Could Bolingbroke, though called a king, ever wash the blood from his guilty hand?"

She examined him as though she were cutting out his face in adamantine. "You have a supple way." She continued to look at him. "There is naught I do not know of those who come within my frame. *I* know what you have said in your plays of kings and tyrants, of power stark and unmistakable as power, of necessities and dangers, of fathers who kill sons and sons fathers, of dying lions who thrusting forth their paws do wound the earth . . . of polished perturbation and golden care." She smiled slightly, and he smiled very faintly in reply, wondering how much else of his she could repeat by rote. "But you have not set my mind at rest, for now I ask myself why did the censor not expunge this play, what were *his* thoughts, how can I ever know?"

At this, Hunsdon spoke with more vehemence than Will had

ever heard in him. "Dear gracious lady, you tremble not as the oak but as the willow!"

She turned on him with such a swift grace that she was all a woman, all distraught and helpless. In a shaking voice, she said, "I warned him he should not touch my scepter!" and her emotion was so stark that no man doubted that she spoke of Essex. "Did he wish to be my Bothwell? That was not the way to do it." She walked away pressing her bent arms against her sides as though to keep herself from trembling. "I have too great a sense of fact to be misled." As she stood by the window, her back to them, the tears fell, as they could see in the glass, and she put up her handkerchief to catch them. "Yet have I risked much, and much would I risk again, grappling with fate. I have let his rashness fly like a bird, for my hawk is swifter than his bird. There is ecstasy in mercy, but in his voice a rapture of doom. Which is greater?"

She turned about and walked slowly up and down. "Men betray and women forgive. Yet if a woman plucks her womanliness away, then can she revenge herself on the perfidies of men and overthrow man at the last."

She looked from one to the other, the tear stains marked against her painted face. Her voice was low and sweet.

"*The hind that would be mated to the lion must die of love.*" Outside in the garden were voices raised, strident and live, and a confusion of dogs answered them. ". . . Though who can blame him?"

She added this with a sudden horrible archness. It shocked and embarrassed all but Hunsdon, who said fondly, "Indeed, madam, he would have been less a man for that."

Her eyes darted to the others, even to the examiners whose faces had taken on the color of old wood. She stamped her foot though the roguish smile still played about her lips. Will bowed his head and murmured, "For a man to give and hazard all for the morning star ennobles him though he may not touch the star."

The archness changed to sagacity, and she touched Will with her fan.

"You have some relish of the saltiness of time. I, too, view eternity in a moment, and may thus sprinkle it with savor. Oh, to die is such a waste of life!" She went back and forth again, keeping her eyes on Will. "I protest upon my soul, I do believe I would have died had I fallen in his power the day he raised rebellion. How long did Richard live after he was surprised in the same manner? The pretense was alike, for the removing of certain counsellors, but shortly after it took the price of Richard's life. You have worked upon my soul with your play. I hate you for it. He that will forget his benefactor will also forget God. Know you that?"

Will felt his mind being gripped and held until it yielded to thoughts that were not his own. He did not know whether he smelled immediate danger to himself and Gus or merely that heady scent of power disporting itself as armed clemency. He frowned and tried to master the constriction in his throat and the palpitation in his vitals.

The Queen was watching him with a smile of provocation. He replied, "Madam, thanks are sometimes too dear at a ha'penny, yet they are perforce the exchequer of the poor and the honorable meed of noble minds."

She drew her brows together and said almost indifferently, "Well, I take thy thanks." Then she stood very erect. "I do assure you there is no prince that loves his subjects better, or whose love can countervail our love. There is no prize so rich that I prefer before this jewel—your love."

The players might convince themselves that she spoke straight to them, and Hunsdon that she spoke to him, and the bird-perches that she spoke to them.

"Love and thanks I count inestimable." It was said with absolute sincerity. "Of me, let it be said that I make merit precious, honor dainty, graces passing rare, and he that shakes my brow daunts not my crown."

She made a swift upward movement of her head which Lord Hunsdon interpreted as her will to leave, and he bowed to open the door. But she paused again. Now she spoke with sharp rapidity.

"I know that treason has been practised, for there are letters to the King of Scotland. And it may be treason too that your *King Richard II* has in years past been played forty times in streets and houses." She paused for a moment. "I fancy that here or sometime, you shall be made to answer this to your smart." She half smiled at Will. "Your words, I grant, are keener than my own, but then I do not wear my dagger in my mouth."

"Madam, I wear no dagger of any sort before my Queen."

"That may be, but I can trust no man at his word." Then she smiled as artless as a child, and looked at them over her shoulder. "Yet, though you are all fools and knaves, you shall eat."

She went toward the door and for a moment she laid her hand on Hunsdon's arm. That smooth man whose emotion was roused only when tranquility was displaced, looked at her with such a flash of heart as made him seem a man of a different temper.

No words were exchanged but he spoke to her with his tenderness, and she drew a deep breath and nodded. Again she turned her head slightly and said with unmistakable but blunted irony, "Farewell, good and honest friends."

"So," Gus said as they reached the garden and the river steps. 'So we are safe." But there was a rising inflection in his flat voice.

"Safe? I would not give a farthing for our safety."

"Hah?" Gus looked at Will swiftly. "Well then," said Gus stoically, "since time and death are neither good nor bad, but things indifferent, we must go at peace with time and death."

Will took him suddenly by the arms. "Oh, Gus, thou art the best man that I know. Give me always such a steadfast man as thee!"

Dickon said, "Well? Well?"

Gus replied with some tartness in his voice, "I fancy we are safe until that day Lord Hunsdon is at war with peace."

"We also improved the time," Will said drily, "noting how a nobleman moves under fastidious stress. Very authentic." He demonstrated. "And gratis. We did not have to pay a shilling to learn."

At dinner they heard a rumor that next day the Great Trial would begin.

After dark Will went home. He stood by the scarred desk reading whatever page lay at hand of his *Prince of Denmark*, and then he threw it down in mingled rage and despair. Only a man with a passionate egotism, a man who could say *I, I, I,* knew the true function of behavior! *Stand up!* Will straightened himself, but with no special heart for the act.

Florio's voice as light and inassertive as a spirit played in his mind. *"It is an absolute perfection, as it were divine, for a man to know how to enjoy rightfully his being."*

He laughed. Let Montaigne speak out of darkness and Florio be his voice. Prove me now herewith.

The Great Trial loomed over the city, investing speech and action. The players rehearsed Dekker's *Satiromastix* all that morning. Each actor had resolved how he would speak his lines, and yielded nothing to another, which was not like them at all. But on such a day how could one afford to yield at any point?

Master bore hard on apprentice. Burbage paced up and down, his short body as tensile as a hawk. He abruptly called his boy Jamie, although he knew that Sly was coaching him, and said to fetch the rapiers. Without regard for the convenience of others, he instructed Jamie in a bout of French swordsmanship that was sharp as lightning. After that he sent him back with a wave of his hand to Sly, and sank into a chair, his mouth open, panting a little, his eyes glazed.

Will sat apart for a time, for Ned, his apprentice, had outgrown him in these weeks. He pretended to be plotting business but he was not. He was sunk in reflection on that power "to enjoy rightfully his being." In God's name, what did it mean when the mind curdled all that it touched?

He compelled himself to watch these nubile boys in order to sweeten his thoughts. They affected him as did some music or certain young animals. Supple as light, androgynous as youth, they shifted between boy and girl as music notes shifted in the scale.

"It is a very good thing," someone said close to him, "that we are doing Dekker's play at this time."

Will raised his eyes to Rob Armin, who sat down slowly, a frown between his eyes. Armin had always a sleepy look, his eyes languid, his eyebrows touseled, his hair apt to stand away from his head in little shocks, but withal of such a pleasing manner that one took him, all in all.

"Why?" asked Will.

"Zooks! Make a war between Jonson and Dekker flame up brightly and it will hide these other things."

"Rob, how fair do you think this trial will be?"

Armin hesitated, and then said with a little smile, "Has there ever been a trial in the history of the world that has not merely set forth what has been resolved before, with witnesses and testimony to say what the great have already determined?"

"Think you so?"

"Has it ever not been so?" Armin asked.

Will said, "Lad, come here." He beckoned to Edmans, whose lips were moving as though in study. When the boy knelt before him, he said, "What are you doing, lad? Those are not speeches of the play."

"I was saying prayers, sir, for this day."

"Sit here by me." Edmans rose and sat by him, and Will put his arm about him. "I who write and you who act are God's dearlings. Each day thank God, dear lad, that you're an actor." Edmans nodded. "For who else can be all men and all things—and well disguised meanwhile."

"Amen," said Armin.

"Who else may cry king today and priest tomorrow; bare old sores and heal them; hold the mirror up to nature; make the age yield its health and sickness?"

Armin was sucking at his lip and smiling with his eyes. "Pray God we may learn that lesson well, and so turn aside this day's blow."

"Sir," Edmans said, "do we act the world or is there something different that I know not of—as these terrible doings that seem —oh!"

Will hesitated for a moment. "When you, John Edmans, stand on the stage, think of the world. Take all to your heart. Let love and observation be your tutors."

"Well, sir, I will try."

Will looked at him with great affection. "What is the proper position of arms and legs for *Be not afraid?*"

Edmans struck a position.

"Ho! That's *defiance!*"

Edmans said with wistful reproach, "Sir, it is the arm and leg position for *I pray all's well.*"

After Edmans had gone to his master's signal, Will said, "Will this day end, Rob?"

"When the sun goes down."

"Shall we send for word?"

"Wait a bit. When we go for dinner, we'll find out all we need."

It came, word by word, as the day went on. Armin summed it up. "Caterpillars do crawl," meaning by that, that obsequious favoritism had laid the course for events.

Yet treason had been practiced, and this fact cut through all the obfuscations of passion, instability, pride and ambition.

They could not forget those great nobles who had come to the plays, drunk with them, and, in the instance of Southampton, given heart and money to Will. As the hours went on, the present was obscured by a carousel of nerves and ale; the tender remembrances became overwhelming as they heard of Essex all in black, Southampton brilliant as the day, knowing their doom before they entered the Great Hall of Westminster, yet bearing themselves with perfect composure. Essex had been like a prince —nay, a king! said those who had not seen him. When Lord Grey, his enemy, had been sworn as one of the judges, Essex had laughed to Southampton. When their indictment had been read, he had laughed again.

How splendidly they saw it in their mind's eye, the brave movements, the proud heads. When Walter Raleigh, whom Essex hated as a viper, was called upon as witness, the Earl had cried, "What booteth it to swear the fox?"

Burbage wept, and all of them sat with wet eyes.

Essex had asked all punishment for himself, making it seem that all his friends had come with him against their will. After he had entangled Cecil, the Queen's first Minister, in Cecil's own net, he had cried abruptly, as though he were a man with nothing to fear, "Ah, Mr Secretary, I thank God for my humiliations. I am indifferent how I speed. I owe God a death."

At the very last, when the frightful penalty for treason—to be hanged, cut down while still alive, disemboweled and quartered —had been passed upon him, he had answered with a princely calm, "I think it fitting that my poor quarters which have done her Majesty true service in divers parts of the world, should now, at the last, be sacrificed and disposed of at her Majesty's pleasure."

Southampton had said only, "Her Majesty being God's lieutenant on earth, I hope she will imitate Him by looking into the heart."

"What of Rutland?" Will asked, "and Bushell, and those others who have been fools but are men?"

The well-clad stranger who had brought these latter details into the Falcon, and who might be a spy to observe their responses (in spite of his own tears), bowed his head and plucked at his beard. At length he turned his head. "High treason, five times more."

"God, I know them all," Will said. "Catesby, Bushell—we played as lads. Those lords—great earls—who else? Cuffe and Davers and two Meyricks—that's more than five."

"Make it as many as you like," said the stranger. "All as mortal as you and I."

"Will we hang by the neck?" asked Will.

The stranger shrugged and bit at his nails. "Who knows? Innocenter than we have suffered so."

"God's passion!" said Dickon hoarsely, "you two are death's jesters."

Sometime later, their own Ned Shakespeare flung himself into the tavern, white as a corpse, yet with his eyes glittering. He was no spy. He had seen the mighty lords with his own eyes. He wrung the hearts of his friends as he leaned half across the table, incoherent yet brimming with speech.

"I saw him, I saw him—oh, there was never such a sight!"

"Well, speak in God's name!" said Burbage.

"My lord of Essex went as swift as a hound, the others were pressed to keep up with him. He bent his face toward the earth. He was first pale and then flushed. He would not look upon any, though many called to him, and all who could flocked after him. I ran as close as possible, and I could see his pale lips through his beard and his eyes swollen with weeping. Even the soldiers seemed to feel what they were doing." Ned wept; he was no longer a youth with impetuous judgment, but a man who had seen the great fallen.

Will's thought turned to Lord William. He listened for a summons, but he heard only in the distance someone singing of a crooked carcass.

"Well," said Dickon, rising at length, "that is done." But he stood silent, caught in Ned's words. Then he roused himself. "Hal, Jacko, Rob—home." Gus and Sly rose too. Will put his arm about Ned.

Ned's fever of words continued to rise and abate till he exhausted himself with all he had seen and felt. When the candle had been put out, and they were in bed, Ned whispered loudly that it was high time they went home. "This is no place for us!" His voice was both angry and frightened. Will did not reply, but he lay for a long time with his eyes open in the dark.

He thought of ambition—legitimate ambition, not the mixed cloth of Essex. He thought of all that a man had been born to expect set aside on an instant. . . . Of a son, say, defrauded of his kingdom by an uncle, say, his whole destiny overturned by a man strong and unscrupled enough to act with lightning swiftness, be confirmed in his usurpation before the heir can so much as say *Villain*. Well, so much Kyd had derived from some old Danish annals, but ambition . . . ah. The helplessness of such a youth, his betrayal agreed to by a weak and sensuous mother. What blind rage must seize him, how he must storm at his own impotence and blacken his thoughts in seeking confirmation of this treachery. Was it a true ghost or was it his own intuition that boldly said *Listen to thy prophetic soul?* Yet to charge a king with a king's murder needed more witnesses than

254

one's own assurance. For the whole court to hear the usurper's confession would serve the ends of justice.

And yet could one listen to the instigation of murder and not lose his soul?

Will drifted half in sleep, ambition flashing like white fire between his conscious and unconscious thought . . . or self-justification, that too was ambition . . . or self-love, or self-pity . . . He roused himself, sleepily amused at how quick one must be to avoid the terrible foolishness of thinking too precisely with the under-mind of one's own sins . . . for then all murder's most foul, revenge a crime against God who alone requites, ghosts become devils, and . . . ah, sleep came on him . . . the very substance of the ambition is merely the shadow of a dream.

All knew that the Queen had retired into the deepest privacy. Some thought she knew nothing of Essex' dreadful doom, and must be told by petition. Will laughed to himself. *She* not know? She knew all, and spun like the Fates.

Dickon canceled one play and then another, shifted about, seeing sedition everywhere, till Heminges, Condell, and Phillips, who had the normal management of these things, were pounded flat by their patience. Dickon talked violently to Heminges, who pursed his lips and flushed, and then came back to argue again with great self-control, merely stressing certain words over and over slowly as to a child. "Let us . . . now then . . . good discretion . . ."

The executions were set for three days hence. Common life went on, beckoning and enclosing all rumors, like the oyster the pearl. The watermen were better than a chorus; coney catchers fleeced the gullible and rode to fortunes. The playhouse was filled daily, but sad songs were sung even in the midst of plays.

None of their great friends came, however, neither Lord William nor Lord Herbert, nor any of their coterie. The lady had not appeared, though Sir Piers attended often. Lord William's deep silence touched Will, who often wondered, out of compassion for one so unused to woe, *How does he?* and wished, for old love's sake, that he might reach to him. But caution like an adder warmed in the sun. Armin said, "Well, let us listen for the purr of fortune, or at least of fortune's cat."

At length Lord William broke the silence and sent for Will. It was a long walk across the city to his home in the Barbican. It led past Paul's Church and up Aldersgate Street, into the elegance of the old days, past the palace at Jews' Gardens, and up Redcross Street into the Barbican, a familiar walk, taken many times.

Lord William's steward said that his lordship would be found in the garden, and added a pleasant greeting of his own. Will saw Lord William sitting like carven patience under a mulberry tree, only to jump up and pace two steps here and two steps there.

When his wild dark glance fell on Will, he stopped short and stared at him. His hand flew to his breast. Alas, poor wretch, Will thought, seeing his stormy eyes which gave no greeting as Will drew near, although his spoil of beauty begged for kindness.

Will bowed. "My duty to your lordship and most humble service."

Lord William did not stir. With his pale face and beautiful wild eyes, he was the youth Will had loved and had prayed might stand always at the top of happy hours. It was an old tender thought and it made Will smile.

The smile was a tinderbox. Lord William cursed and struck his glove at Will's cheek. Will stepped back.

"By what right do you wear a cheerful face when so many hearts are breaking!"

"My good lord!"

"Why did you smile? Only my enemies smile." He turned away and walked a pace up the path, striking with his dagger at the bushes. When he turned back toward Will, he held the dagger gripped by its handle. "And moreover, I take offense at your dress. Look you. You wear a satin doublet, and velvet is slashed into your sleeves." His dagger flicked at the doublet and sleeves. "That is not lawful for such as you. It gives me great offense that you appear in such a flaunting way."

"Where shall I go, my lord, to mend my dress?"

"Go to. Go to. Come hither, sir." Lord William turned away to pace, and turned back swiftly, striking the flat of his dagger against the tree trunk. Then he sat down abruptly and rang a bell. The servant heard it as a summons for wine.

Lord William sat breathing heavily, his eyes closed. At length he opened them and motioned Will to sit beside him, and poured himself a cup of wine. When he spoke his voice was low; the agitation had gone; he seemed weak. He sipped at the wine and looked steadily at Will. Presently his lips moved in the slightest of smiles.

"I beg your pardon. I am most desperately used."

"My dear lord."

"If you have ever known what it is to have your heart torn from its rooted place, and all your dreams to be bloody and nothing bent, then it may be that you can read my present state. I have offered sums up to half my fortune to those who will intercede with her Majesty. She will not see me. My cousin must not die." He rose again to pace. "I have called for you to give me comfort and to say again that he used no words of treason—none, none— that he was always kind, brave, and loyal. I cannot remember what words follow what. I will call for paper and a pen, and you will arrange the words so that they will fall most agreeably before the Queen. Thus Gloriana herself will feel it a duty and a privilege to set him free." He rang the bell again and then he poured another cup of wine and handed it to Will. "It grieves me past enduring to see so many dip their meat in one man's blood."

Will crossed his leg and hunched his shoulders, feeling that sting of agitation which vibrated his nerves when obliged to cramp words to another's use. Would this end as a doggerel in iambic pentameter?

The servant brought him paper and the implements for writing, brought him a little table and some sweetmeats. Lord William withdrew to a bench under a tree and picked up his lute. He cast a young, dependent glance at Will and struck a plangent chord.

Will sat for a long time without putting down a word, and he was aware that Lord William had flung down his lute and was walking up and down the garden. When Will at length wrote down a line, he heard Lord William play energetically with a battledore and shuttlecock and then come forward and stand beneath the mulberry tree beside him.

At length Will glanced up toward the avid eyes and read aloud in a dry voice some words on the Queen's indisputable place in the hierarchy of greatness and on the virtue that grew with her sovereignty: that in her day every man ate in safety, for she was the happiness of England. He ended with words on majesty and mercy:

> "No ceremony that to the great belongs,
> Not the Queen's crown, nor the deputed sword,
> The Marshall's truncheon, nor the judge's robe,
> Becomes them with one half so good a grace
> As mercy our beloved lady."

Lord William nodded his head and nodded again, and moved with releasing tension up and down the path.

"Aye, well spoken. Felicitous. Bravely done! You have pulled the words from my heart." He spread his hand against his breast as though too much emotion would make his heart leap out. At length he stretched out his hand to Will, and at the last, took off a ring and pressed it into Will's grip.

After summoning his servant, he read the words to himself again with moving lips. "Words—oh, jewels—oh, happy man that has words like gold." He suddenly embraced Will. "Oh, a poet is like time; he couples with eternity."

He sent for his steward and ordered him to bring his casket of jewels. When the casket was set before him, he made a selection with great care: a pearl ring, a rope of aquamarines, a ruby brooch. These were put into a small casket of gold filigree inlaid with mother of pearl, the scroll, written out afresh, laid on the top, and the whole entrusted to a young gentleman in his service who was of that appearance and nubility toward which the Queen was most disposed.

Then he embraced Will again. "I have often wished myself poorer that I might come nearer to thee. We are born to benefits; and what better or more proper can we call our own than the riches of our friends? What a precious comfort it is to have so many, like brothers, commanding one another's fortune. To forget all faults . . . Come and dine."

There was a large company at dinner and a noise of fiddlers. Some of the guests Will knew, others reflected Lord William's shifting friendships. But in this fashionable room where the furniture was agitated with a superfluity of carving, the walls paneled in orotund extravagance and all the table furnishings of silver, simple men had little meaning.

Will sat far from the great places. Where he sat the service was slow and the food of indifferent quality. Will studied Lord William, who was partly hidden by the great steeple-salt. Lord William's hat with many plumes nodded as he talked. He was as animated as a waterfall. Will thought with no bitterness, even with a kind of tender regret, Thou art a disease of a friend.

Lord William glanced at Will only once, and then he smiled and nodded briskly. After Will had eaten a little fish and listened to the polite belchings of his neighbor, he withdrew. Lord William took no special heed.

Outside Lord William's gate some half-dozen poor men had settled down to wait for the leftover food that would be brought them by-and-by.

That day Will received another couplet. From whom? Marston, Dekker, Jonson? This one played ingeniously with the names of the lady and Sir Piers Dalglish.

Will felt as though he were past all hurt. How then could he explain the unbearable pain in his vitals?

CHAPTER *Nineteen*

THE next day the Queen ordered the executions postponed, and Lord William appeared at the play for the first time since the uprising. He was effervescent with joy.

The lady accompanied him, and her sister. The lady too was smiling. She whispered to Will, "You have given me such joy I cannot speak—ah, sweet Will."

Lord William confided to Will that he had sent the Queen further gifts of Spanish lace. Will knew, and Lord William knew, that the Queen would accept but do whatever her statecraft required.

During the afternoon, Edmund Tilney, the Master of the Revels, sent instructions to prepare a play for Whitehall on Shrove Tuesday; that is to say, tomorrow. He directed that Burbage come to him in his offices at Clerkenwell without delay.

Dickon was weary enough in all conscience, but when he returned after dark, he took off his jacket and announced that they would work through the night. *The Merry Wives of Windsor* had been determined on. Some must rehearse, others supervise the assembling of traps, costumes, property, and lighting effects which Tilney would send for by barge in the morning. Some properties must be refurbished, a new Windsor oak built, and all the wires, ropes, sconces, and impedimenta for lighting the Great Hall secured and tested.

The next day the Queen reaffirmed the date of execution: Ash Wednesday, the day following. The shock was worse for the reprieve.

"We are then to act beside an open grave?" Will said to Dickon.

Dickon hunched his shoulders and hissed his breath between his teeth, making no reply.

"I have a mind not to go," said Will.

Dickon said shortly, "You are not such a clobber-minded fool."

As night came down, Tilney sent a barge of the Queen's to fetch the players. They were deeply silent. Two of the boys laughed unexpectedly, and Condell silenced them with a blow. The Thames was as simple to cross as the Styx. The lights of the palace were febrile, not gay. The troop of servants in the liveries of great lords had wasted looks, and they killed time in courtyards and corridors.

Tilney himself met them with a private look of grief—and here Will shook himself. Enamourment of death could rot the mind. He took himself with resolution.

The corridors were lined with guards and torchbearers. Tilney, courteous and nervous as was his custom, led them to the stage set up in the center of the Great Hall. Curtains concealed the space below the stage, and here they would change into their costumes. With Gus and Jacko, Tilney made certain that all was in its proper place, and then withdrew to fret at trifles.

Two hours stretched for them till ten o'clock. Armin and Tom Pope slept beneath the stage to kill their nerves, Burbage and Sly walked in the gardens. Will and Gus sat by a window and watched the guests assemble. They talked of things close to their heart, but all disguised in common ways.

The blazing lights that their own wireman had put up, and the massed candelabra required by the Queen at all times, combined in an oppressive heat. The court and the invited guests had that waxen, arrested look of figures used to implement occasions. The scent of flowers, of candles, of fresh rushes on the floor was suffocating.

Lord Hunsdon, with his white stave of office, ordered where the guests would stand or sit on the steps built for this night at both ends of the Hall. At the door the Usher of the Black Rod welcomed ambassadors, dukes, earls, ladies of the high nobility who had been summoned on this night before an execution which was also Shrove Tuesday, the last gaiety before Lent. Gentlemen of the Chamber with golden chains lying on their bosoms, performed further obsequies for the mighty of the land as the hollow cry of pages opened narrow passages in these crowded catacombs.

Room for my lord of Nottingham! Way, sirs, for my lord and lady Montague! into the kingdom of eternal night. The heat and heavy perfumes grew deathly within this gilded tomb.

At length the tall doors at the end of the corridor were flung back and eight pages in white and gold entered with the Master of the Revels. The trumpets sounded and the Gentlemen Pensioners who were the Queen's ceremonial bodyguard and were chosen for bravery, height, and appearance, and the ladies of the Privy Chamber—both men and women dressed in white and gold—made a passage for the Queen.

Old Death herself came in, wearing her skull with paint an inch thick. She too was dressed in white, stiff with pearls, and over it a mantle of black silk shot with silver threads, and on her crimped and curled red wig a circlet of pearls.

She greeted all within her reach with bows and smiles, inclining her head to right and left. Now and then, to a kneeling ambassador, she gave her hand to kiss.

When she was seated in her thronelike chair and the rustling on the steps was halted by her glance, the Master of the Revels raised his stave and the players' trumpet sounded.

The trumpet note had a startling clarity and innocence. It made the dukes, earls, ambassadors, and courtiers the mummers, and the players, men and women. It confirmed Will's heavy thoughts that beneath the paint and garnishments, and the dead hair of the wigs, naught existed save the skeletons. As he stood silent on the stage, the coldness of death reached out to him, and looking out toward the massed tier, he fancied that he saw beneath the skin such looks of terror and impending doom that hell gaped there.

The perspiration ran down his body and once he stumbled against Gus, who himself looked as though he were a reaper of souls.

Will felt anger mounting. That painted and pearl-decked woman had said, "You shall be made to answer this to your smart." Was this her revenge, to make them cavort and sing that they should not hear the sound of hammers raising up a scaffold?

He said this to Gus in a loud whisper when they stood below the stage. "She punishes herself and us and all." Gus, hollow-cheeked, suggested that perhaps she meant to announce a reprieve when the evening was over. Will looked at him sharply. "Think you? Why? On what grounds?"

"No grounds," said Gus wearily. "Only fancy. Might it not be so?"

"Now I wish you had not spoken, for how will we make our way to the end of the evening?"

Gus was sharp. "As we go through life, expecting nothing."

Will put his arm across Gus's shoulder and said, "What a rare comforter thou art, my Gus."

Toward the end of the play he saw that his lady was in attendance on the Queen. From that moment on, he saw only what encroached on her, and on his heavy spirit. There sat his Queen who wore upon her head a fruitless crown; beside her stood his own Daemon of Death, and behind his Daemon stood Lord William.

As he looked, he fancied that he saw beneath the crown corruptible Fortune, that turned Turk, that false housewife, that hermaphrodite, who brings safe to harbor boats without a helm, or scuttles those with compass, helm, and sails. Queen and lady, how they served each other.

Will's intuition was ripe as grain. Beyond the lights of the stage, he saw tiers of sycophants behind Lord William like figures on a catafalque, bowing, blandishing, seeking, flattering, wheedling—and he thought how foolishly he had assumed that two characters in his play of *Hamlet* could set forth the full sycophancy of those who batten on society. Though were he to multiply a Rosencrantz and Guildenstern by the Milky Way, would he come any nearer to the truth?

When the play was finished, and he bowed in his turn, he remembered that now would come the Queen's reprieve, if it came at all.

It was difficult to know why Gus's words had taken on such urgency, for he loved these men condemned to death no better than some others, and even less, in truth. In a desperate kind of way Will recognized this urgency as a part of congested hopes: that mercy should fall on all alike, that hope, as hope, should not always be disguised as a feather in the wind.

The curtain was put aside and Fulke Greville entered. Will felt an edge of consolation, for this man, although a courtier—although the Queen's eyes and ears—was linked with honorable intentions and the green fields of home.

"Good evening, sirs," said Sir Fulke, and he bowed to them all in his quiet way. "The Queen, her Majesty, has commanded that you wait on her as you are."

"Sir," said Will with sudden urgency, "have you news?"

"What news?" asked Greville. "Ah, yes, I understand." He smiled faintly, and had the look of weariness that came on honest men at court. "Lord Essex will die tomorrow and Lord Southampton live."

"Bushell, Catesby—Lord Rutland?" asked Dickon, resuming the jacket of his costume.

"I know not even a rumor."

"So mercy is double-handed, sir?" Will said with agitation.

"I should not say so much as that if I were you," said Greville urgently. "And, sirs, the Queen is waiting!"

Will laid his hand on Greville's arm. "Sir, there comes a moment when a man must speak or die!"

"Not you, Will," Burbage spoke decisively. "Not while we are linked together, in such unsettled times. Mend thy speech a trifle lest thou mar our fortune."

Greville drew back the curtains. "I would say her Majesty has tonight reconfirmed her favor, Mr Burbage."

"Would you indeed, good sir?" Will answered instead. "Might it not be punishment of such costly intent that we pay with our heartstrings?"

"In God's name, show your prudence!" Greville cried softly. "*Con amore!*"

With love . . . when it was Will's turn to kneel before the Queen, he saw how one jeweled foot stirred, not with sharp impatience but as though her whole body quivered. He watched that forlorn small foot for a moment, and as he held her hand to his lips, he felt it quiver also.

She said in a low voice, wearily, "A merry, merry evening, sir. I thank you for gay words and cheerful countenances."

He glanced into her face as she spoke, and he sensed an agony as sharp as dilated love had ever known.

"Madam," he said, "we enact our honor to you."

Her beautiful eyes were fixed on him in such a manner that he knew he must not rise. Her lips scarcely moved when she spoke and yet her words came clearly. "*Jacta est alea.* In God's name, the dice are cast."

He was speechless. He had not even a courtesy to utter. As though she sensed that at such a moment there was no bridge between the human family, her eyes released him.

As he stepped back, he saw his Daemon of Death watching from the corners of her eyes as she whispered to Lord William.

They both were pale, and Lord William had the look of a haunted man. Will turned away. He knew them not. They had both been cast out of his soul.

One of Tilney's men assisted them to pack and stow their clothes and gear. Tilney himself came at the last and paid Heminges twenty shillings; an official from the Office of Works discussed briefly the charge that would be made the players for the stage.

As they came into the courtyard, a young page slipped to Will's side. It was plain that discretion had been enjoined on him, for Will could scarcely hear his words. He bent closer.

"The Queen, sir."

"Aye. What?"

"Oh, hush, sir! You are to come with me."

Gus dropped back. "What must you do?" he asked.

"Go on. I like it not. But I will come by-and-by."

"What do you not like?"

"All commands tonight."

"If your mind dislike it, do it not, sweet friend!"

"It is the Queen. Go on."

CHAPTER *Twenty*

HER court dress had been laid aside. Her cloak covered a dark gown. In her hand she held a bunch of flowers. She rose and gave the boy a coin, and in the moonlight took Will's hand.

But he pulled against her hand and stepped back.

"Why did you send a lying message?" he asked bitterly.

"Would you have come had I sent the truth?" the lady asked. She took his hand again, as stiff as a stick. "Alas, poor fool, did you not half think that it was I? Why should the Queen send for you in secret?" Then she took his other hand as well. "Look you, sweet heart, this is the Queen's business. Thou wilt see. Have I ever lied to thee when it mattered?"

265

"I do not know, but I know how often I have partaken against myself with thee."

"Enough, enough! The Queen bids thee through me."

"What?"

In the wasting light, she lifted her flat little face and studied him.

". . . succor death."

He looked back at the palace, where the lights were going out. Had it ever been answered why a man yields to a daemon of death?

She held his hand as though she thought he might still escape, and went down the Privy Stairs into the barge that bore her father's standard. There she sank back on the cushions under the canopy with a long, humming breath, as though honeybees were gathering. He would not step down from the gunwale.

She said again, "I did not deceive you. The Queen has proxied me to watch tonight, and I will not go alone."

"Watch what?"

"Oh, la!" she said, "come or stay, I care not!" and gave a signal to the rowers. Their sudden movement permitted him to be unbalanced to his fate, and he stumbled down beside her. She smiled and touched his hand. Now his wits and energy were bent on that kind of courteous indifference that concealed a barred and bolted door to thought and feeling.

In the night, death's second self, the silence was unbroken. She leaned back against the cushioned seat, drawing her cloak about her. She put the flowers between them.

The rowers turned down the river. A full moon bathed the sky and washed an eerie lifelessness over forms and colors. In its wasting light, truth was confounded, and boats moving on the river were doomed to a perdition of movement without harbor. No wind stirred. The air was still and stale. At the bow a torch guttered upward.

Although it was night and the tide was turning, they went toward London Bridge. The sound of the rapids around the arches of the bridge roared in their ears. With a cool reckoning, the rowers shot through the arches. She gasped and pressed his fingers. So narrow, cribbed, and cramped was he by his own thoughts that he took no account of now. The Tower, suddenly rearing itself before them in the moonlight, unnerved him like a ghost. He turned to her with a cry, but she pressed his hand and would not speak. Her eyes were fixed on that beautiful and fatal building drawing toward them in the moonlight. He was aghast.

"Put out the torch," she said to the coxswain. He moved forward, a hell-bathed figure.

Every torch that moved on the Tower walls, and there was much movement of men and torches, filled Will with a fiery anguish. He drew away his hand abruptly, and sat huddled against a pole of the canopy, the hand covering half his face, his eyes fixed on fate as it drew near. Oh, comfort-killing night, image of hell.

She knelt, facing the Tower, holding tightly to the side of the barge. "Kneel down, kneel down, and wonder," she cried softly, but he would not stir. "Thou must kneel down and bathe thine eyes for the Queen."

The rowers shipped their oars, and they too turned their eyes to the Tower. They drifted for a long time, lady, man, and servants, all living in a dread alliance with another man's ambitions, anguish, and last night on earth. The blandishments of this alliance were so mysterious and yet so personal that one must be drunk or dead to feel them not, Will said in his soul.

For death lives in our bodies from the moment of our birth, yet it remains a terror of such a black and fearsome kind that a man will sacrifice his honor to hold with age, ache, penury, if he may call it life.

So they drifted, and none seemed inclined to gather up the fragments of his thoughts again. How long she would have held them in this painful league one could not know. The grip was broken by shoutings from the Tower walls, and by a boat scudding swiftly toward them. The Constable of the Tower would take all lingerings amiss tonight, and so the lady's rowers dipped their oars and pulled swiftly for the bridge.

She rose up on her knees and blew a kiss toward the Tower. "For thee, Robin. The Queen's last embrace."

She continued to kneel, watching the Tower as it receded, not changing her position even when they came to the dangers of the bridge.

It was Will who was obliged to take her by the shoulders and draw her back to safety. But he did not hold her. He leaned away, against the pole again. Once more they shot between the arches and emerged into the moonlight.

She sat beside him, leaning forward, her hands clasped tightly in her lap, her little face tricked with her thoughts.

"They say men are most prone to die at the turning of the tide. Where will Robin go?" and when he merely glanced at her guardedly (though moved by the tense and staring figure), she whispered, "How can we know that far land of everlasting dark —for no traveler comes home? Yet one glimpse, one sound, and who would not exchange calamity for a peaceful dagger in the breast?" She looked at him slowly, but he did not take his hand from his mouth.

He saw pass the Bishop of Winchester's palace, his own landing stairs, the light in his own window, and in the Falcon. With each, he put himself safe ashore. Yet he was so blinded by fortuity, so helpless in her gravelike barge, that he felt no shock to find himself still beside her.

O Mortality—Essex' last night of earthly pain. Mortality, farewell. But afterward what land, what bourn, indeed?

She spoke so softly that, though he leaned forward, he did not hear. Glancing at him covertly, she repeated, "That red nest of mice she wears upon her head—it will be the color of blood tomorrow."

He did not reply, but continued to lean forward, his arms against his knees. She went on in her ragged little voice, "She weeps and weeps. Had he sent her one token, I think she would have spared him."

"Why did he not?" He spoke for the first time.

She looked at him with a sidelong smile. "Because he is a fool because he is a man." He shrugged and leaned back.

She was silent for a moment, and then she said in a small hard voice, "I seem to thee cold and cutting. What more can I be, knowing all that I know from the day when I began? There is naught true but statecraft, and we are all lain upon our backs that it may have its way with us. Yet since it is greed and intrigue that doth catch us by the heels, we fall not unwillingly."

He looked at her in the faint light, and his eyes softened in response to her candor. How fatal was this ultimate seduction: humanity and the honest woman she might have been.

She laughed helplessly and leaned back. He saw her eyes close and heard her sigh. Then her hand went out and she released the curtains of the canopy.

In God's name, he must try again to either hate or love her. He must accord her the dignity of one feeling or the other, not the humiliation of fear or lust!

She took his hand again, and talked to him like a child. Yet it was an elf-child, for her low voice was half her own, half some other creature's. "Death, death, death. She did hate him deadly and he is dead. Oh, death . . ."

She was calling on death as she might call on Venus, and death and lust both did the work of darkness. She turned and looked at him, and he felt as though all his rights and dignity were dissolving under her gaze. She said in a low voice, "We must be in love with death tonight. Else we will be harried with this play of bones and see the skulls of dead men everywhere."

"Oh, be silent!"

She fell into a transport of shudders. "I think the blackness would tell me all." She leaned back and dropped her head against his shoulder. She laid her fingers on his and said in a sweet, almost gay voice, "I think if you would kill me now, I would love you through eternity."

"This is monstrous . . ."

"This is a special night when we must be in love with death. And thus go with Robin along the way." She started to sing. It was a song sung when Mary Stuart died. He heard it as her fingers played with his.

> ". . . who lost her head of late
> Doth show that kings as well as clowns
> Are bound to Fortune's fate,
> And that no earthly prince

Can so secure his crown
But Fortune with her whirling wheel
Hath power to pull them down . . ."

"This is enough," he said desperately. "I wish now to be set ashore."

She said, "I will not let you go until you have forfeited some of your good for his."

"But he will die tomorrow and I will not. What can I do for him?"

"Why, all's one," she said. "I see it now—death and life."

"You connive at evil!"

She said softly, "You do protest too much of evil. I suspect you."

"What?"

"That you are half in love with it yourself. You do not weep." She took his hand again and told how as a child she had woven a garland of flowers and then killed her bird to lay him on a flowery bier so that she might find a way to weep.

"I believe you not," he said. "I scarce believe that you have life—I conjure you away!"

She whistled softly. "I live. You know it."

He said bitterly, "Heaven save me!"

"Heaven's not for us. Oh, pell-mell, let us go hand in hand to hell."

With the curtains drawn, only a faint light entered, but he saw her. He saw her as pure innocent evil. Thus innocence and evil canceled out each other, leaving a creature forlorn and empty. Could he hate or fear her then? She existed only by sensation, and when she had created her sensuous means, found them so hollow that she must lash herself to feel again. He saw it all—*all*—in a moment, and it was dangerous to him only as he gave it power. He said sharply, "I will love you well, in my heart of hearts, if you will now set me ashore."

She made no move. Instead she said hummingly, "Have you ever loved me?" When he did not answer, she asked with a sudden sting, "Have you loved my kindness?" He laughed shortly. She put her fingers on his neck and stroked him. "My sweetness?" He did not answer and drew away. "My faithfulness?" After a moment she began to hum again and fondle him. "I'll tell thee what thou hast loved—what I promised and did not give." He stirred but made no move to speak.

"And always the promise will be so great that naught else counts—for it will come." She put her face close to his. "Promise redeemed." He moved to set aside the curtain. "Sweet fool," she said, "a babe would be more cunning than thou art."

It was her pungent assumption that everything was deceit except the body's weakness that angered and confused his thoughts. The assumption was so heavy and assertive that a subtle man, at odds with himself, became his own victim.

He struggled upright. He said quietly, "Unless you are some supernatural solicitor, I'll find my cunning."

Slowly she turned her round eyes on him and touched his cheek lightly with her tongue. "Oh, men, that make such sweet use of what they hate." Her voice held that quality that tried all his members. She could make Death amorous! He refused to speak.

"Adam, Adam." She laughed. It was a cold, old laugh. "I am true to my desires, dear ape. Thou art false."

Will felt a chill creep over him as though he were in his grave. He struggled with the winding sheet, but she—the sheet, the thongs, the worms—was there before his act of struggle. That she was stronger than he, he must deny, else he had no hope of heaven.

She studied him with her black round eyes and with her little face wiped of expression. Before his eyes, in the faint light, she seemed to change as, it is said, a witch can change at her own bidding. She was all female. It was as though her face slowly appeared beneath the paint. It was a curious necromancy, not unlike the action of a player, changing to some new disguise.

Yet this was not play acting. It was a deep thralldom which affected the immortal soul. The practice of deceit began and ended, where?

"How often have I deceived thee and thou knew it not—how often will I do so again. Listen." Although he had known it all

271

before, he listened to her whispering voice in a coldness of shame. He scarcely trusted himself to breathe. All shame belonged to him, for this cruelty stirred as did her kisses. His imagination rotted him. His need for her appetites had been his undoing—undid him now. Words broke from him.

"Oh, thou cruel witch that sports with pain!"

"Ah," she said triumphantly. "I've pricked thee!"

"Oh, if I told thy deeds—oh, my God—oh, strumpet—"

She laughed and stroked his temples. "Aye, and with strumpet's powers, I've vowed to give thee all. I will, when I am ready. Might it be now, in death's dark night?"

"No."

"Have you ever withheld from me? Know yourself." When he moved she mocked him softly. "Well then, leave me—walk on the waters. Do so, but kiss me first."

"Never, never!"

At that her mood changed swiftly. "Ah! Thou tupper. Know that to bear thee near my heart is sweating labor. *I* want no more."

He found his voice. "Good, and enough." As he moved, his arm struck her. She seized it and held his hand in hers.

"Do you not know what love is?" she whispered, "it is war and death."

He began the disengagement of his hand. She leaned forward and brushed her cheek against his. "And when you have pillaged and set fire, then you must hold your conquest with the pain of hell and the cost of the whole world."

"By God's mercy, from whence did you fetch such brimstone!"

Her smile was close to his face. "From my back, defending my belly. From my wits, defending my wiles. From you, in defense of these." She took his hand and held it against her mouth, her lips moving over it lightly. Anguish she could not see, pain she could not feel. Yet she was white and trembling. "Prove me a woman—in death's skull."

He thrust her away, thinking once more that dark and lust are happy friends. Then she wept in a dry anger. "Mountebank, why do you not kill yourself? Or kill me, for love!"

He said quietly, "Lady, I pray you, command the rowers to set me home."

She turned to him. "I love you." She said it with such pitiable sweetness that he set his teeth. She took up one of his hands and held its palm against her lips. He drew it away. She put up her hand and slipped it between the opening of his jerkin and touched his flesh.

"Oh, thy heart—thy heart is pounding like a lover. Yes, oh, yes, yes—"

She pulled him down into her wide smile and the dark night.

Oh, what a double death it is to drown in sight of shore.

He struggled for a choice but there was none. Only hunger, debasement—he was debased and snared. Finish with this moment, struggle elsewhere. He took her violently, stretching her to a full measure of kindled pain, bruising and striking her at the same time that she fought and entangled herself with him. But suddenly with a sharp thrust of cruelty she wrenched herself from him, making a strange inhuman sound, half grunt, half laugh, and toppled him away. Pitched without mercy into his skin and bones, he cried out in anguish.

She said with a studied softness, almost a laugh, "Oh, you are hurt, I thank heaven. Always a man blots me out! But I'll not have it!" She blew upward against her face and put aside the curtains. "Oh, men, oh, monkeys—"

He cursed her.

"Eros," she whispered. "Men—*all but one*—kissing carrion. I'll die with him within me."

"I will destroy you!"

"Enough, enough."

"Oh, never, never, never, never, never—" He covered his face with his hands and wept.

"Destroy me, then I might feel." She struck him with the back of her hand. "But no, you plunder me, you try to wipe out me, myself. But I'll not lose myself! No, a man's a fool. Oh, hell-kite!"

He half rose, crouching, and covered his face. "Oh, I am a strumpet's fool. Tell your rowers to set me ashore."

She studied him for a moment. Her hands were trembling. "Find your own way home," she said. She pushed him with all her might. He tried to steady himself by the pole of the canopy, but when she pushed again he was overbalanced. "Go drown."

The foul black river rushed into his nose and eyes. As he came to the surface, he saw the barge not half a length away, clear in the moonlight. He gasped and shook his head. She was a dark form leaning over the gunwale, laughing and weeping. As he struck out to swim, her laughter overcame her.

"Playactor! Mountebank!" She threw a pillow at him. "Copesmate of ugly night!" She put her cheek against the pole and wept again.

The rowers were hesitating and laughing with convulsive starts.

"Go home!" she cried, kissing her hand and still weeping.

He was swept toward the landing stairs. The rank smell of the river was in his nostrils and the foul taste in his mouth. He struck away the offal. He wished to be lost in the river, hidden from himself and humanity.

When he reached the stairs he clung there for a long time, numbed by the cold, recovering himself in the merciful black. Presently he started to shake. His teeth were chattering. A form stirred on the wharf above him.

"Ho." A woman leaned over, breathing of drink. "Poor boozy. Thou't saved for hangin'. Take me hand."

The next day he was sick, but he drove Ned from their room. That same day, Essex' head was chopped off.

Chop off his vitals. All's the same.

All his vows now were to misuse her.

He knew he could no longer deceive himself with innocence. She could sway him from the very likeness of a man if she chose. She could destroy his power to reason and be honest, she could destroy his choice, she could make all lies seem truth and force him to abuse his very sight.

The shivering seized him. To break this bondage, he must

274

kill her or be killed forever. Or kill himself? Ah, better! To kill himself would put an end to all mortal seeming.

What is there to fear in the tender fork of a poor worm? Are not all odds even? Yet should he not send her to death grossly so that her soul be lost as well? Aye, that he would do, and so wipe out his own humanity and be done with Will.

He thought of ways to kill. I will be found most cunning in my patience, but, hear you—most bloody. Oh, I shall be my age's man, confirmed, proud, subtle, bloody, treacherous.

He wished to go home. Home emerged on a long lonely horizon.

He looked at it from far off—his home in the green country. He could not draw near it nor could he draw back. He groaned. *Revenge, but taint not thy mind.*

Ned refused to be set out of the room any longer. He knocked, and then he kicked open the door. He had a bottle of wine and food, and a face resolutely set against being denied any further. When he saw his brother standing up, he was angry. He said, "You are not sick. And I have brought you gruel."

Will said, "To revenge and not be corrupted is a paradox, Ned. To revenge—"

"I heard you."

"It bears a man to the end of life."

Ned cut the bread. He said with lowered head, "He is dead."

"Who? Who is dead?"

"Why, great Essex."

Death's ambassador.

"She did not let him be hanged, drawn, and quartered."

"God is merciful—not women!"

"He was dressed all in black, save for scarlet. He wore a hat." Ned's voice marveled. "On the scaffold, he said a prayer." He turned toward Will, the knife in his hand, and he spoke desperately. "He confessed all his sins of pride, vanity, and love of this world's pleasure, confessed especially this last great sin 'whereby so many, for love of me have been drawn to offend God, their sovereign, and the world. I thank God' "—and Ned was Essex in

275

some amalgam of youth and tragedy—" 'that I have been justly spewed out of the realm. Oh, God, when my life and body shall part, send thy blessed angels which may receive my soul and convey it to the joys of heaven.' It took three blows to un-head him —oh, Jesu, what a man—and when the headsman held up the dripping head, the headsman cried on God to save the Queen."

"Did he feel the last kiss thrown to him across the waters?" Ned cried, "Do not mock!"

"Mock—at Essex blessed by fortune?"

. . . nor mock at murder which was neither fell nor foolish but the means to a long sleep.

CHAPTER *Twenty-one*

IT was said that the Queen had sat in her private chamber playing the virginal. A messenger had come to her there and told her that the Earl was dead. The Queen had not spoken. At length she had struck a chord and begun to play again.

She spared Southampton. She committed him to the Tower, attainted him and seized his estates. She ordered Meyrick and Cuffe to be hanged; she ordered Blount and Davers to lose their heads. Catesby and Bushell were let off with a fine. From Rutland she extracted a ransom of thirty thousand pounds, a prince's sum.

It was a remarkable clemency, but it did not quiet the people. The great days were over when the Queen could do no wrong. Now each move she made stirred the dark future and deepened the shadows.

Essex' head was impaled on Temple Bar where the dead eyes could look at Essex House. A ballad of his last good night haunted alehouses and dark streets.

> All you that cry O hone! O hone!
>   come now and sing, O Lord! with me.
> For why? Our Jewel is from us gone,
>   the valiant knight of chivalry.

The Bishop of London confiscated all songs in Essex' honor, but he could not confiscate those committed to memory.

The government required a sermon to be preached in Paul's Church setting forth the just punishment of the criminal, Essex, else martyrdom might disturb the delicate balance of state and people. Yet judging the effects, the sermon was not sufficient, for the people stood weeping beneath his head on Temple Bar.

A narrative of circumstances was printed out hastily, taken, word for word, from the original depositions. And government agents, disguised as ordinary men, repeated at market place and pump, alehouse and street corner, Essex' last confession and prayer.

But on the whole, people preferred what they knew; that the times were dark, that the Queen was old, what would come after her? Civil war, or an invasion from Scotland? Or the Spaniards setting fire to the land? Or Armageddon? Or Satan seizing all who were not predestined for salvation.

At the Globe was the same disquietude. If their status was further impaired, they would be ripe victims for extinction. Will's diseased nerves were obscured by the general disease. He lost himself in alleys and warrens, plotting revenge. What revenge?

For in the end, who was the murderer and who the murdered?

Dekker's *Satiromastix* stirred up an effete and noisy conflict with Ben Jonson's *The Poetaster* which the Blackfriar Children were performing, and this gave an illusion of normalcy. The two plays were topical attacks, easily read by those who ran. "The Poetaster" was Marston. He was made to vomit up words in a bowl. Dekker was dimly disguised, and even Gus Phillips was trotted out under a thin cover to receive forty shillings for some doubtful matter or other.

Dickon was angry. He said that forty shillings had almost as fatal a ring as thirty pieces of silver. But Gus shrugged. "Nothing's novel, nothing's strange. Why should we care?"

Lord Hunsdon sent for Dickon. He said that it was desirable for the players to leave London earlier than their summer custom. Let them make their living in the shires until the Queen was herself again. He showed that he was much put out by this, but he would not listen to Dickon's protests, and was short and round in all he said.

Burbage did not conceal his dismay when he brought back the word.

"This will kill us."

"Nonsense," said Heminges stoutly.

"It is a stupid and unwarranted indignity!"

"It will not bbbreak our bbbones."

Burbage stared at them all with an angry flush. "Let me tell you, this is Alleyn's work. He writes certain words in bat's blood on a parchment and ties it about his left arm. Thus he gets what he wants."

Gus said quietly, "Dickon, it is not bat's blood that brought us to this sorry state."

Dickon turned a fiery gaze. "Dekker saw him with his own eyes bind it around his arm!"

Will said, "Dear fool, we'll not take time to find a stronger magic."

"Do you call me a fool? It's the only title you have left yourself!"

"Peace!"

Each man was greatly troubled. Traveling in the provinces was rough and roughly greeted, even though, as the Lord Chamberlain's Men, they had some benefits and prerogatives.

They loved their wives, those who had them. They left behind three dozen children. They had fine houses and comfortable service. They gained no independence and very little means.

Only Will felt relief, an emotion so forceful and uncontaminated that it was close to ecstasy. Jesu Christos, he would be free, he would escape, he would so disguise himself that none might ever find him again.

Lord Hunsdon sent for them a second time. Now he seemed uneasy. He proposed they go to Scotland. Phillips and Heminges started with surprise. Heminges said straight out that Lord Essex had been in communication with King James. Hunsdon said, scarcely moving his lips, "The King is a playgoer. Your position to the Queen is known to him. By you, nothing will be said,

278

done or communicated; but your presence in Scotland will be a peaceful fact. The Scots will know you would not be there without permission." He stroked his cheek and sighed, glancing at them. "The Queen is quite disfavored and unattired. She is fearful of every dish brought to the table. She eats always with a sword beside her. She frowns on all her ladies and walks much in her private chamber, stamping her foot and thrusting her sword into the arras with great effect."

He disclosed himself at that moment, his affection palpitant.

Phillips said merely, "We are your servants, my good lord."

Hunsdon blinked his eyes, and this action in so controlled a man partook of poignancy. "Those who do not care to go to Scotland, for whatsoever reason, will not be held to account. We must know, however, which plays you will perform."

He hesitated for a moment, and then he reached in a drawer and held out a purse. To this he added a wintry smile.

Phillips reported all this laconically as the others were rising from a Lenten dinner. Ned seized Will's arm and compelled him to come apart with him. They stood cramped and noticeable on the street outside the Falcon, frowning at each other.

"Don't go," said Ned, his hands trembling. "If you go, I must go, and it is time we went home."

Ned's hands closed painfully on Will's arm, his eyes were ground with pain, and the sweat lay on his brow. A boy ran by with daffodils in his hand.

Will prised loose Ned's hands and held them like a wrestler. He did not look too intently into his face, for the real need was to look into his own face. Without warning, Ned started to cry like a child.

Will embraced him. "Dear lad, do as you choose. I will not hold you."

But this was not enough. Ned caught his arm again and cried that Will must also go. In London, Will was detestable. Will belonged at home, as he did. Why was Will pretending to be something he was not? Come away home. There he was a man. What did he think his children were doing while he was gone? Who was stealing his revenues?

279

Will stared at him. Oh, home was very much more than going back to Stratford. Ned's anger, derived from so many sources and so uneasy in a mixed company, flared up again. "Do not look like a dunce! Have you made yourself so putrid that you must stay in this offal?"

Will said roughly in a Warwickshire voice, "I'll comb thy noddle with a three-legged stool!" At that Ned flung himself back, striking the side of the tavern and steadying himself, spread-eagled.

"Oh, to damnation—do as you will!"

Will was suffocatingly close to himself. Life had prepared all the precedent steps to this self-knowledge. He put his arm about Ned. "Enough. I must do one more thing. Then we will go home."

Now the players were squeezed and bound together by something more demanding than their love. They were in a dark wood. They had no illusions that by sheer right and justice they would find their way into the clearing.

When Burbage learned that Will was not going to Scotland he became suspicious of Will's motives, and Will grew angry that he did. Yet he knew that Burbage did not truly suspect him; he merely suspected the whole world.

Phillips was regretful. "Whatever will I do without thee?" he said to Will. "Who else will ask and answer questions with me for these many a months?"

Heminges was wistful, for if Will did not go, Jacko said, he would lose those quiet brooding times when he could weep for twelve children and a wife with a man of tender heart and no commitments. Then he spoke his amazement. "But you have a wife and children and you are going to them. Why would I ffforget it?"

Will looked at him and found no answer. It was Condell, tossed up and down in the blanket of leaving his Elizabeth or staying with her, who replied, "Why do you not remind us of home at better times, old Jehovah? I've spent too much money. It was for you to say *enough*. Now I cannot stay. I have no money and two children!"

"My God," said Jacko, suddenly out of temper, "you have no more bbbrains in your hhhead than I have in my elbows. Like as not we'll all dddie among the Scots, so what odds are ttthey, twelve or two children? My Rebbbecca or thy Elizabeth?"

Will thought suddenly that now they would not need his play. He felt some dismay. This *Hamlet* was better than a confessional.

Hunsdon, reflecting the uneasy times, sent twice more for their list of plays. Each one resolved upon wrung Dickon's nerves anew and made him fling fresh accusations at Will of temporizing, cowardice, indifference, Will interrupting to say that Dickon was essential to their success in Scotland, as were Heminges, Gus, Condell, Sly, Jamie. Only a mean actor who had already written all the plays they needed was unnecessary. "Though let us now be candid, Dickon, and say it was your Richard who was at fault, and drives you now away, for you did make him blaze too finely for men to stay indifferent."

This was a fine turnabout, and Dickon accepted it as a kind of apology. He told Will he found it artful—Will at his most ingenious and characteristic, very cunning indeed! Burbage's admiration mounted. He embraced Will with a laugh and said, "By God, I'll have thy *Prince of Denmark* whether I be in hell or Scotland."

Sleep was niggardly. Fresh play scripts must be written out, new furnishings prepared, an empty theatre safeguarded, rehearsals and playing continued till the last. A man need scarcely think.

Gib was all places and all things. He took a sardonic satisfaction that he was puppet master, and watched with cold lone eyes the jerkings of these poor jackanapes.

"How shall we do without Gib?" Dickon cried in Gib's hearing; "I'll not bear what I did last year."

Will answered, "Who but Gib can we trust to stay here and see that all's safe?"

"I'll not have the curtain fall on me again!"

"Gib, train Sam for kingdom-come," Will said. "Make him know he's got no hope of salvation if he fails."

Little green leaves appeared upon the boughs. The boats upon the river were bright with sails. Windmills turning in the fields of Southwark were freshly buoyant. Essex' moldering head still drew the crowds.

They let Dekker have the last play. And at Blackfriars, the Children put on Jonson's *The Poetaster* that same night. It was as good as a bearbaiting. The watermen carried noisy dilettanti back and forth across the river to lay one scene beside another and afterward to drink to some monstrous two-headed beast sired and borne by Jonson and Dekker. This would allow the players to leave London masters of both art and craftiness.

Will was thankful that he had come thus far unthinking, horrors exorcised by making art of them.

Revenge. What would he revenge? His lost innocence? Her purity?

If he held revenge loosely in his mind that might be sufficient, for how does one return like for like, evil for evil, in equal parts? Nay, not in this world, where the web of life is a mingled yarn, good and ill together.

On this last night, after the play, Lord William took possession of the stage and tiring room. Lord William's servants passed wine on silver salvers with the family crest, as though Lord William were at home. The lady stood by modestly with her sister. She wore her mask and all her paint and bore herself with perfect decorum. She had smiled broadly when she saw Will.

Lord William was ebullient, even a little gross and cruel in his gaiety. Every third name on his lips was Rutland. His cousin Roger was safe; all other deaths and disfigurations were no more than scars upon the sea.

Will went to sit on the stairs out of sight. He teased himself that in his best serge doublet and pantaloons, his plain white collar, he could make himself invisible and roam among them terrible as a flight of cherubim. In her ear he would whisper her name over and over until her soul had wakened to live as God desired.

He sat with his head in his hands, brewing his fancies. Lord William's voice came to him high and beautiful, telling how he had spent the morning choosing a horse for Roger. Roger, banished and ruined, worth thirty thousand pounds to the Queen, deserved the best horse that science could insure.

"First they trotted out a black horse and I was full of wroth. With such a color, the beast would be heavy, faint-hearted. For Roger—faugh! Then they brought out a white horse. Faith, I lost my temper. I said, 'Take away all that are of the hue of water, for it is written in his color that he is phlegmatic, slow, dull.' Then they brought out a bay—ah, all air, all sanguine, nimble like Roger. And a sorrel—fiery, hot, choleric. You see how one must know, for, by Hercules, the black was a splendid beast, and the white fit for a Queen. But I bought nobility, the color mixed to show how all elements blend harmoniously to the performance of greatness. My cousin will ride him back to fortune."

Dekker stood in the doorway looking down at Will on the stairs. Will raised his eyes. Dekker said with a half smile on his round face, "Fortune? Who is she?"

Will stirred. "The galled jade who winces."

Dekker gave a snorting laugh. "Aye, she who sells her favors to any."

"A whore." Will pushed himself to his feet.

"Nay, more—a bawd who beckons and a whore who infects. Honest men keep themselves clear of Fortune."

Will patted him on the shoulder and said drily, "Forget not to take thine own counsel, lad."

Dekker grimaced. "Thy flight's not lost on me. But who would not willingly take down all the sails of his ambition and cast anchor on a safe shore—which is to be found no place if not in the country?"

Will said very softly, "Think you so? Yet I fancy there is something first to be earned for that peace."

They stood side by side, staring into the room. The lady, who might be called Fortune's wheel, stood across from them in her monstrous farthingale and flashing excrescence of jewels and pride, teetering on high heels between a smart turkey, a rooster, and Lord William. There she simpered, lisped, jigged, making monsters of men. By hell, she had filled his mouth with offal!

His hands were wet and trembling.

By God, no man needed whisperings from without. He had within himself his own devil.

He coughed and turned aside as though it were no matter. Dekker was watching him with curiosity. Will controlled himself by brushing his pantaloons carefully.

Gib came up. He leaned in the door, his legs crossed. He said to Dekker, "The little mare hath asked for thee."

Dekker, startled and confused, looked three ways. Gib said, "Oh, she minced and was ladylike." Dekker looked at Will. Will lifted his brows and smiled. He pushed him forward.

When he stood alone with Gib he said quietly, "Whatever thy private thoughts, it is not well to call her any name but her own."

Gib turned his dark sardonic eyes on Will.

"Ah, so? You forget I am your liegeman to the death." Slowly, fumbling a little, he took a sheet of paper from inside his jerkin and handed it to Will. Then he turned and looked at the large world on the stage.

The verse was printed.

> Too hot and high he climbed, was doused in swill;
> With chilling fingers mounts the bank and recks
> How Will, with will outplucked will will it still,
> And—

He closed his hand on it. For a moment he did not look up. Then slowly, almost furtively, he raised his eyes and saw Gib watching him.

He folded the paper over and over.

He looked with suffused eyes at her laughing with Dekker. He tried to speak and failed. He opened the paper and held it out to Gib. Gib pushed it away. "I read it. Everyone has read it. It is everywhere."

After a moment, Will said in a makeshift voice, "What shall I do, Gib?"

Gib did not answer for a moment; he studied Will. "Put her where she cannot make monkeys of men."

Will caught at his lip. "Where?"

Gib kept his eyes on Will. "Lock her with bawds and pricks who will give her what she gives to others."

Will frowned. "You have a little touch of hell."

"Lock her where she must submit to rough embraces and brisk indignities without hope of her own way."

Will said, "Are we devils?"

"Not we—she."

Now Will stood outside himself.

"How shall it be done, Gib?"

"Leave that to me."

"I want no more . . ."

Gib said, "In an hour's time bring her down by the Bishop's park." He went off.

Will stood watching, permitting nothing to enter his heart. Presently he went across the room to her.

She gave Will a sudden spring-look with no more menace than the sun's rising. Dekker, spirited as the month of May, had an honest and manly charm as he answered her questions: how, in plays, lightning and thunder were made to leap forth, how ghosts ascended and descended, how fires burned and ordnance spoke with no danger to any.

Lord William, standing like a painted backcloth, wore a doublet broidered all over with bees and flowers, buds and blossoms, sprigs of spring. Yet Will, looking closely, saw that one had been broidered with a worm in the bud.

Will said to the lady, "Madam, I have a token for you before I leave."

She reached out her hand. "Give it me."

"Nay, it is not in my hand."

"Where is it then?"

"Will you come and see?"

She gave him an open look. Lord William said like silk, "Who gives a lady a token graces himself," but his eyes were as curious as a child's.

Will held out his hand. "Madam, will you come?"

She gave him her hand.

He led her into the wardrobe where the boys were capering

285

half-dressed, and he took down a drab gown and cloak. He said to the boys, "Take thy capers elsewhere, lads." They gathered up their jerkins and chased each other up the stairs.

To her he said, "Put on this gown."

She chose to be provoking. "Bare myself in thy presence?"

"Will you have my token, madam?"

"Well, you must act again as my woman."

He unfastened what she could not reach of jewels, ruff, and farthingale, and refused to be cajoled by her fooling. More briskly than she cared was she bundled into the drab gown and cloak.

"Now where?" she said tartly. "This token, is it animal, mineral, vegetable, large or small? Oh, fool, I will miss thee when thou'rt gone!" He did not answer, and led her out of doors through the little entrance at the back. Her voice recovered its lightness. "For thou art very ripe for ventures. Will, sweet Will." Her little voice came through the dark and he tried to close his ears. "When thou art gone I'll think over and over of how we've played together—what games have been. Will, when I have provoked thee—"

"Oh, take care!" he cried. "Here is a ditch!"

" 'Od's pitikins," she said, "what a black world."

They had crossed the field and come to Bankside and turned by the river toward the stews.

She stopped and dragged at him. "Where are we going?" she demanded. "Nay, stop, or I'll scream."

"Who will listen, sweetling?"

Who indeed? It was a world rent by screams and songs on which another added left no mark.

Yet she was keen. Black it might be but life stirred. It stirred in the shore below the road; rats or men. "Give me your dagger," she whispered.

"I will not."

"Could I but see. Who goes there?"

"Ho!" Will struck with his dagger and a man yelped.

"Mind your hand, friend," Will said, "or you will lose it."

She backed against a wall. "God's dines—it's very dangerous—"

"Are you afraid?"

She laughed softly. "Should I be?"

He sunk his teeth against his lip. She screamed a little. "Touch me not!"

" 'Twas I touched you. Come."

"How far?"

"As far as church—"

"Oh, there are eyes!"

"Aye, mortal men have miserable, mad, mistaking eyes!"

She slipped her arm in Will's. "What steep adventure!"

"For God's sake, come!"

It was most urgent that he have no thoughts, and the blackness aided him.

Close by was a sudden scuffle and cry and feet running; then the bell of the Watch and his cudgel thumping. A body would be found in the morning.

Ahead a light showed in one of the stews.

"Out! Out!" The constable knocked against the house. "Out!" A window opened and a face within was level with the face without. They whispered. The hand within dropped a coin into the hand without. The window closed. The constable went on, striking the wall more softly and crying into the dark, "Peace! I charge thee stand, miscreants!"

"Perdy, he reeks of onions," she whispered. "How far?"

"How far is hell?"

"Oh, that I've always wished to visit." She could see in the dark as witches can. "Will, Will—those are men against the walls. What do they there?"

A reply came from the wall in a hoarse whisper. "Thump thee, wench?"

She laughed softly but leaned against Will. "What are their names?" she asked him loud enough for them to hear. They answered lewdly.

Hell, hell! He drew her on. A child ducked from an alley and ran like a hare between them. She screamed. Someone, far off, was shouting. Will caught her as she stumbled. He could bear little more. He went blindly on but she held him back.

"Wait—whist! You would not break the course of love," and

she drew him out of the way of two locked figures. One of them cursed at that moment in a woman's voice and struck her man to the ground. The lady laughed and touched the prone man with her foot. He caught at her.

"Play tick-tack, she?"

She leaned over. "Hug me not. There's thy dish," for the woman had swung around to hammer both the man and the lady. The lady jumped back. "I'll not be touched. Never, never!" She dragged at Will. "How they go to it! Will, you have brought me out and have not kissed me. That's unmannerly. See them there!"

But he had neither eyes nor ears. As Tarquin went remorseless toward his prey, so Will could not draw back. He knew the turning of the lane by the Bishop's park. She laughed. "Speak! Nay, kiss." He tried some sound but it failed him.

Now his eyes saw in the dark. Two or three were standing by the wall. Conscience and his immortal soul cried out. He gripped her hand. Suddenly he made a sound of protest and, holding her hand, began to run.

But the shrouded men considered it a signal. They swooped like bats and, surrounding her, tore her from his hand. Will shouted, "No, no!" but three had her fast and he fell.

He reached his feet in a moment and ran down the dark alley crying, he thought, to wake the dead yet making scarcely any sound.

The last he heard was her voice breaking from a restraining hand. Her voice cried and cried his name.

The night was all black as hell and painted red. He ran up and down the alleys, shouting for Gib in the strange hoarse whisper that was his only sound. Then he sought out the country lanes below the theatre, but the smells and sounds were too sweet. At length he returned to walk the riverbank where the stench assailed. But the river was his nightmare.

To run and run and run the circles of hell was a movement as slow as a crawl. To traffick with evil was to render oneself a legless runner in a nightmare. His senses cooled to hear the night-shrieks in these warrens.

He pounded at brothel doors.

"Gib? Ah, Gib, he's not here."

Will was sure all lied.

The door of the Cardinal's Cap was flung open and a man thrown out. "Pay or be damned! Ah, Will, come in."

In the room were new dirty rushes and foul-smelling candles, the smell of drink, and women with bare breasts. "Gib!"

"Gib? Oh, not here," said Jasper Shore, but his cold eyes were seldom honest.

Will had supped too full with horrors. He had no place to go. Like a sick animal he sought a hole, but there was none. Gib, gib-cat, gibbet. He sank down by the river huddled in his arms, and prayed, *Sweet Jesus, cancel that great bond that makes me man.*

When the candles were at last put out and the sky beginning to lighten, he had taken full measure of himself.

He found Gib at length in Gib's own room, matted with sleep. He seized and shook him. Gib struck himself free and tumbled back to his pillow.

"Go rot," said Gib, but Will struck a light and hauled him up again.

"Where is she?"

Gib did not answer for a moment, stuck with sleep, and then he laughed in snorts.

"Oh, apes. Oh, monkeys." He lay grinning, his eyes closed. Then he opened his eyes and looked at Will, fully awake.

"Jezebel!"

"Speak."

Gib rubbed his cheek and head. "I went to your room. Where were you then, by hell? Only Ned planning on home."

"Gib, in God's name—"

Gib, who read the book of the secret soul in his own fashion, partly closed his eyes.

"Will you hear all or a little?"

Will shook his two fists.

Gib said, "I'll tell thee a little. We gave satiety a fresh appetite."

"What?"

Gib laughed. "We misjudged and miscalculated, friend. She found her trade." Gib said, "She is quite unbroken. I fancy you must kill her."

Gib watched Will with hard patience. At length Will said in a congested voice, "Say on."

"Ah, Will, what story do you want? Let it be."

Will caught his shoulders and shook him.

"By hell," Gib said, "back of the Bishop's palace they know me well. One of his Lordship's geese is the same as another. For money a whoremaster will sell his mother. Why, to look at her was money doubled and trebled. Who lost?" He whistled through his teeth. "You. And poor Moll, Poll, and Doll, good creatures of sale before her. It was a game to her, Will! She went at it like falcon to bird. No subtleties to trouble her. Rough indignities keened her edge. Why, she was home. 'Twas Moll and Doll tore her up and threw her out. When I took her across the river, she laughed all the way."

What Gib saw on Will's face was not to be borne. Gib said softly, "Take off the wrappings round thine eyes."

"To see what? Thy foul and ugly self?"

Gib took the cruel words bitterly for a moment. Then he said with rough gentleness, "Murder thyself no more."

Ned vented his fear when Gib brought in Will. "God help me —thou art—!" Then in a swift glance his youngness found some wisdom. "Why, thou ape of God, come to wash and breakfast. We must go home."

CHAPTER *Twenty-two*

THEIR gear was loaded on the wagons, their room empty of all but dust. Pope, Gus, and their apprentices sat mounted on the street outside. Gib and the stagemen made doubly sure that the stage wagons were safely lashed.

Will kissed the old man and Mrs Nell goodbye. To touch them was, like Antaeus, to touch a gift of life. As Will came into the street, Lord William's servant brightened the dull day. Lord William wished to see him.

Will stood quietly for a moment. Punishment was due. He welcomed it.

Before he mounted his horse, he clasped Gib's arm. "Forgive me."

Gib said sadly, "Perhaps revenge is useless. We're all arrant knaves."

"But say I am forgiven!"

"Oh, all's forgotten too."

Ned looked at him anxiously. "What does the lord want? Let me come with you?"

"No— All is well, dear lad."

Will rode in silence with his friends across London Bridge. Going up the slope from the river, crowds called *Goodbye*. At the Guild Hall they separated, Gus and Pope to add Heminges, Sly, Condell, and Dickon (who would have his own processional of farewells, bouquets and flung kisses), while Will proceeded to the Barbican. In Hampstead, they would meet for dinner.

Whatever Lord William proposed would be a mercy. For Will was, at this moment, amenable to nothing that was not irrevocable and as narrow as a church door.

Lord William was in his study overlooking the garden. He sat at a fashionable gaudy table of inlaid ivory, silver, tortoiseshell and painted wood. Behind him hung a new tapestry of brilliant colors. The window light fell on his dark hair and the ruby velvet of his doublet.

He did not know that Will had entered for he, unlike the Queen, kept his floors with a heavy carpet. He continued with his task of bisecting certain angles of a convolvulus drawn with meticulous care. His preoccupation was so deep that when he looked up, his recollection had to be elicited.

"Ah . . ." he said softly, and then looked down again at the drawing to add one more thing to make it clear. Presently he leaned back and looked at Will with a frown and a smile, both far-away.

Will was not asked to sit down, but he did so.

"Yes . . ." said Lord William laying his long fingers against his throat. He lifted and lowered his fingers against his throat as though a dependable emotion were eluding him. His stillness was deep, and Will returned him quietness for quietness. Their eyes had a common purpose, to study each other.

Lord William cleared his throat. His tone held wonder. "I see. Bones a me. You are a comely man. This had somehow eluded me." He sat with his cheek resting on his hand watching Will. His eyes would be remembered. "But I have been most grossly offended." Will did not reply. "Your silence speaks for you." Lord William stared at him, beating a measure on the table. "Can you say nothing?" But as he spoke he shut his eyes and raised his brows as though to ward off speech. When he opened them again, he did not look at Will. His words came cold and precise.

"My lady and her sister were in my care. When, tired and out of patience, I sent for you, two birds had flown. What could I pretend? I said nothing. I fulfilled what courtesies were left and then, by the devil's codpiece, I fell into a rage. My steward wished to make inquiries but I refused. What cared I? Yet, by Jason's teeth, sir, I did not sleep last night!"

He paused, then, most subtly, his expression changed. He even smiled. He drew in a long breath and said softly, "Toward dawn she sent a message." He hesitated for a moment, then he added with a strong hint of lubricity, "What a queer token you had for her, sir, if I understand it rightly. Not what I fancied at all—if it is clear to me." Now his eyes drew at Will. "But of course she may not have told me all . . . I have a taste for guessing." He paused. "Do you wish to speak?" Will shook his head. "Let me not inhibit you, sir. From one poet to another a gloss is admissible."

Will looked at him, smiling faintly, and shook his head again. Lord William raised his brows in irritation. He said coolly, "I am still affronted—but she sent me something else. Can you guess?"

"No, my lord."

"What would soften my anger? Know you not?"

"No, my lord."

"Why, two sonnets. She swears they were written by you and sent to her . . . not poems, i'faith, to woo a woman . . . but *poems*." He curled his lovelock over his finger in an abstracted way, and spoke with an intimateness so strong that he seemed reluctant to lift his eyes. "Are you married? Have you wife, children, a quail or two?"

Will found his voice. "I have a wife and two daughters."

"By God! I never wondered. A man, like all . . . Eh?"

Will did not answer. Lord William glanced up briefly.

"So please your lordship."

Lord William frowned and smiled. "I knew thee well." He thought of this, still smiling, and then from under the restraining weight of a bronze hand that stood on the table, he took several sheets of paper. He spread them out before him. He seemed to study them for a moment, his fingers stroking the edges. Then, not glancing up, he said, "But perchance, I did not . . . These are the sonnets." He read:

> "Th' expense of spirit in a waste of shame
> Is lust in action; and till action, lust
> Is perjur'd, murd'rous, bloody, full of blame,
> Savage, extreme, rude, cruel, not to trust;
> Enjoy'd no sooner but despised straight;
> Past reason hunted; and no sooner had,
> Past reason hated, as a swallowed bait,
> On purpose laid to make the taker mad—
> Mad in pursuit, and in possession so;
> Had, having, and in quest to have, extreme;
> A bliss in proof, and prov'd, a very woe;
> Before, a joy propos'd; behind, a dream.
>   All this the world well knows;
>   yet none knows well
>   To shun the heaven that leads men
>   to this hell."

He did not glance up, the silence waited for a moment. The sonnet, as private as a bed, lay in the public way. Lord William moved his hand to another sheet and his voice took up the words.

"When my love swears that she is made of truth,
I do believe her, though I know she lies,
That she might think me some untutor'd youth,
Unlearned in the world's false subtleties . . .

". . . hum . . . hum . . . hum . . . it comes back to you?
And then at the end,

"O, love's best habit is in seeming trust,
And age in love loves not to have years told.
Therefore I lie with her, and she with me,
And in our faults by lies we flatter'd be."

His eyelids flickered as though to look up, but he did not. His hand moved to another sheet. Will forbade all feeling. Lord William's eyes traveled across the lines, reading them soundlessly and blowing through his lips. Only at the end did he give breath to the words.

"Past cure I am, now reason is past care,
And frantic mad with evermore unrest;
My thoughts and my discourse as mad
    men's are,
At random from the truth vainly express'd;
For I have sworn thee fair,
    and thought thee bright,
Who art as black as hell, as dark as
    night."

He sighed, his hand remained spread out, his eyes lowered.

"Excellent. Excellent. What felicity: 'Had, having, and in quest to have . . .' " He looked up slowly and his eyes seized Will and would not let him go. "I had no idea . . ." A faint smile took over and it joined his eyes in watching Will.

Only a dumb dignity was left to Will, and a death's joke: that unicorns were betrayed with trees and men with sonnets.

Lord William said, "My affront still rankles. But I must praise thy meter and thy metaphors. Excellent, excellent, though scarcely an homage. Yet . . . exciting. I sense these would seduce. Ah, my anger is cooled and my astonishment heated." He smiled more candidly. "Yet, tell me, there is such an age and difference—servant and lady—yet God knows"—he smiled more openly—"men do not think of such things when the fever's on them. Yet other times, did you not give mind to that? That age of thine and her position? It was this made me start at first . . . until I saw that I must equate man and man. Well, speak!"

Will found a hoarse voice. "My lord, it was I, a year ago, asked you to speak to her for me."

Lord William frowned, still smiling. "Speak what?" Will stared. "What?" The smile faded. "By St Priapus!" His eyes moved over Will as cool as a lake. He said softly, "A woman's love is a trifling thing. Take care. See that it does not come between thy good service and my love."

Now Will, for his honor's sake, must rise and go. He saw how Lord William's brain had, long ago, subdued all moral sensibility and become a law unto itself. He began the move of rising.

Lord William said coldly, "When I give thee leave thou mayest go." He opened a drawer of his desk and put away the sonnets. Then he leaned back and fondled the bronze hand. "If you buy ladies' flesh with any coin, you cannot preserve it from tainting . . ." He studied Will again, with no charm of any kind, coolly interested in another man's passion. "Did you know she is with child?"

After a moment he laughed shortly. "Tongue-tied? Cock's pie, what can you say? Who might the father be? I? Another?" He hesitated. "To please oneself on her does not require one to carry her abroad. She flinched not. By Venus, I'll have no bastards. Let her cry. I will have none of her, and lesser man cannot."

A sharp pang broke Will's icy sheath. Poor lass, poor lass. Here was the man she loved. And that man, impervious to pain, gave her pain, as indifferent as those who cut up animals to test their suffering.

Lord William drew a box toward him. "She weeps to me. Let her whistle. Her brother will take her away—who knows how oft her glass hath cracked—and she'll outlive the scandal."

Will, by a profound effort, rose. The watch Lord William wore on his doublet struck the hour. Lord William looked up with surprise and said agreeably, "So thou art on thy way to the dread Scots. I'faith, greet our King." His eyes held some of the old melting look. He opened the box and took from it a jewel in the form of a daisy, so artful a work it might have danced in a meadow. He rose and held it out to Will.

"From one countryman to another. Perdy, I would give a year of my life to ride across a bonny field when the dew is fresh and the lambs are on the hills. Remember me when the lark sings. And now, a long farewell."

But Will would not take the jewel. "The essential is the only best, my lord."

The journey took two days. Will wished to remember none of it save bird on the wing, fish in the stream, worm in the earth, bud on the tree, sudden shower and sun's quick amends. For they alone would not quarrel with the strife in his soul.

The creation of revenge is a manmade dark where man illumines himself. There his skull glows.

Gus rode beside him, savoring the melancholic wonder of the future. "Will we meet again?" Gus asked.

"Aye. In heaven or hell."

"What if I am bound for hell and thee for heaven?"

"I? Heaven? 'Tis thou, Gus, must hold fast and not let *me* go." He fancied that the damned paid for revenge more than any other sin. Unless it be murder, which stood as close to lust as flame to smoke. . . . Paid with unassuageable remorse.

London was farther than the moon. Each hour drew them deeper into a world where the seasons were the time; where a man lived and died by autumn, winter, spring, and summer. Ahead of him stood his wife.

In the hedges were the hawthorne buds and crab apple; the sloe was tight with blossoms. Along the roadside, violets and primroses were hints of flowers.

At length the Cotswold hills gave place to the Vale of Evesham, and black-and-white houses started up from the fields. Warwickshire was a heart, it was a state of grace. It was his innocence.

Gus watched Sam and Ned cavorting by, playing tricks on the hedgerows and shouting in raw bursts of song. "Five months ago we rode along this very place."

Will attempted to reply but did not. Jamie and Edmans had fallen into a pond and were fishing themselves out to the scoldings of Dickon and Heminges. Gus glanced at Will and presently put his hand on his shoulder and so rode along.

Poor lass, my lady, how perjured am I now to put the blame on thee.

BOOK TWO

CHAPTER *One*

TOM GREENE sought out Anne in the yeling house where the ale was made. He stood a dark figure against the lighted door. She turned her head toward the dark, strong form and smoothed back the hair under her cap. She smiled at him, though she could not see why he hesitated.

The yeling house was filled with strong and pungent smells. It was not conducive to reflectiveness. He came in slowly and picked up the roasted orange that she had been sticking full of cloves to hang in the vat. He turned his swarthy bearded face and said, "The London courier brought a letter from Will. He will be home."

"Ah!" She turned and leaned against the vat. The light from the door made her blink. All she saw was the bright color of Tom's sleeves. He was not looking at her but down at the folded letter. "What has happened? When will he come?"

"He does not say what has happened. But he will be here almost as soon as the letter."

"Ah," she said again, and she was aware that his eyes were studying her.

After a moment he said in his deep voice, "What are you thinking, cousin?"

She gave him a fleeting look. "Why, that my husband will be in his home."

He waited for a moment. "Nothing else?"

Now her glance was even more fleeting. She turned so that she did not have to face the light, and they stood side by side, he not taking his eyes from her. Presently she said, very low, "I wish I knew what he will say and do."

Now Tom spoke in a different voice, as though she must be commanded by him, "You have opened your heart to me. Because you trusted me? Because you loved me, cousin? The man who went away last autumn was beyond your reach, you said." She started to speak, but he went on, his strong voice mastering her. "Well, I think that is what you will find again. Let me speak, cousin, for it is better that you know. I said very little when I returned from London, for I scarcely knew what to put in words." She stirred. "He is a man for whom blood and judgment do not mingle in harmony and self-control." He was silent, and then he put one hand lightly on hers. "There it is. He lives a poor life in London."

"What did thee see! What do thee wish to say?" Her voice was hard.

"I saw that his private life is spent with whores and boozies; his public life with depraved nobility."

"Ah! I do not know what that means!"

"I will tell you what it means——"

"No. I do not wish to hear!"

"I will tell you!"

"No! No!"

His hand closed on hers violently for a moment, then he walked away. But she was aware that he stopped and studied her. "Ask Ned, then," he said softly, "though I think he told me in his agitation and was sorry afterward."

"What! What!" she said.

He answered somewhat sullenly, "A girl, dressed as a boy, has access to his room. And any watcher could tell you of the nets into which he willingly thrusts himself."

She turned in a fury and flung her voice at him. "Be silent! Who hath not sinned? That thee know right well! Who can judge the souls of others?"

"I do not talk about his soul," said Tom quietly.

"Nor reproach them when we ourselves are so imperfect!"

He came to her and put his hands on her shoulders. "Cousin, be advised. Thou too must find some moderation."

"Oh!" She looked at him, her whole body shivering. "Oh, moderation. We are so much more than our foolish ways!"

"Aye," he said after a moment and kissed her gently. "Do not reproach me. Be advised of thy husband. He is not a simple man. Returning at this untoward season suggests some matter out of joint. The mischief that I saw has perhaps been compounded. We do not know. In love and prudence I counsel great discretion. Give him no cause to turn on me or you. Give him no cause to hide his malady."

She looked at him for a moment and smiled with some irony. "Thee be a *man*, Tom, all in all." She put her cheek briefly against his hand which still rested on her shoulder. "Well, that be a good thing, I have no doubt."

He drew away from her, and she looked up at him. "Now thee be angry and I would not have it so." He seemed to wish neither to go nor to stay, and she said softly after a moment, "Why did thee wish to stir me up?"

He answered now with real anger. "So that you do not make yourself a fool!"

She whispered, "I will try to take good care of all foolishness, past or present."

There was some disappointment among the lads that such a fine cry of players did not unfurl their banners, sound their trumpets, and ride into Stratford like the kingship they were. But something understood kept their banners furled. A prudent sobriety would be the best service to Will, who owned the second largest house in Stratford, was the second richest man in town, and had here no need of disguise.

As the dusk fell, they crossed Clopton Bridge with an untidy clatter. The Avon, tenderer than time, flowed beneath them. In the twilight, an ancient man at the bar-gates clutched a small boy.

"That be Wully Shaxper, zur? Ho!"

Ahead of them, on Middle Row, lay Burbage's Tavern, belong-

303

ing to some cousin or other who performed rituals and rites of libation at such times as Richard Burbage returned to Warwickshire. Here they would be privately and decently dined as friends of the second richest man in Stratford. Thus the ambiguity of a situation could have both its ins and its outs.

"Welcome home," said Dickon to Will with a sidelong look. "Be our shepherd, and put us under thy rod, so that we do not disgrace thee." As he spoke he looked so lordly that Will had only laughter.

Ned did not get off his horse. "I'll tell Anne thou art here, and then I'll go home."

Will nodded and smiled. "And kiss Nan well."

Dickon let his voice ring in the twilight, calling for Cousin Burbage, praising the sweet air of Warwickshire, though old Francis Smith's midden pile at the next door took away some of the force of his panegyric. From the stocks a voice shouted a greeting, and Will went across to greet the poor fellow whom the gaoler had left in the dew, feet and hand fast. They shook hands, though poor old Tim Perry was more impeded than Will.

The gaoler came out hurriedly with his key to unlock Tim to his supper and to see who talked with him.

"Why, it be Mr Shakespeare his own self! Ah, Wull, clasp me in arms and mind me of rogues in London!"

The market clock above them drowned out words in its toll of greeting. Dick Quiney, knowing an old friend by a change in air, came out from his shop and grasped hands with proper feeling.

"Have you brought news?" he asked anxiously.

"Ned Bushell and Robin Catesby have been let off with a fine. But Westminster you're thinking of."

"Aye, but glory to God, clemency may blow a good breeze onto Stratford."

"Stratford. Home."

"And welcome!"

Oh, it is a spell of great power, to find thy way home again.

Will rode in the dusk down High Street with Gus and Heminges beside him. A few yards, and home. It was a terrible, long corridor between two doors, with dark above, behind, ahead, below.

In the gloaming, the Gild Chapel rose at the end of the street. Before it was his house with its high gables and three sharply pitched roofs, its handsome wooden fretwork, its brick and timber walls. It was seal and symbol of place in the world. Through the high, mullioned windows, light shone onto the cobbled street.

They clattered to a halt. The door opened and Anne stood framed in the way.

Will came in with a splendid air of "Kiss me all! Why now, how's my sweet chuck?" and the low-timbered parlor took on the animation of homecoming.

Here was all clear light, no shadows. Here was a most subtle sense of the green air of trees. Here no one was personalized. Here all was high and shining. All the pewter plates and vessels on the dresser danced and shone together as though they had an independent life.

"Oh, sweet lasses, kiss thy dad. Ah, Susanna, a lady grown fair and rosy! Judith, my sweet wren, thy childhood's gone! Kiss me again for dear remembrance' sake."

They kissed and clung. With them on his arms, he kissed Anne, cheek to cheek, he kissed Nan Fuller, the maid. Anne kissed Heminges and Gus. Will embraced Tom Greene and Hamnet Sadler, who lived three doors away.

Heminges and Gus kissed all who would be kissed, for they were healthy Englishmen and to kiss was to salute the soul. Anne asked for their wives—she called them Agnes and Rebecca, for she had known them fondly when she had stayed in London before the death of her son—and each child was inquired for, and the new ones described.

The dog was greeted who had wagged his tail from one embrace to another. The cat, who had leapt from chair top to chair top and now crouched with rump raised, was stroked behind the ear. In the window the old magpie with the faulty wing hopped and screamed and her soft brow was cajoled.

Oh, he thought, it was a homecoming as charming and sentimental as a song.

305

Ale and sesame cakes were brought out, and the fair, rosy Susanna sat as close as lichen, smiling into his face. When she asked if he had brought any presents, he cheerfully remembered his saddlebags. Judith and Tom Greene hurried out to bring them in and to make sure that the stable boy had tended the horses.

Judith let the bags slip down beside her father and lingered, scarcely smiling but not wishing to go away. Will took her hand, his shy, lost, half-twin lass, and she smiled guardedly.

He rummaged for gifts and presented them in couplets which were not his most felicitous. For Judith there was a gold brooch, and for Susanna a ring for her least finger; for Nan Fuller a silver pin to wear on Sunday, and for Anne, a poking stick of steel to stiffen the pleats of ruffles not much worn in this half-Puritan town: a gift twice wrong which his blind fool, Paradox, had persuaded him would say both all and nothing to his wife. Or, to be more frank, I chose it because I dared not think at the last.

Anne became suddenly the exact center of his awareness. Though reluctant to make her real, he saw a fair woman of medium height, standing very still with the poking stick in her hands. Her gown was of blue cloth with no farthingale, her apron and her falling collar were white, and white was the cap which closely fitted her fair hair. But he saw no more than that. He kept quite away from her heart or her thoughts.

He embraced her again gaily, and she kissed with spirit. But when she laid the poking stick on the sideboard, he could not read her expression. She smiled at him in her soft sidelong way much as did his daughter Judith.

Will followed her with secret looks, this woman who had beset the underwards of his life. *Lost, changed.* Here in this familiar place, such words failed in meaning. His eyes moved against his will to Tom. He saw Tom glance at her and smile. He saw Tom go up to her as though some subtle overture were understood.

An incontinent trembling seized him. The smell of lavender rose from the rushes and the fire. His need was intolerable to be reassured into peace, as intolerable as his lungs' need for air. He saw Anne go into the kitchen and Tom follow her.

What would he have done had he not been caught in the net of homecoming? He blessed God he did not know. Hamnet was so glad to see him, so warm, that he was enveloped in old love and friendship. Gus and Heminges stood like benign household gods warding off calamity. All these were family men: all, all understood the sacredness of the hearth, but how many of them had kicked at the fire?

Susanna still clung like a vine; her arm was through his, her head on his shoulder. Whenever he moved she moved with him, and he smelt the sweet scent that rose from her cap. Judith had gone toward the kitchen: he saw it; he saw all, he thanked God.

Presently his father and his brother Gilbert came in, and with the embracing and kissing that ensued, one might have thought that Will had returned from the far parts of the world.

He held his father by the arms and looked with the searching eyes of love at the gay weathered face with the bright blue eyes. This man was the map of his childhood. From this man he had derived both strengths and weaknesses. Oh, the yeasty life of his father; had *he* kicked at his hearth? (Should he send his father to see what his wife was doing?) His father's life had been filled with the low-blue of his Celtic soul and the high-red of his public spirit. He had held the greatest honors in the town. He wore the thumb ring of civic office, and had become a gentleman with a coat of arms, though born a farmer's tenant. But none of this explained his life to his son. He alone knew it, end to end, and he kept its secrets.

His father said his mother sent her love, and since she seldom stirred abroad, and moreover had her baby, Ned, at home tonight, she would kiss him by-and-by. Gilbert, who was a man of great taciturnity, clasped hands and nodded, listening with his head crooked to one side as his father asked many questions, most of them about the great Earl Essex. The London courier, Greenway, had brought alarms and raw tales. Sadler drew near to listen, for great events might in some way stir the waters of the Avon.

They talked with great animation in short unfinished sentences. *Where is Anne, so long out of sight?* He was about to whisper to Susanna to fetch her mother when Judith and Nan brought in

307

fresh ale and honey cakes, and Anne the sack for his father. Will's relief sucked in his breath.

"Ah, old dad, sack and all! Like lord of the manor he rules!"

And Tom? Ah, there was Tom, slipping in, so grave and sure.

"Aye," said John Shakespeare, kissing his daughter-in-law. "Here be my doting daughter who knows how to keep well with an old gaffer. Enjoy your cold ale, all," and he drank the hot wine with lip-smackings and loving down-glances at Anne.

Will too glanced at her. She had the winning soft ways of Susanna—or should he put it the other way around? Bright, knowing eyes, and quick smile, but not dissimulating; no, clear and honest, unless there was no trust anywhere.

His troubles fell away. He talked thirteen to the dozen while at the same time, in that mysterious way known only to the searching heart, he watched them all: Anne, where she moved, Tom, where he stood now by the fire talking to Heminges with frowning intentness, the daughters in their eager pleasure; he watched for any sign of secret meanings. Three nights ago, at this hour, he had been dragging a woman to his revenge in the filth of a black night.

It blackened this moment, though God, in His mercy, had brought him home.

He heard bits of talk: his father to Judith, "Oh, what a nice brooch. Put it on, dove." "No." "Then let me eyepiece it. Mightn't it be lost, this fainty pin, in thy pocket?" "No, never." And Gus to Anne: "Mistress, I shall go hence in debt. Keep my friend well and beside you, and when we come for him again, I will thank you heartily." "Is aught the matter that you come now?" "Why, no great matters. He will tell thee . . . Earl Essex." "Would you say more to me?" "Oh, mistress, in all things we need our courage." Will could not keep his glance from turning. He saw—what?—alarm swarm into her eyes.

"I reckon, Will," said Hamnet, "that thee do know the court as well as any man who be not courtier. We've sat here all the winter in the cold and snow, waiting for those great caterpillars at Westminster to give some answer. Have thee one?"

"No. But it will come."

Hamnet cried passionately, "Where be good faith? Nay, look

what us have: villages decayed, men walking roads, slip-string, men of trust crooked, rights and privileges cast down by neglect and greed, and what in their place? Our black lord!"

John Shakespeare glanced at Will. "Peace, Hamnet. Our Will hath still in his ears the clash of wickedness in high places. Let him rest tonight with the decent ways and means of home."

Hamnet put up his hands. "Oh, aye. Enough. Well then, good night. Sweet dreams. Blessings on the house."

In time John went too, and the daughters to bed after many jokes and kisses.

The travel-stained men bathed in tubs of hot water in the kitchen. Then Gus and Heminges went into a goose-feather bed with flax sheets, and all over the house were the sounds that promised a quiet night.

Will lay in his bed listening. No violence came to him, no brutal noise from the streets, no reek of offal . . . only the sunlight in the linen and the lavender in the pillow casings . . . the only sounds wind in the fruit trees and a creaking window silenced by a careful hand.

Lying in his bed in the central chamber where the goodman of the house might lightly hear all that passed and call a warning if danger came . . . Will had half forgotten what it meant to be such a man. Peace? Guilt bound and gagged perhaps; sleep disguising countless woes. Time laid low. Firelight on the ceiling, that token of home and comfort. Why does my wife not come . . . ?

Anne entered the chamber with her candle. He struggled to lift his head and speak to her but the heavy hand of sleep crushed him down.

She stood unlacing her bodice as she looked down at him.

CHAPTER *Two*

THE sunrise bell from the Gild Chapel came through his sleep. He listened to it with his eyes still closed, and to the rise of the rooks cawing against the bell; then to a softer sound, the hour striking. Home . . . He turned in the bed and found himself alone. He lay very quietly for a time, studying the indented pillow where his wife's head had lain, and the empty chamber which she had left.

Where were the raucous sounds of London morning? And the blackness of himself and Lord William, both filthy with revenge? Faint, without force, and far away. Oh, God, was he truly safe?

If he did not think of past woes, of remorse and shame, might he wipe them out? Might his salvation be as simple as that? Early morning held both despair and hope. He had only one vexation; he had not truly looked at his wife. How could he, corrupted as he was?

He rose and went to the mullioned window. Below the window was the garden and beyond the garden was the lane, and by the lane ran the mere which fed the walk-mill by the Avon. The mist that came up the valley had laid soft billows on the early day. Across the lane was the square Gild Tower.

The one-handed dial of the clock on the tower told the time, and the odd little weathercock on the tower told the turn of the wind. Outside the small shop at the base of the tower, the tenant walked up and down watching Will. When Will looked down he waved to him.

In the kitchen, Anne was stirring pottage by the fire, and Tom Greene was sitting with his breakfast. Will heard them as he came to the door.

Anne said, "I think not. Do not say that, Tom!"

Tom replied, "Sh-h-h," for Will came in.

Will kissed Anne on the cheek and she kissed him. Her lips were warm from the fire. There was a tangy smell to her cheek, and the faint scent of myrrh which she used to clean her teeth. It was all sharp in its curious intimacy and Will put his hands on her arms. She stood quietly, her glance, out of those dark eyes, moving on his face. He kissed her again.

Tom Greene was watching. Not stealthily but nonetheless from the corner of his eye, his heavy, handsome face impassive. Will glanced covertly from one to the other, and he did not say to Anne what had been on his tongue to say. Instead he said abruptly to Tom, "Shall we have reckoning of stiles, fences, crops, grass, apples, plums, sheep, and sundries before the day proceeds?"

Tom nodded. "Very good."

Then, compelled in some way he chose not to examine, Will said that he had brought home his money. New things would be bought and done. He did not name the amount but he let them know that it was a goodly sum, for he went on to say with a stiff economy of words that he spent nothing in London save for room and food. The omitted words hung in the air: that he led a circumspect life away from home, that the welfare of home, lands, and family was first in his thoughts.

Tom Greene looked at him and a shadow passed across his eyes.

Tom and Will went into the garden while the day was early. The sweetness rushed to Will. He stopped and made a gesture of greeting. Tom smiled, but not as a kin soul; more as a man who felt greater confidence in pound, pence, and yield as source of blessing.

He said, "The corn is laid, alack, lodged by a tempest. But 'twas no great loss, for I have planted mostly pasture. And see you here, how well the plums have blossomed."

"Aye." Will stood tentatively beneath the trees and looked up into the faint and roseate blue of the plum against the sky, at the apple and the cherry, opening slightly, and Tom brought his attention to the good grapevines, and to repairs in hay barn and stable.

Will shook hands and embraced the stable boy, the cowmaid, Simmy, the old gardener, and Charles, his boy, and told good jokes to all. Old Simmy gabbled in an angry fret of what he had planted and would still plant by moon and sun in his own way, and shot bridling looks at Tom. Tom shrugged. Will laughed.

"Plant to mine honor, Simmy, and let nettles grow where they will."

Then he put his hand against the barn's wattled wall to take full account of repairs. To all these signs of Tom's diligence, he directed those slow appropriate nods which are the honored substitutes for speech.

Tom said in a pleasant cool way that if God spared them the brief white frosts of middle spring, or hailstorms, there would be fruit to sell. Old Simmy said that pruning right had more to do with it. Will reconciled them both, and turned toward the kiln house. As Tom paced slowly beside him, Tom went on to say that now or sometime he wished to give an accounting of Will's holdings of corn and malt so that the Council, which was murmuring against hoarding, would be brought to see the matter straight.

Will only half listened, for Lord William's voice had come to him. *She need not cry to me.* Oh, lass, lass! Tom waited. Will said, "You are a lawyer. I thank you for all."

In the kiln house and the yeling house, Tom went on to talk of malt which had no charm of its own and was made to have none. Will listened with the mind beneath the surface, knowing, from his boyhood, what all this meant and finding in such summation of worldly goods and slight tiddling with the law, an element of that same relief which had taken him last night. He paused to look at his hereditaments with a hungry eye. This house had been built by a Lord Mayor of London a hundred years ago to honor himself in his own town. Will had passed it every day on his way to school; it was now past, present, and future safe under his lock and key. These orchards, this Great Garden going down to the river—he glanced at Tom and saw in his face a reflection of his own possessiveness, that same wonder that Adam must have felt with his first hut of straw.

In the garner house Nan was turning pickled nuts. She laughed because he was going so early about his business, and she so early about hers. He called her a fair lass, and she stood in the door for a moment longer, her hair tumbled under her cap, not yet fit for the day. Her hands were reddened and slender, and she gestured with a raw beauty as she told him where she would put the herbs of grace, the hot lavender and mints and savory had she her way, and the violets, marigolds, and sweet Cicely for salads. The sun lay on her face and she closed her eyes and put out her tongue to lick the warmth.

Argos, the dog, pushed his muzzle into Will's hand and then stood with his paws against Will's chest. Across the lane in the straw-thatched barn, cows were lowing, and in the mere, ducks were swimming to the river. The voices of girls rose in the croft, and smoke was going up from many chimneys. Presently the Sunday bells would ring.

These were all the sounds that framed a state of mind called *home*. It was composed of generalities, sentiments, and ambiguities. Tom said, "Shall we go now to the hundred acres?"

"Aye," said Will promptly, "let us confirm and capture this good life."

The dog danced, and the stable boy brought his muzzle. "Alas, poor Argos," Will comforted him, "all the do's and don'ts of man."

"Yet with a better meaning," Tom said softly, "than in London." He looked at Will directly, his dark eyes studying him, as Will was suddenly aware. He did not ask him what Tom meant; he knew. He had not forgotten Tom's soft cold diatribe against a filthy life. Tom went on, still with his eyes on Will. "Heminges says it is Earl Essex who has sent you home."

"Yes. And great mad foolishness in high places."

"Stratford is a place to wipe men clean?"

Will felt Tom's probing fingers. He looked at him suddenly. "Tom, let there be no ambiguities, no setting on—in the name of God."

Tom turned away, his expression showing nothing. "I set on nothing but thy ledgers, leases, rents, entails, and suits," he said coldly. "I am, if I may say so, a good steward."

The coldness heated Will.

"Then, cobbler, mind thy last!"

He had not meant to speak so sharply, but let it stand! Let all things stand, bad and good, till God the Father harvested the wheat. But, dear God, 'tis only spring!

Tom, with his gaze fixed ahead, said quietly, "Will we be friends, or not?"

Will groaned a laugh. "Friends and kinsmen till death do us part!"

In the doorway Anne had come to watch them go. They did not see her and she did not call to them, but Will turned. She put up her hand in farewell, and he kissed his fingers to her. The early sunlight on his fair skin and russet hair made him look almost a boy, she thought; it wiped away the lines beside his eyes, leaving only the hazel look.

Up Chapel Street shutters were being opened and doors unlocked to bring in the day. Will had gone down this street to school and to church. He had known it when heavy with mud and when the cobbles had been laid. Each house was a friend; none need go a hundred yards hungry or unaffectioned. Few on this street had been farther than Warwick. He knew all their names and ways, their tempers, their spirit, their tastes, their loyalties, their humaneness, but this was not necessarily a fit preparation for the terrors of life.

Mrs Shaw had just thrown the slops surreptitiously out the window (the law being dead set against such acts). She clapped her hand over her mouth, giggled, and reached far out to shake his hand.

"Don't blobchop on me, Wully, I hear tell thee bist come and how be the Queen?"

"She is well as can be expected for a woman who lives in London. She sends her warm greetings to one and all."

"Aaa, that be real heartening, Wully, and thee tell her same." Smiling and nodding she drew in her head.

Not many were in the street, it being the sabbath, but close by the windows were the householders who kept an eye on passing life.

"Why, there be Will!" . . . "Aaa, Wully, butty! Shake me hand!" . . . "Willy, Willy, go thee by with not a word? Come in, there now, and have a pot of ale." . . . "Aaa, I told Bess thee'd be nippin' by and keep a good watch out. Say, Tom?" . . . "Come thee not home a lord, look? Why Dick Quiney and Tom sez thee hobbed with great, wearing thy coat of arms like a smock." . . . "A' thankee, Wull—I still take in me belly-timber though I caunt walk furthern High Cross." . . . "Ah, Will, Will, dolorous times—sure the world's sins is heavy nor God's hand on we. I a' pain in me shoulder, martle bad."

He paused, shook hands, kissed, gave and took, let his ears rejoice in the country speech, yet knowing that every year some waited to see if he wore city airs.

At the High Cross he paused. To go up Henley Street, which was the convenient way to his hundred acres, would be to pass his parents' house, and he did not yet wish to see his mother. He must meet her in the full light of day when he could eye her as closely as she eyed him.

He leaned against one of the pillars which supported the wood and plaster house surmounting the headless cross. At this heart of the town he smiled a little and glanced at Tom. Lord, how their wills met, his mother's and his, how tight she held the secret of her power. He must have the heels of his feet on the ground when she asked her first questions; he must be sure of himself, his confidence without a seam. His smile turned up his mouth. He and she always met with a clash; this put a spur to him which gave more interest than if she were merely a quiet mam. But he could not look to her for comfort; that he knew, and comfort was much needed.

He resolved to go the long way to his hundred acres. Across the road was Condell, pacing back and forth in the sun before the tavern, throwing up his head and lowering it, declaiming under his breath—cramped in this narrow road before the inn. Jamie and Edmans were with him, though playing knucklebones by themselves. Will called, and they greeted him with glad cries. It had been a long separation.

Condell fell into step, his hands clasped behind him, pleasure covering his large handsome face, and the boys raced each other in an esoteric kind of way. Condell's voice did not fit conveniently into a narrow street, but Will thought, Let any bait players and they must bait me. That will give someone a start in his breeches!

They went on down Wood Street. Old Sturley leaned out his window in his night smock and demanded a handshake. He

315

gave them an ode of Horace on the delights of the day. It was delivered in the joyful Latin that old Sturley considered the language of friendship.

Around the village pump a few girls were washing their hair for church, and there too was Ned. He sat at the foot of the Cross, a golden smiling lad. He was talking, singing, showing off, and the girls were answering him as they had done all their lives. All were satisfied. A friend of Susanna ran up to Will dripping like a mermaid for a kiss. She wore a love token and was glad to tell him who had given it and when the banns would be read. Jamie and Edmans lobbed discreet lumps of clay at Ned and the Cross.

Ned sprang up and joined them. He flung his arm about Will and Will about him.

"Content, dear lad?"

"Well, here I've got no master lying on my shoulders."

"Thy teething ring—did our mother bring it out? And how's she?"

"Well. Say! Bidford won Shrove football from Stratford! . . . Mother waits for thee."

"Baby's not enough for her?" Ned aimed a blow and ran on, racing the lads. The bells were ringing again as they came into the meadowland. The sun lay over all with a ravishing commotion of light, and the blackbirds sang.

"Oh, blackies!" the boys cried, and stopped entranced.

Will stopped too. There was magic in the flowers of early spring, the daffodils, the wind flowers, the violets, the primroses, all lifed and limned by light. A thrush rose on a cascade of song.

The fields were laid out in the old fashion of narrow strips; hard to farm, wasteful, but mine own. Last year Will had bought three hundred of these strips which dangled like ribbons from the girdle of the road. He had made a single cash payment. It had impressed himself, his father, his friends, and the Family Coombs who had yielded their hegemony, with their acres, to him.

He did not quite know where his land started but he had the intuition of ownership. Tom Greene set him right by a few yards. Will stood silent, smiling, Ned beside him. The bright wash of day lay over the fields. Beyond them, east, were the greening woods, and west, the downs for cow and sheep, bounded by brown furze and unploughed balks of turf.

Will walked slowly along the road, his head turned toward his fields, accounting more intangibles than hectares and acres, measuring dirt and night and moral squalor against the blessed day. How lovingly the land was adorned. Copses and little streams agitated the feelings with a private emotion all their own. A small jaunty wheatear rose from the shelter of a rock and flew a little way, singing as it flew. He followed it across a field, stepping over the neat furrows. Robins rose from their breakfast.

"Oh, the bobbies!" cried the lads.

"Aye, here as London." He stooped and crumbled earth, letting it fall through his fingers.

Ned sprang ahead, leaping like a country boy. Behind came the others, Tom Greene walking with firm grace over the rough ground, Condell moving like a stalking lord, hobbling like a clown, at length decanting words bottled up too long:

"O, mickle is the powerful grace that lies
    In herbs, plants, stones, and their true qualities:
    For nought so vile that on the earth doth live
    But to the earth some special good doth give."

"Why, what a golden tongue you have!" Will called gaily.

"Will you have more? I can give you a little piece from all his plays. Will, do men truly live in such a place and be content?"

"Aye, for where else do seasons season all for praise and true perfection?"

Condell burst into laughter. "Oh, what a gilded tongue have you, dear master." He stood on a mound and held out his arms as though framing Will. "I've never fancied you in such a part before. I'm struck in amazement. Landowner. King of Compost."

Will did not reply, but he looked at the sky and at the earth, and it was all writ on his face. *If God would be kind and not punish him.*

Tom was speaking matter-of-factly of condition and yield. One field lay fallow, one under winter rye, another under barley, and so on: fallow, wheat, vetches.

317

"Good," said Will, "very good. Well done."

Across the far field a girl walked along the ridge leading a heifer. The sun shone on its dappled hide and on her bare swinging arms. Tom said, "There goes old Prior's granddaughter, and mayhap she's a witch. I keep an eye on old Prior too, for his grazing land is poor by his own neglect and now is flooded and sour. Such times he slips in his cows to graze on thy sweetness."

Will looked grave and forewarned, but when he turned away he was smiling a little, for old Prior knew all the riddles of the countryside, knew where the larks built their cabinets, and he could sing in a bass voice of what the Lord said to Jonah.

A storm had cracked the limbs of a willow tree, and someone had hacked them into lengths. As Tom talked, Will and Ned put them into piles. Over an armful of logs, Will looked at Tom with sudden shrewdness.

"It should be no hardship for my granddad's grandson to preserve this lovely land. Should it now?" He laid on the last logs, and the lads mounted the pile to spread their wings, crow, and fall. "I wish to put a girdle round all mine, till I and mine are safe forever."

"Forever?" murmured Tom.

Will smiled. "A hundred years. There's twenty acres yonder that the Coombses still hold. I'll have it. And across the road, I'll have that too, between the groves, though it be no more than a donkey bite."

"Old Coombs will have *thee*. He's growling at some matters of pound and pence against thee."

Will said comfortably, "I will square accounts." He stood for a moment longer looking at this rich land, with the gentle rise of Cotswolds in the distance. "For I will have all my orchards, gardens, barns, stables, hereditaments, whatsoever, kept intact; all my lands, my fields, my woods, my pleasant walks and arbors, unbroken for me and mine."

Tom said, "Unbroken for two daughters who will need two dowers?"

Will slowly looked at him and slowly smiled. "How shrewd. I had almost forgotten that my son is dead."

Tom tried to make amends. "Has God spoken against a second son?"

A dull flush rose on Will's cheeks, and Condell, stealing a glance, was astounded to see tears in his eyes. With a clogged sort of murmur, Will started back across the fields, striking at the earth with a willow wand. The boys had found a snakeskin and could scarcely credit their good fortune. Ned wandered off to the bound of gorse, and sitting on his heels, watched two long-tailed tits carry feathers and bits of grass to make a nest for their young.

Condell, leaping again among the furrows, sang under his breath a city song called *Shaking the Sheets.* Will said with no expression, "I have also a mind to buy more even than old Coombs can yield. That cottage and small parcel across the mere from my garden, I wish for mine."

"It's a piddling thing," Tom said.

Will replied reasonably, "I have a fancy to look at the river over my own rooftop."

Tom Greene glanced at him. "For that you must swear fealty to the Countess of Warwick, for it is hers."

"Will you see to it, good cousin?"

Tom nodded. He said, "This week, before semiannum comes around, I must talk with you of rents, leases, interests, wines in the cellar, and all accruements that I must give account of."

"Good. I will look forward to that." He would indeed. They were beautiful words.

Church bells were deadly set on them. In the rutty road, Ned and Condell fought a bout with unseen weapons, then Ned ran off to go to church with his family.

Outside of Burbage's Inn, the players sat on a bench in the sun, waiting for their shepherd. They greeted him with loud but decent endearments. The boys showed their snakeskin, which Sam, being some older, took away to keep till after church.

Will marshaled them up and away. Modest and well dressed, they played sabbath parts with perfect competence. Though Sly was slightly drunk he concealed it well, and Armin kept him fast in his gaze.

Will was as conscious of them as of the road beneath his feet.

319

A pack of players in a righteous town . . . his good friends all. He linked arms with Lord Burbage and they proceeded, two English gentlemen.

High Street was full of stir. As though Quiney had been waiting for them to pass, he came out the door of his house and shop in his bailiff's furred robe of scarlet, with his wife Elizabeth who kissed and was kissed by Will, and his son, Thomas Adrian. Henry Walker, chief alderman and deputy bailiff, was almost as grand and glad to see his friends. Will did not go a yard, in fact, without hands to clasp, kisses to give, glances toward his friends to intercept. Elderly women boldly commented on the reckless city life graved on his face, the younger ones took an unfeigned interest in Anne's husband—Anne, poor steady, whose husband left her openly whereas most husbands did so only in their thoughts.

Judith Sadler embraced him heartily when she and Hamnet joined them. She said she had a touch of scurvy but nothing much. "Doctor Hall be a rare hand with scurvy, and so be young Tib a Prior, so I take from twain. Be 'er a witch, think thee? Faith, there be great witchery hereabouts. Yet I trust God."

"Aye, do. That is best," he answered. "There be many strange things that we know not of in our philosophies, but God is highmost."

Hamnet Sadler, ranging beside Burbage, asked him questions of Essex' punishment and consequences. They conversed lowly, and fell out, at length, to walk together.

Dick Quiney, in his scarlet, and Thomas Rogers, the butcher, and Newhall, the constable, and other men, fell out with them, for what Essex had done scarce two months past would be felt in nervous spasms the length of the land. Who could foretell how one's loyalty to established order would be affected, or what great disquiet would send soldiers, frantic for their pay, to haunt the lanes and hedgerows?

Will stopped to gather up his wife, his daughters, his servants, and his two friends. Judith wore her brooch.

"Ah, spiffey," he said to her softly.

Anne walked beside him quietly. This action caught him. Oh,

grace and wonder. Here was his prop and purpose; he was husband, father, householder. This fact could cleanse a man of the smell of pitch. He glanced at her sideways. The sunlight lay on her starched cap and the edge of fair hair, and made a pleasant comment on her complexion. Without looking at her directly, he drew her hand through his arm. Her fingers closed on his arm.

This was safety, her hand on his arm, and distance to keep away foul deeds and rank revenge.

But the talk of fears and famine still went on, too loud for sabbath. "Will the Queen die?" asked Hamnet. "Who steals our wool price that we get so little?" cried Thomas Rogers.

The players were prudent. The cue they had learned by the nature of their business was well learned: that on the tide of men's affairs they rode a leaky bark. Their answers were evasive; Burbage's was given with too much charm. Old Rogers, a fierce Puritan, remembered that these men were actors, of loose minds and faulty judgments, and he said as much, impatient with their answers.

Will started to hum under his breath, and Anne pressed his arm. Dick Quiney spoke soothing words, and Rogers went to walk apart, although he shouted comments on what he could still hear, and presently rejoined them to thrust his head over Will's shoulder and ask if the Queen would die or would she go on as long as sun and moon?

Will said that she was mortal. Burbage added that he believed she had let some passion die with Essex, and with it her sense of destiny and England.

"Who'll come after she?" Sadler asked.

"She says naught."

"Will it be Scottish king?"

"Will it be civil war and strife? Will men be impressed? Four years back, look, soldiers came round church at Easter and bore away all men pert enough to fight."

"If it be Catholic king I will heartily fight," said Newhall, the constable.

Will had nothing to say. He had not come home to talk of involuntary servitude to such masters as cruel times and change.

With his other notorious lacks, he would not lack peace. He smiled, nodded, and turned over his thoughts like a grilling chop.

At this point in the road, those great lay figures, the Family Coombs, emerged from their home which had once been a priests' college. To this scrambled procession, at the head of which was Will and his wife, they gave a lightning glance and bowed with a great crackling of ruffs. Will eased his head from his standing collar and bowed in return, summoning up his charm like quarter-jacks.

Ahead yawned the church door. To assure his peace must be as simple as going through that door. Proceeding down the lane of trees in the mottled sunshine, his friends quiet now save for whispers and old Rogers' voice, the river living and breathing beyond the graveyard, the town unified in the act of worship, were present facts replete with all Christian grace and dignity.

At the church door, Mrs Smith, whose husband owned the tavern next to Quiney, grasped her son Nicholas by the arm.

"Nay, put hat round straight, Nicholas—ah, Mr Shakespeare, welcome—look, afore we go into church."

"Feared of being whisked into the fairy ring?" Will asked sympathetically.

Nicholas looked at him with round agate eyes and a stiff lip.

"Aye," his mother said, "but today be sabbath and no fairies muck about in church. Now there," and she ground the hat onto her son's head.

"Ah, he be a rile lad," said Anne, smiling.

"Ho! It takes every stitchwhile to mind he."

The sound of many feet on the stone floor had an orderly sweetness, like footsteps in heaven. In docile rows at the back Will saw the almsfolk; all the sprightly old heads turned to watch the latecomers, while the beadle roamed, a deadly man for order.

Will's pew was on the south side of the nave, near the pulpit. He marshaled in his manies, while his friends found seats in the public pews. Will sat by the aisle, safe, secure. Across the aisle were the pews of the Bailiff and his Council, and their wives. There sat John Shakespeare in his robe of alderman, but without his wife. Where was his mother? Will looked again, but only Ned, sitting farther back with their brother Gilbert, swiveled his eyes to him solemnly.

By Will's feet, in the aisle, lay buried his predecessor in this pew, and there he too would be buried at the end of his span on earth.

His thoughts were lost for a few moments in a stately contest of pew owners dead and buried, and he scarcely saved himself from laughter. He felt Anne move slightly beside him and he glanced at her to steady his humor. But she was half smiling, and merriment, salted with relief, filled his throat.

To save his decency, he fixed his eyes on the Clopton effigies in alabaster, and waited for the reading-minister to make ready his thoughts. He went with the words of the lesson, joined when the sexton led the responses, waited brightly for the leadership of the small choir in the canticles and metrical psalms, and cast himself with great spirit into the congregational singing:

> The shining Lord he is my light
> The strong God my salvation is;
> Who shall be able me to fright?
> This Lord with strength my life doth blesse;
> And shall I then
> Feare might of men?

When the black-gowned vicar mounted the pulpit for the sermon, Will's spirit had been purged. He listened with fixed attention to the sunlight at the windows, to the fragrance of the wax candles, which cut through the damp smells, to the breathy movements of the congregation, and, by certain spiritual peregrinations, to the words of the Reverend Mr Richard Byfield.

Standing above Will, foreshortened by the pulpit, Mr Byfield was the equivocal figure that straddled past and future. He was not openly a Puritan but he was a terror to recusants. The boarded-up chancel behind him was his natural background. His sermon was vigorous, detailed, abrupt. Will heard a heady promise which he might or might not claim. He closed his eyes. Oh, ape of God, have comfort. Here black sin is wiped away by all repentance of the heart.

323

He was recalled by the thunder of his townsmen's voices.

God gives us strength and keepes us sounde,
A present help when dangers call:
Then fear not wee, lett quake the grounde,
And into sea lett mountains fall . . .
Our rock in Jacob's God we found,
Above the reach of harme.

God take my wonderments, God harmonize my perturbations, he prayed.

He ranged his household in the aisle, kissing and clasping friends as he did so. The players stood in a modest row, hats in hand, but none spoke to them.

Rogers grasped Will by the arm and thrust his face close to his, questioning with his eyes as well as his hissing breath. "If it be the Scottish king who comes after, 'ool he strengthen subsidies, think ye, or ought us prepare petitions now to gie he?"

"Oh, prepare petitions!" Will said urgently, for that would keep them busy for some time.

At the church door, Nan and his daughters broke into a run to see to dinner, and Sam and Ned went after to chase the girls across the grass. Edmans and Jamie vanished into thin air.

In the church porch, John Shakespeare was waiting with Gilbert. Something wonderfully innocent was in the old man's fresh skin and artful blue eyes.

Will and his procession came to a halt before the players, who had redisposed themselves in a neat line just beyond the porch. John Shakespeare went silently down the line of men, grasping each by the hand with no word, but with a little jerk of his head to each. With the last hand, he turned to Will and asked in a low voice, "Come thee now to see thy mother?"

"First I must entertain my friends, father, and see them on the road again. Then I will come directly."

His father said, with no special stress save the quick blinking of his eyes, "She sits at home dead set to wait for thee."

"Give her my love and tell her I will come anon. Dear Joan."
He clasped his sister and her husband, Hart.

"Well, this time it be not plague drive thee home, nor stench of summer. Whatever then?" Joan waited for a moment, her curiosity as sturdy as her little body. When he smiled and wagged her chin, she kissed him again heartily, but gave him a sharp look.

Gilbert waited, very silent, very studying, watching Will with no smile but stepping forward when his turn came. He was a man of thirty-four, unmarried, who scarcely spoke, who dressed skins for his father to make in pretty ways, who listened, read, and kept his counsel. He embraced his brother but said nothing.

He stepped back beside his father, and when John Shakespeare said, "Well, I be off. God be wi' 'ee all," he fell into step without a backward glance.

Meekins, the beadle, acting as whiffler, made way for the vicar, who took Will by the arm and greeted him with a mild detonation. Will knew him as scarcely older than himself, but composed of layers of order, metrical exchange, caution, resonance, sacred theology, and scholarship, while through these stacks of learning gleamed the bright eyes of a man.

As they exchanged their homilies, Will watched an old familiar light gleam in the vicar's eyes and he was obliged to smile, though with some rue. Long ago the vicar had made confession: that he had, when a student at Cambridge, read those two fashionable and lascivious poems *Venus and Adonis* and *The Rape of Lucrece*, and that certain metaphors always leapt into his mind when he greeted this communicant and pew holder, but were kenneled as speedily as possible. He had maintained with great insistence that this mechanism of leap-up, get-down was without emotion, and the light indeed faded even while he held Will's hand and reached for the hand of another man coming through the door. He linked the two. "Master Shakespeare, Dr Hall."

"Aye," said Will, "I have, some months ago, welcomed this gifted man to Stratford. Twice welcome, sir."

The young doctor's face began a smile which reached only to his eyes. He bowed his head and stood looking oddly shy for a young man with such distinction.

"Though young, how wise," Mr Byfield said enthusiastically. "The cries for him come from as far as Alcester and Warwick. He is a jewel, the truly scientific enquirer that no corporate township should be without." As Mr Byfield spoke, his darting glance found the players.

A flush mounted in Dr Hall's cheeks, and he looked with a swift glance at Will, who was smiling.

"Will you not come to supper?" Will said, reaching for his hand.

The doctor bowed. "I wait upon your pleasure, sir."

"Then, tomorrow." The doctor bowed again and smiled more openly. He was a brown young man, brown hair, brown clothes, neither handsome nor plain, of a sturdy and muscular charm.

Mr Byfield seemed scarcely to know what line to take with this handsome, gentlemanly, dignified row of players, blinking slightly against the sun and standing with their hats in hand as though courtesy were their main concern in life.

Presently he lurched toward the profound reality that we are all players in the mortal miming, all wearing the devil's mask until saved by the Redeemer. He said as much and welcomed them with a good stomach, which Will chalked up to his account.

Then Will gave to the doctor the names of these good, kind, loving, decent fellows and observed how he studied the several faces and then, coming to his decision, gave to each his hand. What has he determined? Will wondered with amusement. That we are the marked victims of original sin and therefore the special objects of his mercy?

As the preparations for dinner went forward, Will and his friends walked in the garden, where all decay was honorable and lent to the growing.

He loved this garden without a display of his love. But Heminges knew, and Gus, and they moved quietly along the little sanded paths. At length Gus stood, with his hands clasped behind his back, smiling down at the intricate fancy of the knot garden, palely green.

Gus too, in the body of this death, waited for life. His long thin face had no proliferation of flesh to disguise his longing. Will, sitting on his heels to study the nature of a young vine, saw this expression as he rose. He felt the intensity of sudden recognition. It was almost as though he observed the perfection of friendship for the first time.

He stood by Gus, looking down with him, "Gus, Gus . . ." was all Will said, for he knew how the world contorted all the words and needs of love.

"I thank God you have all this, and your good wife," Gus said. "I will think of all the many ways to be content on our harsh journey into Scotland."

Will said, "Have I done wrong to stay?"

Gus abruptly shook his head. "Peace sits well in your sails. You will tell me of it in rare ways."

"Gus—Gus—I have so much wicked to purge away."

"Aye."

The eating table had been put up and a linen cloth thrown over it. Benches had been set on either side, though the master sat in a chair.

The boys were in a graduated row, the youngest to the oldest. The eldest was Sam and he had effected a complicated arrangement to put himself next to Susanna who sat next to her father. But it did Sam little good, for although she gave him tidbits now and then, her attention was for Dickon, who sat beyond her father and to whom she coursed a witty flow of talk till hushed for grace.

After grace she held her father's hand while daintily managing with her fingers to stuff her little mouth. Her father begged her when he wished to eat. Then she laid her cheek against his shoulder and flirted with Dickon, who responded with such liveliness that Sam ground his teeth.

Will, sharing her little hand, her head, the still childish smell of running and lye soap, felt his heart swell. Her hair tickled his cheek and he laid his cheek against it for a moment, and saw Judith standing by him with a plate of turnips. He raised his head and kissed the hand that held the dish and put his arm around her waist. A flush of happiness rose in her face.

Ned had come so that he might say goodbye to his friends. Everyone was now his friend. His rare sweet smile had become his natural look. Will heard him tell Nan some wild impossibility of London and saw him kiss her soundly. Tom Greene looked at Will with the faint smile that never reached his eyes.

Anne scarcely sat at all. She and Nan and Judith, and now and then Susanna, when eased from her seat by her father, passed food, changed plates, exchanged quips. When Anne sat down it was next to Gus. Her face was bright, her eyes gay. She flirted with him as Susanna did with Dickon. Gus served her from his own plate, putting a choice morsel on her dish, or some tasty bit of salad.

They spoke together quietly, their heads close, their breaths mingling. She asked him guileless questions, putting them with a stammer and a smile, of why they came now from London so early in the year, of how men did and of great lords' demands —and then the full light of her dark eyes left other questions for him to guess and answer.

Gus limped and staggered, leaving her worse than she had been, as he sensed to his dismay. But she was too kind to tell him so, and thanked him with a touch of her hand, saying that to keep a steady house was best for man and wife.

After that he looked at her for a long time from the side of his eyes, though she seemed not to be aware of this.

When the time came for the friends to go, some groaned, some sneezed, some blew their noses, some cursed; only Sly showed a taste for the road. Anne kissed them all. Gus held Anne's hand. "Thou art a good steady. God bless thee." Sam kissed Susanna abruptly and seemed pleased with himself.

There was much wild land between here and Coventry and the roads had, no doubt, disappeared through the winter.

"So it might be well," said Will, as they gathered their gear at Burbage's Inn, "to rest tonight at Warwick and there hire a man to lead you round the sloughs and forest. No Stratford man would know his way."

"It's a damnable cruel life," Dickon said, swinging himself to his horse. "If I come back alive, by God I'll buy myself a little store and bide."

This splendid king of men, this god of London, off to raise his banner among the wild Scots. "A store. Ah, that will be a day to see!"

Heminges embraced Will, comforted perhaps by the store he already owned, and Gus put his arm around Will's shoulder. "Be careful of much," he said, "and love yourself kindly."

"Dear Gus."

They formed a procession so naturally with their laden carts, their furled banners, and their prancing horses that a little crowd was summoned. Ned ran beside them to the edge of town, but Will merely waved. He had a moment's desolation as though it were he who had been left to play a lonely part.

Presently Dickon cantered back, brisk and hurried.

"Old boy, send thy *Hamlet* to me in Scotland."

"Perhaps."

"Try me no further! Fail and there'll be the devil to pay!"

"Win Scotland for the English, Dickon."

"Blast Scotland!"

Quiney had come out of his home to watch, and Cousin Burbage from his inn to wave. Quiney paused. "Look you, Will, what we have here to manage, and Westminster gives us no hope—"

"Dick, I'll stop by-and-by to confound Westminster with you —heartily, very heartily. Now I must go kiss my mother."

"Oh, aye."

Will went slowly up Henley Street. This part of himself he must also face. He said, *Home, home,* as though the words must act with incantatory power.

CHAPTER *Three*

HE crossed the footbridge over the mere. He passed Hornby's smithy and the pair of cottages owned by Wedgwood, the tailor who now stood sewing on his doorstep, right slipper on left foot, and his night smock flowering beneath his jerkin, too busy with the next moment to take much care for the present.

"Ah, Wully, Wully," he gabbled, thrusting in his needle without looking, "Didsy hear Earl Warwick be comin' against we with blunderbuss and old cannon because of croft and Queen be off in her heed?"

"Say! Well, thee'll take thy long needles and I my granddad's old pike and away us'll go."

Wedgwood cackled with laughter, demonstrating a charge with his tailor's needle.

Young Nicholas Smith was swinging on a gate, his sandy eyelashes giving him a cold open look. On the gatepost was an inscription in Latin warning the dormouse to stay the right side of the gate.

Will paused to engage young Nicholas in a further disquisition on fairy rings induced by Nicholas' hat, which was again back to front. Nicholas said some fairies were as big as he. "But I'll know them that they have no feet."

Will said, "Then you have naught to fear. Though mind—never let your mam cut your hair save when the moon is swelling. Then they cannot get bits of it to charm you with."

"Ah?" said Nicholas, curling up his lip. "Be that true?"

"No doubt you are well acquainted, Nicholas, with the writings of Montaigne. He says, 'The evidence for witchcraft appears overwhelming, but I do not believe it because it is incredible.'"

Nicholas promptly fixed him with a stare, practicing his wizardry. Will staggered obligingly and clung to the fence. Then Nicholas swung vigorously on the gate and said, with a flip of his hand toward the neighbor, "Mr a Price was fined a Thursday for midden heap."

"Do you know about Oknos and his ass?"

"No." Nicholas fixed him with his round unshaded look.

"Oknos was condemned through all eternity to weave a rope of hay which his ass ate as fast as he could weave it."

Nicholas rocked with laughter. "Mr a Price be an ass!" He swung wildly on the gate.

"Oh, I tell you no such thing. But when I was a lad, Mr a Price ate up all our outraged efforts as he does now, glad to pay his fines and keep us busy."

Nicholas looked at him shrewdly. "Tell me some more."

Will suddenly felt the eyes of his own mother through his father's shop window. "Another day."

Mary Shakespeare opened the family door to him. She said nothing, but she kissed him and held her hand on his arm as she closed the door. He had the same privilege of scrutiny as she, and looked her up and down, more subtly perhaps but with no less percipience.

She went ahead of him, still silent, her slender figure—and she was as tall as he—moving with an upright grace. Some of her flower scent, which she made in her stillroom, remained like a silk thread to draw him on. She went straight through the low parlor, and the chamber beyond it, and through the little chamber by the back stairs, and into the garden.

Somewhere in the house he heard a person move, perhaps his father or a brother. These rooms were the lacings of his childhood, his adolescence, his marriage. The timber, the lath and wattle, the hooks, the hinges, the splinter pegs of stagbone, the mark of the tools, the finger marks of the craftsmen, were the textures of remembrance.

New Place which he had bought represented a manly resolution, set up for the world's eyes and his own assurance. But this house and home was so bred of bone and blood that he knew if a painted cloth had been added to the wall or a mustard mill taken from the kitchen. This staircase he had trod a thousand times, for his wife and children and himself had, until two years ago, lived in the apartment overhead save those intervals when they were all in London; this garden was their garden, this span of seeing theirs.

The garden was a space of early buds and tender leaves. It stretched the width of the three houses John Shakespeare owned, and reached back to the Gild Pits. It was, as were all loved and tended gardens, the compass of a world.

His mother had turned and was now looking at him as she prepared to seat herself on a rustic bench under the medlar tree. The scent of spring rose from the black earth of the flower beds.

"Thy plants look frem."

331

"They will bear," she said with a little smile.

He bent to a rosebush to examine it for bugs and growth. "Um," he said, "in the autumn this lacked much dunging."

"It hath been sharmed."

He looked at her sideways and smiled.

"Thee and me, we grow good roses."

"Thee and I," she said with an edge of tartness, "grow well whatever benefits us best."

"I'll hear more of that anon," he said, not wishing to at all. "Here is a keepsake for my mother." He took a package from his pouch and handed it to her with a kiss. She opened it with fingers which betrayed her by their trembling, and she drew in her breath keenly. Here lay a cap of blackwork, the red, black, and gold embroidery worked so cunningly into obelisks, architectural designs, scrolls, and flowers that it was a treasure trove of comment.

She shaped it out with her slender fingers. Her eyes were sparkling. "Very pretty," she said, "very pretty," and her caressing hands colored her words.

"Now," he said sitting down, "tell me who has kissed who and why; what Joan has made of her children, how Gilbert fares, where my father has erred."

"Those things thee will learn for thyself. Now let me see thee. Stand up and walk about." He did so good-humoredly, but taking sharp note of the mulberry tree in passing.

"This hath been badly pruned. And who had the pleaching of those hedges?"

"Never mind. Thee hath lost some flesh. Why be thee so pale?"

He laughed and looked at her, sitting straight and elegant with life redolent in her flushed cheeks and sharp eyes. "Why, for sickening after home—and to hear thee rail at me."

"No," she said, "there is something in thine eyes that I like not." He stared at her for a moment from eyes made abruptly blank. "What hath ripped thee?" He was very still. "Some matter at Court . . . or some other thing . . . Or thy cousin Catesby in his sad travail?"

He started, then he laughed abruptly and began to walk up and down. " 'Cousin Catesby,' mother? Robin Catesby does not own me as his cousin."

"Yet he be own cousin to my cousin, Edward Arden."

"Mother, heaven has guarded me well that no one else has known—for Cousin Edward was hanged, disemboweled and beheaded, and Cousin Robin has a strong smell of treason upon him."

She turned and turned the cap slowly in her hands. Then she said in a compressed voice, "Yet they be thine by blood."

He leaned forward to whisper, "Then let us keep it a secret, that naught may come of it."

She flushed slightly, and kept her eyes lowered so that he would not see that tears had come to them. But he knew, for he knew her idolatries. He came and sat on the seat beside her, putting his arm along the back and touching her shoulders with his fingers. "Now confess," he said, "why thou, pretty and healthy as a girl, did play crafty-sick this morning." As he spoke he wished he could withdraw his words, for if he wished honesty from her, he would get it.

She looked at him fixedly for a moment. Then she said, "How could I greet thy motley friends?"

He answered coldly, "Why, as a courteous lady whose good manners act as poncet box between them and her gentility."

"Ah," she said softly, "let us not have hard words of what is done. If I fail in good manners, it is not for want of breeding."

Through the years he had schooled his tongue, and now he sat back, swinging a crossed leg and frowning.

He was invaded by the terrible din and clatter of remembrances which came like untrained dogs to their dinner, and by her extremest need to go through the ritual of what might have been, what has been, what must come after. How she of gentle birth, coupled with a yeoman, had invested her hopes in her eldest son and had spent herself night and day in leading him toward the single aim of lifting the Shakespeare strain as high as the Arden and then carrying it beyond. But when the time came for the

University his father was bankrupt, and when the time came for marriage he was already committed to a woman pregnant three months. These were blows that could be measured only by the terriblest hurt of all, that he became a licensed vagabond.

It all seemed now so old, so lost in life as lived that he wondered only at his mother's failure to find a means to greet his friends. He believed that she would have liked to do so.

For she had faced her life, he thought. She had taken pride in her husband's sure-footed rise (until, by her telling, his Celtish temper and his enemies' devices had toppled him only for him to rise again). She had pride in the son who had, after all, become a poet, found his intimate footing with great men, spoken with the Queen, and might still effect the quartering of Arden arms with the Shakespeares of Bosworth Field. Life had been shaped to a design not unlike the one that she had fancied. It seemed to him, in a rush of insight, that she performed the present ritual almost as a placating gesture, to insure some stability to all the uncertainties upon which decree and rank were raised.

"What do you think if I made a bid to buy the town tithes? Would they not bring something like three hundred pounds per annum?"

"Fie, fie, more." And then she laid it out before him, how this and this carefully invested would yield thus and so much. He had a great respect for her acuteness. She handled money as though its primary function were to multiply, and the mysteries of pounds and pence were as plain to her as the mysteries of her kitchen pans. She sparkled with her careful annotations, and Will unclenched his hand.

Playing a measure on her shoulder, he observed, "Between you and Tom Greene, I will become the richest man in Warwickshire, and you will live to see inherited your wishes."

At that she carefully laid aside her words, as though they were some needlework, and looked at him reflectively.

"Tom Greene. How is it that thee have set him in thy house?"

He was surprised. "Why, that is no secret. To leave so many duties of so large a place unmanned, fields unstewarded, no proper head except in London, was perfect foolishness."

"Unmanned indeed! Why then not Gilbert or even your father?"

"Gilbert does not wish to sit in my place or bear my fardels. This is no surprise to thee, dear mother. We spoke of this when I arranged it so." She raised her brows, then she frowned and sighed deeply. "What do you wish to say with all those sighs and heaves?" he asked reluctantly.

"I do not like Tom Greene. His tongue is smooth. He keeps peace too readily. I judge him guilty."

"Of what, in God's name!"

She hesitated for a moment, and then looked at him with the full effect of her light brown eyes. "I think he would leap into thy office had he half the chance."

"Into my office," he repeated stupidly. And then he asked on a queer breath, "You do not mean with my wife?"

"I mean that I like him not, and I forecast thee must beware."

"Mother, mother, mother, are you casting down my nest and scattering my chicks and calling their dam a whore?"

"Fie on thee! Watch thy tongue. I said no such thing. Nay, though I had no joy of Anne when first thee brought her home, that is Susanna's age away. All the years that we lived in this house together, I saw that she was a good mother and a good wife, however much love we lacked between us. Nay, I ask thee merely why thee set up Tom Greene."

He tried to master annoyance, anger, and a mass of tired old doubt. The anger mastered him. He stood up. "What can thee point to that is wrong?"

She sighed. "He hints. He suggests. He does not speak straight out. When you press him for a clear answer to some confusion, he slips away."

"Oh, fie!" he said impatiently. "You are a daunting woman to some men."

Then she was angry. "God help thee! I have a brain that leads my heart. That I cannot say for thee."

He kicked at the path. With his mother he had no help of anger. With her he must put on a different face if he did not wish to be made into a boy again. "Tom has been most careful of accounts. He has not puffed up himself. He has been very prudent. If he chooses to speak subtly, what is that to me if in money he is clear and open?"

She answered directly. "He has let it be known, with sidelong looks and apt gestures, that a woman dressed as a boy has intimate access to thy rooms in London."

Her words delivered the kind of blow before which he was most helpless. The blood rushed to his head. His rage swept up before he could control it. Heaven had kicked swill into his face. He did not know whom he should hate most, his mother or Tom Greene. He began to speak and stopped. He felt his personality melting under her gaze. He shaped an indignant gesture and did not carry it through. Abruptly he sat down.

"Upon my honor, you have gored me shrewdly."

Her distress leapt into her eyes. "Will, before God, should it not be I that tell thee?"

After a moment he nodded and said with a cheerless attempt at humor, "Aye, if a man be porter of hell-gate, he should have the turning of the key."

She was silent. Then she said, plucking at her new cap and speaking carefully, "Stratford eyes such matters not as London does. Folks are deep set against a codding spirit. A fornicator is known to all." She hesitated. "What I know of thee, I know. Thee hath a certain transparency for me. Speak without fear."

He glanced at her and smiled obliquely. "Oh, madam, I am the blind goose that comes to the fox's sermon." Her head jerked up. "I am afeared of thee."

The color left her face. She looked at him so wanly that his compassion was enlisted. He put her hand to his lips.

"Should *I* step forth to whip hypocrisy? Tom would say that I myself should be cut first. Yet I will take care and see that he does not cheat me by act or hint."

"So I be to thee a fox . . ."

"Dearest, I spoke out of my distemper!"

"I reckon not." To his irritated remorse was added the signs of her withdrawal into that proud loneliness and estrangement which had been her private habitation as long as he remembered.

"Mother," he said softly, taking her stiff hand, "fie upon pain.

Fie upon wounded hearts and woeful pride! I make no doubt that to thee I am as clear as water, as soft as putty. I daresay there is no man more bound to his mother than I." His voice was soft and quiet. "It is you have laid your print on women, and my inmost soul has said that whatsoe'er they wish of me is theirs to have, because my mother says so. Is that not very foolish? That my mother should have taught me such a—codding thing?"

She would not pick up his words. "Thy mother taught thee that a man's estimation of himself can make or mar him. I taught it well. Thee be not marred."

"Mother, mother, what else must I say to thee? Would you have me false to myself? Is it not best I play the man I am, and name my sins, so many and so grievous?"

She refused to yield him a jot. "If thee do not o'erreach thyself with too much striving . . ."

He said with tenderness, "But I learned from you ambition."

"But not dissembling with thy nature, so that that honor which lies with thy friends in London be not thrown down here in this place where thy gentility hath root and branch. Tell Tom he lies in his teeth." Then she added with a smile, "Beat his head below his knees."

He was startled. Then he saw how she was watching him. "Woman, woman, you have a tongue with a tang."

"I'll kindle thee to do it!"

"What must I do?"

"Be very cunning."

"Mother"—he touched his brow—"I do not wear my motley here."

"Good, that is what I mean to say. Forget all motley. Be cunning, shrewd, and untrusting. Thy great friends—"

He was aware again of her iron will that was so much at odds with her pretty ways and soft voice.

"Mother, mother, what are you doing? Do you not know why I came home?"

She was very silent, even her breath seemed still. "Why?"

"Because all my weaknesses sought me out. My flesh, my hopes, my great friends. Mother, the mighty are fallen."

"Do not lie to me. I inform myself of what takes place. Some

337

have fallen—who were not thy bosom friends—but most have not, who supped with thee and asked thee favors."

He felt a dry despair. How could he dispossess her of a treasure that was so worthless? He remembered, not with his mind but with some other part of him, the humiliations inflicted by his great friends, the cool debasements. She was saying in her soft melodious way, "I feared at first for thine involvement when we heard of the great Earl's fall and of thy questionings, but I found out that the ear at court was not turned away from thee, that those who are most powerful still held thee in regard, and why not, since thee be kin."

He was bewildered. "Powerful kin?"

She looked at him with the flash in her eyes that, with her, passed for importunity. She said with no evasiveness, standing it square before him, "Fulke Greville."

He had a terrible desire to laugh or to leave her. For her to threaten such mischief toward him filled him with a weak and hopeless anger.

She went on swiftly before he could speak. "I am Arden. The Ardens are blood kin to the Beauchamps, the Nevilles, and the earls of Warwick. Sir Henry Arden's grandson was put in custody of Joan Beauchamp, Lady Bergavenny—" She began to draw with a stick on the walk a pedigree table. He stood up and spoiled it with his shoe.

"That is enough," he said. "Within this month the Office of Heralds has challenged our right to arms and rank. What can so easily be set aside is not worth the having, mother."

He wished not to remember her face, nor the long silence. What he administered was just this side of a mortal blow.

She sat like a carven figure, the color drained from her face. Then she searched his face with her eyes. At length she stood up, knocking the blackwork cap onto the ground, not knowing what she did. He retrieved it, glad for an action, and followed her to the house. With all his might he held his ground, contending against the ancient childish fear that he had displeased his mother and must make amends.

338

But she said nothing. She stood by a table in the parlor, patting the edge softly. The color had not returned to her face. He knew now that she was badly frightened. When frightened, she always had her way.

He was in a poor mood to talk to Quiney, but he went to it, for Quiney offered him civic distress, not personal.

He looked into the window. There was Quiney still Sunday dressed, reading a great Genevan Bible in the family parlor, thinking on it aloud to his wife as he marked a place.

Will listened and looked. All was set in order, the low timbered room and prosperous family with good connections in the county, and a self-respect made in England.

He hesitated for a moment, for Quiney's voice brought back the summer-winter recollections of his boyhood when to be a boy had the simplicity of the everlasting.

" 'If the firstfruit be holy, the lump is also holy; and if the root be holy, so are the branches. . . .' " Quiney's voice was rich, the man's honor stocky and true, like himself. He had held all the honors of a corporate township. Had he been molded out of Mary Shakespeare's body, he would, no doubt, have multiplied those honors and made safe and sure her claims to a coat of arms.

Will turned away.

He went down Middle Row to the river and stood for a long time by the water. Should he put down a law to Tom—that all is true, yet here at home it is a lie? that Eden's serpent is a playful beast who will not sting until his tongue is out? that I am black as pitch yet you must see me clean and happy?

The cows in the croft surveyed him with a resolute concentration and moved toward him with the singleness of his mother. He went on hurriedly, but he could hear their quiet movements and breathing when he stopped again. Oh, let be. Let rest. He had come home that nature might bring together what fortune separates.

He stood surrounded by the breathy cows who kept him in their curious gaze while they cropped. In the end he was glad of them and of the slowly moving river.

339

When it was twilight, he came into the Great Garden by his river door.

CHAPTER *Four*

WILL looked through his own tall window and saw Tom talking to Susanna. Tonight he would in no way address Tom Greene. His old fears might be wide awake, but peace was more important than old fears.

He went into the garden and watched the house martin preparing for the night under the eaves by the solar. The stillness laved him. He wished nothing but an unconditioned present, locked to an utter quiescence, bounded by a total stillness. He was absolute for his purpose.

In the twilight he saw that the dog violets had opened. He knelt on his heels and touched one with his finger.

A light in his bedroom flickered and grew brighter. He strolled once more around the knot garden, and then through the window he saw that the parlor was empty. He entered the house and took his candle from the table, and mounted the stairs.

Anne was leaning over a chest in their room, in her arms some colored stuff or other. She looked at him sideways and smiled. Her cap was off, and the candlelight glowed on her fair hair.

"Hast thee eaten supper?" she asked.

He shook his head. She laid the cloths in the chest and straightened up.

"I will bring thee a morsel."

"I am not hungry, dear heart."

She studied him. "Thy mother hath stirred thee up."

He frowned slightly, and then he sank into a chair before the fire and gave her a quick soft look.

"My mother always stirs me up. It is not fathers who are powerful, it is mothers. When I say it is dark, I mean it is light. This is known as the equivocation of poetry." He smiled as he balanced a fire iron reflectively.

340

She gave him a merry sidelong look and shook out a garment to put into the chest.

"How unjust." Then she closed it and drew up a stool to sit facing him by the fire. "She hath no one to oppose her. It is lonely to be queen of Great Nothing when one is keen and could rule." He did not reply and she went on tentatively. "Gilbert does not listen. Thy father listens but does not always heed, though I think he would not do without her." His fingers met together over his mouth. He studied her till she was aware of his eyes. Then she looked at him quietly for a moment. "My husband . . ."

He did not move. Presently he took his hands from his mouth and began to unfasten his jerkin. He said without expression, "My better half . . ."

She flushed faintly. Her brown gaze rested on him. "We have said naught to each other since thee came home."

"No," he agreed. Then he added gently, "The house hath been filled with people."

Under the coruscated surface of his adultery, revenge and guilt, where was this woman, his wife? Oh, peace—take no soundings—if he had not peace with her who had lived beside him for eighteen years, he had nothing.

Eighteen years, in which he had grown to be a man redolent with sin.

He looked about the room, at the four-posted bedstead with its curtains, flock bed and feather bed, bolsters, pillows, blankets, sheets, hillings, its heavy carved back panel and canopy over all: a world; at the carved locker at its foot, at the carved chest, the carved wardrobe, at all the surfaces where man's cunning hand had put its mark for harmony and order. These had been his for only two years of those eighteen.

He glanced at her briefly, but her face was not an open book so he turned away, reluctant to undo the clasp. Peace. Let no dog bark.

Yet another glance slipped. She was alive with something secret —what? Dared he know secrets? Secrets seldom led to peace.

As he felt the comfort of the fire, he said, "It was my lord

Hunsdon sent us to Scotland by the Queen's order, to stay out the moil of Lord Essex' plot."

"Ah," she said, "I wondered."

He leaned against the hard chair back and closed his eyes.

"Thee bist not on the road to Scotland . . ." she ventured.

He laughed abruptly. "My punishment lies elsewhere."

Still he did not look at her. She stared down at her clasped hands, wondering when she would dare say the truth . . . that she was a woman in love with her husband who had grown cold to her. *I love thee* is so simply said, yet were she to say it and receive no answer, such a cry would be drawn from her, such a desire to throw herself at his feet, beg for reassurance, that she would lose whatever she might have.

What *did* she have?

The woman in boy's clothes! Oh, she was not so great a fool as to think his lip was virgined away from her . . . yet faithfulness was not alone a woman's duty. If she asked and knew, if she grappled with something real and seen, then might she deal with it as she had dealt with other fears? Yet if she took it upon herself to ask, and learned, and could not bear it, then she would have only herself to blame for an unassuageable pain. Oh, what courage it took to kiss away kingdoms.

He had opened his eyes and now looked at her pensively. "I have a play that must be put down," he said to answer questions that he heard unasked. She nodded again. She wondered what to say because all things she wished to know led in a dangerous circle.

His clasped fingers lay across his mouth, but his eyes were watching her. He had said *his better half*. If one half was rotten would the whole be affected; or was it, vice versa, that the good half cast the bad one out? *Are you good? Are you honest? Do you love me?*

He said no more, and she began to speak. "The girls—" for they met in a great love for their children.

He replied quickly before she could go on, "Susanna is like yeast. Judith is like a sacramental wafer. Why?"

She answered that Judith trembled before each new day of life, a child still cut in two, half of her in heaven with her brother; that Susanna was reckless to engage in life, be married.

His eldest child, his golden-haired! He asked in dismay what tongue-tied lout could she possibly have eyed. Anne hesitated for a moment, then replied with a smile, "She fancies Dr Hall."

"Christ's body!" Then he corrected himself. "Merciful God! Why, he's my age!"

"Twenty-seven."

"Nine years less! And he?"

"He be a grave and courteous man. Perhaps he doth not know."

"With Susanna?" He laughed, all bemused. "In God's name, I asked him here to supper!" Then he was by turns perturbed and engaged, wide-awake, thinking of his daughters, outraged and charmed, sentimental, amused at himself. At length he sat staring at Anne. "Why did I know naught of this?"

"What should I have told thee? That the spring was in the earth? Why, Judith too hath Thomas Adrian Quiney dancing as a sweetheart." She added, throwing away an edge of caution, "But thee was too far away and silent to tell this to."

He bent over so that his voice was muffled. "If I write, another must read to thee. What should I say for Tom Greene to read aloud?"

She hesitated, and he was, in that quiet chink between his defenses and the rude world, able to see her fair and bonny. Oh, caution is peace! No word and no move is peace. No questions, no replies, no past, no future; there only is peace.

She turned around on her chair and reached behind her in a gesture which recommended itself to a man's eyes . . . except that he was most particularly not a man! She sat very straight with a book in her hands. She slowly read:

" 'The same followed Paul and us crying out and saying, These men are the servants—' " He rose and put his arm about her, kissing her on the cheek.

"Lovedy, this is very brave and gallant! Learning to read! What does thou need to know from books, dear heart?"

343

She laid her hands flat on the Bible and her warm brown eyes were clear. "Our Lord's words." Then she hesitated and looked at him. "*Thy* words. Thy letter . . ."

"My letter!" His one solitary protest against that wide void— he did not remember clearly what he had written, only the need. Now he was embarrassed, touched, troubled. He shook her slightly by the shoulder. "Is this thine own teaching?"

"Tom hath been my teacher." She saw him frown and his brief unguarded look. Her own brows drew together. "And Judith's also." He turned away. She coaxed. "She longs to read like a starved child for food."

He trimmed the rush light. "Let it be thy learning that teaches her."

"My sweet Will, what matters who be teacher so we learn?"

He shrugged slightly. He was so disturbed by unreason that he could not defend himself. *Daughters scarce younger than his lady with all their senses roused, violation waiting like a pit before them.* Anne saw and struggled with the mystery. She was determined not to be cheated of the sweetness of his kiss. She caught at her lip in an effort to understand the inexplicable. He laughed a little saying, "What ado!" and walked about as he untied his points.

She sat without moving, the firelight on her face, "Thee did set me a conundrum in thy letter: that a man and wife being two are one."

He stopped, and after a moment replied with a little laugh, "Did I not call thee my better half?"

Briefly she turned to him her languorous half-closed glance of shyness. He stood beside her for a moment, his fingers lightly stroking her temples; then he took up the Bible and opened it at random.

He thrust it at her. "Read me that." He walked away as she slowly read what Elijah said to King Ahab. His attention was not on the words but on himself, his intemperate, foolish ways, his unkindness, yet what could he do? Any gentle action would tip her into his arms, for it was all or nothing. And all or nothing in no way took account of his compound confusion: revenge, remorse, guilt, doubt, dismay—and an absolute resolve for peace, that is the tomb. With which of these would he touch his wife? He stopped abruptly to reaffirm with his eyes the fact of this room in the context of the whole.

She hesitated over a word, and the silence restored his attention. He came to her side and bent to see the word.

" 'Abundance,' " he said. She repeated it, and went on to the end of the verse. There she stopped.

After a moment he said, "We will read together, by-and-by."

Her head remained lowered. But she took the promise and held it as carefully as a child.

She was forty-four years old and she too had been married for eighteen years. She had been the mother of three children, one dead; the pain of that death still rankled in her heart. Yet because her husband was her heart, all dead and living children were a part of him, like hand or hair. Because of this, love was whole, it was not disparate. It was compounded of words said yesterday, flowing back to a gesture made today, recalling a laugh that was to come tomorrow. It was the rain that fell on them together, and the seeds that they had agreed to plant in the garden. It was also love, freely given and taken in word and act. She knew that it was so because she knew it.

She rose to take the hillings off the bed and fold them, to shake the bolsters, to hang up his jerkin and lay out the night smocks. She set up great shadows against the plastered walls.

Will watched her shadow for some time through half-closed eyes, hearing on one side of him the crackling of the flames and on the other the boards creaking as she moved. The shadow gave him peace, for the movements were undefined, in contrast to the substance.

The chapel clock sounded firm and resonant. He did not stir, only his white shirt gave the illusion of life where the glow of the fire leapt upon it. He let his eyes close. He slept in the chair.

She came softly to his side, loosening her long hair and combing it as she looked at him. Presently she went to the window and set it open, staring into the starry night.

She did not know what betokened, save that something was

345

amiss and she not able to inquire. Oh, heart, would I dare, were permission given? This was a rank foolishness of love: love timid! But then she knew with all her instinct that it was not timidity but some private wisdom that said to risk all might be to lose all. Perhaps her purgatory must be acquiescence with what she had, however meager. But why? Why?

All she asked was that Anne be wanted for that she was Anne. If Anne had ceased to be a part of Will, then where was Anne?

In almost every house in Stratford at this hour, husband would be untying his points, unlacing his shirt, wife undoing her bodice, turning back the sheets on the bed, as matter-of-fact as sweeping the garner, no eroticism induced by the slow off-casting of day. And when they got into bed, each from his own side, and stretched out his body and hers, and let them be loosened in the bed, there would be some talk of common matters, a texture woven into home; one would yawn and say some sleepy thing, perhaps a joke, for taking a quittance of day released body and spirit somewhat of its duties and anxieties. Then with love and some urgency the act of husband upon wife would become a natural consequence of being one in some design of the whole.

Whereas with that girl-boy, what could proceed the act of man and woman but hot blood, hot eyes, limbs, starting flesh, a world of effect without root or flower?

Yet . . . here in this house, this room, truth had become in some way equivocal. Natural purpose was obscured and action moved heavy and disengaged as in a dream. The husband, played by Will, sat log-limbed by the fire, slowly taking off his shoes. The wife, played by Anne, set great shadows against the plastered walls, her hands performing some act of housewifery with no more shadowy shape than fins.

Will, seeing her through half-opened eyes, felt drugged with relief that time is the friend of all—thank God, he had time! And he stumbled bedward with a sleepy joke.

She put out the candle and came into the bed beside him. The fading firelight cast great spurts of light. She longed for a tender word which rejoiced that she was Anne, a word that he was glad to be again among these hollows of companionship, a bed private but not secret, hallowed to that vow that did incorporate and make them one.

She did not stir, for his little joke lay between them. But unless she spoke she would not sleep all night. Her voice was very soft and held a touch of laughter.

"Susanna do think that bitty ring thee brought will put doctor in mind of marriage. She plans how he will slip it on her finger, unbeknowing her craftiness, and then be made to like how well it looks. I'faith, she hath thought it out very weathertight."

He laughed. He shook with laughter. He was seized with tenderest irony. It rocked him so gently with laughter that he could turn and find a peace-filled hollow, gasp "Ah-h-h," and laugh again, while that sleep that shuts the eye of care came gently down.

Anne took his hand, his fingers closed sleepily over hers. She kissed his shoulder.

The chapel bell clanged him out of drowsiness. He clutched at day. All he faced was peace; his relief was like a sparse tide thinly covering the shore.

He sprang from bed, staggered, sank back. He would carefully quarter out this day: so much for property and business, so much for family, so much for friends, so much for putting words to paper.

To be resolute for peace and order was the sign of a tranquil mind. The past was dead and gone, lady, dead and gone.

Yet he still sat, watching the sunlight creep along the window ledge. He said aloud in a soft reasonable voice, "Get brimstone in thy liver. Arise. Accost. Bang-bang."

The little bell from the tower rang for school. As he heard the shrill responding sound of boys, he rose with a deep sigh and slowly enclosed himself in his garments.

In the kitchen, Anne was cutting cheese and bread, and Nan, pretty and sleepy, was sitting on the settle with her knees high as she spooned pottage the short distance to her mouth. Old Simmy the gardener, and Charles his boy, sat at the table with their bread and beer. Anne glanced around when he entered, and smiled, smoothing back her hair. Nan put her feet flat on the floor as a gesture of deference to her master.

Domestic felicity was the good English name for tranquility. He drew in his breath as he looked about this pleasant room, stone-floored, black-beamed, built for a man's honor. He went to Anne and kissed her cheek. Next he accepted, with a quip and a grace, the mug of beer from his own yeling house which Nan, clutching at her milk, handed him. With the mug and a laden bowl, he went to the open half-door and delivered a eulogy on the day.

Any fool knew that a cheerful manner was a powerful magic. He longed with all his soul to show his love for all.

Old Simmy growled that it was bad weather for the beans, and for the artichokes he'd not give a broken farthing.

"Simmy, gaffer, thee do plant and they do grow. What I want of the garden this year—" And he brought his beer to the table and laid out all his thoughts in such a firm yet tactful manner that Simmy believed they were his own. When the gardener left, Will said to Anne, who was moving about the kitchen in her slow way, "Why do thee not speak?"

She glanced at him startled, but even so, the quality of her brown look did not change. Her eyes were slightly closed and it gave her a languorous manner.

"Of what, dear heart?"

"Why, of the day, of events, of people, of work."

She smiled and went on with her business. "We be alive. Day is bright. Selah!"

He was annoyed and amused.

"It hath not been known that thou wouldst say two words when one would do."

She smiled slightly.

"Be that a fault?"

"Sweetling, I want the rose of May in all its glory. To hear two words from thee would not be a fault." She laughed quietly.

"Joan, thy sister, hath some Provens roses for thee to plant. Will thee fetch um?"

"Too late."

"She says it be not."

"I'll call, but I say it is too late to plant them safely."

He looked at her as though he scarcely saw her, his mind's eye filled with roses. "Thou art good for baking bread, not for horticulture."

"I am good for more than baking bread," she said with spirit. "Mind my comfits and my suckets, candied ginger and sugary nutmeg."

He looked at her with humor and smacked his lips. "Aye, and some very searching wine."

She straightened herself, drawing together her shoulderblades and taking a wisp of hair from her eyelids. *More than that—I am Anne.*

His eyes on her deepened. Something turned and moved below the light. He put his hand on her shoulder and kissed the lobe of her ear.

"Presently I will go up to the solar and lock the door."

"What must I say to thy friends?"

He frowned, already in that locked room.

"Why, that I am doing accounts."

"Sweet heart, I will lie for thee."

"Where are thy daughters? Slug-a-beds! Good Nan, call them instantly. I'faith, thee must show a firmer hand, dear wife. If you do not, I shall set them tasks to do."

"Ah, they talk all night of thee, and London—or Susanna does."

"It will not do." He put his hand against her cheek.

"I see that. As thee say."

Tom Greene had come in. For a large man, he was quiet in his movements as though he wished to give no trouble. He said "Good morning" in a manner that left them free to answer or not, and he stood by Nan as she put pottage in a bowl.

Will said "Good morning" belatedly and glanced at Tom. For a brief moment he saw him as Herod in the mummery plays, all menace. What power Tom held! Then Will blinked and could not reconstruct the impression he had had.

Yet an ache remained in his mind as though it had been bruised.

He said to Tom, "I must talk to thee about the malt. After dinner, good cousin?"

Tom bowed slightly and said, "Cousin, I have no doubt it will all yield to thee as most things do."

Will turned toward the door with a violent irritation. He said to himself in a fury, Set aside, Will, set aside. Fool. Dolt. Simpleton! speaking both of himself and Tom. But he turned around pleasantly. "Aye, that is the mark of a good master, is it not? to make all yield smilingly." And he went out closing the door quietly.

Tom looked at Anne over the rim of his mug. She stood rather lax in the center of the floor, as though beached, one hand, with a wiping cloth, hanging at her side.

"He is a contrary man," Tom said. She turned toward him abruptly and was aware of his dark eyes very sure and certain, and of something quite worldly and knowledgeable on his swarthy face. He went on firmly, keeping her in his gaze, "There is more behind their banishment than Essex' uprising, I feel sure. But then there is more to Will than just the man." Her eyes asked him questions that she would not put in words, and he answered quietly. "He is a poet. I recommend this to thine attention."

She still said nothing. He looked at her as though he knew her well, and spoke slowly, not taking his eyes from her.

"He has set me in this house to rule for him when he is absent. I use my judgment. I should not have told you what I learned in London. I did it from compassion, that you should not be left naked to the world. But you do not know what to do. Indeed, what wife would. He is a contrary and passionate man—who is a poet."

She threw him a wild look and fell to washing up the mugs in a wooden tub. He blinked at the look and came forward to add his mug to the three that she was washing. She knew that he stood beside her, looking down at her swift hands and then at her. He spoke with a humorous inflection. "I too have written poetry. I know how poetry affects a man, especially when the words are rendered with voluptuous intent."

She glanced up at him.

"Am I not thy friend?" he asked. She nodded, and then she smiled very like her daughter, Susanna. "And, being thy friend—"

She said quietly, "Speak no more."

He was not at all put out. He stooped and kissed her cheek.

Judith came into the kitchen and lingered, reedy and wondering by the door. She was wearing her gold brooch. Anne spoke to her in the quiet tone she gave her children.

"God be with 'ee today, my darling."

Judith came up abruptly and kissed her, and bowed her head to Tom.

"My father?"

"Aye. He says thee must be brisk and about. And right he be. Now eat thy breakfast and take thy spinning so that he will not have to speak again."

Judith stood close by her mother, frail with prettiness. She was silent, but Anne knew that standing close in this way was as though she had put full speech into words.

"What be it, sweetling?"

"Father comes—but he goes again." Her eyes were as dark as the corners of the kitchen.

"Well, that be the world. Be glad he comes."

Judith said very low, "My brother sits in my heart and whispers to me."

"Love, love, he went away to God, being so perfect. Thy father will bide. Now eat thy pottage and give not a windy night a rainy morrow."

In her heart she thought with some despair of the unruly blasts that wait on the tender spring.

CHAPTER *Five*

THE solar had a key in the door. Will turned it and put the key in his belt, as though the door were now double locked. He was alone with quill, ink, paper, the sun, the garden, the magpie with the faulty wing.

What a dear room. All was well. It was a room made for a man's reflection. Here his star would dance, his prince be nourished. Last year, a comedy; this year the devil's jokebook unless he turned it to his own account. His sister's rose would go there beside the eglantine. Unless it would be best against the wall.

He rose to look down more closely. Then he saw that the grape trellis had not been cut back, and he was much put out.

Yet his indignation was so shallow that he began to smile when he saw the wilted old gardener creep into sight, troweling the borders and lifting himself as though revived by the sight of the dog violets. Will watched, his gold-brown eyes, his whole face, alight with pleasure, this little cup of life which held the old man and the flowers enough, enough. Returning to Stratford was as though returning from the grave. All had a vernal gait, all smacked of song.

Old Simmy crept vernally round the hedge, and the iron which Will had put into his liver spoke metallically. Bang-bang. He sat at the table, his back to the garden though an ouzel, sitting in the topmost branch, had in his tone all the wonder of bird. How does a prince venture the killing of a king? Will gazed at the grain of the table wood and presently ran his nail along it. The magpie hopped nearer and spoke raucously. Will replied.

This prince who grew under his hand was proud; Will knew the stuff he wore, his perfumes, his bibelots, his callous and kind heart, his skill with calligraphy and sonnets, his very mold and form. He was loving to his friends, courteous to his servants, cold to his mother, cruel to his mistress, the very flower of this age, bedeviled by agonies both dead and living . . . and *there* the secret lay.

Will scarcely moved, not his eyelids nor his breath, while he thought of this great mystery of living ghosts.

Since the devil has power to assume a pleasing shape, what can one say of living agonies except they are the devil? Why, sure, ghosts do appear, no believing man discounted them, but dead or alive, it was their heavy hands which must bear the burden of death, damnation, and hell.

So this woman's son, Hamlet, being cruel and kind, wholehearted, sinful, passionate, ambitious, and loving (the epitaph of every woman's son), is commanded by a sepulchral voice to take a bloody vengeance; but he cannot bring his mind to lift his hand, and shows thus much his courage. His own deepest shock—his, Will's—lay in the knowledge that he had yielded to the culminating lust of revenge. All else was slight to this. Will had sought revenge.

To kill a king was to kill God's anointed, and in the allegory of life were not all men kings and princes? Did not all men struggle into their sea of troubles and struggle out again?

The offal in the river had been less decayed than his act. How shallow was his peace! How shallow, how wiped out. Stratford corrupted, home diseased.

He tried to master himself with sensible reflections, but his peace was cracked. He fumbled with his pen, patted the top of his head, smoothed at his beardless chin, examined the condition of his shoes, stroked the head of the magpie, whistled at the bird in the tree, and at length wrote down three lines with firm resolution.

But the bucket proved to have no bung, the water had run out, and Will was filled with his own stare.

He sat for some time making circles with his pen which could be words if only the sense were added. He knew in the catharsis of this time that setting out words is setting out thoughts is setting out the spirit's language, and is, at length, seeing quite through the deeds of men into their very souls.

He was a little shocked that his understanding of the nature of man had not worked in his own behalf. He thought about it for some time, here in his bolted room.

At length he saw how poor Will-o'-words might, like Jesus in the proverb, be given short weight by the baker's daughter and, in a just rage, turn her into an owl.

He laughed and laughed, all quiet by himself, and then he raged, softly treading the floor, for if just nature held the mirror up to him, she should, in courtesy, permit him to see himself face to face, for from what other source did the poet draw?

First he must leave his cell! He drew the bolt and went softly down the stairs. Then he must, by his own strength, cast out his weakness. The mending was in his hands.

He eluded the eyes of all but Argos. They set up the street on this pristine day in this arboreal town to fetch the roses. Will talked to Argos, praising him for virtues and reminding him of the antique nobility of the name he bore. Argos was pleased.

Will could scarcely comprehend such a flood of light. London was night. Like a catechism, he recited the dispensations of grace in this world of Stratford: ploughing, seeding, reaping; blossoms and fruit; houses, stables, and barns; dog and cat, and all the affections which the heart could give, a bounty with no winter in it.

Virtue drives out vice as one nail drives out another. He had no choice. He had tried all else: exorcism, absolution, restitution, return to innocence. They had all been full of promise, but now he stood once more naked of his own respect. To fool myself would forfeit strength.

Let me be a good father and husband, and so find my way back home—yet my uncleanness smells to heaven! Ah, self-imposed agony has at least the virtue of some moral strength.

It was an hour when most men were in their shops or fields, and women at their tasks. The streets were empty. It was a pretty town of small houses with thatched roofs, or of grander houses of carved wood and plaster, gardens and orchards.

To a loiterer under the High Cross, Will called, "God to thee!" and went down Henley Street. He passed his father's shop, and there stood Gilbert by the window examining a hide for some flaw or other. Gilbert's expression did not change, but he jerked a little nod, and said a word within. Will heard his father's voice, rich and rolling, calling even before his face appeared.

John Shakespeare was a whittawer, a glover, and out of the soft skins dressed by Gilbert he fashioned purses, girdles, fine gloves, and, on municipal occasions, parchment. Glovers were almost as powerful as tailors and millers in the Queen's economy. A glover stood up very tall, not only here but everywhere.

"Come thee to beard us?"

"Nay, to share and share alike. Joan hath roses for me."

"Ah, hers be sweet roses."

Will stood by the open window. "By my faith, I forget how fair are the days and the roses of Stratford."

"Be there only nights in London?" asked Gilbert, impassive.

Will did not answer for a moment. Then he replied with a smile, "Only nights."

John Shakespeare asked craftily, "Thee should be more about this town, taking part in all. Keep it clean and orderly and healthy and prosperous. God knows how heavy it lies on us that do. It's 'care for all' the motto here, as thee may forget in London shimble-shamble."

Will looked at him with caution.

"Might there be too much prying, father?"

John Shakespeare turned on him the eyes of a young badger. "Ah, if all be in together, who be there to spy upon? Opening a door, thee'll find thine own self looking out at thee."

Will said, "I feared as much." He smiled at both. He savored the familiar smell of this shop, aware that Gilbert, still standing by the window with the hide in his hand, was watching him without looking. The house beyond was silent. At this hour his mother was doubtless in the garden and Ned building bridges to everywhere. To find his own self looking at himself, why, there's the rub. His father said gently, holding out a pair of scented gloves, "Eyepiece this—be it not as good as London's?"

"Better."

"Aye. Virtue be here. Take hold on it, lad."

"Oh, father, father, that's why I'm home!" Then he smacked his knees and rose. But he paused. "Has my mother said aught?"

His father replaced the gloves carefully and stood leaning on the counter. "Of my heraldic do-das, look? Oh, aye. She be marvelous distempered." He spoke lightly. "So tell me, man to man, what cause a them to fault us?"

From his cool voice one might have thought he was talking of a fine for letting his ducks wander. Will told him. John stood, elbows on his counter, pulling at the tip of his nose and smiling slightly. Will knew his humanity, which asked few questions unless he thought to get true answers.

"Well, by our blessed Lord, what comes goes of worldly honors. Though I be not unmindful how it touches her."

"It has not yet gone, father?"

355

"Ah? Be he good friend, Camden?"

"It is not a matter of friendship, but of words—words put down in my play, adduced—what men infer who look for shadowy meaning. Is reality real? That's what they ask. Is truth true, is Elizabeth James, is England indivisible, is a prince justified in killing a king, does God speak through eclipses of sun and moon?" He laughed. "All this of me."

"Plays be lies," said Gilbert.

"Why, thank thee, Gil." He touched his shoulder. "Then I have naught to fear."

"That was not what I meant."

Their father interposed. "Thy mother'll overget it, and I—"

"Will she, though, father?"

"Lad, see thy mother through me. That be best. We be both knowing, sound, and shrewd; neither of us be weak or yielding. We be both tacticians, look, and we admire each other. She'll undo thee, as thee do think, going behind thy back to have her way, as she hath done to me; but all in all, her weaving be so tight that it saves thee much when tempest blows."

Will frowned and smiled at the same time, seeing on his father's finger the heraldic ring with its emblem of spear and falcon. What would his father do if the decision went against him? Hurl the ring into Avon and go his own way? Will said, "Much I must take because my father tells me."

John Shakespeare did not overlook the tang. But he replied, "Aye. Though we do not kiss the cow, look! Shog off now, and I'll thank God thee's home."

Will did not say that in this town there was no dignity in being a player or a writer of plays. His father knew it. It was a lonesome fact that although it was not the player had the coat of arms, it would be the player lost them.

Joan had begun to sweep the parlor—inward, so as not to sweep away the luck of the house—but she was very glad to see him. She cried out that "the room's all on a mulloch; it wants fettlin'," but in a moment she threw up her hands and took him into the kitchen. There the baby was going around and around in the

356

baby-minder like a little donkey, and her son Michael was making her laugh with a doll on a stick.

Will lifted the baby to dandle and caress her, and Michael slipped a small remembering hand into his pouch for licorice.

Joan talked without stopping. "Be not baby pretty? Favors Ardens, mam says. Mind what Michael say? 'Where did baby come from? Out of me ma's panzy-bed?' Oh, Will, shit, shit them puppets out o' chair. Now then, where be Hart? Michael, don't mess along now, fetch thy father! Oh, Will, he be such an aunty little brat, but what sweet lad be not? Tell me now, Will, how fares with thee? London now? What reckon thee of Susanna's swain—i'faith—he'll not let her die unkind! Doth he doher face yet?"

Her sweet little voice paused, and she was rosy with interest.

"Oh, Joan, you have not changed a mite. *Doher* face! How should I know whether he hath kissed her? She's a child."

"Not so! She'll have babies in a year, if banns be read."

Her husband came in, a thin young man who somewhat ran to nose though he had also a piercing eye. He pumped Will's hand with both of his and kissed him on both cheeks and said, "Well, well, well," firm and resonant beneath his wife's running little voice.

". . . I say to she, 'Gie o'er or a' done—there be those as know along of witches' tales—and I judge her guilty of most *calamitous* slander . . .'"

"Wife, wife," said her husband, "how thee do cank!"

She turned round-eyed to Will. "*Do* I talk too much?"

Will kissed her with the baby under his arm. "It is like a little stream to my ears; purl, purl, purl."

"Oh, Hart do go on at me," and she kissed her husband heartily. "Michael, now there, has thee thanked thine nuncle for licorice?"

Michael was a gentle little boy, an aunty brat only to his doting mother. He was russet-haired and fair of skin, like the Shakespeares, and sat very low and happy, sucking at his comfit. He nodded and smiled at his uncle with his eyes.

357

"Michael, I will tell thee," said Will suddenly, "how we will spend the day. You and I will look for birds' nests though not touch them, and watch the silverlings in river though not fish. We'll lie in meadow and sing and tell good tales and make our world anew."

"Oh . . ." said Michael. "And baby too?"

Baby had her toothless gums fast around a loop on Will's jerkin. "Baby too if thy mam says yes."

"Oh, oh," said Joan, "now thee can see that stagger-bob born out of old cow and baby'll taste her fill o' meadow grass—swarm not up thine nuncle! Oh, oh, I'll fetch thee summat to put in stomach while thee lies and tells thy tales."

She went off as pleased as Michael, and Hart told Will of hatters' troubles, though none were too bad. Too many hatters, that was all. Who could wear all their gear?

Baby was cleaned and tidied, hugged, kissed, and given a sweet; Michael was kissed and instructed and then called back for his short coat which Joan called a slop.

Argos was waiting. The day was fair, the four were friends. They went north along the footpath to meander with the stream. Michael wished to carry the baby and did so for a space of time, telling her things of common interest, of the wood anemones which closed with the wind, and what the buttercups said when held beneath the chin. She was a knowing baby.

In some truth and tenderness, these children were his own. They were a living past of summer days when Anne and he had taken their babies by the river and into the fields. No day in April ever came more sweet.

Michael asked gentle questions and pondered the answers quietly. The change of the seasons was still new to him and all he saw was fresh. The stream wandered as aimless as a dream, and under a heavy willow, half islanded by the stream, ewes browsed with their newborn lambs.

The meadow grass was short and Michael put down his slop for baby to sit on. But she crawled away, slapping at the grass with her hands, dribbling and crowing with a freshness that was even newer than Michael's. He ran after her to bring her back but stood for some moments with her hanging from his hands while he watched a mouse watching him.

"Her hath babies," he said softly, "all pink."

He brought his own baby back to Will and returned to sit on his heels, quiet as the grass, to watch the mouse's nest.

Will heard the meadow pipit. He heard each separate note as it rose straight up, and then he heard the different song it sang as it plunged to earth, ruddered by its upturned tail. He heard things not heard before. He saw the buds on flower and bush. He saw each bud as it were itself alone. He held a stalk of fritillary level with his eyes and reflected on its grace and oddity.

He lay on his back, and the baby thought he was a mound of earth. The dappled sky was so innocent it had never yet been crossed by tempest. He watched it with his soul, for he did not trust his eyes to see aright.

Argos came from some wandering and sat down to pant beside him. The baby clutched at Argos and drew herself to her feet. Michael climbed a young willow aslant the brook and sat in its lowest branches. He told what he saw in the stream below, all stones and little fish and reeds made soft by the water. Above him, a nesting warbler paid no heed save that she spread her feathers to cover all her nest. After a time Michael leaned back against the trunk and sang sounds without words. Will and the baby slept. Argos also slept.

Will waked to find Michael sitting beside him patiently.

"Why do fish swim, nuncle?"

"Why, to get where they are going."

"I do not swim to get where I be going."

"Thou art a boy."

He asked after a time, somewhat sadly, "Why not a fish?"

"Because thou art not. There is no other answer."

"Baby?"

"She'll not swim either, save perhaps on summer days."

Michael hummed under his breath. "Now I be hungry."

The meat pie was divided between those three with teeth, and the baby was fed the curds which had been wrapped in an old cabbage leaf, and bits of bread crumbled up by Michael.

359

Then Michael lay back. "Thee did promise to tell a tale, nuncle."

"Aye. What shall I tell?"

Michael dreamed. "Sad tales be best, of sprites and goblins."

"A sad tale let it be."

He told and he remembered at the same time, like words and music, separate but going on as one. Remembrance of things past had no element of time. Sprites and goblins were as light as cobweb, and what had been came back the lovely April of its prime.

All good was one. *So let this virtue be my dispensation.*

Michael was pleased with the tales, and told one or two of his own in thanks. Will asked a secret riddle which must not be told to any other. Then they listened to a yeorling and Will taught the child its song, "A little bit of bread and no che-e-ese."

When it came toward late afternoon, Will said they must go and see his fields. Michael went ahead, and there was a method in his forthright leadership. Before Will knew where they were, they had come onto old Prior's land.

Sour and unwholesome it might be, as Tom had said, but it also held something wild and winning. Here beasts did leap and birds did sing, save for the nightingale who leaned her breast upon a thorn and wept her song.

By the cottage of wattle and daub, old Prior's granddaughter was milking her ewe. With her cheek against the sheep's flank, she watched them with bright eyes, in silence.

Michael was laced with smiles. He stood close. Tib and he smiled at each other. Will guessed that they were secret friends. When her bucket was full, she straightened up and nodded at Will. Michael then leaned against her shoulder. She lifted the bucket, heavy as it was, and tipped it up for him to drink. Will loved the light grace with which she moved, the child's lifted face. She said no word, so Will said, "Godden, lass."

She put back her tangled hair. She was wild and pretty—fifteen or sixteen perhaps, as all fair women were at one time. Tom and others said she was a witch.

Will asked, smiling, for her grandfather. After a moment more of eying him, she put out her hands for the jiggling baby.

"Him go to fall a tree."

Will offered her a sweet. She took it saying shyly, "God 'ild ye."

Michael said, "Mine nuncle tells tales as sad as thine, Tib."

"Ah, by Gis!" She put her pail carelessly by the door, the baby held against her shoulder. The ewe wandered away while Tib wiped her free hand against her ragged skirt. In her eyes was now a power of speech, but her tongue was somewhat lagging.

"Do he tell of paddock here, and where he takes I?" she asked with a soft look.

Will saw then a sleepy toad pulsing his throat beside her. Michael squatted down beside the toad. "Where takes him thee?" he breathed, and she sang, crouching down beside him, "In a sieve, in a sieve, thither sail. Like a rat without a tail."

Michael sang after her on two high notes, "I'll do—I'll do—I'll do." They crouched there, two children by the blinking toad, singing to each other. A gray cat with a smiling tail came out from the cottage. Michael called it by name, "Graymalkin."

Now Will knew that they must go away, for these were witches' words and must not be cut too deeply in Michael's mind or his mother would be badly set about. Will might say *No* to belief in witches, but some lures must not be yielded to for good sense and self-respect. Did he speak for Michael or for himself? Necromancy meant black night, evil battening on evil.

Tib's was a benign witchcraft after all that he had known. He held out a handful of sweets to the girl. She took the sweets, saying with a wide smile, "I be partial to suckets."

He took back the baby. "Come along, Michael, it's home for us. See baby's fist plugged in her mouth?"

Michael held out his hands to Tib. She took them and they danced in a circle, and then she gave him a gay push and said, "Peace, the charm's wound up."

Will said to her with a little bow, "God be at your table."

"God b'w'ye." Then she picked up the toad and called after

361

them. Coming close she held the toad in the light. "Eye he," she said. "Be he not beautiful?"

Will saw. All the toad colors were jeweled in the light. The delicate tracery of design was more lovely than filigree. Her act was touching. He looked into her harebell eyes. She said softly, "Fear not. Fear not."

Her words seemed not strange at all. He had waited for them. He smiled and stroked the toad's cold head with his finger. A magpie watched them from a hazel tree.

"Thank you, Tib."

She nodded and stood back, the toad between her hands. Then she said reprovingly to Michael, "Michael—Master Magpie!"

Michael tipped his hat to the magpie and said, "Godden."

At the stile, Michael caught up with Will. "She be my friend."

"Aye, I see. Shall it be a secret between us?"

"Like thy riddle?"

"Very like my riddle."

Joan took back her young with awed and cheerful cries. Will embraced her.

"Thy tender lambkins are now king and queen," he said.

"Oh, see baby's garland!" She gave Will the roses he had long since come to fetch and swept away all his doubts of time and planting.

Nicholas Smith was swinging on the half-door of his father's tavern next door to Quiney. Will said, "Good evening, Nicholas," and Nicholas resumed their conversation at the precise point it had been left yesterday, his round face without expression.

"If Mr a Price be an ass, what be Mrs a Price?"

"Never mind, Nicholas!"

"Shall I tell thee?"

" 'Fore God, no! Will you have a sugared ginger or a licorice?"

"Well, both? Mrs a Price be—"

"Who's that poor fellow constable be wagging finger at?"

"Miller's Walt. Istaday, he hit Geo Fleming in jaw."

The fellow in the pillory was bearing the lecture of the constable with weary fortitude. His eyes were closed, his cheek laid against his wooden yoke. The constable was lecturing in a kindly way but it did not hold attention.

Out of the corner of his eye, the constable saw Argos, and without a change in voice said, "Dog unmuzzled, Will. Tenpence there."

The fellow in the pillory opened his eyes, clucked his tongue at Will, spat, and shut his eyes again. This put the constable into a proper rage.

"Thee malt worm! Thee'll lie by heels or I be no true man! By gog's wouns, scrabblin' along, dropping out with all thy neighbors!"

Will waited for no more. He handed over his tenpence and ran home, remembering suddenly that Dr Hall had been asked for supper.

As he came in the garden door with the roses, he heard Susanna's voice like a bird and the doctor's grave and measured. Susanna saw her father, but did not pause in her soft breathless account of how the great actor, Richard Burbage, contrived certain effects whereby gods came down from the heavens and ghosts rose up from the depths of the earth, and severed heads appeared on platters and fire burst out and consumed nothing. She explained how it was done. Even Will listened in some amazement.

As for the young doctor, it was clear that he was helpless. Caught between delight in speculative hypotheses and frank dismay at such juggling with empiric fact, he was dumb before his intellectual honesty.

But Susanna was agleam. Her imagination was lighted by a thousand fantasies. She watched him demurely with her head lowered, and she wore an expression round her mouth so like Mary Shakespeare's that Will intervened out of pure compassion.

"Welcome, sir, I am very glad to see you. And you, my love, will go and help your mother."

"Oh, no!" she protested.

"Love, did you not hear what I said?" Then he called to the old gardener for a spade. He himself earthed it for the roses and

363

talked gaily all the while, though old Simmy leaned against the wall, snuffling with disapproval of position, depth of hole, spread of roots, quantity of water, and prospects for the future.

Will was keenly conscious of this young man on whom his daughter had set her heart. That she had done so was like a woman. God grant he used her gently. When the last earth had been loosely set about the bush, and old Simmy sent off with the spade, persuaded that the bush had been planted exactly as he wished, Will walked with the young man around the knot garden. As they talked of the lavender, thrift, hyssop, germander, and savory that filled the interstices of design, he took his measure.

John Hall's face was a very port and haven. His brown hair fell somewhat long against his plain collar, his eyes were gray, his shape tall and slender, his hands strong and thin, his manner reserved, not shy, his expositions keen, not forward, himself conscious of his own worth but not bold.

As compelling as a falling man's cry for help was Will's need to cement together all the virtues of this home and place, and set them between himself and the rude world. This young man was a part of that virtue. He had a dispensational quality, as though disinterested human devotion would not be all-in-all to him; as though his wrestling with the health of others would be in the strength of love.

Yet he was untried, Will sensed, passion waiting, penitential tears still contained in sacred vials.

Will asked him questions proper to a father and also informative to his own nimble curiosity. John Hall said that he had taken his medical degree in France. Before that he had, at sixteen, matriculated at Oxford from Balliol, taking his B.A. three years later, and his M.A. from St Edmund's Hall. Before that, he was the son of a Worcestershire gentleman. His future? Why, all the world lay waiting to be liberated by scientific thought, and no mystery, save the mystery of godliness, could intervene between man and this open door. He was brave and new.

Ned came for supper. Nan was the flower for this honeybee. Ned was now his own man. He had a washed country look

about him, and his eyes, the color of a thrush, were always turning toward her.

After supper they had sweetmeats in the garden and listened to
the nesting birds. At dusk they returned indoors, where Susanna
played the virginal and Judith sang, her light voice floating onto
the clear air. Will sat, his hand covering his mouth, and his eyes
fixed on his daughters, those precious motives, those strong knots
of love, those abstracts of all that do contain the whole.

The doctor (Will's eyes slowly turned) sat listening with attentive quietness; the light shone on his long hair, his eyes were
speaking as his mouth could not—this young man's face was very
contiguous to the times, being both spiritual and sensuous.

And then, Will, very private, looked at his wife. She sat somewhat apart in a stiff chair, but there was no stiffness in her manner. Her hands were in her lap, her head upright, a slight smile
on her lips. That was all he allowed himself—a sense of curve.

At length John Hall sang, looking at Susanna, whose fingers
found the keys without her eyes. He sang:

"Come tread the path of pensive pang with me, ye
    lovers true.
Bewail with me your luckless lots, with tears your
    eyes bedew.
Aid me, you ghosts, who loathed life, your lovers
    being slain,
With sighs and sobs and notes of dole, my hard hap to
    complain.
Farewell, my lords and friends, farewell my princely
    state.
Behold, behold, I yield to thee, my ghost, ah see, I die,
    I die, I die,
Ah, ah, alas, I die, I die."

Susanna was rosy with pleasure.

Ned sang, his eyes on Nan, and then the elders sang, of whom
John Hall accounted himself one. He shared a music book with
Tom, while Anne and Will shared another. The children played
the viol, cittern, recorder, and virginal.

Ye that do dwell in pleasures plenty (*sang Anne*)
And dwell in music's sweetest airs, (*the men replied*)

Whose eyes are quick, whose ears are dainty, (*and all intricated and wove their parts*)
Not clogged with earth or worldly cares (*sang John Hall*)
Who now is dead, yet you his fame can raise (*sang Will and Tom in firm baritones*)
Call him again, let him not die,
But live in music's sweetest breath. (*sang Anne and John*)
Place him in fairest memory, (*the voices twined, repeated and emerged*)
And let him triumph over death, (*Anne sang, and Will affirmed*)

Together and separately, they wound happily to the end:

O sweetly sing, his living wish attend ye,
These were his words: the mirth of heaven, God send ye.

They smiled and complimented each other. Nan shook out her recorder and giggled at Ned. Susanna struck a last chord on the virginal. From the street came the voice of a neighbor singing the end, and calling, "Good night, all!"

Will walked home with John Hall. They walked slowly by the Bank Croft. The moonlight lay on the willows and the smooth river. To Will, the sounds of infinity vibrated in the ear which knew star upon star.

John Hall was moved to more speech in the dark than in the light. His light voice stirred the air as he expatiated on mortal man's power to transform henbane, plant juices, oil of lilies, shavings of ivory into mysteries of medicine. He told with a quickening voice of strange effects he had witnessed when ancient cures had been filtered through this modern knowledge and become still more mysterious. Will said nothing, sharpening his own self-knowledge against this eager mind. Their footsteps were loud; in the dark a song thrush sang.

John Hall spoke of science as though it were exact, and he spoke of all that did not yield to empiric fact as falsities. Then he turned his head slightly, and in the dark Will sensed his hesitation before he spoke of plays as falsities.

Will laughed. Here was the first man in Stratford, outside his family, who had mentioned his profession. John Hall waited courteously, but Will merely laughed again and put his hand on the young man's shoulder. So John Hall asked in his cool scholarly voice how fantasy could be reconciled to Christian ethics.

"Or disguises to the pursuit of truth?" Will asked. He hesitated for some time, watching his own beckoning thoughts. At length he said, "I will not answer, for there is more mystery here than in thy henbane or ivory shavings."

"Well, sir, I do not mean to be discourteous."

"Indeed, indeed, I understand. Shall I say this: that all of us are living parables, seeking by indirections to find directions out? Why man is evil and woman corrupt, what spells we put upon our minds, why spring is sweet and winter harsh, why all, in reverse of this, is also true. Can you answer that?"

John Hall replied with some diffidence. "I feel God has set forth His holy law, line upon line. This we must scan, and not men's philosophies."

All the sweetness of the evening had roused in Will some agitation that made him speak with more passion than he meant. "Ah, but what of humanity? Can one come by natural progression to the liver and the spleen, and omit the conscience? And thus, anatomized, may we not see what breeds about the heart?"

The doctor walked in silence. Will could discern in the faint light that his face looked young and troubled. What would John Hall say to his kind of sin? Will pressed his advantage.

"To see this is the poet's function. Yet to see this requires self-knowledge, humility, and love. I have no scalpels such as you save the cutting edge of my own mischance. And what do you say of the foot above the head of the sons of men? What do you say of all the broken tears, all the past joy and present laughter, that conjoin and make a man? If this be not empiric fact, then when I strike myself no blood will flow.

"Well, sir," said John Hall quietly, "I am young, but I have seen the open griefs. How to heal I will, in love, pursue."

"One can ask no more."

"But, good sir, I am perplexed, and I will say it plain, that a maiden like your daughter should believe in imagined things—

367

effects done upon a stage that are not true in fact." Will waited. The young man was struggling with himself. "For our Bible tells us plainly that we must pull down imaginations and all the high things that do contend against the Lord of Hosts."

What could he say? Break his daughter's heart? Will both smiled and grimaced in the dark. At length he said with warm courtesy, "Good friend, how can I answer without some thought? You've given me much to chew upon. Will you, dear sir, let your kind heart think on what I've barely offered?"

"Well, sir, I must at least return your courtesy." But he said it with a little stiffness.

When Will came home, he found Susanna mooning in the garden. He said nothing but drew her hand through his arm and mooned with her. At length she sighed.

"Oh, mankind . . . is not mankind very lovely?"

CHAPTER *Six*

THE days had no clear mark of Monday, Tuesday, Wednesday. They traveled in their own orbit. Keep all quiet. Keep thy home under thy own life's key. Keep thy wife in thy mind's eye to study of good and all. Make no move. Then, by God's grace, you will be clean at last.

What did his wife think? He would not conjecture. With haste and shame he prayed that eighteen years had given her the power to read his mind—yet, dear God, not too precisely!

To fall asleep night after night in his chair was not to deny her, by premeditation, her conjugal rights but to buy himself their peace.

When he stumbled sleepily to bed he would be alert enough to see if she had gone to sleep. But always her eyes were open, watching the fire, and when his hand slipped into hers, her fingers closed on it.

Tom said to Will, as though offhanded, that he, Tom, might have the Town Clerkship if Coombs said the word.

"Indeed, well, good, Tom. Proud we'd be."

"I'd be thy steward as long as I was needed."

"Well, I thank you, Tom, and I know your loyalty."

He did indeed. In his heart, he knew it very well. He would not yield to any other thought! He said, almost to himself, "I am the master in my own house, and that's enough for me."

His play concerned him deeply. It moved by fits and starts. Never before had he discarded so much thinking to be thought anew. A man's whole life stood within the center where truth is hid.

There! He smacked his hand on a day's work. Rest in peace. Yet when he reread it, he had not quite said what he thought had been put down. Well, try again. It was his compass. What would life be without this special dispensation? He stood with the old magpie on his hand, looking out at the garden which also had its true scope within himself.

Yet this town, too, held his chart to peace. Taken all in all, each separate soul and body could lead him to the whole.

He idled in Quiney's shop, where all the soothing bolts of cloth, the silks, the wools, the Milan fustian, the medley cloth and tuft taffeta, suggested how civilized man had learnt to set himself apart from beasts. It also rendered coherent certain protests against such fusty minds as their Black Lord's.

"Look you," said Quiney, "it be not, in point of fact, *enclosing* public land for private use that we fight. It be the past pressing on our times. Why should I or thee or Hamnet or Jack a'Daws, who've made our way by our own good sense, yield to a lord of the manor who sets himself against us? Our charter says we be free men. I'll tell thee a thing. I have thought to go away. I have bought land in New World, acres and acres and acres, look, to speculate. But now, if a man like thee will contrary the lord, I will bide."

"Oh," Will groaned, "I came home for peace, Dick."

"But it be a world with no peace save as men make it so," said Quiney in his lonely voice. "It be groaning with change, and there's such suffering on highways that not only are men rich yesterday, now vagabonds, but calves and hogs and geese be also homeless."

"What would you do?" asked Will, little liking the thought that poor dumb beasts were also at the mercy of groaning times.

"We must appeal to have our appeal heard. I make no doubt it will be heard to our good if it be heard. In this, I and thy father be somewhat alone on Council, for Council is growing too fat in the head with fining its own aldermen for failing in brotherly love." He smiled a little at Will's laugh. "Aye, we're a cantankerous lot, and rather pay a fine than say a brotherly God-to-you at end of Council meetings."

Will said again, "It's peace I want, not stirring up."

Yet he went off smiling, for the individuality of his town was a strong warp in the weft. Though, in truth, individuality had its sting also . . . he kept somewhat clear of his mother, for there was a fine here to pay that they understood each other so well.

He gave much thought to his garden, to planting, to buying, to leases, and soon he would go to John Coombs for more land. All this might somehow build a bridge from evil to good.

From one sleep, that had in it many dreams, he went without his breakfast to the river. In the mists of the river were the swans and their cygnets, the little ones in a nervous joy of swimming, the great parents plucking at their breasts and cleaning their wings. As he watched, the pen swam toward the middle of the river, flying in the water, as it were, lifting her wings somewhat as though to catch a breeze, while the cob lifted himself on great beating wings to fly with a loud agitation of air just above the surface of the river.

Will walked on along the river toward the church, watching the cob's flight as it went higher and seemed to take the mist with it. It was a power of upward going. Below the church was the town windmill, and riding on its slowly turning sails were the miller's sons. They shouted like boys in elfland, and he watched them gladly, rising with them on the sails.

The miller was helping Hamnet Sadler hoist some bags of flour on a cart, and paused to wave. Will stepped across to speak to them. The miller was a large quiet man who had a good word for all. With his sons singing aloft, he smiled and said, "Would we be lads again had we the chance?"

"Oh, yes," said Hamnet, but Will was not so sure.

"I think," the miller said, "I'd rather see than be a child" and he motioned to the meadow where Tib a Prior was wandering with her ewe beside her like a dog.

"Ah, but she be more like changeling child," said Hamnet, frowning.

"She be child," said the miller.

"Aye," said Will, "I thank God I contend as a man, not as a child with all the evil still to face."

Oh, he'd find his way, just give him time . . .

On market days he sold with his father like a good monger to show where he belonged. His father took it naturally though Gilbert was a little put out. The market day before Easter, John Coombs stood picking at a pair of gloves.

"Well, Will . . ."

"Well, John, and good day. Will you have a pair of gloves, finest of their kind?"

John Coombs was a man who always did some steely smiling, like a plane joking with its length of wood. "I have business to talk with thee, Will."

"And I, indisputably, with thee, John."

"Tomorrow?"

"Tomorrow I go fishing."

"As you will. My pleasure waits."

"And mine on thee."

John Coombs went off, having bought nothing, his hands clasped behind his back.

Gilbert said, "Thee hath not fished for many a year."

Will said, "Why, Gil, why should I bait a little fish that harms me not? Shame on thee!"

Gil ducked his head with amusement.

"John Coombs is not my master."

Across the way he saw Anne stopping by a stall. He looked as though seeing her afresh. There was a guilelessness about her, not forward, yet not meek. It came to him suddenly that to render all harmonious and coherent was a function which some women considered as important as childbearing.

Next day was Good Friday. He walked with his daughters in

371

the woods to see what was in flower, and returned to eat hot cross buns and add one more to the cluster hanging from the roof beam in the kitchen.

The cluster was a venerable placation to household gods, elves, sprites, and Queen Mab. Benign but superstitious. Coombs's traffic with the devil Lucre was not so benign, nor his with the fiend Revenge, but Tib a Prior's witchery had a little taste of hot cross buns.

By all such patient peregrinations as these, he might in due time reach his true home.

London lived over the edge of his mind. But it was there. How did the lady think of him? He could not guess, nor himself think too precisely on the cost of revenge, bastardy, or the brutality of a noble lord.

All answers must be the acts of revelation, and thus by neither good nor bad was truth disclosed. Self-recognition was the prism. By God, he said to himself, knowledge of truth is won through suffering and sin, and redemption through looking into the fiery pit, as he had done. Nay, more, ghosts, those poor dead specters of tradition, by their obverse figuration threw off the cerements of death and beheld the infinite. Salvation lay in this infallible essence of life. It made small and it made great, and always at its center was man, in form and moving express and admirable.

Easter Monday his mother sent for him. He went loiteringly, using the good excuse of Heaving Day to defer her questions. Old Rogers was lifting Judith Sadler off her feet and claiming a kiss in token of the Lord's being lifted up to glory. In Will's path was old Mrs Shaw and he swung her aloft where she cackled from a long life of such fun.

"Mind tomorrer, Wully! 'Ool be thy turn to be heaved. Faith, women plan feast o' beer un goodies stretched clean cross road t'catch ye one and all."

"I'll be there," he said, and kissed her old bright cheeks again for good measure.

Around the High Cross certain great kissing fellows had settled in to spend the day, and Will wished them gladness.

His mother said, "Have you heard?"

He wasted no time in persiflage. "No word, good mother. Peace." She groaned. "Aye. Amen."

He did not stir her up by saying that he might never hear, that being the world's way. The Shakespeare gentility might be stripped away unknown to either.

In her soft reasonable voice, she said, "I've set out that when Greenway comes from London with any mail for thee, he's to come straight to New Place."

Will drew in his breath. She went on with a composure as double-faced as his. "For we must know the worst before we can set at work the best."

"The best?"

She laid her slender hand on his arm and looked into his eyes. "Aye, power to meet power."

As she spoke, his fingers stroked and stroked at the lines on his brow while he selected, discarded, grappled for words which might reach her. He looked at her charming round face, the slightly tilted nose, the very round eyes with the deep lids, and said, "Take heed, mother, that I'll make no move to stir the black dung of London by any questions."

She acted as though she had not heard him, and continued to weave strong plans until she betrayed herself by a quake in her voice.

He murmured, "All Penelope's yarn merely filled Ithaca with moths."

"What did thee say!"

"Peace, mother."

She grew very angry, and then she burst into tears. He took her hand and talked to her calmly.

"I know the world of splendid giving where gifts are bought and bartered. It is a world as hard and yellow as gold. Think of me as I am, quit of that world. Think of me as I might become if thy dear plans held sway."

Her round deep eyes did not leave his face. He continued to hold and stroke her hand. "To buy myself from them would be to sell myself."

"From *them*?"

"Aye, those who lie in wait to smirch all honest men." He laughed harshly. "For even the rich are not sure of their rights, mother, and the high-born are, on no account, sustained by their greatness in this world of which thee know naught and I, all. They set one against another, and he who comes to play the courtier—and this is what thee do ask of me—loses his right to be a merry chapman, for the game of power requires a coldness of the heart and mind. I know them, mother. They deal in offal."

Her eyes had remained fixed on him, and as his light voice fell silent, her gaze dropped to his hand stroking her hand. She sat very still. Presently she murmured, for him to hear or not, "Thee were ever yet too gentle."

He laid down her hand quietly and rose.

Of the world he was forewearied.

Now night after night he slept when his head first touched the pillow. Anne continued to lie awake, watching the fire. She knew the sleep he sought was oblivion. That she was and was not his wife struck her sorely. To her the truth was very simple: *I love my husband.* But to him, it seemed, it was not simple, and here she lost her way. That he hated her she did not think. That he was cold she did not believe. That he had ceased to love her became her terror. To love a man for twenty years was to invest love with the length of life which only death could part. *But what of all the time after death?* She laughed with silent irony. Well, that too . . .

From such drugged nights he wakened before dawn, thought of her with a rush of bitter sweetness, and always found her gone. Each morning he rose by himself and went out to watch the day begin.

This April morning, he idled down the sleepy street, thinking of that day when his prince would find a means of redress. Not naked revenge, but himself larger, somehow, than events. He set out for the Market Cross to see what buds had come to the chestnut tree. There in the early light the beadle was whipping old Tim Perry in the pillory.

Meekins struck with no great fervor, but the blood ran down

374

the old man's back and Tim's face wore a look of such obliteration that the very man himself seemed to have stepped aside.

He saw Will as the beadle put down the whip, and on the confusion of his features, a stark pride emerged. Meekins said, "Godden, Will," and fastened old Tim's shirt about him. "Now then, stand awhile."

Will halted below Tim. Tim said, "Oh, Wully, cum thee to end of days with better honor."

Meekins answered stoutly, "Tim, we beat thee to honor thy godliness."

The confusion of Tim's features was increased by a laugh that held no mirth. His eyes were on Will. "So he sez, but I think a light burn blue for me last night, and that, as all know, be end."

Will said with a sudden terrible urgency for himself and poor mankind, "Tim, I'll be surety for thee. I'll feed and house and work thee kindly. Come with me!"

Tim shook his head, and there were tears, whether of rheumy age or sadness, in his eyes.

"Thankee kindly, Wully, no. M' fate I bring upon m'self."

Will came into his home and locked the door onto the street. He stood all alone in the hall . . . his fortress. Within the enclosure of the walls, each pot and dish, and condiment, each leaf, each flower, bird and crawling thing, and glass in windows, must be defended like a siege. For if he did not find a true repentance, how could he claim his own?

He touched the mule-chest, he touched the paneled walls and the hangings. Susanna came down the stairs and he touched her hair and cheek.

He went to the solar and sat there through the day. He heard the chapel bells call his father and all to Council meeting; men sitting to judge their peers. With sudden rage, he cursed such judges.

He thought of men's tricks on men. He knew them all. He would not be caught unawares.

Having come to the end of the afternoon with little to show, he went into the garden to soothe himself with a book. There Susanna brought her knitting to coax him to read to her.

Susanna was in love with all men because she was in love with

one, Will thought as she laid her head against her father's neck.
"Oh, such love-dove," he said rubbing his cheek against her hair. "It's not always thee treat thy father so."

"Read," she said sweetly.

"I've known thy prickles. What would thee coax from me now, honeybee?"

"Read."

"This?" he said of the book. "But it's not even in God's English."

"Then," she said, settling against him, "make it into God's English from whatever naughty tongue it be."

"My dearest, it is French, out of very choice Italian." The chapel bell began to ring. "Hark, there go home our elders, having separated our tares and wheat until next Council meeting."

"Never mind that," she said, "what is this book called?"

"It is called *Hecatommithi*. The tale I read is called 'The Moor of Venice' and is not, I fear, fit for Christian maiden's ears."

"I do not know what you mean. Read on."

So he limped with his small French into English, skipping here and there, thinking with a sharp and practiced mind how out of this sow's ear he might contrive a leather purse, suitable for a play.

When he had finished, she lay against his shoulder, shredding a leaf which had fallen on her knitting.

"Ah, poor lady," she said in a voice quite like her mother's, "I would not let a man behave so foolishly."

"Would thee not?" he answered gently, "and how would thee mend it, my sweet peach?"

"Why, by making him stand to and see what a wicked man was his enemy."

"Evil does not always come so clear, my darling," he said.

She thought for a moment. "I would know," she said, "if my love were engaged."

"Perchance it was merely thy body. Then what, chuck?"

She did not answer quickly. "My body will not teach my mind," she said softly.

He kissed her hair. "Then thou wilt teach the world."

She sat up straight and looked at him somewhat shyly.

"You are very wise and clever, are you not, father?"

He replied with his arm around her, "That is a flattery crude enough to touch an anxious heart."

Tom came into the garden through the gate, not seeing them. He was a man in a temper, and when he saw them sitting in a loving pose, a certain darkness crossed his face. Will greeted him with the touch of irony he could not master.

Tom did not reply for a moment. He stood irresolute, his gaze lowered, one open hand twitching against his thigh. Then he said in a quick jerky way, " 'Tis wait and wait and wait again. The Council will postpone Judgment Day."

"Is it thy clerkship, cousin?"

"Aye." He mimicked. " 'Why, Tom, it just did not come up. Now I wonder why?' Geld a codpiece!"

"Oh, Tom, Tom! Though patience be thy tired mare, she'll plod on."

Tom did not care for the laughter in Will's voice. He looked at him for a moment and then said with a nice venom, "Well, chew on this: the Council has taken time to bar plays from Stratford. What do you think of that?"

Had Tom planned his thrust, it would not have been more precise. Will searched him with his eyes. Then he frowned.

"Barred plays? Why?"

Tom shrugged.

"Why *now?*" Will asked.

Tom laughed shortly, as though the vagaries of why and what were beyond his need to know. "It is the temper of the times. What will come, men say, if we do not make our peace with God? Civil war and all riot, the papists in the seats again. Stratford is very prone to such a temper." He added, "Mr Byfield preaches sermons that make one wonder whether the very stones will not tempt men from God." He stooped to examine a gooseberry bush.

"But plays—playactors—*I*—tempt men from God?"

Tom shrugged. "I do not say it, but 'tis said."

Will asked abruptly, "Who is my enemy?"

Tom put out a restraining hand. " 'Tis not John Coombs!"

377

"Then it is someone very like. This is no trick in a corner. Who is John Coombs's creature on the Council?"

Tom shrugged. "I do not know, cousin, but John Coombs is not strong enough to sway the clerkship to me."

"Oh, you fool! He will wait until he has you more and more within his grasp, and then he'll reach and hook you." Tom looked at him angrily, and Will asked after a moment, "What is the Council's action?"

Tom replied sullenly, "They have resolved that no more plays are to be given in the Gild Hall, and that any member of the Council who takes it on himself to license players will be fined ten shillings."

It was a squeezed humiliation, and Will in a gesture that he scarcely understood looked about him at his house, his gardens, his orchards, his barns, as though they stood in proxy to some godliness in man. Susanna was touched by his expression. She picked some violets and put them in the opening of his jerkin.

Tom studied Will under lowered brows.

After supper, Will went to pick a quarrel with Quiney. Quiney, as head over this town, had betrayed some article in the encyclical of their life together.

"That thou—thou, Dick Quiney—could so stab at me that the name of God was used to my hurt and confusion—this confounds me to a deep amazement!"

Quiney's anxiety deepened in his kind eyes. Then his face reddened and he sighed. "Oh, Beelzebub! Playacting? Nay, confusion's cure lies not in confusion. Be peaceful, Will."

"Ill-gotten words!"

"The times—the times!"

"Oh, hellfire, I live in the times. I curse them every day."

"Ah, Will, do not roil thyself. Thee be Stratford born and bred —this action's not at thee." Will sat drumming his fingers on the table, his head lowered, his eyes closed. Quiney said, "Will—" and was shocked, when Will briefly opened his eyes, to see them filled with tears.

Quiney sat staring at his friend. "These be also great and glorious times when each man's conscience is his book, and the future—" he faltered, for Will opened his eyes again, and smiled in such a way as made Quiney cry, "Hell's ramparts! I did not vote so, nor thy father! And it was not against thee, but against unnaturalness—men in women's clothes, and painting and bawdry and disguises, and things which are not, in place of things which are!"

That Will lived in this town was sure; to end as his own master was his sure intent. These were fixed stars. When he got home, he said to Tom, "Tomorrow we will go to Coombs and talk of land." Land was sinless and honorable.

To Anne he said nothing, for in a convoluted way he would not believe that plays and players related to a life in which she had a part. And more, that this day's events had to do with punishment and penance and the blind ways of fate which, by too much talking, would multiply their toll.

Suddenly she spoke without intending it. She said, "How God must love thee, Will, to make thy heart so good."

It was no less a miracle than the burning bush.

He put his arms about her and drew her to him till she was close as his breath.

"My dearest soul, I cannot smile and talk and turn any more. I cannot look for peace where it is not. I cannot find my way alone. Will you take me with all my sins, dear love?"

He pressed his face into the curve of her neck.

"Ah," she said, "what sins? I know not any."

He put his mouth on hers. "I'faith, I come home to you."

Old lovers have ways to find each other. They remember only the good and forget the bad. There was much sweet joy to remember.

At length he whispered, "Oh, heart's dear, may every tempest bring such calm."

CHAPTER *Seven*

THE next day was keen and clear like his own soul. *A man and his wife being two are one.* It was no longer a conundrum.

Tom reminded him about John Coombs.

"By heaven, yes. What joy sublime. Come, dear Tom. Let's make old Saturn laugh and leap with us. I have come home and here I mean to stay."

Tom, by his expression, showed some curiosity, but Will was at too great an ease with life to banter him. He said, "The Coombses are leeches, Tom. Remember that when you're tempted to set them up too high. For three generations they've ruled the countryside, except for such families as the Cloptons and the Lucys who, no doubt, preceded God to Stratford. Ten per cent interest on all loans, that's their rule, unless the need is dire, when the interest's set at twelve. Oh, Tom, smile! I sat in school with John Coombs, and I fancy when I began to buy their land he was tickled somewhere in his cool usurous parts, planning how he would play the game of taking it away from me. Well, if he does not succeed, he'll merely shrug: I'll say that for him; he's mean but he's not evil. Shall I go on? Would you hear more?"

Tom smiled. "If I become Clerk, shan't I learn it all?"

"Not as well as you will from me. 'Twas he induced his father, brother, uncle to accept my cold coin. He does not always trust his brother in business ways, for Thomas suffers from that special illness of our age, poetic fever, and his uncle William, sitting so high and grand in Parliament, and his father John, collecting rents and making leases for the Earl of Warwick, have rarer things to think on. But John the younger, he's got no wife, no private life, only loans, per centums, appraisals, and so it pleases him to control, defeat, and encourage the rise of all new men in this town. Because you are my loyal cousin, he believes he will also have a grip on me who has eluded him so far." He looked at Tom. "Oh, be cheerful, sir! You're worth all this to me and him."

Tom barely smiled. "I would not do his bidding."

"Ah, did I say that? You'd serve the Corporation well, and that means Stratford. Tom, laugh! Devil's teeth, man, you live now in the only other house in Stratford that's as grand as the Priests' House, and so you can take the Coombses' measure."

They paused for a moment on the Old Town before the Coombses' gate. The house, which had been a priests' college in the days before the old king, Henry VIII, was out of sight behind the trees, but the grounds, in new spring grass, lay as inviting as all good intentions. Will threw his arm around Tom's shoulder for a moment.

"I pray you, cousin, watch how it is done by him and me. And be my friend, as I am yours."

Thomas Coombs's son Thomas was beating a servant, and he greeted them with a flushed face; his sandy brows and eyelashes started out with peculiar whiteness. He blinked and smiled, but his expression had a thickness that took away the natural comeliness of youth.

Jerking at his small ruff, he contrived to release a nod. "Aye, aye, come within."

He kicked at the servant and sent him off, and animated speech broke from him as he pointed to a monstrous springless traveling coach that groaned with each movement of the servants as they took the luggage from it.

"Father's uncle come from London there, and he dare not go to Warwick till they catch that outlaw who feeds on coaches. By the devil, I'd hunt him down and hang him in a cage from a tree for birds to peck at! Say, you come from London now!" And an expression which Will knew well on other faces moved slow as treacle across Thomas' own, an expression of bawdy tales remembered, and disreputableness exploding as limbs and parts in his mind.

Will bore with it, nodding and smiling as young Thomas led them across the dark stone hall and managed to convey in this brief journey a contempt for Stratford, a knowledge of the wide world, and an intimate command of the salacities of Oxford life.

When he threw open the door he revealed a row of Coombses. Will's smile brightened at this formidable undertaking.

But no vivacity of greeting appeared on any face, though Thomas the elder rose from his place by the wan fire, set aside his massive goblet and advanced with a heavy tread. His head moved up and down as though ruled by a mechanism, and this, together with a limp hand, was his welcome. Yet he was pleased. He nodded to Tom Greene; and to his son he said, "Wine."

His gratification when any Stratfordian, great or less, came to him was well known. He showed it by a deepening coldness that came close to heat. In this instance, a poet greeted a poet; it increased the occasion. He returned silently to the fire and gestured to a stool. Chairs, except for the master's and his brother's, had not found their way to the Priests' House. The row of Coombs faces, set in relief against the say curtains, the portrait of the Queen, the tapestries of *Poverty* and *The Murder of the Innocents*, all turned in one direction.

Will bowed smilingly. He longed for jokes and games. He was quite unaffected by the power resident here, yet charmed by the sight of men and women.

The parlor had been the priests' common room, and in spite of rich hangings and paintings, it preserved some of the austerity of the ecclesiastic way. Indeed, the shift from ecclesiastic to economic authority had, Will reflected, not perceptibly altered the climate of the place. His ear observed the modulation of voice, as though God had given them a final message, and even in the shift of eyes to the open door, there was something cool and otherworldly.

They were a handsome assemblage, clothed in modest splendor. The heavily wrought features of both men and women, although lacking in sensitiveness, had a forceful character.

Uncle William and his wife sat with a small oak table between them, partaking of a meal which was composed largely of the dead limbs of animals which they held in their hands. Uncle William had a linen tablecloth fixed under his ruff, and by his right hand a quart tankard. His wife showed a more dainty spirit with a pint pot.

Young Thomas brought two goblets of wine to Will and Tom and hitched forward another stool with his foot. A concerted lifting of goblets followed in a silence that was challenged only by the creaking of Mrs William Coombs's stool.

This lady was weathered, empty-eyed, smelling slightly of old clothes and the winter; she turned with drumstick in hand to see what disposal these men made of themselves.

Will sat before them all, one leg crossed over a knee, easeful, chatting, measuring the moment. He had meant John Coombs to speak first, but any such course seemed now highly trivial. This world of sacrosanct usury, entailments, leases, and rents, struck him forcibly as a world that trifled with humanity in ways even more ambiguous than the world of Lord William. He did not wish to be too well informed of its rules.

He stated his wish courteously and simply, buried half his face in his goblet, and observed Tom Greene's expression as he did so. Obsequious. Eyes and manner pleading with the Coombses to take nothing amiss, to exert their good pleasure that we poor dogs may live. Will frowned. A man must be either yea or nay . . .

Thomas Coombs did not answer, so there was a weight of silence. John Coombs smiled a little, a faint muscular twinge beneath his mustache, and he beat a slow liturgy with his fingers on his arms. William Coombs, the largest and heaviest and most imposing, ran his tongue over his lips and wiped his beard with the cloth. Then he fetched up a sigh and studied his nephews with a lackluster air.

The two ladies had no reason for comment, but the younger— the one of a more modest bestowal, who had *not* been married to Sir William Pickering, Keeper of the Great Seal, but had been raised from simple stock to the Coombses' bed—she had put down her stump work and was now watching Will with an unobtrusive blinking and a faint animation around her mouth and cheeks. Her two sons were playing chess by the fire, and kneenudging each other for the next move, so inattentive were they to the game.

Will felt a sudden complete indifference to the whole matter of buying and selling. Wife, home and peace were so superb that all other things paled beside them. The sense was so complete and obliterating that he began to rise. But Tom Greene's shocked living eye, and the sudden fearful clanging of the iron chamber clock with its buttresses and vigorous bell, recalled him to the temporal needs of courtesy.

Thomas Coombs's eyes had by now traveled to meet his brother's, and John was smiling openly. It was he who spoke, in a high, thin voice that contrived to be very human.

"Ah, Will, Will, Will, buying and selling like the children of men? Why, how will thee end? How will thee cherish Stratford acres in London?"

"Ah, John, John, John, do thee not know that man lives in his mind? I'll have these fields with me in London."

"How much?" said Thomas suddenly, looking at Will with the full measure of stare.

"How many acres?" Will replied.

"Of that parcel, twenty and some."

Will named his price with no tone of barter. Thomas accepted it. John laughed shortly. Tom Greene looked grateful and relieved. Thomas the younger checked his brother, Mrs Thomas picked up her stump work, Mrs William wiped her mouth and looked sleepy, though she, who had been married to Sir William Pickering, Keeper of the Great Seal, had forgotten more about finance and exchange than Thomas Coombs would ever know.

Will started to rise. John motioned him to sit again. "Thomas forgets my name must be on this bargain." Thomas Coombs opened his eyes wide and looked at him, then sighed faintly and pressed his thumb tips together. John laughed very low.

Will said with perfect good nature, "I've named my price, John." John waved his hand. "Ah, the price is too low, but 'twill pass. God's dirt. Nay, I wish to ask a question that hath been in my mind since Stratford men went up to London carrying a grievance against our lord of the manor."

Tom Greene looked alarmed and pale, when John's wintry eye fell on him. "Indeed, thy esteemed kinsman was among them."

Tom opened his mouth to speak, and then thought better of it, and closed it tight as a bailey. Will smiled, wide awake. John added smile to smile, and settled himself with a quiver almost sensuous in its content. "Our lord of the manor has exercised certain prerogatives of enclosure. Law is on his side. Where do thee stand, Will?"

Will, friendly and clear, studied him for a moment. "I have not thought very much about such things, John. Now I must think." He settled himself, fingers pressed against his mouth, eyes lively and gay. Thinking entailed gazing at John with a slight smile, and John, with unblinking pale eyes, gazed back in return. After a moment, Will took his fingers away from his mouth.

"I have thought. I know how men can be bamboozled and lose their way. I am no lover of the lord of the manor and I itch to play pranks. Enclosing! Fie, John, save in the hand of God. Why, Stratford men are true men, living in a modern age. How could they yield in such a matter as taking the rights of pasture from the community?"

John continued to smile and glanced at his brother. Thomas stiffened the lines between nose and mouth, but his eyes seemed to be looking at something far away. John rose.

"Thee do not need those twenty acres, Will."

Will stood up. "I see that I do not. That was a close escape."

Tom Greene looked bedraggled, his black beard showing hairily against his white face. He turned forlorn eyes onto John, who did not shake hands.

But Thomas did. Thomas had risen, taken a volume from the table, and held it out to Will. He then pressed his hand.

"From my pen. I should be glad of thine opinion."

Will responded with appropriate ejaculations and hand clasp, reading aloud *One Hundred Moral Emblems from the French by Thomas Coombs, Esquire,* nodding as though he grasped its rich import.

Walking up the Bank Croft Lane, Will still held the book open. He laughed with some affection. "He hath given me six copies, each time with the same presentation." Tom Greene did not reply and Will glanced at him. "You are much put about, cousin. I went as much for you as for myself, and see what I have done!" He burst out laughing. Tom could not laugh. "I ask your pardon, Tom, though, faith, such great carven figures should be toppled over. Tom, Tom, I promise this will not affect your chances!"

"How?"

"Well, you must treat with them separately, not as part of me. God's bread, man, don't underrate yourself. All I ask is that naught be done *against* my good. For I've come home."

"Oh, not against thy good, Will!" Tom cried in an agony. "The clerkship lies in John Coombs's hands. I've set my heart. Truly it would not impinge on thee."

"Why John? Would not others do as well?"

"No one else has the Corporation plate in pawn as has John! He can fix the screws."

Will crowed with laughter. "I think he will not fail you. I think he will now make you sweat a little more, and ask some things of me through you, but he'll support you in the end. Who else is there in Stratford with your legal learning? The Corporation should be on its knees to you."

Tom expelled a breath through his teeth. "Will, what way could he touch thee?"

"No way, save as a peaceful tree is troubled by a hard wind."

At Chapel Lane, Tom Greene went in by the garden door, and Will went on to Quiney's.

Entering the shop, he said cheerfully, "I've come to find out what mischief we can make for the black lord. I'm full of game and sport."

Quiney looked up from a deaf old lady he was waiting on, and his kind face was visited by light.

"Well, praise be God that brings all things to hand!"

He left his son, Thomas Adrian, to shout at the old lady, and took Will into the sunlight of the garden. He spoke eagerly.

"I told thee we must appeal to have our appeal heard. I have formed the opinion of going again to Fulke Greville and putting it once more square to him. Think of all his honest ties to Stratford: himself justice of the peace, his father Recorder, his cousinship to the Earl of Warwick, his help in the past. If thee were hand in hand with me again in this, I'd be much comforted."

Will looked away from Dick into the boughs of the mulberry tree. Greville was a name like Rutland, or Hunsdon, full of prickly souvenirs—though nothing like Lord William.

"Go to London?" Will asked with caution.

"No, to Alcester, whither he hath come."

Dick was watching him with a contracted brow. Dick was the friend of his youth, bound by ties as unbreachable as they were different from the ties with Gus Phillips. His tongue would swell in his throat before he would lay naked before Dick the reasons why Fulke Greville put some weight on his spirit.

Rising, he walked around the mulberry tree, examining it closely and singing, "Ten in the hundred the Devil allows; but Coombs will have twelve he swears and avows. If anyone asks who lies in this tomb, 'Oh,' quoth the Devil, ' 'tis my John o'Coombs.' "

Thomas Adrian, standing cross-legged in the door, laughed aloud.

Quiney said, with a slow smile, "What be that?"

"Epitaph for John Coombs, by W. Shakespeare, defrauded of twenty acres. It is also a snap of my fingers at fellows who cast long shadows on good men. When must we ride to Alcester?"

Quiney's freckled face was alight. "Tomorrow."

That night he wrote on his play until his candle guttered. The play had set its course and all was well. It was as alive as himself and his peace with home. When, later on, he lay beside his wife, he whispered for a long time of thoughts and plans, and she murmured sleepily. Their hands were clasped. He kissed her lingeringly. How could a man want more happiness?

Quiney, wearing his bailiff's chain, said very little as they took the road that led through the forest of Arden. He observed merely that "it be mizzling day. Wind's going downhill."

But as they rode through the neglected countryside where the wild apple and pear were struggling in a confusion of growth, and the hawthorne was entangled in hedge, he broke into words.

"Our black lord's steward, look, brought this morn a fulminous missive that may or may not be grief for all." He lifted his head and surveyed the melancholic land so rank with spring. "I be sick unto death of fighting daffy men."

Will made no comment. He was moved by Dick's love of the rights of man. It was a love that must be defined more by instinct than law. Dick was a Christian and a Protestor who said God gave man his singularity, not crown or state or church gave it.

387

Dick's face with its freckles had always a boyish look. It was now turned toward the sorry fields. "That cottage there—it be naught but sticks and dirt, and all because of men like our black lord; though this be the Golden Fleece of England without which mankind would have starved."

"Aye, I see it now," Will said, though he also saw the mayflower coming into bud, and the gorse yellow as gold.

Sir Fulke's home, Beauchamp Court, was not a park. Sir Fulke had forborn to enclose his land. They rode through the arch of the gatehouse and down a road through the rough pasture which came up to the house.

Beyond one saw pollarded trees and pleached vines which told of walks and gardens. The house was open-faced, with tall windows in the Tudor style. It was made of Cotswold stone which had a honey look.

Dick went to the great door and pulled the bell. Will stood with his back to the house and looked off north and west where the land rolled in good pastures and hedgerows as far as the eye could see.

This Greville was a great family. Grevilles and Nevilles and Beauchamps had ruled Warwickshire in one way or another since the days of the Norman.

The servant who came, wearing the blue coat and yellow worsted stockings of Greville livery, had himself been a Stratford man and welcomed the Bailiff and Mr Shakespeare. They waited in the paneled hall and examined a lively tapestry of Venus and Adonis. Presently the servant returned, and they went with him to the study where Sir Fulke was playing chess with a very old lady.

Here sat London, cap à pie. The scent Greville wore, the rustle of his garments, the rosette at his knee, the velvet cap with the rich jewel, the cultivated expression, were the incarnation of that world of silken power. To present oneself, hat in hand, was to slip back into the comportment and servility which Will had cast off when he returned to Stratford.

Will put his hat under his arm.

Greville rose with the courtesy of the country. The old lady looked at them with sharp moist eyes and rested her mottled hand against her wavering chins. Greville shook their hands and named them to the old lady. Neither by expression nor movement did she acknowledge their response.

Sir Fulke said he supposed they had business with him to ride so far as Alcester. With bows and murmurs to the old stone lady, they went to walk in the sunshine, though her eyes followed them beyond the window.

Will murmured a variety of pleasantries, and kept his eyes fixed on the sensible country trees. The personification of Fulke Greville was accompanied, like a masque at court, by Elements, Symbols and Qualities that Will knew only too well. He had last seen Fulke Greville the night his lady had taken him onto the river. The mucky taste came back to him so unexpectedly that he put his handkerchief up to his mouth.

Greville was himself a man of singular goodness and, through this irony, a leaden echo was heard by Will, as though the wicked world, able to lay its finger on such a man, could make reverberant its terrible power.

Will was aware that Greville was looking at him as though familiarizing himself in some manner. Will thought that Greville might look at him in the same way if his mother carried out her rash threat to intercede.

The three men walked beside the ancient yews. Will paced silently, his hands clasped behind his back, attentive to Dick's laconic account of their black lord's latest threat. For Dick there were no sycophantic memories. He moved sturdily, his hat on his head again, his small clear eyes fixed on Greville. He concluded on a hard tone. "Thus hath he put it on a line. And such a rage doth great hurt and harm, not only to the Corporation of Stratford, but to every son of Adam."

Fulke Greville nodded. "I know his rages." His thin features were pursed, his intelligent and experienced eyes measured Quiney and behind him the Corporate Body of Stratford. He was a man of modern sensibility, aware that his kinsman was already dead and buried though the poor old man knew it not. Yet there were delicate coilings of precedent and prerogative which must be taken into account, in order that peace might be kept in these fractious times.

He paced and pondered for some time between the yews. He asked questions of Dick and studied him with his careful glance, having added, subtracted, and deduced for the Queen many times.

At length he stopped short under a medlar plum and said that the rights of the Corporation must be protected; he would speak with his cousin.

Dick's face smoothed like a young man's. He laughed and looked at Will. Will smiled and nodded and said, "Many thanks to you, sir," and put on his hat, thus hastening that process whereby the bear of London reverted to the bush of Stratford.

Sir Fulke now said with a gentle heartiness that they must drink a stoup of wine. He put his hands lightly on both their arms to direct them toward the house. He delivered a quiet panegyric to the country and said, in an offhand way, that London had quieted in a measure from the lamentable rebellion of Lord Essex. He added, more for Will than Dick, that Lord Southampton remained in the Tower and had been heard to regret all the hardships felt by the innocent.

He turned aside to examine the gardener's work in a bed of tight green tulips. "Ambition is, indeed," said he, "the shadow of a dream. Some philosophers opine that the gods curse men by granting their ambitions." He looked at Will. "What think you, sir, who have written of ambition?"

Will smiled. "I see that it requires much attenuation to keep it wholesome."

The old lady still sat in the study. She did not glance up, but she stirred at intervals to move a chess piece against herself. With the wine, Sir Fulke's geniality flowered, though all his change was gentle. He put out his small hand, palm upward toward Will, and said in his closet voice, "My ears are hungry for noble words. Will you not try a speech, sir?"

Will kept his hat skewered on. "What speech, sir?"

"Why, let us taste of Dido's lament. Or some newer thing— that would be an honor undreamt."

Will gave him Dido's lament as being a thing of harmless inconsequence. Then, on an impulse, he remembered some lines he had written the other day out of an angry mind.

"That nature, being sick of man's unkindness,
Should yet be hungry! Common mother, thou
Whose womb unmeasurable, and infinite breast
Teems, and feeds all; whose self-same mettle,
Whereof thy proud child, arrogant man, is puff'd,
Engenders the black toad and adder blue,
The gilded newt and eyeless venom'd worm,
With all the abhorred births below crisp heaven
Whereon Hyperion's quickening fire doth shine;
Yield him, whom all thy human sons doth hate,
From forth thy plenteous bosom, one poor root."

Dick looked startled. The old lady hawked and spat into her handkerchief; she fixed Will with relentless rheumy eyes. Greville put on a look of courteous gravity and nodded several times. He commented on the words "Hyperion's quickening fire doth shine; Yield him." He pointed out the copious variation and use of sound which lay within the competence of poets, and expatiated with charming vivacity on the use of consonants, analogy, simile, metaphor, metonymy in the service of poetry. He kept his eyes on Will.

Will answered briefly, but with a friendly scrutiny of this man. His protest made, he could now afford to study him. The lines had been offered with questionable intent, but Sir Fulke had given no sign of offense and had turned the moment to Will's benefit. Then Sir Fulke rested his chin on his hand and became lost in some retrospection. Dick slid forward his legs to rise. Sir Fulke looked at Will and spoke as though they were alone in the room.

"Your patron, and I fancy friend, Lord William, has been arrested."

Will stared at Sir Fulke. *Lord William. Arrested.* What a mad conjoining of words! Arrested? That golden youth! For being cautious and careful, and a generous purveyor of money for the Queen's use?

He frowned and stared at Sir Fulke, who added in his small voice, "He hath been charged with siring a child out of wedlock. And for refusing to marry the lady."

Every caution that Will had ever known came down on him like a fog. After a moment he asked carefully, "How can this be? The lady?"

Sir Fulke's smile was discreet, even merciful. He said, "The lady's identity is no secret, alas. But the greatness of her family hath enjoined silence."

Then indeed was the fountain of Will dried up. Anything that he might say would be so true and so unrecognizable—as familiar objects are themselves while distorted by nightmare— that he had no choice but silence.

Revenge. His revenge and Lord William's revenge had united to create Lord William's arrest. And yet all he could see at this moment was her face when she told him of her only true love.

He stood there, to all intents a model of discretion, but his eyes did not leave Greville's face. "Sir, I am struck with amazement. I know not what to say. Speak for me, I beg you. Where is he lodged? What is his health?" And then, after the faintest pause, "How is the lady?"

Sir Fulke rose and moved a chess piece overlooked by the old stone woman. He said quietly, "He is lodged at Fleet gaol. His health is good: he has the governor's apartment." He added somewhat tartly, "He seems in no way discommoded. His food bills are princely. He is, however, very much put out." He too indulged in a faint pause. "She has left London." Sir Fulke bent his head a little so that he looked obliquely at Will. "Lord William has caused a bit of doggerel to be printed." He paused as though assembling it in his head.

"For if with one with thousands thou'lt turn whore.
Break ice in one place and it cracks the more.

"This has not made it easy for the Privy Council to mend matters with her father. For you will, no doubt, be alive to the implications of these lines. Lord William is suggesting that the paternity is in some doubt."

Then, as though he wished no more said or exchanged, he rose abruptly, pulled at a tapestry bell rope, and held out his hand to Dick and to Will.

"Good day, sirs. God be with you. I will care for that matter."

Will rode, sunk in the pale light. Dick glanced at him, and after a moment said quietly, "There can come no good of vexing thyself."

Will did not answer. He thought how revenge redounds. He did not think directly of her. She was well able to care for herself, though he could not keep away the remembrance of a mettlesome spirit that now and then shone through the predator she had become. He thought of a baby brought unwanted to a world—but all such thoughts must be stopped in mid-feeling, for with him she had no more a place. His wife had closed the door and held the key, and he did not wish it changed.

When he reached his stable, he did not get off the horse for a moment. He put his hand against his chest. His heart was beating as though he had run all the way with a host pursuing him.

He entered through the kitchen where the smell of supper was rising from the spit. He greeted Nan and then, dusty and hot, paused by the parlor window. In the garden Anne sat idle for the moment, though her sewing lay on her lap. Tom Greene stood, as graceful as Hercules before Omphale, reading aloud to her and her daughters. There was animation in his look and manner; now and then he glanced down to smile at Anne.

Will threw off his gloves and went into the garden. He greeted all and took the book from Tom. Tom was startled, glanced at Anne, relinquished the book, and then took a step forward to point out the line.

Will was a better reader than Tom Greene. He made the most of it. But in six lines they were called to supper. Tom Greene smiled slightly and courteously offered to relieve Will of the book.

Will handed it him, scarcely aware of the hand that stretched out. He had suddenly thought, The lady is barely three years older than Susanna.

393

CHAPTER *Eight*

THAT he had breathed for a moment the silken world of Sir Fulke carried no penalty unless he wished to impose one on himself. And in this he would not be his enemy. After supper he sat in the kitchen and thought that what Sir Fulke had laid before him had been abstracted from a world which, at the moment, had no command on him. He owed it nothing but Christian charity and a certain knowledgeable caution.

Here at home he had found himself: husband, father, master, and diligent compeer of those poor, good fellows suffering in Scotland.

All this was true as truth, solid as the kitchen stool on which he sat. He had no other obligations whatsoever, and all the subtle and complicated riggings of his imagination must strangle themselves in their own lines. He loved his wife and she came in to stir the pottage that would be their next-day breakfast. He rose and put the purring cat on the floor. "Thank God for wife and kitchen pots," he said softly, and kissed her on the sweet curve of neck.

"Thank God for husbands who do rule in peace."

At that a rough pounding at the door laughed at peace and sounded like the Judgment Day. He was amazed, but Anne laughed, and Susanna, rushing into the kitchen, could scarcely contain herself.

"Oh, it be May Day Eve, father!" she cried unbelieving that any could forget. "Oh, oh, what boughs be they nailing to the door? Oh, Judith, can thee not see!"

In the hall Judith was making shy and valiant efforts to see out the window by the door without being seen.

"Oh, look again! What if they do make a joke of me!"

Tom, coming out from the parlor, teased her. "Why do thee think that thee alone live here?"

"Aye," said Will, "can they not be honoring thy mother or thy

394

sister—or Tom, or thy poor Dad—plum for glum, or thorn for scorn?"

But she was sure. When at length Judith came on tiptoe, wreathed in smiles, to say they'd gone, Susanna flew to the door. What bliss! Pear for fair. They all stood on the street to admire the bough. Susanna kissed them all, and told her sister and her mother that John had surely meant it for them as well.

"And will we go into the fields, father, before the dawn?" Judith asked, standing close and looking up at him.

"Why, what could keep us home! Unless we sleep too late."

"I will not sleep," Susanna said, laying all her knitting out, "so rest you well. Pear . . ." She looked at her mother slyly. "Dare, fair . . . pair."

Will waked her while it was still dark, and kissed her cross and sleepy face.

Only the staid, elderly, and Puritan remained at home. Down the dark street were merry whispers and bursts of song. Across the dark fields and into the woods they went, friends and lovers knowing each other by some still-peering. Silence was a rite, but the clumsy and eager fell over roots, some swore, and some muffled their laughter. There was much kissing, and some goings-on to confirm the sinful heathenish purpose of old May rites.

Will found a rock on the edge of a field and drew Anne down to sit with him. They held each other's hands in silence. Presently she put her head against him and watched for the morning star. In the wide field and the dark, with only the walls and ceiling of heaven to crib, the heart was at one with God. In the deep dark, where bird, flower, beast, and man were still, she lifted their clasped hands and kissed his fingers.

Along the horizon a faint suffusion of light was greeted by the waking of birds.

"Good dawn to thee, heart." He kissed her. "Fair day, peaceful night, and many days and seasons."

"Calm and content," she replied, "be thy guerdons."

The first color appeared in the sky, and with that sign the

395

silence was broken. The dawn was hailed with drums and cow-horns, fifes and old trumpets, voices bursting loose from the silence and shouting songs to the day.

Over the fields, into the woods and groves they streamed, shouting with joy. They cut the birch boughs and the sweet-smelling may as though winter and spring had given place to summer eternal.

Will cut his boughs with pleasure, singing across to his neighbors, and Anne bent to bathe her face in the dew in honor of the Day.

On the edge of the field stood Tib. Her gray cat and her ewe were standing with her, and in the early light, with mist still in the pockets of the meadow, she looked fleet and airy. Someone cried, "Fly away, witch!" spitting in her direction. Old Rogers' granddaughter, Rachel, cried, "Whist, aroint thee!" and quickly cut some twigs of rowan to make into crosses for the tails of the cows.

Susanna came up to her father. "Rachel says witches meet and have great power this day and night. Be Tib a Prior a witch?"

"Ah, whist ye!" said Anne. "That be naught to chatterpie about."

Will looked at both his wife and daughter. "I'll tell thee something now. Thee are to be most kind and courteous to Tib a Prior whatever others say. Come now. Hand in hand, we'll speak to her and say good morning."

"Oh, father!" Susanna drew back and stretched sideways toward her friends.

"I have told thee. Come."

Anne hesitated for a moment, then she said, "Thy father speaks."

Tib stood without moving though she picked up her cat and held it close. "God give you a good day," said Will, "and a happy summer."

Tib said nothing but she dropped a curtsey.

"Doth thy cat purr?" Anne asked. Tib did not reply, but she stroked the cat behind the ear and a roll of purrs came forth like a staff of music.

Will smiled. "And to thy grandfather, good yield and fruit. All blessings to you both."

Susanna stood arm's length away but her father's grasp was stern. She said faintly, "Good den."

Tib smiled then and said, "God 'ild ye all."

Walking back across the field, Will kissed Susanna.

When the village returned to breakfast, it seemed as though the woods were moving, so laden were the arms fetching summer home. The children would soon adorn the branches with ribbons and bright-colored rags, or bend them into garlands and sell them for pennies on the street. There would be no work today, but dancing from all ends of Stratford and across the river.

With dinner past, Will went up to the solar. Had he a choice he would be exactly what he was, a setter down of thought and feeling, a translator of himself and other men. He fancied there was no joy to be compared to that. And what he put down would not remain trussed in words. Actors would cut the bonds.

Dickon, Heminges, Gus had their own thoughts and bodies. He talked aloud. He set Heminges to enact steely-jawed old councilors, and how they set traps for the unwary in a fashion that both life and the exigencies of the play would accept. He imitated Dickon's breath-span, his way with arms and head. He contended with Dickon on the fall of a thought, and the thought of a word, and whether an actor had passion to spare at this point.

Dickon's voice infused one scene and rejected another; Will did not protest. He himself was an actor. He sat thinking of Dickon, that consummate transformer of passion and thought; of Dickon, his prince, brought to a pitch of readiness. "Enact and testify," he whispered, "for you have the sum, man."

Suddenly Anne knocked on the door.

"Oh, Will. It be Sir Fulke. Come by all means!"

Will came in haste.

Sir Fulke had passed from the Great Parlor, where Anne had left him, into the garden. He held a ribboned May branch in his hand, for which, one deduced, he had exchanged a penny. He held out his free hand, and a faint scent of musk attended the movement. He wished the joy of the day and said that since business had brought him to Stratford, he had used the occasion to call on the Bailiff. Having found Mr Quiney absent, he had taken this liberty . . . Sir Fulke gestured and inclined his head.

To come, in fact, was a compound of condescension, country ways, and the position of New Place, and this was not lost upon Will.

Sir Fulke went on, "I wished to inform the Bailiff of a moderation in the attitude of the lord of the manor. Though, to be sure, my cousin's moderation is never a matter of the firmest assurance. It is merely the occasion for a quiet hope that reason, sedulously and winsomely presented, may prevail."

Anne brought them the cowslip wine and cakes of May Day. Shyness gripped her tongue, but her brown eyes were lively, and Sir Fulke found several ways to offer his respects. When she had returned to the house, he chose a seat on a bench that encircled a tree, and Will wondered if he had given his true reason for coming.

"It is a sense of public duty," Greville said, sipping his wine, "that is most woefully lacking in these times. When our feudal suzerain passed away, what took its place? Private interest and private conscience." He spoke with no great stress, as though his own life of public conscience put this outside his direct concern. Then he added with greater bite, lifting his beardless chin out of his ruff and turning his dark eyes toward the leafy boughs, "Each degree must be kept to a proper regard for the good of the realm. No man is alone."

Will replied, as cool and languid as Sir Fulke, "Take but degree away and the string is untuned."

Sir Fulke, well-tuned to irony, moved his gaze to Will. A faint smile glinted. He said, "Where would go the wild seas or how fare the majestic heavens fretted with fiery stars, were they not held in place and order within the commonwealth of God?"

Ah, plain speaking, plain speaking! Will implored silently.

Greville murmured, "Yet we live in days when some men are scarcely friends with their own shadows."

Will offered a cautious syllogism to the effect that God had not willed a world where truth and light were denied to men. Greville nodded gravely and picked up the crumbs of the cake with his small fingers.

"Methinks," he said, "that we will look behind and chide ourselves that we mis-saw these times. Methinks they are the call for men to trim their lamps."

Then Will said with a boldness unfamiliar to such a man as Greville, "They that dally with words may quickly make them wanton."

Singing on the street came across the garden wall. Greville shot at him a look like an arrow. "I make them wanton, sir? How can that be when I know that words can be our executioners? Why, sir, I destroyed a modest drama of my composition when Lord Essex fell. The words would not have commended themselves to such times as these." He studied Will for a moment in a courteous, oblique way. "When Lord Essex fell, there was a fall indeed. Who was not touched? Who does not still stand perplexed of friends and enemies alike? . . . on Temple Bar, his head still molders, to caution and remind."

From within doors came music of the May dancers, who had entered from the street and were dancing through the rooms to bring the luck of the summer. Their singing voices, and the eager cries of cowmaid and stable boy running to the fun, curled around the quiet garden.

Will said with an effort, "Indeed, sir, as you know, you are speaking to a man who stands in such perplexity." Greville looked at him with great kindness in his eyes, and touched his mustache in lieu of reply.

At length he said, "I know a part of your perplexity. I am very sorry, sir, that you are troubled by matters that affect your family standing."

It came so suddenly that Will was swept by all the old humiliations that a mother can inflict upon a child. He pressed at his temples with his fingers.

"Then, sir, I judge my mother has made good her threat to speak to you."

Greville was distressed. "Go to, go to, sir. I beg your pardon. Your mother is a lady for whom I have a most wholesome re-

399

gard. Many a time has her sound wit laid claims on me. Nay, sir, I beg you, consider this matter fairly. How often do our remedies lie within ourselves? That is what your mother sees. Nay, hear me out. Plain speaking is a virtue, and your mother is a wise woman."

Will would, with relief, hear him out, but he rose and walked about to do so.

"There is so much matter here that we must peel it as we do an onion." Greville's gentle voice was firm. "William Camden, now. He owes me much, even his position. I will speak with him, for it may be that some part of his enemies' machinations within the College of Heralds can be rendered void by another more easily than by himself."

The dancers came dancing out the kitchen door to circle the gardens on their way back to the street. They danced around Greville and Will, bobbing bows and curtseys. Sir Fulke rose to bow to them. On they went, without pause in their singing, dancing out the garden door, and their voices could be heard until they danced into the Almshouse.

Sir Fulke smiled. He lifted his own May bough to smell the leaves and sap, and glanced at Will over the leaves. "On such a day of general rejoicing we should wisely match our tempers to the time. Though these days are bleak, the brighter days will come. Of Camden, sir, one must reflect that certain fortuities also impose restraint on him. One must consider the best ways of dealing with such matters." He glanced at Will and added softly, "For example, Lord William proposes to be reckless in his own defense and give several names of men who may be more guilty than himself. You see how the onion peels?"

Will sat down slowly on the bench. Greville kept his eyes averted and presently went on in a lighter tone, with a hint of that amused irony that colored his mind.

"Lechery may hold fashion, but by too much speaking Lord William will squander his defense."

Will endeavored to speak, but Greville, with a practised urbanity, did not permit any statement that would require a positive response from him.

"I think Lord William will be restrained. A man in his position knows the duty he owes his Queen, who is preceptress to her maids. This is being brought again to his attention, forcefully."

He made a gesture preliminary to rising, and he looked at Will with a sudden sweetness. "Gentle sir, rouse your spirit. Let us grant it is amiss to tumble on the bed, but discretion must be our moral now. To find the truth in this affair is most unlikely, and we have a woeful lady to consider and as much dishonor to abrogate as means to do so, considering her close position to the Queen. Let me have your hand." He turned toward the house. "Will you require my servant to fetch my horse?"

Will gave the order. When he returned, he found Greville examining an almond tree.

"Tell me how this grows so fair?" Told, he turned to examine the garden as a whole. "Your young limes could be coaxed into a bower. At Cobham, I have seen trees so beguiled that branches grew from the trunks in tiers, strong and cunning enough to bear stairs and platforms and fifty men concealed. Yet I have no such taste."

They had almost reached the door to the parlor when Greville stopped. He stood for a moment with his glance turned aside and his teeth holding his lower lip. Then he looked at Will, put his hand on his arm, and drew him away from the door.

"Sir, there is something else I am obliged to say. The Bailiff's presence constrained me yesterday. I should also make clear that for three days I have been under instructions to send for thee. My delay owed to a certain conflict within myself. But thou art no crack, and so I speak."

He used the homely word for "lad" as though to ease the way between them.

"The lady of whom we spoke has asked for you. She hath spoken of you in a kind and honorable way. She is a lady much cast down." He hesitated for a moment. "She is nearby, at Coughton Court."

Will did not move. Greville went through the parlor door. Will said urgently, "Sir Fulke!"

Greville paused, but he did not look at Will. "She is very

importunate. It is the Queen's express command that she be not crossed in any way so that we may mend matters that much quicker with her father."

"But discretion, my good sir—!"

"Let it be your tutor. It hath great resource."

Will returned to his solitary room. In the distance could be heard the pipes and viols of the Morris dancers who came each year from Bidford—the fool, the hobby horse, the man disguised as a maid . . . He was quite clear he would not stir abroad one step.

He was filled with bitter unreasoning anger which held a touch of terror. That authority should lay its evil hand on peace and home was more than he could bear: anger that it should so presume, and terror that he should be sent against his will into her house of spells.

His anger was the worst. He sat staring at the table, at the flat faceless outline of words remote from tears and anguish. Oh, deception of words. Oh, despicable copulation of lies with truth! Words which came from the mouth against words which came from the breast!

Some knowledge, he believed, was unbearable and so a man went mad. Discretion was a bawd. He thought for one effervescent moment that to become a part of elemental, irrational life would be salvation, for it was the humanity and divinity of man that lashed him to the burning wheel which turned and turned without an end.

This play had become his evil conscience, for it misled him. A man who thinks too much is a man who has sealed his bargain with the devil, and *there's* an end.

He remained in the solar that evening, refusing his supper. Obstinately, sullenly, he sat in the light of a candle and wrote not a word. He had made his peace with honor. He would be resolute for honor, think only of his wife, his children, his home. He would not yield to discretion, pity, compassion, or the Queen's command.

At length however he had no choice but to go quietly and

secretly out of this prison house to borrow the night for a dark hour or two.

He went without direction. The river ran through his mind nervous and chattering, and he welcomed, for company, all the unseen spirits of this May Night. He stumbled. Ah, the Council Hall! He trailed his hand along its side as he had done when a boy.

A dog barked and ran toward him. He whispered and there was a great silence as though all attention had been lost in sniffing. Here was a brick wall, blind men saw well in the dark; here the home of Susanna's beloved and the betrayal of the nobler part to the gross body's treason. Presently his foot felt the church's grassy sward. By what indirections does one find direction?

He paused for a moment, his eyes better friends with the night, and moved toward the graveyard. Here among these stones was the grave of his son, that dead half-twin. To die a child had a special grace.

Do not feel remorse. Do not become entangled in subtle griefs. Exorcise regrets. This was his litany. *Be firm, be constant.* But in the world of darkness, Flibbertigibbit, and Obidicut, Hobbididance, Modo and Mahu, and all spirits that in crossways and floods do lie buried, all devils, witches, and Robin Goodfellow, all Pinch and Patch, Gill and Grim, Sib and Tib, Lick and Lull, took on her likeness. They slipped into the orifices of his brain and there distilled that cunning poison which turns a grave into a wedding bed.

He found his son's grave and put his hands upon the mound of earth. Hamnet, prince of curds and cream . . . oh, blessed dark where I can neither see myself or be seen.

He stood up and went toward the church. He put his hands on the walls of the charnel house. Dark or light, the grave, the bone house, the riverbank where his slipping foot stirred some little creature, were all places where a man may rot and rot, and find an end.

He could not remember how his son looked. He sat down on the bank and wept.

Yet he saw *her* eyes. They brimmed with tears. Their youth, their fear, their brimming were unaffected. The remembrance of those overflowing eyes when she told him of her one true love possessed him, as did her last cry in the black of Southwark. Oh, he had helped her down the slopes of hell!

The perfumed, stayed, and wigged darling came to him as he had seen her last. He looked at her with a disrobing eye, not for lust (he was as cold as a dead fire) but for the girl beneath the tears and sighs. But one should never look beneath the skin unless one is prepared to meet the Maker. And one should never search for the soul of another unless protected by the most austere self-sovereignty. Of all rash and lonely truths, none is to be feared so much as that first glimpse of the human and divine. For, alas, one artful smile, one personated question, one importunate move corrupts the divine and leads to that path where forever after I, poor dunce, must tread between conscience and the fiend.

Oh, the quickening with kisses. The disguise of kisses. The rush of memory of kisses.

He had heard the alarm clear enough: beware, beware. Look to thyself who searches for souls. But for such as he, alarm had always been a snare so beguiling that he had run to its embrace: alarm to hope and fear, alarm to love; tocsins quickening him toward that alluring fear that truth must indeed be askant and strange, but always true.

Oh, this was a supernatural solicitation, a very potent magic!

He smote at the grass. He must cut out this malignancy or he must give up hope. Alas, those wounds heal worse than men do give themselves.

His wife must save him.

But what would he tell her? That he had been commanded to go to the woman who had laid a sickness on him? She would say, "Do not go." He would reply, "The Queen commands it." She would then look at him from the sides of her eyes. "Why art thee afraid to go?" And how would he answer? That he dared not trust himself?

He did not know whether this was true. Or whether his fear came from the bitter knowledge that his home, his wife, his children, his lands and orchards were as vulnerable to authority as he himself.

Two days ago his world had been all sun. Now it was black as London night.

CHAPTER *Nine*

HE told his wife nothing, nor did he cast off his deep depression. Anne asked no questions: a foolish woman! Yet it might be that heaven would grant that equipoise which permitted him to step between the devil and the deep sea and so come safe to land with nothing set awry.

But Anne knew. That is, she knew some new fear had come into the world of home. She asked herself slow careful questions. At length she said to Will in her soft voice, "Sir Fulke be a very courteous man. How good the house was fettled. What came he for?"

He waited a shade too long. "Oh, some tenant's drunkenness. He is justice of the peace. Nothing. Tom could have managed. Nothing, nothing."

Yet in the middle of the night she waked and saw that he had gotten up and was sitting in the moonlight by the window. She did not speak, but she lay there wondering what to do.

He would not go to the lady: that was clear. When a week had passed, a letter came from Sir Fulke. It said merely, "Dear Sir. The Queen must be obeyed."

He took it with him to the solar and locked the door. Here like a man in a prison cell, he remembered the world. He heard the voices of friends come and go, heard the voices of wife and children. These were the rooftrees of his house.

The play that lay beneath his hand levied its stamping, snorting armies against the secret forces within the soul. Oh, it was a monstrous battle, fought in the dark and in secret. He flung himself to his feet. As he did so he glanced out the window. In the garden, Tom was slowly pacing the sanded walks, writing on a tablet which he supported on his palm. Recording for the King of Kings or counting the sands for Will?

A man without a wife, sitting day after day beside another man's wife, must, he supposed, have snow-broth in his veins. But when excitements of the reason and the blood beat upon the citadel what defense had poor two-legged man? *Oh, I have seen the hungry ocean gain advantage on the kingdom of the shore!* There was no mystery here to him, and since this was so he reckoned up the cost beyond its measure, heaping it.

The letter crackled in his hand. He offered it to the magpie, who tore it slowly between beak and claw.

Commanded as he was, he addressed himself in reasonable terms. "If I ride to the lady and speak as a Christian man to her disheveled state, such charity may clear my blood of both remorse and fear."

This was intellectually cooling. It was the blessed opposite of hot blood, hot thoughts, hot deeds, and all that came with the eating of Venus' doves.

He also thought, with some relief, that she might wish revenge for his revenge, and so offer him a blessed penance.

In any case he had no choice.

He took up his riding gloves and started down the stairs for the stable.

The day was English, tremulous and changing. Along the bank, the broom lay like sunshine, and in the woods, bluebells grew with the primroses, and the white chervil foamed by the roadside.

The road he traveled, between fields and patches of forest and across streams, took on a curious transmogrification. It became an essence of his wife. On that tree was imposed the lift of her head, and it would always be so however often he rode this way; that hilly pasture would forever partake of her expression between light and dark.

Coughton Court was owned by Sir Robert Throgmorton. It lay in a wide and spacious park, and around the stone of the building was a lush greensward with flowering bushes, topiary conceits, and fanciful arbors cut out of yew hedges. A plot of saffron lay in the sun. Ivy clung to the walls of the house and nodded into several open windows. There were gardeners and grooms in plots and stables, and a small army of servants could be presumed out of sight.

A gentleman servant took Will's horse when he dismounted, and another, by the prescience of long habit, opened the door. Will asked for her ladyship, but it was Sir Robert who came through a studded oak door into the Great Hall.

They were strangers to each other, for the Catholic Throgmortons had no politic ties with Protestant Stratford, and lived too far away for casual jaunting.

Sir Robert was a grizzled man of more than middle age, short and brisk. He inclined his head in greeting but did not offer his hand. There was no aloofness in his manner, however, and his gray eyes were kind.

He gestured toward a chair which faced the mullioned windows and the greensward beyond, and he gestured again when a servant brought in the wine. At length he nodded briskly and broke the silence.

"The matter is of such extraordinary delicacy, sir, that one angles for words and casts them back like undergrown fish. Well, let us try out these minnow-words. My lady has asked for you. I questioned the propriety of interchange with any man save myself, but Sir Fulke Greville has assured me that you are a man of honor and of the chastest disposition toward her." He cleared his throat as a courteous invitation for comment. Will did not avail himself, so Sir Robert proceeded, his bright eyes still pursuing their kindly physiognomic inquiry.

"The lady, in her distress, is under my protection. The protection should be of her father or brother, no doubt, but I am not free to discuss that matter. She has been woefully misused. Her betrayer is in prison. The Queen requested some obscure asylum. My collateral relationship to the lady and my irregular position as a member of the True Faith combine in the queer maze of our lives to cast my home in this role." He hesitated once again;

407

Will tried to give no sign of his astonishment that the lady had a connection in Warwickshire. Sir Robert rose. "That she has asked to see you and no one else has prompted my present loquacity. I understand no matter of this, my dear sir, but I have the highest regard for Sir Fulke and a tender concern for her ladyship."

Will bowed. "Your kind and generous heart must be your greatest guardant, Sir Robert." His own heart was beating in a manner which put a severe restriction on his movements. He thanked God for that pellucid charity of Sir Robert that saw, heard, and spoke no evil. He wondered, suddenly, why Sir Fulke had gone to such pains to guarantee his innocence and what, indeed, Sir Fulke thought in the intimacy of his own mind.

Sir Robert opened one of the long windows that led to a vista of gardens and arboreal retreats. He stretched out his hand.

"If you will proceed straight ahead, my dear sir, a minimal search will disclose her favorite bower."

The scent of flowers and bushes was a prologue to innocence. In the country air was no hint of reproof or retribution. Will saw a glimpse of a green cloak, then the line of that artless profile.

It affected him as he had been afraid it would. He half turned to go, but her waiting woman, who was reading to her, saw Will, and rose to curtsey.

The lady turned around. Her eyes grew so large that he thought for a moment she would faint. Her mouth moved, but no sound came. He stood still, at a distance, and she searched him with eyes growing calmer. As he watched, he saw her movements reinvested by the old spirit and her expression change as though wax had slipped into a mold.

Slowly she smiled with her wide childish mouth. A flash crossed her face. She remained huddled in her great cloak but she held out her hand.

He came forward determined to set the key. "Madam and mistress, a thousand good morrows!" He kissed her hand and sat down where her waiting woman had been sitting; he smiled and smiled and nodded, and picked up her hand to kiss again.

Her square little face was unutterably familiar. She too was smiling like a guileful child. She had said nothing and continued to examine him. She made an abrupt gesture of dismissal to her woman and they were alone.

She took off her cap and shook out her springing hair. He had said all that he need till she spoke. He picked up the book her woman had been reading and saw it was Chaucer's *Troilus and Criseyde*. She breathed deeply for a moment, her breath quavering, and then she spoke in the husky little voice that was the trumpet of elfland.

"There are two lovers," she said nodding at the book, "who play false to one another."

He smiled and read aloud at random.

> "He gan at him-self to jape faste,
> And seyde, 'nece, I have so greet a pyne
> For love, that every other day I faste'—
> And gan his beste japes forth to caste;
> And made hir so to laughe at his folye,
> That she for laughter wende for to dye."

She did not take her eyes from his face. She said, "There are so many Shakespeares in Warwickshire, how could I find thee, rustic man? Faugh! Thou dost smell of straw!"

She covered the lower part of her face, but her eyes were filled with a swelling light. He did not reply. He laid down the book and folded his hands over his knee. Presently the light in her eyes faded. "Why did you not search for me?" she asked.

He smiled in his pleasantest way. "My lady, I have been shut away from the world since I left London."

"Why then have you come now?"

"Did you not send for me?"

She shrugged and suddenly was close to tears. She was stripped of all capriciousness and evil; he was shockingly reminded of Susanna. The tears came. She said in a muffled voice, her face turned aside, "Though I had my way with you, you were always kind. I trust you."

He realized with consuming dismay that she had not linked him to any plot of revenge: he had here no hope of penance.

In a moment she looked at him darkly. "I sent for you because I thought that you would make me laugh."

He looked at her gently and laughed.

"Dearest lady, there is naught that is not made for laughter. Let us like true Christians crow with mirth at sudden sorrow."

Then she said sharply, "Would you have laughed had I come coffined home?"

"Why do you speak of coffins?"

"Because I wish that I might die."

He searched her face. Her eyes were brooding. She spoke in a low rush of angry words, of snares laid for her, of coney-catchers who dealt in flesh, meaning, he supposed, that she considered herself seduced, of black-hearted villains whose evil deeds must most horribly end with rats and toads and slimy things.

Her bitterness surprised him. He had imagined that she would take her fortune as a sort of japery. That she was burnt and cut made him wary.

He said, "Dearest lady, you have good and loyal friends who will see that your person and future are safe with honor."

"Oh, thou fool!" she said. "What an infinite mock that a man should have the best of eyes only to see the way of blindness." He sat with his chin against his hand, waiting. "I would that God had nothing else to do but seal my curses. I would make the air ring." Then the tears came again into her eyes. "I love him and he hates me. He will go to gaol rather than marry me. Was ever a woman more cruelly served? Have you ever loved?"

"Why do you always ask?"

"Do I?" She studied him a moment and then she drew the hood of her cloak over her head. "I ask to measure my suffering at his hands." Then in the old ironic way, she said, "How fares your wife? Does she dance as high and well as I?"

"My wife is well, I thank you, and my two daughters."

She laughed softly. "Ah, yes, I forget what a well-stuffed family figure you are in truth. What color eyes hath your wife? Is she fat or thin?"

He said, without expression, "One might pick a thousand salads e'er he light on such another herb as she."

"Well," she laughed, "I should misdoubt a love that compared

410

me to a salad. Ah, you are vexed, foolish man. Does thy wife know of me?"

"I will not talk of her."

"And why not? Show me this paragon and I will ape her, joint by joint." He was silent. She flung herself back against the seat, her hands clutching at the marble arms, incredulity struggling with chagrin. "Tell me," she persisted, and there was something like alarm in her tone, "were all thy vows to me writ in water? Or is it that my body swelling no longer tempts you?"

He knew that to pause now was to answer matters of great consequence awry.

"My vows to thee were to love thee well as I did see it. But mine to thee, and thine to me, put them in two scales. How will they balance?"

She continued to stare at him with all her senses. "Mouth-made promises may be broken," she said passionately.

"Aye," he said smiling, " 'tis serviceable for both."

She wept, not moving, and he watched with great reserve.

"Men's vows are women's traitors!" she softly cried. "I spared thee the onus of my shame."

"Why?"

"Link myself with a base-born man? Never, never, never!"

Both Lord William and the lady had slammed a door to any accountancy of his for so great a sin. Both had employed the same bolt of *base-born*.

He looked at her with a sudden fierce detachment. Perhaps the function of some women was to teach men, by reversion, how to be civilized. He could not a restrain a smile. The lady saw it and flung herself to her feet.

"How I believed thee! How I put discretion, decorum, peace of mind aside for thy promises!"

He said quietly, "My lady, if we vowed to weep seas, live in fire, eat rocks, tame tigers—why, that was a monstrosity of love."

She stopped and leaned against the yew, a bright figure, flowing green. "What a supple way you have, you rustic man. What arts you do employ."

"Learned from young Eve."

"You smile and mock me," she said, "as if I meant naughtily."

"Do you not?"

She said with sudden gaiety, "Thou wifed man—I'll unsmock thee."

"Not if I take care."

"Take care—with me?" And then she sighed deeply, as though the memory of her injured life had grappled her again, and paced to and fro. "Take care—from me, with me. Oh, what will become of me? Oh, men are vile and if I had the steeping of them all in red-hot flames I should make their anguish more than they could bear! He chose prison—not me!" She turned on Will, her pride fighting with her tears.

Oh, my injury sit as gaoler to my pity! he told himself.

"Thou art a little wren," he said gently. "Never was a larger bird so brave. Naught can defeat thee. What is but as 'tis valued? Be thy own true self."

"And what is that?" she asked mockingly.

He made a profound effort. "A lady most fair and tender; a lady whose sublime variety could make her goddess."

She looked at him so enigmatically that he barely knew her. Then, though cumbered by her long, enveloping cloak, she raised her arms above her head and clasped them there. "Oh, I could be as happy as the Queen of Heaven if mischief had not ploughed and cropped me so."

Now was the time to go. He stood up and said, "By your leave, dear lady—"

"Oh, you men will never tarry!"

"You will catch cold and curse me."

"Go, go." She threw her hand over her eyes, and then half withdrew it to give him a speculative glance as dark as a willful child's. "But come, come, come again." She seized his arm and clung to him. He could smell the sun and wind in her dark hair. "Bring me thy verse and thy play." She held his arm in the way that gave her such a lichen power. It was spontaneous, her whole self given in some spasm of need and affection. "Bring me thy lute. Bring me thy quips and thy merry voice. Make my life bearable!"

"Madam—!"

"I will be served. Mark you that!"

She waved goodbye, full of smiles and grace. As he rode home he thought that to reason well on a misdeed is to wipe it out. Sin is pardonable if a man sets himself a penance and resolves to sin no more. He put her in a sonnet form to keep her at a safe remove. *That you were once unkind befriends me now . . . But that your trespass now becomes a fee . . . mine ransoms yours, and yours must ransom me.*

Against his will he remembered that speculative glance, darker than a child's. In a most provocative way, there leapt onto the saddle of his mind certain words on marriage in the Book of Common Prayer: "A remedy against sin and to avoid fornication: the mutual society, help, and comfort that the one spouse ought to have of the other . . ."

Yet he carried himself very carefully, as a man charged with being a drunkard is on guard to walk very straight. There would be no clandestine meetings, no secrets from the countryside.

At supper, he talked with lively animation, concerned with each. He made solicitous plans for the next day in which all would share. Susanna grew effervescent with the prospects.

But suddenly he was seized with such a sense of evil that he groaned. It came down as cold as death and pervaded all the room. His heart became like ice. It was that black spirit which brings the smell of terror and works its deadly arts in the night. No priest or ministering angel has power to subdue it. Man: what help has he!

He sat swaying slightly, clutching the edge of the table. Anne looked at him and half rose. But he smiled at her, or his daemon did, got up, and stumbled from the room.

Susanna looked at her mother in stricken wonderment. Judith made no sound, but her great eyes followed the lurching footsteps going up the stairs. Tom frowned at the table.

Anne murmured some consolation to her daughters, and then rose and followed him. But the door to the solar was locked.

She came into the bedchamber and sat down by the cold hearth.

She knew neither what to think nor yet how to plumb her dismay. Faith was all she had, and it was a very little child. Presently she read, with her finger moving, how the son of the widow of Nain was raised from the dead. She read it again. It quieted her spirit. Her eyes came to rest on the bunch of meadow flowers that Tib a Prior had left for her at the kitchen door. She would not move until he came. She fell asleep in the chair.

She waked with a jerk that set her cap askew. Will was sitting opposite her, his eyes on her unblinking, infinitely sad. She smiled slightly and straightened her cap.

After a while, when the silence had grown deep, she drew on her breath to speak—but what would she say that would not unleash the dogs of fear?

Presently she reached for her knitting and calmed herself thinking of the widow of Nain. Death rifled . . . death of hope, of love . . . daily dyings set at naught . . . the bier made void. Nothing almost sees miracles but misery's blind faith. Think of Mary when the angel came. What doubts—what faith without sight!

He saw her smile. After a moment he spoke in such a husky voice that she hardly knew him.

"Give me a sign."

She looked at him with wide eyes.

"Of what?"

He ground his teeth and shuddered.

"A sign. Give me a sign."

She was not frightened but bewildered. Elijah had asked for a sign and God had answered him. "What will I give? All that is mine is thine."

He said hoarsely, "It is only you can do it."

Oh, this should make her heart leap. So indeed it did, but from apprehension, as a child might by some strange word rouse a parent's awe. She knew she must be bold. Words were forced past the constriction of her throat.

"Tell me what—and how."

At that he cried out and flung himself to his feet. Then he went back and forth, stumbling, his hands over his face, his voice bloated and unrecognizable.

"There is no bottom to my evil. Naught could fill it. Every sin that hath a name is mine." His voice was clogged and inhuman. She thought, He has gone mad! and grasped the arms of the chair. "I would o'erbear all—all—that opposed my will. Do you hear? All would merely be a sauce to make me hunger more."

"No, no!" she said strongly. His erratic lunging did not cease but he took his hands from his face, and at that she moaned, for he was deathly pale.

Will said so softly it could scarcely be heard, "Hell is my home. All scruples are as black as pitch. Curse me and cast me out."

Her eyes searched him. Her hands still held her chair, but her fear was gone. She sensed that he wished her to castigate and drive him out so that his punishment would precede his crime.

She knew no crime toward her but one. But toward himself? A good man's principles were his life. To kill his soul was to kill himself.

She believed that any word she used would be taken by his fluent tongue and turned against the truth. She sensed that though he begged her help, he would fight with all his power if she gave it; that he was in the full fell grip of that spell which came upon a man when he feared what he most desired—or perhaps desired what he feared, so that the punishment would be a more exquisite pain. What could shatter that flinty surface, shake up, rouse up, trumpet up, pulverize, this stone-hard man-thought? Can it be, she thought, that it is stronger because it dare not admit a single question or importunity, and so is like a moat impregnable?

She framed some words but they were so poor she put them by. To wait required a special gift of silence. She picked up her knitting to quiet her hands. He began to speak clearly and slowly.

"How think you of sin, dear heart? God's temptation or the devil's lure?" From his look, he meant to tease her unready speech.

She smiled. "Thee be sharp, my dear."

415

"Ah, what a groaning it would cost thee to take off that edge."

For a moment she fought against tears. Then she said, "I love thee . . ."

"Poor wretch. Have you never wronged a man, nor woman neither? Held no tainted thoughts? Begged no boons that had a poison in them?" As she tried to answer sensibly of human frailty, he chopped on in his soft voice. "How got thee thy first daughter born too soon? Nay, now—what do I know of my own house? The man I set in my place, doth he have my place?"

Her knitting faltered and she stared at him. He put his hand across his eyes. After a moment she said scarcely above a whisper, "Thee be most unkind."

He had lost her! He could not lift a hand to summon her back. Adultery, fornication, and all uncleanness lay to the blood like leeches. The horror of love's passing was equal to the horror of death.

He cried out with dim words against himself and her. At length the tears came to her eyes and she said she would hate him if that was what he required to prove that lies were now honored in this house.

Then he talked wildly of unnatural beasts and portents, said that if she was incapable of seeing when foul is fair and fair is foul, then heaven itself had turned away its face, and they were doomed to hell.

At that she stood up and went to the clothes peg to take down her cloak. So strong was her action that he could only watch with held breath. In her cloak she stood by the chair looking at him with a pale face.

She said, "I do not know what has happened. Until I know, what can I do? Will not my husband tell me what is this great amiss?"

For a moment he tried to find some words, but then he shook his head. "It is my daemon . . ."

She said, "Let thy good angel throw him out!"

Then he laughed softly. Presently he put out his hand, open palmed, for her to take or not as she saw fit. After a moment she took it.

CHAPTER *Ten*

NO one could pretend that there was peace of heart. Day by day no music played. He sealed himself away as though salvation lay with ink and paper. When they sat at meals he was quieter than his habit but his gaze moved over them all, time and again.

Anne found that his eyes were often on her. Sometimes she thought he saw her, and sometimes not. A violence lay close to the surface of his love, and it was a violence filled with such crying out against poor forked man on a cleft stick that she begged him to speak plain.

But when she begged, he fell into a bottomless silence.

It was Judith roused him to some speech. She came to him and asked in her soft voice, "Why caunt all love and bide close?"

It was a sweet blow. He said, "Dearling, who lacks love?"

Then she looked at him fully with her honey eyes. "I want not that any speak deadly to the other."

"None do, none do, I promise you!"

She looked at him and the shadow of a frown passed across her face.

"For love's sake, sweet heart, be at ease."

The lady had said she would be served: but not by him! If Fulke Greville intervened again, he would tell him plainly: "Let this be treason, still I will not go."

When a week had passed, Anne came to him where he worked in the garden. Behind her was the lady's waiting woman.

He rose slowly. He was helplessly aware that his expression of shock and dismay spoke more clearly than words. He made no effort to greet her; he looked down at her hard smile and knowing eyes as though she were the Mother of Harlots, the Scarlet woman of Babylon.

She made no effort to be discreet beyond the act of coming

417

close to him and looking at him on the bias as she squinted against the sun.

"I am told to say that I will come each day until you come."

To kill dead this vulgar smirking woman was his bounden duty. She waited for a moment, her smile not fading, and then she raised her brows, turned, bowed her head slightly to Anne, who stood nearby, and went away.

After a moment, Will's glance leapt to Anne. He said with an effort, "You see that I am bidden."

"Where to?"

He could not lie but he could not tell the truth. He threw down his trowel and struck both hands through his hair.

"It is the Queen," he said, "quite off her head."

Anne did not answer for a moment, and when she did her tone was unlike any he had ever heard from her. "Poor woman," she said with sudden irony.

She turned toward the house. The opposite of love is not hate but fear.

"What did you say?" he asked, putting his hand on her.

She had spoken aloud without knowing it. In her mind she had asked herself, How can we do more than give and hazard all we have?

His heart told him that tragedy—and also salvation, perhaps— lay in the fact that both he and his wife abhorred the ignoble. Neither could escape loyalty and affection.

He saw how the adulterous queen of Denmark, having violated the marriage sacrament, had reduced all human contractual relationships to empty forms. Thus she had made her marriage vows as false as dicers' oaths. But to take the vow anew, that should insure a threefold cord.

He went to Quiney to communicate with a man who had certain tried weapons against black lords and ladies. Dick was busy and said he would join him by-and-by in Smith's Tavern.

In the dim pungent public room of the tavern were his father, and Smith, old Rogers, and Hugh Field, the ale taster, and young Nicholas, who was polishing pewter in a lackluster way.

"Ah, dear boy," his father said, "I was on way to find thee. Not moren minute to finish tale." He turned again to Rogers, a gay, unmalicious zest on his face. "There he be—'tis schoolmaster and smith, I speak of," he explained to his son, who had sat down smiling, "going along like two folk along of their fall-out—there be schoolmaster, tippy-toein' past, no more to be seen than a leaf. But Jem Hornby can eye him through brick walls, and out he nips with horseshoe sizzling at end of tongs, and beats up air with fiery curses. There be poor Alex Schoolmaster, like stuck fly, can't go forward or back, set an' all not to irk the foul fiend."

"It be no laughin' matter, by God," said Rogers sourly, "for it be strong drink that becalls Jem, and it be better far, look, to brand his brow with what he be!"

John Shakespeare had paused courteously in the midst of a great laugh and now nodded with an open mouth, brimful of laughter. "Oh, I be not laughing. I be merely observin' in jocose way. And, look, there be pity, an' all, for poor Alex slowly heatin' himself to apoplexy. So I put arm around Alex and say, 'Oh, Alex, butty, this be sneapey day for man with cold as bad as thine. Why, hark to thy sneeze!' Poor Alex knew naught of sneeze, but he be mighty choice over Jem's tongs and glad to give sneeze or two by way of fare-thee-well."

Will was laughing. "Oh, father, keep the peace! What matters opinion of right or wrong?"

"Opinion?" said John Shakespeare. "Why, that can be worn both sides like a leather jerkin. But peace—that's got *one* side."

Old Rogers stood up, shaking the table, upsetting the chair. "Well, I hold wi' some and not wi' all their cogmaggin. Some be just mankind witches, whether they wear breeches or skirts. God be wi' 'ee."

Nicholas took his place with his pewter and rubbing cloths. The ale taster admonished Smith in a busybody way of some quality ale he had served, and went out with a goodbye to all.

Will looked at his father. Shrewd, honorable and very human, he was a good rooftree. Will longed to lay his head on his father's shoulder and show him, in stark hieroglyphics, his life of surprises. But thirty-seven years of father and son intervened. A

419

father's rise and decline and rise again had played on his son's life, and had defined certain responses.

Love swarmed into his mind. His father hated cant and hypocrisy, refused to bend his knee to a world which set each man's thought in its place; he had many irons in the fire; he loved the swings and roundabouts.

Will said, "Play cards with me, father."

"Aye, dear boy. Nicholas, please fetch the cards. But speak first. Thy mind hath somewhat in it of a sour taste. I see it in thy face. To communicate be healthy."

"Why, father, have I not all things to make a man happy?"

"No, for then thee'ud tuck up thy toes and someone else 'ud close thine eyes."

"Father, mayn't a man sometimes be lost and amazed among the thorns of the world?"

"Thou? Oh, lad!" When he stopped laughing he said, "Well, thee a' come home safe to bide. Bide."

"Lugging myself with me?"

"Oh, be sprightly, lad, as thee were born to be. Aye, thee was always a sweet crack. I ask no questions, for I have no heart for dusty answers which fool and lead thee by the nose as though thee be an ass. Thankee, Nicholas. Will, I'll play thee two games of gleek. Wilt thee have a hand, Nicholas? I have no doubt thee do play better than one twice thy age. When we finish we will go to thy mother, Will."

"We? I'd rather bide, father."

"Look, lad, her mind be working like a saw—twelve cards dealt, Nicholas—and she hath cut several good weapons in thy warfare with unscrupulous men."

"Father, she says I am kin to Greville," said Will.

His father riffled the cards and smiled. "I make no doubt she could persuade him if she fails of thee."

"Father, she has already made mischief. Put a bridle on her!"

His father smiled and yielded a trick to Nicholas. "Well, I'll say I have not seen thee—for, by Gis, I scarce know thee, dear lad, riding such a wild fancy as that: put a bridle on her!

Nicholas, thee hath cheated. Where will thee look when God sees it?"

Quiney came in, the rain on his shoulders, and stood with his hand on Will. "Greenway courier just came in from London—and Westminster's answered right! I think we've most pulled our black lord's teeth."

What cries of joy! Quiney went to fetch a pint of ale, and later he drew up a stool with his foot. "If that be true, then we can turn our hearts to other things. Petition for a proper road, eh, John? Think thee? Wool must be got out better than it has been. We fight Coventry traders on our own highway." He was happy and buoyant.

John said, "Tell all!"

But Quiney had scarcely wet his throat in a preliminary way when the door was opened and a surge of men came in. They smelled of horses and the wet day.

Quiney sprang up. "Robin Catesby, on my honor—and Ned Bushell—'fore God! Welcome!"

John got up to shake their hands, and Smith came around to pump their hands also. For a moment Will found himself becalmed, in a dead spot. Catesby and Bushell: they were London, they were Essex' fall, they were dark nights and dark doings, they were violent men.

He sat quietly for a moment, head turned away, watching Nicholas cheat. He had last seen Bushell led by torchlight from the Queen's barge. Then he looked obliquely at their high color and vaunting ways.

Quiney's emotion was brimming over. "Why, by God's grace, we'll drink thy freedom with thee!"

He pressed Smith away and drew the ale himself.

Catesby, shaking out his cloak, was in some far-fetched way an Arden, and Bushell, who had been Gentleman-Usher to Essex, was Catesby's cousin, and was linked to Quiney by some sort of marriage—all so collateral that it took the iron will of a Mary Shakespeare to strike to the heart of it. Will put a smile on his face and rose to greet them on his way out the door.

Robin Catesby seized Will's arm. "Will, not going?"

"Not till I have shaken thy hand!" Will said shaking hands heartily. "And thine, Ned Bushell. And praise God misfortune is behind thee. And now I must be off."

"Nay, nay, there's no door so unfriendly as to let thee out!" Bushell said.

Quiney held out the pots and spoke with stern emotion. "Come, touch pots, all. Will, drink to freedom."

"By the Mass, yes!" Catesby said in his bold voice. "The devil's pit did burn beneath us, but straight out were we plucked, and, by the True Faith, deposited to plan another day."

"Whist, Robin!" said Bushell with a grin.

But Catesby was used to rule. He said loudly that by the Queen's league with Satan, the True Faith was scourged while at the same time she filled her purse with gold dragged by red-hot pinchers from such faithful Catholics as his own father, and he would say so.

Quiney and Smith made anxious gestures, John Shakespeare cuffed Nicholas, and Will moved again toward the door.

Bushell laughed, though to an honest ear it had a dishonest sound. "Why plotting and counterplotting are all that the old woman knows. We loyally abet her. What else keeps her alive?"

Will said "Goodbye!" in a cheerful voice, but Catesby put down his pot.

"Wait." He came and stood with his back to the door. His color was high and his expression fed by his own excitement. "Hath it been told me right that you have a mind to hang about our uncle's place?"

John Shakespeare's eyebrows crept to his hair line. Will frowned.

"Your uncle's place?"

"You are neither a witty fool nor a foolish wit. And try neither dormouse valor nor insolent courage, for you will find the cost well beyond thy means."

In the room was a full silence. Only Nicholas, shuffling the cards, made any sound.

Will said calmly, "Robin Catesby, you are mad."

Bushell's attention had a sickly sweetness about it. His smile was fixed. Nicholas laid out the cards as though commenting on the future. Bushell said, without raising his head from his supporting hand, "We came a purpose to seek thee, Will. Our uncle's place is Coughton Court."

Will had a sinful desire to laugh. He had forgotten this collateral detail. His father's eyes were on him stealthily. Quiney sighed like a bellows and chewed at his lower lip. Smith leaned on the counter and listened to add up his sums. When Catesby spoke his tone was soft.

"Willful women win, but if their tuppers tempt with too much ticktack, then must the cock be pratted."

"Lord, Lord!" said Smith in stark amazement.

"Why, you could make your living writing lascivious epigrams," Will said with narrowed eyes.

Bushell responded on his cue. "To have a lovely creature in thy naked arms is more than epigram."

Then Smith interjected, "Not in my house—not in my house —such language!"

Bushell said, "No more. He hath been warned. He is no fool."

But Catesby flamed with violence. "No fool? Did he not fail and betray our lord of Essex in every way he could?" He raised his pot of ale as though to fling it.

Will was white. He went out on a rage. He heard the pot strike the door.

When he came into his own house he locked the street door. He was shaking with anger and violate pride.

The rain was still raining. His wife sat by the kitchen fire spinning. In the stillroom, Ned was loitering with Nan, who was singing in a small high voice as she worked.

The little voice was woefully thin but wonderfully true.

> "Western wind, where wilt thou blow?
> So weary falls the rain,
> The small rain down can rain,
> Christ, if my love were in my arms
> And I in my bed again."

Anne looked at him with narrow sidelong gaze.

423

He looked at her blindly as though he did not see her. He heard Ned kiss Nan and say, "Sing again."
Like a mourning dove, her words drifted into the kitchen.

"How should I my true love know
From another one?
By his cockle hat and staff
And his sandal shoon . . ."

His lady had been innocent once, until cruel night and vicious expedients had laid her by the heels. Whether he had ever loved her or not was of no consequence. Ah, he loved only the world remade without cruel and ignorant men. Ignorant . . . knowing neither good nor bad . . . that was to be without morality . . . like youth. How young had she been when expediency had first lain upon her?

Yet his daughters were helpless with their virginity lying upon them. Youth was a pander. It built the engines of lust and war. Catesby had the boiled brains of nineteen and the violence of a full-grown man. He called out suddenly to Ned, and the still-room was filled with silence. Ned came to the door.

Will looked at him, and because neither spoke, Anne looked from one to the other.

Will smiled and Ned, leaning in the door, said "Master?"

Will spoke with a half smile as he stroked the cat. "The universal wolf at last eats up himself."

Ned frowned and then made a mocking sound. He returned to the stillroom, where he could be heard giving Nan a comic explication.

Anne's spinning stopped. She turned her face toward Will and it was white. "Thee do never say A is A and B is B, but always speak in riddles. It be more—" She shivered.

What he could not bear at this moment was A and B. All must be amorphous and full of verbal opulence. Simplicity would flay him to a skeleton.

He stood up. "Ned will whore her." He smiled. " 'Tis in nature. All men do if they have a chance. No maid is safe. Is that plain enough for thee, dearling?"

"Why, plain to him who sees it so," she answered, stepping on the treadle nervously.

He stood in the middle of the kitchen. Somewhere there must be a place where no opposition beveled his straight line. He started abruptly toward the door.

"Come back," she said above the whirr of the wheel. He was so startled that he turned his head. "Come back," she said more quietly, stopping the wheel with her hand.

She looked up at him with a little flutter of panic and said, without raising her voice, "Thee do act coxey and contrary. In God's time such acts must end in humble pie. But that is God's business. I will not have lewd words spoken before my daughters, nor harshness set up so high in this house."

He stared. Her brown eyes did not falter yet her hands were trembling. Silence had fallen in the stillroom. In the kitchen door he saw Judith standing sideways so that she need not look straight in. He stared again at Anne. Now she lowered her gaze.

Astonishment put an edge to his voice. "Do thee rail at my authority, dearling?"

"God is my authority." She sat pressing her arms hard against her sides, her eyes blinking swiftly. She thrust away the wheel. "Let thy rage crack!" Then she flung up her hands and slapped them against the sides of her face, and continued to slap at her cheeks, crying, "Oh h-h!" until she burst into tears.

They were all dismayed. Ned came and sat hunched on the table, his hair shaken over his forehead. Judith looked from the corner of her eyes but did not move. Tom appeared behind Judith and, lifting his brows, looked from one to another.

Will hesitated, then he came and stood before Anne. He said softly, "Why, chuck—"

She looked up wildly. "Do not speak to me! Why, all—all—oh, 'tis monstrous! 'Tis all *I will, I won't, my sorrow, ask me not!* But what is going on? Oh, mercy!"

He could not remember ever having seen her thus. He was at such a loss that he tried a dozen words in silence before he spoke: "Wife—lovedy—!"

"I hate all dishonest men, and women too," she cried. "I hate those who cower. I hate those who hint and pretend." She was clutching at the spinning wheel but her moving eyes saw the white and startled faces of the children, Ned, Nan, Judith, their eyes all turned like spaniels to see: *Is it me she hates?*

She fought to both hold and subdue her anger; and then she heaved a sigh and rubbed her hands against her skirt. She sat for a moment longer, breathing sharply. At length she said in a quieter tone, though her voice still trembled, "Brighten thy faces. The storm hath past."

Ned jumped off the table. "By Adam, that was a spin in the air. Kiss me, Sister Anne," and he kissed her on both cheeks. "Thou hast no fleas about thee for company. Alleluya!"

Judith stood behind her mother's chair and traced with her finger the fold of cap. It was Will who did nothing. Anne looked up at him swiftly. There was no shrinking in her gaze. As she rose to go to the fire she said with a trace of coldness, "What thee said was not wrong, but it was not right. That false tone troubled."

He did not wish to think about false tones, or true, in any way whatsoever. He felt as though he had been flung into a vat and stirred until he could no longer think. Meeting Tom later in the stable, he struck out at him with the first words that came.

"A man should be what he seems. Thou dost seem an honest man."

Tom was taken aback. "Why, cousin, out of a lifetime's knowing me, what is this *seems?*"

"I am master here. I will have no stirring up."

Tom carefully stooped to pick up a bridle which had fallen to the ground. When he straightened, his face was flushed. He said angrily, "Then shall I whip *down* for you Robin Catesby?"

Will said "Hah!" as though he had been struck. He picked up a whip and smote the post so hard the whip protested. He went away to curse himself, the Corporation of Stratford, and all things else that were too subtle-potent to bear the light of day.

Life was determined to grind from him all complacency.

He spread out the pages of his play till they covered the whole table. What mummery for mummers is here to speak to fools?

He walked around the table several times. Paradoxes, enigmas, extremes of good and bad. A son who hates his mother and loves his father; or perhaps it is who loves his mother and hates his wife. Battles that would not stay won. All asked to feed on death that death once dead there might be no more dying then. O, he was a witty man with words! Almost as witty as Mr Bushell and Mr Catesby.

Poosh—fie! Mrs Innocent Simplicity had said coxey and contrary. 'Fore God, he would no longer contemplate the small nerve ends of love or hate. What must he, must be man-sized.

He longed for the company of actors. Actors would shake this remorseless play and make it yield. No play had ever before demanded of him *all* judgment, *all* imagination, *all* reconciliation, *all* vehemence and passion. It was beyond credence!

Design upon design arranged the affairs of men in time and place. Yet he must be whipped by God to wrench life *through* to the exhausted end, *through* as the price of a peaceful sit-before-the-fire. It only proved that God was stupider than men!

Actors had the insight, they translated and revealed, they mastered imagination, they did not fart themselves or make servile defecations of wondering too precisely upon the event. Oh, he would enact to prove no man need go down to hell to find his heaven.

But then he put his hands over his face and groaned. For, under all, he divined, was man in godlike state. What other purpose was his link with God? Unless, by John Marston's book, he was a beast, no more; begot by bastards, by bastards learned; in mind, valor, everything, illegitimate.

How would I be if I were such a man who thought too much why black was black and white was white, or why my wife dumped my dinner in the fire? He struck at his head. Now you do mock yourself, you coxey man! O, what an ass am I!

O, let us remake goodness in the image of God! But the key-lock still eluded his agonies of plotting and contriving.

Actors were free to show you suffering and remain unaffected. In them the mystery of the imagination was as narcotic as a

427

Delphic prophecy and as well put on as a new gown. But the poet was a dozen men within, a dozen forms and colors, and *all* himself.

Who else beside Tom would speak of Catesby?

By angry sweat and heaving, Will at length arranged an exhausted line of thought which saw in the wrecked designs of man the trial of God to test his metal. He wrote a scene which he did not tear up.

Good! Thus events have the rule of men and men must yield to the mysterious design of all-wise God. To this, man must bring what pity he can offer, what constancy, what solace, not knowing where he goes. By this, compulsion may be seen as duty; mystery as a man's strength, and black as white. To be a writer is to be his own priest. He praised God shakily.

The next day, the lady's waiting woman returned. Nan fetched him, and when he came out, the woman said nothing but grinned from her seat on the horse. He motioned her away, but she laughed and steadied her dancing horse. He then ordered his horse saddled, and fetched his lute and odd scraps of poetry. She rode ahead but looked back now and then.

He hated the humiliating means, but he went not unwillingly, for he had an extreme desire to assert that freedom which Mr Bushell and Mr Catesby had so cunningly abused. He had the courtier's weapons for both defense and attack, lute, verse, and song, and by these wise means he would make sure that she exercised only such arts as courtesy required, while he remained the best courtier of them all.

This is all that she had asked and all that he would give, good servant of the Queen.

Coughton Court welcomed him. The servants smiled. The doors swung open. The gardens were wreathed in airy fancies, and everywhere were sweet smells and beckoning delights.

He went on through the magic air until he found her. She was playing pall-mall, knocking a ball through a wicket, against a servant. This must have tried her spirits sorely, for when she saw him she threw away her mallet and ran to hold him.

Today she wore a scarlet cloak, with flowers in the fillet that bound her hair. She put her arm through his, to assist his simpleness, and they walked about the lake until they came to a marble bench. She took his lute and played a song, and then she sat with her chin in her hand to study him where he sat upon the ground.

"Nay, thou must have a pillow against the damp," she said tenderly. "Now I will tell thee all the whys I sent for thee . . . because you make me laugh, because you make me cry, because you make me beautiful, because you make me rough and ready . . . because you tell me jokes, because I am I. Ah, my dear, my sweet, life must spring up with no more thought than a rose. Is this not what thy poems say?"

He smiled and nodded.

"Then listen more . . ."

And she moved upon the bench and told him wondrous things out of a quick and merry fancy that knew the dark side of the moon. She touched his face with her little fingers. She held and kissed his hand in ways no heavier than a thistledown.

He called her sweet heart, played and sang, for love's gentle spring doth always fresh remain. The heat of the day was taxing, but the garden was full of scent and murmuring bees. She wove a garland and she put a flower behind his ear.

"Oh, see how beauty's rose need never die. When music's to hear why hear we music sadly? Sweets with sweet war not, joy delights in joy," she said.

This was a rich concoction, but he had been living on very simple fare: one feast was not gluttony. He played his lute again and sang.

> "Was this fair face the cause, quoth she,
>   Why the Grecians sacked Troy?
> Fond done, done fond,
>   Was this King Priam's joy?
> With that she sighed as she stood,
> With that she sighed as she stood,
>   And gave this sentence then:
> Among nine bad if one be good,
> Among nine bad if one be good,
>   There's yet one good in ten."

God loved him. He had become twenty-four years old again, the right age for a man. He had been much abused by his own tossed spirit and by the gross earth's gross calumnies.

He took off the garland and put it around her neck. What is this curtsey worth, and these doves' eyes?

Well, well worth the stooping for!

Sir Robert, in addition to the servants, bowed and smiled in farewell, a gentle good old man who graced him through the door.

"How fair she is," Sir Robert said, smiling and twinkling. "Come you tomorrow, sir?"

"Why, all tomorrows are ours to multiply!"

"Oh, true indeed! You are like a father to her."

Will became very still. He, an old magician, knew a rough magic when he heard it. His eyes were compelled to turn. Sir Robert had a look that was so full of guileful childishness that there was not a jot of truth in it. The good old man stood there smiling, and then he reached over and took the flower from Will's ear.

Will turned away abruptly. The spun sugar was not as well made these days as in the past. It melted faster. "Ask me if I am a courtier, sir. It will do you no harm to learn." Sir Robert did not reply.

He mounted his horse and rode down past the sickly saffron. Oh, dolt. Oh, Will-a-dreams. He was very courteous with himself, for it is a wise man who does not draw his own attention to the dunce cap that he wears.

Presently he got off his horse with his poor lute about his neck and wandered in the field, dragging his faithful nag behind him.

Never, he thought sadly, had a man fooled himself with so fixed a soul. There was no innocence pure and simple . . . unless Mrs Innocent Simplicity had some special knowledge.

O envious and calumniating time, have I deserved to lose my birthright to play the fool? . . . to have my choice of seeing or no sight?

O time that fumbles all illusion into such loose farewells.

That she was cunning, wily, faithless, tuned too sharp in sweetness, false, and love's similitude brought no ounce of comfort. For so was he, and all occasions informed against such artful spirits.

His mare dragged at the bridle and led him to a stream. There she drank loudly. Will stared at the stirred water, and then he slipped into an untidy crouch. The horse munched grass.

In the agitated stream no image could be found. His fingers touched his face but told him nothing. Suddenly he was quite put from the understanding of himself. Fear was in his legs, his arms, his back, his blood swelling like a sea. Terror said that nothing based on time had any hope, and time was all. My mind . . . my mind is like a fountain stirred and I cannot see the bottom.

In what had he believed? Simplicity, family, friends, justice, God, a tranquil mind? As the fish to the osprey, so were they to that dread monarch against which he had no hope of winning this unequal strife.

Ah, poor Will, I'll have thee beaten for being old and wise before thy time.

When he came home it was twilight. He sat in an obscure place in the garden.

As he saw the candles lighting in the house, he rose. He put his hands over his face. Henceforth I'll wear thee as mine enemy. Yet how will I know thee to salute thee with my fist?

When he came in, Anne was standing dishes on the cupboard shelves.

"Oh, my dear," she said, "thy supper!"

"Give me that mirror that was thine from me."

"Mirror?"

"Aye, my gift, my gift. Give it me, if you please." His hand was half across his face.

"Are thee hurt, dear one?" she cried.

"For God's sake, give me the mirror!"

"I have no mirror. That be long ago."

"Not so long—not so long. I gave it thee. What didst thou do with it?"

"Why, broken—or I gave it—aye, Tom wanted one for some matter."

He struck her face.

She cried out and her eyes blazed.

He said, "I gave it thee. It was a gift."

She stood with her hands against her cheeks, her eyes hot.

He walked about. "I am thirty-seven years old. Most done. That blow was alms to bribe oblivion." He shook her slightly and said close to her face gently, "Give thou too some alms against this monster of ingratitude, old lady."

She looked at him as though she had not seen this man before. He turned and groped for the stairs.

I struck her for being my partner in time's relentless march. Some time I shall sleep out, the rest I'll whistle.

The war within was now the war without. He sat alone in a cold and dark chamber.

CHAPTER *Eleven*

ANNE stood without moving until the blood resumed its natural course.

He was her husband. He was not a man whom she need petition or wait for. What nearer debt in all humanity was there than the wife's to the husband, or the husband's to the wife?

When the household had gone to bed, the daughters kissed, and blessings exchanged of Tom and herself, she started toward the stairs.

In the dark above the stairs, she saw Will standing as motionless as the stairpost, staring down, as the cat twisted in and out his legs. He watched the cat for a moment, and then he struck with his foot. The cat uttered a cry and ran down the stairs.

Then Will saw Anne, and they looked at each other in silence. He turned and went toward the chamber, and she slowly began to mount the stairs.

She put the candle obscurely, so that the light was mostly shadow. The room was cold, for the window was open and creaking in the stir of air. He confronted her, a sickness on his face.

"Have you found it?"

"Found what?"

"The present that I gave you when you were young enough to need it."

She turned away to the clothes peg and said calmly, "No, I have not found it."

"You will tell me who has taken it before we sleep tonight."

"I will not, for I do not know. And that's the end. I will not be struck again, neither by the devil nor by thee."

From the side of her eye she watched his queer lurching gait. In her compassion was some bitterness that she must shift from her protective stance, where she had chosen to see and name no evil, to that disenthrallment which left no kindly obscuration.

The tomb-like room and the creaking cold were adjuncts to her misery. She wished for light, but when she turned to lift the candle to a shelf, she saw him watching her as though the very life of his eyeballs was contingent on her stillness. So she sat down slowly, holding her night smock in her hands. She was lost somewhere in the shadowy reaches of the mystery of man, and she knew her way only by instinct.

Her silence goaded him. "How can I punish the wife who betrays me? Speak! What is there here of man or woman?"

She spoke slowly. "Who has the right to read the souls of others?"

"It is not my soul I show to thee, but the man who is most unwillingly humbugged by any."

"No," she said wearily, "I think that is not it. Thee hath not been humbugged. I think thee would be very glad indeed to keep all as it has been, except that I also be a woman."

"Also?"

She looked at him with her great brown eyes for a moment.

"Be she not a woman too?"

"She? What she?" The dullness left him. He became effervescent with a dancing anger. "The cuckolded husband is neatly topped."

She said only, "Do not speak to me that way."

"Should I not speak to my wife howsoe'er I like? She hath a beauty you know nothing of."

Anne spoke with difficulty. "She must be fair, when with your blood you daily paint her so."

"Oh!" he cried in a voice more like his own. "Women are so simple. They can hop only on the strings tied to their hearts."

She gave no sign. She took off her cap and released her hair, and she unlaced her bodice. He lay back against the bolster and put his arms behind his head, watching her with eyes as quick as ferret's, and speaking swiftly as though to ward off blows.

"Oh, God, a woman's appetites—nay, the soiled horse hath greater temperance. Why, God goes only to the girdle of a woman. All else beneath is the foul fiend's."

She laced up her bodice as slowly as she had unlaced it. He covered his eyes with his arm and whispered hoarsely, "There's hell—there's darkness—below the girdle. Sickness, death and damnation, and God deals with us as flies."

"Speak, do not rave," she said, very low.

The silence swelled.

She said softly, "Thee be friends with both truth and lies. Thee must choose."

He looked at her through his half-closed lids.

"Will you betray me again?"

She looked up startled, but then she smiled faintly, though she gave no other sign. His voice staggered on.

"Can a man bear the truth? Is there not a pity that is truer than the truth?" When she did not answer he asked, "With all our sins upon us, can we stand revealed and live?"

"This be poison!" she said.

He tried to cut a way for himself in another fashion. "Do you not know that men are always caught where weakest?"

"Aye."

"It is easier," he said, "to do a thing than to give thee warning."

"Aye," she said with another faint smile toward him. "Fear of trouble makes thee lie to me."

"Lie? No, i'faith, not lie. 'Tis a jointure with life, and one cannot tell the difference."

"That is an idiot's tale."

He lay very still. The creaking window was lost in the tolling bell. He fell to sudden shivering. She rose and brought the candle from its hiding place. Leaning against the end of the bed, she looked at him. Then she went to the chest and brought out a coverlet which she put over him.

Violence, blood, redness, rawness danced behind his lids, thunder, lightning—free powers wheeling like the sun. The time had been that, when the brains were out, the man would die. But not now. Truth, honor, and good deeds were baits to send the taker mad but not to end his life. By transferring his wakeful phantasmagoria to his night dreams, he might perhaps forget the taste of tears.

But hollow sounds, reverberating in an empty place, laid such terror on his lonely soul that he started up to dream again. He heard his own voice.

"When I love her, I hate her. Who can control his fate?"

"And sometimes I hate thee," she said quietly, "for the way thee hath betrayed me. And thee hate me for thy bad conscience. But do not let the hate separate, nor the fear. Do not let it separate us! It is a part of union as is the love."

He groaned and flung himself sideways on the bed. Her soft voice went on, "Do not turn away. Do not hide thyself or fancy this will slip away, what I am saying. Do not drift, waiting for the voice of God. God speaks. Do not reproach me for using words of God. I must, and you must listen tranquilly."

His hand was still fretful, but he was silent.

"Look at me," she said quietly. He became very still. "Look at me," she said more heartily. She saw his eyes open. "Thee must see me for what I be," she said. "Anne. I love, but I be not deceived in me or thee."

He lay there with not a breath moving, the slits of his eyes showing him little. A woman . . . her conclusions had not destroyed him as he had hoped they might.

At length she stirred, and took her hands away from the bedpost. He said in a muffled voice, "Will you betray my weakness? I have put it in your hands."

435

"No. But neither will I give thee pap."

As she stood alone the next morning in the buttery drawing cream, Tom came to the doorway. He held papers in his hands to show that he was on his way elsewhere and could not linger.

"Cousin," he said, "as we love each other, may I speak plain?"

"Aye, do."

"Call the doctor for thy husband."

She looked at him quietly. "Why?"

"I will speak to thee bluntly. His incontinence will do harm to himself and all."

"What do thee mean?"

"This incontinence steps into high places. High people wish to bring him low."

Her look deepened. She leaned against the wall. He was not unmoved by the grace of her movements nor the quality in her eyes, and she was aware of this. But she did not reply for a moment or so.

"These words because he struck me?"

"Not that alone, cousin. Men strike their wives. No, it is his dangerous playing with the honor of the great. He hath been warned."

"I do not understand what thy meaning is," she said. "Much that be plain to thee be lost to me who do not know high ways. But what I know is my guide, and I can follow no other."

"Women must listen to men," he said sharply, with almost a jealous anger.

"Not always. In marriage, only two understand—and sometimes only one—who holds it dearest."

"Thy unworldliness will snare thee, cousin."

She turned her eyes suddenly on him. "Thee be not a wife. How can thee know as his wife? Must I take revenge on myself, who am so simple that I must be constant to my heart?"

He frowned, for he saw how winning were these ways of hers. She put out a hand and laid it on his arm. "However noble be thy pity, cousin, it be thy pity and must remain thine."

He answered crisply, "Thou hast grown to be a talker, cousin."
She flushed slightly and took her hand away.

"I must be on his side, whatsoe'er it be. I must put away my tears and pain."

He laughed shakily.

"Cousin, thou art a woman easily deceived. That is a misfortune for a woman whose husband is so full of hot blood and deceit."

"Oh!" She suddenly flung out her hands. "Oh, cold man, what do thee know of passion!"

He was startled out of himself. He looked in a sharp new way at this woman tossing her head back and forth. He put his hands on her shoulders and drew her back to him in a fond and friendly way.

"Cold man? No. Neither now nor any time. But I would never be made a fool by lust."

Alone, she tossed her head back and forth again. Tom had shaken her composure. He knew that alien world in which her love lived most of his life and which now hung above her like a hawk. Her heart drained sickeningly.

What should she do who had nothing but her faith? Go to Tib? And why not? Nature's mysteries were no less compelling than the world's. She was most disturbed that he went secretly to Coughton Court, yet what questions could she ask of his deft evasiveness? He was the skittish horse which was unwilling to go by the scene of the secret murder.

She came out into the sunlight and saw Susanna dreaming in an apple bough.

"Where be thy knitting?" she said.

"Oh, la, I forgot."

"What man will care for a careless wife. There thee be, burning daylight. Graceless girl!"

Susanna looked down with open mouth. "Why, mam, I be saying my catechism. Iffin—"

But Anne was close to tears. "Iffen and offin—wait—mess along! Lose thy joy through ignorance!"

437

She came into the bedchamber to take down her cloak. Oh, but her faith could not fail her. She sat down in her cloak and took up the Bible. She held it for a moment without opening it, and when she opened it, looked for the words of hope.

But not a word did she know. Not one was clear to her. They were all strange and unlearned. It was a mockery so sharp and cruel that she flung the book across the room. It fell with a heavy crash and lay with its pages broken. She put her head against the wall and shut her eyes: *Tib, dear child of grace* . . .

Will went to Coombs. He would build a buttress as high as heaven of land and place to make him and his secure forever.

But he did not speak to Coombs because, standing just outside the open window, he heard Tom's voice. Tom asked Coombs bluntly who diddled with the clerkship. John Coombs mused and took a turn about.

"Some say the Shakespeares are recusants. There was, I understand, a confabulation with those papists, Robert Catesby and Edward Bushell."

" 'Fore God, no! It was quite another—" Tom stopped, not knowing perhaps how to say a bad thing in a good way.

John Coombs was waiting, half turned.

Tom struggled on. "It had to do with—God a mercy, John, it had naught to do with treasonable religion!"

John Coombs was studying him sideways in an iron-gray manner. "And thou, Tom? We are a forthright town, wanting naught to do with ways opposed to church and state. Art thou very steadfast in a uniform faith?"

"As a rock."

"Searching out all evil works, all devil's spawns, all feats of darkness, all—"

Tom said sharply, "I am an honest man, and you well know it, John; conforming in all matters that pertain to the public good. I would serve the town well. There's an end."

John Coombs smiled. "Why, Tom, thou dost rear on thy hind legs. Good."

As a girl Anne had joined in the dancing on Midsummer's Eve, in leaping the bonfires and driving the cattle across the dying embers, in strewing the ashes over the fields.

On this night the devils flew through the air on animals not seen by God-fearing men and gathered in woods to invoke the dark spirits. But she need only lie in *his* bed and the devils would come.

Before dawn she rose, took down her cloak in perfect silence, and stole out the house.

The dawn was inexpressibly sweet. The singing of birds increased with the light. The rising mist on the river and meadows showed a new day complete.

She drew up the hood to conceal her face, and went swiftly along the river, by the drift lane, through the hawthorne brake, to her husband's fields. On the edge of the field she stirred a corncrake. In the early light, on old Prior's land, she saw Tib dancing, her ewe and her cat gamboling and frisking with her like creatures newborn. She stood as silent as a tree, her heart beating so fast she thought it would fling itself out of her breast.

In time Tib saw her. Tib stood quiet, though her beasts gamboled still, and a smile broke on her face. Anne went toward her slowly.

"Good dawn to thee, Tib."

Tib made a curtsey like a step in a dance. The fields were alive with birds. Tib had been dancing among the pink yarrow on its woolly stems, and the eyebright, small and white, the blue tufted vetch and the pimpernel. From her pocket she took wild rose hips and put some in her mouth as she watched Anne; the rest she held out on her palm.

Anne thanked her. She said huskily, "Tib, thee do work many charms, do thee not?" Tib did not reply, but she took the cat up in her arms. "Can thee not call heavenly peace?"

A song thrush at that moment set out a chorus of singing. Tib gave a sweet low cry, and a hare leapt from the meadowsweet and joined the ewe in eating grass. She cried again, and a fox stole by the hare and nuzzled it. She cried again, and a green gilded snake came from the long grass with a little mouse riding its back.

Tib looked at Anne with her harebell eyes, and Anne fancied that their color would be seen even in the dark. Anne put her hand against her throat to still a throbbing. Tib gave her an open smile and cried again. A merle flew to her shoulder and leaned down to part the cat's fur with its beak.

Anne whispered, "Do thee charm them all to the improbable?" The tears stood in her eyes. "Can thy innocence make honors of impossibilities?"

Tib spoke for the first time. "Thee hath a stone in thy heart?"

Anne nodded. Tib stood very still, looking at her for a moment. Tib seemed no longer a child. The ewe and the cat and the birds fell quiet. Tib leaned down suddenly and picked up a small pink stone that glinted in the light. She held it in a cupped hand, and said in a voice which had lost its childish tone:

> "Fire will not burn thee
> Seas will not drown thee:
> A rock at sea art thou,
> A man at land art thou.
> On the side of God and His powers
> Thou art the red rowan tree
> To cause the wrath of men to ebb."

Then she stooped and picked some yarrow with her free hand. With the pink yarrow and the pink stone in her hands, she spoke again.

> "If eye hath blighted,
> Three have blessed,
> Stronger are the three that blessed,
> Than the eye that blighted:
> The Father, Son and Holy Ghost;
> If aught elfin or worldly hath harmed it,
> On earth above,
> Or in hell beneath,
> Do thee, God of grace, turn it aside."

Three times she said this, her eyes fixed on Anne, her hands holding flower and stone. Then she said, "Now tread feet on pearlwort and come to me."

Anne knew the efficacy of the trailing pearlwort against the powers of darkness; it was the first plant in all the world on which the Lord Jesus had put his baby foot. Tib gave her the yarrow and the stone.

"Yarrow boil and give he to drink. Stone wear in thine own pocket." From the woven halter of the old ewe she drew a green thread. "Thread sew in his garment to make all fresh and new."

Then she picked up the ewe's halter. The birds flew to their trees. The cat wound its tail around Anne's leg. Tib did not say goodbye, nor did Anne thank her, for thanks or coin would have cut the charm. Anne watched her running toward the cottage, the ewe and the cat bounding before her like two fawns.

Anne put the stone in her apron pocket and drew up the hood again. She went home swiftly. She boiled the yarrow in water and added it to his ale. She sewed the green thread to the seam of his shirt. The broken Bible she hid in the chest beneath the stairs where their Sunday clothes were kept.

His wife became obsessive to Will's thoughts. Her silence, or her strength, or her calmness, whatever name he gave it, frightened, consoled, and angered him.

That trust was not perplexed in the extreme, that time brought summer when briars had leaves as well as thorns, all this must be conjunctive to his life and soul.

His prince must break from his prison cage. Though his thrust might carry him beyond the peaceful custom of these summer days, yet he must act, for some things must be acted before they can be scanned.

He wrote down, *There is no shuffling in heaven. There the action lies in his true nature, and we ourselves compelled, even to the teeth and forehead of our faults, to give in evidence.*

Chaucer's Criseyde had learned the footliest race of all, how to keep her balance. It was a prize that hoodwinked time.

He thought of Criseyde and her Troilus. Boccaccio had made her a whore. Chaucer had made her a tender time-server. But truth was something else again. Truth kept a balance, and forced malignant time to work in one's behalf. Was this not a woman's art? His mother knew it. The lady knew it. His wife knew it. His daughters showed a dawning knowledge by indisputable signs.

He loved and regarded women. Most of them moved straight on, whether for good or bad, but with courage and, at best, with moral strength.

To cast off, howsoever, to act, to uncripple his dragging steps and knock a window through the stale unprofitableness of his self-war. To find his prince's answer might be to find his own.

To dance a jig in the village street, to drink the river dry, to jump over the church tower, to speak without fear, unpack his heart, make confession of his true state, see truth and be it—be no longer a man who stood in pause where he should first begin . . .

He knew no other way to break the ice which sealed him in.

And yet how did he dare?

Yet dare he must. Jump over the church, that was it. He laughed. Poor Will-a-bedlam, raving.

Break the spell, break the spell. Who has ever endured the pure truth? That is, if he knew it to be the truth.

I am a penny-server.

I do other men's business.

I am expedient, dishonest.

I have betrayed where I was trusted.

I am a rogue and a slave because I will not make a true confession.

I am asleep and will not waken, though my dreams are bad.

No one understood Will as well as Will.

Coming swiftly into the kitchen, he kissed his wife and said to Susanna who struggled sleepily with breakfast, "Today is thy mother's birthday."

Anne looked up. "Why, no."

"Why, yes. You are reborn in my deepest heart. That is the truth. Henceforth this day will be the celebration of thy birth." She smiled and made some joke about not having a year added to each. He said to Susanna, "I went to write her a poem but could find naught to rime with lady but baby, and she is no child, thank God for us."

442

Anne listened, drawing the ale.

"For thee, dear lass, this market day will be remembered when old tales are told. We'll take a lance today against all tyrants and usurpers."

"Tyrants and usurpers," said Anne, "in our sleepy town?"

"There's the tyrant Custom, and the usurper Lies. I've done with both."

"Will, have a care."

"Oh, not where truth is concerned, dear love." To Susanna he said, "Thy mother, she will stay at home and make all safe and ready while we gather gifts to lay them at her feet."

Susanna clapped her hands a little warily. But her natural gaiety won with some help from her curiosity.

Will stood up to fetch his best jerkin from the chest beneath the stairs. Anne remained very still; her only movement was the creeping of her hand to touch the stone in her pocket. Susanna looked at her mother and whispered, "Be all well?" Before she could reply, Will had come back, and he had the broken Bible in his hand. He held it as though it were a live thing struck down and still not dead.

"Why, this be thine, love. How come it so?"

It did not occur to her to lie. Yet she found it hard to speak. At length she said, her eyes watchful of them both, "I heaved it across the room."

"Ah!" Susanna gasped.

Will made a swift gesture to her daughter. "Go thee now, and fettle up thy room."

"Oh!" But his gesture was so stern she fled.

He put the broken book on the table and said to Anne, "Dear heart, why?"

"Because it failed me." Her voice and eyes were resolute; she would yield in nothing. "And this has not." She took the stone from her pocket.

He stroked the broken book. His heart was thudding. Her gaze moved only from the book to his face. At last he looked at her.

"Because of me?"

She nodded.

"And the charm has worked?"

"Well, thee hath not cried out in thy sleep these last two nights."

Broken faith or broken book; each was each. With sick despair he added one more item to his list of sins.

He did not move to kiss her, for she stood as stiff as the stone in her hand. He put the book back into the chest and called Susanna.

Susanna was very grave. Her glance flew to him.

As they stood on the street outside the closed door of the house, she whispered, "She heaved the *Bible?*"

He took her hand. "At the devil, lass! It hath been done before. Come, smile, we have our task to do."

At the white meat stall across the road, he bought one egg. "First we shame the guise of the world," he said to her, "by lifting our orb of state."

They stopped at every booth. Oh, he was young, gay and handsome! On Tinker's Lane he bought pans to hail their coming, and Susanna struck them daintily and laughed with all her friends. Down Rother Street the sun still held, and he performed a stately dance called *Lady Carey's Dump* around the Cross . . . If she went to Tib a Prior it was to a blessing witch who caught some measure, though darkly through a glass, of nature's good. He thought of the old man in London with his dear ways and wisdom. Oh, but to know that his wife had been moved to such extremes sat on him like an homunculus! . . .

Girls and boys joined hands and danced a roundel, and one dear lad thrust flowers in Susanna's hair. Down Wood Street they went, where a faggot joined the egg as scepter to the orb. He said, "My wife is queen." He said, "Married men, all, love thy wives and they'll love thee always!" He was greeted with jokes, both good and frisky. Everyone was bright on market day.

At each stall he explained it was his wife's birthday and he bought a present for her. Susanna began to be less willing. At the village pump, he kissed each woman who was washing clothes, and hailed her as a true woman and loyal wife.

444

And so they were and kissed back heartily, for his natural elegance allowed him to play the fool but never look the part. A few wondering friends—old Mrs Shaw and Judith Sadler—joined the coil of idle youths behind him; his brother Gilbert, at their father's lumber stall, frowned and said, "What do thee, Will?"

"I'm beginning at the beginning and working through to the end. Can the world support it?"

Susanna held tight to his arm.

A little voice at his side said, "Suckets? Hast thee any?" and there was Tib, the little witch, disguised now as a shepherdess, for she was leading her old ewe to milk and sell the milk out of a battered mug.

"Why, little witch!" he cried, "thee must have suckets and ribbons and spells aplenty for thy kind heart and true ways. And a garland for thy ewe and a comb for thy wild locks."

"Nay," she said, "it be only suckets I be partial of."

He bought her an apron in which to carry the candied sweets and ginger and sugarplums, and when he told her that she must take a lance with him against usurping lies, she gave him a swift keen glance. He said to her, "Set thy charms upon the air while I perform my antic round."

"Ah," she said, in her soft childish voice, "thee do need no charm. Thy strength's thy own."

"Oh, Tib," he said, "that be conjuration and most mighty magic!"

Michael stole up under her arm, and she fed him a sucket. Then in a sudden brisk voice she said abruptly, "Peace, thou foolish man," and went off with Michael at her side.

At Perrott's Tavern, Will saw the tyrant, Coombs, leaning on his staff, and he told him in bad Latin that he cared not for his face which had Usury written on it. John Coombs replied, with no temper, that 'twas not his face was his fortune.

Through all the later journey, Susanna clung to Will. In her apron, which she held up with one hand, were all the birthday gifts. Long ago the egg had been broken and some gifts stealthily dropped behind. But she wore the bangles like a gypsy, and on her shoulders lay enough ribbons to deck a maypole.

At some point, Judith slipped up beside Susanna. Will heard with his sharp ears Susanna's hissed counsel. "The other side— the other side. Take thee there his arm."

Judith held him with both hands upon his arm, her head lowered. Will glanced at her. Her face was pale. It was high time she learned that life must be taken hold of, not yielded to.

Jokes ran from him like a millrace. He left behind jokes-repeated, and presently they were following him like old bawds, an embarrassment.

He knew well that here and there friends did not laugh but frowned. He preferred the frowns. *Have courage, Will, to be God's fool, for God looks on the heart.*

Hamnet Sadler said, shaking his head, "Will, Will, spend not thyself on such antics."

"But I am a penny-server," said Will.

"Not you, Will," said Hamnet heartily. "Come home to dinner, thou honest man though a little drunk."

Will shook his head. "I am not drunk with liquor."

Quiney stood in his doorway gravely. Will addressed him with a painted text he had bought to hang upon a wall. He read aloud the text. "'*A virtuous woman is a crown to her husband.*' Give this to thy Elizabeth, with the kiss no man takes from thee."

Quiney stood holding the painted wood, his kind eyes sad. "Come in, Will, and give it her thyself."

"Not so. I've betrayed where I was trusted."

"Will, Will, say not that to thy friend Quiney!"

"Fond man, remember thy wife."

"Father, it be dinnertime," said Susanna.

"What, hungry? Why, thou wilt feed and hunger once again. Foolish girl. We're not half done for, yet." Impeccable was the word for him, in voice, manner, gesture, comportment.

Joan came up to Judith. "Go home, lass. Gie me his arm." But Judith shook her head. Will's eyes traveled from one to the other. Joan marched to Susanna. "Scud, lovedy."

Susanna went, and Joan said, "Now, Will, thee do make a fair Bobb a thyself. It be no one's birthday save Bardolph's Ben.

Thee'll get polt on conk iffen thee buss so steady. Come betimes."

"Go!"

"Ah, peace. How much booze hath thee had?—though, faith, I thought thee never drank too much."

"Joan, you have misheard: to fear the worst oft cures the worst."

She said, gripping his arm with five little fingers like locks, "What be there to fear!" She did not ask a question. "Anne, she coasteth to thy cry. Leave her to grope no more."

He was so put out of countenance that he said, "Why do you speak true so suddenly?"

"Because I know thee for a lawful man who'lt not disgrace our family."

"Oh, thou hast misread, Joan. I am expedient and dishonest."

"Oh, thou cobloaf! Thee'll pay sauce with shame. Come, come!"

It was all said close to themselves. Judith was listening with lowered head and eyes seeking Joan. The procession had acquired a herald; a spry, leather-lunged fellow whose name none knew, who went from market to market, selling trinkets, broadsheets and ballads. He knew all and told all, both lies and truth. Will's jokes were snatched up by the fellow and his broadsheets waved as though the jokes would be found therein.

Will said loudly to Joan, "If the Hart do lack a hind, if the cat will after kind—" and she sucked in her mouth and slapped him well, while the fellow shouted:

> "If the hart do lack a hind
> If the cat will after kind,"

and waved his broadsheets.

Ned was at cudgel play, but he let his adversary win, and lounged by Will to let all see that what united was stronger than what set apart. Thomas Adrian, shirt torn, eye brusied, left his wrestling for love of Judith's paleness.

Will bought a tray of beads and bangles from the herald, and gave a token to every woman at the Market Cross. He made a

447

couplet, praising humankind, to go with the gift, and Ned conveyed each with a bow that could only be executed by an illicit player in a canting town.

The pedlar repeated the couplets in urgent tones, and begged Thomas Adrian to set them down in a clear hand. But Thomas Adrian would not be taken from Judith's side.

Then Will suddenly cast a cue to Ned from *A Warning to Fair Women*. Ned caught it deftly, and the market place was treated to that unlawful enterprise, a play. The scene was much applauded. When it was over, Will looked about. He saw his father come down from his stall under the High Cross, and he saw Henry Walker, Head Alderman, watching him with a lingering pleasure in the scene just past.

Will went to Henry and gravely counted out ten shillings for a fine. "They'll take this from thee, Henry, as fine against me."

"Oh, no, no, Will!" Walker backed away. "High spirits on market day!"

John Shakespeare said, "It was a play. Thee did not stop it, Henry. Take his foolish money." Poor Henry Walker. It set a bad tone. Quarrels broke out. Constables were soon crying, "There now! There now!" and rattling their clubs.

Something in the look of John Shakespeare, who had had so often the culling of his town, made Will hesitate. In a soft voice, he said, "Does not the end crown all, father?"

John Shakespeare said calmly, "Thee be sick and must be cared for. Ned, speak within doors to the good Smith and lure out a tray of ale for friends and all. Now, Will, sit here on Cross."

Will sat down with a composure that seemed unflawed. He said quietly, "Not sick, father. My long sickness of health and living now begins to mend, and nothing brings me all."

"Thee be darkened in this action, son. Let us have no more mysteries." He was very firm.

As the tavern maid, Betty, passed the ale, Quiney came over to drink a pot in the company of his dear friend, and he brought the miller who was always a kindly man. The ale was drunk in silence, and one by one the minions slipped away. To those who were left Will said sadly, "Look for no more ale and cakes here, you rude rascals." And then, to those left, he said more quietly still, "Chew upon this, good friends. Simple truth's miscalled simplicity, and captive good attends on Captain Ill."

Judith cried, "Do not speak in riddles, father!"

"Love, love, how can I speak more plain?"

His father said shortly, "I say, leave off this disguise which antics us all."

Will was suddenly very tired but his courtesy did not leave him. "Dearest father, shall I forget myself to be myself?"

"Aye, if yourself's remembrances wrong yourself."

Will said sadly, "Father, I've spoken naught but truth from the beginning to the end, but no one has believed me save little Tib a Prior."

Henry Walker worked his mouth industriously as though clearing it of a meal, and glanced angrily at a loiterer, who grinned. At length he muttered, "Take him home, as thee be a good father," and went off angular in his concern.

"Aye," said John, "the holiday is over, Will. Shall I come with thee?"

"Why? I am not sick."

"Then end this playing-day. Come, Ned."

Will rose. "To all, goodbye. Betty, farewell. Thank thee for thy good ale." Judith was weeping against his shoulder. "Oh, Thomas Adrian, heed. Thee must never follow bouncing Bets with their jolly buttocks, but comfort the faithful who weep."

His daughter now had all his love. He put his hand against her cheek. "Lovedy, thee must not weep. Shall I tell thee a story? Of Neptune, whom the Welsh folk call Lir? Nay, wait! He had two cruel daughters who were the rough winds. But the gentle zephyr was his third child, and it was she who prevailed in the end. Is that not good? Do you not say so, Thomas Adrian? That Judith is my gentle zephyr, and I put away all foolish ways for her?"

"Very good," said Thomas Adrian.

"Then let us go home and make our peace with common sense."

449

Thomas Adrian went a street with them, but when Judith showed she was no longer crying, he touched her hand and returned to his father.

Will said nothing. He held Judith's hand. He was sad and tired and ashamed.

The street was empty. Market day was over and suppers were toward. Judith reached up and kissed him. "Now thee look like *father*," she whispered. On Chapel Street were only the old ewe and Michael, Tib, Tom Greene, and Newhall, the constable. But Tom was shaking Tib, and Michael was kneeling beside the ewe, his face half hidden against her side.

Will went forward slowly and no one saw him. Tom shook Tib till her hair fell about her brow, and he cried softly, "Confess! Speak, thou wretched ronyon! Nay, confess, confess, and somewhat save thyself."

Her face was shut against the world of men. She let her head be flung back and forth, but her eyes, with their odd blue light, held to Tom's face. When Newhall saw Will, he nodded.

Will tore Tom's hand from one arm of Tib, but Tom still held her by the other.

Tom looked with blazing wrath; then, seeing Will, he cleared his brow but swung Tib nearer to him with the hand that gripped.

"What does this—?" Will began, but Tom spoke at the same moment.

"I saw, I watched! She cast charms, and in the graveyard danced with her beast and this babe, this child of Joan's, now soiled! It is past endurance; constable knows how to act."

" 'Tis past *my* endurance," Will said quietly. "Leave off thy hands."

Tom said, "Newhall, take her."

Will seized Tib so swiftly that Tom's grasp, being loosened, was shaken off. "Now run," he said.

And run she did, having snatched up the ewe's halter. Michael, crouching all alone, was very still and low till Judith crouched beside him.

Tom cursed. Newhall said, in fine fettle, "There now, Will, who gave thee leave to take law in thine own hands?"

"Oh, by God's lid, vex me no more! War on children if thee have no better part, but not where God—or I—can see thee!"

Tom stood angry and silent, but Newhall was hurt in outward ways.

"She be no child! By gog's wouns, he who hath truck with her, be a rare fool, an' all. I be waiting for such evidence as Tom be quick to see!"

"Matthew Newhall," said Will, "to dance in graveyard in full day hath no charm in it. I'll say so to all who ask."

Newhall, still smarting, said coldly, "*Thee* did have some fire-new charms today, some thought. As the devil loves fools, think on that!" and he went off, rank with his abused authority.

Will said quietly to Judith, who sat as crouched as Michael, "Take thy cousin to his mam. Make light to her."

He and Tom were alone. They stood like wary dogs waiting for the first to move. Tom turned sharply, and went home.

Will came more slowly, aware that one or two looked out their windows. He was weary past enduring. By firm resolve, he did not stumble.

Tom was waiting inside the open door. He closed it when Will entered. He said, "Cousin, perhaps thou hast not heard that this town has turned a hard face upon witches."

"Has his wolfship Coombs licensed you to hunt them?"

"I know not what you mean," said Tom, "but it is the duty of us all to rake out witches."

"I like it not, neither hunting man nor beast. And that you know right well. And there's an end."

Anne had come into the parlor door.

Tom answered quietly, "Some say thou art very apt in feats of darkness."

"And some say there is a man in the moon. Will you say aye to all that John Coombs speaks?"

Now Tom looked narrowly and took careful account. He replied with a cool manliness. "Dost thou think any man can rule me? Either Coombs or—Shakespeare?"

Will made a little sound of surprise. "Well taken, cousin. But a clerkship in thy purse might speak, might it not?"

Tom threw away discretion. "I am sick to death of thy poor

faith. I'll have no more of it. From now, make thine own mess of ledgers, rents, and lawsuits."

He turned away in a rage and then turned back in a gesture of such dramatic fitness that it could only come from outraged integrity. He held out his bunch of keys.

Will took the keys. Tom went to the stairs. He said to Anne, "I am sorry, cousin."

Will saw her and half-smiled. He put the keys in his pocket. She turned toward the kitchen and he followed.

He stood by the table in silence for a moment, and then he drew an embroidered kerchief from his pocket.

"There is thy gift, love; all that is left."

She took it and held it in her hands. She looked at it and smiled a little. He watched her for a moment.

"Thy goodness share with thy birthright, sweet simplicity."

She did not look at him, but smiled still.

"Love all, trust a few. Keep thy husband under thy life's key . . ."

She said nothing, and he wished that she would speak.

CHAPTER *Twelve*

NEITHER Will nor Tom found much substance in the awkward parts they had chosen. Rents, ledgers and lawsuits affected Will with awful distaste. He wished life's pieces to be undisturbed until he had mortised them forever. Tib had not been troubled again, and she brought him a bunch of meadowsweet.

As for Tom, he had given away even the keys to the house, so that he was now obliged to test doors to find one unlocked, or stand below and call.

Quiney told Will that John Coombs had let it be known that he was pleased with Tom's diligent act toward a witch and held out a positive hope.

"Sure, you do not believe the lass is a witch, Dick?"

"I believe only in the corporate good," Quiney answered with a slight smile.

"I am sorry that I spoke to Tom with bad grace, yet it made me mad."

Late at night, Anne heard Tom softly calling. She came down in her night robe to let him in, unable to hold back some of her laughter at the plight he had made for himself.

He smiled ruefully. "I'm like some poor unmindful outlaw sneaking home." He took her hand. "Cousin, speak for me. Faith, I've been a fool, but he made me mad. Thou art a saint, but not he. Where is he now?"

"In solar," she said, smiling still, so that she looked young as Susanna.

He put his hand to her cheek. "Bounteous cousin, whatever shall become of me?"

She patted his cheek with her fingers. "Ah, Tom, it will pass. How foolish be thee and he in thy pride. A woman would never shut all doors behind her."

He laughed a little, feeling suddenly free of care. "By God, dear Anne, thou dost make me think of wives with ardor. Shall I find one rare as thee?"

Now it was she who was ruefully amused. "Oh, ask for better'n me, Tom, else life will be worth a mere penny."

He put his hands on her arms and drew her close to him to look with a spring of affection into her face. She continued to smile to conceal her ruefulness, and made a little joke at which he kissed her.

"Well," she said, "that be a comfort, and I thank thee, Tom." Then he kissed her again and she drew back, the smile fading from her face.

"Nay," she said softly, "that kiss be no comfort."

"As I am a man," he replied gravely, "I could not forbear. Good night, cousin."

"Good night," she said without moving, and then as he stood a little off looking at her, she added quietly, "I will speak of thee with Will. Have a good heart."

Above stairs, on the landing, Will had seen all but not heard. There, before his eyes, rose up the bitter conclusion of all spells and enthrallments. He went away softly.

He stood in their room by the window, gripping the ledge. When she came in, she did not see him till she had once more gone to their bed.

She laughed. "Poor Tom, locked out again. Dearest Will, gie him back his keys, or dup the door. Humble him no more."

He held to the curtain, his face half turned toward her. How tender was her voice. Feelings that could scarce be called emotions swarmed out of black pits. Words failed, reason failed. He ran his tongue over his lips.

"Ah," she said, with a sleepy teasing in her voice, "thee have so much and he so little. Leave off thy pride."

He tried to speak but he could only blink his eyes against the tears. She saw none of this in the shadowy room, and turned on her side with some teasing still.

"I'll gie him the keys," she said. "He well loves peace and a home. I'll save thy true pride." His silence roused her. She raised herself on her elbow. "Will, what be amiss? Come thee—"

But he stood without moving and she, confused into wakefulness, watched, in the leaping light of the candle, the still figure with his back turned to her.

There must be no death of love, never, never, never. No spell of witch, black or white, must break the anagram of wife to husband, husband to wife. For his soul's life it must be found that simplicity and kindness, love and loyalty were not enthralled.

He stood in his window next day and watched Tom pacing the path below. He would not see a man, and yet it was the man he saw. How well Tom carried himself, how manly, comely, virile were his looks; with what grace he moved. Suddenly Will whispered with great violence, "But do you think that I shall make a life of jealousy?"

If spells were needed, he would find the most potent of them all! He thought, with a bitter sweetness, that perhaps his emotion stood in proxy to that deep love which would forever put quietus to the lady.

Anne, seeing one step and then another, took the keys and gave them to Tom. Will knew that Tom had resumed his place, for in a courteous way, Tom told him of some lease or lawsuit that must be tried.

Will nodded and said, "Thank you." He was indeed most thankful for any grace that did not bring a counter ill. For he must now move to that dead center where Will had heard Will's cries for help.

In this town, he had known the clock, the bells, the graveyard, the swans, the ululating pigeons, the market cross, the ducks that waddled to the river, the men, the women, but he had not known himself.

There was one more thing that he must do. Whatever the sad spell on me has been, I hereby cast it off. And by that token, I cast off all the names that I have given it: expediency, the foot above my head, false time, and all the gins, the snares, the subtleties that bear good, kind and sovereign names, like *Greville* and *the Queen.*

He fetched his horse. He took no lute, no verses, only certain absolute words.

"Today my lady is not well," Sir Robert told him wanly. "She hath suffered giddiness and indigestion, the dauntless dear. But now she will be more spritely with a good friend to cheer." He himself looked brighter. "My sweet lady, is she not a honey bloom? Be gentle, sir, for she fetches her breath as short as a new ta'en sparrow."

His gray eyebrows were frayed, his eyes weary; in his old velvet surcoat, he had an air of being overused. He was himself Will's escort.

In her apartment a fire burned even on this warm day.

She was sitting with her back against the window plucking idly at a cittern. She was creamy pale, with her lustrous dark hair about her brows. Her eyes were dark and restless, her mouth as rich in curves as a cherry, her body laden. Her waiting woman, who had always a jolly hard expression, was embroidering and singing to the music.

Sir Robert laughed to see how glad they were to meet.

For the lady's face flushed and she slowly set aside her cittern. Will kissed her hand and, sitting on a chair nearby, picked up the instrument and struck a chord. "That," he said, "is to make you smile."

"Amen, amen, amen," Sir Robert said and closed the door. But she did not smile. She pressed deeper into the pillows.

Will said gently, "I am sorry you have not been well."

She replied in a small shrouded voice, "When you do not come, this place is no better than a gaol."

"Oh, dear lady, you are the apple of Sir Robert's eye."

"Did she withhold her leave for you to come?"

The waiting woman made a chortling sound from her place by the fire.

He said, "Indeed, not so. She sent me."

She was plainly startled, and then she partly closed her lids and leaned back her head to smile.

"Ah, tell me her message quickly."

He told her, "I will not come again. Lay this harsh simple *no more* to thy heart, and so be free. We are no longer coiled. The clasp's been broke."

He knew she had heard him by the way her eyes searched his face. But she did not speak and gave no special sign of response. He put aside the cittern and stood up. "Dearest lady, what has been good is good forever; the rest's for death. Farewell."

He thanked God that she said nothing and showed a way for him to leave without delay. But she stirred and her head knocked against the window glass. "Oh, yes," she said very softly, "the odds are gone." She said it with great poignancy. He asked, "What odds, dear lady?"

"The odds of me against the world." Her face was pale. He saw her great eyes reflected in the glass. She started to sing huskily, not bothering with the tune:

> "The fox, the ape, and the humble-bee,
> Were still at odds being but three
> Until the goose came out of door
> Staying the odds by adding four."

Her expression moved almost as though the child had moved within her. She went on in a toneless little voice, "He cursed me

456

and lies still in prison. What shall I do? Beg to have him brought to me, trussed like a goose?"

Then she slowly moved her head to look at Will.

"Why, Will, dear Will, thou art frolic and fancy, games and song. Kiss me for that."

"No."

"Then kiss me goodbye."

"No." He smiled.

Her gesture was sweet, her eyes were soft. She wiped her forehead.

"Then stand you there, and I will pelt your heart with that true affection that I bear to you."

He moved away. In the distance, a horn sounded and the halloo of men. He said, "Whate'er betides, I will not see you again."

She closed her eyes and her breath came hard. "I have no one in the world but you. You have been my friend, my counselor, my lover—now I need your perfect love for his hate's too much for me to bear. In God's name, how can you treat me so! My sweet Will who does not let a dog suffer!" She moved her head suddenly back and forth. She said on a whisper, "I die, I die, if I am set aside!"

"Lady," he said, "let us not adore our errors!"

"I ask that you hold me in your heart of hearts and do not let me go."

"All good's remembered!"

"Then kiss me!" She put up her hands.

"Lady, I'll come no nearer now nor ever."

"I ask your kindness!"

"I give it you."

"My God, I will not suffer so!" She turned her face to the window, and the ineffable profile spoke more vehemently than words. Then she turned again to him. "Why look you so green and pale at what you once did freely? Are you afeared to be the same in act as in desire?"

He would not believe that this remorseless girl was stronger than God.

She lifted her hair with both hands and moved her head slowly from side to side. "God needs the devil, and so do you, proud, stupid man. Thou art as tied to me as a lame man to his crutch."

He knew well that all his still and mental parts were being assailed by another's will, a will so rapacious that it devoured all in sight. But he said, "Not so, lady, on my solemn word."

"Thou art no *man*," she whispered. "Thou art so afraid of me that thou art ashamed of thyself." Her whisper was a groan. She was watching him, and she said quietly, "If you hold away from me, I'll scream you to dishonor. I'll bring that good old man, and others too, and say that you misused me."

"In God's name, spare us both such madness."

With a sudden expression of fear, she said, "We did buy each other with a thousand kisses."

"They were forged lies, dear lady! Believe me for the good of both."

"Lies? They are real as I. Kiss me and tell the truth. Oh!"

He was jarred by the spasm of pain that went across her face, the anguish that broke into a groan. She cried hoarsely, "By Gis, the very dice obey thee!" and her groans shivered the air.

He hesitated still, and then he saw her pain was real. His humanity, like spring in the earth, cracked his reserve. Her fear was like a child's and he went toward her. The waiting woman ran to the door and threw it open, shouting, "My lady—come to my lady!"

Her face was bright with sweat and in her eyes was an absolute terror. He held her tossing body. Her groans were screams, and her breath a terrible heaving, and she thrust him from her with an unnatural strength.

"No, no—I'll have those odds again!" As Sir Robert ran into the room she forced herself to a sitting position.

"Drive him out—he hath set a spell! Drive him out, he hath bewitched me!" and she fell back in violent panting.

Sir Robert, bewildered out of his senses, looked from one to the other. The waiting woman, shrewder than the others, screamed for the doctor.

Sir Robert cried, "My dearest little rose of May—step aside, sir, leave the room. Ho, help for the lady! How do you, sweeting? Ho, fetch wine, the doctor!"

The waiting woman struck Will a blow as she rushed from the room. It was a man's voice from the doorway that set his course straight.

"Poor Will," said Catesby, cold in face and voice. "Poor Will. Doth love's quick pants in a woman's arms come to this? Poor Will. Violent ends for violent delights. Will's task is done. Begone, Will."

It was the repetition of his name which raked him. He drew his dagger. Catesby's eyes blazed.

"Why, thou upstart!" He struck Will's arm a blow that flung the dagger across the corridor. "Now pick it up and be gone!"

CHAPTER *Thirteen*

THAT a man could be sick for several days and yet have no fever caused alarm.

But he was not sick. He had withdrawn into the only secret place where he might bring all to a just end.

John Hall said to Anne, "It is his head, I fancy. Let him smell only sweet savors, and drink this balm of lavender, rose, and foal's foot. And of borage, too, I'll boil a cure for melancholy. Let him not cry or sing high or shout out, and give him a hot posset at night."

She was very still, but she quietly wrung her hands. This touched him deeply. "All that's small and trivial hath been done away," she said.

A thousand loving answers welled in his heart. But he was no more made for compound speech than she. "Aye. What's true abides."

Will watched his wife as she moved about the room. Music rang in his head. My wife . . . my wife . . . Vibrations of music were as tangible as light.

He listened, dwelling in his mind on the consuming wonder that an importunity which had held him night and day, clawed at his body, possessed his mind, owned him as wholly as the devils had owned the Gadarene swine, had faded inconsequential as a vapor.

459

This wonder now consumed him. All the passion for which he had forsaken discretion, peace of mind, and marriage vows had become a dull amazement.

In humane gentleness: welcome. Yet what of poor mankind, where'er it be? Dearest souls, thy cause doth strike my heart with pity!

He heard a storm, but there was no storm in the sky. It did not break for many hours. He cried out in whispers for poor souls who did fly backward, for lamentings heard in the air, and strange screams on the wind. The tempest in his heart held all the world's sorrows and they knocked at his door.

He cried out to Anne that Tib was at the door. She went, but there was no one there. He raised on his elbow again and cried that some poor naked wretch knocked for shelter—some poor young lass travailed to be delivered. Hear! She would not go, but sat on the bed and held him in her arms. She whispered that he would see: the greater the misery, the sweeter the miracle.

"Thee be my Will, rooted in my soul."

Then she took all the magic things, the herbs, the charms, and burned them in the fire. She threw away the stone. After that she took the broken book to Tom and, weeping, asked his help. A compassionate man, he taught her the words which said that God does not give for bread a stone.

She would be Tom's friend forever!

John Shakespeare sat in the room asking questions that had nothing to do with illness. Ned sat in the embrasure of Will's window, telling him who passed below, frowning toward the bed, leaping to any move beneath the covers.

Once Will, watching him quietly, said, "How goes it with thee, lad?"

"Oh, alack," Ned cried, springing up, "how goes it with thee?"

"Art thee contenter, lad?"

Ned held his hand. "I'faith, get well, and I will be thy man through all."

Many came to inquire, and only one or two linked his sickness with his antics on market day. Most thought of some kind of spell, of which there were many kinds and few remedies. Who and how had he offended? Old Mrs Rogers fell into a shriek before the inevitable, inexorable nature of the curse on poor Will!

John Coombs inquired, sending for Tom.

Tom told Anne that Coombs, standing at his window with his back turned, had asked, "Is it a true illness? Or is it witchcraft, of which there is more and more about?" "A true illness. Dr Hall is attending him." John Coombs had chuckled. "It would have been better had thee said witchcraft. Now I must be very hesitant about any legal transactions thee hath set me to. For a man, once ill, may go suddenly to God."

Tom's anger still flushed his face. He added bitterly, "I see there is no earthly justice."

As far as Will's body was concerned, he could get up and move about at any time, but by no effort could his mind venture from the cell of this bed. Here he was safe concealed until a last mystery yielded up its answer. Here, at the heart of the house, lay its truth, and the honorable contest of truth with lies.

Quiney came in. "Myself it be." Then, with a frowning love, he said, "Will, how goes it?"

"Well, well, well."

"I must ask thee, Will—oh, plague and pox—!"

"I lie on fire. Come to the matter."

"Be it—oh, hell-kite!—Council's action against players that hath o'erwrought thee?"

Will lay back against the pillows and saw Quiney with affection.

"Nay, Dick, for how can I play the player any more, and hide from me the true nature of my life?"

"Devil's dam, that be quibbling."

"No. Disguise shall, by the disguised, pay with false exacting."

"Oh, good now, I know not such twitty words! But thee, I know, are worth more than all those sanctimonious old fools."

"Dear Dick. I'll praise any man that praises me. Yet, by all that's holy, I know thee for a just and loving man."

Quiney was moved. He said nothing, but his rare smile appeared. "Be about, Will, for we've thrown devil-take-him to our black lord."

"Oh, I shall not miss that."

461

A scent of flowers seemed to enter the room, a step came, light but resounding, a presence breathed, the door opened, and Mary Shakespeare entered.

She was smiling, keen, and beautiful. Her eyes were fixed on her son.

"My dearest boy," she said, and kissed him with warm assimilation of touch and smell, lips to cheek. "How be thee?"

She dismissed Quiney with a charming move. Quiney said goodbye and Anne stepped into the room.

Mary Shakespeare looked at her, and Anne sat on the bed by her husband. Mary Shakespeare stood the other side of the bed, looking down at him. There was irony in her gaze.

"For God's sake to me," she said quietly, "what trouble and dubiety is here?"

Will opened his eyes straight into his mother's gaze. "Oh, mother," he said, "where is thy wonted pity?"

"For what, my son? That thou hast put thy kerchief on thy head, and so proclaimed thy sickness? What sickness?"

"I am unwell, mother."

"Tush, of what? Going to and fro in the market place?"

Anne stirred on the bed. Will heard the faint agitation in her throat, and felt the warmth of her side against his shoulder.

"What have I done that my mother should chide?"

"Thee hath misused thy commodity of good name. Thee hath made thyself a laughingstock."

He was silent for some time. At length he resumed the restless movement of his legs beneath the covers.

His mother rubbed her long fingers up and down the bedpost. She said in her clear voice, "A good name is a commodity used in all transactions that do with men's opinions. When the question of our coat of arms is yet unsettled, one takes extra care of his assets." She lifted her head, moving it slightly as though she sensed or smelled some strangeness. "There is something amiss. Something—I know not what."

Will said softly, "It is thine iron will, mother. It is without compassion."

Apart from a sharpening in her eyes, his mother gave no sign that she had heard. She said, "I know the world that thee, poor fool, takes into such small account. I have no illusions that it will wait till a man like thee makes up his mind."

He looked at her with interest. What a remarkable woman she was. How he loved and hated her. He said softly, "Mother, mother, I can chop logic as well as thee."

"I doubt it." She moved suddenly and came to kiss him good-bye. As she stood close to him, and Anne's fingers, withdrawn, lay briefly against his neck, she said to Anne, "The truth is, that I blame thee for much."

Anne did not understand for a moment that Mary Shakespeare was addressing her. Then she was incredulous. Her hand flew to her breast. Will lifted his head and looked at his mother.

Mary Shakespeare was surveying Anne dispassionately. "Though I have no doubt thee be a good wife in the common way, thee hath not the gift that feeds a man to his own uprising nor sees what ambition means." She added coolly, "For that he needs a helpmeet fitter than thee. But alas, what can we do?"

It was calmly said, with no stress or anger. As she went out the door, she called for Susanna.

After a moment Will laughed and fell back. He did not at once see that Anne was white. Then he made a wry grimace and took her hand. In a moment, he tugged it gently. "Dearling, smile." She turned away her face. Then he pressed her hand tightly and drew her down against him. He stroked her back.

"Dear wife—dear heart. Forget, forgive."

She smiled faintly. "She hath never said this much before."

He said again, his hand still stroking, "Dear heart, forget, forgive *all* affronts."

He gave a welcome only to John Hall; for with this grave young man, an oblique healing went on beneath the masquerade of medicine.

This day, the third of his illness, he waited for the doctor with a passive eagerness. Susanna brought him in. She looked flushed and happy; life was very full, her father ill, her lover brought to the house each day, her own womanliness called to account.

She laid a bouquet by her father. "Ah," said Will taking them up with a faint smile. "Known as kiss-me-at-the-gate." He looked from one to the other. "Well, well-a-day. Sit thee, sir. And kiss me, love, and leave us."

This had not been Susanna's plan. She put a good face on it but took away her flowers.

Will said, "What cure is there for decay?"

"It is suspected," said the doctor, "that circulatory—"

"Ah! Is naught eternal?"

"God," said the doctor.

"May not the lost and dead return?"

The doctor was cautious. "There is some credence put in ghosts, but caution is best exercised in a world of doubtful fact."

Will lay silent for a moment. "It was not of ghosts I thought —though some do haunt. I thought of daughters, wives, sent to death but not killed, the miracle." Then he turned his eyes on the doctor. "But they say miracles are past, and we have our philosophical persons to make modern and familiar, things supernatural and causeless." He laughed quietly and smoothed at the bedclothes. "In London, there is a good old man, as close to me as my conscience. I see by him we make trifles of terrors; ensconcing ourselves into seeming knowledge, when indeed we should submit ourselves to an unknown wonder."

The doctor stood looking down at him, his young face compassionate. "Thy heart is sorely charged, sir. Is a doctor thy remedy?"

"Hah? Can you not minister to the mind? Why should it not be in your mercy to pluck up all rooted sorrow, erase all hidden fears?"

The doctor sat down. His face, with its singular blending of the flesh and the spirit, his simple hair falling to his simple collar, his eyes most knowing, turned to Will. "In that, the patient must minister to himself. Be his own doctor and divine."

Will was silent for so long that the doctor rose to mix some brew or other. Will said then, "Shall I tell thee what I see? I see, through the hollow eyes of death, life peering. But the skull—it is our prison house and within it lies our strange and self abuse."

"Dear sir, are we not all men, and all tempted in all ways? We are yet but young in deed. But I dare believe there is no tragedy so great as when a good man yields to baseness and forgets he is a lamb of God."

"Say you so? What is, is not. What is not, is. Od's puttikins, sir, knock, knock, knock."

The doctor laughed. "I would we were all of one mind, and one mind good. Then fate would knock in vain, and there would be a desolation of gallows."

"Yet first must be endured your ignorance that finds not till it feels . . ."

"There be also the modern scientific mind, sir. To search, it pushes back the mysteries a pace. In a world much given to fearful speculations and giddy fears, I beg that what we cannot prove we then disprove."

Will looked at him reflectively. "The truth—if my prince from himself be ta'en away—nay, let me see. Bear with me, sir. Must a man always go graveward to snatch at the truth?" He fell very silent. "Yet if, by thy book, darkness be the only ignorance . . . though ignorance be dark as hell . . . well, well. Is this not an infinite mock, that a man should have the best use of eyes to see the way of blindness?"

"Thy prince? Is this a play?"

"Aye, a play, but true in heart."

The doctor said hastily, "It is natural man, nature's child, who does not use his eyes."

Will laughed a little. "How will you physick me, who has been nature's child?"

The doctor looked down with some amusement. "By not losing my way with thee, sir."

Alone, Will put his arms behind his head and watched the gathering twilight. In the landscape of his mind, the comprehensions of life stood to one side; apart from them was ranged the self-born, disengendered, unparented evil, black as ignorance. Between them lay the amazement of the poet, where words clashed in his head like swords.

He rose the next morning and announced himself well enough to go to church.

In the reflective garden, after dinner, with the hot light of summer falling on the full growth, he said suddenly, "That cat —is that not Tib a Prior's?"

"Aye," said Judith. "She be afeared that toad and cat be chivvied by rude men set on some mischief. Yonder's toad."

The cat looked at him with half-closed eyes and the toad with pulsing throat. In the heat he felt cold.

"Who will touch her? Tom?"

The tears sprang to Judith's eyes. "No. Some others creep about, call her witch. Herself she'll fly away, but these she'll not have hurt. Do these do her bidding? There be great load of fear toward them, yet they look so pretty. Even mother wonders some, but says we must obey thee, who are ever kind, and keep them safe."

"What says *thy* heart?"

She lowered her head and smiled.

He picked up the cat. "I'll go to Tib," he said.

Judith asked, "Hath she devil's mark on her?"

He saw that she had some fear, although her gentle heart loved the little beasts.

"No, she be not Satan's trull. 'Tis more like a kind fairy."

He had scarcely set down the cat again when the silent, scented young man who waited on Fulke Greville found him by Nan's direction. The young man, who was of a noble family, said that Sir Fulke begged the honor of Mr Shakespeare's company without delay.

Greville belonged in the company of the snares, the gins, the subtleties which he must now call by their true names. Yet a kindly snare which might perhaps release the hare.

They rode in a world of pimpernels in the waste places, of tansy in the meadows, and Grass of Parnassus by the streams. They rode too in silence, for one did not abuse this silent fair young man with questions.

But thunder clapped without warning from a sky grown surly and the young man crossed himself as instinctively as he might sneeze. He cried, "By heaven, thunder on the sabbath is the devil's voice!" and his coolness did not return.

When they reached Beauchamp Court he took Will to Sir Fulke's study, that shadowy room which was hung with baleful tapestries of the chase and which smelled of wax candles, roses, and carnations.

Sir Fulke was busy at his desk. A secretary took away a letter and sprinkled the page with sand. Sir Fulke started, greeted Will, affixed his seal, and then gave his hand. About him was that air of slightness, nothing urged, all shrewdly tentative and contingent which gave him scope to ply his gentle arts.

While the young gentleman poured the wine, he gave Will a sheet of paper with a poem written. "Give me your opinion."

Will read it, leaning against the window, with the light on his russet hair and his fine, subtle face.

When the young man and the secretary had gone, Greville rose and, with a faint smile, waved away the poem. He put the head of a carnation in the wine before he handed it to Will. Then he sank into a chair by the window through which came the smell of hay, and rubbed his forehead with one finger. His expression gave no hint of stress, but when he looked at Will it was to study him for a moment.

The scope of study was large and penetrating. Will bore it with an open look, standing still and studying Sir Fulke in return.

Sir Fulke said quietly, "As I do honor you, sir, I speak. It is just that you should know Sir Robert Throgmorton came to me this morning."

Will nodded. Sir Fulke gazed out the window, stroking his thin mustache, his dark eyes reflective.

"He is a tender man, a babe, perhaps, but withal faithful and kind. With one hand he held that balance which I gave of you, and which, i'faith, he enjoined to his own knowledge, and in the other that love of her ladyship who is to him a wayward daughter." He turned his eyes on Will and studied him again for a moment, the smile still sweetening his face.

"It would be ungracious of me to speak more than I must. So I beg you, sir, to say naught till I am done. The lady has offered certain vigorous charges toward which Sir Robert, in his distress 'twixt Scylla and Charybdis, knows neither what to say nor what to do. She hath talked like a woman out of her mind, but for three days she hath been in labor—in advance of her time—and women are then prone to imaginings far from the world of men. Sir Robert has permitted none but her doctor and her waiting woman to hear her wild talk."

Sir Fulke rose abruptly, and walked to his desk. Then he stood with hands clasped behind him gazing out the open window. "I did not put on Sir Robert to speak more than was essential. He and I know that words invested with speech cannot be withdrawn." He turned to look at Will, and his fingers played with his ruff. He moved the vase of carnations, stirring the scent. "I am one of her Majesty's servants. A course directed by her Grace's will must not run out of hand. Aphorisms or explanations at variance with that determined course can, on occasion, serve only to breed mischief. It is the skill of a good servant to judge such an occasion."

His dark eyes remained on Will for a moment, both kind and cool. He then sat down slowly and lifted a poncet box to examine.

"Knowing the lady—knowing also, dear sir, the world and the devil—I told Sir Robert that she was, in her sickness, mad. I counseled him to be ruled by me. After some hesitation, he agreed. There matters stand. We are united. United, however, we have still to rule the lady. It is perfectly true that once she is well and returned to her wonted place, refreshed by city life, she may have no wish to remember her shame. But her lively temperament offers no firm assurance. She may not even yield her child to be sent away, though she may also hate it deadly. Who knows? So I ask you, sir, to consider with me some form of concordat that may be acceptable to her."

He paused. For a moment, Will wondered whether it was his cue to speak. He wished to fling himself on a tide of self-recrimination, self-abasement, fate and fortuity, but he had the good sense to refrain. He did ask, in a voice which needed clearing, "How is she, sir?"

"She is alive; though her travail, which hath not ended, hath cost much blood. Her youth and her doctor's skill are much to be praised." Then he added with a fixed note in his voice, "What would you call a firm compact?"

Will cleared his throat but words failed him. He tried again. "Sir, I will ask no questions. I will simply address myself to your chair. Any compact, I judge, must affect me, else I would not be here. But what possible compact can hold between me and those in high places? I will never see the lady again of my own will, but in London to refuse a command from greatness is outside the scope of my competence."

Greville considered him for a moment in a sympathetic way. "By this, I infer that you are not wholly persuaded of your own detachment were you obliged to answer such a summons."

"Dear sir, I am persuaded. But I live in this earthly world where to fear is laudable."

After a brief tribute of silence Greville said, "I can reassure you only in part: that if you decline a summons, the consequences will not be to your disadvantage. Now, you are also here, dear sir and particularly—because what you know of the lady is not known by me nor by Sir Robert. You have some knowledge of her heart, of what inducement might fall most winningly upon her ears. For there is one other urgent thing, good sir, which presses on all this: a great lord lies in prison who must, by commonest good sense, be set free." He crossed his legs, rested his chin on his upraised fingers and studied the toe of his shoe. "I beg you to consider well, and speak."

Will considered. He considered heaven and earth, the seven seas and the five senses, salt, pepper, and the savor of tears; considered all women everywhere, his daughters, lost, lost on hillside and in the sea, his mother, his wife, the lady, her curling hair and her dark look and her wild heart, and all the fears which heaven must harness and ride into the calm of salvation. He too studied the toe of Fulke Greville's shoe.

469

When at length he caught Greville's eye—for their eyes lifted and met at the same moment—he said with an irony so felicitous that Greville showed a poet's joy, "Find her a husband who loves her beyond all other things, and will beat her daily unless she loves him too."

Greville nodded. "Failing that, sir?"

Will shook his head slightly and replied very low. "She hath much need to be loved for herself and her bitter knowledge. Can such love be squeezed into agreement?"

Greville spread out a hand. "In a sense, we do so with all diplomacy. I will see what I can do—about a loving husband."

"Stronger than she—"

"Oh, indisputably. There is such a man, in the court, who loves her dearly. Sir Robert's kinsman is coming from Coughton Court to resolve expediencies and disposals, that is, young Catesby, who must be finely handled, and I wish not to have so frail a thing—for, indeed, sir, I know that with such a woman, the threads of her good and evil are woven into a proud and reckless heart—I wish not to have his headstrong ways rip at this frailty. For, think you, mere husband she will accept?"

"Not in a million years."

"I thought not. So I must write it down in some manner that he cannot spoil, and yet will urge on her with proper spirit." He became brisk. "So be it. You, sir, must take your leave, for I see I would be a great fool to have you meet. Accept my thanks, my regards—"

He got no further, though his hand had reached out to Will's, for Catesby came into the room.

Greville's servant made dismayed, explanatory gestures. Greville pinched his mouth and opened it to speak.

But Catesby brushed aside all but the barest greeting. About him was an evil splendid beauty, the kind of violence shown by one of those creatures raised by magic. Will scarcely knew him. Catesby said, "I came in haste, for I did not wish to let slip away this bed-presser—this copesmate." His tone was violent as he looked at Will. He held in one arm an object wrapped in a length of cloth which he thrust at Will.

"Take thy gifts. She wants no more of you whate'er betide. Open it up." The flash and fury was of a man in some way beset.

But Greville, made prescient by his long training in ambiguities, was seized with alarm. "On no account!" he said, moving forward with a fleetness he seldom displayed. All his slightness fell away. He was robust, contentious, and absolutely authoritative. "Mr Shakespeare, do not so! Give it me. This is madness. Do not yield to it!"

For a moment Will had been confused. Now he put the swathed object on Greville's desk and the three stood taut as wires. When Will moved, Catesby laughed like Lucifer.

"Still thou wilt not escape, Will. I'll pursue thee like the black fiend, with the dead in my arms."

Greville was shaken in a way not seen before. At that moment he was stripped of all that had borne him through his life; he was helpless and revolted and filled with a shrill panic. But he called up his careful training, and it responded like a faithful dog.

He said in a voice congested, but his own, "Sit down. I beg you both, sirs, sit you down. Nay, sit you down! Now, let me say clearly that it is not by wild and untenable charges that a lady's honor and future will be assured—"

Catesby broke in roughly, "Wild and untenable! By the Holy Whore, she shrieks in agony, and with each shriek names her betrayer."

Greville was used to dealing with unruly men. He said firmly, "A noble culprit lies in the Fleet, charged with fathering her child. One mischance may be compassioned a maiden, but an incontinence of two is beyond our means of redress."

Catesby answered shortly, "Not beyond mine."

"Sir, I direct you, in the Queen's name, to take no action!"

"That is what you say. But I shall strike him"—Catesby sprang up like a ferret, and before Will could draw back, struck Will's face with his glove—"for each time she hath called for him!" The glove was heavy and stiff with sweat and bit at Will's cheeks. Will did not draw back. "And she hath called these three days. Oh, thou clapper, thou coper, thou tupper, thou fleshmonger! If no other man will strike for her then I will!"

Will bore it with angry joy; expiation and a kind of revenge against misfortune were tangled and torn within him.

Greville turned aside, knowing that so much must be expended so that they might, in coolness, find their way to the future.

Catesby struck again, and then again; but soon he was uttering half cries, and his rage was failing. He struck a final blow, cast down his glove and leaned backward on the desk breathing like a man who had run a race. His eyes were glazed.

His unseeing hand touched the bundle; with a final blaze of fury he dragged it forward.

"Thou black ram, take *this* into thy naked arms! Ask thyself when is a soul not a soul—unbaptized, unaneled, unhoused."

Will did not resist. Whether this was cruel jest or a grisly fact was now of little consequence. Whether true or false, just or unjust, its metaphor was the dead past which must be buried.

Will's face was burning in lines where the blows had fallen. The pain still made his eyes smart with tears. Greville watched from under lowered brows; then without a word he rose and brought him a cup of wine.

He said quietly to Will, "Now thou wilt go, my friend, and God be with thee. In the name of good, bury now this madness with no further ceremony."

He went toward the door to open it himself. " 'Tis left us to insure the lady's future honor. I fancy we must talk like Christian men."

Catesby cried like a last blaze on the hearth, "The honor and future of a dying woman?"

Will stood in the doorway, his back to the room. "*Can* she die?" he asked out of gritted teeth.

It astonished him that it was still the day. Surely only hell and night brought such a monstrous birth to the world's light.

Oh, pity, thou sky's eye that sees all things, pity . . . not for himself, he was purged and empty, but for all naked newborn babes, all ministering life, all gentleness; oh, pity. By conscience and grace, I cry against all deep damnation.

What is measured is pressed down and running over. Why,

death has as many parts as a play. Dark images of thought become truer than the forms of living men.

The quiet waterways of streams brought sky to earth. He came toward the river where the waterfowl rustled in the reeds by the river. Here, beyond the church and the miller's home, lay the sheep downs bounded by long heath and brown furze. He would not ascertain what was in the bundle, for dark deeds must not be helped by any action too precise. He dug a hole in the earth with his dagger and his bare hands, not a large hole but deep as a grave. There he put the swathed bundle, whatsoever it was, in the name of God, and pushed back the earth.

He sat down by the river, voided of all thought save empty rest.

In the river, the submerged plants swayed and spread to the rotting current. What judgment can encompass human acts? If he did not boldly venture into the countries of his soul, he would be held like some poor dolt by a postern gate too narrow to give him passage to eternity.

If the imagined terrors were so great, how could he bear the unimagined which cast him into regions beyond the reaches of his soul?

He sat into the twilight, so alive with death that only life could reclaim him.

His horse had gone. He did not know at what moment she had lifted her head and trotted home. He rose and went slowly toward the church and the road.

In the heavy dusk, he saw Anne coming down the road. They did not speak, but death was pushed back a step for that he was no longer alone. After a moment, he put his hand on her shoulder, and they went toward home in silence. Love is the search to be done with the conditions of mortality. But first it is courteous, patient, vaunting not itself, hoping all things, enduring.

Anne said, "Look, the unfolding star calls up the shepherd!"

He said with a faint laugh, "How may that be?"

He felt that she frowned. "Difficulties are simple when they are known."

Dearest Innocence. His thought was rueful. He said quietly,

473

"May I, from such a rough work as myself, shape out a man?"

She answered with a touch of humor, "Praise God who alone has the answer."

CHAPTER *Fourteen*

TO bury the past was not necessarily to uncover the present. The landscape of the mind on which he looked seemed barren and crepuscular. That which called itself Will shifted, dissolved, floated like an empty ship on an empty sea—now himself, now indistinct as water is on water.

He returned to his play of the prince of Denmark as a fixed place in his watery sky.

Of all the kindnesses to men, Almighty God gave nothing rarer than the joy of work, unless it was home and love. Nor no worthier conflict than that between the poet and the man, for in this struggle could be tested the metal of the soul. He had no doubt that this was its design and that naught existed save as thought. It gave him a fierce joy, as though after the bare winter came the spring.

Here am I king of infinite space though bound by the walls of a room. Here I love my wife and children with no flaws or hesitations.

He fixed his thought on Anne, not as a living woman but as an abstract of life invested with the power to transform that barren landscape where the buried lay.

Toward late day, he went to the meadow by the river where he had dug the grave, but already the trampling sheep had obscured the spot for one who did not look too closely.

He bound two sticks together as a cross and thrust it in the ground, and bound two other sticks which he cast into the river to quiet all spirits of rivers, streams, and wells that his irony could conjure.

Last of all, he asked, *Has the lady died?*

He cast another cross into the river.

Early the next morning, the toad in the garden considered

him with its great golden eyes. He sat on his heels before it.

"Thou art loathesome in the world's eyes, full of diabolic mischief and uncleanness. What hast thou to say to me?" The light shone on its mosaiced skin. "Oh, Tib!"

He had forgotten. He went in haste.

Coming down High Street, he saw her in the pillory. An early-morning crowd of boys was watching as the beadle whipped her. She did not weep, and her only move was the convulsive natural one when the whip struck. She held a bunch of flowers in one of her pilloried hands.

He ran to the beadle and caught his arm. "In God's name, Meekins! Thee would not beat a child!"

Meekins shifted slightly and struck again. Tib quivered. The eyes of those whom he had known all his life waited with some expectation.

"By Jesus, stop! What be her fault?"

Meekins said heavily, "One say she hae cast a spell. Step doon, Wull. I see devil a kammed thy face."

Tib turned her harebell eyes and partly saw the bruises on his face. She smiled and blinked. Will ran across the street to Quiney. Meekins called with no rancor, "Thee gleck, yet thee be marked."

To Quiney, who was still at his breakfast, Will protested with all his heart. But Quiney could only come to stand gravely in the doorway and shake his head.

"Will, it be a matter of the law. Sarah Bardolph says Tib hath charmed away a hen. Tib says she stole it. We take the lesser evil and whip Tib for stealing. Praise God for that."

"This cuts to the brain!"

"Thee hath seen such sight before."

"Never before as now! Look at their codding spirits. See! They whip and watch to lust with her."

Quiney turned his look on Will. He said with a grave humor, "Why, thee do talk of the devil, Will. Mustn't we leave him out for thy Tib's sake?"

"By God, yes. For a man may see with no eyes how the world goes. Change places, and handy-dandy, which is the justice, which the thief?"

475

"Peace." Quiney put his hand on his arm.

"Tib, you did not steal at the devil's bidding! The prince of darkness is a gentleman—he steals only in the best company. And you are poor and cast away! Rascal beadle, hold your bloody hand! Why do you lash the lass? Strip your own back."

Meekins paid no heed, and continued his slow strokes, and Tib, her bright face catching at a new thought, went with the blows as though she scarcely felt them. The lads looked keenly. Quiney said sharply, "Will, good friend! Thy face be marked."

Will put his hands swiftly to his cheeks. "These are her stripes I take as well."

Quiney turned away with some impatience. "For God's sake, learn when thee must wait. Take a lesson from thy face."

But Will cried, "Shame on him who strikes for faults of his own liking!" He flung a handful of coins among the boys. "For every whip and scorn, there's penance. Bend down, bend down."

Quiney's expression was knit, his lips thrust out. "In God's name, Will, the longest day comes to an end."

Will flung more coins. "Good friends, pity's sleeping. Wake it up."

Meekins put away his whip and stood impassive, watching. Tib's eyes were as bright as a child's as she watched these gay coins roll. At first the boys did not move save to observe where they went. Then two or three stooped to the coins, and one or two held out their hands as though to give them back.

Will cried, "Take note! Such chinks buy, in this world, the baby's right to beat the nurse: all's topsy-turvy."

Quiney said sharply, "Have done, Will! Must we be angels in one day?"

Meekins unyoked Tib and, not ungently, shoved her forward. "Scud, now. Rear up thy own biddies."

One boy had squatted down to work a coin from its hiding place, and held it out to Tib. She took it. In her other hand, she still held her wild bouquet. She scarcely looked at any. She seemed more than ever a child, though some of the mischief had wilted. She licked her lips and smoothed at her wild hair.

"Tib a Prior!" Will called to her, but she gave him only a fleeting look like a little fox, and ran with all her might toward home. Some lads lingered still to see what next would chance; but Quiney made a forthright gesture, and they dispersed.

Halfway in his door, he studied Will.

"Will thee not set thy self in order, Will?" he asked with a smile. "I need thee, butty, all in a piece."

"How I solicit heaven, I myself best know."

Quiney watched him gravely as Will went toward home.

They'll touch her again, Will said to himself. How do we mend the world? Tib a Innocence. The fairy child of Mrs Simplicity.

Oats and barley, day and night, rain and sun; Will made a litany. Think not too precisely, for innocence is flayed in this gross world, and all ghosts are sinners, since they wish us to repeat what's dead and gone.

He put his hand against the solar door, his safe abiding place. Here lay his confessional play . . . his *homo sentiens* . . . his *quod erat demonstrandum*. Someone was in the room. He felt a blaze of anger no less when he saw it was his wife.

She did not hear him, for she was bent above his desk. The magpie's cage stood beside her, and she held the bird's seed on her open palm. Her whole attention was fixed on a page before her.

Will stood silent, suddenly moved by the passion, courage, and vulnerability in her bared expression. Her slow finger followed the words, her lips moving on a sharp drawn breath as she said, "Oh, lad, what mischief—"

The magpie hopped and scolded for its interrupted meal and rattled at its cage. Will came forward and she looked up, startled but in no way put out.

He stood across the table from her, looking at her and covertly at the page she read. She blinked her eyes once or twice and smiled. He smiled too. In an odd flash she felt as though all that was known, loved, and hidden was being claimed by him.

He turned to the magpie and put his finger through the bars.

477

It pecked in frustrate anger and she put the seed into its bowl. The bird noisily struck away the chaff for the substance, as Will said softly, "Have you read so before?"

"No." Then she put a palm hard against the page, as though asserting a right. "But I told thee why I aimed to learn my letters."

What clear, strange eyes she had, she whom he knew so well. "What did you find today?"

She teased briefly, with a little flush. "New words."

"What else?"

"Pain."

He answered shortly, "Why, so it is hurtful—the imagination."

"Words put down must heal or hurt."

"Ah, Mrs Simplicity, hast thou got so far?"

She lifted her head against the light from the window. Her hair, her complexion, her lips were her own, no disguise. "There be here a man set against himself by love's betrayal. And a ghost who's no true father, for he be a sinner to ask for blood. Why doth he not see, this young man?"

She put the cage back in the window and gathered up her dusting cloths. "Sure this young man sees how wicked things play with him to his misfortune, yet he turns even from his own true heart that tries to warn him." Abstractedly she wiped the globe of the world—though how one could know the shape and the places of the world baffled her. She looked at him with her sideways look. " 'Tis not from the heart one turns away—for where else is the divine concealed, and we have hope to end our sorrow?"

Will could say nothing. He watched her with lowered face, his eyes on her, his lower lip thrust out. "Say on," he said softly.

She laughed a little and put the back of her hand to her face. "I know no more. See, I have read only where I know the words."

"Shall I read it you?"

"No." She looked at him with some shyness. "For then I might not know what to say."

478

"You!" He felt suddenly swept by a conviction that this woman knew all and could tell all. She flushed, and because he watched as intently as he did, he understood the flush better now than at another time.

"I mocked you not, my love. I think you know all when I know little." He put his hand against her face, and then he went to stare out the window. "Say on."

"What could I say, and all?" She laughed softly. Then she gathered her voice. "For some fear of thine, thy prince hath been left too forlorn."

He turned to stare at her. "Fear of mine?"

She did not answer, but turned toward the door. He could not allow her to remain in possession of secret and intolerable knowledge. He said sharply, "No, do not go!"

"Is he not writ out of thee in some part? How does one know the sky is blue save he sees it of himself?" She looked at his white collar, somewhat frayed, then at him.

He made a wide orotund gesture, but she closed her eyes for a moment and then said with no special stress, "This prince, he hath but slenderly known himself. And he be afraid to know more."

"Jesu-God! Well, Mrs Simplicity, what will you make of the rest?"

It suddenly amused her. Her eyes gleamed like Tib's. "Will he shake off that old mole in the cellar? The witch of Endor could scarce do more to muddle him."

"I have set a play to catch a man."

She smiled and thrust out her lips. "T'faith, the world does not wait for a man to resolve his moans. The world goes on as best serves its needs, and he must come along with it."

At that moment, nothing was real but this woman and this place. All meaning was here. Legs, arms, ears, eyes, genitalia, births, graves, whips and chinks must, by God, become the anatomy of self-knowledge. He and she were the only ones in the world. He shut the door and went without a word to take her in his arms.

479

"Let kissing," he said, kissing her, "be the greatest discord our hearts shall make."

She kissed him with the joy that came to all her kisses. But even as he felt their warmth, something of herself drew back. Her instinct told her she was not at this moment Anne—that she was some bell calling home, or some landmark, but not Anne. He was aware that she drew back; and though he kissed her again, he let her go. He asked with some pain, "For my misdoings, could you be cruel to me?"

She did not answer, and he went to the window and leaned his forehead against the glass.

She came behind and put her arms about him, her cheek against his back. "Is it cruel," she asked, "to think on thee awake and asleep?" Then she asked softly, "What does a man want of a wife?"

He shook with awful laughter. What indeed but the whole world! She was stricken, but she did not let him go.

"Thee must speak," she said, her cheek against his back, "with thy poor bruised face."

That stopped his laughter. She had looked at him briefly, the night before last, her mouth part opened, but she had asked no questions, offered no remedies. He said unsteadily, buying a little more time, "What does a wife want of a husband?"

She pressed her arms about him. "I will tell thee." He heard her clearly, though she held him with his back to her. "That I be Anne, in no sort or limitation. That I be taken all in all, not cut up in little pieces and some cast away. I love you. What is that to you?"

He stood with tears in his eyes.

Her arms released him slowly. He did not wish to be released. He tried to speak, but he had too many words at his command. When he turned, he found he was alone.

He thought of the uncharted wilderness that a woman such as she so boldly entered, of the mysteries for which she had no guide, of the forlornness which surveyed all.

By God, Mrs Simplicity had the virtues of his own golden

girls—Juliet who persisted *When wilt thou send?* Rosalind who wooed on trees—this wife of France, here in the book by his hand, who kept her husband to his vows by stealing into his bed as another.

When woman wooed, what woman's son will leave her till she hath prevailed?

He walked about and about, yet he could not leave this room. Life was tangible here though not fully seen. He stopped and stared at the bird, quiet now, cleaning its feathers. No doubt it was a woman-bird—no doubt in the world. Who else would be so insistent on her large rights and detailed tasks?

Oh, the high stakes, the high stakes! A passionate and profound woman must adapt and bestow moment by moment with no sure guide. The stakes were risk and promise, truth, not myth; they were the authentic word spoken, the true move enacted, the generous hope confirmed.

He did not know what to say or do. It was all a measure of self-recognition. He wanted everything on the moment; health, wealth, love, prosperous fields, prayer, and the hot sun on his head. Yet words would not do his bidding.

Judith came to the door and called. He flung it open and embraced her. She said, muffled in his arms, "My grandmother hath sent for thee."

"Aye, now *there* is a woman—indefatigable—unswerving—"

"Immediately, she said."

"Where is thy mother?"

He had a world upon him. It was light and yet it bore him down.

"I do not know." Judith held in her hand a rough corn doll.

"Ah, the corn maiden," he said. "I did not know the harvesting would end today. Look at her! Is she not a goddess? See how, sweet, fair, and womanly, she holds our fortune."

Judith said, "It be only the last sheaves tied like an old dolly."

"Where's thy scope, fondling, if imagination lacks a shape to act in? Old dolly, perdy! 'Tis a *she*—the corn spirit who will not die."

Judith gave him a fond look. "Then I shall hang her in thy study. Father, thee will go away."

"Must I?"

"Do not mock me. Thee hath always gone."

"Fondling, be cheerful. Think of each thing well."

"Thee will not take us by surprise?"

"No."

"It is very hard that wives are left forlorn."

He smiled. "Have thee said this to Thomas Adrian?"

The tears came in her eyes. He sighed for his little joke. She said so softly he could scarcely hear her, "That be not what I mean."

He said quietly, "Dearling, do thee know I love thee?"

"Aye."

"Then remember this: will any love the daughter who hath not loved the mother?" She shivered slightly and then she kissed his hand. As she ran off, he saw that she was smiling.

Mary Shakespeare wore a black damask dress, one she reserved for funerals or fine occasions. She kissed him. She poured him out a cup of wine. She called his father.

She had such beauty and grace that it would be folly to deny her claims. She was indominable, not to be cracked or broken.

Her husband came in, and they made a glance together that was compounded of their unsentimental but enduring love.

At last she sat down and folded her hands tightly in her lap. She had at no time smiled, so he did not know whether this was a feast or a funeral. She cleared her throat and then released a long, inexplicable sigh, as though scarcely aware of what she did.

She took a letter from the bosom of her dress. He received it from her with a faint remembering frown. Then he saw that, though signed by Camden and addressed to him, the seal had been broken. He looked at her.

"Aye," she said in a clear voice, "Greenway gave it straight to me. For, dear boy"—and then the color flooded her face and her eyes filled with tears—"I had to know better than thee." Her hands, with two rings upon them, came up to cover her face.

Will looked at his father, whose mouth was quivering on the

verge of some unapproachable laughter. John Shakespeare motioned at the letter.

Will read that the Shakespeare coat of arms had been confirmed in the name of "John Shakespeare, who has been worthy to receive them as a magistrate in Stratford-upon-Avon, a justice of the peace, and High Bailiff, married to a daughter and heir of Arden, and of a good substance." Camden added in his own script, "And to William Shakespeare, a pregnant wit of these our times, whom succeeding ages may justly admire."

It was bountiful toward all three. Will rejoiced with his father and his mother, with no grudging spirit, heartily. They ate and drank, and suddenly his mother looked like an old, contented woman. She sighed and sighed, stroking the damask gown.

"So," she said, looking at her husband and her son, "I have prevailed for thy good, and the name of Shakespeare. Now will the name be safe."

Will smiled and kissed her hand. When he left, she did not cling to him.

His father followed him to the door. "She hath never before opened a letter which did not belong to her," he said.

"I'faith, she hath not now, dear father."

His thoughts went to Greville and all the hosts of greatness and of darkness where the lady would be found, dead or alive.

Judith sat with her mother shelling peas. She talked in little bursts of animation. Will stood in the parlor, hearing. She did not mention Thomas Adrian, but every third word bore his print. This shy, lost, half-twin lass had found her grace equal with wondering.

"Aye," he heard Anne say, "loving so, some dear bodies find each other as though they were God's spies. They are the happy ones."

He came into the kitchen and kissed his wife. He did not mention Camden's letter: he already scarce remembered it. He sat down and ate raw peas as they dropped into the bowl till Judith took the bowl away and handed him a recorder.

He sat playing softly, and Judith sang.

The men and women of his mind's art would from henceforth

be in the full fell grip of life, standing with all their goodness and their sins upon them like wonder-wounded hearers. His lady, oh, dear young strumpet, did she live?

Anne rose to stir the pot and set the peas to cook. As he watched the firelight on her face, he thought that all was an act of revelation. Even the harlot and the libertine might earn immortal longings.

He tried to speak to her but he could not: a man with too many words at his command often misses the word with the simplest charactery.

CHAPTER *Fifteen*

NEWHALL, the constable, knocked at the door of New Place. "God-dig-ye-den, Will, I a come for witch's beasties."

"Witch's beasties?"

"Tib a Prior's cat and toad, God watch me!"

Will stepped into the street and closed the heavy door behind him. It was a Lammastide day full of sweet smells of nature and some mucky ones of men. He smiled at Newhall and took him by the arm.

"We'll walk and talk on such a lovely day. How be thy garden, Nick?"

"Oh, no," said Newhall, "none of thy billin, Will," and he stood heavy as a stone. Then Will noticed to his satisfaction that one of Newhall's eyes grew lower than the other. "Thee hath harbored what law may call a familiar of devil's trull, and there's an end."

Will considered. "This is fool-begged, Nick."

"Fool-begged a thee." Newhall stared down at his belly. "Law hath taken note of certain things and will move with further charges."

"By innocence, I swear the only charge is laughter."

Newhall licked at his lips and tapped his mace. " 'Tis no man's good to mock at witches nor us as must aroint them."

"To get goal for goal of the devil will be my way."

"Bist sure thee's not bargainin' with devil, Will?"

"Good now, Nick, I'll raise the place if aught be kindled against me!"

"Ah, Will, it be thee do kindle!"

Will thought discreetly. "Well, let us walk, Nick, for sure thee know an honest man will not yield in matters of this sort without a reason."

Some interest was being shown in the conversation by Hamnet Sadler passing. He stopped to listen.

"But a cat, Will, and a toad," Newhall was saying, "that's all I be here to take. Worthless things, save to the devil."

Will felt his anger heat. "They're worthy gifts of God to me," he said. "A cat's purr has its weight in goodness, and the toad is jeweled. Come, Nick."

Newhall moved with pondering slowness, a heavy mind turning. Sadler sighed, rubbing his forehead.

"It will be sworn she christened the cat," Sadler said.

"Better than some men."

Newhall's face was now mottled. Sadler whistled a tune. Old Rogers, passing, groaned.

"Will Shakespeare," Newhall said in a voice hoarse with outrage, "iffen I ud not known thee all my life, look, I ud have no more truck with thee save as I be bound. But now, I must save thy soul."

Will said sharply, "My soul, good Nick, must shuffle for itself. I'll give up no harmless beast to be used against a harmless maid."

"She be chance child," said Rogers.

"So are we all bastards in our ignorance! Nick, in God's name, let us not outdo each other in our crudy ways. I too have known thee all my life, and here's my hand. Go to, now, let us speak as friends. We know blobchops twit, but must we heed their gossip?"

The blood had not yet left Newhall's face. Mrs Shaw paused with her basket. Newhall said in a suffused way, "It 'ull be sworn that she a been carried in air to dance, sing, cull and perform other acts of venery with such boys and men as she desires and they no chance to ward her off."

Old Rogers sketched a cross that no one was supposed to see. Mrs Shaw said, "Oh, I'd not go nights past her hut, ever so."

Will's anger made him very clear in the head. "Dancing in air? Nick, wert thou watching? Thou shouldst have joined hands and got off some of that fat belly."

Newhall was staring fixedly at Will, the only expression on his face a rendering from the heat. "I 'ull swear that Watch and I a seen her dance all night, naked, save for unguents made from flesh o' babes."

"What wert thou doing watching a naked lass?"

Sadler said, "Now, Will, becall him not!"

Newhall stared with professional fixedness. "What do thee say, Will, to bull-beggars, urchins, elves, hags, fairies, satyrs, pans, fauns, silens, kit-with-the-cansticks, imps, calcars, change-lings—Robin Goodfellow!—the sporn, the man-in-the-oak, the hellwain, the firedrake, the puckle, Tom Thumb—"

"Fie, fie, so much devilment in Stratford. Is law asleep?"

"All—seen all!"

"Indisputable as the ass's head, good Nick."

Mrs Shaw said, "Think thee, Wull, so? I be sure hit's been her terrifying my cabbages."

Newhall permitted himself a sigh and a wipe at his face with a handkerchief. "She a also hanked Bates's cow; and for me, I find of this, foot irks me after speaking with her."

"Nick, good friends, for sorrow's sake, feel good pity."

Newhall said, "She'ull be used no more'n her desserts."

"Ah, who would then 'scape whipping?"

"Will, a last word. If it be resolved to examine her, then yield cat and toad thee must. But now, think. We be strong in custom, Will; this town be thine, thy father's town, thy mother's, thy children's—and well to pay thy breath to time and custom when by so doing thee doth link thyself to Almighty God."

Will did not answer for some time. Then he put both hands on Newhall's shoulders. "The devil knew not what he did when he made man politic. I thank thee for thy counsel, Nick, and now hark to some of mine."

Newhall stirred and set his face without expression.

"In thy book, we are fools by heavenly compulsion, drunkards, liars, adulterers by an enforced obedience to starry superstitions; and all that we are evil in, by a divine thrusting-on. From all that hath beset me, I name this folly and ignorance."

"Gie me beasties," Newhall said.

Old Rogers suddenly cried, "Hark, all! Thunder. It be God thunderclapping out of clear sky! Will, mind!"

Mrs Shaw waved her knitting. "It be not thunder. It be the devil—look! Oh, Wull!"

"Constable!" Hamnet cried. "It be not the devil. It be our black lord!"

The thunder of hooves at the end of the street brought parity to Newhall's disparate eyes. A great black horse was galloping like an apocalyptic beast down Church Street, bearing a great black-browed man in black shabby velvet, while behind him rode a flock of black men-crows on great gray horses. Lord of the manor, black lord and his minions, they passed looking neither to right nor to left, and smelling of sulphur.

"Where's Dick Quiney?" Will cried.

"By Jesu, where be whole corporation!" cried Newhall starting in a shaking lumber down the street, striking his mace against the houses as though to summon men to Judgment. "Call men, Hamnet, Henry, Will! Rachel, fetch thy husband."

Will came after him swiftly, and called to the faces thrust out of the windows. "The black lord and his men!"

"Damnation!" said Shaw, opening the door for his wife.

"Hell's fire!" said Reynolds. "Fetch Walker!"

"He'll have seen," Will cried, "for they went down Sheep Street."

"Get thy father and old Sturley!"

Will ran.

As he came down Henley Street with his father, Gilbert and Ned, and shovels for all, John Shakespeare said, "No man can play God any more! That's what black lord do not know, poor fool. We fought for our rights and we have them." He called out to his neighbors, "Come not unarmed. The madman is here. Bring thy shovels."

487

"And thy wits," Will said.

In Butt Close, certain patriotic Stratfordians had been practicing their weekly archery for the Queen. They had met the first assault of the black lord, not with arrows but with stark amazement. The lord had ridden his horse onto the close by the river, scattering the archers until they understood his intent. Now the archers were throwing away their bows and hurling themselves into the business of catching their cows. Will and Ned ran to their assistance. But men afoot were at the mercy of the lord and his minions, who, wheeling and trotting up and down the causey and along the bank, were scattering cattle and pigs and harrying men. Will, flinging himself on the ground to avoid a horse, caught a terrified pig. But most of the animals ran this way and that, some splashing into the river and trying to swim to the other shore, others running in dumb terror into the lanes, while the dogs barked from the edge of the lane or rushed out to herd the cattle.

The black lord roared a command comprehensible only to his men, and they fell to digging trenches for the enclosure, as though gold lay under their mattocks. They cast their glances to right and to left, however, for now the Stratfordians armed with shovels and wits were swarming onto the close. John Shakespeare shouted for them to throw back the earth as fast as it was dug.

The black lord was riding down the men who were racing across the close to leap into the river and guide the cows, and he was also riding down his own men, shouting, "Dig! Dig!" as he beat them over the shoulders.

But he could not be all places at once, and his black horse was trembling and whinnying with his sharp turns and plunges and his inchoate cries. At length it stumbled at a hole his own men had dug, and threw off its master.

The black lord lay for a moment like a huge doll, perfectly still.

Thou poor bumbling old wizard, Will thought, starting across the grass toward him. The old man sat up without Will's help, grass sticking from his hair and the back of his doublet, and watched for a frenzied moment as Hamnet Sadler threw back the earth that had been dug for a trench.

488

The horse stood trembling and shaking its bridle. At the edge of the close, John Coombs stood impassive. The black lord lifted himself to one knee, picked up his velvet cap, and hoisted himself onto the saddle.

The fall had quieted him. He sat looking like an ancient monument, uttering a few sharp cries that were lost in the clash of the battle of shovels. Stratford men had charged with their mattocks and had been met with the mattocks of the lord's men; and now Quiney, who arrived on the run, was shouting into the uproar.

"Forbear! Lay down thy shovels all. Sir Edward, command thy men—let us talk!"

John Shakespeare cried, "John Coombs, whatever thy heart say, help now!"

Coombs surveyed the battlefield, the casualties, the bloody head of the apothecary, and Gilbert Shakespeare limping; he took the bridle of the black lord's horse. He brought him into the lane without a word, and stood beside him, pale and cold, looking at Quiney.

The black lord reared and braced his feet against the stirrups and lifted his whip, but Coombs talked to him with barely parted lips. It took some courage thus to show his alignment against the town. His only move was the involuntary jerk when the horse shook its bridle.

John Shakespeare was shouting, "Hold back thy spades for this time!" Quiney drew near the shivering horse.

"Let us speak with good reason, but with words, not with blows!"

The black lord did not look at him. The grass still sprang from his hair and his doublet, and in his beard hung a flower. Quiney said angrily to Coombs, "For God's sake, this be no decent hurly-burly!"

" 'Tis thy work," Coombs said, " 'Tis thee bit thumb at thy lord."

Quiney grasped the black lord's leg and shook it. "Sir Edward, let us talk like men, not devils!"

But the black lord kicked him away without looking down. This action brought back his voice. "Dig!" he shouted, and, rearing up his great horse, shook it from the custody of Coombs.

Coombs reached out to grasp it again, but was compelled hastily to step back, for the black lord, refreshed by his silence, was rearing, thrashing, and shouting as though all the armies of hell were rolled into one.

Quiney cried to his son and to others for help to restrain such an abuse of good reason, and he sprang for the black bridle.

But the black lord jerked away the head of his sorely tried horse. Quiney fell; a flailing hoof caught him in the temple.

He sank down like a rock; he lay as hard and still as a stone.

The black lord barely paused and did not look down. He cried "Avaunt!" to his men. They cast away mattocks and spades and ran to their horses. In a moment, they were riding like a great cloud down the street.

Thomas Adrian fell on his knees by his father. Coombs stood very quiet, looking down. Will looked at Coombs as long as he did at Quiney, to measure this man.

Coombs drew in his lips tightly; his eyes had a flash of sadness. He said nothing. He sighed; then he turned and slowly looked at the men of his town. They scarcely took note. They had moved like slow water to see the disaster. Coombs stepped aside and went alone down the street.

"There be no doubt he be dead?" Sadler asked in Will's ear.

"None."

"It was like the devil come . . ."

Quiney lay as he must have lain often in heavy sleep, but with no flutter of breath. No one wished to pick him up and thus confirm the worst. No word was spoken, though several drew in their breath whistlingly. Thomas Adrian wept, and at length Sadler stooped and straightened Quiney's legs. John Shakespeare picked up his cap.

Will put his hand on Thomas Adrian's shoulder. "I will go first and tell thy mother."

John Shakespeare said, "We'll fetch doctor nonetheless. Ned, taste thy legs!"

Elizabeth Quiney did not weep, though she cried out. When Will put his arms about her, she dug her fingers into him, as though she must still find life in the flesh.

"Oh, Dick, oh, Dick," she moaned, "who would kill the best man in the world?" When the heavy footsteps of Quiney's friends were heard, she turned toward the door.

Dick's head lay against his son's shoulder, and his legs were borne by Hamnet. He was laid on his bed, Elizabeth took off his shoes, and then she wept, and begged all to tell her how the devil could have such power.

In Will's house, no supper was eaten. All sat at the table, save Tom, who was absent, and Will built a mound of crumbs to break down again and again.

O, our lives' sweetness, he thought, *we the pain of death would hourly die. Die, pain.*

He looked with his hazel-flecked eyes at wife and children, life's immanence.

The passing-bell was tolling, and its slow sad knell submerged them as though the town had sunk beneath the undulant sound.

Tom came in with twilight. He looked about him swiftly, his expression composed but withdrawn. Will examined him with sharp lights in his eyes. Poor Tom, always trying to keep his balance in a world of stupid loss. Was expediency less evil than pure evil? Who killed Dick?

Tom said, "Neither priest nor doctor could be found, though Mr Byfield has at last arrived. Walker thinks some charge should be put against the lord, but some say if he did the work of Satan, what charge can be sustained?" He said it coldly, as though his opinion lay elsewhere.

Susanna asked leave to go into the garden, though before she went she asked Tom sadly, "Where be the doctor?"

"Tending patients, I have no doubt."

Soon they heard her playing at the virginal, a sad hymn under the tolling bell.

Anne put fruit in a basket. "I will spend the night with Elizabeth."

Will nodded. His eyes remained on her as she went from the room.

Do not die. He felt he could never have said this in words, for where would he have laid the stress? He counseled Judith, "Lock safe the little beasts of Tib a Prior." She looked alarmed. He smiled, "Sweet heart, I am dead set against all dark deeds darkly answered."

When Anne had gone, he went to the solar. He could see Susanna walking in the garden. Presently Tom joined her. Judith had gone with her mother to sit with Thomas Adrian.

He stood in the dusky window looking out at the iron-gray twilight. He dwelt, without thought, on Dick's loving-kindness. So he had died—in loving-kindness. To know a man well was to know oneself.

There was a holiness in the imagination. It did not create illusion. It approached reality. O world, world, but that thy strange mutations make us hate thee, life would not yield.

So a man is a mirror of himself, and himself the mirror of all. It is the intensity and exactness of his self-knowledge that makes him true. The words of Montaigne leapt into his mind: "Knowledge is hurtful to him who has not the science of honesty and goodness."

The bird fussed sleepily, and he took it on his finger and looked at its sleepy lids and ruffled feathers. He brushed his lips against its head.

Tom and Susanna left the darkened garden. After a time Will saw a candle throw its light from the parlor window. Something of his being blossomed into life, and he looked around as though a form had taken shape in the room.

Before Will went to bed, Tom came to him. Tom said, looking at him candidly, "It is wise you know there be much talk of witchcraft in Quiney's death. But let me say, with all my strength, that I have tried to damp it down."

Will frowned, "In God's name, Tom, how can men be such fools?"

"Have you never feared sorcery, Will?" He said it in a somewhat sardonic tone.

"Aye, but I think not quite this sort."

"What difference? Witchery is very potent, very cold. Think of desperate, helpless fear, as the curse makes its way toward you—

the inevitable which you cannot see until it strikes. The emptied bowels, the sinking of the heart, the clammy hands, the abject terror, the quailing suspicion of all oddities and small mischance."

Will said sharply, "What are you doing? Are you casting a spell?"

"It is said that Tib a Prior cursed Quiney for watching her be beat and saying naught. The lass is in gaol."

Will was silent for some time. He softly beat against the stairpost. He said under his breath, "The monster Ignorance, how deformed he looks."

"I suggested to our new bailiff that the devil is known by his horns, and that our black lord wore no horns." Tom said it with the new sardonic tone.

Will turned abruptly and started up the stairs. "Thank you, Tom. I am much obliged to you."

Next day Anne told of sitting with Elizabeth and of things that were toward. She did not say much, for to her such a death watch should be crystal clear to all.

What came most keenly as he sat in the window listening was Anne's clarity; her emotions had nothing stale upon them. Elizabeth's grief was no one's else, but heard by each as his own, to strengthen the bonds of humanity and enrich the substance of love.

Anne was saying, "She wishes to be buried with him when death comes. She begged all." Anne was transparent with sleepiness, but her fingers lifted with her knitting. She added, "She anguished for it." He nodded.

Anne leaned her cheek against the window. "She cried out that she wanted naught but the furnishings of their room. Heirs may have all else that's new—the second best are where they lived their lives. When they took him away, she wept and wept and would not leave the mark his body made. She would not go to the new mourning bed. And so she fell asleep."

"Sleep thou," he said, touching her and lifting her up to walk to her bed.

"Oh, to breathe the day . . ." She lay down dressed, though he took off her cap. He saw her lips move and leaned over her. She murmured, with her eyes suddenly wide open on his face, "And I too—buried next thee—and all else." He put his hand on her eyes.

All day, as he carried through the acts of friendship to Elizabeth, his thoughts laced back and forth where poet and man were the same, and sensibility closer to truth than to paradox.

Elizabeth was ashen calm, sitting now in the mourning bed to answer the condolences of friends. The house was hung in black. Thomas Adrian wept; Judith fixed him a soothing drink and held his hand in silence.

The doctor was still away and his housekeeper knew nothing.

All talked of Quiney, and of Tib a Prior. Could it be? . . . was it? . . . and tales were told of how curses worked their way relentlessly, and of the infallible signs attending.

Henry Walker, who was now bailiff, gave his rough comfort to Elizabeth. "She be safe locked up."

"Is it true, Elizabeth," Will said at last, "that thee are so superstitious grown? Where's comfort?"

She burst into tears. "Ah, Will, ask not so. Who would kill him save he be bewitched? Ah, me, let us save others afore it be too late!"

"Elizabeth, dear woman . . ."

"Oh, Will, I heard her, myself, say that she kept a man sitting all night long on a cabbage he came to steal. *He could not rise up!*"

"And I remember when thee thyself hung a red petticoat in the window to keep away the smallpox scars . . ."

She wept again, sitting bolt upright in the black bed. "Oh, Will, Will, he was the best man in all the world!"

"Indeed, indeed."

He went away greatly saddened, and stood for a moment outside the gaol. Dick Quiney's identity had been unswerving; a man who had known himself well, unbewitched.

To say *This is I* is to be no more time's fool. *This is I, Hamlet the Dane!* Well, leastways, Will could perceive that his prince had not only his right to a choice, as he had foreseen long ago, but also the right to his own self. But to claim it was another matter.

All day he gave thought to the fell customs of abuse, to the dark working sorcerers that changed the mind and Beelzebub who was the liar and the father of all lies. Sounds were sharper that day, light more intense, the smell of the gillyflowers in his own garden rose as though all the flowers of the world gave up their scent. Between daylight and dark, identity was incarnate; the lion rose out of the contour of the hill, and the great serpent of creation heaved in the fields. All was one, legend and fact, to be unraveled in truth.

Why, man could no more evade his soul's catharsis than night could evade day.

He thought of Tib, but he made no move to go to her. He seemed, in some odd fashion, unable to relate the free child to the village fears. Tib herself was at freedom in the moonlight.

He sat for a long time on his heels talking softly to the toad; its eyes were filled with unplumbed knowledge.

Dick's funeral was as fine as any seen in Stratford. In the Quiney parlor, Mr Byfield spoke of his virtues. On the coffin stood a jug of wine which was passed as a loving cup. Then, in his fur-trimmed scarlet robe, Dick was carried on the Corporation pall through the street to the church, his hands crossed on his breast. The embroidered face cloth had been taken off, and his waxen countenance was like a stranger's beneath the purple panoply.

Will walked after the robed Council members and the singing men. He walked beside the miller, who held high place in town and hummed under his breath a psalm to living things and carried his branch of rosemary as emblem of the soul's life. Behind came the almshouse folk in their new black gowns. The tolling bell did not cease till all had cast their branches into the grave and the grave had been heaped with flowery garlands. Then the bell burst into a cadenza of hope eternal.

At the feast which followed, Elizabeth sat back against the black cushions of her chair, touching no food, but listening to the music, her eyes following the dance as though comforted by life's presence. Neighbor pinned rue on neighbor, and all kissed one another.

Will sat beside her, holding her hand on his open palm, coaxing her with fruits, speaking now and then of Dick to her ashen stillness. When she broke into a storm of words and wailing, he nodded and kissed her gravely.

"If I might lie tonight in the grave, how happy would I be in the sweetness of death, holding his hand."

"Aye." What private knowledge might there be of stirrings beyond the shadows of the grave? "We were boys together." He moved her hand tenderly to the tune of the lutes and pipes as he went with Quiney as far as he dared.

"I never loved another man," she said.

The new bailiff stood to comfort her. "Dear heart, tomorrow first thing will we take truth from witch. We a brought in a pricker, a deadly man for finding out a witch—very choice."

Walking down the street, Anne looked at Will. He said, "I will do something, as God's my own!"

"Aye."

"Since first I could distinguish between a benefit and an injury, I have not found a man who knows how to love himself in such straits as these." Then he hesitated for a moment. "Dear heart, hast thou still thy charms and spells?"

"No."

"What shall it be that we do?"

"God knows." She put her arm through his. "Thee had once the dowser's gift. Hath it left thee?"

He looked at her. "What do you mean?"

"It is the gift of finding."

"Take a hazel branch and go into the dark? To find what?"

"Ah, Will!"

There was something wonderfully mysterious about her face in the twilight. He laughed a little. "How like a woman, not to say."

When they came to the house, Tom was already sitting over papers. He still wore his funeral clothes, and they gave him an air of settled authority. Sitting ramrod, his white collar casting up light into his handsome face, his pen scratching even as he glanced at the door, the dog lying beside him, the house very still, he became a focus.

The dog wakened to scratch itself and go to sleep again. Tom ran his hand through his hair and spoke to Anne as though they were alone. There was a ring in his voice which he made no effort to hide.

"The clerkship is mine."

"Ah, Tom!" she said, and stood above him smiling.

He nodded, his eyes on her as he fiddled with his pen. "God knows I wish it had not come by Quiney's death. That is a blot on the time." He looked sideways at Will. "Coombs hates me now. Am I cleansed?"

Will put out his hand. Tom took it hastily and then, brushing at his hair again, said, "For Quiney's death, and the consequences, the Corporation must have legal counsel with no delay. I would it were not in this manner, but being so—" He frowned.

Anne leaned down and kissed him, holding his cheek against hers. "Thee be honorable and just. God lets all see."

Then Will said tightly, "I wish thee success, heartily, yes, faith, heartily." Tom looked close to tears, so precarious is relief. Will said in a freer voice, "And I ask thy mended judgment. Good cousin, forgive for all affronts."

Afterward, Will said to Tom, "Secure my rights in Stratford, Tom, and I will make it well with thee."

"Thy rights?"

"All must be unassailable. Of New Place, now. Search the deed, I pray you, before your clerkship asks too much of you. I want to know all things. Do I own it? I had scarce bought this place from old Underhill when he died; his son had poisoned him, no doubt bewitched." He laughed. "So son was hanged, and next heir is not yet of age. Who owns this land by a hanging? I? or the Crown?"

"Why, thy money and thy deed."

497

"Search the deed, good cousin. And then too I will buy the lease of town tithes on corn, grain, blade, and hay, from the three villages. There's much to be said for power."

Tom studied him. "Half tithes on wool from Stratford goes with the lease."

Will smiled slightly. "And lay reader into the bargain, to speak in church and be buried in the best place."

Tom laughed a little. "Is there thy reason?"

But Will grew grave and sighed. "No. I am commanded home, and though I be abroad, and wounded much, and tossed at sea, home be my heart."

Tom still had his eyes on him, and said with his new taste for irony, "I must love thee and sue to know thee better."

Will smiled. "You will see to it? And take my thanks, good cousin? For you have borne affronts most patiently. Give me your hand."

Anne, with Susanna, was setting bread to rise, since household tasks were all askew; Nan was preparing lye for the next day's washing, when a knock came at the door. Will went.

It was the doctor.

"Come in, come in, good friend. We've looked for thee in vain. Come, we'll have a feast."

In the door, John Hall shook the rain from his hat. "No feast, dear sir. This sad news. May we talk quietly alone?"

"Aye, sadder than most. Come and sit down."

He brought him into the little parlor and shut the door. The long wet twilight stretched beyond the windows. John Hall, looking tired and pale, let out a sigh.

"I am very glad to see you, sir, very glad indeed," said Will.

John Hall said, "Tell me, sir, I beg you—"

Will told him the manner of Quiney's death and of the funeral. They spoke of a good man's virtues as a marvel in a naughty world.

"I am very sorry," said John Hall. "He gave his love and friendship without receipt."

"And now it hath pleased the devil, Ignorance, with his fat rump and potato fingers, to pester our townsfolk with charges against Tib a Prior."

"The lass who blesses and harms not?"

"Aye, and by my hopes of heaven, sir, this ignorant devil is the greatest sinner of all, for he comes disguised as a saver of souls."

The doctor sat frowning, lost in thought. Will's voice was tired. "These good people I have known all my life, and loved. Yet now I see them move, without a backward glance, against a lass. Alack, fear and ignorance are everywhere unkenneled—and not least within us witty ones who are so full of eloquent inventions."

The doctor looked at him. "Is that thy finished thought?"

Will smiled. "No. I do remember a humanity in which I have a sort of faith. This town has loving hearts."

The doctor said drily, "I should not repose too great a faith in that. These are days when God is somewhat lost in clamor." Then he added, "Tib a Prior has many a time gathered herbs for me."

"Does that make her thy confederate?"

"No, but it might make me hers." He drew in his legs to rise. "I will see what moderation I can exercise on saucy fears." He remained poised to go, but stayed.

He gave a little sigh and sank back into his chair. He sighed again as though to draw in some fresh beginning, and said quietly, "I have been to London, sir. I bring you a message."

All poetic hyperboles were suddenly like painted ships upon a painted sea. Will sat very still.

"Her ladyship, my patient, is safe in London. I saw her to her brother's home."

"You were that doctor?"

"I know no other from Worcestershire to Warwick."

"You heard, day by day—"

"As I am a doctor, dear sir!"

"You kept her from dying."

"Leave her to God, sir."

"What did she cry out?"

"Sir, this is not fitting for me to talk of. I came to give a message. Will you hear it?"

"Oh, oh, what scorpions are in my mind!"

The doctor was silent, and then he said with a little touch of irony, "The sun shifts from the poet's bower."

Will paced unevenly, so stripped by shock and shame that he was not his own master. The doctor rose and took him by the arm.

Will cried, "She is all alive again! What did she cry out?"

"What does a human cry out but his own amazement before the throne of God?"

"Speak!"

"Sir, by no right can I speak nor you hear. She spoke to God."

"*Can* she die?"

"Dear sir, she might be moldering seven fathoms deep, and still not be dead to thee unless thou take bell, book, and candle."

Will covered his face.

The doctor's lip was thrust out, and his cool eyes were narrowed. He blocked Will's path as incontrovertibly as a rock. "Leave thy false gods," he said with an acerbity that was free of courtesy or comfort.

Will struck his brow. "Here is the gate that let my folly in and my good judgment out!"

"I have no doubt. But, most loving and good friend, all's dark and stumbling till we come to self-knowledge, humility, and love of God. From the rack of this tough world, let us now see."

"I see! I see!"

"See better, sir. The time is free."

Will stood by the window, staring into the black. He turned to John Hall. "If I say it is not Will who does what he would not, but Will ta'en from himself—then is Will guilty?"

The doctor hesitated. "Good friend, let me answer thus: there was much tenderness for thee in what the lady cried. It was not all black as sin." He picked up his hat. "And now I give my message. Sir Fulke Greville says to you: *Semper eadem*."

Will smiled slightly. *Always the same.* "I thank you, sir. Of you, I beg good pity."

John Hall clasped his arms. "Nay, I give thee more: my good love." He seemed to hesitate for a moment, and then he reached into his pouch and took out a letter.

"This is yours, sir."

Before he received it, Will caught the scent. He did not reach out his hand. John Hall said with a little smile, "It is not the deadly hemlock."

Will took it and put it in his pocket. At the door, the doctor said, "Would it not be wise to forgive thyself and her?"

Will told neither his wife nor his daughter that John Hall had come. Anne studied his face for a moment, and sent Susanna off to bed.

He sat in silence for a long time, she glancing at him now and then. At length he whispered, "Pity, unloose the saving grace of sight."

"Aye," she said, wrapping the last loaf in a cloth. "I've been thinking how Tib came to Joan when she was brought to bed. A gentle lass. She loosed all knots in the house and dupped all doors, that baby's birth might be easy. That was good kindness even though superstitious."

He looked at her. The scent on the letter rose up suddenly. He took it unwillingly from his pocket and turned away toward the fire to read it.

"Great friend, dear lover. *I* am now the married woman. My husband is a gallant captain, though he hath no title to his name. He loves me well. I wait for thee."

He folded the letter and sat with it in his hand. Anne did not stir behind him. At length he turned and rose. "Dear heart, thee must put this in the fire. Then by God's grace it will stay consumed."

501

CHAPTER *Sixteen*

AT breakfast, Tom gave Will a letter which had been left the night before at Smith's Tavern. Will felt and turned it round and round.

"Another letter," he said with a shaking laugh. "It is not from London." He considered it anew. "So dirty, it comes afar."

"Break the seal," Anne said.

"What if I care not for it?"

"Best know and weep."

He opened it and laughed. "Dickon Burbage." He read it aloud.

" 'Dear Will, good friend. By God's grace thou hast been spared the barbarous Scots, cozeners all from whom we must be very wary, rutting thievish roads, loud weather most foul and in conclusion this is the time that the unjust man doth thrive. In a fortnight we turn home by our lord's orders, and will meet thee at the Aylesbury inn at ides of September. See thou to that. I am greatly provoked by thy contrary silence. Where is the play that by all the devils though God sitteth highmost we die if thou defraud us of? Greet thy good wife.' "

Tom laughed. Will folded the letter and looked at his wife half smiling. Anne was silent, her hands on the back of a chair. All she had abstracted was *September* . . .

He thought of all that was incomplete, not least his play. He thought of what lay in wait for him in court and theatre and Lord William's demesne, where God knows what must be said and answered. London was like a heavy fardel which stood in the corner by the door. He would not heft its weight until he must.

He was lost in thought. The washerwoman came, and went with Nan; Tom rose to go somewhere; the daughters came to breakfast, and still he turned and turned the letter slowly.

Anne thought again, *September*.

His obligation was as wholesome as milk—to finish a play for his fellows, a task he had readily discharged again and again. By taking too much pleasure in unanswered questions, the over-subtle man can o'erreach himself.

He hesitated, and his prince hesitated. Which was first?

God, take note. I have allowed this prince to see his ghost before the murder. Brutus saw his ghost only after the deed. Is that not one notch for Thee?

This prince was the son of a warlike king and a voluptuous mother. Violence was as close to lust as smoke to flame. Could he between now and the ides of September answer a dilemma independent of time: of a man born of this ancient union, a man perplexed in the extreme, but catching some glimpse toward?

Anne sat down at the table beside him though the household was waiting for her. Susanna set about to crimp her hair, for Tom had told her that John Hall was back. Judith sat staring at her pottage and then looking at her father, who, she had learned, would go away.

Anne said softly, "Doubts be traitors."

He heard her after a moment and looked at her startled. She smiled sidelong and added in her low voice, "They make us lose the good we oft mought have, frightened from the attempt."

He smiled and frowned, picking up her hand and holding it against his cheek.

Somewhere a door slammed and voices were raised. Tom came in looking pale. He stood very straight, barring the door to the constable. He said, "Will, law has come for witch's beasties."

The constable spoke provokedly over Tom's shoulder.

"Gie ovei, Wull, wo a enough of foolery. Pricker's come."

Judith burst into tears.

"Witch's beasties?" Will rose slowly. "I know what you will do. If they run to her, as indeed they will for they are hers, you will call her witch. It's past reason. Aroint you, sir!"

Tom said, "It is the law, Will."

"It is black superstition, and I herewith declare it outlaw." He put the letter in his pocket, put back the chair against the wall, and kissed his wife as though off to business. "I'm sorry if I offend thee, Nick, but there it be. And now I'll say goodbye."

Constable stood, gnawing briefly at his lower lip. "Well, then, must I get summons."

Anne said to Judith, "Don't scrum, lovedy, eat slowly," though Judith was not eating anything at all. Within her heart, Anne was wringing her hands.

"Do thy duty, Nick, and God rest thy soul."

Newhall said heavily, "It be souls concern us. I 'ull argue no more. To Justice and back." He went off in a heavy rage.

Tom stood in the doorway, his eyes staring at the floor.

"This is our town, Will. It is strong in custom. Must we not bide for better or worse?"

"Egregious murderers." He looked at Tom. "Do you believe in witches?"

Tom raised his eyes to Will. "Do you?"

Will walked up and down, and stopped abruptly beside Judith, who was weeping. Tom looked at Anne.

"Do you?"

Anne stirred. Susanna came and put her head against her shoulder.

Tom looked again at Will. "Cousin, on witchcraft, be advised. They have found a devil's mark on her."

"Aye, her lap, no doubt! You are an honest man, Tom—how can you yield yourself to such obscenities?"

Tom lifted his brows and sighed and turned away. "This town is mine now, winter or summer. I must make my peace."

"Hah—the monster Custom whom all sense doth eat. Tom, his habits are of the devil!"

Tom said quietly, "I like the devil no more than you."

"Oh, amen, amen—lest the devil cross that prayer of thine."

Anne said, "Newhall returns and—what, Will?"

"Dearling, does God make honors of man's impossibilities?"

She took off her apron. "I will go along a thee. The more to witness, the better for the child. Daughters, do not burn daylight. Be brisk. Answer any with very large discretion. Surrender naught."

Tom said nothing. The whiteness of his face testified to his divided thoughts. He stepped aside, and then he followed after.

One cross of the street and there the business was, so close it could not be overlooked. A crowd had gathered in the street before the Gild Hall. The old folks from the almshouse had brought stools into the sunlight, where they worked their old gums and told all.

Children played in the dust, the younger soon forgetting why they were there, the elder hanging to all rumors. Nicholas Smith came up to Will, throwing a ball from hand to hand.

"Witch overlooked mam's cream istaday. Butter ood not come. I dropped in sixpence, and it come like you said."

Will paused. "I have misused thee, Nick. I must make amends."

Joan was close by the door to the Hall, Michael clutched to her. "Oh, Wull, Wull—Michael scream all night—weep and weep! She hath hanked him. What can I do?"

Will held Michael against his side and Michael burst into tears. Will said softly to him, "Love thy friend well, Michael . . ." and to Joan, "Look bright, for the love of God. Where is father?"

"In. I thought she be only white witch, Wull! When she was little lass, she gie me charm t' make my hair curly."

Anne put her arm around Joan, and her cheek close. "Do not thee hank, Joan, ever so. Bless, rather." Then Joan wept.

Will saw his father in the crowded Hall. Everyone who could push in had pushed, and the two serjeants in buff leather who waited on the Bailiff pressed back as best they could with their silver maces. But Will forced himself through all impediment, and Anne, her hands on his waist, came after.

John Shakespeare, with a seamy brow, looked at Will and said nothing. Gilbert also looked and said nothing. Ned could not be seen. Nor Tom. Many kept away, not liking this in one way or another.

The silence was like the inside of a waiting drum.

The sounds were all of people's fearful thoughts and gross wonders. Some whispers and some shuffling feet broke the heavy quiet in a hesitating way. Henry Walker, as magistrate and bailiff, sat in his arm chair, chin cupped, his gray and kindly eyes like steel.

Will looked for Tib. He hardly knew her, so childlike did she seem, with her head shaved and sitting very small on a stool. Her body was bared to the waist and bleeding in many places.

The pricker, a wiry, jumping man who was not known in Stratford though famous all around, charged twenty shillings for his long brass bodkin and his choice findings of witch's marks. His name was Mr Simkins and he stood nearby staring at her fixedly. She had many marks, little moles, and red spots and blue—all suitable for suckling her familiars—but they all bled, and true witches' marks were bloodless.

The pricker chewed his lip and summoned all his cold cruel knowledge. Among so many marks should be one that did not bleed.

Suddenly he leapt forward and thrust the long brass pin into her elbow. She jerked her arm and hissed her breath, but the pricker cried, "No blood, look you all, no blood! There be devil's spot. Aroint the witch!"

He moved rapidly on his toes, effervescent, looking at all faces for his reputation.

Henry Walker rose slowly. "Is that so? Now must we do it pat. Alas, Tib a Prior, why did thee summon devil dressed like lord of the manor?"

Tib breathed in little broken cries. She held her elbow for a moment. She dabbed at the bleeding spots on her body and cried softly, "Oh, oh, oh," as though taking in her nakedness for the first time. She thrust her arms into her shift. "Oh!" she said more boldly. "Devil works for pricker!"

"Tib a Prior," said Henry Walker sadly. "Thee be witch. Confess."

"If I be witch, I could fly home along old ewe. Who milk she? Tell I that!"

"Tib a Prior, we a many ways to make confession."

She turned like a little animal with the hunters close.

"Look!" the pricker cried. "See how she searches for her imps." He turned to speak to all. "No tears! That be sure sign of witch."

Henry Walker said, "Where be her beasties?"

Newhall called over the heads. "He ull not gie um up, and I caunt no ways find summons for thee to sign."

Will laughed, and so drew attention to himself. Henry Walker said, "William Shakespeare, gie o'er."

Will said, "I have no witch's familiars, Henry. I'll have summons on thee for such loose talk of my household."

John Shakespeare was saying *Whist* as earnestly as he could.

Will said sharply, "Whist thee, father. How look I that I should lack humanity? Henry, let us use good reason. There's been no witch in Stratford long as memory holds—leastways not this kind. Why must we be burdened now?"

Henry Walker said mildly, "That be impious talk, Will—it might be held. Times are changing. Witches be everywhere. Armageddon is at hand. These are days of mortal peril." A moan rose to a shriek and spread into a squirrel-like chittering. "Law is law. Charge be made and held, who can gainsay it till innocence be quite clear, but her guilt is much more likely."

"Oh, these are fears which feed upon themselves and so must die of hunger!"

"Here was proof infallible," said Walker. "What say you, Mr Simkins?"

"Aye, aye!" Mr Simkins said in his low suspirations. "And if ye yield to devil whispers like that man's, it must all be done again, so sneapey are the ways of Satan. Weigh her against the church Bible! There's infallible."

"Oh, no!" John Shakespeare lost all caution. "That you'll not. Little lass like her ull weigh less than that great monstrous tome that can scarce be lifted. Feed her bitter herbs and let it go at that. It be good purge and does harm to none."

"Swim her!" called a loud voice.

Will said sharply, "What foolish, dreaming superstitions have made all these bodements?"

"Whist, Will, they mean no harm—only salvation," said Gilbert.

"That's hypocrisy against the devil."

Someone cried shrilly, "Thee 'a' no religion, Wull, if thee dunt believe in witches!"

507

"Who said that?"

Anne whispered, "Oh, say no more, no more."

"But see, see how it doth work; the wounded reason casting a spell of such deep damnation that the heart is griped."

"Aye," Anne said, very low. "But the child will make enough mischief for herself. Wait, I beg."

"Swim her!"

"Nay, set her in a black room!"

"She put murrain on cows."

"I seen her sittin' on withy tree a-puttin' on her shoes!"

Mr Byfield, the minister, pushed his way to prominence.

"We be Christians," he said in his theological voice, "and wish to save the lass. It is only right those testify for her who'll do so. Lifetime knowing counts for much. But Moses said no witch should live. The Emperor Augustus—"

"Who be he?" asked someone in a rich ironic tone.

"—and Alfred the Great ordered death for enchanters, wizards, witches. Witchery is a presumptuous effort to ape the divine will. In Christian love, her guilt or innocence must be tested, *in Christian love*, good friends! Her innocence must shine as clear as noonday sun, else she is guilty."

"Oh, Will, wait," said Anne, "oh, wait." With remarkable diligence she had her way, and said, against his shoulder, "It be only the devil will hear thee now. Wait, in God's name."

Tib a Prior sat hunched, a lostling. Her feet were planted hard against the floor, her fingers plucking at her shift, her eyes closed tight.

The Bailiff listened to the pricker's whispers and looked gray and dry. He turned to Tib. "Will thee not say truth, Tib a Prior?"

"I byunt witch," she replied, quick as a catapult.

"Ah, Tib, mind thee not the time I could not get my horses past thy door, and thee laughed at me?"

She laughed now, bitterly. "They watch for sweeties I always gie 'um when Biddle owned 'um."

Henry Walker stared. He said desperately, "Yet thee did say, 'God bless thee and horses' and that be a witchlike speech, as all know."

"Oh, I'd curse thee now, iffen I could!"

The Bailiff called, "Constable, give thy deposition once again."

Newhall did so in a loud weight of words. "So help me, God— seen flying—heard saying—and that Quiney'd be sorry—"

"Fetch the rope, and in God's name we will swim her."

Tib pressed her arms against her sides and blinked her eyes against the tears she was too proud to show.

Walker said heavily, "Constables and serjeants, take note. Do duty."

He went ahead through an opening lane, but it was on Tib that eyes were fixed. Each good man and woman who lined the lane spat carefully at her as the serjeants and constables brought her through, and all made crosses of their fingers.

Will said, "Father, you will come, and miller, where is he? I think he will speak a word for her—and doctor, where by hell is he?"

"I'll fetch," said Gilbert with holy promptness.

The crowd was a solid thickness, breathing like men, but in no other way human until it reached the street. There some rough handling broke out, together with violent chatters. But over most was a deadly stillness. As the movement went toward the river, Bart Hiccox could be heard loudly and incoherently relating of a whole coven he had once seen, leaping to its feet when the devil, eight feet high, piped on burning chanter reeds of hell while below spread out a burning lake on which the sinful danced, *seen with my own eyes!*

Joan pushed forward, lifting Michael just off the ground, for he would not take his face from her skirts. She pressed close to Anne, her lips moving though no words came. Anne put her arm about her.

Will saw that Mr Byfield was holding back for him. Mr Byfield fell in step, blinking his eyes against the sun. "Mr Shakespeare, witches' marks, *mala fama*, inability to feel pain, these are providential discoveries of dark crimes. It is but rational to think that the devil, aping God, should imprint a sacrament of his covenant with—"

"I've heard tell," Will replied, "that skin of elbow hath little

509

blood, also that shock may hold back blood. The child's a nymph, she has country tongue and eyes, as some folks have had since spring and winter were begun. What things she does are done in kindness. Naught else can be proved. Thy granddam had such old wisdom, and so had mine."

"White witches," said Mr Byfield forlornly, "oh, good sir—or blessing witches, as some call them—are even more to beware of than cursing witches. They can deceive the very elect. Their works look *very much* like God's."

"Oh, sir, such thoughts can make men die before they sicken."

But Mr Byfield would not hear of this. He persisted in a low voice, "Some say witches are proofs of science, very queer adductions, I must say. Others that they are papists in disguise. Odd, that, too. Most witches are sullen women, old—ah, sweet Lord, it takes a careful mind." He was pale.

Will said hardly, "Shall I name the devil's work for thee, sir? Lying, slander, dishonesty, lust, envy, cruelty, hypocrisy, hate, adultery—"

Mr Byfield gave him a distraught look. "Sir, do you teach me my business?"

The air was fretted with pushing, shouting, and uneasiness. The great body of people went down past the stocks (where a poor fellow begged to know all details and wrung his frustrate hands) and past the gaol where the beadle fetched a coil of rope.

Ahead, by the river, the shouting increased. Will pushed forward until Hamnet Sadler caught his arm. "Oh, Will, I like it not. Seems very shifty. Against reason, somehow."

"Then let us act on that!"

The bridge was in danger from so many people. Will and Hamnet pushed onto Butt Close. From there they could see Tib standing on the bridge wall clutching at the shoulders of two constables, her eyes fixed on the river below. The rope had been tied about her waist, in case she sank with the weight of her own innocence.

Will heard a call from Gilbert and the miller. The miller was a calm man. He said, "They'd say making bread was witchcraft if they could. I know all tricks of black ignorance. Where be little maid? Hah! Henry Walker, I be here to say she be a good lass. Let her be!"

"Too late!" said Henry Walker in some relief as he gave a sign for constables to send Tib spinning through the air.

The splash was large for one so small.

"Oh, God, let her not kick!" cried Hamnet. "Sink she must, to be pulled up to the throne of grace."

Tib came to the surface, tossing her head. Angrily, she wiped her eyes and thrashed her arms to swim.

"Tib, Tib, take a breath and sink!" the miller cried.

The beadle ran along the other bank with a long pole to thrust her from the shore.

"Hey-ho! She floats like a cork, bob, bob."

"There be witch, sure as ever was."

Henry Walker was holding the rope laxly, his face furrowed. Boys were running along the bank. Some seemed almost friendly, as though this were a game. But others threw stones at her. One struck her on the head. Her hand went up, and for a moment she disappeared. But she reappeared, wiping away the blood. She did not seem to hear the cries of her friends, "*Sink*"; or perhaps her stubborn little spirit would not let her yield.

She thrashed with arms and legs, her frightened face watching the pious poles that kept her from the shore. Presently she was crying.

"Witch she be," old Rogers cried, and Henry Walker began to pull on the rope.

But then the crowd along the close yielded sharply. Thomas Adrian, pulling off his shirt and thrusting off his shoes, plunged in from the bank and swam to her. He seized her and went down. Bubbles rose. Murmurs rose and ran along the banks. Hamnet looked at Will, and the miller ran to the bank. It was an eternity before the heads bobbed up again.

Thomas Adrian flung back the water from his hair. Tib was panting and sobbing for her breath. He trod water to hold her up.

He shouted to Henry Walker, "See you, see you! She went down like a plummet. I had to pull her up."

The pricker cried it was a deadly ruse. He had his cohorts who joined in his protests. But there was a faint smile on the Bailiff's face. He hauled on the rope; Thomas Adrian jerked it from him. "Leave go. Nay, leave go! Throw crudy rope in water. Leave go!"

Thomas Adrian said something to Tib, and she put her arm about his neck. He swam them both to shore and brought her dripping up the bank to John Hall.

John Hall wrapped her in a blanket; Anne wiped her face. Thomas Adrian spoke to Will with a quick lift and lowering of his eyes.

"Father would hate it, just."

Ned leapt on his back, knocked him down, and wrestled him dry. There were some murmurs and some shouts that truth had gone awry. Nearby someone said, "Aroint the prickers, I say— mealy men. Out—out!" Judith Sadler came boldly and kissed Tib.

Will turned to Anne and asked her with his eyes.

She said, "Doctor says hot comforts and possets. Aye, John, I thank thee, with my heart. Come along, lass."

Tib shook as though with ague and drew up the blanket over her face.

They came onto bankside through the watchers. Some turned away but most were friendly. Their friendliness was no doubt genuine; no doubt they were glad she was no witch. No doubt one might justify a hope built out of compassion.

"What went on below my lamentations?" Will asked with a modest irony.

Anne looked at Will sidelong and smiled. "Thee'd have come to the same answer in a little time," she said. "I went to Elizabeth and put it clear. She has good sense and loving heart now grief be quiet. I also reckon that Thomas Adrian knew what-for Judith would give him if he did not act."

Will unlatched his gate on bankside and closed it on the stragglers who followed. "Jig's been danced, friends. Goodbye, all."

To Anne he said, "Dear heart, upon such acts the gods themselves throw incense."

"Oh, Will, Will—so many words."

512

He looked at her in some surprise. He hesitated. Her eyes were lively.

"Do thou thy task and I'll do mine," he said with humor.

Will stood a candle on the table in his bedroom. The day had been lifelong. He saw himself reflected in the window; any man going to his rest.

There is the shadow of a shadow cast by the image of my thought. What truth is there save in that divinity which shapes my ends? By light I see myself, yet not myself but truth and love, tempest and shine.

He nodded to see the lighted form nod too: oh, yes, oh, yes, the greatest of your having lacks a half to pay your debt to all humanity.

By such a way lay peace, though much fear might lie between himself and peace, much good unraveled to be knit again. To end the fear, to knit the raveled skein . . . the light figure had no walls nor doors behind him . . . *there by the grace of God go I.*

When she came into the room, his Anne, married eighteen years, no longer girl, familiar as the grass yet fresh with attributes, he did not turn for a moment. Her image in the window was enough for him.

But when at length he turned, he saw her by that art that doth mend nature. He saw her as both herself and him. She smiled and came to him and put her arms about his neck.

He felt a passionate tranquility, a buoyancy of life.

"Oh, my dear, my dear, my love, oh, my dear . . ."

She laid her mouth on his and he put a gentle hand on her neck. She saw his face and he saw hers, servants of themselves and of each other. The dark needed no candles now, for the dark was light.

CHAPTER *Seventeen*

A WET and ragged gentleman came out of the rain into the Aylesbury inn. He sat in the chimney seat and looked in absolute wonder at twelve men and boys who came down the stairs. They embraced the landlord, kissed his wife, drew the heat away from the fire, commanded the air. He hunched himself, gnawed at the side of his finger, and watched them all with small flashing glances. By cock, he'd not yield a buttock's worth.

He lifted his flashing black eyes and called for the drawer in a North Country tone.

Alas, poor man, he was the victim of his own pride. He was shabby; he had no more than a pound in his purse; he was on his way to London to ruin his brother in a lawsuit: suspicion and caution must be his two angels. So, when the drawer came for his order, he hesitated, clutching his poor ruff and clearing his throat in a thunder. It was Will, balanced in front of the fire, who said with a bow, "Two sacks, if his lordship will permit me the honor."

His lordship, disconcerted, doubtful, delighted, grunted and looked about sharply. All, all were gentlemen, he saw now, even the boys; lords' sons, or old gentry.

His new friend paid for the sack, as he had feared for a moment he might not, and they toasted each other gravely in silence.

There was such confusion that the dog barked without stopping, and such movements of going and coming that the smell of new rushes and herbs rose in constant sweet breath from the floor. The North Country gentleman looked with loneliness at the landlord's wife when she came to the fire to stir up the pot. She comforted him with a word about dinner.

This gave him leave to unhunch his shoulders and peer at his new friend, and his friend's friends, from under his brows. Every kind of woman's son was among them; tall, short, fat, thin, young, old, all shaped by the hand of life so that nothing offended.

All were captains, he ventured to think, all led, even the lads who played knucklebones by the fire and spoke to each other in tones of sweet music.

As the trestle tables were pushed together, the tall, short, old, young were driven back to the walls. There some did push-ups with exceptional grace, and two mimed a duel with poker and fire stick. Presently the landlord clapped his hands.

"Knives out, stools up."

In the silvery confusion of voices and knives, of the melodic sound of the landlord's wife filling and passing dishes, the North Country gentleman felt alone and very hungry: more than one meal a day was too dear. But Will called to him, lugging forward a stool, and said, "The best place at the table for his lordship, our guest."

The landlord said grace, and the youngest boy sat with his knife dipped toward his food. *Amen*, and the clatter began.

Overcome by his need to deal honorably with such honorable men, the North Countryman said sadly, "I am no lord."

"Indeed?" said Will.

"I am a *gentleman*. My brother's the lord."

He brooded. His hand did not move toward his mouth. Will waited.

"He hath six soons, great lads . . ." the passion of this knowledge overwhelmed him. Then he raised his small fierce eyes to Will. "My broother hath a great croomplin' waste o' castle, and ne'er gie me due. Thur's nobbut England lak so—men croomplin', strugglin' to stay oop. Six soons. I'm home froom t' wars. I've three wounds and one poorly mended. Doth me Queen need me? Me kinsmen? Me horse? Oh, woe! *Me God?*" He considered his knife point and he thrust it into a piece of meat. "Not a one."

After a moment, he looked sideways at Will. He had told him all, all his whole life, the life of Englishmen in these perturbed and baffling times. Now he expected a courteous return. "Tha and thy friends be twelve. What be t' badge tha wear?"

Will bent his head to the emblem on his breast.

"It is the Lord Chamberlain's badge, sir. We are his servants. His players."

"Is that so now! God Almighty! Playactors? Flummery-mummery?"

"Aye, that."

The North Countryman sank into deep silence. At length he looked straight at his friend. "I tuk tha for a gentleman." He felt the warmth of his full dinner. "I hae been t' plays. And when this rude world o'ertuk me, I had learned t' mimic speeches."

"Say!"

"Aye, heartens one." He did not look up again; he wiped his knife on the edge of the tablecloth and thrust it into his belt.

At length all were content, guests, landlord, and the dog that had stood profitably under the table. The Edward board was ordered out for a digestive period of shove-penny. Burbage was saying to the landlord, "And three farthing dips, if you please, for better light, so I and others can moon over this contentious play of Will's." He laughed and caught Will. "It shall be cut to smidgins tonight, old lad, and tomorrow set to memory as we ride. Oh, alack, alack, think you how tardy-off we come? Turns me blood to ice. Alleyn now, 'tis said—" He jumped, for the North Country voice whipped into the air.

> "On every side drop captains to the ground
> And soldiers, some ill maimed, some slain ootright,
> Here falls a boody sindered from his head;
> Here legs and arms lie bleedin' on t' grass
> Mingled with weapons and unboweled steeds
> That scatterin' o'er spread t' purple plain.
> Till Don Andrea, with his brave lanciers
> In their—main battle—made—made—"

Condell's voice slipped under the lost word and bore it on:

> "—so great a breach
> That half dismayed the multitude retired
> And Phoebus, waning to the western deep,
> Our trumpeters were charged to sound retreats."

To this, Ned replied:

> "Thanks, good lord general, for these good news:
> And, for some argument of more to come,
> Take this, and wear it for their sovereign's sake."

The North Countryman threw back his long hair; his eyes flashed, his nostrils flared, his very soul neighed.

"Oh, roundly spoke. Oh, fine, fine. 'Eavens aboove! Oh, joost!

Ale for all! Oh, dyin' dooks! Oh, ringin' words!" Then he made an incomparable gesture. Seizing Burbage's arm, he cried, "I'm thinking, I'll pay ya t' gie me t' rest o' tha play!"

Burbage paled. Heminges reddened. Such a fine gesture must be respected with the whole heart, but all had seen his frayed doublet and shabby ruff. All had heard him speak of his blasted hopes. The North Country gentleman caught the hesitation, and his pride ruffled. He went to the hearth and he spread out eight shillings, one by one, in a row.

He sat down in the chimney seat and lighted a pipe which he took from the wall. He watched his own twitching foot. Burbage rose to a display of country thrift.

"For four shillings, sir, we will give you a better play than that. We will read you, new and copied out today, a play by your friend Shakespeare."

The gentleman did not look up. He nodded. He took back four shillings, and was seized by a giddy joy.

Burbage said to his fellows, "Parts are writ out, lads, with some et ceteras. Author will make distribution. I'll comment here that it is not quite what I expected; but it has some nice effects. I, the actor, am much called upon, for this author's a subtle rogue, a finder of occasions for our talents. Now, I'll speak what goes first, and you, Sam, and you, Ned, will follow after."

He cleared his throat. Then he paused, rose, clutching at the loose pages, and bowed with exquisite form to their patron.

" 'Elsinore. Before the castle.' "

" 'Who's there?' "

" 'Nay, answer me. Stand and unfold yourself.' "

" 'Long live the king!' "

Oh, singularity of man, who of all beasts can strike life into speech! Will listened, each telling scene remembered out of that life within, that joy of poet—though not phrased perhaps exactly as he meant! The frustrate months were gone when he had wrenched this play from black night and open day.

The landlord and his wife sat as silent as wood. Countrymen coming in for their ale hushed themselves and tiptoed to their mugs.

As Will listened, he was suddenly aware that his play had no ready conclusion: each man might see himself. The countries of the soul lay across its road.

He smiled. God knows, they would wait for him!

Within the round of this play and the square of this room, anguish, wonder, and amazement fell on willing ears.

"Aye, aye," a farmer cried, holding his brimming tankard.

And a ploughboy wondered that men dare trust themselves with men. The landlord's wife wept for all poor discarded sons and cast-off maidens everywhere.

The dark deepened. Night grew heavy. Men should be asleep. The dog slept. Dickon, the consummate actor, came to full height with this prince.

> "How all occasions do inform against me,
> And spur my dull revenge! What is a man,
> If his chief good and market of his time
> Be but to sleep and feed? A beast, no more!
> Sure he that made us with such large discourse,
> Looking before and after, gave us not
> That capability and godlike reason
> To fust in us unus'd . . ."

At length Condell spoke the concluding words of Fortinbras:

> "Take up the bodies: Such a sight as this
> Becomes the field, but here shows much amiss.
> Go, bid the soldiers shoot."

No stir broke the silence. Then the dog wakened and looked from one to another, striking the floor tentatively with his tail.

The North Countryman lifted his head; his whole body shuddered. "Ah," he said. "It struck me here!" He smote his breast.

He pushed himself to his feet and walked stiffly back and forth with short steps, shaking himself now and then like the dog.

The players wiped their faces and looked at Will. Gus nodded; Heminges did not hide his tears. The North Countryman pointed his pipe like a dagger at Burbage.

'I'm thinking that's t' story of me, ambition slighted, hope tricked. Oh, there be a true man and all his questions. Wull, wull, a man's virtues as wull as his faults cast him in turrible consequences. By heaven—ah!"

Burbage frowned and leaned his head back. "Yes," he said, "I am willing to testify to life's unanswered questions set forth in this play."

Gus Phillips disengaged his legs from the stool and suggested that Will had said a final word on the human value, that a man's virtue consisted in his readiness: 'twas all.

"Is that so now?" The North Countryman rocked on the balls of his feet. "I am a mon who has sought more meanin' in t' cannon's mooth." Then he tossed his head and wiped the sweat on his forehead. "Ah, well, what does one know? Tell me —you, stoic—was this prince always true t' himself? Did he not go forward an' back, bandagin' his eyes t' light, luk some I could name? I'm thinking he'd better have killed that wicked usurper without all this shiggle, shaggle."

The landlord suggested that the play told of the greatness of man pitted against the power of fate. This was thought on, although Armin averred it was not fate, perhaps, but that holiness of the heart's affections, and that perplexity of imagination that dreamers make from their dreams.

Condell, to the astonishment of all, ventured to believe that it said, He who seeks revenge will be killed by revenge.

Burbage sat upright and called for some food. He declared that the true nobility of a great mind could not be subdued by life or death. Here was a prince, a piece of work noble in reason, in form and action like an angel, a princely paragon, a courtier, soldier, scholar—the very ripeness of this time—the expectancy and rose of our own state—

"And mad, mad as a daftie!" the North Countryman said angrily. " '*Sweep to my revenge!*' Aye, so would a canny man, but what does he?" He struck his hand against his breast, and his chin fell against his ruff. "Oh, t' doot, t' doot, must he doot so much? 'Tis very hard on me own uncertainties."

Will leaned forward. He studied the shape of his shoes, he admired the precise play of the animals who lay close underfoot;

the dog who languidly cuffed at the cat, who washed her face and, when ready, replied to the dog.

The play was the wheels of a cart. It bore forward those who believed that their own legs alone did the journey.

He smiled with sympathy at the discomfort of the dog, and consoled him with a murmur. He heard Phillips' voice, warm as a setting hen; dear Gus, who would understand all. He listened. Gus's words were calm and shrewd, making both surprise and truth of this play.

The North Countryman had usurped the hearth. "Now, take ya that speech: Am I or am't I—take I arms or don't I—what shall I do?"

Will turned his eyes to this rough man with his unkempt beard and his shabby clothes. Toughness begat tenderness, strength impregnated weakness. Out of the teeming and bountiful realm of the soul, this man, these men, these women, these animals, this rising smoke, this wind and rain—out of all this, life stood forth.

The North Countryman was close to tears. He thrust his voice at Will. "Let me tell ya, sir, thou hast mixed thy truth wi' lies. All a mon can do is go nobly to his fate an' take a swipe at some." He was growing giddy with his thoughts and the heat of the room. "Oh, we live, we live only to hold off that bloody monster, death, wi' all his terrors. Oh, what a turrible woorld, what a lamentable fate. Ah, that ghost told all."

He sat down abruptly in the chimney seat and passed his hand across his eyes. Then he said in an altered voice, looking at Will, whose eyes were on him like a friend's, "I hae been quite carried away, I'll grant ya that." He seemed to sink without protest into his weathered face and ragged beard. He whispered, "There are woords imprisoned in thy woords. I hear them beatin'." He sighed. "Speak again, once more, you, sir," he half turned, pointing to Burbage. "Speak again t' lines aboot t' sparrow fallin'." He listened with his eyes closed. "Ah, Jesu, *what pain t' leave this world too soon!*" and he burst into tears.

The players sat looking at their thoughts. It would be a poor world that could not weep at will. Burbage motioned Ned to strike up some music.

The sweet viol went along with the weeping. It held close the heart of wind and rain, the heart of poet. Will sat very still, his eyes on the weeping man, his expression warm and tender. Within himself was the world, sad and glad, hungry, thirsty, longing, loving—all the living. *Ah, the living, the living, they shall praise Thee as it is this day.*

At breakfast the next morning sat Greenway, the Stratford courier. Will and he greeted each other with an embrace. "By heaven," said Will, "I never thought to see a Stratford man so soon. You are hope for a homesick man."

"Well now, just," said Greenway rummaging in his saddlebag, "there be letter for thee, Will. I thought not to deliver it till London, but why not now?"

Will took it with some curiosity. The script was unfamiliar. He opened it and looked at the name signed. Then he went away alone.

"Dearest husband.

"This be first letter ever I have wrote. It be for thee alone, so forgive mistakes.

"Dear sweet husband, my love is in the grain, and bears both wind and sun, and thine to me.

"Thee did say old lovers have ways to find each other. Aye, for all in my heart is thine. What's built anew grows fairer than at first, more strong. I speak to thee from center of my soul, and thank thee there. Hourly joys be still upon thee. In love, thy wife."

After a moment he put it under his jerkin near his heart.

With the dawn, Dickon rallied his friends. God's teeth, what a life!

Heminges roamed up and down in the mud, minding the comfort of all. Gus paid the landlord, who asked anxiously, "You'll sure go to church? Law'll take after me!"

Smoke went up from cottage chimneys, and on a hillside a ewe bleated as though heralding the dawn of the Saviour.

Will rode with his memories. Phillips rode silently, glancing at him now and then. Burbage rode like a king and sang aloud. All the others looked fresh and merry, and cantered as though they were the horses.

Here by the road grew the bramble and the yellow toadflax. Will said to Gus with a smile, "Back we go, stenches, aches, and confusions. Mankind has scarcely been born."

Gus gave back his smile. "Mayhap we've only gone round a corner; is that not a great thing?"

"Aye. If powers divine behold our human actions, as perforce they do, God grant they look with kindly eyes upon our corners."

"Good friend, amen."

They had passed through a deep forest and into the open. They had picked blackberries and apples. The sun had been up for two hours when they heard behind the small thunder of hoofs. Burbage took up his ancient pistol and Heminges readied his pike. But Gus, looking over his shoulder, called out a greeting. The others drew on their bridles and slowed themselves to a halt.

Their patron, the North Country gentleman, rode beyond them and wheeled about. But their greetings died in their throats, for he pointed a pistol at them.

"I want back me four shillings," he said, the shabby plumes of his hat catching the light.

"But, sir," protested Burbage, "we gave you their worth."

"Aye, I'll grant you that. But it's mornin' now, and I'm cold sober to t' daylight, and thy crafty art hath made fools o' men befoore. I'll thank ya t' give it back with courtesy, or else I mun take it at me pistol point."

Some of the horses danced with a clatter, and the North Countryman's with them, but he kept the pistol steadily fixed.

Will said, "Give it him." He added in a friendly way the words of Fluellen, " 'There is figures in all things.' "

Phillips rode forward, plucking the shillings from his bag as he did so.

The North Countryman said, "I thank ya an' I wish ya well. I'm hopin' for your souls though I doubt your salvation. For what hope a' ye from lies and foon? 'Tis the hard facts ya best believe: do nae ya believe four shillings, when all experience says an empty purse." Then he made a sudden compelling gesture to Will. "Git ya doon, sir. Git doon. Git doon off your horse. I luk ya well. I've a little giftie for ya."

Will, everlastingly curious, dismounted and stood smiling in the mud, bridle in his hand. Then the North Countryman drew his sword and Ned and the younger men shouted.

"Nay, no fear. I mean to honor his sagacity and insight. That's better than four shillings. For he makes you look within, and though that's hard, it bears a little stamp of greatness." He put his sword on Will's shoulder. "Rise up, Sir Oracle."

Then he turned his horse and rode back through the dark forest. They could see him fumbling to reach his moneybag and put away the coins.

ABOUT THE AUTHOR

HENRIETTA BUCKMASTER was born in Cleveland and has lived in New York City most of her life. She is the author of a number of distinguished novels, most of which have been published in England and also translated into other languages. Her most recent novel, *And Walk in Love*, was based on the life of the Apostle Paul. Before that came *Bread from Heaven*, and *Deep River*, which won the Ohioana Award. Her nonfiction book, *Let My People Go*, is a standard work on the abolition movement and has recently been reprinted in a paperback edition. Miss Buckmaster has been invited to the MacDowell Colony for several summers and has also received a Guggenheim fellowship.